About the Author

L.P. Blower grew up in West Sussex and joined the Royal Navy in 1961, where he spent 25 years in conventional submarines during the Cold War era, retiring in 1986.

Now an OAP, he enjoys writing for pleasure, walking the South Downs, and birdwatching near his home, which he shares with his partner.

With my best regards

[signature]

B TGRODE
(AUTHOR)
(LP BLOWER)

Please visit the Guernsey Sailor page on Facebook to post any comments

Dedication

I dedicate this book to every man who ever went to sea in a conventional submarine.

Author's Note

The main character in this story was based on my Grandfather George Deseria Torode, who was born on Guernsey in 1896. In 1982 I began to write an account of his life, but unfortunately, he died just after I had begun, and with him went many of the tales of his life in the navy, which he would relate to me when I used to take him out for many a Sunday lunchtime pint. He joined the RN in the January of 1914, eight months before the start of WWI. He served as a stoker during both WWI and WWII, before finally retiring in 1945. With not having much documentation I shelved the project.

I later became interested in the Gallipoli Campaign, and especially with the submarine involvement. Everything I read was very precise and factual, and I began to wonder what many of those sterilized characters were like as normal men. So, I decided to write this tale from the view-point of a crew member. That was when I decided that a fictionalized version of my Grandfather would fit the bill. Fortunately, I have managed to remember some of Granddads tales, some of which have been included within this book.

The book of HMS E11 campaign in the Dardanelle's entitled Dardanelle's Patrol tells the story exactly from Martin Dunbar Naismith himself, and I have had to use many of the facts from this book to animate the story from the point of view of the men who served under him. I have not copied anything exactly.

I have attempted to blend the fact with fiction in this tale of the failed Gallipoli Campaign of 1915. It is an attempt to humanise, and bring to life some of the characters who fought so bravely to achieve a victory, but were let down by the incompetence of their commanders. Alas it all happened over a century ago, and many of them are now largely forgotten.

Although much of the action that takes place is factual, many of the characters are fictional, and they only represent the heroic deeds of those brave men. For the higher-ranking members in the tale, I have used their real names, but in no way have I tried to mis-represent their character. It is an attempt to write a fictional rip-roaring tale, much of which did actually happen.

Rest in peace granddad.

L.P. Blower

THE GUERNSEY SAILOR

AUSTIN MACAULEY PUBLISHERS™

LONDON · CAMBRIDGE · NEW YORK · SHARJAH

A CIP catalogue record for this title is available from the British Library.

ISBN 9781528987226 (Paperback)
ISBN 9781528987233 (Hardback)
ISBN 9781528987240 (ePub e-book)

www.austinmacauley.com

First Published (2021)
Austin Macauley Publishers Ltd
25 Canada Square
Canary Wharf
London
E14 5LQ

Table of Contents

Synopsis

The story begins on the granite cliffs of Pleinmont Point on Guernsey in 1910, where the death of a friend evokes a hatred that is to have disastrous consequences in the years ahead. On the 4th of August 1914 World War I starts, and George Torode heads off across the English Channel to join the Royal Navy. On the voyage he meets Gladys Rumsey, who promises to write and await his return. On completion of his basic training he falls foul of the dubious delights of the naval city of Portsmouth, and finds himself drafted into the embryonic submarine service.

This is the story of the coming of age of a young Guernsey-man in a time of conflict, who survives the sinking of a training submarine after she hits a mine on the surface during a storm, and following his recovery is sent to join *HMS E11*. In the spring of 1915, they form part of a small flotilla being sent to the Mediterranean to bolster the submerged capability of the Allied Fleet in its attempts to penetrate the Dardanelles during the Gallipoli Campaign. There he meets his hated enemy in an extremely unusual situation, and has to fight for his life.

Each reader will be taken on a roller coaster ride as they experience everyday life aboard a WWI submarine, and the formidable dangers they encounter on a daily basis. They will sweat with the crew as they attack the city of Constantinople, and gasp in terror when the unpredictable tides of the Bosphorus nearly cause their destruction. Other allied submarines are lost, and E11 nearly becomes one of them.

The lives and loves of George and his crewmates are recounted in human detail during this time of great danger. After volunteering to take part in shore raids against the Turkish mainland, he is badly injured. A long convalescence on the passage home allows him the time to reflect on the past nine months of conflict. Will Gladys still be waiting for him as he arrives back in Portsmouth on Christmas Eve 1915?

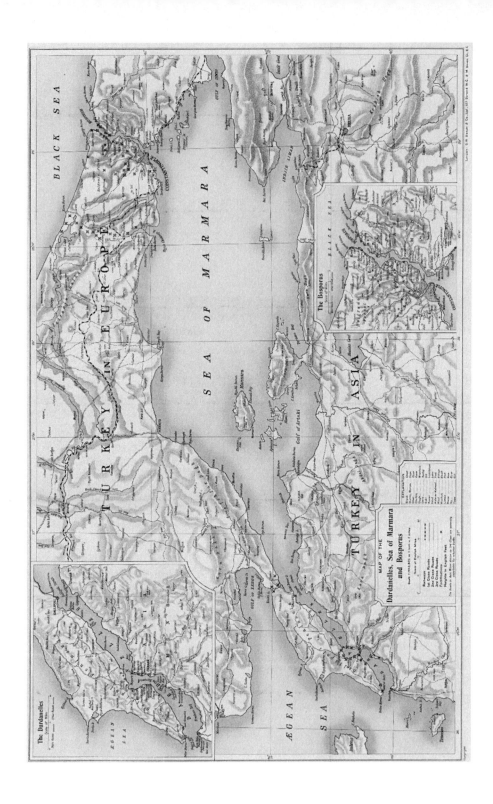

MAP OF THE
Dardanelles, Sea of Marmara
and Bosporus

The Dardanelles

The Bosporus

Chapter One

5th of May 1910 on the Island of Guernsey

The town of St Peter Port nestles gently into the hillside on the eastern fringe of the Island of Guernsey. There is a tranquil calm as the latent heat of the night slowly becomes the coolness of the early dawn. The sleeping town stands deserted, save for a cat padding its way down the High Street, returning home from nocturnal adventures. The front windows of the houses standing higher on the hillside all have their upper windows flung wide open, not to admire the view, but to catch any chance zephyr being wafted ashore off the sea. The temperatures have been very high of late.

Looking eastward from the town, one can see the Islands of Herm and Sark erupting through the mirrored waters, their black silhouettes showing stark against the fanning aura of the dawn light blossoming over the Cherbourg Peninsula. These tidal waters that daily fill the granite walled harbour, also surround the towering ramparts of Castle Cornet standing out at the end of the south mole. An ancient bastion that has protected the inhabitants of the Island for over eight hundred years. The lack of activity around the harbour adds to the silence, as it patiently awaits the rising waters of the next high tide. The tidal ranges here are amongst the largest in the world. It was from this old harbour that many of the old Guernsey families sailed forth to pioneer many of the far-flung settlements around the world, during the last century.

A ridge of high pressure has been lying dormant over the Island for the whole of the past week, creating hot sweaty days and humid uncomfortable nights. The lack of any breeze this morning suggests a repetition of yesterday, but it is at this hour that one can enjoy the most comfortable period of the whole twenty-four – a time to luxuriate in relative coolness. The dark shadows of the High Street lay deserted, and it would be a few more hours before the ferry arrived from England, bringing out the newspapers and mail.

High above, the stars begin to melt away, as the eastern sky morphs from indigo to blue. The stillness is suddenly disturbed by the first contributions towards the dawn chorus, as birdsong quickly fills the air with avian pleasure. Flying high above the harbour, a lone black back gull glides with its wings spread wide, soaring across the rooftops on an inland sortie. The bird's head moves lazily left and right, searching for the edible anything that would provide breakfast.

On the northern fringes of town, La Vrangue winds its way up from Le Grand Bouet, a narrow road which rises steadily up towards the Island interior off Les

Banques. This road is a turn off from the St Sampson coastal road that provides travellers heading south with a viable alternative to going through Town. Towards the top of the climb travellers pass a tiny hamlet, standing off to the left, almost hidden amongst the trees. Closer inspection of this vegetation reveals the symmetry of grey slate rooftops, broken only by the up-thrust of red brick chimneys. It is a small terrace of four cottages surrounded by a stand of verdant oaks. Built long ago before permanency preceded profit, these dwellings are already over a century old. The houses face onto a granite culvert, a concrete monstrosity that runs down from the top part of town. Its prime purpose is to drain the rainwater from those upper reaches, which is deposited into a large stone trough. This water supplies the domestic needs of those who dwell here, but a well provides their drinking water. At one end there is an overspill which carries the excess water away towards the roadside gutter, from where it can freely run down towards the coast. During this recent dry spell, the supply has dwindled dramatically.

Ranged in front of each house there lies finely tended garden plots, each with a varied selection of sprouting vegetables. The meagre water supply from the trough has been keeping them alive. This emergent summer bounty is arranged in regimental lines, and will supply essential sustenance to all the incumbent families. The distinct lack of any visible weeds bears testament to all the hard work that had been invested.

At the far end of these houses there stands an apple orchard, creating a division between the end of the terrace and other market garden businesses beyond. At the rear of each house, there are more plots that run out towards a wooded copse of oak and ash. Lines of stout poles rise up from the dark soil, each forming an inverted V, the tops securely tied at the apex by ginger coloured string. Already the winding tendrils of the runner beans are racing to be the first to propagate. These four dwellings are known collectively as the Torode Cottages.

The black back gull dives, swooping low, its threatening menace evoking an instant response from the rookery that adorns the top branches of the oak trees. The birds caw loudly in alarm – corvid klaxons that destroy the morning peace. Lying directly beneath the trees, there stands a large chicken coop, where a rooster, seemingly taking the cacophony as a personal affront, pompously marches out from his wooden dwelling to belatedly announce sunrise.

Lying up in his bedroom, the sudden blast of noise causes a young man to open his eyes wide. He rises immediately, making his way over towards the window. Not thirty yards from where the proud cock stands in the early dawn light he can see a vixen, moving through the shadowed trees as she stealthily darts back towards her den in the woods with a rabbit dangling from the corner of her jaws. Her cubs will eat well.

With her disappearance, the young man watches as the hens begin to emerge from the coop, filing out in matronly strides in response to the cockerel's reveille. The birds spread out and begin scratching at the dirt, their beaks incessantly stabbing at unseen titbits on the ground.

Far above him, the gull begins to climb ever higher on an unseen up-draught, rising far above the gentle hillside forming this part of the town. Sensing its destiny, the bird catches sight of the sea as it levels, and turning begins a slow glide back down towards the harbour. Years of experience have told this ocean wanderer that the fishermen would soon be returning to the harbour from their night out fishing out in the sound, and once the filleting begins on the quayside, there would be pickings a plenty.

Out beyond the ramparts of Castle Cornet, the upper arc of the sun has already breached the dark undulations that is the Cherbourg peninsula, as it begins to illuminate the smaller rocky islets. Around the orchard, the warming rays reflect off the hundreds of dew laden situated amongst the darker recesses of the ditches and hedgerows beyond the orchard. Steamy white mists can be seen rising from the dew laden grass, denoting the onset of the evaporation process.

Fully awake now, for the fourteen-year-old George Torode this is easily the best part of the day. He had lying semi-conscious for over an hour, watching the slowly changing shadowy invasion moving cross the indentations on his distempered ceiling until the cock-crow finally provided him with the impetus to rise. He is extremely careful not to make a noise, because he can hear the soporific breathing of his young brother in the other bed. He gathers up his clothes and tip-toes towards the door.

Another raucous burst from the cockerel made him jump, and spurred his movements. Emerging out onto the landing, he could hear rhythmic snoring through his parents' bedroom door, as he approached the top of the stairs. Feeling confident that he had not woken anyone, he carefully made his way down the bare wooden staircase.

With the disappearance of the gull, the consternation of the angry corvids quickly subsided, allowing him the pleasure of listening to the natural wonder of the dawn chorus. He was proud of the fact that he could recognise quite a few of their calls. He could hear the lilting warble of the robin, as it vied with the rich throaty bliss of a blackbird in full performance.

At the bottom of the staircase, he looked out through the window next to the back door and he could actually see the blackbird that was singing. It was sitting atop the runner bean poles. Although they do not sing all the year round, these birds live on Guernsey all year round.

His sole attire was a pair of underpants, because last night had been far too hot for pyjamas. He was carrying the rest of his clothes in a confused bundle. He walked through the door into the long room that served as their kitchen and dining room. Dumping them down on the seat of a wooden chair, he walked towards the front door, clicking the latch. His legs rose high as he walked barefoot out along the brick path. They were very cold under his feet as headed out towards the stone trough.

All through this spring the weather had been unusually dry, and he thought and it was high time that they had a decent rain-storm, as the plants that he and his father so carefully tended were starting to need of a good drink.

He stretched his arm over towards the wooden box, fingers grasping for the cake of soap. His father made this tray especially for the family bath nights, where he and his siblings would be washed before bedtime. It had a small slanting roof, which prevented the soap from being dissolved by the rain, when it did come. The bar was an unattractive, rough-hewn lump, that his father had made by boiling the discarded fat obtained from the local butcher to produce a tallow, which he then blended with salt, a dash of lavender oil and liberal amount of carbolic acid. He poured the resultant mixture into a long rectangular mould where he allowed it to set hard. When more was needed, he would get out his pruning knife and simply cut off another lump. George had carefully watched the whole process from start to finish, and now felt sure that he could turn out some decent soap, should he ever be asked to do so.

Standing on the cold flagstones surrounding the trough, he splashed his face with water, rubbing the carbolic bar around his neck and behind his ears. Wetting his hair, he rubbed hard as he lathered the soap into it, his fingers massaging his scalp. The coolness of the morning air against his wet skin made him shiver. He had to lean well down into the trough to dunk his head into the water, rinsing out all the bubbles from his hair, and re-emerging he let out a loud gasp. His eyes began to sting, but another splash quickly cleared them. He reached out blindly for the towel, and grabbing it, he quickly used its coarse fibres to massage his skin back to life.

He returned to the long room and began to dress, donning his father's old short sleeved collarless shirt. His father had bought a new one last April for the Easter Church service, and George, being the next in line, had inherited his old one. He had worn it every day since to show the world that he was approaching maturity, with the exception of the once a week, when his Mother wrenched it from his upper body to include it in the family laundry.

The wearing of his father's shirt, along with him being the eldest of his siblings made George feel very grown up. It was the first hand-me-down that he had ever received from an adult, and in his mind it provided the irrefutable proof that he was edging towards manhood. The new hair growth around his genitals convinced him that the foolish pursuits of boyhood would soon be a thing of the past. The cotton fabric flopped loosely over his wiry frame, the hem almost reaching down to his knees. It looked more like a dress than a shirt. After having washed, he was quick to notice the musty body smell emanating from the material – the result of him sweating in yesterday's heat, as he had toiled in the garden. He still wore short trousers, but then so did most of the boys of his age. It was only the sons of the affluent farmers and shopkeepers in town, who wore the long flannels to school. George didn't mind, as shorts were more comfortable at this time of the year. They were grossly misnamed however, because they reached down below his knees, but they were still better than long trousers.

Last Christmas he had received the best present of his life – his first ever pair of long trousers. They were now his best and strictly reserved for Church on Sundays, baptisms, weddings and funerals. Even on those solemn occasions, he was never allowed to run out and play in them.

As a direct result of him wearing shorts, his legs were firm and deeply tanned, the skin looking like the stretched leather of his father's fireside chair. Wire tight tendons stretched as he raised each leg high to step into them. Buttoning up the fly, he looked down through the gap between his tummy and the waistband, where he could see both of his feet. So, there was no struggle when he tucked the shirt in and pushed the material deep down below his hips. A pair of grey webbing braces prevented them falling about his ankles. He treasured these braces, as they had once belonged to his great grandfather, who had died of mal de coeur just five years before his birth. His father told him some wonderful affectionate stories about the old man, and now these braces provided him with the only tangible link to his departed ancestor. His father had told him that the old man had worked as a forgeron (blacksmith) down in the parish of St Martin for most of his life, and George could see from the glint his father's eyes, that he was proud of him. His son, George's grandfather, had died at the early age of just thirty-nine when he had been killed in an accident up at the quarry and the old man was drawn back out of retirement to help bring up his family.

His father, George Samuel Torode now worked as a master Stone Mason at the same Island quarry where his father had died, and had been doing so from the age of ten, when he was taken on as an apprentice stone-cracker, gradually worked his way up.

George used his thumbs to adjust the straps on his braces, positioning them comfortably on his shoulders. They were attached by buttons of varying sizes; not exactly fashionable, but preventing any embarrassment. He hopped on one foot, as he pulled on his polished hob-nailed boots, his toes curling involuntarily as they met the cold unyielding leather interior. Kneeling, he made short work of tying the leather laces.

Finished, and he peered into the mirror, checking his toilet and flicking his hair into some form of semblance. Its dampness from his wash prevented him achieving anything near perfection. It was not ideal, but it would do, he decided. After all, he was not going to meet anyone of importance who would be likely to report any discrepancy to his mother.

Feeling reassured, George made his way towards the back door. If his mother were up, he knew that she would have called him back and would have made him comb his hair properly. A sudden pang of guilt made him stop, and partly out of duty to her, and partly from knowing deep down he should have done it properly in the first place, he hastily ran his fingers through his fair wavy locks once more – honour satisfied! That would have to do, he thought!

Outside it was pleasantly cool, but in the darker shadows it was quite cold and he shivered involuntarily walking in the darkened lee of the house, as he made his way out towards the garden shed. On emerging back into the first rays of the sun at the end of the garden, he immediately felt its warming kiss against his chilled skin. It was a long back garden, nearly fifty yards in length and was already showing the promise for all the hours of hard labour that he and his father had invested into its preparation and planting. He knew that in a month or two the family would be enjoying the freshest of salads for their evening meals, but was he also aware that constant vigilance would be required against the unwanted attention of the birds, slugs and aphids. Already the blackbirds could be seen hopping across the newly dug earth, between rows of newly planted lettuce, ever hopeful of a big juicy worm. He really liked blackbirds.

On reaching the wooden shed, a ramshackle construction badly in need of renovation, he heaved and tugged at the heavy door. The metal hinges had long since rusted away, still awaiting the fitting of new ones, as promised by his father. Old frayed lengths of rope had been tied in place of the metal, to provide a pivoting point. He pulled it open, the bottom edge carving a perfect arc in the dust at the entrance. Inside, George began his search. The interior smelled like a mixture of turpentine and sawdust, blended with the resinous air of varnish, but there was an omnipresent mustiness in the air, that hinted at an undetected dampness. He had a rough idea where the object of his quest lay, and headed straight for the spot. Cobwebs brushed across his hair as he moved forward, the damp smell growing stronger as he passed a stack of old Hessian sacks. In trying to avoid them, he bumped into a badly rusty scythe, which fell from its hanging nail, clattering down onto the dirt floor. He coughed in the disturbed dusty air as he began to sort through a heap of old coats, newspapers, overalls, and leather aprons until at last he could see the canvas haversack that he was looking for. It was just out of reach.

His father had told him that it was the very same one that he had worn during the Boer War, whilst was serving with a mobile shore battery from *HMS Juno* of the Royal Navy. His father said that he, as a Guernsey-man, had used the old Island battle cry of Diex Aix (God be with us) when they went into action. It was the same as the one that Guillaume le Batard had used before his victory at the Battle of Hastings. A lot of the Islanders had formed part of his army.

Reaching through another clinging veil of cobwebs, long since abandoned by their creator, he gave another choking cough as the dust began to tickle the back of his throat. Adjusting his position, he finally reached down and claimed his prize. He gave it a good bang against the side of the bench to remove the desiccated debris from all those webs; the husks of woodlice and other insect detritus rained down towards the floor. Triumphantly he slung it across his shoulders, quick to make a slight adjustment to the straps. His chest expanded as he took a deep breath, feeling like one of the King's soldiers who was about to begin a patrol of the Khyber Pass, or face an onslaught from the Zulu hoards. He ducked down through the low doorway of the shed, and with his shoulders pulled back in a military manner, he swung his arms as he marched back towards the house.

On reaching the back door, he stepped back into the scullery, picking up his sandwiches from the table, which his mother had carefully wrapped in yesterday's newspaper. There was one round of sliced boiled egg and another containing some dark preserve. He stuck his finger into the sticky spread and licked it with relish. Mmm... Blackcurrant Jam – his favourite! There was another boiled egg still in its shell. More than enough!

Fitting the neatly folded parcel snugly into the rucksack, he filled an empty stone cider jar with fresh water and rammed home the cork stopper, placing it carefully beside the wrapped bread. Going outside once more, he went around into the wooden larder, which stood outside on the north wall and picked out an onion and a small slab of cheese before returning to the kitchen. Glancing up at the clock on the mantelpiece above the fireplace, he saw that it was ten minutes to five.

The other two had better be ready, he mused; it was a long walk down to the cliffs, and he didn't feel like hanging about waiting for them.

Just outside the back door, as if trying to make amends for his earlier negligence, again the rooster loudly announced the hour which served to provoke the rooks in the tree tops into another eruption of cawing. Ornithological mayhem reigned once more, just as George finally walked out the front door and down the garden path. Raising the latch on the wrought iron gate, its rusty hinges moaned soulfully as he passed through. His grandfather had made this gate in his very own forge long before he had been born. There was a metallic clank as the latch dropped into its slot, and he gave it a slight push with his backside to confirm it was shut.

Looking up, there was not even a wisp of a white cloud in the sky as he set off.

There were now a full flock of gulls circling high overhead. Not black backs this time, he knew that these were herring gulls from the red spot on their beaks as their raucous plaintive cries evoked images of the sea, which is to be his eventual destination on this glorious morning.

As the distance from his home increased, so the tree-top mayhem from the rooks gradually faded as he walked up the Vrangue towards the crest of the hill. Here it turned off into a lane lined with long grass, mosses, and edged on each side by low granite stone walls. An occasional house stood sedately back off the lane, each possessing a well-tended garden providing proof of occupation. After half a mile the lane began to narrow into track with two dried rutted lines of compacted grit running parallel to the central line of thick lush grass. Dew glistened on the tufts, reflecting the sun's rays, dazzling any casual observer. More lush greenness erupted from the side ditches, where the steam vapours rose, climbing lazily skyward before disappearing as the sun's rays ate them. The moss-capped walls looked soft and spongy, whilst out in the fields beyond, there was a kaleidoscope of spring flowers opening to ingest the early morning energy.

A little further along the lane he saw some tall trees that cast elongated shadows across the path. Walking into those shadows beneath the mighty oaks, he could see a sprinkling by bright pools of mottled light splashed across the track. On either side the low walls gave way to earthen banks that guarded some pleasing white and pink blossom of an apple orchard. The air became filled with a scented aroma. Looking up, he could just see a perfect blue through the canopy leaves, knowing that later today on his return, those same branches would provide a welcome parasol against the heat.

George was feeling on top of the world and he kicked a stone enthusiastically, watching its erratic passage, as it bounced along the path ahead of him. Today was going to be just perfect.

This month had begun hot and sunny, but due to the lack of rain, it was beginning to cause some concern on the Island. It had touched ninety degrees on the mercury thermometer in the local store yesterday, and George had not tarried there too long between his deliveries. He had a job there in the afternoons after school, riding on the shop's trade bicycle six days a week for the princely sum of half a crown. Not that he ever saw any of the money. Every Friday his mother was waiting for him when he arrived home, immediately claiming the fruit of his labour as his contribution towards the family household budget. There were other advantages though – like his being free on a glorious morning such as this. Today being Sunday, his Mother had reluctantly allowed him to miss the church service, so that he could go off on his adventure with his friends. His father had been against the idea at first, but his mother had words with him, which had changed his mind. He had not mentioned exactly where they were going as she had made his sandwiches, trusting him to get up and get himself ready. Her faith in his abilities had made George feel quite adult.

After twenty minutes he had reached the carrefour (crossroads) at Croix de Ballieul (Bailiff's Cross), and turned right to set off down the long slow descent that would eventually take him to St Andrews Church. The church itself was set in a shallow dell, with the banks on each side covered by masses of spring flowers. Pink campion vied with the orange of the dandelions, white cow parsley, along with the deep blue of the last bluebells, with a light yellow of speedwell, bringing a bright pallet of colour to the dissolving shadows.

He walked through the village of St Andrews, and noted that many of the residents here had planted their gardens with flowers instead of vegetables. He had learned a lot about horticulture since he had been helping his father prepare and plant their own gardens. Many of these village gardens had tied bunches of early flowers for sale, bursting out from the rim of a half-filled pottery jug standing on small tables at the roadside, some were positioned on a tray on the top of their walls. People were entrusted to leave some money in the honesty box if they took them away. This area of the Island was particularly noted for its beautiful flora.

As the village road dropped down further towards the church, he could see his two friends waiting by the stone wall, near the lych-gate. Soft moss crowned the granite walls of the churchyard that encompassed a flotilla of gravestones. At the end of the nave there stood a square bell tower surmounted by a low pyramid spire. It was known locally as St Andrews of the Sloping Apple Orchard.

Ahead of him, the two boys had not noticed his approach, as both leaned back lazily against the wall. One of them was reading the newsprint in which his sandwiches had been wrapped, and the other was actually engaged in sampling his lunch! Both of them were dressed casually like George, and he could see that they were carrying more equipment for their joint venture. The taller of the two had a coiled length of line tied neatly to the securing strap of his bag, while the other had a larger bag.

"Mornin' George," mumbled Arthur Collenette, through a mouthful of his sandwich, using his rear end to push himself free of the wall.

"Mornin' Arthur," he replied. Then speaking to the other boy, he said, "Mornin' Matt."

The third youth, a pimply boy whose pink cheeks provided the combat arena for a severe case of acne, grunted with his head still bowed over the newsprint.

"What's that you're reading then, eh?" asked George.

"The Germans are building more battleships again, George. My grandfather says that there will be a war if they don't stop trying to build a bigger navy than ours," he replied.

George had heard about the arms race, but was certain that the Germans would prove to be no match for the Royal Navy. Last year there had been some of the elder lads from their own school, who had travelled over to join up. George knew that it provided them with a steady and secure job, whereby staying here on the Island only made one's future prospects of work more precarious. Most young men, if not being apprenticed under their father, or going over to England to join the navy only had a choice of going to the quarry, or becoming an agricultural labourer. The thought of any form of conflict seemed far too remote on such an idyllic day as this, so the notion was quickly dismissed from their minds.

"Where's it to be then, eh?" asked George. "Shall we find somewhere along the south cliffs, Pleinmont Point, or maybe go around the point into Rocquaine Bay?"

"Pleinmont Point," said Matthew Marquand, rather too quickly. "My uncle was fishing down there yesterday, and he said it was swarming with all kinds of seabirds."

"Then that is where we shall go," said George decisively.

These two boys were his best friends. Well, Matthew Marquand was actually his best friend, but although Arthur always followed them around. George secretly held several concerns regarding him. He was a strange lad, who just seemed to turn up uninvited in everything he and Matthew did together. George did not mind too much, but thought it a bit rude that he never actually asked. One misgiving that he held against Arthur was that he was not always a loyal friend. He was a rather good-looking lad with fair wavy hair, but at school he never supported Matthew and George whenever trouble had loomed. Instead of him backing them up when they found themselves in trouble, he had stood back and let them face wrath of their teacher, when a little white lie would have saved them both. He always seemed to take the side of authority, even at the expense of placing his so-called friends in deep trouble. George had thought him to be too honest at first – there were boys with strong convictions who were like that – but he soon realised that a true friend would have stood behind them. George had not trusted him much after that incident, especially as he and Matthew had ended up being caned. It appeared to George that Arthur needed them, more than they needed Arthur. His attachment was more accepted than asked for, and as the two friends never seemed to object to his presence, so Arthur continued on towards full inclusion within their clique.

George had known Matthew Marquand all of his life. Their mothers were good friends. The boys sat next to each other at the same desk during lessons within old Mr Jeffries class at school. The elderly master had tried to split them up once, but the resultant rebellious behaviour, with the disruption to the class had made him revise his decision for the sake of peace. That had been the first time that Arthur had been seated on the same bench as them, and seemed to assume that it gave him licence for inclusion into their friendship.

Arthur Collenette lived over on the western fringe of St Peter Port, on Les Rohas de Haut in the parish of St Andrews. Although it was not that far from George's house, it was a little out of his way, and so they had arranged to make their way individually towards this meeting point.

Arthur had not known his father. He had been killed by a sniper's bullet at Spion Kop during the Boer War, leaving his mother struggling valiantly to bring him up single handed. She was a woman known throughout the community for her hard work ethic. Maybe it was the lack of male supervision that caused her to indulged his every need, selflessly trying to meet his ceaseless demands.

Another of the main reasons that George had doubts about Arthur, came when he began displaying an irrational jealousy after Mrs Collenette had recently remarried. Arthur had ranted and raved, displaying nothing but hated towards his new stepfather. It seemed irrational, and something that George had found hard to understand. He had acted like a spoilt child.

Mr Henry Bichard was a gently spoken man, a very likeable person who worked very hard at Best's Brickfield in St Andrews. After his marriage to Mrs Collenette, he always appeared to be full of good intent towards his stepson. George thought that he certainly did not deserve to be treated the way he was by Arthur. The man tried hard to meet all of his needs, in a thankless attempt to cement a bond between the two of them. The financial fruit from his labour was poured into the Collenette household, which certainly put an end to the years of hardship. He had been the first new man in Mrs Collenette's life since she had been widowed all those years before. They had met at a spring church social evening just over a year ago, and after a decent interval of courtship, they had married last Christmas. She seemed extremely pleased with her new husband, and he had been more than happy to take on her son as his own. However, he quickly found that his stepson extremely resentful and difficult young man. Arthur remained defiant, adamant that he would have none of it. He had been totally unwilling to make any compromise with the usurper of his mother's affections. His hatred had grown worse over recent months and George was getting tired of hearing of his incessant tirades against the man. He inwardly became sure that Arthur was becoming obsessional, and it created an uneasiness within him. He was sure that no good would come of it.

Matthew Marquand's early life history had been much the same as Arthur's. His mother was a teacher, who ran a small private school that stood behind Roseland House. As a direct result of his mother's fine education, Matthew was easily the brightest of the three of them here today. Never one to boast, he was always ready to assist his two friends with their lessons. A quiet unassuming lad, whom some would say was easily led. His father had been lost at sea in a storm when his fishing boat had floundered in treacherous weather just three years beforehand. His mother contained her grief by working hard and by always being busy, and as a result Matthew had learned how to look after himself. He did have an elder brother who was always out at work for long hours to support the family, and as a consequence he hardly ever saw him. So, he was thankful for the friendship of his two companions to fill his lonely life. Although Arthur was the odd one out, the three had worked through their differences to become companions, forming a tight unshakable camaraderie that is common amongst young adolescents.

As they walked through the fields on this particular early May morning, the early brightness quickly developed into heat, and their initial carefree gait quickly faded into a determined trudge. They made their way along the dusty roads and leafy lanes that led them ever south-westward, squeezing between the parishes of St Saviour, Forest, and St Pierre du Bois. They knew the shortcuts and the edge of a farmer's field, or going through a hedgerow failed to prevent their progress. Next came the parish of Torteval, where they could see the church with its round tower and tall spire. They began clambering over stone walls, heading towards the high ground that marked the southern cliffs. The climb tested their leg muscles before eventually emerging out onto the cliff-top track. Sweat beaded their foreheads, as the sun climbed ever higher towards its noon zenith.

The three of them stopped for a breather, sat down on the grass and looked out over the wave motion. Great mounds of liquid heading in from the wide expanse of the Atlantic. These rocky granite cliffs, had borne the brunt of many thousands of storms over the centuries, battering the Island during the winter months. Even in today's fine weather there was some white water at the base of the cliff as the waves lined up to self-destruct against them. These waves were not as high or as powerful as those in the storms, but they still possessed enough force to cause a lot of spray.

"It really is a great day, isn't it?" said Arthur. "Three Guernsey-men off on an adventure."

"That isn't exactly true, Arthur. Your name has only been here on the Island since the 1600s, when the Huguenots arrived here, having fled here from nasty old Louis the fourteenth and the Edict of Nantes. My family name has been here since the Vikings settled here in the 900s. So, its two Guernsey-men and one recent immigrant off on an adventure."

Arthur grunted, not liking George's reasoning, but knowing that he could not argue the point. It had been a long walk, but after just a couple of minutes rest they stood and started off westward. It was not long before they could see the Mont Herault Watch House standing bleak and alone on the cliff-top in the distance. Their destination was getting closer, and they increased their strides with renewed vigour. Wading through the long grass their shins and boots became soaking wet from the dew, but they did not care, their ultimate objective was almost within sight.

George had been in town yesterday and after he had made his deliveries, he noted that waters in the harbour had been flat calm, but now that they were over here on this side of the Island, the sea today seemed a lot more agitated. There was a light south westerly breeze shaving the surface of those great mounds of energy, coming in from the deep ocean. He always felt small and insignificant when witnessing these majestic monsters, stretching out as far as the eye could see. He inhaled deeply, breathing deep of the ozone laden air. This was certainly going to be a day to remember!

The three boys walked past another of the deep jagged gullies that cut into the cliff face and could feel the pressurised impact of each wave as it hit. The roar was drowned by the incessant cries of the sea birds. Each thump was followed by an exhalation of spray. From then onwards, as they passed by every crack in the cliff face, the boys were totally awed by the sheer majesty of nature. George savoured these moments.

"When you see these waves hitting the rocks, it makes you feel small doesn't it, eh?" he said.

The others nodded – knowing exactly what he was trying to say was true – as each of them staring down into the void in spellbound fascination.

After another few minutes of walking the granite edifice that was Pleinmont Point loomed up before them. This was what they had come for, and their eyes immediately began searching the cliffs for a good spot to start – looking to see where the nesting gulls were most prolific. The cliffs were much steeper here, with their dark granite faces dotted white with bird droppings. These hard-craggy stone faces, with their crenelated crest that were thatched by lush green tufts of grass, they were the age-old monuments to the grandeur of Guernsey.

High above them, a thousand of gulls wheeled in apparent confusion. Some diving, while others hovered, seemingly motionless on the up-draughts, as if they were dangling on a piece of invisible string. Gulls are ruthless greedy birds, always searching for a weakness to take advantage of, or to raid the unguarded nest of a neighbour. Away from the cliffs, other species of seabird were expertly riding the capricious air currents, being blown about like autumnal leaves in a November gale.

They all took deep breaths of the ozone laden air, and their heads began to swim in anticipation of the excitement to come. As the three friends neared the cliffs, they looked out along the vertical faces, quickly spotting the nests they intended to scavenge. Noting that there were several narrow ledges, each providing a home to countless seabirds. George knew that their eggs would make good eating. This was the sole reason why the boys had come here today. If they were as successful as George was hoping they would be, then his family would be living on omelettes for a week. The roar of the sea had disappeared completely, taking second place to the screams of the voracious gulls, terns, kittiwakes and countless other species – the noise was absolutely deafening. This was indeed the nesting season, the time when eggs were laid on these precarious rock ledges and for those with a stout heart and a head for heights, it was a time of plenty. The boys thrilled in expectation.

"Over there, eh!" shouted Matthew, his finger pointing to the thin crack in the sheer cliff face, which tumbled down into the sea at the furthest tip of Pleinmont. "There'll be loads of nests out there, and it doesn't look too hard to get down to them from the top."

Arthur, who had been lagging behind, ran to catch up with them, his eyes turning towards the direction where they were both looking. The sight of the sheer precipice made his heart falter, he hated heights, but not wanting them to see that he was afraid, he smiled and he nodded.

"Looks as good a place as any to start with," he said confidently. "Let's go, eh."

In ten minutes, they had rounded the last small cut in the cliff face and finally walked out onto the grassy summit directly above their target. It was a raised headland that provided breath-taking views over much of the south west of the Island. To the north they could look down on Rocquaine Bay, where the Cup and Saucer, an old defensive position from over a century ago stood in the middle of the bay. They set down their bags and equipment, and began assessing the job in hand.

"OK, who's going first?" asked Arthur, feeling more than reluctant to go himself.

His relief was almost tangible, when he heard George's eager response.

"We will, won't we, Matt?" George looked at his friend, relieved to see his own excitement reflected in the boy's eyes. "You stay up here Arthur, just in case anything should go wrong. Once we've filled the bag, you can throw the rope down to us. We will tie the full bag to it, and then you can haul it up full with eggs. Be careful that you don't hit the rocks, as you draw it upwards."

As his anxiety began to melt, Arthur quickly nodded his acceptance of the plan. Without further ado, the two lads emptied the contents of their rucksacks out onto a single patch of grass. Hopefully, by the time it came to eating their lunch, both of the bags would be filled with eggs. Hitching the first bag over their shoulder, George and Matthew edged themselves carefully towards the edge of the drop. Both boys had already taken the precaution of removing their hobnailed boots, wedging them into a cranny for safety. It would be extremely dangerous trying to find a foothold with those rounded steel nail-heads skidding and slipping against the granite. Barefoot was definitely the safest way.

George led the way and with a backward grin to his friend, he disappeared over the edge of the precipice. He was closely followed by Matthew. Their descent was not as difficult as it looked from above. Both the boy's bare feet seemed to grip firmly on to the protrusions, much like having an extra pair of hands. George recalled the words of advice that had been given him by his uncle. It had been delivered last year on the first occasion that he had been taken gull nesting.

'When you're climbing you must always have three of your four limbs secured. Move only one hand, or a foot at a time, and make sure of its security before relying on it, and only then change to your next hold.'

He had relayed this advice to his friends on the way down through the parishes, and now they each considered themself to be proficient rock climber. Arthur, however still found it very difficult to control his vertigo. George and Matthew were fully aware of his inner fear, but they had never made any detrimental remarks, or tried to demean him in any way.

Thirty feet down from the top from the top edge, the two boys had reached a ledge and were edging their way along. Matthew now led the way as they inched out further towards one of the main groups of nesting sites. Agitated birds began a whirling dance in the air around them, screaming their protest. Their issued threats were an effort to divert the boys away from their obvious intentions. Some of the larger varieties actually stood their ground with their wings spread wide, adopting an aggressive posture, determined to defend their nest against the alien invaders. However, one sweep of Matthew's arm sent them all toppling off the ledge, falling only a few feet before soaring majestically upwards, their wings catching the rising air. Stretching forward, Matthew leaned out towards the first nest.

"Here's the first one," he yelled, holding up an egg in triumph.

He carefully placed it into his bag, before he reached back to claim another. George soon reached his position, and followed his example. Each egg was treated as a prize, something special that was laid in the bag carefully, so as not to crack, or break it. The sheets of newspaper that had been used to wrap their sandwiches, was now being used to cover each layer. before the next load of eggs.

The boys' upper torsos quickly became covered by a salty mist, dampening their skin, but not their spirits. George could feel the heat of the sun beating down against his back and soon felt trickles of sweat ran down to mingle with the moisture. It all became a heady whirl of birds, spray, the incessant scream of the gulls, combined with the roar of the waves. It completely filled their senses. Thrilled by the sheer excitement of the moment, time began to lose any meaning; it flashed past and the contents of the bags soon began to bulge. Finally, it was full enough to be sent up. They had only been on the cliff-face for thirty minutes.

"Throw down the line, Arthur," shouted George. "We've got two bags to come up."

Above them the length of line sailed out over their heads into space, until it reached its full length, then falling back down to rest against the rock – just ten feet from them. George was the nearest to it, and edging carefully back along the narrow ledge, he claimed it, tying the end to their bulging bag.

"OK Arthur, haul away. One bag coming up – be careful, eh!" he called. "We don't want all our hard work being smashed against the cliff."

Slowly the bag jerked its way upwards above their heads, before finally disappearing from view. The line quickly reappeared, tied to the other empty bag. Over the course of the next forty-five minutes another full bag was sent up, which made the boys decide that it was time for a break. They began climbing upwards, following the last rucksack as it rose out of sight, giving each other a satisfied grin.

"We've done well," said Arthur as they appeared, his arm sweeping across the array of eggs nestling on the grass behind him.

"I hope you've been keeping a good look out on those big gulls, Arthur. Coz they'll pop in and steal the eggs while you're not looking," George warned.

They brushed the wetness from their clothes, getting back ten yards from the cliff edge, moving over on to the softness of the drier grass.

"After we 'ave 'ad something to eat, 'e will head off home, eh," George said, with his stomach grumbling from the lack of a proper breakfast.

The boys settled themselves down, and George and Matthew took long swigs from their water bottles. Arthur had eaten his sandwiches before they had set off. Matthew had eaten one of his, and George had taken a good bite out of one as well. As they lay sprawled out across the grass, Matthew and George reached over and grabbed what was left of their lunch from the grass. The sheets of newspaper that they had been wrapped in, were now being used to now protect the eggs. The two of them began to munch ravenously, as Arthur sat apart, a look of envy in his eyes.

A shadow swept over them. Looking up the sky was beginning to show a significant gathering of cloud, the first they had seen all of this week. Despite the sudden gloom, the air temperatures remained high. It was beautiful spot, being perched up there on the cliff-top, but there was no shelter, or trees, especially when the sun was radiating down at full power.

Having finally finished his sandwiches, George stood up and looked both ways along the cliff-top path. There was no one in sight in either direction, so he removed his shorts and the others followed suit. To feel the warming kiss of the sun's rays on their already tanned bodies was absolute bliss. Despite the early season, they had gone swimming a week ago in the almost deserted bathing cove at Fermaine Bay. It was well hidden, and could only be reached by a narrow winding path that twisted its way down the steep hillside. There was a hotel half way down the steep track, but it stood back amongst the trees and very few of the guests ever ventured right the way down to the beach. There on that hidden beach they could go out into the placid water completely naked and after their swim they could lay back on the rocks to let the sun's rays dry them. It was so different around this part of the Island. Here the sea would pick you up and dash you against the rocks like a piece of driftwood.

The distant hoot of a ship's siren attracted their attention, their eyes searching the line of the horizon. Far off to the south-east, Matthew spotted the tiny silhouette of the daily steam-packet. A pall of thick black smoke belched from a slender cork-tip funnel, curling away over towards the French mainland on the light south-westerly breeze. It was on its regular run from St Helier, on the Island of Jersey, heading up towards St Peter Port, before then it then sailed back across the English Channel to Weymouth in Dorset. Faintly smudging the horizon, just beyond the ship, they could see the faintest tip of Jersey. The ship brought out the mail, supplies for the shops, as well as passengers. When it left St Peter Port later that day it would be laden with fruit, flowers, and vegetables to be despatched on the first train up to the Covent Garden Market for sale in London tomorrow morning. They had to raise their voices to be heard above the incessant shrieks from the birds all about them.

"One day I'll be on that ship going over to England," declared George confidently, enjoying the expressions of incredulity on the faces of his friends that his words evoked.

"Why should you want to go over there then, George?" enquired Matthew, as hardly anyone ever left the Island more than once, or just maybe twice in their whole lifetime. So crossing the Channel would be a major event.

"Because I've decided to go over and join the Royal Navy when I leave school. You have to go over to the mainland to do your training," said George looking at the steamer, fully aware of their amazed expressions.

It was true that many of the Islanders never left Guernsey, although during the last century many of the Island families emigrated, starting new lives out in the far-flung outposts of the Empire around the world. So, in him declaring his intention to leave the Island so early in life, it was definitely something to be admired. His friends looked at him enviously, as neither had yet made any decision about their future, or what career they would follow. Arthur was rather lazy and had not given the prospect of any form of employment a single thought. Most of the young men on the Island followed their father into his profession, but George had no intention of slaving away in the stone quarry up in the parish of Vale. He often took his father his packed lunch up to him, and would inwardly cringe when he saw how hard it was to cut out just one of those huge granite blocks from the wall of granite. The men all sweated profusely, even in the coldest of weather. Each man who worked there was at the peak of physical fitness, their muscular bodies displaying the power within, but that peak would quickly decline by their mid-thirties. The constant hard toil took a tremendous toll on those muscles and bones, and was responsible for the numerous accidents. Very few quarrymen lived beyond the age of sixty years. He remembered his father telling him about his grandfather, also named George Torode, who had died in one of those accidents aged just 38 years, leaving his grandmother alone to bring up five children. If it had not been for the compassion of his great grandfather Daniel Torode, the family would have ended up in the workhouse. Instead of enjoying a well-earned retirement from his forge, the old man had worked on into old age to provide for the family of his son. Old Daniel Torode had died in 1893, just three years before George had been born. His self-sacrifice had saved the family from destitution.

George turned to the others and asked them to think about what they would like to do when they left school. Strangely enough, and much to George's surprise, Arthur said that he expected to be employed at the stone-quarry. He added that working as an agricultural labourer, like his stepfather on one of the small farms, was not for the life for him. He wanted a man's job. George knew for a fact that he had never been up there, and was completely ignorant of the hardships endured by the men who worked there. Matthew on the other hand, said that it was his ambition to be a teacher, just like his mother. He was certainly intelligent enough to do so, he thought.

Having finished their lunch, the two boys laid back and stared up into the blueness of the sky between the increasing cloud cover. More gulls crossed the void as they circled above their heads, staring down expectantly, almost cannibalistically, eying the clutch of eggs that lay between them. The more daring tried a tentative swoop down on any of the discarded tit-bits of bread from the sandwiches, but they had to be extra quick to beat the hungry Arthur!

"Do you want to have a go over on the cliff, Arthur?" George asked, with the slightest trace of a smile at the corner of his mouth. "I noticed that two of the eggs are cracked and will need replacing."

"You know I don't like heights, George. I'll stay up here if you don't mind," he replied, embarrassed at having to admit the fact publicly.

George nodded. "No problem, Arthur," he said. "Matt and I will go over once more."

In an attempt to change the subject, Arthur turned his attention towards Matthew.

"What did your Ma put in your sandwiches today, eh?" he asked.

"Cold sausage and mustard," Matthew answered proudly, knowing that he had been the only one with a sandwich containing any form of meat.

"Yeh, and we know where that comes from, don't we, eh?" jeered Arthur, his voice taking on a nasty sarcastic tone.

It was generally known around the town, that the local butcher was sweet on Matthew's mother, and there was seldom a day when Matthew did not have meat for his lunch. However, he was fiercely protective of her reputation, and would not have a thing said against her.

"You take back that remark, Arthur Collenette, or you will get a punch in the mouth," he said, scrambling to his feet.

A sudden panic stabbed Arthur. The thought of any pain made him quiver. The affair was common knowledge for goodness sake! Why was Matt acting so aggressively? The thought of being punched sent another shiver of dread through him. He began to panic, his brain trying to think of a way out of the situation. He needed to think of a way to avoid conflict which will also enable him to save face. How on earth was he going to bluff his way out of this predicament? Not thinking, he resorted to bluffing.

"Do you think that you're big enough to give me one then, Matthew, eh?" he said, wishing immediately that he had not.

"Get up and you'll soon find out," said the smaller of the two, rising to his feet with his fists already held up in a pugilistic stance.

George raised himself up on his elbows to watch the two of them with some amusement. He was always game for a bit of horseplay. Young Matthew might not be so big height-wise, but he could look after himself all right. This time Arthur had opened his big mouth once too often, and he would either have to take the consequences, or back down and apologise. He popped the last bit of the boiled egg into his mouth and began to watch developments.

Arthur was now very well aware that he had gone too far and was feeling very afraid. He had never been a fighter and could already imagine Matthew's hard knuckles hitting him about the head. The thought terrified him. He hated pain. How on earth could he get out of this without losing any face? If he didn't back down, he knew that he was certain to get hurt. The alternative was to be branded a coward by both of his friends. He was now wishing that he had kept quiet.

As Matthew squared up to him in readiness to fight, Arthur took a deep breath, closed his eyes and launched himself at Matthew's midriff. He had figured that if he could encircle his friend's arms and pin them to his waist, he wouldn't get a thump. Then he could just hang on until Matthew calmed down and saw sense. Unfortunately, as he rushed forward, Matthew was far too quick for him, nimbly side stepping and swinging a well-aimed blow that caught Arthur full on his ear. Almost before the pain had registered in Arthur's brain, Matthew followed it with an upper-cut that sent him sprawling headlong across the grass.

Arthur lay still, taking deep gasping breaths, his senses were reeling, and he could feel a trickle of blood running down from the corner of his lip. His tongue flicked around his mouth, tasting the salty metallic tang of his own blood. As the stars began to clear, he looked up and saw Matthew standing over him, seemingly ready to give him more of the same. Utter panic and desperation now engulfed Arthur. What was he going to do? He looked towards George only to see a broad grin on his face. Then, his eye caught something lying on the ground, and an ugly and malevolent thought flashed through his mind. This was a possible outlet. Both of Matthew's feet were apart, but standing on the length of rope that Arthur had used to haul up the eggs. Arthur's eyes flicked down to it, returning instantly to Matthew's face. This could definitely be his way out? If he managed to grab it and give it a big pull, then Matthew would be sent flying, and that might just be enough for him to gain the advantage. Then it would be honours even, and it would certainly give Matthew a good fright.

Slowly his hand inched out, his fingers surreptitiously encircling the rope. He struck with the speed of a striking cobra, grabbing hold of the rope and yanking it with all his might. Matthew's feet were whipped out from under him, forcing him to stagger backwards, his arms wind-milling in an attempt to regain his balance. The downward slope just behind him only served to increase his backward momentum towards the cliff edge. The rim loomed, swallowing him whole as he disappeared into the void.

George stared wide eyed in momentary disbelief. Suddenly he leapt to his feet and dashed over towards the empty space where Matthew had just been standing. Half sliding, half skidding, he raced down the grassy slope towards the rocky outcrop at the cliff's edge. With his feet resting against the top of the rocks, he craned himself out, almost too afraid find out what he would see if looked down. A hundred feet below him the sea was thrashing itself into frenzy, but he could see no sign of Matthew. He was praying that his friend had missed the rocks, and was down there somewhere having simply fallen into the sea. He began scanning the water for any sign of him – but there was absolutely nothing but the white foaming water. Then he heard a faint cry, just distinguishable above the noise of the waves and guttural cries of the gulls that surrounded him.

"Help! Quick – George, for God's sake. Help me!"

George leaned out as far as he dared, his hands gripping the clumps of grass immediately behind him. He strained forward, leaning over once more and then caught a glimpse of Matthew about twenty feet down the sheer face of the cliff. He could see that his fingers were covered red with blood, but somehow, he had managed to grab hold of a chunk of rock that jutted out from a ledge. As George looked down, assessing the situation, he could see the wide-eyed look of terror etched on his friend's face. Beyond him, he saw that his feet were dangling free in the air, with just the water and rocks far below him. A quick search left and right revealed that there was nowhere that Matthew could swing up to, so he was unable to climb out of his predicament.

George felt the grass roots that he was holding beginning rip beginning to give way, so he eased himself back into a safer position. Immediately he moved closer towards the edge of the drop and without thought for his own safety, he began to climb down as quickly as he could.

"Don't worry, Matt. I'm on my way. You just hang on, I'll get you out of this," he shouted reassuringly, as he descended.

"I can feel this rock is loose and it's starting to give way George. There's nuthin' else I can see that I can grab 'old of. I'll have to stay still and not try to climb, as I can feel it move slightly every time I try," his voice was trembling with fear. George was only ten feet away now and getting ever closer.

"I'll have you back up on top in no time, Matt," his voice soothing, as he tried to hide his mounting anxiety.

He got himself into a position just feet above where Matthew's hand held the rock. Sending his foot out on a mission of discovery, it finally found a tiny ledge and his toes groped for a foothold. His hand was scratched as he reached for a new hand-hold, sending a shower of small stones over the edge, just missing his friend. Ramming his hand into a crack in the rock, his fingers held on tightly as he lowered himself down towards Matthew's extended hand. He was only inches away, but despite him stretching out to his fullest extent, his hand still did not quite reach him. He quickly realised that he would need to get a better foothold that was a lot lower, if he was going to reach Matthew, as looking up at his supporting hand, he could see that his knuckles were white, standing out white against his tanned skin. Using this leverage, he began probing about blindly with his foot until he finally found a small crevasse in the rock wall that would take his weight. He let his full weight down onto it. It held firm, and his fingers sought a new hand hold that would enable him to move his outstretched grip lower. There was another small split in the rock face and plunged his fingers into it, immediately forming a clenched, vice like, grip. Almost crouching now, he extended his free hand down lower towards his friend, realising that he himself was now leaning out over the hundred-foot drop. He was only an inch away from Matthew's hand, and by juggling his position slightly he made sure of his own security. Then he forced his body out into the void to be able to get lower. This time their fingers touched, and very slowly his hand snaked down, his fingers encircling his friend's wrist, until he had a firm grip.

"Can you manage to hang on to the rock with just one hand Matt? If you can, then you will be able to get a hold of my wrist with the other," he heard himself say, amazed that his voice sounded so calm voice. "Once we have a firm grip, I think that I can haul you up. Do you think that you could manage to do that, Matt?"

Matthew started to answer, but his words were masked by the roaring arrival of another crashing wave immediately below him. He slowly released one hand from the hold on the rock, reaching out to clasp the wrist of his would-be rescuer.

"Good Matt. Well done. Now I have your weight, I can haul you up enough for you to grab a new hold. Can you do that Matt?"

Matt grunted once more, but he was unable to get a good grip on George's wrist, and had already released the rock as his other hand sought the safety of George's wrist. He quickly realised that he could not get hold of it, and reached back towards the jutting rock to get a better support. As he re-applied weight, to his horror the rock gave way, falling down into the sea. Matthew screamed in horror as a small avalanche of stones fell towards him, leaving him dangling, with only by George's outstretched arm holding his wrist. The suddenness of the extra weight almost pulled George from the cliff face, but he tightened his own grip on the rock that he was holding. The tremendous force that had suddenly been placed on his shoulders became absolute agony, and he could feel the blood pounding through his veins. His muscles begged for release from the strain they were enduring, and sweat began pouring from his body, running in rivulets down his face and dripping off the tip of his nose. The two boys were welded together, both unable to move, forming a macabre tableau in the moisture laden air. George gazed down into the frightened eyes of his friend. His terrified pleading look was unmistakable. Where was Arthur?

"Arthur! Get down here and help – and bring the rope – QUICK!" George screamed.

There was no answer. He repeated the call, and then again for a third time. He whimpered in frustration, at the lack of response. That stupid bastard caused this situation – where the hell was, he?

Every sinew and muscle strained beyond its limit and then some. George felt frightened as he began to realise that he was not going to be able to hold on to Matthew for very much longer. Where WAS Arthur? He was their only chance.

"There he is!" Matthew shouted from below him. "Right over there on the top cliff path – running – heading east."

George found it difficult to crank his head around far enough, but finally caught a glimpse of Arthur running hell for leather, away from them. Why! He knew that it would be absolutely useless trying to attract his attention in this incessant noise; the distance was far too great.

30

The bloody coward's running for it! thought George disbelievingly. He was leaving them to their fate. Having seen evidence of that fact, George began experiencing real fear, and an ominous dread slowly crept into his mind. He was not strong enough to hold his friend for too much longer, finally realising that Matthew might not get out of this in one piece. If he was going to die, then George decided that he would give everything in his power to prevent it from happening. He would never stop trying.

His brain tried to think of a way that he could make one last ditch attempt that would be enough to save his friend. With his last remnants of strength draining away, he knew that they would have only one chance, two at the very most. He quickly reassessed the situation, and came up with a plan.

"Listen, Matt. I'm gonna try and get you up to this ledge where my feet are, eh. Do you think that you could grab a hold of it, if I pull you up close enough?"

"We've got nothing to lose, George," Matt replied, his voice began to sob with fear. Then, as if suddenly coming to terms with his predicament, he said, "If I don't get out of this in one piece, then please go and tell my Ma that I love her."

George looked down to see tears of realisation welling in his friend's eyes.

"Now that's no way to talk, Matt. You just hang on to my arm nice and tight and we'll be home for tea, just you wait and see," he hoped that his voice sounded more confident than he felt inside.

At that moment George detected a slight flicker of weakness in his friend's grip, quickly realising that Matthew's strength was also starting to falter. Then Matthew's hand slid an inch down his wrist. George tightened his grip on his wrist to compensate, sending a hot pain up his arm that felt like a branding iron.

"Hold on tight now Matt, one last big effort, and we'll have you up here. I will lift you as high as I can, and you grab hold of the ledge that my foot is on. On the count of three and we will both go for it – OK?" said George, knowing that time was rapidly running out for both of them.

"OK," said Matthew, trying to force a grin of confidence. "I'm ready."

"We both go for it on the count of three, Matt," said George.

The boy below him nodded.

He took a long deep breath, filling his lungs with oxygen and mustering all his remaining strength.

"One – Two – THREE," he screamed through his teeth, as his whole body strained with the tremendous effort. Wire-taut tendons were being stretched well beyond their limits. His arm and shoulder muscles bulged like never before. A great groan of physical effort exploded from George's throat. His arm pulled upwards with every ounce of strength that he could muster. Then he could feel one of Matthew's hands groping out frantically for the ledge. There was a sudden pain in his foot, as Matthew's fingernails raked across the bare skin of his ankle in their panic to find a hold – but they had missed the rock ledge.

It was only seconds before all of his power was gone, and despite trying to stop it, slowly his arm began straighten. Matthew's weight was too much for him. He knew that he could not hold his friend up any longer. His whole arm had gone numb and with the lack of feeling he was unable to assess how much pressure he needed to hold his friend's wrist.

Sweat poured from his brow to join his tears of frustration, as he fought against the inevitable. His panting exhalations quickly turned to spray, as his saliva and

31

sweat were panted out into the swirling void below. The attempt had failed and poor Matthew was hanging back down once again.

Looking down George could see that his friend's liquid eyes held the frightened realisation as to what fate had in store for him. His tears were flowing quite freely now. The pleading look had gone, replaced by the certain knowledge that he was living his last moments on earth.

They stayed suspended like that, each knowing that neither had the strength to alter the situation. Their grip was slowly slipping, but there was nothing that either of them could do about it. Suddenly, Matthew's voice became strong and firm, a resentful tone exploded from his mouth.

"George – you make sure that bastard Arthur gets what's comin' to him, eh," sobbed Matthew.

"I promise," George heard himself saying. "I promise you that, Matt."

Then the inevitable happened. Their grip broke, and Matthew's body just seemed to slip away. George's arm was so numb that he did not even feel his hand slip – he just experienced the sudden release from the agonising pressure. One moment his friend was there, and the next he was gone. George stared down unbelievably, watching his friend falling away, getting smaller and smaller as he went. He could still see the terror in his friend's eyes, as he fought against this inevitable conclusion. It seemed an eternity before Matthew hit the rocks below. He didn't bounce. His body just stopped falling, lying very still where he had landed in a grotesque pose, as if he were a discarded doll that had been thrown down in a tantrum. One leg lay at an ugly unnatural angle, and his unseeing eyes were still fixed upwards towards George.

"I promise you, Matt," cried George at the top of his voice, but Matthew was beyond hearing him. Tears were still running down his face and dripping off his nose, carrying his grief straight down towards his friend's broken body.

At that moment another huge foaming wave came crashing into the crack in the rocks and across the rock on which Matthew had landed, sweeping him away. To George looking down it was confusing – one moment he was there, and the next there was nothing – it was so surreal; it was as if Matthew had been wiped away – as if his life had never been.

George's stunned brain wrestled with reality, as he realised that all sounds had disappeared. He could no longer hear the cry of the birds. The waves still came crashing in, but they were silent – he could not hear them. Realising that he was still hanging there on the rock face, everything seemed to have been a bad dream, and all that he would have to do was wake up for this nightmare to end.

He shivered, shaking his head, trying to clear his thoughts, when a stabbing pain in his shoulder reminded him realise that he was not out of danger himself. Looking up he could see that his arm was still holding on to the rock, but everything in his arm had gone completely numb. He could not actually feel if he was gripping the rock or not. He turned his head towards his other hand, which was still hanging down, pointing to the position from where Matthew had just fallen. He clenched his fingers. Sensation slowly began to return with the loss of Matthew's weight, the blood began flowing back, causing an initial stinging tingle in the limb. He tried to move – tentatively grabbing at another hand hold to ease his own body weight from his numbed arm. As soon as he let go a terrible pain flooded through his arm, as the numbness wore off and blood came flooding back. He closed his eyes against the agony, knowing that he would just have to endure it, because at that moment he could not move.

It slowly eased, and with the frail amount of strength he had remaining, George very slowly managed to claw his way back up towards the cliff-top. On reaching the crest he staggered forwards, falling down and flopping over onto his back, and began sobbing uncontrollably. His mind drifted away as everything went black.

When he came to, his body was shivering. He did not know how long he been lying there, but as full consciousness returned, his whole body began to shake uncontrollably, not from the freshening wind, but from coming to terms with what had happened. Complete mental and physical exhaustion drained the last vestiges of his body strength. How could such a beautiful day have ended so tragically? His mind answered his own question as an image of Arthur running along the cliff-top filled his thoughts. Then he lost consciousness once more.

He had no idea as to how long he lain there. A sudden chilling effect from the freshening wind finally brought him back to consciousness. The bright sunshine of that morning had completely disappeared, replaced by threatening dark clouds and increasing winds. The often prayed for break in the hot weather now looked as if it was arriving. The slate grey clouds were dashing across the island from the south-west like mournful spectres of death.

He took a deep breath, forcing himself up to stand on his feet. After a quick search, he eventually found his clothes and boots. His mind began going through the whole terrible series of events once more, before coming to the realisation that he would have to go and inform somebody of what had happened. Matthew's body would need to be recovered from the sea. Quickly dressing, he set out to find the nearest farmhouse to report the incident. He could still feel the tears of loss that were still running freely down his face.

He was still crying as he walked back along the cliff path, a little boy once more, frightened and alone. In trying to recall what exactly had happened, he remembered seeing how Matthew had stood threateningly over Arthur, having just thumped him about the head. The next thing he could remember was Matthew's spinning arms, as he toppled backwards over the edge. How on earth had that happened? Had he tripped? The one absolutely certain thing was the fact that Arthur had run away, leaving them both to die. If he had he stayed and assisted, then Matthew might still be alive. If he had thrown down the rope, then it might have just been possible to have made a rescue. Instead he had run. He had betrayed them. An inner anger seethed inside, and at that moment he felt as if he could kill Arthur. Remembering his promise to Matthew, and he became determined that he would honour that pledge.

Soon he could see the Mont Herault Watch-House perched on the cliff top ahead of him. He knew that it was empty, as it had not been used for many years, but he also knew that there was a farmhouse in the fields not too far beyond it. He would be able to raise the alarm there, and then they would instigate a search for Matthew's body.

As he stepped away from the cliff path, he turned and descended, heading straight towards the farm. After a few paces he could see somebody emerging from the old building, and head up towards him. George felt the relief flooding through his body, and broke into a run to meet the man. It was an old man. He had a lined windswept face encased in white hair, a leathery darkened skin that had experienced a hundred storms. His face screwed as he looked at George with enquiring eyes.

"Help me, please. My friend is dead," cried George.

"Are you Marquand or Torode?" asked the man.

"George Torode," he replied. "It's Matthew Marquand that is dead."

At that, George finally broke down and sank to his knees. He knelt there, his body racked by sobs, his heart releasing his grief for his dead friend. As he cried something in his brain began asking – how did he know our names?

"You'd better come back to the farm, lad. We had your friend here over an hour ago. I've already sent him up to St Andrews for the Constable to organise a search party. I think that you will find yourself in a great deal of trouble young man."

Trouble – why? The old man's words puzzled George, but he let it pass. When they reached the warmth of the farm kitchen, George was handed a hot cup of tea by the farmer's wife. He had not drunk any liquid since his water bottle at lunch time, and it proved to be very welcome. There was a fire in the hearth and the lady led him over to a stool, from where he could feel its warmth. She had clucked, tutted, and made sympathetic noises, but said nothing that was constructive. The farmer left him sitting there, and disappeared outside.

Within the hour the Constable arrived on his bicycle. He was ceremoniously preceded into the kitchen by the farmer, and the two men looked imperiously down at George before sitting down at the table. The policeman told George that he needed to take a statement from him. The farmer's wife had made another pot of tea, and passed over a plate of sandwiches that she had made – but no one felt like eating.

"At least one of you lads has had the presence of mind to report what has taken place. I've already taken a statement from young Collenette, and I understand from him that it was through your stupidity in fighting on top of the cliff that caused your friend to fall over the edge. To go gull nesting on those rock faces was a silly enough thing to do in the first place. It's hard enough to climb out there with safety ropes. You were all asking for trouble." said the Constable.

George could hardly believe what he had just heard. The policeman had made it sound as if Arthur was a hero, and yet it had been Arthur who had started the fight. He tried to protest and to tell what had really happened. He told them how Arthur had deserted them both, and how it was largely responsible for Matthew's death, but the stern stare on the Constable's face told him that he was wasting his time.

"You should be grateful to Arthur Collenette, instead of trying to besmirch his name, young man. He saw you both squabbling on the cliff-top, and actually witnessed Marquand fall to his death. If it can be proved that you pushed him, you will be facing a murder charge. Or at least one of manslaughter," he glared fiercely at George.

George became completely lost for words.

Continuing, the constable said, "There's a boat that is already making its way round the bottom of the island from Rocquaine Bay in an attempt a recovery of young Marquand's body. It is going to be difficult with the weather worsening. Because of your irresponsibility, I now have the unpleasant duty of having to go and inform Matthew Marquand's poor mother that her son is dead. I understand he was her youngest child, and she only buried her husband a while back – poor woman."

This was not good. George had been cast as the villain – by the actual villain. He dropped his head into his hands in frustration.

Later that evening George's father arrived at the farm, having come down on his bicycle to collect his son. They walked all the way home together in the darkening twilight in total silence, and on arrival he was sent straight up to his room. As George lay stretched out on his bed, a crammed series of conflicting emotions flooded his mind. He tried to come to terms with what had happened that afternoon, but the worst thing was the realisation was that he would never see Matthew again, which made him feel sick inside. He recalled that final look of inevitability in his eyes, reappearing every time that he closed his eyes, and prevented him from sleeping. So he began turning his thoughts over and over, trying to think of anything different that he could have done which may have affected the outcome, but took some assurance that he could have done nothing better. He was confident that he had given his all in trying to save his friend. If Arthur had helped them with the rope, the situation would still have been touch and go, but Matthew might very well have been saved. He started seething inside when he thought of all the lies that Arthur had told everybody, making him appear in the worst possible light. The injustice of it all boiled within.

Then he suddenly vision of that rope appeared in his mind, and it brought back the memory of exactly what had happened. It had been Arthur who had pulled the rope from under Matthew's feet. It was Arthur who was definitely the culprit.

Just then he heard heavy deliberate thumping footsteps on the stairs, giving him a feeling of foreboding. He could hear the tinkle of a metal buckle belt being unbuckled. The door to his room slowly opened and the ominous figure of his father loomed over him, with his belt wound around his hand.

George received the thrashing in silence. It wasn't the red welts across his backside and legs that was the cause of his tears, it was the frustration of knowing that a coward like Arthur Collenette had turned the tables on him, and he felt a total impotence of doing anything about it. Nobody was listening to his account. Each cutting lash of the leather across his tender skin branded a hatred for Arthur Collenette, and he knew deep down that it was going last for a lifetime. It should have been Arthur who was receiving this beating. George made a vow that night that he would definitely honour Matthew's last request, and in doing so he would not only avenge his death, but redress the injustice. No matter how long it took, one day he would get even. Arthur was going to pay the price for his cowardice. George learned a very important life lesson that night.

The incident was never spoken of again in the Torode household. No charges were brought against George, but the Coroner at the Inquest delivered a scathing rebuke against him, as Arthur repeated the lies under oath. An unjust verdict of *Misadventure* was brought in. Arthur Collenette had tactfully been moved to another school the day following Matthew's death. Matthew's mother said that she forgave George, but her eyes told him otherwise. In the days that followed, Arthur always kept a safe distance between George and himself, should they by chance bump into each other. George kept his patience, knowing that eventually Arthur would be made to pay his debt to Matthew.

****

There was another occurrence just over two years later, which endorsed George's suspicions about Arthur's true character. Arthur's stepfather was found murdered on the Vale Road on a dark moonless night in the October of 1912. He had been working late and had promised to help a friend move some furniture, but he had failed to arrive. The following morning, his body was discovered by a postman, out on his early round. The back of his skull had been smashed in. From the deep wound, the police thought the murder weapon to be a spade or an axe, and it was very probable that the victim would have been somebody who was known to him. The only comfort was that he would never have known what had hit him. The police suggested that he had known his attacker, because there were no signs of a struggle and he was struck him when his back was turned. The murder caused quite a stir on Island, as crimes of that nature were a rarity. There were no clues as to the assailant's identity, and the only people who knew of his movements that night were his wife and family. Despite an extensive investigation, no one was ever arrested for the crime, as the police could find no leads, or even provide a motive for the murder.

However, for some unknown reason, George had immediately suspected Arthur, aware of the hatred that he bore for his stepfather and having himself been a victim of his fearful resentment that would override sane reason. Lies just rolled off his tongue. George knew that Arthur would never show any signs of guilt for his actions, just as he had never shown any remorse for his desertion of Matthew and himself.

He also knew that it would be useless for him to try to voice his concerns without any actual proof, as he would only be accused of trying to take his revenge on Arthur. He certainly did not want to be the recipient of another beating from his father.

George had attended the man's funeral, and as he and his parents had filed had slowly past Arthur's pew, he had purposely looked at him directly at him. There was not a single tear, or a trace of sadness in evidence. At the graveside George shuddered when he noticed the faintest trace of a smile on his lips, as the coffin was finally laid to rest. Arthur looked across at George with an arrogant sneer, plainly showing that he had thought himself his superior – and the fact that he was untouchable. Later, as they had filed out of the churchyard, Arthur remained impassive as he tended to his grief-stricken mother, but there was something else that George had noticed. He noticed the strange remoteness that filled Arthur's eyes. It was the look of someone who had managed to achieve a clever plan, and had and got away with it. George shuddered – it was a devilish expression, an almost satanic glow of triumph. He remembered seeing that same look on the cliff top at Pleinmont Point, just before Arthur had yanked the rope that had sent Matthew to his doom. From that moment onwards George knew that Arthur Collenette was a murderer, and might well be insane.

Chapter Two

Tuesday 4th of August 1914
in St Peter Port, Guernsey

"Its war!" declared George's father, as he walked in through the front door, waving his newspaper in the air. "We're at war with the Kaiser! He didn't accept the ultimatum that Herbert Asquith had given him. He will pay for his arrogance. You mark my words."

The tall thick set body of the handsome Guernsey-man filled the frame, blocking the view of a glorious evening sunset. George Samuel Torode had just returned home from his day of labour up at the Vale Stone Quarry, but this once in a lifetime piece of news had wiped away any sign of fatigue. It was teatime on the 4th of August 1914, a date that was to be forever ingrained in human history.

His wife Jeanne-Marie Torode nee Allain was about to serve up the evening meal, which she had spent most of the afternoon preparing. She stood at the fire-place, continuously stirring the contents of a huge iron pot. There was the occasional sizzling sound as some water droplets dripped from the rim of the lid down onto the hot metal range, as she held it clear from the utensil. She had six young mouths to feed, and despite the warm summer weather, she had made a large pot of vegetable stew, complete with a squadron of fluffy suet dumplings that floated on top like icebergs in a brown sea.

It had been a good summer so far, and the garden continued to be a good provider, but the only meat that the pot contained had been provided by a sacrificial donation from a rabbit, who had very obligingly stuck its head through the noose of the snare that George had set down by the copse of trees. He had only begun setting traps after noticing that some of the lettuce leaves were being eaten, employing them purely as a defensive tactic. Today, his actions had proved to be beneficial. The welcome addition of the meat would not only provide them all with extra protein, but it also saved some of their precious vegetables for another meal. George and his father had invested a great deal of hard work in protecting the tender shoots from slugs by sprinkling broken egg shells strategically around each plant, and by strategically hanging lengths of string between cleverly placed poles to prevent the birds from eating the raspberries. Pests come in a variety of forms, and any invasion would place their winter supply in jeopardy.

George Samuel left the door and went across to the stone culvert at the front of the house, where he washed his hands, face and arms. He returned and sat down in his favourite chair, and eased off his boots. In his stocking feet he rose and sat down at the head of the table. The children were lined up on each side.

"Bon jour mon Cherie," he said to his wife in Guernseiaise, then changed to English. "I met Patrick De la Rue on my way home. He works in the telegraph office in town," he continued, "He told me that war was officially declared at eleven o'clock this morning, so we have already been at war for nearly seven and a half hours. The Kaiser's taken on more than he can chew this time, eh. They are going to send out the army to Flanders from the mainland. I bet you anything that the Guernsey Militia will be called up, and that they will be sent over to France straight away. It seems strange to have France as our ally doesn't it, eh! There is already a call for more men to join up. Apparently General Kitchener says he wants a hundred thousand men recruited by next month. A hundred thousand men – can you imagine?" he repeated as if the figure was beyond infinity. "You remember General Kitchener! It was him who showed the Fuzzy-Wuzzies and the Boers, and now he will be showing the Germans not to meddle with the British – you just mark my words!"

Jeanne-Marie had been born in France and she resented her husband's derogatory remark about having the French as allies. She could still remember the build up to the Boer War, after all it had only been fifteen years ago for heaven's sake, and now there was another conflict brewing. She had seen how the Guernsey men had queued at the recruiting stations, remembering this same sabre-rattling rhetoric being spoken back then. They had used the same jingoistic words, all full of bravado and excitement to give themselves a false confidence to mask the nervous anticipation of the unknown yet to come. Way back then the conflict had taken place far away – so distant from the Island. South Africa was almost on the other side of the world for heaven's sake. When she had read the reports of the war in the newspaper, it was as if she were reading the d'Guernesiaise printed review of a new theatre production that had taken place here in town. Her English was still not that good. She had been born in Pont Melvez in Brittany and as most people on the Island were bi-lingual, either English or d'Guernesiaise speakers, she had not bothered to learn too much English. She had just enough to get by on, but she was proud of the fact that all of her children could speak both languages fluently. Inwardly she silently doubted her husband's prophecy, but she kept her counsel. During the Cape conflict, just a few thousand Dutch farmers had stood up against the might of the British Empire, and had provided a very good account of them-self. The casualties had been appalling, and she and several more of the young women of St Peter Port, had helped to raise money for the convalescence and rehabilitation of the wounded men, who were constantly being shipped home. Back then it had all seemed to be very dramatic and exciting, but that war had never actually touched their own lives. She was fearful that this time it was might be a lot different – this time it was against the whole of the German and Austro-Hungarian empire, the two biggest countries on the continent of Europe. They were four times as large as Britain in area, and had a far greater population. The Germans were close cousins of the Dutch – weren't they – and those Boers in South Africa came from Holland originally – didn't they? The Kaiser was the cousin of the late Queen – so why was he now threatening Britain? Why did he want to start this war? Even with France on our side, the combined land area of both was less than half the size of Germany. Together with Austria and Hungary militarily, they were formidable. Allied with France, Britain was going up against extremely difficult odds. She had read that the combined armies of the Kaiser were three times the size of the French and British combined. She knew that Russia was allied to France, and that they had already declared war, so that may help and swing things in our favour. Russia's involvement would make the Germans fight on two fronts, but even a fool would quickly realise that it was not going to be the walkover that her husband was predicting. If the Germans showed half the spirit of those Dutch farmers in South Africa, then it was going to be a very bloody affair indeed. Germany was also a much stronger country than South Africa, and this time the conflict would be taking place much closer to home – and that frightened her. She gave an involuntary shudder. Yes, this was going to be much different war, and she felt fearful.

Young George sat beside his mother, and he was rather enjoying the surge of excitement that was coursing through his veins. This was going to be the start of a great big adventure for every man in Britain and the Channel Islands. There was going to be a huge upheaval right across the British Empire as men rose up to stand against this threat. He knew that he too would be leaving his Island home, and the thought of conflict filled him with a need to be part of it, but as he looked across the table at the anguish etched on his mother's face it made him hesitate. She had the look of a woman who was about to lose her men. He hated the thought of doing anything that would hurt his mother, but he just had to be part of this, probably the biggest event ever to take place during his lifetime.

All of the children were sent out to wash their hands at the stone trough before the food was served, and there was a cacophony of scraping wooden legged chairs on the bare floorboards, repeated as they re-seated themselves around the oak topped table.

George's younger sister Florence was late to the table, and received a suitable scolding. George loved his younger sister dearly, and as he turned his head looked across at his youngest brother, Arthur, a thought of his name brought the image of Arthur Collenette. Oh, how he wished that his brother had been given a different name. It had now been over four years since the loss of Matthew on the cliffs at Pleinmont Point, which had been followed by the murder of Arthur's step-father. As he looked at him, he could see that his brother's face was a picture of innocence, and thankfully nothing like the other Arthur.

He waited until his father had finished the rebuke of his sister, before he took his usual place. George Samuel continued to expound more prophesies as to the outcome of the new conflict. George's younger sisters, Victorina, Florence, Jane, Ida, all sat in silence with frightened, bewildered expressions. None of them were really sure what their father was actually saying – or indeed what it all really meant. The younger ones were not even sure what a war was!

George certainly knew. He was eighteen years old now – nearly eighteen and a quarter actually – the eldest child of this family – and he was definite that he wanted to go. Unlike his siblings, he knew exactly what was happening, and had already made the decision that he would join up at the earliest opportunity! He would make the whole family proud of him, but at that moment he kept his counsel, as he was sure that any announcement would produce an immediate refusal from both of his parents.

His Dad was right in what he had said that men could not sit around and let the Germans have their way. For years the Germans had been challenging Britain's supremacy, both at sea, and abroad across the Empire. Ever since the turn of the century they had been building up their naval fleet, which could now almost match that of Britain. Several attempts to disrupt the trade from Africa had been reported in the papers, where the perpetrators had obviously been the Germans, but Britain seemed powerless to prevent it. They would certainly be putting a stop to it now.

The Guernsey Militia might even try and recruit Dad, George thought. After all he was as strong as an ox, and only forty-four years of age – he might just still be eligible to enlist! What was the upper age limit to join the forces? This news meant that his childhood ambition would be realised sooner than he had anticipated. Even if war had not been declared, he was still determined to go over to England and join the Royal Navy. From leaving school up till now he had been working in the Vale Quarry for past two years, intending to apply to join up at the end of this summer. This declaration of war would just hurry things up.

The aroma emanating from the stew-pot was heavenly. Jeanne-Marie used an iron ladle to serve it out into earthen bowls, with a kitchen cloth carefully wrapped around the handle to prevent burns. A steaming bowlful for each of them was passed down the table, which was quickly followed by a doorstep size lump of bread, cut from the home-made loaf. Everyone was hungry, but they dutifully waited until their father finished saying grace before tucking into the food.

The evenings were starting to show the first signs of drawing in as the twilight shadows were getting that little bit longer as the sun set that little bit earlier. Gone were the balmy evenings that stretched out the daylight hours beyond ten o'clock, but tonight they were being treated to eating their meal by the red and orange hues of the setting sun. The prayer finally came to an end, and at the signal from their father – they all began to eat.

The newspapers for the past ten years had been full of reports about the arms race that had developed between Britain and Germany. Indeed, it had been the main topic that had dominated the British broadsheets, but during the past year, events had escalated. Just a few days ago, George had read that the British Navy now had twenty-nine battleships at sea against Germany's twenty – although Germany had another seven of these mighty monsters under construction, while Britain had over twenty more on the stocks. That is where this war would be won or lost. George had already decided that it would be at sea – and that was where he would serve. He could just imagine himself on a great battleship, manning one of the huge gun turrets, while his ship sailed out to fight the enemy. He was so excited that, despite his hunger, he could barely eat his food.

As he managed a spoonful, his eyes flicked up to meet those of his mother, who was staring at him with a strange expression filling her face. Jeanne-Marie turned her head, and looked away. It was almost as if she were taking notice of her eldest son for the first time in a long while, realising that her little boy had grown up to become a man. She could see from his excited expression that she was about to lose him to the conflict.

Slightly perplexed, George smiled and complimented her on the meal.

His father gave him a sharp look. He was the only one who was ever allowed to speak at the table, and every meal was usually a somewhat sombre affair. It was frustrating as George could barely suppress his exuberance, and was bursting with enthusiasm, but another stern rebuke from his father quickly subdued it. He wanted to discuss everything about this earth-shattering event with his father, but his parents always ate in silence, so their true thoughts on what the future held would remain unknown for the present.

The following day every newspaper banner was emblazoned with the story. Huge headlines declared 'WAR'. Having taken a keen interest in Britain's gradual descent into conflict, by regularly reading the reports in his father's newspaper, George was eager for the latest reports. Strangely, it had been ever since that dark day when poor Matthew had fallen to his death, that George had developed his keen interest in politics, and had been an avid reader of his father's paper. Matthew had always relayed the current affairs of the world to him, and when he had gone, he missed receiving them. Reading the political reports, he found it amazing the way that those in power seemed to be able to wield international events to their own advantage. It had been the Kaiser who had initiated the arms race in an attempt to gain enough sea power to be able to usurp Britain's monopoly in world trade. For the past twelve years the Germans had been stirring up trouble right across the globe, in an attempt to destabilise the global economy of Great Britain. It had begun when Otto von Bismarck, the Iron Chancellor, had used the Triple Alliance of Germany, Austria-Hungary and Italy to dominate Continental Europe and now they wanted to control world trade. Germany had become a powerhouse of industry, but had quickly found that trying to export its output was very difficult, because Britain held the monopoly on world trade. Despite all of the tension, even in those early days of the twentieth century, conflict was only narrowly averted by tactful diplomacy. The Germans might have a superior army of on land, but they had been quick to realise that they were no match for the Royal Navy at sea. To overcome this deficit, the Kaiser had ordered that German shipyards begin to build a High Seas Fleet, that would match that of Britain. With the Minister of Marine, Admiral von Tirpitz, Germany instigated a previously unmatched building programme in order to challenge the British supremacy. It quickly became obvious to Whitehall that from the rate of construction, and the sheer number of battleships that the High Seas Fleet was aiming to build, it could only be used for offensive reasons, because defensive operations did not require such numbers. Once this fact had been realised, then the United Kingdom's dockyards were also placed on full production in order to keep that one step ahead, and they soon began to match the German output, ship for ship.

During that first decade of the twentieth century Britain were becoming increasingly annoyed by the aggressive German disruption to its commercial interests around the Empire. German controlled territories had been issued with orders that prevented them from coaling any British ship, and any non-German passage by ship through their territorial waters became very restricted. British ships faced aggressive action by German Naval vessels. Embargoes and heavy import taxes were placed on British goods, and civil instability mysteriously sprang up within British overseas possessions, especially when they abutted a German imperial possession. Each year the tension increased and the conflict drew ever nearer.

The Royal Navy had been despatched to the outer limits of the Empire to quell any disquiet. Nearer home, the tension within Europe was becoming volatile, likened to a gunpowder factory where the workers continually smoked cigarettes and pipes. Then last June, on the streets of Sarajevo, someone had thrown their lighted cigarette stub into the powder keg when on the twenty eighth of that month, as the heir to the Austro-Hungarian throne Archduke Franz Ferdinand and his wife were riding in an open top vehicle on a visit to that city in Bosnia-Hertzogovenia, a Serbian anarchist stepped out of the crowd and fired shots from a revolver that killed both of them. The fact that this atrocity had been committed by Serb national, who was fighting for the whole of the Balkan region to be returned to Serb control, caused the Austrians to despatch a stern ultimatum directly to Belgrade. This missive caused all hearts to flutter right across Europe, but there appeared to be some reason for optimism when Serbia had responded in a conciliatory tone. Unfortunately, on the twenty fourth of July that optimism vanished when Austria firmly rejected their reply, when it finally became obvious to everybody that Austria was hell bent on war with Serbia. In them doing so, it meant that Russia would support Serbia, as her long-time ally, so it seemed that nothing was going to prevent conflict. Due to the threat of war from the arms race, there had been so many treaties and alliances made all over the continent by most of the European nations. Now with this increase in tension, most of those countries began to prepare for mobilisation, simply as a precaution.

The two squabbling nations caused a domino effect that accelerated every nation in Europe towards total war. It was like a scene from a tragic play. As Austria announced war against Serbia, Russia immediately ordered general mobilisation in support of her treaty with Serbia. Both the German and British fleets were recalled from their summer deployments and exercises. The British Grand Fleet was ordered to sail immediately for Scapa Flow, in the Orkney Isles, as a precaution. It arrived there just as the Kaiser, whose Germany was allied to Austria, answered the Tsar's mobilisation with a declaration of war against Russia in support of Austria. At the same time, he also sent an ultimatum to Russia's other ally France, warning her to stay out of the conflict. France ignored the order, and endorsed her treaty with the Russians by declaring war against the German and Austrian alliance. At this time, it appeared that Britain might avoid getting involved, as they only had treaties with Portugal and Belgium.

In less than ten days war had broken out right across continental Europe. The lightning advance of the German Army through the Belgian Ardennes, as a direct result of France's declaration, then forced Britain to fulfil her guarantee of upholding Belgium's neutrality, and a further ultimatum was issued to the Germans requiring them to recognise Belgium's neutral status. This had been totally ignored.

That had been yesterday, and that was why Britain had reluctantly declared war. If Britain was at war, then all of its overseas colonies would certainly be drawn into the conflict in support of the motherland, and they would also send troops into the conflict. With an empire that covered a quarter of the globe, it ensured that most of the civilised world would become embroiled in the approaching carnage.

****

A hot August sun shone down from a clear summer sky. It was another one of those extremely humid days, apparently too hot even for the seagulls, who were normally found scavenging for any discarded scraps lying in the gutters around the harbour of St Peter Port. Despite the shimmering heat, the whole town was abuzz with the latest news, and speculative rumours abounded, all completely unhindered by facts. Already there was a recruiting station being assembled in the Civic Meeting Hall on Smith Street. Standing outside, a crowd of curious onlookers had assembled to watch the proceedings. All seemed to be eager to catch a glimpse of the first

Guernsey man to enter and sign up for the conflict. Smith Street ran straight uphill from the High Street, and was lined on both sides by two and three storied buildings, most of which traded as shops. Brightly coloured flags and bunting had been strung across the roadway, giving the area a carnival atmosphere, but it all hung down in rather flaccid despair from the lack of any breeze. Moving amongst the people was an enterprising Union Jack and Guernsey State flag seller, who was doing a roaring trade. Several members of the local Salvation Army Band arrived, and after milling in some confusion form a rough semi-circle outside of the Meeting Hall. Music sheets were handed out and they began playing a selection of stirring hymns and patriotic pieces. The evocative chorus from Jerusalem was blasted out in oom-pah passion, then followed by Rule Britannia with the resounding beat of the bass drum echoing off the rendered walls.

The discerning crowd noticed that the euphonium was lagging slightly behind the rest of the band, but none the less they were becoming enthused, nodding and swaying in time with the music. The crowd grew rapidly and the children were waving their hand-held flags in time to the beat of the drum, like a forest of highly decorated metronomes. Union Jacks were being draped out from every first storey windowsill, giving the grey rendered walls a much-needed splash of colour. Lamp-posts had been festooned in red, white and blue ribbons looking rather like patriotic barber poles. Newly pasted posters adorned every available space, and blanked every shop window, each one displaying idyllic views of the English countryside with slogans inviting any viewer to *Come and Defend This.*

Over at the meeting hall, everything seemed to be ready when a barrel-chested sergeant, dressed in a bright red jacket with brass buttons, emerged to declare to all that they were open for business. Almost immediately an unexpected cheer erupted from the crowd, as two of men walked over the road to enter the hall. The excitement on their faces evident as each turned to wave before going in through the door. It was all so terribly uplifting.

Being on a steep hill, the crowd was being swelled by pedestrians coming into town to shop from their dwellings up on Haut Ville. Such exciting days such as these were extremely rare on the Island.

The inside of the meeting hall was rather dim and gloomy, which was interrupted by two sunbeams coming through the windows, filled with glittering particles of dust. Yet more bunting and even larger union jacks failed to brighten the claustrophobic stuffiness. A whole series of military figures strutted about the floor space in purposeless splendour, while other more junior members were sitting at tables that had been erected for the purpose of signing up recruits. A lone expectant chair was placed in front of each.

A giant portrait of King George V and Queen Mary stared down imperiously from a frame positioned above the main doorway. Two huge chalk boards stood on easels. They too had posters pinned to them, declaring that the country badly needed her men to fight the new foe.

In the road outside, young girls were now shamelessly kissing each volunteer on the cheek as he made his way towards the entrance. The flag-seller could not keep up with the demand, with a tidal wave of patriotic fervour sweeping through the crowd. Newspaper vendors were doing an equally splendid trade, as people were eager to read first-hand reports of the latest developments on this, the first full day of the conflict. Despite the infancy of war being only one day old, everyone was expectant, eager to read about the first British victory. There was a widespread consensus that this coming conflict would show the world that Britain was still the greatest country in the whole of God's creation. After all, beating the Germans should not take too long, and everything should be over and done and dusted by Christmas!

Another huge cheer from the crowd went up as the first newly recruited man emerged from the Hall. The young man stood on the top step nervously, obviously not used to being the centre of attention, but the roar of approval made him thrust out his chest. He waved his enrolment papers to great applause. He was being treated like a hero – despite the fact that he had not yet been fully indoctrinated into the service. Everyone crowded around him, wanting to shake him by the hand. Another huge cheer greeted a second man who appeared in the doorway behind him, looking equally embarrassed. The newly recruited men had to run a gauntlet of back-slapping from well-wishers, as they went downhill towards the High Street to inform their parents that they had enlisted.

Having made his way up the hill from the Torode Cottages on La Vrangue, George Torode stood in the small square near La Greffe, looking down the hill towards the crowd. He tentatively moved forward, and made his way down into the mass of people surrounding the hall. He had purposely not gone to work today, after hearing of this recruitment drive. He gently eased his way through the heaving throng, craning his neck as he tried to catch a glimpse of the unfolding proceedings. Looking down the hill over the heads of the mass of people, he was surprised to see just how many had turned out for the occasion. He felt a little guilty about his absence from the shop, not being one to purposely miss work. He had been in two minds as he knew that he would be docked a whole day's pay for not being there, but the thrill of yesterday's news had kept him awake for most of the night. Looking about it seemed as if the whole Island was here in Smith Street, and he now felt reassured that his decision had been a good one. The human throng stretch all the way down to the High Street, spreading out right and left in both directions. He had never seen so many people at one time, and he became excited. He just could not help himself from cheering along with the crowd, even feeling obliged to reach out and pat the back of each man as he went in.

The members of the Salvation Army brass band were playing ever more patriotic tunes. The thump, thump, thump of the bass drum seemed to reverberate inside his rib cage, as if beating courage into his very being. It all became a heady whirl of pride and passion and he didn't know if he was being swept along on the tide of patriotism, or if it was simply a nationalistic obligation. Whichever it was, the splendour of the occasion tripped all of the intended responses within him, and he just knew that he wanted to be part of this whole glorious affair. He wanted to be part of this great adventure that would remain with him for whole a lifetime. Before he knew what was happening, somebody had kissed his cheek and hands were pounding his back as he mounted the stone steps to enter the portals of the Meeting Hall. He could hear cries of 'Good show!' and 'Well done lad!' as the door closed behind him. As his eyes adjusted to the gloom, he realised that suddenly everything around him had gone very quiet. After leaving the glaring sunshine outside, it had become dark and gloomy. The static air was hot and stuffy.

Suddenly he could feel a huge figure looming over him, and turning he was confronted by the imposing figure of an army sergeant with big ears. That was the first thing that George noticed about him. His bright red jacket bulged in front of his eyes, as a moustachioed face peered down imperiously from beneath the peaked rim of his cap.

"Congratulations young man. You've done the right thing. Come over to the table and I will sign you up."

George looked around the large hall, noting that there were at least six or seven tables, each was being used to take down the details of a new recruit, but now he suddenly felt disappointment and deflation creeping through him. Before he could turn to go, the sergeant had grasped his arm in a vice-like grip and was leading him over towards a recently vacated table. As he sat down on the chair George became aware that the sergeant with big ears was asking his name.

"You 'ave gotta name, ain't you, son?" he enquired in a broad Cockney accent.

George was amazed at how much quieter it was inside the hall – it was church-like, almost solemn. It was more than a little bewildering after all of the excitement of outside in the road. He looked at the waxed moustache of the soldier.

"Y-y-yes sir," he stammered. "George Torode."

"… and 'ow do you spell your surname, George?"

"T-O-R-O-D-E," he replied.

"'Ave you got a middle name, George?" the sergeant asked patiently, as he proceeded to write on the enrolment form.

"Yes sir, it's Deseria," he said, also spelling his middle for the sergeant.

"Cor, that's a mouthful, ain't it? I shouldn't mention it too much in front of your new mates, as you might get your leg pulled a bit. It's French, ain't it?"

George nodded and replied, "My mother is French, but Guernsey now."

At that moment a young man rose to his feet, over at the adjacent table. Another burly Sergeant stood and shook hand. "Welcome to the Army, Lad. I know that a clever lad like you will do well in the ranks."

George suddenly realised that he was signing up for the Army.

"I want to join the Navy, please sir," George said.

"Do you now," said the Sergeant, giving a sigh of resignation. "Well, I'm signing up for the Army at this table, my son. You will do well in the army, a bright lad like you."

"But I don't want to join the Army, sir. If I can't join the Navy, then I'm going home," said George indignantly.

"OK, OK, don't go losing your rag, boy. If you go across to that desk over there," he pointed towards the edge of the stage, near a door marked EXIT.

"The navy are recruiting there."

Sighing, the sergeant began ripping up the enrolment form he had just wasted. As he stood, there was already another volunteer waiting to take George's chair. He walked across the hall to the table by the stage. There was a Petty Officer sitting there, and recognising the uniform George gave a smile of satisfaction. The man looked hot, running his finger around the inside of his starched collar; George thought that it must be quite uncomfortable in full uniform in this airless hall.

"Good for you, lad! I'm glad to see that someone has stood up to those bloody arrogant Pongos at last," he said, as George sat down in the chair in front of him.

"What's a Pongo?" asked George.

"The bloody Army, that's who – you know the old song – 'where the Army goes, a pong goes,' You must have heard that before," he said, disbelieving that there was anyone in the world who was not aware.

George hadn't got a clue what he was talking about.

"It's also the name of a type of ape," added the Petty Officer informatively. "You will be learning a lot of new expressions once you're in the navy."

'At least that Sergeant's big ears fitted that bill,' thought George.

"Those Pongos got here first thing this morning, and their Sergeant Major positioned me right over here out of their way. Plonked all of their own desks right across the room in front of the entrance door, and so far they have grabbed everyone who has come in. You're my first recruit. That is if you've come to join up in the navy – you have, haven't you?" he asked hopefully.

"Yes," said George, to the man obvious relief.

"Well, you've picked the finest service my lad. We are the Senior Service after all. You're over eighteen, aren't you?" he asked, still unsure that he was going to get his first volunteer.

"Yes, I will be nineteen on the eleventh of May next year," replied George.

"Good. That's ok then. We'll begin by taking down your particulars, if you'll pardon the expression," said the sailor, grinning at him. He picked up his pen, dipped it into the inkwell and prepared to write.

"Right then, what's your name?"

"George Deseria Torode," he replied.

"That's an unusual middle name!" said the Petty Officer. "French, isn't it?"

"It's grandfather's name, over in France. My mother's father's name – he was French from Brittany – it is not very common here on Guernsey," explained George.

"Date of birth," continued the recruiter.

"Eleventh of May 1896."

"That makes you eighteen and a quarter – good. What's your address?"

"Number Two, Torode Cottages at La Vrangue. It is over the hill, at the back of St Peter Port."

The man wrote down the details and suddenly stopped, and checked what he had written.

"Your house name is the same as your surname – you're not 'aving me on are you lad?"

"No sir. That is its real name. It was built a long time ago. My family have lived there for over a hundred years."

At the end of the questions, the sailor asked George to check the details he had written down to make sure that he had completed the form correctly. When he nodded that it was all correct, the man smiled.

"Alright then, if you'd like to sign on the dotted line, you'll receive the King's shilling. It's a whole day's pay actually. It's a little more than a shilling; and with it you get a free steam ferry ticket that gives you a ride all the way over to Southampton. There will be a meal provided for you on the ferry – so you won't go hungry. I have to tell you that you have just made the best decision of your life today. Enjoy your time in the navy. We need bright young men like yourself, and I am sure that you will do well."

****

When George got home and told his mother, she was far from pleased. She ranted and raved in her Brittany French, saying that his father would never allow him to go, and without his permission he would be barred from joining. She said that she would make sure that he would not give it. The age of majority here on Guernsey is twenty-one, he was not even old enough to vote, let alone join a service in which he may get killed. Until he was twenty-one, he was still their responsibility, because he was still technically a minor. He was only just old enough to enter a public house for goodness sake – not that George could afford to buy a drink. How would he manage? Why, he couldn't even darn his own socks. As for washing his own clothes, he had absolutely no idea where to start, and there were many other inabilities of which he was completely ignorant. She itemised each on her fingers.

He could see that she was upset, and as her reasons for him not going started to dry up, George could see the despair and defeat in her eyes. She finally realised that she had lost her eldest son to the war. Throughout the tirade George had stood firmly impassive before her, with a defiant determined look. He had never dared to defy his parents before. She fell silent and looked at him with pleading eyes, silently begging for him to change his mind, but as she looked at him, she knew that she had lost her little boy. He had grown into manhood, and was now beyond her control. In the realisation that she had lost she broke down sobbing. George suddenly felt terrible for having made her cry, but knew that he would probably never get another chance to leave the Island and see the world. He had to take it. None the less he stepped forward and gently wrapped his arms around her, feeling her body yield as she accepted the situation, trying to compose herself. Although she was much smaller than him, she reached up and cuddled him close, cradling him against her ample bosom; knowing full well that this would be the last time she would hold him as her child.

"*Ma mere. Je dois faire partie de l'aventure,*" he did not speak to her in her native language very often these days, but felt that this time he needed to.

"It will not be a great adventure if you get yourself killed. You must promise to write home at least once a week George. We will write back to you, and let you know how things are here at home. It will get very lonely for you otherwise. Always remember that this is your home, and that we all love you. We will be waiting here for you when you return," she said, drying her eyes with a handkerchief.

Then as a final act of capitulation, she said, "*Je suis tres fier de vous, George.*"

When his father arrived home, there was a re-enactment of his wife's response. He stormed around the kitchen stating that he would refuse to give his permission. After calming him down, his mother led him out of the room and when they returned, he seemed much more subdued. There was an embarrassing silence, until his wife nudged him forward. He coughed – and held out his hand – wishing his son all the luck in the world. He too said that he was very proud of him. George never knew what his mother had said to him, but his handshake was the nearest that his father had ever come to actually being affectionate.

****

The steam packet that would take him over to the mainland was due to sail the following Friday. Once a week it made the circular tour from Weymouth or

Southampton to Jersey and Guernsey. Very occasionally it would put into St Anne's harbour on Alderney, but it would not be doing that on this trip.

On his last morning at home, George was feeling anxious and somewhat trepidacious about what lay ahead as he packed the small suit-case that his father had loaned to him. Friday finally arrived and the whole family were dressed in their best clothes as they made their way down the hillside. Winding their way through town towards the granite lined harbour. The ferry stood patiently at the quayside awaiting their arrival. It was high tide which had forced the sides of the vessel high above the granite walled edge of the harbour wall. The steam packet had just arrived into the harbour from Jersey, and would only be staying long enough to disembark those going ashore, before loading produce and embarking those going over to England. George could see the mail sacks were being unloaded into the back of the horse drawn postal van as he stood nervously with his parents. They were standing amongst the many other spectators who had also gathered there. A loud puff of smoke belched from the tall funnel, and George looked up to see the dark cloud spiralling skywards, realising that this would be the last few minutes that he would spend with his family for a long time.

In the past George had seen many of these vessels come and go from this harbour, but this would be the first time that he would actually board one and sail away from the Island. His father and uncle had often allowed him to accompany them on fishing and crab potting trips, but his uncle's clinker boat was not even as big as one of the life-boats on this metal monster. He knew that it had been whilst on those local fishing trips, that he had developed his taste for the sea. He enjoyed the feeling of isolation, the total peace and reflective solitude, away from the hustle and bustle of life.

When they had set off from home this morning, his father had insisted on carrying his suit case for him. George tried hard to recall another occasion when he had ever seen it used before. It had certainly been very dusty when he had extracted it from beneath a pile of old newspapers down in the shed at the bottom of the garden.

Looking about at the gathering crowd, he could see that there were several family groups amongst the spectators. George recognised a couple of the boys from his old school. They must be joining up just like me, he thought. Beyond them, a little further along the quay, was the local Salvation Army Band shuffling into their allotted positions, each member tuning their instrument before enthusiastically launching into the first number. He was used to seeing them play every Sunday outside the Holy Trinity Church – albeit with the euphonium player being slightly behind in his timing. Their exuberance on display via puffed red cheeks of the tuba player, which was only exceeded by the extravagant swinging arms of the three tambourine wielding women. They sang such patriotic songs such as Pomp and Circumstance, and Rule Britannia.

The crowd began to swell, and George and his family quickly became engulfed in the throng. An impatient nervous atmosphere filled the air, and as he looked about he suddenly realised that the departure from his family was being repeated by all of these other people, who were also sending their sons off to the war.

His own family had gone quiet, none of them quite knowing how to handle the departure of one of their own. His brother and sisters had starting to become bored, and began pinching each other. A loud rebuke from their father stopped them, when a loud hailer blared from the top of the gangway. It instructed the passengers bound for England to embark. The announcement evoked frantic hugs, kisses, and much shaking of hands. George went over and hugged his mother. A soldier, smartly dressed in a khaki uniform with puttees up to his knees, marched down the quayside calling for all the new recruits to board immediately. Each of his siblings wanted to kiss him goodbye. Finally, George retrieved the suit-case from his father, and wrenched himself away from his mother's arms, he shook his father's hand, turned and headed manfully towards the gangway.

He noted that a strange lump had developed in his throat, which made him question his rash decision in Smith Street, but a determination not to be beaten forced him forward. Looking back at his mother's tearful face made him dither for second longer, but after taking another deep breath, he bounded up the gangway, making his way in through the gaping metal doorway that was cut into the side of the ship. Suddenly, he was away from the noisy mayhem on the quayside – the crowd noise and oompahs of the band replaced by a loud hum of machinery, that seemed to reverberated throughout the vessel. It was considerably darker down between the decks, and an artificial electric lighting had replaced the bright sunshine on the quayside. In this unfamiliar environment George felt somewhat disorientated, until his eyes became adjusted to the gloom. Suddenly the soldier from the quayside was standing before him.

"I am Corporal Isaacs of His Majesty's Catering Corps. Make your way up to the upper deck where you can wave goodbye to your loved ones. That is the ladder over there. Once we clear the harbour, I want you to come down to the main salon, where you will receive your meal for the voyage."

Just as suddenly as he appeared – the soldier disappeared. George stared around him; any thoughts of his family momentarily forgotten, as he struggled across the passageway towards the near vertical ladder that led to the upper deck. Climbing the metal rungs was difficult, especially having to drag the suitcase up behind, but he emerged back into the brightness of the day. Shielding his eyes from the glare, he joined the throng of humanity that lined the rail at the ships side, walking behind lots of hunched backs until he eventually managed to find an empty space. There were over a hundred people down there. After searching the faces, he quickly located his family, and frantically began waving for all he was worth. His brother and sisters did him proud, waving so hard it seemed that they were trying shake their arms from their shoulder sockets.

After five minutes his arm was starting to hurt, and the ship had not given any indication of movement. The aching muscles began to curb his enthusiasm. Just as he stopped, there was a sudden shock blast that erupted from the steam siren, heralding the ships departure. Below him, a team of harbour stevedores eased the heavy gangway away from the ferry, pushing it back onto the quay. There was a rumbling vibration through the metal deck, which tickled the soles of his feet. The eyes of spliced Manila ropes were removed from the huge metal bollards and dropped into the water. George watched as the seamen on the foc'sle quickly retrieved them, manually hauling them aboard. He thought that he may well be doing a similar sort of job in the near future.

There was a rumbling vibration, which quickly increased in intensity as the big ship slowly began to ease itself away from the quayside. George looked back towards the quay to find that his family were still waving. He waved back, a small tear appearing at the corner of his eye, which he quickly wiped away, hoping that nobody had noticed.

The band struck up the Guernsey national anthem of *Sarnia Cherie* as the vessel backed off towards the centre of the harbour. As the sternway increased, a brick building at the end of the granite jetty suddenly blanked his view of the family and a mild panic attack gripped him. Was that the last time that he would see them? The lump in his throat returned and he was very close to tears. He turned to see the backdrop of St Peter Port filling the hillside above the harbour. This was his home – it had always been his home – and it would always be – but had he done the right thing? Wiping away another tear, he looked around to make sure that nobody was watching.

"You look sad – are you leaving your family for long?" the soft female voice came from behind him.

Spinning around, more in self-consciousness than surprise, he saw a pretty girl of about sixteen standing near one of the wing passage doorways. Wisps of her fair hair were blowing in the freshening breeze, as the steamer sailed out through the gap in the outer harbour wall. George could see Castle Cornet go flashing past, and then they were out into the sound between Guernsey, Herm and Sark far beyond. He stretched his neck to make one last check, trying to ensure that he could not see his family, before he finally turned away from his search to face the girl. His first impression was that she was very beautiful. Suddenly he felt embarrassed, awkward and not quite knowing quite what to say.

"There will be one more quick chance to see them as we pass by those buildings over there," she said, pointing to the cluster near the quayside crane. "So, I would get ready to wave your last goodbyes. We shall be out of sight of them after that."

His eyes scanned the quayside once more, and then as the buildings flashed by, there they all were, standing in the small gap between two of them. He waved for all he was worth until they were gone. That was it – the last he would see of them until his return. When would that be?

Beyond the buildings the full panorama of the town was spread out over the hillside, displayed in all of its majestic splendour. The pyramid spire of Holy Trinity, the Town Church where he had been baptised, lay directly beyond the southern reaches of the harbour. He quickly recognised all the familiar landmarks, picking out the various hotels, and prominent buildings. Old Government House – The Salvation Army Hall – La Greffe – they were all there. When he looked back towards where his family had been standing, they were gone, having melted into the dark human mass that smudged the top of the stone jetty. Maybe they could still see him. He waved even harder – just in case. Gradually, the quayside disappeared behind the outer harbour wall. When would he see them again? He made one final search, but they were gone and his attention returned to the girl standing behind him. He was glad to see that she was still there!

"Parting is such sweet sorrow," she said and then. "Do you like Shakespeare?"

Trying hard not to show his ignorance, his brain searched for an impressive reply. He knew perfectly well that Shakespeare was an English play-write, but that was about all. Then he quickly remembered his schoolmaster Mr Jeffreys quoting tracts from his works in class and luckily there was one quote that he remembered – it was from *Romeo and Juliet*. Of how frustrating that he could not remember it all and so he simply replied, "Yes. *Romeo and Juliet* – that is one of my favourites."

Then, trying to change the subject he said, "I am off to join the Royal Navy – I'm going over to Portsmouth to begin my training." Then he said without hardly pause. "I've just been saying goodbye to my family."

"I saw you waving," she said, then added brightly, "My Father is also a sailor. In fact, he is the captain of this ship. Every now and then he takes me for a trip across to the Islands. I am very lucky because I get my own cabin. He would never have brought me this time had he known that war was going to break out before we arrived back home."

"The Captain!" said George incredulously.

"Yes. We live in Portsmouth, well Southsea actually," she continued. "Maybe we will be on the same train from Southampton down to Portsmouth!"

"Oh. Does this ship not go straight over to Portsmouth?" George blushed at being forced to show his ignorance.

"No, I'm afraid not. We will be landing at Southampton. Normally it goes across to Weymouth in the summer, but on the last three sailings they have been using Southampton. I think that the naval base at Portland has been placed on high alert, and Portsmouth is obviously very busy with the navy at the moment. Now that the war has started, the ferry company will probably be using Southampton all the time. We used to live in Weymouth – in Cove Row – which overlooks the turning basin within the harbour there, but we have recently moved to Portsmouth for that very reason. My father and I will be taking the train down to Portsmouth. I expect that the navy will have arranged transport for you, otherwise you could have joined us."

George had to suppress his gasp, because he could just imagine what her father would say if he found out that his daughter was consorting with a common naval recruit.

"Yes, I expect they will be sending transport to pick us up. I'm really looking forward to learning how to become a sailor, and then to go off to fight the Germans."

"Maybe my father could give you a few tips before we reach Southampton. He's been at sea all his working life," she continued. "He is up on the bridge at this moment. Would you like to go up and meet him?"

George's eyes rolled upwards. He felt certain that her father would certainly not want his daughter mixing with the likes of him. How could he explain it to her without damaging her naivety? Looking at her again, he noticed how her blonde hair fell about her face in gossamer strands, she really was a very pretty girl. Her skin was lightly tanned, which enhanced its flawless quality of its smooth appearance. She wore a straw boater hat with a scarlet ribbon, pinned to the back of her head. A cream bolero jacket covered her pink and lilac cotton dress. George could not help but notice that she wore white stockings and a pair of white pumps. She stood there demurely, holding her hands in front of her.

"Look miss – er…" he stammered.

"It's Gladys Rumsey," she said with a radiant smile on her face. "I do think that it's so old fashioned to have to be formally introduced to someone before one can hold a conversation. Don't you?"

"Well, yes I do, but Miss Rumsey," he began. "I really don't think that your fa…"

"Please call me Gladys," she said, interrupting him in full flow. "I don't hold with all that formality. It is all so Victorian. We are after all living in the twentieth century. All of those silly old-fashioned attitudes should have died with the old Queen. What is your name by the way?"

"George Torode," he answered, forgetting his train of thought – forgetting everything. Then struggling for something to say, he said, "My sister is named Gladys."

"There we are George Torode – we have managed to formally introduce ourselves, and already we have a connection."

"Come along, Gladys," said an old tired, but somewhat impatient voice, behind him.

George turned to see an old frail looking elderly lady, who was leaning heavily on a walking cane. She wore a dark heavy weave black shawl that was draped around her shoulders, almost hiding her face. There was some dark silk frills that lined the rim of her bonnet, which she had firmly tied beneath her chin.

"Gladys, you know that your father doesn't like you talking to strangers."

From the glare that the old lady gave him, George was left in no doubt as to whom the word Strangers had been directed.

"Oh, but Aunt Lucretia, this is no stranger. May I present Mr George Torode of Guernsey," said Gladys.

"You know this BOY?"

"We have been introduced – yes," she continued.

"Well, I still think that you had better come up to the cabin with me. If your father were to appear, I don't thin…"

"He wouldn't mind one little bit, Aunt. George has very kindly invited me down to the Lower Salon for tea and cakes. You would be very welcome to join us, if you would like to."

"I er – that is – oh my headache is getting worse. If you promise me not to tell your father, I will go up to our cabin and relax for a while. You must promise to come up and wake me at least an hour before we dock."

"I promise you Aunt – now you go up and have a nice rest. I feel sure that this sea air does not agree with you."

"Yes, that's probably it. I deeply regret my decision to come. If you'll excuse me then – I am pleased to have met you Mr Torode."

With that she turned and climbed up the wide metal steps rather unsteadily, heading towards the cabin situated on the deck above. George would not have wished a headache on anybody, and felt more than a little bit guilty about the internal delight he was experiencing. Gladys turned and smiled at George.

"There, she will be asleep in five minutes, and I am now free for a while. What are we going to do George? Are you going to officially invite me down to the Salon for tea and cakes?"

Standing out on the exposed deck in the freshening wind, it had caused the temperature to drop significantly, and George suddenly felt quite cold. The wind was blowing almost head-on to the ferry as it began to clear the sheltered waters of the Island of Guernsey, and began to head north-eastwards up towards the Island of Alderney and the English Channel beyond.

As Gladys had already spoken of it to her aunt, George decided that he would indeed ask her below to the Lower Salon. After all, his father had given him five shillings to last him until he received his first pay packet. Tea and cakes would not cost that much – would it?

"I'm not really supposed to go down there," whispered Gladys secretly. "Father is a firm abstainer, and does not approve of alcoholic drinks of any description. There is a bar down there you see."

George was slightly puzzled as to why she had told her aunt that he had already asked her down to the Lower Salon, and now seemed to be trying to find excuses as to why she should not go. Women were strange creatures, but he just knew deep inside that he really wanted to spend some time with her.

"Please don't worry Gladys, because I will look after you and ensure that nothing untoward happens. At least your aunt will know where you are, and to be quite honest, I really do need something to eat," replied George.

She agreed immediately, and they started to make their way down to the next deck. Gladys led the way, as George had not a clue where the salon was located. As they reached the bottom of the steps, there came the pungent aroma of cigar smoke and alcohol, which hit them both like a sledgehammer.

He opened the main entrance door, and was immediately confronted by the loud buzz of conversation as they entered the confines of the salon. They could hear some voices being raised, clearly heard above the ambient din. A raucous cackle of laughter erupted, as someone loudly appreciated the punch-line of an unheard joke. The salon was a large area, that stretched from one side of the ship right across to the other. George could see the round portholes on both sides, each containing concentric brass fittings. From within these shadowy claustrophobic confines, the sunshine outside lit the glass on one side to create glowing orbs. There were a lot of passengers enjoying the chance to relax with a drink or three.

The dim interior was furnished with long buttoned leather seats, that ran down both sides of the salon. The leather had discoloured patches, the victim of recent spillages. In the centre, encircling the vertical metal stanchions that supported the deck above, were more seats covered with the same intrinsic leather. Fitted around them were several round varnished lacquer-topped tables that that had been bolted to the plain wooden deck. Each table had four high back wooden chairs, with a dirty tartan fabric covered seat.

From the rather rowdy singing taking place in the far corner, there was obviously a party in full swing. Many of the passengers had retreated to dubious shelter of this haven upon sailing, and as George looked about, he could see that most of the seats had already been taken. A champagne cork suddenly exploded, the cork ricocheting off the ceiling to the great delight of the onlookers. Excited screams evoked extended arms holding flared glasses.

Over in the opposite corner stood a trestle table, covered by a white linen table-cloth. The Corporal from the Catering Corps, who had checked George on board, was standing smartly behind it. He was dispensing packs of sandwiches wrapped in grease-proof paper to a line of nervous looking young men.

'They must be the other new recruits like me,' thought George.

He carefully observed as one of the men carried away his wrapped meal. The man's expectant look of anticipation crumpled like a punctured balloon into one of utter disappointment? George could see that the large thick slices of white bread that had been hastily buttered, and filled with slices of beetroot. The malty white slices were stained by huge red patches, where the juice had leaked through, making them look they had been shot and bandaged. The man's nose wrinkled in disgust, and George could only empathise with him.

George immediately made a bold decision, and he carefully led Gladys straight past the table containing the unappetising sandwiches, over towards the on-board service counter. In doing so he had to manoeuvre her around a very large gentleman, who was swaying alarmingly as he sang a risky ditty to a grinning audience of four. George could not decide if the man's unsteadiness was due to the slight motion of the ship, or to the effects of the beer that was slopping out from the top of his glass. An exuberant swing of his arm caused yet more to slosh out of the glass, and Gladys had to draw her skirt away from the frothing cascaded. George carefully navigated her around the danger.

There were oil lamps, hung on gimbals' that protruded from the bulkheads, to keep any flames vertical within their glass cage. Despite it being the early afternoon, George could see that they had been lit, but these lamps were purely for decoration, because the salon now boasted the new electric lighting, which had been fitted on the ceiling directly above the centre of the bar. This is a definite sign of our modern times, George decided. He stared curiously at the lights, having only seen them a few times in St Peter Port, and tried to figure out how the brightness was produced without the use of a flame. The service counter loomed.

It was attended by a steward, who was valiantly trying to keep up with the heavy demand. George invested some of his precious pocket money in a pot of tea and a plate of cakes for himself and his new-found friend. They managed to find two chairs in an alcove near the entrance door, and once seated they recommenced their conversation. They were soon revelling in each other's company.

Eventually all of the cakes had disappeared from the plate, and their tea pot was empty. Time seemed to have lost all meaning, and when George looked over towards the large circular clock positioned above the bar, he noticed that there was only about an hour and a half before the ship was due to dock. The smoky atmosphere down here was making him feel drowsy, and having spent most of his money, he invited Gladys to take a walk around the upper deck with him to get some fresh air. They rose together, and left the salon, before climbing the ladder to the next deck. Gladys stopped at the spot where Aunt Lucretia had ascended the ladder up to her cabin, and produced a key. She opened a narrow locker door and retrieved her coat, before locking it once more.

"It's a private cupboard for the ship's officers, where they keep their all-weather great coats," she explained.

By getting out into the chilly breeze, the ozone laden air quickly cleared his head and George hunched his shoulders against the unexpected coldness. Fortunately, the stiff breeze had eased and the surface of the sea appeared fairly calm. The late afternoon sun was quickly melting into the evening twilight as it descended below the cloud packing the western horizon. George gave the sea a quick search around, but it was completely deserted. It was the first time that he had been surrounded by water, and out of sight of any land. Their only escort in these waters were two seagulls, who kept perfect station on the port quarter. Glancing up at the towering bridge superstructure, George observed that there was an extra look-out sentry stationed out on the bridge wings. He could clearly the man, and noted that his binoculars never left his eyes. During the course of such a pleasant afternoon, George had quite forgotten about the war – quickly realising that a German submarine could easily torpedo them! This thought made him carefully rescan the horizon once more, this time searching for a U-Boat's periscope – but thankfully, once again, there was nothing to be seen.

"Look," he said, pointing towards a dark purple line on the north eastern horizon. "That' must be England. There is a flashing light as well."

Having never seen it before, it was a piece of pure speculation on his part. He had said it to sound knowledgeable, but his effort was short lived when Gladys replied.

"Well, almost! It's the Isle of Wight, actually. That flashing light you can see is Saint Catherine's Point Lighthouse. I've made this journey quite a few times, you know."

"Of course," he replied, somewhat crestfallen. Then thinking aloud, he mused, "I wonder why it's flashing if we're at war?"

"Mmmm… good point George," she replied, impressed by his thought. "I really don't know, but I'll pop up and ask father if you like!"

"No, it's not that important, Gladys," he said. He had absolutely no desire to meet her father. "Look – as its quite chilly up here, would you like to go back down to the lower salon and I will buy you a soda water, if you would like one?"

She did not want to go down immediately, and they stood together at the rail watching the land mass rise steadily out of the horizon. Soon the vessel was making its way up past the white chalk cliffs of the Island, and off to his left he could faintly see the landmass of England in the distance. They could see several of the glowing lights along the Bournemouth beach front, and some pin-points of the smaller towns along that part of the coast.

Then Gladys shuddered, finally accepting his invitation to go below once again. She took his arm this time. Her touch was like an electric shock, and he felt his heart pounding. He felt like a king with her on his arm, as they descended the stairs.

"Are you feeling alright, George? You look a little flushed. You're not sea-sick, are you? Oh, you poor thing," she was genuinely concerned as she guided him over towards a seat. The wind had reddened his cheeks, it had completely spoiled his moment. They quickly found a seat. As he tried to assure her that he was in fact very well, then George became uncomfortably aware of the looming presence of a figure standing beside him. Turning his head very slightly, he noticed were the four gold rings sewn on the sleeve of a navy-blue uniformed jacket, dangling level by his right eye. He had an ominous premonition as to whom the sleeve belonged. Gladys' joyful greeting confirmed his guess.

"Hello, Daddy! This is Mister George Torode. He's on his way over to join the Royal Navy."

"WHAT do you think you are doing down here, young lady? WHERE exactly is your Aunt Lucretia?" he said in a thunderous voice.

"It's all right, Daddy. George has been protecting me. Aunt Lucretia has a touch of the mal de mer and is lying down in our cabin – she has a terrible headache. I've been perfectly safe with Mr Torode here, who has been the perfect gentleman," she said guiltlessly.

George's neck slowly sank down into shoulders, as he forced himself to rise to his feet, turn, and face the blatant hostility that was emanating from the old seaman's eyes.

"How do you do, sir," he mumbled, holding out a nervous hand. "I am very pleased to meet you."

The Captain totally ignored him, as if he were a fly on the wall, looking straight past him as he spoke again to Gladys.

"Come along and get your things ready, my dear. It's time you went up to your cabin and woke up your Aunt Lucretia. We shall be docking in about an hour. There will be a lot more security at the dock gates now, and we don't want to miss our train," the deepness of his booming voice only enhanced his forbidding appearance. As he turned and strode away, George's sigh of relief was audible.

"I'm sorry he was so rude George, he's still so very Victorian in his attitudes," she apologised.

"You'd better go straightaway, Gladys. Maybe we could meet again at some time in the future, eh? That is… if you would like to? Portsmouth can't be that big a place – can it?" he enquired.

"Yes, I'd like that very much George," she said shyly, her face brightening at the idea. "I'll give you my address, then when you get some spare time you could come to tea."

She took a card from her reticule and gave it to him.

"There you are George Torode! We have an assignation on your first spell ashore," she said in a matter of fact tone.

George had never had an assignation before, and the thought of having one with Gladys pleased him immensely.

"I've really enjoyed your company Gladys. You can count on me to get in touch. I don't know when that may be, but I promise you that I will definitely come as soon as I possibly can," he said fervently.

She blushed slightly, lowering her eyes.

"I've enjoyed being with you too, George, and I'll look forward to seeing you again, whenever that is."

They parted with a gentle, but formal shaking of hands. At the last minute, she darted forward and pecked him on the cheek, then fled up the staircase towards the cabin deck. He slowly raised his hand to his cheek and touched the place where her lips had been. Then he stared down at the card in his hand. He would keep it safe. Carefully, he placed it in the leather wallet that had been given to him as a going away present by his father.

After she had gone, he went back up to the upper deck and stood alone at the guardrail. He watched the illuminated dots of the shore-lights sailing smoothly past in the evenings fading light. It was much colder now, and he turned up his collar as he shivered. Ahead of the ship, in the far distance, he could see the loom of glowing lights that he thought must be Portsmouth or Southampton. The lights cast a bright arc in the dark sky above the city – not that George had a clue to the fact that it was to be his eventual destination, because as he watched the ship turn sharply to port, it started to head north up Southampton water. He crossed over to the other side of the ship to be out of the wind. A great red-brick Victorian edifice, that he would later learn was the hospital at Netley, was the only building that he could make out in the gathering gloom. It wasn't long before the illuminated wharves of Southampton suddenly materialised out of the rapidly darkening evening.

The ferry docked quickly and efficiently at nine thirty, just as the darkness really began to set in. There were few stars, as the onset of thickening cloud coming in from the west had brought about a premature sunset. A gangway was placed in position by the dock labourers, and soon the file of passengers began to disembark.

George retrieved his suit-case from the lower salon, and made his way towards the gangway. His eyes darted around, hoping to catch a glimpse of Gladys, but he never saw her. As he stepped ashore, the one thing that he did notice was a wizened looking naval Petty Officer, who was obviously waiting on the quayside to meet George, and his fellow new recruits. He was standing beside a navy-blue truck that had RN painted in bold white letters on the side. At the back of the vehicle was a canvas tarpaulin that was stretched over a tall metal frame. 'A mobile tent! Is that our transport?' thought George.

As he made his way towards the man, George did manage to catch a final glimpse of Gladys and her Aunt. Her father was escorting them both across the open space of the dockside, towards a waiting taxi cab. George lean forward, wanting to see if she turned for a last look, but a gruff voice gathered the men into line, as the Petty Officer began calling out their names. When his eyes returned to the spot, it was to see the red lights of the taxi just as it disappeared around the corner of a dockside building. George's heart sank with the uncertainty of not knowing when he would see her again.

"George Torode!"

The sound of his name brought him back to reality.

"Here, sir," he called.

"Wake up Torode! There's a war on, you know," said the NCO.

There were only seven other recruits; George recognised three of them from Guernsey. The other four must be from the other Island, he surmised. Guernsey folk always refer to Jersey as the Other Island.

"OK you lot – make your way into the back of this 'ere lorry. You're going to be travelling first class tonight, and you are lucky enough to 'ave me as your chauffeur. Conductin' you all to the execution site, I am," he added, laughing at his own sick wit, seeming to delight in their nervousness and uncertainty.

The men picked up their bags and suitcases and headed towards the rear of the vehicle. The Petty Officer kept up an onslaught of sadistic comments as to what fate had in store for them. They each climbed up into the canvas tent. This would be the first time that George had ever travelled in back of a truck. He had once travelled around the Island in one of the four-in-hand horse-drawn excursion cars, which had been a business run by his uncle, but this was going to be much more exciting.

After climbing up and over the back-boards, each of the men sat down tentatively on the wooden slatted seats that dropped down from the side boards. The dark canvas tarpaulin would give them some protection from the elements, but it would also serve to block any views as they travelled. They would have to be content with looking back through the open section at the rear, to get their first impressions of southern England.

Once they were all aboard, the Petty Officer made his way forward, climbing up into the front cab, yelling to his assistant to start cranking the engine. There was a thunderous explosion, quickly followed by a billowing cloud of acrid smoke that quickly began to rise through the floorboards of the truck. Someone had had the presence of mind to hold up the canvas screen at the side of the lorry. Slowly the smoke cleared, but not before everyone was coughing. The NCO in the front could be heard laughing. Once the engine had settled and was ticking over, they could all hear a loud annoying rattle. The constant stench of the carbon-dioxide gases was still seeping up through the floorboards, irksome, but not enough to provoke more coughing. Suddenly without any warning, there came the crunching of metal on metal, as the gears were engaged. The truck suddenly jerked forward, creeping at first, before picking up speed as it headed towards the dockyard gate.

There was a smoky discolouration that distorted the black sky over the dockyard buildings, giving the recruits an impression of it being a heavy industrialised area. They stopped at the gate, where a policeman checked the Petty Officers papers, and soon they were outside into the streets of Southampton itself, driving through the central hub of the city.

Electric street lighting was a phenomenon that the Island men had not seen before, and it came as an awesome surprise that the main streets here were lit-up as if it were day-time. There were more tall buildings here than George had ever seen in one place – and some of them were more than four stories tall. Southampton came and went very quickly, and the urban sprawl quickly gave way to rural solitude. The almost total darkness of the countryside lanes provided them with fresh clean air, which thankfully blew away all traces of the obnoxious gases, but now it became really cold and he started shivering. George was not so sure if he was enjoying this new experience.

The sudden bumps at hump back bridges threw the men all over the place, and they had to hang on tightly onto their seats for personal safety. The maniacal laughter from the front cab never ceased. George felt his body being pounded and bruised, having to brace himself on the corners to prevent him being thrown from his seat. However, the thrill of the wind rushing through his hair, as they flew along the country roads of Hampshire, was an excitement beyond belief. By standing one at a time, the recruits could look out directly over the top of the cab, but the force of the wind brought tears welling into their eyes. The roads ahead were very dark and narrow, lit only by the lorry's head-lamps. None of the young recruits had the faintest idea of where they were. Their driver would often lean out from the side of the cab, and look back at their wide frightened eyes. He grinned sadistically, as he rammed his foot onto the accelerator. As the truck reached the crest of a hill, one of the recruits standing yelled for the rest to come and see. They all found themselves looking down on the faint glow of lights far off in the distance. Something told George that those lights must be Portsmouth. He just hoped that his intuition was more accurate than it had been when he had been with Gladys that afternoon, when he had sighted the Isle of Wight.

Soon they were driving through the streets of Portsmouth and George stared out in wonder. Again, the presence of electric street lights made everything as bright as day, as the truck approached the centre of the city. Almost every building they passed made those in St Peter Port look small by comparison. It was now nearly ten o'clock in the evening and yet people could still be seen strolling about in a leisurely manner. There was a sea of blue uniforms, so many sailors littering the pavements in untidy groups. Many could be seen lurching from one pub to another. As the truck turned down into Queen Street to head up towards the Royal Naval Barracks at *HMS Victory*, some loud cries drew their attention towards the side of the road. A group of three drunken sailors were shouting raucous advice to them, and gesticulating wildly.

"Jump off while you can mate, it's not too late!"

"You don't know what you've let yourself in for!"

Their friend turned to urinate in the narrow passageway behind them.

They quickly disappeared, and after a few hundred yards the truck began to brake as it manoeuvred sharply right towards the Main Gate complex of the Royal Naval Barracks. Four great square red brick pillars supported black wrought iron gates at the entrance. An enormous guard-house stood over to one side. The open gateway was guarded by two armed uniformed sentries, with bayonet fitted rifles. They raised them in a threatening manner and challenged the approaching vehicle to stop. The lorry shuddered to a halt.

A Chief Petty Officer emerged from the adjacent guard-house, towing a thin sub lieutenant in his wake. The recruits stood warily, picking up their bags and suitcases. Their tormentor climbed out from the cab, came around to drop the tail-gate. He told them to jump down. Mingling into a group, they stood uncertainly on the cobbled road.

George stared in some awe at the two sentries in full dress uniform. They sported white belts with shining brass buckle clips, with white gaiters which were laced up to their knee. Black serge chin-stays held their caps securely on their heads. They were each equipped with a Lee Enfield .303 rifle, complete with a loaded magazine clip, which they held across their chests. George could see the shiny glint of cold steel of the eighteen-inch bayonets. He realised that he had finally arrived at his destination!

Their driver had become uncharacteristically quiet, as he held out his sheet of orders for inspection by the Chief Petty Officer. He saluted the young Officer as he appeared from behind the senior rate, but he spoke directly to the Chief.

"Detail returning from Southampton, Chief. I've picked up a new draft of recruits from the Channel Islands."

He stood to attention with his chin drawn so far back that it had almost disappeared into his starched collar. The Chief Petty Officer consulted the lists on his clip file.

"Yes – here we are. This lot are part of the 143 recruitment. They are billeted in Keppel Block tonight. Get them bedded down for the night, Petty Officer. They will be dealt with in the morning," said the CPO, in a broad sharp Ulster brogue.

'Dealt with,' thought George. They are making it sound like we're cattle going to the slaughterhouse. He remembered the sailor's comments on the street corner just a few minutes ago, and then thought that maybe we are!

"Right you lot," continued the Chief, addressing them as a group. "You are going to be given a bed for the night. Follow the PO here, and he'll show you where it is. There will be someone who will meet in the morning, and he will tell you all what to do."

They picked up their luggage and began to follow the Petty Officer, who led them up a tree-lined avenue that stretched out into the darkness of infinity. They all realised that were now within the Royal Naval barracks. A series of sturdy imposing three storied red brick buildings rose up in a procession on their left. Each of these blocks stretched back at least a hundred and fifty yards, so far that they disappeared into the darkness of the night shadows. At the lower floor entrance of each, there was an illuminated set of double-doors facing directly out onto the roadway. A stone lintel over each doorway was engraved with the name of each particular block. Frobisher was followed by Drake, before they stopped at the third and George could just make out the word Keppel above the door. They were herded through the double doors, and into a bare bleak foyer.

Inside the entrance hall, the walls were divided, half painted in white distemper from the ceiling down to brown glazed tiles that rose four feet up from the floor. The white paint failed to lighten the gloomy atmosphere. The space was lit by a single hissing gas mantle, that hung down from the ceiling just inside the doorway. A wide staircase disappeared around a corner, as it rose upwards towards the next floor. The flag stone floor amplified their footsteps, as they made their way across towards the small kiosk marked with the legend – Block Office. It had been roughly partitioned off the hall by some white painted wooden studwork. There was a large glass window in one side – but the interior looked dark and deserted. The PO knocked loudly on the only door and walked in. He emerged thirty seconds later accompanied by a drowsy looking rating, who was rubbing the sleep from his eyes, and tucking his white front into his bell bottom trousers. The dishevelled sailor took a quick look at the new arrivals with an expression that hovered between contempt and pity. He walked straight past them, heading towards another door at the end of the hall bearing the words – Bedding Store. Keys rattled in the lock, before he managed to open it.

"OK you lot, one at a time. Come in and collect your bedding for the night. Welcome to Jacob's Mansions, your home for the foreseeable future," he said, yawning widely again.

He was referring to the series of accommodation blocks they had just passed when they had walked up from the main gate. Each of these buildings had three storeys, and each floor contained two huge dormitories. Each dormitory slept some 240 men in hammocks. The blocks had been built just over ten years before to accommodate the men, who had previously been billeted in the wooden hulks from Nelson's era. There were still some moored down in the northern section of the dockyard. These were the wooden remnants of the old navy that had supplied the accommodation needs of Britain's main naval port for over seventy-five years. Some of these hulks had been moored in backwaters around Britain to act as prisons during the last century. These new accommodation blocks had been built as part of the redevelopment of the three major naval ports of Portsmouth, Chatham and Devonport between 1902 and 1903. They formed part of Admiral Jacky Fisher's naval reforms.

"I'll leave them with you now, Scouse. You will make sure that they are each given a bed, won't you?" said the PO.

"Yes, and I'll tuck them in as well PO," said the Liverpudlian, with a vain attempt at a smile.

The PO turned, and without even a word of farewell, he vanished out of the door. The group suddenly felt very alone, with their one familiar face having departed. Each man looked around bleakly at the Spartan starkness that surrounded him. At that moment every one of the recruits was thinking of the home comforts he had left behind. Each of them made their way into the store where they received a pre-determined issue of one pillow complete with a pillow-case, two sheets, one blanket and a counterpane. For this set of luxuries each man had to sign that they had received their quota in good condition in an issue book.

Once they had all been equipped, the sleepy rating re-emerged from the store and locked the door behind him, before leading them up the broad staircase. It became increasingly darker as they ascended. There were two flights, each of twenty steps before reaching the first landing. There was a single gas light that lit the first floor, but they didn't stop there. It became difficult as they ascended the second staircase trying to carry the bedding, along with their individual cases. On the second floor, and four flights of stairs later, they halted as their guide pushed open a set of swing doors. The cavernous space inside was lit by a single gas light, which had a red glass filter. The satanic glow it created did little to help them see where they were going. There were sounds of snoring men, only exceeded by the stench of sweaty socks, as they each edged into the darkness. The sailor placed his index finger to his pursed lips.

"Quiet lads, or you might be wearin' a boot as an earring," he whispered. "Go right down to the bottom of the dorm, and find yourself one of the metal bunk-beds with an empty mattress, make up your bed with what I have given you and get yourself turned in. They will issue you with your kit and hammocks, tomorrow. If yer want the heads during the night, there is one on each landing. Over there," he said, pointing. "Good night."

'What are heads?' thought George.

"What's the heads?" enquired one of his fellow recruits, as the man started to descend the stairs.

"Shut up," said a snarling voice from somewhere behind him in of the darkness.

When he turned back the guide had disappeared.

There were long narrow aisles between the endless rows of hammocks, all of which appeared to be occupied. Each hammock was slung between rows of metal bars that stretched laterally across the mess-deck. Moving on tiptoe, the new recruits followed each other into the near darkness. At the far end of the dormitory they finally found the series of metal framed bunk beds, stacked one atop the other. Reaching them, they stopped. It was too late to ask any questions, as their erstwhile guide was probably already back in his own bed. The incumbent natives around them didn't appear to be friendly, so the recruits began to dither, very unsure and none seemed to know what to do next. George was now wishing he had not signed those enlistment papers, but he broke the spell by placing his suit case on one of the bottom bunks. Following his example, the others began to select a bunk, and began to undress. After making up his bed, George climbed in, and tried to settle down. The coarse scratchy fibres of his blanket started to annoy him, before he realised that he had not placed the sheets on first. He got up and unmade the bed, before reassembling it, which proved to be much more comfortable. It certainly wasn't home, but at least he was warm, and there was a moderate degree of comfort. Vaguely satisfied with his lot he soon drifted off to sleep, dreaming about the lovely girl he had met on the ferry.

The alien wailing that woke George, made him sit up in alarm. He jerked up into the sitting position, hitting his head on the metal springs of the top bunk, making him fall back onto his pillow. His mind was reeling, as he tried to analyse the shrill high-pitched notes that were blasting into his eardrums. It's a bloody bugle, he thought.

His eyes slowly focused on the forest of metal bed legs that surrounded him, and with them came the realisation of where he was. Looking beyond, he could see lines of bulbous white sausage-like bundles five feet up in the air, all arranged in neat rows. Bare hairy legs began to appear from the edges. The dormitory began to buzz as sailors lowered themselves down from their hammocks, and bunks and headed off towards the washroom. Very soon there was a continuous procession of men, each carrying a towel, passing by his bunk. Following their example, George took his own towel and soap from his suit-case and followed the tide of men. The washroom walls were rendered in a white coloured cement, standing at the far end of the landing. Next to it were the toilets, which George heard one man refer to – as the heads. He was learning already. The washroom was big, and stretching from floor to ceiling. The floor was bare wood and scrubbed as white as wood could be. Positioned around the walls, and running down the centre, there were long slate slab tables, supported on metal trestles. Running down each of the slate slabs was a shining copper water pipe, with taps extending outwards at intervals on both sides.

A series of white enamelled metal bowls had been placed at intervals under each of the taps. George soon found that the taps only ran with cold water, before quickly noticing that over in the corner of the washroom stood a cauldron of hot water, that was bubbling away on a pot-bellied stove. The fire within the stove obviously made that corner of the wash-room warmer, because that was where most of the men had congregated. George watched the procedure as sailors picked up one of the bowls, filled it with a ladleful of the hot water, and then adjusted the temperature by filling the bowl from the cold taps. He quickly followed suit, enjoying the fresh feel of the soap against his skin before he rinsed his face. A sudden wave of nostalgia swept over him as he realised that he was using the soap that his father had made, which immediately made him think of home. The men standing alongside him were shaving, although there were many others who sported full beards. He felt slightly intimidated, as he only needed to shave once a week. He didn't possess a cut-throat razor anyway. Following the example of the others, he emptied his bowl of dirty water down a sluice sink, and then returned the bowl to the slate slab. He then refilled it with cold water and cleaned his teeth before re-joining his little group who were gathering nervously by the bunks they had slept in.

All around them men were donning uniforms, while others were lashing up their hammocks. George watched the chaotic scene in wonder, noting that it was a set procedure, which began with all of the internal bedding being tucked inside the hammock, before the sides were drawn in and lashed together by a rope that looped around the bundle several times to produce a completely water-tight cocoon. The sailors made it look easy, but George knew that it probably wasn't. Each of the hammocks were then taken down, and placed neatly into a huge metal basket, that looked like rows of giant white cigars arranged in a box.

George asked one of the passing men what they were to do. He said that he was off to breakfast, and suggested that if he were hungry, that they he should follow him. The others quickly fell into line behind George.

Breakfast turned out to be a hit or miss affair. They joined a queue towards an area of the dormitory where the Leading Hand in charge was holding court at a long wooden table. Some of his lackeys had been over to the galley to collect steaming buckets of porridge, trays of crispy bacon, and yet more trays containing fried eggs, that looked like white lily pads swimming in a pond of grease. At one end of the long table several loaves of bread were being sliced and buttered. The rations were being dished out in accordance to rank, or according to the Leading Hand's personal whim. His friends received bacon and egg, while lesser mortals, and that included new draftees, received a bowl of porridge. George and the others were the recipients of a great glutinous dollop that was plopped into a bowl. It came with the addition of a big spoonful of sugar, which when stirred in made it almost edible. The long scrubbed wooden mess tables were packed with men, so the newcomers had to eat whilst sitting on their bunks.

The food was extremely bland – but it was hot and filling, and it quickly dispelled their hunger. Afterwards the plates were washed and dried by their users in the buckets of hot water provided. Then, after the plate had been inspected by one of the Leading Hands, it was dried, and returned to the china pile on the table. Shortly afterwards there was another bugle call, which George found equally irksome. Instantly the mess began to empty, again leaving the recruits feeling at a loss as to what to do.

"Where is 143 recruitment?" screamed an urgent voice from down near the doorway, at the far end of the mess.

George stood and raised his hand, instantly feeling very self-conscious as many eyes turned in his direction. By him raising his hand, it had marked him out as a newcomer. He felt that it was a bit like being back at school, and asking to be excused to visit the toilet – that moment when everybody turned and looked at you with silly grins. Then it occurred to him that this place was not unlike being at school, because it was just as regimented, and just as formal. After all, this was a type of school, where he was going to learn how to be a sailor.

A Leading Seaman marched down the white wooden walkway between the bunks and empty hammock bars, halting in front of them. George had never seen a more highly polished pair of boots.

"Right, you lot – pay attention. My name is Leading Seaman Andrews and from this moment onwards you will call me – Leading Hand. I am going to be your instructor for the next twelve weeks, and we are going to get on famously, because if we don't, then your life is going to be absolute hell. You will all do your very best at all times, or I will make you wish that you had never heard of the navy. This morning we are going to get your issue of kit and hammocks. After that we can begin to turn you into sailors."

Looking down at his clipboard he said, "Right, answer your name when I call it out."

He was a slightly built man, but he looked very smart in his blue uniform. His white cap was pitched at a jaunty angle on his head, and his sharp chiselled features displayed a confidence and self-assurance that George had noticed in most of the men on the mess-deck that morning. The recruits started to move out of the accommodation dormitory, making their way down the wide staircases and out through the entrance hallway into the fresh morning air.

It was a bright, but somewhat cloudy day. The tree-lined road they had walked up the previous evening was awash with uniformed men going hither and thither in purposeful determination. Squads of men were being marched off to unknown destinations. They passed a smart group marching with symmetrical efficiency. More new recruits began to emerge from other blocks, and were ordered to join the Channel Islanders. They all stood together on the pavement, looking extremely awkward with their civilian cases and bags at their side, as they desperately tried not to get in anybody's way.

Leading Seaman Andrews reappeared, having been going around each block collecting his flock, and began herding them together like the good shepherd. They huddled for mutual support in their civilian clothes, making them stand out like sore thumbs. Beyond the avenue of trees, George could see a great open expanse of flat tarmac, its centre bulging up in a slight rise. Making it difficult for him to make out the white caps of men on the far side. It was rather like an extremely large black version of a crown bowls lawn.

"That space you are looking at out there is the parade ground," explained Leading Seaman Andrews, pointing to the tarmac area. "That is hallowed ground, that is. The first thing you have to remember is that you do not walk across it for any reason. There is only one time that you will ever be allowed to step onto it and that is when I take you out there for drill. At all other times, stepping onto it will bring down the wrath of God onto your puny shoulders, and if any of you ever needs to get somewhere on the other side, then you 'ave to go all the way around the edge. Your first drill will begin this afternoon and it will continue every day for the foreseeable future. Do I make myself clear?" he glared at each of them in turn.

"Yes," they mumbled.

"Yes, LEADING HAND," he screamed.

"Yes, Leading Hand," they repeated, in shocked chastened tones.

"Right, let's get you into a formation. The Navy has a language all of its own and the sooner that you begin to learn it, then the better your lives will become. We are all going to attempt to march across to the Slop Room. The Slop Room is the clothing issue store. In the navy, it is called the Slop Room – Is that clear?" he said.

"Yes, Leading Hand." They were beginning to learn.

Their transformation had begun. He began to arrange the men into three ranks, adjusting their positions according to height. He eyed them, and then he moved one of the men in front of George. Another check and he seemed to be satisfied.

"That's it," he declared. "From now on, every time you are told to 'Fall In' you will do so in exactly the same position that you now occupy. So remember who is in front, and who is on each side of you. I do not want to find anyone who does not know what his position is within the squad. Do you understand?" he bellowed.

"Yes, Leading Hand," they chanted as one.

"Good!" said Leading Seaman Andrews. "Pay attention to what I have to say. I'm going to give you your first marching orders and I don't want to see any silly mistakes. People will be watching you, and silly mistakes makes everyone laugh at you, because real sailors do not make mistakes. I know that you haven't been shown how to march properly yet, but for now I want you to try your very best to keep in step with the man in front of you. OK then, here we go," he said. "Listen carefully to every word that I say."

Raising his voice again, he shouted, "143 Class – HALT! That means that you stand at attention, with your feet together, arms at your sides and head still, looking straight ahead."

He spent another two minutes walking amongst them. He adjusted some of their postures to meet his stringent requirements. Once they resembled something like a squad, he stepped back and tried another order.

"143 Class – Will move to the RIGHT in threes – 143 Class, Right Turn."

All of the men did as they were told, except one who turned had left. The man looked confounded, and quickly reversed his position.

"There is always one," declared Andrews. "What is your name, sailor?"

"Christopher Powell," said the luckless individual.

"Powell, LEADING HAND," screamed Andrews. "I don't want to know what your mother calls you."

"Powell, Leading Hand," repeated the luckless Powell.

"Powell, you don't need me to tell you what an absolute pillock you look, do you? Now get yourself level with those around you."

There was a titter of laughter from Powell's new classmates. Andrews resumed his abrasive manner, and shouted. "Quiet." There was an instant stunned silence.

"All of you listen carefully to what I am saying. You are all going to make mistakes. Powell is just the first of many. None of you will never laugh at anyone in your class again. When we march, you will lead off with your left foot and swing your right arm forward. Just for your benefit Powell, your left leg is the one hanging off your arse on this side," he shouted, as he thumped Powell's left hip. Finally, he issued the order they had been waiting for.

"By the left – QUICK MARCH."

They moved off as one, and although keeping in step quickly became a problem for some, they managed to keep relatively together as a squad. Leading Seaman Andrews stared incredulously at Powell who was somehow managing to march with his right leg and right arm moving forward at the same time. Arriving at the Slop Room he barked once more.

"143 Class will come to the halt – 143 Class HALT."

Powell crashed into the man in front of him.

"I can see that you and I are going to have a very stimulating time together, Powell," grinned Leading Seaman Andrews, speaking into the man's right ear.

"I am sorry Leading Hand. I am not very good at this sort of thing, am I?"

"If you are looking for sympathy Powell, you will find it in the dictionary between shit and syphilis. You are right however – you are not very good at this, but believe me when I say that you soon will be."

Moving to one side of the squad, he tried them with another new order.

"Move to the left into file – and I will be watching you this time Powell – Move to the left in file. LEFT TURN."

They all breathed a sigh of relief when Powell got it correct.

"We are now going to get your kit. This is the first stage of the navy's attempt to turn you into real sailors. After today, at least you will all begin to look like one. It's not going to be an easy job sorting out all the pieces of unfamiliar kit, but at least you'll look the part when I have finished with you. When you've been issued with it, you will come back to the position you are standing in now. With intelligent men like you joining up, I bet the Kaiser is quaking in his boots. He is probably wishing right now that he could turn back the hands of time, and regretting the fact that he ever started this war. It is up to men like you to show him the error of his ways. I am sure that once he finds out that Powell has begun his training, he will be seeking an unconditionally surrender. A grateful nation will be forever in your debt, Powell. The King himself will want to shake your hand. You all might think this is going to be simple, and that being a sailor doesn't require too much thought. Well, I can tell you right now that the coming weeks are going to be hell. You will curse your mother for having given birth to you. But I can assure you that the more you try, then the less of a hell it will become, and your miserable lives will gradually become a lot easier. Because when I've finished with you, real sailors are what you are going to be."

It was not as bad as George had feared it was going to be. He was still feeling a little apprehensive, but if it continued as it had so far, then he had the feeling that he was going to enjoy his time in the navy.

Chapter Three

Assignation

George and his class had completed their six weeks of basic training at the Royal Naval Barracks. This was then followed by another six weeks of specialised training in gunnery and armaments, which in turn was interspersed by fitness training, and initiative exercises. The class had been marched and drilled on a daily basis, both taking place on the hallowed parade ground and along the roads of Portsmouth to the Gunnery School at Whale Island, which stands on a small Island towards the top of Portsmouth Harbour. There they underwent a vigorous series of assault courses, which were designed to push them all to the limit. Shore based gun-mountings allowed each man to practice the loading and unloading procedures of several types of naval armaments. Many of the shells and cartridge cases were extremely heavy, and several of the practice dummies were dropped before they finally got the evolution correct. They even had one practice on a twelve-inch mounting, which came complete with hydraulic rams, on which each man took turns in operating.

There were some quieter periods however, when they were shown rudiments of how to sail a whaler, one of the many boats carried aboard the larger warships. They were cast adrift in the fairly placid waters of Portsmouth Harbour, and told to put the new knowledge into practice. They also underwent the muscle sapping exhaustion of rowing the clinker-built cutters in the creek near the Fountain Lake Jetty, at the top of the dockyard. Early every morning an hour was spent in the huge gymnasium of the barracks, undergoing squad fitness training along with cutlass drills. George thought it a little outdated to swing a cutlass, but was told that he may be part of a boarding party, and may well have to use one. Obstacle courses, cross country runs, and seamanship exercises had filled every spare minute that could be squeezed into their day.

It had not been long before George could feel a physical change occurring within his own body, as he was forced up towards reaching the peak of physical fitness. Every night, as he lay in his hammock, his muscles burned – strangely itching for more exercise – making him feel confident that he could handle anything they chose to test him with.

The main reason that the whole class still remained an intact cohesive unit through the trials and tribulations was largely due to the dedication of Leading Seaman Andrews. George could remember moments in the early days when it looked like they might fail, but they quickly found that by helping each other, and standing together as a team, they could achieved their objective. By the end of their basic training their instructor had turned them into his private nautical landing party. They had become a strong cohesive unit that worked well together and for each other. George realised that this same ethos could be applied to the crew of every ship within the fleet. It was how the Navy worked – by good teamwork.

Leading Seaman Andrews had been a terrific instructor, once they had gotten to know him, but many of them found out that he could be a tyrant if they got on his wrong side. He had taken the time and trouble to ensure that they all got through their training successfully, including the luckless Powell, who despite the extra hours spent practicing on the parade ground, still found marching a challenge. Maybe it was his inner co-ordination?

Following their final inspection, they were each pronounced fit to take their place aboard any ship in the fleet. It had all culminated with a large parade of the six classes who were passing out on the same day, and they smartly carried out a military march past in front of the Commander–in–Chief of the Portsmouth district. Everyone knew that they would shortly be drafted, sent off to their individual postings. George felt a surge of excitement when speculating on where he would be heading!

After arriving back in their mess-deck after the parade, Leading Seaman Andrews announced that each of them had been granted leave until midnight. He also informed them that he expected them all to attend a celebration party in a local pub that evening. A huge cheer had erupted, as this would be the first time that they had been allowed any freedom since their arrival at the barracks.

During the rigours of the training, George had thought about Gladys several times and he just hoped that she still felt the same way about their friendship, because the enforced absence had made him keener than ever to see her. He realised that he was being allowed a whole twelve hours of total freedom in which to do whatever they wanted, without being told what to do. The freedom of being able to step outside of the confining boundary of the Barrack Gates, to mingle with normal people, would be a pleasure in itself. As he had arrived at night, he would now be able to see what the city of Portsmouth actually looked like. Over the past twelve weeks he had become very acquainted with the road route between the Barracks and Whale Island, but this was a tiny fraction of the metropolis. It was a city of a hundred thousand people and it would be nice to see what the rest of it looked like. Besides his weekly letter home, he had written several letters to Gladys, telling her about all of his adventures during training, but he was longing to tell her in person.

Unfortunately, he would not be able to stay with her for too long, as he had been ordered to attend their celebratory passing out party that evening. He worked out that he would be able to make his way down to Southsea, find Gladys, and spend some time with her. Allowing himself four hours, then he would still have time to make his way back in time for the party.

George thought the service a strange place, because the Navy, in its infinite wisdom had just spent three months turning raw recruits into a single reliable team of men only to split them up and send them off to the four corners of the earth. George thought that it would be much more sensible to draft them all together to the same ship within the fleet, where they could continue to work together. He knew that was not going to happen, but the prospect of being sent to some exotic location had them all in a state of eager anticipation. Every one of them was eager to go to sea, wanting the chance to put their newly acquired expertise into practice.

During Stand Easy (the morning break) a Petty Officer walked into the mess deck and pinned up their drafting appointments on to the notice board. As the doors shut behind him, the men surged forward and crowded around it; fingers began stabbing a name, and tracing along the lines of type to reveal the ship they had been drafted to. There were some great whoops of delight heard as the names of some of the great battleships were shouted out as a destination. Powell was off to join a cruiser that was part of the West Indies squadron – lucky blighter! Leading Seaman Andrews said that it was probably because he looked like he was dancing to a calypso when he marched. His ship would be based at Bermuda – and George was very envious. Some of the other men were going to equally exotic locations such as Shanghai, Cape Town and one even as far away as Australia, but most of them were being sent to front line combat vessels within the Home Fleet. One of the Jersey men who had come over on the ferry with George, was off to join one of the latest Dreadnoughts. Another was joining a fishing trawler that had been converted to mine sweeping duties in the Channel, a post that nobody envied. George watched the disappointed expression spread across the man's face.

Standing on the outside of the throng, George patiently waited for his chance to get to the board and once there, he eagerly sought out his name from the pages. Eventually he spied it, his eyes followed his finger along to his assignment. What! He couldn't believe what he had just read. Had his finger slipped from the line? Horrified he rechecked his name, and his destination draft. It must be a misprint, he thought. His third re-check confirmed that there was no mistake. Submarine Service!

Out of all the different types of ship serving within the fleet to which he could have been drafted, he had been selected for the Submarine Service. He immediately went and sought out Leading Seaman Andrews. When he complained to him about his posting, he was informed that there had been a huge increase in demand for the recruitment of submariners, as the building programme of these underwater craft had been stepped up tenfold. In normal peace time conditions, most submariners were hand-picked volunteers from men who had served at least four years within the surface fleet, but due to the outbreak of war they were now taking new entrants to train directly. As a result of this decision, George would be travelling across the harbour to join Fort Blockhouse at Gosport on the 5th of November 1914 to commence his underwater training – and to make matters worse that was tomorrow!

Standing there in utter dejection, George bitterly regretted his hasty decision to enlist that day in Smith Street. Everyone knew that submarines were death traps – it was common knowledge for goodness sake. He had read articles about several of the disasters in his father's news-paper, where the crewmen had died horrific deaths, suffocating and entombed within these metal coffins. Some of the older members of his mess dormitory were only too keen to embellish these stories with a series of particularly gruesome tales. The consensus of their reminiscences was the fact that one or more submarines had been sunk, either accidentally or otherwise, every year since the Royal Navy's first submarine named Holland 1 had been launched back in 1901. Most had gone down with the loss of their entire crew, leaving them virtually no means of escape, even todays modern versions provided little chance of getting out should the unthinkable happen. Hundreds of men had perished inside these steel tubes as a result the trial and error policy that the Admiralty had seemed to employ during their development over the past fourteen years. Most of them had died slow excruciating deaths as their oxygen had slowly disappeared, while the luckier crew members had been drowned instantly. He remembered reading his father's newspaper that back in January when there had been one lost. *HMS A7* had failed to surface for some unknown reason during an exercise. The local and national broadsheets had printed a name list of the unfortunate crew. Some of the teething problems in these boats, during those early years, had been caused through sheer incompetence, or just a plain ignorance about how the sea conditions affected the boats manoeuvrability. Other causes had been because the naval designers themselves had simply got things wrong. There also existed the very serious hazard of being run down by surface ships, whose Captains were unused to seeing such low-lying vessels. After all, it was a new science, and as with all emerging technologies there were bound to be casualties. George was very well aware that the Wright brothers had only taken to the air some thirteen years previously and that several of those early pioneering aviators had met tragic ends through teething problems with the design of their aircraft. George didn't want to be a casualty because of a teething problem.

Somehow, being sent over to Gosport on Guy Fawkes Night only served to place a bitter icing on a foul-tasting cake. George made a last-ditch effort by stating an official complaint in front of his Divisional Office, but it simply resulted in something that he had been ignorant of being pointed out to him. He was told that he should have read the small print when he had signed his enrolment papers. On the first page it clearly states that he agrees to serve in any of His Majesty's Ships, and that word ANY included submarines. George felt that his life had reached a new low point.

Having already made his decision to try and locate Gladys, and not wanting to let this bad news get him down, he quickly got dressed in his best uniform. Many of his friends were also getting ready to go ashore, but he declined their invitations to join them for a drink in the pubs along The Hard, telling them that he would see them that evening. Once outside, he walked purposefully towards the Main Gate, grasping the precious leave pass in his hand. As he neared the gate, he could hear the hustle and bustle of Queen Street long before he reached the large guard house building, which he had learned also contained the barred windows of the detention cells for miscreants. He had heard stories that this was where the drunks were thrown on their return from shore leave. George had no wish to visit the place, and certainly had no intention of getting drunk.

All of the men going ashore were standing in a huddle, and as the town hall clock could be heard striking the hour at midday, they were told to *Fall In*. They all lined up in three ranks, before being inspected by the Officer of the Day. Two of them were sent back to polish their shoes to a better standard, and another had failed the inspection due to dirty marks on his cap, but the rest were allowed to proceed ashore.

As soon as he stepped outside the Main Gate, George was met by a flurry of activity that made the water-front of St Peter Port harbour look like a sleepy hollow. Above him, the sky was somewhat cloudy with splashes of sunlight breaking through the omnipresent cloud. The plaintive cries of gulls, blown inland off the harbour, quickly reminded him of the proximity of the sea. Until now, marching through the Dockyard, and along the brick wall of the barracks towards Whale Island had been the one of the few times he had actually left the confines of the barracks. This would be the very first time that he had set a foot out into the city of Portsmouth. In fact, it would be the first place that he had ever visited away from Guernsey. At first, he felt somewhat self-conscious in his uniform, and more than a little awkward. Although he had gotten used to wearing it, it had always been in an environment where everybody was dressed the same, but out here he realised that he was the odd one out, as most of the people on Queen Street were wearing civilian clothes. He stood just outside the gate at the edge of the pavement, and took in his first glimpse of life in Portsmouth.

Motorised omnibuses and electric trams rattled by, all crammed with people, with a cacophony of honking horns and frightening klaxons warning the unwary of their approach. These mechanised monsters ploughed their way past the horse drawn delivery carts, and brewer's drays. The loud whirr of their electric motors vied with the clip-clop of the animal's iron shoes echoing against the cobbles. The pungent whiff of horse dung assailed his nostrils and he turned his head in the direction of the smell to see a fresh steaming pile in the road behind the loaded dray that had just passed by. This assault from the noise from of the street even dulled the cries of the ever-present gulls that were circling overhead.

George leapt back from the kerb-side as another city bus careered past. A girl wearing a bright red scarf, which draped down over the side from the open top deck, caught his eye. She was pretty, and her scarf was blowing in the breeze like a regimental banner. He saw her looking down in his direction again, and was a little surprised when she gave him a little wave, before turning towards some unseen companion.

From immediately behind he heard the groan of metal on metal, and as he turned, he saw that the huge black Barrack Gates were being opened. He could hear several orders being bawled, and before he realised what was happening, he had to move out of the way as a whole ship's company of marching sailors emerged. Each man was carrying his kitbag on his shoulder. A policeman stepped out in front of them into the traffic, holding up his hand to stop the vehicles. They squad marched smartly through the gates, before the stream of navy blue turned right, down towards the dockyard gates to join their newly refitted ship. They were followed by several carts being pulled by more sailors, that were filled with their hammocks. As he watched George felt that he was now an equal with each of them, and with his newly acquired technical knowledge, he felt that he had truly become a child of the twentieth century. The start of his big adventure was just about to begin – if only he were not joining the submarine service!

Forcing his mind back towards the present, he became filled by a strange excitement as he set forth on his first excursion into Portsmouth and a relief of finally leaving his environment of the past three months. As he began to pass the populace, his concern about being conspicuous in his uniform quickly disappeared, mainly because nobody seemed to turn a hair. Sailors had been going ashore in Portsmouth for over five hundred years. Why should he be any different from any other sailor? As he was now part of that proud service, he turned to his left and started walking towards the group of taller buildings standing above a line of trees that formed the town centre. His confidence began to climb.

He had not walked more than fifty yards before a new problem reared, as he realised that he was not too sure where to go. Across the street stood a tented stall that was selling hot roasted chestnuts, and the smell of the hot coals and charred nuts drifted on the wind. Taking a deep breath, he crossed over the road and asked the vendor for directions. On this side of the road, standing out in stark comparison to the ratings' dreary accommodation blocks, stood the imposing grandeur of the Officers Wardroom. At the gateway entrance, with its fancy ornate ironwork gates, there were two more armed sentries who stood guard, each man standing in front of sentry box. Although it had been built of the same red brick as the Barrack Blocks, the architect had obviously been given a much freer bigger budget in his design. There were carved lintels, elaborate archways, complete with Doric pillars. After arriving in the navy, George had very quickly become well aware of the great social divide that existed between the officer class and the ratings of the lower deck, and the opulence of this building plainly displayed that disparity. He thought it to be unfair because every man – officer or rating would be fighting in the same vessel – each placing his life on the line for victory – maybe this was the way of the world.

As he walked eastward along Queen Street the pavements were crowded with people and sailors in a colourful clash of uniform and civilian attire. All along the street there were other vendors earnestly trying to out-shout one another in their enthusiasm to attract business. Each seemed to be doing a roaring trade, providing everything from seafood to shoelaces.

He thought how nice it was to see women again, and he realised with some amazement that other than the nurses in the sick-bay, there had been no women in his life during the whole of his training. Overhead, seagulls continued to squawk their grumpiness to the world, always keeping a watchful eye out for the unattended edible anything. Several barrow-loads of fruit and vegetables were vying for trade beside a stall selling matches and tapers. He stopped and noticed a small posy of late autumnal blooms, which he bought. The stall holder wrapped them in brown paper. They were not as colourful as the summer flowers, but the perfumed smells made George think of Guernsey. It had seemed such a long since he had been home, but then realised that it was only three months since he had waved goodbye from the departing ferry.

Heading up the street towards the city centre, above the ambient roar he heard the tooting whistle of a steam train. Beyond the eastern end of the barracks wall, just past the imposing splendour of St John's church, stood some hand-wheel operated railway gates, which he could see were just closing, shutting off the road to the traffic flow. During his training George had heard these trains several times a day, as they came off the main line between Portsmouth and Southsea Station and the Portsmouth Harbour Station, to make their way down into the Royal Naval Dockyard at the Unicorn Gate, but this would be the first time that he had actually seen one. He stopped and waited, as he was somewhat curious. A long line of goods trucks rumbled and rocked their way down the slight gradient, hauled by a dirty steam tank engine, puffing loudly and send a column of white smoke high into the sky. Each wagon had a fluttering red flag flying from the roof to indicate that explosives were being carried. The groaning metal of the rails was an indication of their heavy load, and as each truck passed by it caused the ground to vibrate beneath his feet. The clunkety de clunk, as the wheels jolted across the rail joints resounded in his ears. At the head, the small tank engine looked somewhat incongruous to be hauling these heavy loaded wagons, but it seemed to be coping well. They clattered on into the dockyard to deliver their deadly cargo to the waiting warships. Once the long line had past, a railwayman appeared and began to strain on a giant hand-operating wheel, which slowly opened the gates, releasing the impatient queue of traffic that had amassed on either side.

George could see a mass of people heading towards him, and wisely decided to run across rails before the surge of vehicles bore down on him. Standing on the safety of the pavement, he looked westward, back down Queen's Street. Beyond the Barracks there lay a procession of public houses, theatres and music halls that stretched all the way down to the harbour frontage area known as The Hard. He knew that the dockyard gates stood at the northern end of this area, which along with the Harbour railway station formed the eastern edge of the harbour itself. Somewhere down there was where he would be meeting the rest of his class tonight for the farewell party. The Dog and Duck was the name of the pub.

Turning back towards his main purpose, he noticed a building ahead that was much taller than those around the Commercial Road area. He quickly realised that he was viewing the upper part of the imposing splendour of the Town Hall ahead, built in white stone, and towering up above the trees that formed the verdant oasis of Victoria Park. The clock on the tower read a quarter past twelve.

He felt total freedom, and have the ability to do anything. With his newly established position in life as an Ordinary Seaman, he realised that there were a great many things available to him that he had never been able to access before. The temptation to enter a public house and buy a pint of ale came to mind. He had never been into a pub on his own before, and knew that the age limit to drink alcohol was twenty-one. It was something that he did not agree with at all. After all, if he was old enough to die for his country, then he should be able to purchase a pint of beer, but from what he had heard on the mess-deck, the publicans of Portsmouth usually turned a blind eye if the man was in uniform. Voting was another contentious issue, as over here on the mainland one also had to be twenty-one before they could even choose their parliamentary candidate. It did not work that way on Guernsey. The Island was Bailiwick, which was an ancient feudal form of government, many of the legislative positions there were hereditary, where land owners, or those who held fiefdoms effectively ran the States Council. The States were in fact the eleven parishes on the Guernsey, including the Island of Alderney. He suddenly missed the Island, as a wave of nostalgia washed over him. He decided that he would not to buy any beer. What would Gladys think of him, if he turned up with beer fumes on his breath? Besides, there would be plenty of opportunity to buy a pint tonight at the Dog and Duck.

After deciding to abandon his visit to a pub, he made his way through another set of wrought iron gates, and took the short cut that had been recommended by Leading Seaman Andrews, heading towards the Town Hall square via Victoria Park. The trees provided a welcome sense of peace and tranquillity, as he left the hustle and bustle of the busy thoroughfare behind him. Some conifers supplied the greenness of needles, but most of the deciduous trees had seriously begun to shed their crisp brown leaves, and the pathway was covered in a rustling carpet. Looking up at their bare branches, George could see them silhouetted against the autumn sky. They reminded him of the plan view of a gigantic river delta complex. At school, he remembered sitting beside Matthew, as Mr Jefferies had drawn a diagram on the blackboard, trying to explain the natural formation of a river during a geography lesson. The smaller shoots of these trees looked like the tributaries that were running into larger branches, which in turn thickened as they joined the main body of the trunk. A squirrel suddenly scampered across the branch he was looking at just as a passing cloud converted the bright blue sky into a dull grey, spoiling the silhouette definition, the shadow making him shudder and hunch his shoulders. Even with him wearing his coarse-knit sea jersey, instead of the standard white front, the exposed skin around the neck felt the icy fingers of the air that blew down from the Arctic regions; a harbinger of the cold season to come.

The sceptics, who had forecast that the war would be over within three months, had already had their prediction shot down in flames by what was taking place out in the bloodied fields of the Mons valley. The French were also suffering terrible casualties further south. Nobody had envisaged the terrible effects of the machine gun, or the sheer intimidating size of the German military machine. The opening engagement of the conflict had already made the cavalry obsolete, as both the lancers and their mounts were mercilessly mown down. In these initial exchanges the French Army had attacked with flags flying, accompanied by a full military marching band. They had also been mercilessly mown down, making all subsequent attacks much more cautious. Having lost of over a hundred thousand men, the Allies had finally halted the initial German advance, and prevented them reaching Paris. The British and French armies were desperate for reinforcements, to just be able to hold the enemy. The two enormous armies now faced each other over the new extensive excavations of their protective trench systems.

With the consequent shelling by both sides the flat farmlands of Picardy, that were once filled with poppy and meadow flowers, had been churned into a hellish moonscape of mud, craters, the sodden slough interrupted by the stumped torsos of denuded trees. Forlorn, dispirited soldiers were now living up to their knees in mud, and for many death came as a welcome relief from the misery they were being forced to endure.

After reading in the newspapers about the senseless slaughter taking place in France and Belgium, George was now extremely thankful that he had insisted on joining the navy on that day he had enlisted in St Peter Port. Over there in the front lines, life for the average Tommy Atkins was absolute purgatory and with this current stalemate, he saw little chance of an early termination to the conflict. If one side managed to win a few precious yards, an immediate counter-attack would invariably recover it. Each attack was paid for with the blood of hundreds of the nation's youth. Fit young men like himself, who now will never to be blessed with the chance of growing to full maturity, or of ever have a family of their own, or able to fulfil their childhood ambitions. These fallen heroes lost not only their lives, but each death seriously reduced the professional strength of the army. New recruits were just emerging from training and were now being sent to reinforce the front lines. National and local papers had begun publishing the names of those who had perished. A series of faceless names on the ever-growing list of casualties, leaving only their kinfolk to mourn their passing.

George was beginning to see the futility of this conflict, and had already tried to calculate his own chances of surviving it, because by him soon to join the submarine service, knowing that his life expectancy had had been significantly decreased. The great adventure that he had envisaged, was turning into a nightmare. Over the past weeks he had read every newspaper that he could get his hands on – although not that many were available whilst he had been in training. From what he had read, it was Germany who was holding the upper hand. Britain and France had done well just to hold them back. The Allied Generals did not seem to have an answer to the machine gun, other than to use the old tried and tested tactics of sending hundreds of men forward against them. It all seemed such a senseless slaughter. Perhaps the significant turning point that was needed would take place at sea! George had convinced himself that would be where his big adventure would turn the tide, and eventually bring about an Allied victory in this war.

Every winter fashion was being paraded on this changeable autumn afternoon, with a mixture of light furs, bright scarves and long warm coats adorning the trendiest women. There were even a couple of pessimistic umbrellas being paraded, as obviously some did appear to trust the weather. Despite the drabness of the autumn colours, the blueness of sailors in uniform were prevalent in providing some colour. Some strolled through the park with a girl on their arm, while others were just out for a bit of fun and freedom. The relative peace within this small green oasis in the middle of the city gave George a feeling of well-being. As he got nearer to the Town Hall, he began to calculate his next move, as he knew from some earlier enquiries that it was a long walk to Southsea. Leading Seaman Andrews had tried to give him directions, but had suggested that he catch an omni-bus. George thought that it could not be that far, and that by him walking there he would save his money, but after half an hour at a brisk pace it seemed longer than he ever imagined. After he had cleared the town hall square area, it seemed that he was walking past one long terraced street after another, with every house looking very much the same. The constant repetition began bore him, he became a little disorientated, and tried to assess where he was. He knew that if he continued south-ward he would eventually reach the sea – would he not? Should he ask his way? He continued.

George had never seen so many private vehicles on a road before, and he had been sent scampering onto the pavement for his personal safety on more than one occasion. Deciding to keep to pavements, he again once more to think of the disappointing start to this war. Recent newspaper reports, although extolling stories of personal heroism from the battlefield, were failing to mention the huge losses that were being suffered. The population had expected a speedy end to the conflict, and the longer it progressed then the greater their concern would become.

Only recently he had read with interest the report of a naval fiasco that had occurred in the Mediterranean around the time that he had left Guernsey. At the start of the conflict, the chance of an early victory at sea had been lost through indecision, and a series of bad luck judgements. At the beginning of August, a few days before war had actually been declared, two German battle-cruisers, the Goeben and the Breslau under the command of Admiral Souchon, had been coaling at Brindisi harbour on Italy's south east coast. They were being monitored by a force of British Battle Cruisers under the command of Admiral Sir Berkeley Milne, and a squadron of armoured Cruisers under the command of Admiral Troubridge. Without any warning the German ships slipped out of harbour under cover of darkness, leaving the British to hunt high and low for them. After shelling the ports of Philippeville and Bone in Algeria, the Germans had disappeared once more. Admiral Souchon's cunning had become apparent when it was officially announced that the Goeben and Breslau had entered the harbour of Constantinople in Turkey, and that both of the units had been officially sold to the Turkish navy. As he had read the report, George could not help but think that all of these place names sounded rather romantic. To his young mind they evoked mysterious and exotic lands. Fabulous locations like North Africa, Greece, Italy, Turkey, and ancient cities like Algiers and

Constantinople. Who knows where and what places he would be visiting before this war was finally over!

George's day-dreaming had taken him as far as the Queens Hotel, a large oblong block of an hotel that guarded the top of Osbourne Road, and looked out over the wide expanse of Southsea Common. He looked out over the grass and could see the shimmering waters of the Solent and the Isle of Wight beyond. He was amazed at the large number of ships that were anchored out there. He could also see the four great round stone towers, rising up out of the water, relics from another long-forgotten war. They had been built during the last century to repel the threat of a French invasion, who strangely, were now our allies.

His mind returned back to his present quest, and he reached into his jacket pocket for the scrap of paper containing Gladys' address. As he reread it, he noted that he was now standing at the top of the street where she actually lived. He had been walking for nearly an hour, and had managed to get himself lost on two occasions, admitting to himself that he had only arrived here by sheer luck.

Feeling a nervous anticipation, he began to make his way along the street, his eyes searching the door numbers. Working out how the sequence of the numbering system, he predicted where her house was well before he reached it.

Stopping at the gate, he stood staring up at the polished brass knocker and letter-box mounted against gleaming black paintwork of the wide wooden front door. Nervous was the only word that described how he was feeling. Taking a deep breath, he pushed the gate open, and started to walk up the path. Half way, having decided that he would simply announce his presence, he suddenly remembered her father, which had caused an involuntary hesitation, and he began to dither.

His nervousness reminded him of the time Matthew had dared him to jump into the sea at St Peter Port harbour at low tide. It had been from the top of a brick storehouse that stood at the end of the stone jetty. From where he had stood that day, down to the water had been a drop of nearly forty feet, as the tidal ranges in the Channel Islands are some of the largest in Europe. He could still remember his hesitation. His dare-devil spirit had wanted to jump, but caution against injury had held him back. What if there was an underwater projection that would spear him! Or maybe a submerged rock that would snap a leg! He was feeling that same hesitancy now. Would he be chased away by her father, or merely be rejected by Gladys, and have the door slammed in his face?

Just as he had on that roof-top, he had taken a determined deep breath and stepped forward. He walked up to the door, noticing that his hand was trembling as he reached up for the brass knocker, but none the less he gave it a good rap. It had been more from an internal determination than any confidence that he possessed. He stood on the door-step waiting through what seemed like an eternity. The urge to use the toilet came upon him, but it disappeared as he heard footsteps approaching from the other side of the door. He removed his cap, nervously fiddling with the rim. The door opened revealing, not the steely eyes of Gladys' father, but those of the diminutive figure of a uniformed maid. She cast an appreciative eye over the young sailor.

"Yes?" she enquired with a coquettish smile.

"I've come to see Miss Gladys Rumsey," he said in a dry rasping voice. Coughing nervously, he looked at her expectantly.

She gave a shrug, closing the door on him, and he heard her footsteps receding down the unseen passageway. He stood there in the cold wind blowing in off the Solent – the urge to relieve himself returned. The next set of footsteps that he heard, were certainly not those of the maid. They sounded more of a shuffle, a much slower and a gentle gait, punctuated by the clunk, clunk of a walking stick. When the door was opened this time, it revealed the diminutive form of Aunt Lucretia. She looked as pale and frail as George remembered from their brief meeting on the boat.

"What can I do for you, young man?" she enquired.

"Do you remember me, ma'am? My name is George Torode. I met Miss Gladys and good self on the Channel Island ferry three months ago. I've come to pay Gladys a visit – that is if she is in."

Suddenly the looming figure of Captain Rumsey filled the doorway behind the old lady. George cowered.

"What is it? What's all the noise?" he demanded, looking from one to the other.

A strangled gasp came from George's throat, it had never felt drier. He looked up at the Captain's intimidating presence and managed to stammer that he wished to see his daughter. The older man's face showed utter disdain, but George's resolve stiffened, and he became determined not to be put off – so he repeated his request in a more determined manner. The older man seemed lost for words, and did nothing but stare at him. He did not invite George to enter, and nor did he speak. It was developing into a standoff of wills, as each of the men seemed to be trying to outstare the other. George was determined that he would not to give in, and it appeared that the Captain had exactly the same ambition. George could feel himself begin to weaken inside, and it came as a sheer relief when he heard Gladys' voice calling from the top of a staircase.

"Who is it Daddy?"

Suddenly she was at her father's side, her face peeping enquiringly around the big man's sleeve.

"George," she squealed delightedly. "How absolutely lovely to see you."

George's face broke into a shy smile, his expression quickly moulding back into one of defiance, as he gave her father a fierce stare. He felt like saying, I told you so, but thought better of it. Ignoring the captain, he turned his whole attention back to Gladys. He handed her the posy of flowers that he had bought. She took them and plunged her nose into the tiny blooms. He could not help but stare at her. She was definitely as pretty as he had remembered, and was wearing one of the most attractive dresses that he had ever seen. A powder blue creation, with the top half covered in white lace that ran up her slender neck.

"Why on earth are you standing out here in the cold, George? Do come in, come in. How nice of you to call. Has your training finished at last?"

She took his arm, pulling him past the unbending figure of her father, and her rather non-plus looking aunt. George found it difficult to squeeze past the captain's bulk, as he seemed determined to make his journey as awkward as possible. Then, as if sensing defeat, the big man's determination finally crumbled and he stepped back, moving aside to allow the sailor entry. Seeming totally oblivious to the battle of minds that had been taking place, Gladys began bombarding George with questions, as she led him towards the drawing room.

"You look very well, George. Naval life certainly seems to be agreeing with you," she said, as they sat down together.

The room was very well appointed, and as he was directed towards a chair, George could hear a mumbled conversation taking place out in the hallway behind him. Then quite suddenly they were joined by Aunt Lucretia. She made her way towards a cushioned seat in the window alcove, and nervously sat down. George surmised that the captain had sent her in to be a chaperone. There was no sign of the captain, who seemed to have disappeared, but he suspected that he would not be very far away.

Despite the old lady's presence, George soon began to relax in Gladys' company. She was so exuberant, inquisitive, and eager to hear all his news. He felt totally vindicated for having come, and began to answer her by recounting his tale of naval life, making her laugh at some of the exploits, giggling when he told her about the first day of his training.

"That chap, Powell certainly seems to be accident prone, doesn't he?"

George looked across at the old lady, whose head was gently nodding down towards her chest. They grinned at each other in a conspiratorial fashion and lowered their voices to a whisper. Just as he was running out of stories, she came to his rescue by changing the subject.

"Have you heard the terrible news today, George?" she asked, her mood changing as quickly as the question, and she became somewhat sombre.

He had to admit that he had not heard any news today. Leading Seaman Andrews had given them a severe bout of physical training before breakfast, and he found that his muscles were still aching in places. The parade had followed and then the disappointing news about his draft had filled his morning. The rest of his time had been spent getting his kit packed and ready for his posting across to Fort Blockhouse. There just simply had not been any time to read a newspaper. In fact, the last newspaper he had read that been one that was abandoned on the mess deck table three days before.

Gladys rose and crossed the room to the low table in the far corner, and picking up that day's newspaper, she handed it to him. He looked at the headline and saw that it had been written in a large bold typeface – SOUTH ATLANTIC SQUADRON SUNK AT CORONEL.

"Isn't it terrible?" she declared, before he had a chance to read the full report. "All those poor men lost at sea, and dying like that so far from home."

As George began to read the article, he was thankful for her respectful silence. The report served to reinforce his earlier pessimism about the Navy's apparent ineptitude so far in this war. The West Indies Squadron under the command of Admiral Sir Christopher Cradock had been drawn south in pursuit of a German force that had been carrying out offensive operations against Allied shipping in the South Atlantic.

Wasn't the luckless Powell due to join a ship in that squadron? The ship that he was due to join may well have been one of those that had been sunk.

Cradock's squadron had managed to transit through the Straits of Magellan, emerging out into the Pacific following the receipt of intelligence information. The German force was both superior in quality of their ships, and in their fire power. It was inevitable that the two forces would meet. The action had taken place only three nights before off of a small bay on Chilean coast named Coronel. Cradock's force had consisted of two armoured cruisers, an armed merchant cruiser and one light cruiser. Originally his squadron had included the old pre-dreadnought battleship,

Canopus, but she had been plagued by engine problems and had fallen behind, being too slow to keep up with the main force. At 1620 on the 1st of November smoke was sighted on the south eastern horizon and just twenty minutes later Captain Luce of *HMS Glasgow* reported that he had sighted the Scharnhorst and Gneisnau in company with the Leipzig. With a slight advantage in speed, the British might have had the chance to escape towards the south, where they could have sought the protection of Canopus' powerful twelve-inch guns, and in doing so they would then have complied with Admiralty orders not to engage a force with superior firepower. At that moment Cradock's argument had been that he would lose contact with Admiral von Spee's German squadron, and that would have given the Germans the freedom to strike anywhere in the Pacific at the time of their choosing. He knew that he had no choice but to stay in contact, and logically reasoned that he did not need to sink the Germans, but simply cause them enough damage to force them to seek repairs in a foreign port, where they would be then interned for the duration of the war.

At 1818 the *Good Hope*, *Monmouth*, *Glasgow* and the *Oranto* were in single line ahead on a south-easterly course that would quickly bring them within range of the Germans' guns and Cradock signalled to his squadron that he was going to engage the enemy, but it was not until 1900 that the action actually began.

Von Spee had also spotted the British, and had purposely taken up a position towards the east of the British force to place Cradock's ships in a position where they would be silhouetted by the setting sun on the western horizon. The range closed to 12000 yards. The initial exchanges began, and Scharnhorst's third salvo put *HMS Good Hope*'s forward gun turret out of action, and the Gneisnau's opening shots quickly set *HMS Monmouth* ablaze. The fight continued as the darkness descended, and by 1945 both of the damaged vessels were in obvious distress. Five minutes later there was a tremendous explosion as *HMS Good Hope*'s forward magazine went up, which quickly reduced her to a blackened hulk, lit solely by the faint red glow from the fires that blazing within her hull. *HMS Glasgow* and *HMS Oranto* both turned, and fled south towards the protection of Canopus, it being impossible for them to help any of the survivors due to the total darkness, and the heavy sea that was running. To remain would have been suicide.

Von Spee signalled to his light cruisers to go in search for the surviving British squadron, but all that they managed to find were the wrecks of the *HMS Monmouth* and *HMS Good Hope.* They also found it impossible to affect any rescue of the crews, and so the German gunners despatched them both to the bottom. Both ships went down with all hands. Von Spee then turned his squadron northward towards the wide expanses of the Pacific in the knowledge that he was master of all he surveyed.

George carefully laid the paper down on the table, his face shocked and expressionless. The war was going from bad to worse. The Navy seemed to be losing ships at an alarming rate. Just five weeks earlier a single German U-Boat, the U-9, had sunk three British cruisers in just one morning, causing the loss of over 1,500 men. What a cry of outrage there had been in the national papers, accusing the Royal Navy of having lost its Nelson touch?

"I've never even heard of this place – Coronel," said George.

"Colonel – colonel who?" mumbled Aunt Lucretia at the window, who seemed to have emerged from her doze.

George did not answer and looked to Gladys for a lead.

"It wasn't a colonel anyone, Aunt. We were talking about a place called Coronel in Chile, where a sea-battle took place recently." Turning back to George, Gladys said, "Come on! How would you like to take me out for a walk? I'll show you the sights of the Southsea promenade, if you would like to see them!"

George was happy to go along with any suggestion, so long as it prolonged their time together. As he started to rise, she held up her hand.

"Wait there for a moment while I put my coat on. I'll just go and tell daddy that we are going out," and she crossed the room, disappearing through the door. George heard Gladys calling out to her father and he was not surprised by the immediate response and the predictably negative answer. He had obviously been eavesdropping in the next room?

"Definitely not," boomed the captain's voice.

"Oh Daddy, don't be such a fuddy-duddy. This is 1914 for goodness sake. We are only going for a walk on the Common. You can come if you must."

"Hummmmph – Well, provided Lucretia accompanies you – then you may go," he agreed reluctantly.

George sat on the edge of his seat, twiddling his cap nervously until she reappeared. Gladys came in wearing her topcoat and carrying her hat and began pinning up her hair and skewering it in place with a hat pin. Then she helped her rather unwilling aunt to get ready, before they all set off.

They slowly made their way down towards Southsea Common, a great expanse of grass stretching all the way along the Solent shoreline. George was thankful to note that the weather had not changed, and that there were still some small patches of blue to be seen through the cloud. They quickly reached the promenade road, and carefully crossed it. Walking onto the grass they headed up the mound towards the Southsea Castle, emerging at the edge of the stone sea wall, which lay about a hundred yards from the castle itself.

Standing as close together as convention decreed, Gladys and George stared at the heaving steel-grey surface of the Solent water that stretched out from the shingle beach below them. The Isle of Wight rose up darkly, like a giant breaching humpback in the distance, dominating the southern sky-line. Stretching from Bembridge westwards to Cowes, the island vaguely reminded George of his last view of Guernsey from the ferry. It was just another Island, after all.

There was a sudden flash of brightness against the darkened silhouette, which on inspection revealed the presence of a destroyer under way, way out in the centre of the Solent. Smoke belched from two of her three funnels as she turned to port around the Outer Spit Buoy, and began to navigate her way into the deep channel approaches leading into Portsmouth Harbour. Two plumes of white water produced a double fountain flying away from her bow as she headed almost directly towards them. George could see a line of white-capped sailors manning her foc'sle, dressed ready for a ceremonial entry into the port. The warship loomed larger and larger as it approached, before suddenly heeling hard over as she turned to port to round the Spit Elbow Buoy. Her racy sleek lines were fully on display to them as she sped past, her tall masts raking backwards as she headed up towards the Round Tower at the harbour entrance.

"I wonder what ship you will be on, George?" she said, as her hand moved up to clasp his elbow.

Her touch thrilled him and he held her hand snugly under his arm. In his eagerness to see Gladys, he had quite forgotten to mention his unfortunate draft. He watched the destroyer until she entered the harbour. Over on the far side of the same entrance, he could plainly see the defences of Fort Blockhouse that formed part of the submarine squadron that was based there. That was the very place that he would be heading for tomorrow morning, in order to begin his training. He turned to Gladys and slowly he related his misfortune of getting a draft order to join submarines. She was genuinely shocked. Worry lines furrowed her brow, and there was obvious concern in her voice.

"Aren't they very dangerous George? Every time I hear any news of them, it's invariably bad. The war must make it doubly so."

"I'm afraid I don't have any choice in the matter, Gladys. I have to serve wherever they send me. We can't pick and choose where we want to go. The navy doesn't work like that," he replied ruefully.

A group of protesting seagulls squawked and cawed above their heads as they struggled against the stiffening breeze. The group of three walked northward along the esplanade. Maybe it was the sound of the gulls, or the feeling of dread about his future that brought the image of Matthew's face to appear in his mind's eye. He shivered, remembering how the grip of their handhold had broken that final time. George knew that if Matthew had lived, he would be right here with him serving in the navy. They had always done everything together. Then he recalled his promise to Matthew – that he would exact revenge for him. By God, if he ever met Arthur Collenette again, he would get what he deserved.

"Are you all right George, your face has gone quite white?" Gladys said, tilting her head up at him in concern.

Before he had a chance to respond to her question, Aunt Lucretia spoke to Gladys.

"I feel exhausted my dear. I am going to have a sit down on that bench over there, which should keep me out of the wind. So please don't go too far."

George's heart leapt. He had wanted to get Gladys by herself all afternoon and was now presented with his chance, steering her away from the old lady's watchful eyes, as they headed towards the ornamental gardens. His heart was beating fast as he looked down at her. She looked so sweet, but her face was still etched with an expression of concern for his safety. Leaning forward, his lips gently brushed hers. Her eyes widened in surprise, then softened, and slowly closed as he drew her to him. His inexperienced kisses became surer and more passionate, until she forced him to break away, gasping for breath.

"George, you mustn't! It's too public!"

Once they had both calmed down sufficiently, she asked again what he had been thinking about a moment before. Her perception surprised him, and he thought for a second before he haltingly told her the full story, starting with that dreadful day's gentle beginning, right through to its tragic conclusion. She listened quietly until his voice finally tailed off, choking with emotion. Her hands reached out and cupped his face and her heart went out to him in his grief.

"Are you a Christian, George?" she asked quietly.

"I go to church every Sunday," he replied. "I have to admit that I am not really sure what I actually believe."

"I didn't ask that, George. I want to know if you believe that Jesus died on the cross for us and promised everlasting life through his resurrection."

George looked at her in amazement. He had never paid much attention in church and to be honest, he had found it somewhat boring. He believed that the soul of a body did not actually die when death came, but was not sure what happened to it after that. He was not sure about there being a heaven either.

"Yes – I suppose so," he hedged.

"Well, if you do George, then you must forgive Arthur for his sins. No matter how gravely you view his part in what happened to your friend. You must forgive him George, and try to put all of this behind you. The devil will live in you until you do."

George was shocked.

"That is something that I can never do Gladys. I will carry Matthew's terrified face as he fell with me until the day that I die. I made a vow to him just before he fell, and I will not go back on my word."

"What happened to Arthur after that day?" she asked.

"I don't really know, Gladys. He moved schools, and I rarely saw him after that. I think my parents made provision so that he and I never came into contact. I certainly did not see him, which was just as well." He thought about telling her about his suspicion of the death of Arthur's step-father, but then thought better of it.

"Well, that probably saved you from getting into trouble, so maybe it was a blessing. You mustn't carry on with this hatred George, you must learn to forgive. Otherwise, it will only ruin your life."

"How can I ever forget the fact that he ran away from us, when he could have saved Matthew? He was a coward, Gladys, and he is going to pay for it some day in the future."

"Well, we mustn't let it spoil our day together," she said sternly.

Smiling, he grabbed her hand, and together they made their way back to retrieve her elderly relative. Having done so, they went back towards the ancient fortifications of Southsea Castle. A small lighthouse surmounted the ramparts to guide ships up the narrow channel off Solent Water. The nearness of him was having a strange effect on Gladys, and she tried overcome it by recounting her local knowledge of the Castle.

"This castle was originally built around the time of Henry VIII, you know," she said informatively. Her heart was still pounding with excitement from his kiss, and she was sure her cheeks must look red, as she felt so warm. She decided to stand directly in the breeze, hoping that it may cool her. "He is supposed to have stood here, right at this spot, as he watched his flagship Mary Rose flounder out there in the Solent."

"You must have been paying attention at school that day," said George teasingly, giving her hand a gentle squeeze.

The cool breeze was not working. She smiled, embarrassed now, her eyes not daring to look into his. As for George, he was feeling on top of the world. Gladys was the finest girl that he had ever met – not that he had met that many. In fact, she was his first.

They walked on in silence for a while, past the Castle and down the promenade towards the pier. There were a few other people out, daring to brave the chill that had developed in the breeze. Two children were attempting to fly a kite out on the

Common, but each launching of the bright yellow toy had ended in failure. George couldn't resist the challenge, and letting go of her hand, he dashed over to their assistance. Very soon the kite was a hundred feet in the air, the children screaming in delight as they struggled to control the pressure on the guideline.

"You're just a big child yourself, George Torode," she said in a mocking voice. "I know exactly what to buy you for Christmas now."

Her remark suddenly made George wonder where he would be at Christmas. It was only six weeks away. He then realised that he would probably still be training to be a submariner.

Southsea gardens lay just beyond. A pergola, covered in twists of wisteria vines wended its way decoratively over the path and lawns.

'It must look splendid when in full bloom,' thought George.

The borders had been freshly dug and were clear of any weeds. There were many other shrubs and evergreens standing tall, giving cover to the smaller more delicate plants.

Suggesting that her Aunt might have another rest, they deposited her safely on a seat out of the wind, and made their way discreetly into the foliage. Once alone, he drew her to him again. Her hands were eager this time, raking against his chest in want. He held her there, placing his arms about her slender frame. Gradually she surrendered, as he increased the pressure until she melted in his arms. His mouth covered hers. Her legs almost gave way under the wave of emotions sweeping through her. Her yielding body went limp in a complete surrender to his kisses, his arms holding her tightly. Suddenly a wave of panic went through her. Whatever was she doing, there might be someone passing who knew her father.

"George, stop," she moaned. "Stop, stop."

She eased herself from his embrace.

"We mustn't."

He stood there feeling somewhat foolish, as she straightened her hair. He felt a little unsure as to how to react next. Did she want him to kiss her, or not? This was all a bit new to him. He knew that he just wanted to hold her close, and kiss her again and again. Why was she backing away, did she not want him to? She had seemed to be enjoying what he was doing just now – why had she stopped?

"What's the matter, Gladys?" he asked. "I thought you liked me as much as I like you."

She looked flushed and bewildered. "I do like you George, but it is too public."

Suddenly he said, "I love you Gladys. Will you wait for me until the war is over?"

He could not believe he had just said those words, and then realised that it was true. He was absolutely sure that he did love, Gladys. He had never felt like this before, and he very much wanted her to be his girl. Then he became suddenly aware that he had an erection, and earnestly hoped that she had not noticed. It was straining hard against his bell bottom trouser flap. Did an erection mean that you love someone?

Looking back, he realised that he had always felt this strongly about Gladys, ever since their first meeting her on her father's ferry. Why else would he feel like this?

Her hands reached across the space between them, and he reached out and grasped them. She slowly raised her head and looked straight into his eyes. Her face became very serious, as if she were about to say the most important thing of her life.

"I love you too, George, and I will wait for you," she said.

Then suddenly, she was in his arms once more, and this time she didn't resist, indeed she wanted to stay there for ever. George just knew that he did not ever want to let her go.

Chapter Four

The Dog and Duck

George left Gladys on her doorstep with a promise of his undying love. Both of them had vowed to write every day whenever it was possible to do so. She had clung to him, not wanting to let him go, neither knowing when they would ever see each other again. Their parting kiss was no more than a peck, as her aunt had been standing close by. Poor aunt Lucretia had been utterly exhausted by the walk, and had eventually been forced to go into the house, but Gladys had spotted her father peering disapprovingly through the curtains of the lounge window. Her lips had quivered against his skin, lingering a second too long, loathe to release the contact.

"Return home safely to me my love. I will pray for you every day. Always remember that I love you. Goodbye my darling, stay safe," she had whispered, tears welling in her eyes as she turned, and ran up the steps into her house.

He stood there as the door closed behind her, a lump forming in his throat. His erection was still partially evident. Did that mean that he was missing her already?

As he walked back towards Portsmouth, George's mind was filled by a cluster of conflicting emotions. Ever since he had left home, his life seemed to have been in constant turmoil. Everything at home had been so quiet and orderly – so routinely normal. His mother and father had provided him with a protective security, which had completely disappeared the moment that he had boarded that cross-channel ferry to Southampton. Since then he had been on his own, no longer able to seek his parent's guidance or advice, having to make all of his own decisions. He was quick to realise that he had been told what to do all his life, but he now by him making his own decisions, he was becoming independent. The navy had partially taken over the role of his parents in providing him with the domestic security, all of his food and accommodation, but within the system he was very much his own man. Using his initiative was what Leading Seaman Andrews called it. The hard training had ensured an onset of maturity, forcing him think for himself, which in turn had produced a greater freedom. It was not long before George realised that he enjoyed being independent. He enjoyed being in the navy. At times he found himself thrilled and amazed by his new-found confidence, but there had been other times when he had questioned his somewhat hasty decision to join up. He had experienced feelings of homesickness for his family and Guernsey, which had been quite common amongst his comrades during those early days, but the non-stop dawn to dusk routines of navy life had not provided the time to be nostalgic. He had retired just after the sunset bugle each night feeling utterly spent, and never failed to fall asleep within minutes. Although he loved his family, he was now aware that he was able to live without them – in three short months he had become a man.

There was something else that was troubling him as he made his way back towards The Hard, because he had become totally confused by the magnitude of the welling of emotion, he had just experienced, along with the strength of his feelings towards Gladys. On the doorstep she had told him that she felt the same as he did, and that filled him with joy.

As he walked, he began to resent the existence of the war, and the fact that he had to serve in the navy, as both came between him and his desire to be with her. On the other hand, he then thought that if the war had not happened, he would not be here in Portsmouth, and he would never have met Gladys. He knew that his new confidence had emboldened him in his advances towards her, but he also realised that he had meant every word of what he had said to her. Once this war was over, he knew that he would leave the navy, because in Gladys he had found true love, and she now possessed all of his hopes for the future. He knew that he wanted to protect her, but his desire was being hampered by the frustration of not being able to see her as often as he would have liked. She had now become his main reason for surviving this conflict. None the less he still liked the service life, and decided that he would enjoy what the navy provided until then. At the moment he felt very light hearted as he skipped along the pavement, filled with knowledge of having such a beautiful girl to call his sweetheart. He still could not get over the fact that she seemed to be truly interested in him. She had said that she loved him, and would wait for him to come home. That had made him feel so elated – he was on top of the world.

Eventually he slowed his pace as he came to a cross roads, and stood there trying to remember which road that led him back towards harbour area. He asked a passer-by and was directed towards the road that led off towards Old Portsmouth. With each step his mind drifted off on another fantasy, dreaming of what the future might have in store for Gladys and himself. Could he have been lucky enough to have found the girl of his dreams on his first real date? As if in a trance, staring straight ahead, still deep in thought he became oblivious to his surroundings. He was just so thankful at having had this unforgettable afternoon together. If only this war were really to end by Christmas, then would be able to see much more of her.

The pedestrians that he passed looked at him curiously, each perplexed by the wide foolish grin splitting his face. As the distance from Gladys increased, so the strands of his naval life slowly returned. The images of Gladys eventually began to fade, and his mind began to think about the party with his classmates later this evening.

He felt quite cold as the wind whistled down the long narrow street of terraced houses. George's body shivered in acknowledgement, and he hunched his shoulders, increasing his pace once more in an effort to keep warm. This wind had certainly gotten worse since his walk this afternoon, and there was now an icy edge to it. The evening twilight was overpowering the last vestiges of daylight when he heard the first faint snatches of music and singing. He looked about for the source, and saw the entrance to the Medallion Music Hall across the street. There was a queue waiting to go in for the next performance. Despite these bleak times, people were still going out to enjoy themselves. Life seemed to be going on as normal around the city. Maybe some poor Tommy Atkins, sitting in a trench in France would not agree, or the lookout aboard a small destroyer riding out a storm in the western approaches might have other ideas. They were the men on the front line of active service. He would soon be one of the servicemen whose dedication permitted these people standing in this queue the chance to enjoy them-self. Gradually George's dreamy thoughts of Gladys faded completely, as he was forced to negotiate the traffic on the roads.

Retracing his footsteps from earlier, he passed a greengrocer's shop that he had seen on his way to visit Gladys. The earthy smell of the fresh vegetables wafted up from the thin packing crates, and the shoulder high stack of sacks of potatoes reminded him of home, when he had helped with his father's vegetable plot in the back garden. Looking through the shop window, he could see the mounted clock on the far wall over the counter showing the time as being ten minutes to seven. He realised that he did that there was not much time to get to the celebration party. It was due to begin in the 'Dog and Duck' in Queen's Street at seven-thirty. Forty minutes – how long would it take him to get there?

Leading Seaman Andrews had made the necessary arrangements, as the pub landlord was a personal friend of his. George continued on purposefully, walking determinedly in an effort to keep himself warm. Other people were hurrying home for the night, all of them now wrapped warmly in heavy coats, scarves and mufflers. He deliberately walked past the turning that led off to Old Portsmouth, heading as he had been directed on towards the shore-based Torpedo School and Gun Wharf Quay at *HMS Vernon*.

Passing the twin brick towers of the establishment main gate, he glanced through the metal bars, catching sight of the duty Quarter-Master sitting forlornly behind his desk. A flickering oil lamp lit window. George walked on under the main line railway viaduct, just as a train rumbled loudly overhead. Steam hissed rhythmically, as the engine headed on towards the city centre. His legs were just beginning to feel a little tired, and his feet were cold and aching. Withdrawing his hands from the flap of his trousers, he blew his hot breath into them before stuffing them back.

From the viaduct he passed by St George's church and emerged out on to The Hard. Ahead of him, and to his right lay a row of public houses whose frontage overlooked the Portsmouth Harbour Railway Station and the Gosport Floating Bridge terminal? Gas lamps glowed and illuminated each side of the road, making an iridescent avenue of light that shone all the way down to the golden orbs surmounting the pillars standing each side of the dockyard main gates. Out towards the harbour he could see spray from the wind-blown wavelets slapping against the cobbled fore-shore. He began to pass the first of the public houses.

Just after his arrival at the barracks someone had told him that those balls on the dockyard gates were actually made of solid gold, but he had eventually found out that they were shaped stone orbs, that had been covered with gold paint. This was the first time that he had actually seen them for real, realising that he had been the brunt of many jokes in those early days. You quickly learn to become less gullible in the Royal Navy, or you suffer the consequences.

He felt some relief from reaching The Hard, as he knew that he was not too far to his destination. Queen Street ran to the right from the Dockyard Gate – and he could now see the corner lying at end of the row of these public houses.

Reinvigorated by this reassuring fact, he increased his pace once more. As he hurried past each of the hostelries, he could hear loud honky-tonk piano music blasting out the latest music-hall favourites. From the slurred choral accompaniment, the patrons were enjoying the offerings of the hostelry. He looked in through the open doors, noting any sign of a bar had been completely obscured by a sea of blue serge. Laughter and babbling voices filled the air. Each of the pubs looked to be lively place.

Suddenly there was an eruption of noise ahead of him, when a group of people came spilling out of the doorway of the last pub before the corner with Queen Street. The hanging inn sign declared that it was called The Apple-Tree. The sprawl of humanity grew rapidly, spreading out into the roadway in front of the dockyard gates. He could hear someone shouting angrily, as another voice began screaming insults. Many of the patrons emerged from the pub doorway to watch the confrontation, and most carried on drinking from the glasses in their hands. Slowly the crowd split into two factions. Everyone seemed to be arguing.

To be able to reach Queen's Street, George realised that he would have to make his way past this rapidly developing fracas. Suddenly, somewhere within the centre of the crowd a fight developed between two drunken sailors. A natural human ring formed around the combatants, with the spectators screaming encouragement to one or the other. Fists were swinging with little effect, with both men being totally intoxicated. As he neared, George could see that the object of their dispute was a heavily painted, sluttish looking girl – but after another ten paces he realised that she was far too old to be classified as a girl. She stood between the two men screaming some of the most profuse Anglo-Saxon words that he had ever heard. The two sailors nodded, and attempted to carry on with their farce of a fight. The object of their affection stood with her legs firmly apart, arms akimbo, with a smudged crimson explosion below her nose, awaiting the victor. Taking a closer look at her heavily lined face, and toothless features, George thought that, had he been one of the pugilists, then he would have deliberately lost the contest! He began to make a very wide semi-circular course around the mayhem, breathing a sigh of relief when he reached the far pavement. Now he had a clear pathway up Queen Street. He was just thankful to leave all that trouble behind.

He smiled to himself, because whilst he had walked along The Hard he had been propositioned three times. With the first he had felt a little embarrassed, but he also felt strangely proud of the fact that the prostitutes had considered him as a prospective client. His stride had quickly developed into a discernibly cocky and confident swagger as he walked away from the corner.

The lights that lay ahead on either side of Queens Street amazed him. It was a brilliant avenue of light. There were only a few lights in the whole of St Peter Port, and in comparison to these Portsmouth streets, they appeared to be quite dim. He stared in wonder at the bright glowing orbs of the vehicular traffic headlights as they approached. They came along the road, flashing past him in a whirlwind of carbon dioxide and petrol fumes. There had been so many new innovations since this century had begun. Electric lighting was virtually unheard of during the Victorian era. Motor cars were becoming commonplace, and up in the sky, flying was swiftly becoming the norm. At sea the great battle-ships were now being driven by oil, although there were still quite a few of the old coal burners – but everything was developing at a great pace.

An ethereal tenor's voice grew out of the shadows, filling the night air. George noticed a musical hall off to his right. He had never seen so many drinking establishments.

Another three hundred yards along the road and the 'Dog and Duck' public house appeared. A painted sign was suspended from an iron gallows bracket, mounted on the high brick rendered wall above the entrance, depicting a Springer spaniel retrieving a shot fowl from a waterlogged reed-bed. George breathed a sigh of relief when he finally reached the door to the Public Bar, but he suddenly stopped. He realised that he had never actually been inside of a public house before. Standing there he felt nervous, willing himself to enter, but at the same time there was something in his conscience that held him back. Most young men went into their first Pub with their father. The prospect of doing it alone suddenly seemed very daunting.

"Get out of the way if you ain't goin' in," growled a voice behind him.

A group of sailors, wearing cap tallies from *HMS Greyhound*, filed past him through the door, and as the last man went through – George followed. The glass panes set in the doors were made of frosted glass, and completely masked the interior. His senses were immediately sent reeling at being confronted by a wall of noise and tobacco smoke. As the closed the door behind him, the sudden rise in temperature hit him like a sledgehammer. The compacted mass of human body warmth left no room for any air to get cold. He rose on tip-toe as he searched the room for his friends – but was unable to see them as the far corners were obscured. The place was jam-packed with servicemen. They were mostly sailors, but there were uniforms of every shape and colour. He had fully expected to be ejected for being under age, but to his surprise he was totally ignored by everyone, which made him feel a little bolder as he squeezed through the throng to get to the bar. Smoke hovered overhead in thick grey gossamer clouds, and the smell of burning pipe tobacco was enhanced by the omnipresent hoppy odour of spilt beer, furniture polish, and wet saw-dust.

Looking through the bobbing heads, he could just make out the line of spirit bottles on a shelf, standing as a backdrop behind the counter. The tops of barmen's heads could just be seen dashing to and fro, as they desperately tried to meet the incessant demands of their customers.

There was an eruption of excited cheering that came from over in far right-hand corner of the barroom, and was quickly followed by a series of shouted lewd remarks. This produced a burst of even louder encouragement, which quickly became deafening. George was naturally curious as to what was happening, but was unable to see what was actually occurring.

Another quick search to his right and left failed to find Leading Seaman Andrews, or the rest of his classmates. He looked up to a huge pendulum wall clock, seeing that it was just before seven twenty. He felt pleased, because he had made good time coming back from Southsea, and was early by nearly ten minutes. Maybe they had not arrived yet!

Fighting his way forward, he squeezed himself in beside a fifteen stone stoker, who was singing a familiar lullaby to a plump young girl sat on a stool beside him. On the other side were a group of three Petty Officers drinking pints of beer, with whisky chasers. As he stood there waiting to be served, he noticed that the song that the Stoker was singing had unusually sexually expressive lyrics, and the girls face had an excited expectant grin, as she awaited his next tuneful crudity. George could see that the girl was continually patting away the hand of her crooning suitor, who was trying very hard to grope her knee. Another loud roar erupted from the far corner. Again, George's curiosity was aroused.

"Whadya want, sweetie?"

A five feet tall buxom blonde bombshell with bulging breasts that were straining the material of a white blouse, awaited his order. Her dyed blond hair was a desperate attempt to hide the greying strands, and her teeth were yellowed from smoking. She had definitely seen better days, thought George, but she had a pleasant enough smile. Her face wore a bored expression, honed from a life-time of working in pubs. It was very busy tonight, and she was doing her best to keep up with the overwhelming demand. Looking along the counter, he could see that working behind the bar of a public house on Queen Street had taken its toll on most of the staff in one way or another. All of them were well beyond the age of being called up into the armed forces.

She stood there with her hands on her hips, and repeated her question. As she reached down under the counter for a pint glass, George's eyes became transfixed by her breasts, until he suddenly realised that had risen and was now speaking directly to him. Her question took him aback for a second, and he became embarrassed as he realised that he had been caught staring, and that that his naivety must appear to be obvious. Did it indicate to her that he was under age? His mind went blank for a moment. He didn't know what to order! What did his father drink?

"Bitter, Mild, or Stout," she said by way of encouragement.

That was it – he remembered that his father always drank bitter, so he ordered a glass of the same. As she began to pull the pump handle, he felt very relieved that she had not questioned his age! As the glass was being filled, he began to feel the return of the confidence that the whores on The Hard had given him. The barmaids bulging leg of mutton arms flexed, making short work of the task. The pint glass of the light brown effervescent liquid was crested with a foaming head, which she placed on the bar before him.

"Thruppence three farthings my luv," she said, smiling as she held out her hand for payment.

Reaching into his pocket, he counted out the coins, and gave her the right money. She winked at him, and turned away towards the till. He lifted the glass tentatively to his lips and took a sip. It tasted so sour that it caused his face to crumple in disgust. Was that how bitter should taste? How on earth did his father drink it? If that was bitter – he had taken an immediate dislike to it. There was a horrible vinegary taste, which made him shudder.

"Terrible beer in 'ere, ain't it, mate?" said a voice at his elbow.

A sandy haired sailor stood there, grinning at him. His cap, which was pitched jauntily on the back of his head, had a cap ribbon that bore the same name as his own – *HMS Victory*. Not Nelsons old wooden hulk at Trafalgar, but the Royal Naval Barracks of the same name.

"It's definitely the worst bitter in Queen's Street, and that's a fact. They tip the slop tray in yer pint, unless you watch the bastards. Old Bill the landlord 'as never been known ter clean 'is beer pipes. That's the main reason why it tastes so 'orrible," he went on. "They're all furred up."

George had had all his queries about the beer answered in one breath. He looked at the man in front of him, who was dressed exactly like himself.

"My names Fred Chapman," said the sailor, holding out his hand to George.

Another prolonged loud cheer went up over in the corner, followed by a loud round of clapping, whooping, and whistles.

"Glad to meet you Fred. I'm George Torode," he replied, then indicating with his thumb. "What is going on over there?"

"It's a pissin' contest, George," said Fred. "Old Bill 'as offered two of the local Pros five bob for the first one ter fill a pint pot wiv 'er piss."

"Do you mean that they are actually doing it over there in the bar!" he asked an incredulously. "Is that why they are all cheering?"

"Old Bill knows 'ow to pull in the customers," said Fred. "It was deserted in 'ere at opening time – look at it now?"

George's curiosity got the better of him, and he stood on tip-toe, craning his neck over the huddle of humanity that barred his view. He could just make out the heads of the two women standing amidst a circle of navy blue. So, he stood up on the brass foot-rail that ran around the front of the bar. It raised him a good foot off the floor, and could just about see what was happening. He coughed involuntarily as the drifting tobacco smoke up there slowly began to contaminating his lungs which were gasping for clean air.

There were two women squatting down, holding pint pots underneath themselves. Both of the whores were throwing gins down their throats as quickly as their grinning supporters could buy them. The spectacle made George feel quite sick, and somewhat disgusted. He climbed back down and stood with his new-found friend, who was just draining his glass.

"I don't know how you can drink that muck. It made me feel quite ill," George said.

"Then yer won't mind if I see yer pint orf?" said Fred, picking up George's glass.

"Please, help yourself," he said, glad to be rid of the vile liquid.

"I will get you a bottle of brown ale, George," said Fred. "It's the only way you will get any decent beer in here."

He stood up on the rail once more, and looked about the barroom once more, searching for his class-mates. The room was lit by gas mantles that were fitted within bulbous glass globes hanging down from the ceiling. There were four lights spaced at intervals. The once white ceiling was a dark yellow, after being constantly subjected to the tobacco smoke that billowed up like funeral pyres from a hundred pipes around the bar.

"'Ave yer just finished yer training then, George?" Fred said, as he wiped away the wet residue from his mouth with the back of his hand, gasping for breath just long enough before another prolonged draught from George's glass.

George nodded that he had, but his attention was once again diverted by the sounds of a growing argument coming from the pissing match supporters over in the corner. One of the women had tried to knock her opponent's glass over, and a catfight had ensued – much to the sailors' delight. A large bald-headed man appeared from behind the bar, and proceeded to break up the scratching, hissing women, by hitting them soundly across their ample buttocks with a besom.

"If you ladies want your money, one of you had better fill her pot. Neither of you will get anything if you carry on fighting."

They ignored him, and continued their scrap, both grunting and screaming as each fought the other for supremacy. He gave them another whack, which brought yelps of pain. They finally parted with a begrudging, grumbling obedience.

'That must be Old Bill,' thought George.

Both of the women were still yelling insults at each other as reluctantly, they had retracted their claws and retrieved their respective glasses. The contest recommenced.

"Wot draft did yer get, George?" asked Fred. "A lot better than mine no doubt – I'm orf ter join them steel coffin boats across the 'arbour in Haslar Creek. I start my submarine trainin' termorra."

George couldn't believe what he was hearing.

"That's strange Fred. I'm joining Fort Blockhouse tomorrow as well," he blurted.

They both burst out laughing, and shook hands, united in their common fate.

"Looks like we are goin' ter be mates, dunnit?" said Fred. "It's good to meet yer, George."

Learning the fact that some other poor wretch would be sharing his misfortune, made life just that little more bearable for George. He picked up his glass and looked at the couple of small mouthfuls that Fred had left him to drink. In the bottom were what looked like some lumps of cork, or could it be small chunks of wood that swirled within the acidic mixture? The sight made him think better of it, and he replaced the glass on the bar. Seeing George discard his drink, Fred quickly reached over to claim it and drained the glass. He went to the bar and ordered another pint, and a bottle of brown ale. On his return, Fred handed the bottled ale to George, and proceeded to down half of the pint that he had just bought.

"Cor that was good – yer don't know what yer missin'."

"Where are you from, Fred?" asked George.

"Cor blimey George, ain't it bleedin' obvious from me accent," laughed Fred. "I'm a Londoner ain't I? A real Cockney Sparrer ain't I? A good ol' Eastend boy fresh orf me dad's barra, and now servin' in 'is Majesty's Navy. I didn't fink that they'd shove me in those coffin boats though. I'm a trained Snob, I am. I thought I'd be sent to some great big battle-wagon ter mend the Admiral's shoes fer 'im."

"Snob?" asked George inquisitively. "What is that?"

"Blimey George, don't yer know nuffin'? A cobbler – a shoe repairer. You should 'ave a dekko at me work, its real neat. I 'ad nearly finished me apprenticeship before I joined up, I did. I can make a lovely pair of boots, I can. Ol' Mr Joyce, the one wot's bin trainin' me, says I can go straight back to 'im and finish orf me trainin' once this lot is over wiv. Wot you bin doin' George?"

"I was working in a quarry on Guernsey before I joined up. I didn't have any regrets about joining the navy until I got my draft this morning. That hit me like a sledgehammer."

"'Ave yer got a girlfriend, George?"

"Well, yes I have Fred. I only left her a couple of hours ago. She lives down in Southsea. How about you?"

"Yer, I bin goin' out with this red-head. She 'aint got no 'air – just a red head," Fred burst out laughing at his own joke. George thought it was quite funny too.

As they laughed, they were interrupted by one of the biggest cheers yet. Grown men were now screaming with excitement, and shouting themselves hoarse. Standing up on the bar rail once more, George could just make out that one of the two women was nearing her goal. One enterprising seaman started offering odds of ten to one on the other prostitute achieving a miracle.

"YES – Scotch Annie's the winner!" screamed someone in the audience and to prove it Annie held up the full glass of amber urine. Much of the contents slopped over her hand and dripped down onto the floor. A crescendo of congratulations from her supporters crowned the old hag's triumph. She was completely surrounded by drunken sailors, patting her wherever there was a space to pat. Three of the men grabbed her unceremoniously and hoisted her up onto their shoulders.

"Oooooha – weere's me faive bub," Scotch Annie screamed, grinning through a mouthful of decayed enamel.

She swayed from side to side as the men fought to keep her overgenerous weight aloft. The glass quickly lost more of its contents, which fell down onto those holding her aloft, but nobody seemed to care. Many more hands were thrust up to keep her in position, some remaining longer than was necessary, groping her ample flesh. The heaving human mass then started to totter slowly forward. Once confidence was established, they began to steamroll ahead, apparently intent on a circumnavigation of the public bar in a lap of honour.

In an already crowded bar, it was inevitable that something unpredictable would be bound to happen – and that it would only be a matter of time. The nearest table was toppled over, sending glasses and sailors sprawling across the floor. The disgruntled men scrambled out of the way to safety on their hands and knees. The sound of their broken glasses could now be heard crunching under the feet the front rank of the bearers. A human press of patrons in the bar, were desperately backing out of the way of the swaying juggernaut. Some actually dived out of the door, and out into the street to avoid being mown down. Others remained trapped against the bar, with their hands clasped over their genitals – fearing for their marital prospects.

The next table loomed, and had quickly suffered the same fate as the first, but this time one of the sailors didn't fall to the floor. He was a thick set beefy red-headed Scotsman, who quickly regained his feet, and defiantly faced the giddy group – a Celtic bastion defying all of them to proceed any further.

"Gert out of the way," slurred one of the giggling sailors, supporting the crone, who was now waving a completely empty glass about her head.

Everything happened so quickly. The Scotsman's arm shot out like lightning. His clenched fist smashed into the mouth of the sailor, whose oral cavity burst into a red smudge. A lightning second blow from a left hook sent him crashing to the floor like a pole-axed steer, spitting blood and teeth. The sudden loss of one of the integral supporters of Scotch Annie, caused her to lurch dangerously sideways from her lofty perch. The whole mass toppled over, and she landed on her back on the top of the bar, sending every drink within reach crashing behind the counter. Her urine-soaked body followed the drinks over the edge, and she disappeared down behind the woodwork. Her waving legs were still protruding above the rim, as she struggled to prevent herself from being hurt.

Suddenly the Scotsman was being reinforced by many more malcontents from the bar area, who were angry at losing their beer, moving in behind him in his resistance to the juggernaut. The drunken supporters of Scotch Annie became aggrieved at losing their mascot, and stared back angrily at the primary cause of her downfall.

Everything in the pub went deathly quiet. The tension in the room became electric. It was a powder keg waiting for a match. No-one saw who threw the empty bottle at the red headed Scotsman, but it was enough to set off the fuse. In a matter

92

of seconds, World War One was concentrated in the public bar of the 'Dog and Duck' in Queens Street, Portsmouth. The protagonists were Scotch Annie's Army, versus the Beerless Malcontents first fifteen. Fists flew. Chairs rose and fell onto white capped heads. Table legs snapped under the weight of wrestling blue serge. Floorboards were awash with the foul-smelling urine spilt from Annie's broken glass, and the pints of beer from twenty glasses, which formed congealed lumps in the sawdust.

"Come on mate," said Fred. "Let's get owt of 'ere. The Crushers will be 'ere in a couple of minutes."

"What are Crushers," asked George, ducking a china ashtray that whizzed over his head.

"Yer don't know nuffink, do yer George? Crushers – the Naval Police Patrol – that's who," said Fred. "Unless you wanta end up in the jug ternight, let's get owt of 'ere."

George was just about to enquire what the jug was, when Fred grabbed his arm and dragged him towards the only quiet spot in the room, over by the far wall. Both of the young men stared about in wonder, as every furnishing in the bar seemed to disintegrate before their very eyes.

To prove the adage, that discretion is the better part of valour, Fred edged very gingerly along the wall towards the entrance door and George did not need to be told to follow him. Ducking swiftly out the door, they started off down the road at a brisk pace, heading in the direction of the dockyard gate. They reached the next pub after only fifty yards, and Fred steered George straight into the illuminated portal. The painted sign on the wall outside declared it to be the 'Landport Music Hall and Lounge', but once inside it seemed to have the ambiance of a funeral parlour – certainly a complete contrast after the furore of the 'Dog and Duck'. The gas-lights here were a lot dimmer for a start. Someone was playing a beautiful piano piece over in the shadows on the far side of the room. George immediately recognised it as Claude Debussy's Claire de Lune. It was his Mother's favourite piece.

The two of them made their way over towards the bar. Looking about the room George noticed that it was much quieter, and that several of the tables only had two occupants. He also noticed that there were a lot more women in this pub, compared with the last. Most of them were sat at the tables in the company of a lone sailor, but some of the more hard-faced females stood brazenly at the bar, with a come-hither look, that dared any man to approach them. They were much prettier than Scotch Annie and her friend in the Dog and Duck.

"This seems a bit more like it, Fred," said George, his eyes looking left and right as they ordered their beer.

"Just be careful mate, these women don't talk ter yer fer nuffin'. If yer want ter talk to 'em, yer 'ave ter buy 'em a drink."

"What's wrong with that, eh?" asked George naively. "It's only polite."

"That's all right in a normal pub, but yer get fleeced here – that's why. It'll cost yer the earth," explained Fred. "Just stand here and watch what 'appens to those mugs over there sittin' at the tables, while I get the pints in. Just make sure that you don't talk to any of 'em before I get back."

While Fred was ordering and paying for their drinks, George watched as one of the barmen toured the tables with a tray containing an array of liqueur glasses. Each glass was filled with a darkish brown looking liquid. Any of the girls with an empty glass in front of her had it swiftly removed, and immediately replaced by a full one. Her companion of the moment was then charged a sixpence for the service. Fred appeared back at his shoulder carrying two pints of bitter.

"Try this bitter George. It's a lot better than Old Bill's. That's only cold tea in those glasses," said Fred, handing him a glass. "Costs a tanner, it does. Nearly as much as these two pints put together."

George noticed that most of the girls looked as if they were bored stiff by their companion's conversation. Between them they must have heard every chat-up line ever devised at least a thousand times. There was no sign of a welcome, or friendliness on any of their faces – most just had an expression of utter disdain. Men are egotistical and therefore – completely gullible. Each of those eager young sailors, with their faces brimming full of confidence, thought that their luck had changed as they sat with the girls. George noticed that every one of them was young, and therefore must be as naive as he was. The older more experienced naval hands knew how things worked here, and they stood over here at the bar well out of the way.

"They've got as much chance of getting' orf with those gals as Rip Van Winkle 'as of getting' insomnia," said Fred.

Surveying the scene, George thought that the whole thing looked rather sad. All of the pubs on Guernsey were full of men, who went there to have a chat with their friends and maybe tell a joke or two. They liked to pass a jovial, relaxing couple of hours over a pint of beer. Women were only allowed in the saloon bar, and only then if they were accompanied by a man. Here it seemed that every type of persuasion was being employed to extract as much money from their customers, whilst giving as little as possible return. Occasionally a sailor would stand up and refuse to pay – realising too late that he had become a victim of the extortion. Anyone who disagreed with the system, or who reckoned that he had been conned out of his money, was expertly dealt with by two heavies, who appeared from nowhere at the slightest sign of trouble. The trouble-maker was simply picked up by the two men and physically ejected out through the door. If the man continued to cause problems, then it was not uncommon for him to receive one or two pacifying thumps to his head to help him on his way. There were not many who attempted further protest after that.

As he watched the proceedings George unthinkingly took a mouthful of his drink, and was pleasantly surprised to find that it tasted a whole lot better than the muck being served up by Old Bill just along the road. Enjoying the taste, he took another mouthful, and found that it was the best pint of bitter ale he had ever drunk.

"I was supposed to meet my class tonight in the 'Dog and Duck' for an end of training party at seven thirty," said George. "Why don't you come along, Fred? What time is it now?"

Fred looked at the clock behind the bar.

"It's seven forty-five, or as you being a new trainee should say – 1935 hours. In the old navy they would have said – just past Three Bells of the Last Dog Watch."

They both chuckled. George was amazed at how much had happened in the last fifteen minutes. Queen Street certainly was a heady mixture of conflicting attractions, but he realised that it could also be quite a dangerous place – but that was probably half of its attraction! He took another swallow from his glass. This was good beer. He was beginning to feel good.

"Give it anovver five minutes fer the walkin' wounded to 'obble orf 'ome ter their 'ammocks and then we'll venture back an' see if yer mates are in there," suggested Fred. "Seriously George, I know the 'Dog and Duck' is an absolute dive, but yer can always guarantee it's gonna be a lively evenin'."

"I bet the press gangs did a roaring trade in there during the last century," laughed George.

"Last century? The way this war is goin', that may well be the way the navy recruit more sailors in the very near future."

It was a quarter to eight when they re-entered the grime encrusted portals of the 'Dog and Duck'. Inside it was a lot quieter, and there were a lot less people, although the place was beginning to fill up once more. The bar staff team were sweeping away the last of the debris from the fight. Most of the broken tables had been hurriedly cleared away and some rough replacements had been set out. The wooden floor was still damp, and the smell of urine prevalent. A fresh layer of sawdust had been sprinkled down, with little effect.

Looking around the bar, George noted that well over half of the original clientele had disappeared. Most of those missing were probably nursing bruised heads, incarcerated in the stark comfort of a naval detention cell. Most of the pipe smokers remained, having relit their briars to produce the familiar bitter sweet aroma. George stood on tiptoe, his eyes scanning the heads of Old Bill's customers, as he tried to pick out his classmates. His gaze centred on the lone individual at the bar, as he recognised Ordinary Seaman Powell from his class. Leading Seaman Andrews had said that he reckoned that Powell could easily qualify for being the most awkward man on the planet. George watched him as he stood there expectantly, as he was totally ignored by all of the bar staff. He got impatient and started waving an empty glass, trying to attract the attention of the buxom barmaid that had served George earlier.

At least one of his classmates had made it here, thought George. Powell looked up and caught sight of George, and immediately gave an enthusiastic wave, but in doing so he knocked over the beer of the sailor to his left.

"Come on Fred, one of my mates is down the far end of the bar," said George.

"'Ello dearie, d'yer want something you've never 'ad before?" The stench of the old woman's breath made George retch. Her clothes stank of urine, as she looked at him through gin glazed eyes, from under her head of matted hair. One of her rouged cheeks had smudged – or was it a bruise? She looked pathetic.

"No fanks," said Fred, "nobody volunteers for leprosy."

"Soot yerself, luvvie," said Scotch Annie.

As they threaded their way through the sailors towards Powell, there came some cheers of derision from over to their right. A group of sailors were sat around one of the few surviving tables, and were shouting and waving at them. George saw that the rest of his class had arrived too.

"Late again George, can't get anywhere on time, can you?" shouted one.

"You've got some catching up to do matey, as we are all on our second pint already." called another.

"But you lot can't have been here longer than five minutes," said George.

"That's right – you have some catching up to do."

"You owe the kitty 'alf a crown, George." said another member of his class.

Someone shook an empty pint glass under his nose. It chinked loudly, filled with silver and copper coins. George was amazed. He and Fred had only left this place less than a quarter of an hour before, and in that short time his class had arrived, downed two pints of beer each, and Powell was ordering more. He tossed a half crown piece into the beer mug.

Leading Seaman Andrews sat at the head of the table with a strange lopsided grin on his face. George put it down to the several empty spirit glasses that stood on the table top in front of him. He certainly could not have been in there longer than twenty minutes and yet he had already done a good job at attempting to empty the rum bottle behind the bar.

"Hello, Leading Hand, would you like a drink?" asked George politely.

"You can call me Andy tonight, George, and in ansher to your kind invitation, yesh please – a tot of rum," slurred his venerable leader.

"This is my mate Fred Chapman. Is it all right if he stays with us tonight?" asked George, as he edged towards the bar.

"Hello, Fred," said Andy. "Coursh you kin 'ave a run out with ush. Just make shure you put 'alf a crown in the kitty though. Oh, and mine's a tot of rum by the way."

Talking was starting to become a challenge for Leading Seaman Andrews.

George purchased a double measure of rum, blushing as he received another wink from the same diminutive barmaid. Returning to the group, he immediately noticed that there was a full tray of filled pint glasses that stood in the middle of the table. It was simply a case of help yourself, the quicker you drank, then the more you got. Every time the tray was in danger of becoming empty, Leading Seaman Andrews despatched the amazing Powell to the bar to refill it. Andy attempted to stand, but started to sway alarmingly, so then thought better of it. So, flopping back down into his chair he raised his rum glass to them all. George grabbed a glass of bitter and found that it didn't taste half as bad as that first one that he had bought.

"Cheers mates, you're all OK, you are. You are all proper sailors now, who will do their bit in the coming months for King and Country, and I'm proud to have met you," said Leading Seaman Andrews, his tot of rum following the fate of a dozen others.

The tinkling of an upright piano started up across on the far side of the barroom. After the pianist had played a few practice notes, he went into a tune and was quickly surrounded by several sailors. George vaguely recognised the bawdy number that had been popular around the music halls and pubs during the summer on Guernsey. The curly headed pianist completely disappeared from view, as he was instantly accompanied by swaying singers, all loudly singing along. The noise level in the bar rose significantly as everyone raised their voices, all trying to make them-self heard above the music.

"Fred here is joining submarines with me tomorrow," shouted George to the others across the table.

"I don't envy you shipmate, they're death traps," said the amazing Powell, as if he knew what he was talking about.

"It's one of those little death traps that could take out something the size of the *Inflexible*, which you are now joining Powell," said another of the class. "Look what happened last September. That Hun submarine captain in his U-boat… What was his name?"

"Kapitan Leutnant Otto Weddigen," volunteered George. "The U-boat was the U9."

"Yeh, that's it, George," said the sailor. "Well, he sank the Cressy, Hogue and Aboukir, in less than an hour in that tiny vessel with a crew of less than twenty, and fifteen hundred men went down with those three ships."

"Well it will certainly alter the future tactics of the Admiralty," said George. "Nobody has ever really taken the submarine seriously as an offensive weapon of war before. From now on people are going to hear a lot more about them. You mark my words."

"You will make the difference, George," said another. "Good luck matey. You are certainly going to need it."

It was true that submarines were becoming the weapons to be feared at sea, certainly as much as their own crew's feared serving in them. George wondered if he was trying to bolster his own confidence, or simply trying to justify the fact that destiny had dealt him a cruel blow. As he watched all the others of his class nodding their heads sagely, he suddenly felt a little twinge of prestige – but they still gave George that – rather you than me – look. None the less, he thought that he could see that there was also a hint of a grudging respect in their expression. Maybe it would all work out for the best!

The evening in the bar wore on in a never-ending series of jokes, tall stories and reminiscences from the course, all accompanied by a lot more drinking.

At one point in the proceedings a band could be heard playing outside in the street, which had threatened to drown the piano, along with the accompanying singers. The thump-thump-thump of the bass drum shook the windows, and made the pint glasses vibrate, rattling in time on the back shelf of the bar. The blare of trumpets, tambourines and clarinets tried their best to soothe the heavy beat, but the stalwart drummer was undeterred. Suddenly it stopped, to reveal the tinny sound of the tinkling tambourines, that were still being shaken to good effect. Almost in sympathy, the pianist in the pub had also finished playing. The sudden quietness made everyone stop talking, as they realised that they were shouting unnecessarily, and looked at their companion in embarrassment. Just then the doors of the pub burst open to reveal a surprise attack from an offensive unit of the Salvation Army, complete with tambourines, news sheets and collection tins. Christ's advance infantry unit was determined to invaded these halls of Satan and do battle to save the souls of the godless. A loud cheer went up from the defenders.

"Good ol' Sally Ann."

"Fight the good fight."

"Fuck off."

A heady mixture of friendly bonhomie, fused with abuse, was hurled in their direction, instantly testing the resolve of General Booth's finest. Undeterred and wearing the determined smile of righteousness, they charged into their soul salvation mission with resolute enthusiasm. Tins were being rattled under the noses of sailors, as their bloodshot eyes tried hard to focus on the unfamiliar noise in front of them. News-sheets were being handed out to any who would take one, each proclaiming a message of sobriety and good living to be found within the church of Christ, with temperance being the watch-word. One sailor willingly accepted one.

"Thanks, I was just goin' for a crap," declared one recipient, as he disappeared in the direction of the toilets to the cheers of his friends and waving the leaflet above his head.

Notwithstanding, the Christian Cavalry continued with their task with an ever-increasing gusto. From the determined expression on their faces it appeared be a complete impossibility that they would ever fail. Their chance of victory soared above the stench of stale ale. From the end of the bar emerged the bleary-eyed Powell, wearing a lop-sided stupid grin. Without warning he suddenly dashed over and pinched the peaked Salvation Army hat, as the man's attention was diverted. The owner suddenly spun around and seemed very eager to reclaim his property.

"Come 'ere sailor – give that 'at back," panted the Soldier of Christ. He was a short, thick set man, with greying hair at his temples. George guessed that he was approaching his fiftieth year, and thought that Powell was being stupid.

The luckless Powell came skipping over to the table holding his trophy aloft, grinning like a Cheshire cat. George could see that he was very drunk. He had a maniacal stare as he stood giggling with the hat. The man approached him, and Powell being taller, began waving the hat over his head to prevent its recapture, until the last possible moment. The owner eventually caught him, and was showing a lot of patience. He snatched back his hat with an understanding smile. Seeing no harm done, the man saw the funny side of the prank, and turned back towards his comrades.

At that moment, to everyone's utter amazement, Powell followed him and poured the contents of his glass over the man's head. The claret piping on the man's black uniform suddenly darkened, as the liquid soaked through to his shirt underneath. The man froze in mid-stride.

What happened next, nobody could confirm for sure, as it all happened so quickly. One minute, Powell was standing laughing uncontrollably at his idiotic deed, and the next he was flat on his back on the floor, out for the count. He lay with the stupid grin still locked in place, but being slightly distorted by a rapidly developing red bruise at the corner of his mouth. The short Salvationist was rubbing his knuckles, apologising to those of the class who were still awake, before turning and heading for the door. Miraculously, a pathway opened before him, and he strode down it, walking passed the amazed faces that were staring open mouthed. A silence had descended over the whole bar, which broke as the door was shut behind him. A loud raucous laugh burst from behind the counter.

"You matelots will never learn, will yer. Nobody 'as ever got the better of Mad Mike O'Kerrigan," chortled Old Bill.

"Who the hell is Mad Mike O'Kerrigan?" asked the class as one.

"Before he found Jesus, Mike was the best darned bare-knuckle street fighter in Southern England. Could have turned professional so he could, but he gave it all up to follow the Lord," said the Landlord. "He still has a bit of work to do with 'is temper though."

From behind George there came a muffled groan, and he turned to find out what had caused it. At the far end of the table he saw Leading Seaman Andrews sliding down from his chair, disappearing down beneath the rim of the table. 'Blimey,' thought George, 'am I a slow drinker or what?' He had tried to keep pace with his peers, but had quickly realised that he could not match them. Despite the fact that he had not imbibed as much as they had, he felt that his brain was beginning to become a little confused. Already realising that his own voice had begun to slur his words, but he found it amazing that he could think without slurring. Despite trying to concentrate when he spoke, he found that he was unable to form the words correctly.

It was funny being able to study oneself like this, discovering the effect that the alcohol was having on his brain. As he looked about, he felt that he had manage his alcohol consumption pretty well. Especially when he had observed the body of his course leader, lying on the floor. He reckoned that he still had plenty of room for a couple more beers as he raised his glass, and emptied the contents in one long draught. Fred went to replenished it.

With the sudden demise of two of its main members, the celebration lost much of its impetus. Some of the class began to head back towards the Barracks, and two of them managed to rouse their erstwhile leader from his stupor, and support him towards the door. It was definitely the sensible thing to do, with them all going on draft tomorrow morning. They were hoping to get a good night's sleep. Fred suddenly appeared carrying two more full glasses.

"Time Gentlemen Please!" yelled Old Bill, ringing the bell of some long-forgotten warship, that hung behind the bar.

"Well it's nearly time ter go, George," said Fred, cramming his cap onto his head. "O'ill drink this, and then give the last of yer mates a 'and ter carry any of the walkin' wounded back ter the barracks. Are yer comin'?"

His beer disappeared in four gulps.

"Yep," said George, through experiencing a sudden bout of hiccups, and seeing his full glass of beer, he decided it would provide the cure. "I'll follow you just as soon as I get rid of this last bit of beer, Fred."

The pub slowly began to empty, but some of the more reluctant regulars were attempting to get another drink. He drained his glass in eight gulps. As the last of George's class disappeared, and he made his way towards the door, when a voice at his side made him turn.

"Would you like another beer sailor? I've got plenty up in my room."

His friends were suddenly forgotten, as the thought that another drink suddenly appealed to him very much indeed. Trying to focus his eyes on the origin of the invitation, he became alarmed that there was nobody there. He looked left and right – still nobody. Then when he looked down, he found the face of the buxom barmaid looking up at him. He thought that she was really quite good-looking. Very short – but very good looking. There was nothing wrong with short people! He should have noticed her before. What a nice girl – well, lady – to invite him home. He started to nod his head, but it got a little out of control, and he nearly lost his cap from his head.

"Come on then, me ducks," she said. "You can escort me 'ome. I'll just go and get my coat."

She returned wearing a dark coat, and slid her arm through his, as she guided him towards the entrance door. Once outside, they crossed the road and turned off Queen Street into a quiet side street, well away from the procession of sailors who were heading back towards the barracks. By them moving away from the illumination of Queen Street, it suddenly became very dark. It was also unexpectedly cold, and George breathed in deeply in an attempt to clear the muddle from his head. It proved to be a bad mistake, because the intake of so much fresh oxygen immediately made him feel nauseous, as it quickly replaced the nicotine that filled lungs. They stepped off an unseen kerb, which caused George to stagger forwards, and in trying to regain his footing he became giddy. His teeth began to chatter, and he thrust his hands into his trouser flap for warmth. An involuntary series of shivers attacked his upper body and shoulders. His head sank down into the confines of his blue uniform collar.

"Don't you worry, me luv. It's not far to my place. I'll soon 'ave you nice an' warm," said the barmaid, guiding him across the road.

"Wot's your name?" asked George.

"Doris," said the barmaid. "Yourn is George ain't it? I 'eard one of your mates callin' to yer."

George grunted a yes. Doris was now using both of her hands to steady him, as they walked along the pavement. George felt a lot safer with her guiding him.

What a nice thoughtful lady Doris is to help me, he thought. It was good to meet someone who cared, after all these past weeks of relentlessly bullying. Doris was nice, but Gladys was an even nicer girl. He was absolutely sure now that he really did love her, Gladys not Doris. He decided that he would tell Doris all about her, when they were having a drink together.

They turned off down a narrow alleyway and it became inky black. Only a cloudless blanket of stars was discernible between the towering rooftops, but it was very dark down here. A searing pain suddenly shot through George's right foot, as he had stubbed his toe against some unseen obstruction. It was another kerbstone.

"Ouch," he yelled, unable to stop himself toppling forward helplessly.

She just managed to prevent him falling into the puddle, but lost hold of him as he began dancing on one foot. He crashed back against the brickwork of a gable end wall. Doris struggled to hold him upright. She began speaking to him in soft soothing tones, trying to reassure him and take his mind off the pain. Eventually they moved off once more, with her encouraging him onwards towards her home.

"There's a good lad, take a good deep breath and then you'll be awlright. It's not far now," she cooed.

The pain in his foot made him limp, and he lurched heavily against her support. Reaching down and grabbing hold of her shoulder, he could smell the cheap perfume that mingled with her distinct sweaty body odour that rose up from the collar of her coat. By the third inhalation of this caustic mixture, George could feel the bile beginning to stir in his stomach. He started to wretch. Stopping once more, he leaned one hand out against another wall. He was gulping fresh air in great gasps in an attempt to keep the contents of his stomach where they should be.

"Go on my luv, you throw up. You'll feel a lot better afterwards," said Doris, holding his hips.

Using both hands to support himself now, George did not need a second invitation as a fountain of vomit cascaded against the wall, the ricochet splashing back over his trousers and shoes. The brim of his cap suddenly dug into his forehead, as the front hit the wall. He took more gulps of fresh air, like a drowning man trying frantically to stay above the surface of the water. A second burst of vomit burst forth. Not as violent as his first attempt, but with just as much in volume. He suddenly felt extremely empty. Thankfully all the pressure that had been trapped in his stomach had gone, and he could feel the fresh air beginning to clear his head.

She certainly knew what she was talking about, did Doris.

After another minute or so he stood erect once more. Doris was fussing, concerned about him. She seemed such a kind person. He decided that he was definitely going to tell her all about his Gladys. He was sure that she would be very interested.

Wiping his mouth with the back of his hand, they set off once more, arm in arm. Despite the cold air, his mind began to wander. He tried to focus on earlier in the day, when he had been with Gladys. Why did this bloody war have to come between them? Although, if it hadn't come along, then he would never have met her, so in one way he was glad. Did he say that before? How could he feel glad and sad at the same time? He didn't know what he meant, he just felt confused. I do hope that Doris doesn't mind, George thought, but I really don't think I fancy another drink just at the moment. I'm so tired I could sleep for a week.

The next thing he remembered was Doris speaking to him, but he couldn't quite make out what she was saying. He was vaguely aware of the sound of tinkling of keys being inserted into a lock. This must be her house!

Suddenly they were in a hallway and the cold breeze had gone. At least he was out of that biting wind, but it was still cold and damp in here. He could feel the grit on the soles of his shoes, as it crunched against the bare wooden floorboards. They started to climb some stairs. In total darkness as she led him up a staircase, but it was not easy climbing in the dark. He tripped – knowing for sure that some of the steps were higher than others. He could hear the clomp, clomp, of his own heavy footsteps echoing in the hollowness of the stairwell. They seemed to be climbing forever – it must be a long way up, and he could feel himself getting out of breath. Up and up, until they finally reached a landing. It was so dark and he knew that he would have to go where she led him, because he could not see a thing. He heard himself panting for breath.

Another key rattling noise, and then he was moving forward into a musty smelling room. Every noise suddenly became muffled, as he stood alone in the darkness fighting to keep his balance. He could hear Doris fumbling about in front of him. Then there was a spluttering ignition from a match, which made him jump back in surprise. As his eyes fought to focus, he suddenly could see the outline of the spirit lamp, as the flame touched the wick. A glass shield was lowered into place to produce a dim light that projected their elongated shadows out towards each corner of the room.

He could see a huge bed off to his right, and he could also see Doris, who was standing beside it. It certainly looked so inviting – the bed – not Doris. She advanced towards him, her arms reaching up to grasp his shoulders, trying to turn his body around. As he did so, his head continued to spin like a top, and he became giddy once more. He could feel the edge of the bed against the back of his legs, and then felt himself falling backwards after losing all sense of balance. Pillows, or at least it was something soft, hit the back of his head. It was a welcome relief. Oh – it felt so good. Very quickly all consciousness faded. In his ethereal consciousness he could hear Doris shouting something at him very loudly. Why on earth did she sound so cross? The last thing he remembered was the comforting feel of his blue jean collar against his cheeks, it had risen up behind his head to enfold his ears. What bliss.

****

As some vague threads of consciousness returned, everything around George seemed to be totally peaceful. He felt warm and comfortable, and the blanket around him felt good, but when he tried to move his head it caused a dagger point stabbing pain between his eyes. The severity of the pain surprised him at first. On his second attempt it was not so much of a surprise, but it still caused him to fall back down. Not wanting a repeat of the pain, he simply laid very still.

Trying to open his eyelids was proving to be equally difficult, as they seemed to be welded shut. That was alarming, but he would just lie still for the moment and hope for a natural improvement. It was as he lay there that he realised that he could not swallow. The dryness in his mouth revealed just how parched his throat was. His sandpaper tongue rasped against the roof of his mouth, and traced along the inside of his furry teeth. He desperately tried to cough up some saliva, to no avail. After several attempts, he eventually managed to do so, his tongue running this liquid around his mouth and his teeth. He felt relief as he began to recognise their unnatural texture.

He felt absolutely horrible, knowing that he just wanted to curl up and hide away from the world. It was unusually quiet, but could hear a strange rhythmic tapping. He normally awoke early, well before reveille, but he did not recognise this sound. Maybe it was even earlier than he thought. He enjoyed the warmth and solitude of his bed, but everything was so quiet. There was always some sort of noise in the dormitory somewhere, someone snoring, someone farting, or someone else going to the heads at the end of the landing. Then he realised that something was not quite right!! What was it that was not right? Some built in natural instinct alarm in his brain was trying to tell him that something was very wrong indeed. It began with a mild uneasiness, but it quickly developed towards panic proportions. A sudden feeling of unknown terror shot through him. He reached up with his fingers and forcibly opened his eyes. He immediately grimaced as previously unknown pains stabbed through his brain. The light coming through the curtains was piercingly bright. It felt like a knife entering each eye socket. His head felt as if it didn't belong to him. It was November and the mornings did not get light until seven thirty. Normally it was dark when he woke up, yet strangely, it was quite light now. Why was that? Then he thought about the curtains – they did not have curtains on the mess-deck windows. Who put these ones up? His mind struggled with the anomaly. Focusing on the source of the tapping noise, he could make out the shape of the clock on the mantelpiece above the fireplace. He didn't remember a clock, and there wasn't a mantle-piece or fireplace either. Where the bloody hell was he?

The urgency of the need to relieve himself suddenly outweighed his foggy curiosity, and he leaned forward in an attempt to sit up, but every muscle froze in terror as his hand touched the warm softness of human flesh. His eyes widened when he saw the mass of blonde hair spread across the pillow next to him. Frantically, he tried to remember what he was doing here. Where was here? Where the hell was he? He turned his head quickly left, then right. More, previously unscaled heights of torture were being reached by the sharp movements, as his brain was sent crashing into the inner walls of his cranium. Where was he and who the bloody hell was this beside him?

The clock came into focus once more – 7.25! Oh my god. Oh my god 7.25 and he wasn't in the barracks!

The full implications of his predicament suddenly became fearfully apparent. Several huge intakes of breath eased the initial panic, but his leave pass had only been given until midnight. Even the attempt at basic mathematics, when his brain tried to work out how late he was, ended in pain. It made him seven and a half hours overdue and he knew that he would be in a great deal of trouble. Seven and a half hours of being absent without leave, and he still had to get back to the barracks. His breath came in short gasps, as more panic began to take hold, desperately trying to think of what to do. He was fully awake now, and he started scrambling around the floor in a desperate search for his shoes. His pulse rate was racing, but disregarded it, as he knew that he had to get back to the barracks as quickly as he could.

There were his shoes, underneath the dressing table. One of his socks was still missing. It took another two precious minutes of hunting before he located it beneath the bedclothes, down where his feet had been. Trying his best to brush his uniform into some semblance of decent order, he found his badly bent cap on a chair. The front rim was grossly distorted. Bending forward, and trying to tie his laces produced more waves of nausea. Just standing up produced a heady whirl of giddiness, and he fell back onto the bed. He straightened his collar and adjusted his land-yard. That would have to do, as he pulled his cap onto his head.

"Fuckin' big waste of time bringin' you 'ome last night, wasn't it?" said a sleepy, disgruntled voice from beneath the quilted eiderdown.

Doris! The image of the buxom barmaid suddenly flashed through his tortured mind. It had to be her – hadn't it? What had happened? He certainly did not have time to stay and find out. All that mattered at that moment was getting back to the barracks as quickly possible. Another thought then crossed his mind, which only added to his many worries. He was being drafted to join the Submarine Service later on today, and he had not fully packed his kit yet. He was in a great deal of trouble.

"Goodbye," he muttered, as he headed for the door. He was going to say thank you for a nice evening, but thought better of it.

'Oh Lord, if you make everything OK, I promise that I'll never drink again,' he vowed in silent prayer.

Chapter Five

C301

It was the fourth of January 1915, and despite the public disappointment that the war was still raging on after Christmas, the New Year had brought no evidence to a cessation of the hostilities. The Yule festival had come and gone, and the only heartening story had been a report of an unofficial Christmas Day truce. It had occurred when the war weary soldiers from both sides had sung carols together. They had simply climbed out of their respective trenches and had met together in No Man's Land to exchange cigarettes and play a short game of football. After a cordial couple of hours, they had shaken hands and their officers had ordered by them to return to their respective defensive positions to resume hostilities. To George it was an indication that the basic good was still evident in the common man, but it was the body politic that perpetuated war. The New Year of 1915 had passed and it seemed that the conflict was hell bent on continuing. Ever more troops were being sent over to France. Kitchener's new recruitment campaign was working after employing a new concept where whole streets of men, classes from school, and those from the same town were all joining up together into their regional regiments. These groups were becoming known as the pals' brigades.

Behind the main trenches that faced each other, there existed a whole series of excavations that cross-crossed these once productive farmlands, they were being used by reinforcements to relieve those on the front line, and to bring up supplies and ammunition. The almost incessant shelling by the artillery of both sides had turned the countryside into a sea of mud, which now stretched for nearly four hundred miles from Nieuwpoort on the North Sea coast of Belgium, right the way down to the Swiss border. The British were based in the northern sector, and the French manned the middle and southern sectors. The opposing forces stared at each other across a void, that in places was only one to two hundred yards wide. The simple act of raising one's head to view the enemy, would bring instant death from a sniper's bullet. The mirror periscope was being widely used to observe safely.

After those initial battles of 1914, which had halted the advance of the German military machine, an impasse now existed. No side seems to have the advantage. Old tactics were producing heroic charges across No Man's Land, where each attempt produced nothing but slaughter and terrible injuries. The use of modern automatic weapons was proving to be devastating, scything down the advancing infantrymen like harvested corn. The sheer loss of life has been appalling. Casualty lists, published in the national and local press, were giving cause for concern in both Parliament, and amongst the general public.

There was one success at sea that occurred in early December of 1914, when Admiral von Spee's cruiser squadron had returned from the Pacific to the South Atlantic, intent on attacking the coaling station at Port Stanley in the Falkland Islands. However, as the Germans approached, they suddenly spied a squadron of Battle Cruisers of the Royal Navy, who had been sent down there to track them down. The Germans had been spotted as they approached, and the British sailed out immediately, and set off in hot pursuit. Just after lunch, Admiral Sturdee ordered his force to open fire and the battle commenced. Of the German force of eight ships, only two managed to escape, and Admiral von Spee was killed, along with his two sons. The British casualties were light, and this victory reinstated the Royal Navy prestige, giving them back their dominance of the South Atlantic.

****

Two rain soaked bedraggled figures stood ten feet above the surface of a tempestuous sea, both clinging on to the periscope mount, with their feet straddling the top of their tiny conning tower of the small C-Class submarine – *C301*. Both men were clad in black oil skins, with a southwester hat tied securely beneath their chins. The systematic battering from this force ten gale was mercilessly venting its fury on them.

His Majesty's Submarine *C301* had sailed early that very morning with six trainees embarked from their Gosport base. There had been no indication, or indeed any forecast of this approaching storm. After diving, the whole day had been spent testing the knowledge of the trainees. When the time approached for them to return to the surface, the external conditions had deteriorated badly and within the course of an hour this storm had hit them. Instead of taking the northerly course needed to return to base, the captain quickly realised the present danger that his frail craft faced in these conditions. Heading north would place these mountainous waves on to their beam and their force could easily roll the boat over. So, he brought the boat around onto a south-westerly heading to stem the fury. He knew that diving was also out of the question as most of their battery power had been used up during the day, so they had no option but to ride it out on the surface.

The sole protection for the two watch-keepers on the bridge was a sodden white canvas screen lashed to the wire guard-rails. It served to deflect most of the on-coming waves, but each time the bow drove downward, water rose up and flooded their position. Both men had their heads bowed low against the stinging onslaught, which was making life an abject misery. Each had tied him-self to the immovable metal-work, to prevent from being washed overboard. As each hammer force wave hit them, both were forced to cling on grimly until the awesome power had subsided. Some of these horrific waves submerged them completely, and they were forced to hold their breath and pray.

The Commanding Officer, Lieutenant John Nolan RN and his lookout, Able Seaman Rogers, had tied the best bowline their service experience permitted, because a poor knot would mean being snatched away to certain death in this maelstrom. Their freezing hands were numbed by the wind rasping mercilessly across their exposed skin. They clung on, waiting for the right moment to release their grip. Then they had a few seconds to blow some hot breath into their fists to keep the circulation moving before the next wave hit them.

The motive power required to achieve forward motion was placing a terrible strain on their solitary twelve-cylinder petrol engine, that was driving the single propeller. There was a discernible groan that could be heard reverberating through the boat as the pressure of each wave hit them. This overt display of meteorological violence was making everybody feel small and insignificant, because out here, thirty miles from the nearest point of land, you were nothing, just another piece of flotsam that was being battered by a storm.

Every time a big wave engulfed them, water poured the open hatch, raining down into the boat. The men below were fighting an endless battle to keep the ingress under control. They had rigged a large canvas bag directly beneath the hatch to collect most of each deluge. With the severe motion, preventing spillage was impossible, and the men worked like Trojans scooping it up with buckets to dump back into the bag. From the nearest pump connection, a flexible hose had been fitted, and was running continuously. In the engine room the ballast-pump was trying to cope with the continuous demand, by attempting to pump the water back into the sea. This canvas bag was known affectionately onboard as the Bird Bath.

It was a never-ending task, but succumbing to fatigue was not an option for anyone. Strangely enough, down inside the boat the briny liquid was relatively warm to the touch, but up on the bridge, once one's skin became wet and exposed to the icy chill of the gale, the body temperature quickly plummeted. Unfortunately, this chilled air was also being sucked down the conning tower, to provide the air needed for the engine that was driving their boat. It was essential, because if the engine were to fail, they would have to return to their battery power to drive the electric motor. This would not last for long, and there existed the very serious risk of the boat being turned beam on by the waves with the same fatal consequences.

High above on the bridge, the two men were suffering their fate with a resigned fortitude. They were constantly being submerged by the waves, and each time it seemed an eternity before it finally drained away, but it was in fact only a couple of seconds before the boat won its fight for buoyancy to stay on the surface. The big danger was that both men faced the threat of hypothermia as the wet wind hit their soaking bodies. Fortunately, their oilskins covered most of their exposed areas, and with rolled towels wrapped tightly around their necks to seal in their body heat, they stood a good chance of survival. The freezing onslaught honed their senses, giving them the stamina to fight the storm and keep their boat safe. With each passing, they would instinctively check on the other, both grinning with relief to find his companion still there, a common bond that is experienced by sharing mortal danger. In a situation like this, rank lost all meaning; they are simply two men who were fighting the elements, both defiant in the face of death.

Inside the boat life was absolute purgatory for the crew, most desperately pumping the bilges as their small craft fought to make headway against the force of the gale. It was an uncomfortable ride for everyone, and it had been so for the past three hours. The influx of water down the tower was incessant. Everyone was wet and cold from the freezing wind coming down through the small opening. It was a howling gale, which was whipped through the boat to create utter misery. Water dripped off pipes, paint-work and people. With each roll, it sent the contents of the Bird Bath cascading over the edge, across the deck to join the rest of the mobile sludge. Those who were not on watch fighting this ingress, rested wherever it was remotely dry. The trainees had been instructed to keep out of the way and let the crew do their job. Everyone was avoiding the metal deck, which was awash with a mixture of human vomit, oil and freezing salt water. Trying to sleep in the violent motion was an impossibility, because the men were forced to hold on tight to whatever was within reach to prevent themselves being thrown across the compartment. Some had chosen refuges where they could jam their bodies into narrow confined spaces, thus allowing some form of rest for their tired muscles.

The trainees aboard included George Torode and his friend Fred Chapman had all been in high spirits as they left the protection of their base, that lay within the sheltered waters of Haslar Creek, a branch off Portsmouth Harbour. Their transit out to their diving area had been made in a reasonable moderate sea. They were excited because today was the culmination of all of their submarine training. They had quickly arrived at a position twenty-five miles south of St Catherine's Lighthouse on the Isle of Wight without any difficulty.

The class were then supervised by the crew, as they were then made to dive the boat and keep it on depth, and whilst dived show their ability in operating all of the boats systems and machines. Following a successful day, they would graduate as fully fledged submariners. Everything had gone very well. On completion of the dive, they had intended to get the trainees to surface the boat under supervision, but the worsening weather conditions prevented that. Normally before sailing they would have received an adequate weather warning, which would then have given the time to return to base, or to seek shelter in the lee of some headland. This deep depression had come in very fast, catching everyone totally unaware. The end of January was always the time for sudden storms, a so-called cyclonic phenomenon.

The sea was not the only peril they had to face out here in mid-channel. A German U-boat had been spotted in these waters recently, despite the preventative defensive measures of the Dover Patrol and recently installed boom nets and minefields that had been laid across the narrows between England and the French coast. The crew's only comfort came from the sure knowledge that the German submariners were probably feeling just as miserable as they were. They also knew that any attempt to fire a torpedo at a target in this weather, would be like trying to hit the bulls-eye on a dartboard whilst wearing boxing gloves. This somewhat doubtful assurance allowed them to concentrate on their own battle with the elements.

George Torode felt himself luckier than most. He had managed to jam his body between the wire cage that protected the electrical breakers of the battery panel switchboard, and a T frame that provided the internal strength to the pressure hull. Wedged in vertically allowed him to relax his tired muscles, that had been fighting the erratic non-stop motion. Looking out from this self-imposed incarceration, he feeling utterly miserable. Mal de mer was a terrible affliction, but with him now being held firmly within the submarine construction, he no longer had to fight to keep himself upright against the ever-rolling motion. So, when the boat heeled hard over, he was now carried over with it. He felt that the heaving forces acting on the boat were beginning to combine with the heaving forces within his stomach. He concentrated on keeping himself where he was, as the ever-changing gravity was constantly trying to dislodge him from his sanctuary – he was feeling terrible! The steamy fume laden mist that filled the engine room mixed with the carbon-dioxide that escaped from the engine, to form a bleary curtain in front of his eyes. He could just make out the on-watch stokers at the forward end of the Engine Room, also struggling against the rolling motion as they went about their duties.

The overpowering throbbing roar of the petrol engine began to numb his mind. The spinning propeller shaft was just three feet below his perch and below that he could see the dark patches of oil and water slopping around in the bilge. The rolling motion made the foul liquid ride up the side of the pressure hull, to leave rounded brown smears against the paintwork. The pungent acrid stench this produced, reduced the internal oxygen level still further, and did little to make George feel any better. He needed fresh air, because the bile from his stomach was rising and falling in his throat like a blacksmith's hammer, although he had not actually been sick – yet! Was this going to be his fate, dying out here miles from his Island home, and far away from his new-found love?

The continuous rocking motion was making him feel extremely drowsy. Maybe I could try and sleep standing up, he thought! He closed his eyes, attempting to obtain the sanctuary of oblivion, knowing that sleep would provide the chance of escape from his torment. Another excessive roll to starboard and he smacked his head against the cold steel of the 'T' frame – he gave up the idea.

As he looked forward, along the interior of the submarine, all appeared to be complete chaos. There were no bulkheads and he could see weary, pallid faces, with red-rimmed eyes were peering back at him from every nook and cranny. He could just make some of them out through the fume laden smog filling this end of the boat. He could just see the form of the recumbent Fred Chapman up near the tubes at the forward end of the boat, recognisable by his unruly mop of fair hair, he was stretched out across two seats that had been lashed to the side of the boat. George knew that he was not asleep, because he noted see his hands were firmly gripping the support legs. At least Fred had found a relatively comfortable spot in which to curl up and die. They would both be on watch in half an hour.

Up in that bow section, some lay prone on the spare torpedoes, others on the wooden boxes of canned food and the luckier ones had curled up on the soft bales of damp cotton waste. Personal possessions surfed across the deck, as the water splashed to and fro, the owners totally oblivious – quite willing to leave the items to their fate. Perhaps they just didn't have the strength to care. Fragments of broken crockery had joined this cascading miscellany and with each roll they were being smashed into ever smaller pieces. The deck was very slippery and dangerous.

The boat shuddered from stem to stern, as the bow ploughed into yet another giant wave. Those on watch instinctively groped for the nearest handhold, to prevent themselves from being thrown across the tiny compartment.

"That's another milestone we've hit. The skipper must be drivin' too close to the kerb," said one of the on-watch Torpedo-man sitting at the electrical switch gear, on a bench close to George.

He was monitoring the electrical gauges that were located not two feet from where he was jammed. As bad as he was feeling, George couldn't help but chuckle at the remark.

The act of laughing made him feel a little more human, but he knew that it would not last. Retreating back into his self-imposed purgatory, his mind began to wander back over the past two months. The submarine course had begun ignominiously on Guy Fawkes Night, when he had joined Fort Blockhouse whilst being under punishment, following that disastrous leaving party at the Dog and Duck. He had quickly completed his joining routine in the Master at Arms Office, still feeling a great deal of shame about the incident. That terrible morning, he had made a promise to himself that he would never again get so intoxicated that he did not know what he was doing. This oath had followed the spine-chilling warning that he had received from his Divisional Officer. He had been told that he could have been shot for desertion for being absent without leave in a time of war. To an impressionable eighteen-year-old, these words had branded themselves into his brain. He could have cried with relief when the barracks Commander had only awarded him one month's stoppage of shore leave, supplemented by a series of minor extra punishments, such as extra drill and extra work.

Once he had been ingratiated into Fort Blockhouse community, the first four weeks of his course had been particularly gruelling. Like the rest of his class, he had the normal workload of daily instruction, but when it was over, he had been faced with the additional extra punishment duties to be completed before he thought of going to bed. There had been little time for him to study his notes, and after a very short time, the fatigue started to make a difference.

That was when Fred Chapman had come up trumps, proving himself to be a real friend. He had patiently sat with him each evening, helping him to write up his notes in readiness for the next day. He also took the time to explain many of the things that George's tired brain had missed during the day, and assisted him in preparing for the final written examination. Each evening he helped him to lay out his kit for inspection by the duty officer on his rounds. This had been a tiresome time draining punishment, and Fred had proved to be a good friend.

Despite those long tiring days, the submarine training course had been an inspirational voyage of discovery for George. He had learned about some beguiling mysteries, such as the hydraulics, and the principles of buoyancy. Electrical theory had followed, and he was soon able to draw out the internal tank and pump systems of a C Class submarine. High-pressure air systems were no longer baffling, and the surfacing and diving arrangements became so much clearer. He was told that he would have to be totally familiar with all of these new specialities, and a hundred other systems before he would be accepted into *The Trade*. Each new subject was handed on to him by an aged instructor, who with unlimited patience took the time and trouble to check that every member of the class had completely understood what he was telling them, before proceeding onward to the next system.

The Trade, was the submariner's term for the knowledge and expertise that was needed to work in these submersible craft. The ability to take them to sea, work them safely underwater, and fight the enemy. Serving in the surface navy, a rating only had to familiarise himself with his own particular part of the ship. For a stoker it was the Engine room, and associated systems. For the seamen it was the upper deck, and their own speciality, such as the weapons – guns or torpedoes. The submariner had to know everything aboard his vessel, and thus he was considered to be a tradesman – hence *The Trade*.

It was heady whirl of new sciences and proven theoretical principles, a strange new mechanical world that he was being inducted into. As the course had progressed, so he discovered that he was actually enjoying his newly gained expertise. He became proud of his new knowledge, and despite his tiredness he began to thirst for more each day. He now knew lots of previously unimaginable things. There were things like the construction of the submarine batteries, and new terms such as the batteries being connected in series or parallel. He learned the working components of a diesel engine, and the principal of a petrol engine, the theory of hydro-dynamics involved in the diving and surfacing a submarine. He soon learned that these craft were not at all the death traps that he initially thought them to be. They were wonderful intricate masterpieces of naval engineering, although he could see that the escape facilities certainly needed to be improved as the newer designs came into service.

His punishment thankfully came to an end after the first week of December and suddenly George was free. He was able to devote all of his time and energy towards his studies. Christmas had come and gone with very little in the way of seasonal cheer, other than a chicken dinner being served on the big day by the base Captain. With the passing of the New Year, he was looking forward to starting the next stage of his life as a fully trained submariner. He was desperate to serve in his first sea-going draft, and he just had to pass the final sea-exam aboard a submarine.

That was where he was now. The class had been told that they had all passed the course before they surfaced, but due to the worsening conditions, they had been excused surfacing the boat. There was no room for a mistake in the evolution, and so the crew had brought her up.

Another rivet busting thud, shook the tiny vessel. Through the misty fumes, George could just see a sailor approaching from the forward section of the boat. He was wearing a sodden pair of bell-bottom trousers, and carefully made his way through the boat carrying a metal tray that was piled high with sandwiches. Each consisted of huge rough-cut slabs of bread, buttered, with a slice of corned beef, or herrings in tomato sauce mashed in the middle. As he approached, he made for rather a comic figure, side-stepping, first leaning one way, then carefully juggling the tray the other, constantly fighting against the acute motion. Dirty water splashed over his boots, spraying the blue serge with every roll. George recognised him as the boats appointed cook for the day, although the very act of cooking on that small portable electric hotplate in this weather, was an impossibility. He proffered his wares under the noses of the on-watch stokers, who were standing at the front of the engine, but found no takers. After his inspection of the contents in the sandwiches, one of the men had leaned over and grabbed a bucket and was violently sick. The cook's gaze searched around for any more customers, and finally located the switchboard watch-keeper. Seeing a possible outlet for his culinary efforts, he began the perilous journey around the engine on the deck-plates towards him. If the boat rolled the wrong way, then he would be thrown against the hot piston heads of the engine. He had obviously done it before, as he made it look easy. The tray of food arrived, and after another refusal by the switchboard watch-keeper it was stuck unceremoniously under George's nose, allowing him the chance to select from the array of delicacies. George had seen that faced with the appetising choice of sandwiches or nothing, most of those afflicted with severe mal de mer had picked the latter. He noted that the slices of bread were very thick, and appeared to have been hewn from the loaf by an axe.

"Want a sarnie?" enquired the sailor.

George shook his head, as he could already feel the bile rising from his stomach rise once more, at the mere thought of it.

"You really should try and keep something in your stomach, lad," the man persisted, offering him a lump of plain bread from the bottom of the pile. "Take it from me. You could end up with an ulcer, or something worse, otherwise. Even if it makes you vomit, at least give your stomach will have something to throw up."

George took the lump from him, more to keep the cook quiet than any need for sustenance, hoping that he would go away and leave him to suffer in peace. To placate him he took an initial small bite, forcing his face into a stunted smile and a grimace of thanks. The sailor nodded happily, satisfied that he had accomplished his duty in supplying another satisfied customer. To George's relief, he squeezed his way past him, heading back towards the stokers.

George returned to his inner sanctum of self-pity and despair. With the dry bread in his mouth, his tongue began mixing it with the vast amounts of saliva that had already accumulated. He rolled it around his mouth, pleasantly surprised by the taste of the yeasty goodness. He was amazed at how good it was, and the food soon made him realise just how hungry he actually was. Slowly the bread dissolved, and he quickly bit off another chunk. He felt his head begin to clear, and the lethargy of the sea-sickness began to dissipate.

Maybe that cook knew what he was talking about, he thought, as he finished the crust off. If the cook were to return, then he would ask to have another slice – maybe with a piece of corned beef.

To his surprise the cook did re-appear, and he was more than happy to accommodate George's request before slowly heading forward once more. George began eating ravenously as the sea-sickness abated.

At that very moment, up on the bridge, with their heads lowered against the elements, neither of the two watchmen caught sight of the black spherical ball that was lying semi-submerged in the water – just three hundred yards ahead of them. Its presence had only been briefly revealed for a flicker of a second, lying deep in the trough of the wave. Covered with ominous thorn-like projections displaying its designed purpose, it bobbled like a rebellious balloon tethered to the end of its mooring wire. The submarine's bow reared up high into the air, as it reached the crest of yet another wave, seeming to hover there for a lifetime before plunging down. They were now less than one hundred and fifty yards from the mine.

Feeling much better, and in serious need of a breath of fresh air, George disengaged himself from his self-imposed incarceration, carefully making his way forward. His feet clanked along the metal deck-plates, as he struggled to remain upright, and keep himself clear of the engine. People looked up, watching his passing with disdain, they were the faces of prisoners at their cell doors, watching a fellow inmate heading off to the gallows. He was feeling very stiff and seriously wanted really to stretch his legs, so he pushed against the constant dampness of the air-stream, making his way towards the open hatch and bird bath below the conning tower. Although very wet, the cold air was much fresher here, and George began to feel almost human again, for the first time since the storm had struck. Around him several of the crew were using buckets to bail the water from the control room bilges, tipping it back into the Bird Bath. He reached over and grabbed a spare pail to lend a hand.

Just at that moment, the bow of the boat plunged downwards into another trough and George felt his stomach fall with it. It reminded him a little of the lorry ride down from Southampton, when the driver had driven too fast over the hump-backed bridges. It was at that exact moment that the shock wave of the explosion blasted through the boat like a sledgehammer. It threw George backward like a rag doll, his body crashed into the dividing curtain that isolated the chart table. The material caught him like a football in a goal net, before his body crashed to the deck, losing consciousness for a few seconds.

All around the Control Room there was pandemonium. Back in the engine room the petrol engine could be heard spluttering, giving a series of stuttering coughs as it began to die. All of the lights immediately flickered, and finally failed as everything went eerily quiet. The downward rush of the wind suddenly ceased, as the engine finally died. A single battery powered emergency lantern provided the only discernible illumination. Clouds of billowing smoke could be seen coming from the forward section of the submarine, and it rapidly filled the boat. Then sharp acrid fumes sent every man who was conscious, into a series of hacking coughs. The dim emergency light gave the interior a crypt-like appearance, and the shadows created eerie spectres.

George came to, and as he picked himself up, he could just see that several of the men around him were badly hurt. Many were lying at awkward angles, with blood pouring from the various points of impact. One unfortunate had been impaled on a screw threaded retaining bracket that was protruding outwards from the pressure hull. George could see the man's terrified eyes, as he looked down incredulously at the metal rod sticking out from his lower chest. His life blood was turning his dirty white sea jersey a dark crimson.

The smoke was becoming increasingly dense, making it difficult to see anything in the small compartment, possessing a foul-tasting acrid stench that filled the air. He could feel it scorching his lungs with every inhalation, noting how it had changed from the smell of explosives. Gone was the smell of cordite – leaving this strange metallic pear drop odour, that was making his chest feel as if a furnace had been lit inside. His eyes were filled with stinging tears. Alarm bells began to ring in George's head; he had recently learned about this phenomenon in the electrical section of the course. It has got to be chlorine gas! It is caused when sea-water enters the battery tank, and mixes with the electrolytic acid in the cells to produce a very toxic gas that is extremely poisonous! If he stayed down here, he knew that he would die very quickly. The boat had also begun to take on a weird angle, leaning heavily to starboard with the bow going down as if it were diving once more. After that terrible explosion, then maybe it was!

"Eer y'are George, grab this mate." Cough, cough. "It must 'ave bin a mine wot we've 'it." Cough, cough. "They'll probably abandon ship any second."

George turned to see Fred, who was coughing at his elbow – just like he was. Despite his obvious distress, he was looking calm and determined. In his hand he was holding out a life jacket. Donning it quickly, and tying the straps around his waist, George followed Fred through the dense smoke towards the ladder that led up the conning tower hatch inside the bird bath. He climbed over the edge of the bird bath and placed his foot on a rung. Then from above, they could both hear someone screaming – "Abandon Ship."

"Go on George, after you mate."

The angle of the boat was increasing dramatically, and as George began to climb he noticed everything below him was disappearing in the poisonous gaseous fog. He instinctively held his breath, as he noticed that his own arms were becoming invisible as he reached the rim of the top hatch. He could hear someone choking behind him. It must be Fred, he could feel his weight jerking on the ladder, at he went up the last rungs. The fumes were so acidic that he was completely blinded by his own tears. He emerged out into the open air, and the wind quickly whipped away most of the discomfort. He gulped down the fresh air to relieve the furnace in his chest. Stepping out onto the bridge, he took in another huge lungful of the sweet clean air. The blast of the wind soon cleared his head.

Then a wall of sea-spray hit him, and he became drenched, its force causing him to shiver, and make a grab at the nearest handhold. He shivered violently in the bitter cold, as his soaked clothes stuck to his skin. The cork inside of his life-jacket failed to provide any insulation. He faintly heard the voice of the boat's captain, Lieutenant Nolan, coming from nearby. He was surprised to find that there were some more of the crew already standing just in front of him. His face was ashen and dripping with water.

"Keep close together, men! Keep together when you get into the water! She's just about to go down! Remember to try and stay together in the water, or you'll be washed away! I want everybody to tie your life-jackets together once you are in the water. It will be easier for a rescue boat to spot a group of us. Abandon the boat! Over you go men!"

He repeated these words of encouragement calmly to each man, as he had appeared at the top of the conning tower. George made his way gingerly over towards the periscope stand. Seawater was washing around his calves as another wave broke against the tower, and he used the wire guard-rail for support to see what he should do next. He looked around for Fred, but he must have gone over the side.

Just ahead of him the captain was leaning heavily against the side of the periscope standard, still trying to make sure that his men were getting off safely. George glanced down and could see that his right leg had been horribly shattered below his knee. The blood covered shredded fragments of his trouser leg, hung loosely below his oilskin. Hanging on tightly to the wire, George made his way round the bridge structure to support his commanding officer by placing his shoulder under his, and pulling his arm around him. He could see that the man was in a great deal of pain, his face was pale and gaunt, looking as if he were about to pass out. The water had now risen up to their waists and George could see it pouring down the open hatch from which he had just emerged. Through the water he could see an up-stretched hand and face, that disappeared as it fell back into the darkness of the boat. Then another hand appeared, being forced up against the influx – groping frantically for the upper rung of the ladder – and then it too was gone. There would be no more men coming up from below.

The next sequence of events happened so quickly that reality seemed took on a dream-like quality. The surreal spectacle that was unfolding before him certainly did not seem real, a drama from another world – George began to feel very giddy. He took in another huge lungful of fresh air, because he knew that if he gave in now, he was going to die.

If anything was going to concentrate George's mind, it was the bite of this freezing cold wind. It tore at his exposed skin unmercifully. By sucking in more of the fresh air, he could feel it clearing most of the toxic poisons from his lungs. Still supporting his captain to remain upright, he tried to think how they were going to get off the boat together, because he could see that the captain was now past making decisions. George slowly edged the wounded man to the front of the bridge, fighting to keep his balance. That was when he noticed the terrible damage. As the bow was lifted by another wave, he saw that most of it was missing. It was just a mass of twisted jagged metal. The bow went down again, never to reappear as the damaged section plunged deep under the water and simply carried on down. A quick check aft, and George could see the stern starting to raise clear of the boiling foam. There was no time to waste. He saw two more men leaping into the water, and watched as they swam frantically away from the boat. It really was every man for himself – but he knew that he could not leave the wounded man behind.

He scanned the bobbing heads in the water for Fred, to make sure that he was OK, but he was nowhere to be seen. A quick glance around the bridge structure failed to locate him – he must have jumped over already! The water was now up to his chest, and he could feel the boat slipping away beneath his feet as his life-jacket began to take his weight and support him. The air was absolutely freezing and he shivered uncontrollably. Holding the now semiconscious Lieutenant Nolan, George simply stepped off the side of the bridge with him and let their life-jackets take their weight as he swam side-stroke – dragging the injured man with him. At a distance of ten feet from the conning tower, a huge bubble burst upwards, forcing the two men further away from the craft, as a wave of frothing spume covered his head. George inhaled deeply through his teeth as he broke the surface, breathing a sigh of relief to find that he still had firm hold of his captain's life-jacket.

Strangely enough, once he had got into the water his shivering stopped, and as he towed the lifeless body of his captain away from the craft, he was amazed that the sea water was strangely warmer in, than it had been out of it. It had been the wind chill on his wet skin that had caused the intense cold. Swimming on his side with one hand, he dragged the inert body of Nolan with him until he joined up with the group of seven or eight other men, who were already in the water. On reaching them, he stopped swimming and hung exhausted in his life-jacket, letting his feet dangle down into the unknown darkness. As he turned to see the faces of those who had got off the boat safely. He didn't recognise anyone immediately, and another closer check, confirmed that there were none of his classmates amongst them. Where was Fred? There must be others in the water somewhere that had not joined them yet. He reached out and tied himself and Nolan to the nearest man's life-jacket.

The whole group of survivors turned and watched silently as the stern of the submarine climbed ever higher, like the minute hand of a clock approaching the hour. The conning tower and periscope had already disappeared, as she commenced her final dive. George noticed a lone figure jumped off the bridge into the water as it went under. Maybe that was Fred! Whoever it was, he was going to be the last person to abandon the craft. Anyone else who was still aboard would now go down with her. Over the roar of the waves, there came a terrible rumble as the boat slid out of sight forever. A white bubbling caldron filled the space where she had just been. This foam was quickly dissipated in the storm, and a strange calm oily patch of sea provided her headstone. A voice startled him.

"Keep together, men! Make sure that you tie the straps of your life-jackets together! A large group of us will be easier to spot!"

Lieutenant Nolan had regained consciousness, and as with any good captain his first thoughts were for the safety of his men. The man next to him mentioned the fact that George had brought him safely off the boat. Nolan turned and thanked the young trainee.

The rest of the men in the water swam towards their leader, and after they had all arrived, George finally realised that Fred was not amongst them. It was impossible. George had actually seen Fred heading towards the ladder ahead of him, before everything had clouded. He just had to be in the water somewhere. There must be another group of survivors out there somewhere. He craned his neck around, trying to catch a glimpse of his friend in the heaving sea, but it was too dark, and not a sign of anyone else. It only seemed a few seconds ago that Fred had handed him the life-jacket. Fred was always so clear headed. He always knew what was going to happen, long before George did. Could it be possible that his friend had just died, and that his body was already down there in the cold depths beneath them?

In the next ten minutes, after a head count, there were just ten survivors – all now tied together, bobbing up and down in the tempestuous sea. Only one other member of the crew had managed to join them after the boat had sunk. George realised that he was the only survivor from his whole class.

The air was cold around his head – colder than George could ever remember. Cold kills! He was told that, during his first aid training. If they were not picked up soon, then they were all going to die from hypothermia. He knew that he had to keep his body as warm as possible. That sounded stupid swimming here in the English Channel in January, but he began moving his legs. If he kept working them – as if walking underwater. He thought that the effort might be enough to raise his internal temperature, or at least keep it at a level which would keep him alive. Above him the sky was totally black, with a thunderous black cloud cover that masked the stars and moon. None of them were going to last very long in these conditions. He became determined that he was going to survive as long as possible, but realised that any control might be snatched away. There was so much more that he still had to do with his life. He wanted to marry Gladys for a start.

Three hours later, and the group had become very quiet as they remained at the mercy of the sea's fury. Each of the men's mind had withdrawn from his frightening predicament, withdrawing deep inside with his own thoughts, as they contemplated imminent death. Each was thinking of how their passing would affect those closest to them. All were totally exhausted, which started to make them feel drowsy. Then someone started singing. It was a hymn. George recognised it from the Sunday service after the parade at the barracks.

"For those in peril on the sea!"

He thought of how incongruous it seemed, singing it here in the water, whilst facing the greatest danger that any of them had ever experienced in their life-time. Yet at the same time the choice seemed so right.

"From rock and tempest, fire and foe. Protect them where so e'er they go," George joined in.

As the hymn ended, Nolan encouraged his men. It had been he who had set the first man singing.

"Well done lads – Let's have another…"

"What exactly 'appened, sir?" interrupted the Engine Room Chief Petty Officers? "Did one of our torpedoes explode?"

All heads turned towards the captain, awaiting his answer, each of them knowing that this was the question that he had wanted to ask.

"A mine, I think," said Nolan. "It all happened so bloody quickly. I'm pretty sure that it wasn't a torpedo. Whatever happens out here tonight, we must all stay together, because if we get parted, we will have less chance of survival. Being massed together will give any rescue vessel a greater chance of spotting us. Now who is going to sing the next song?"

The next few hours were an absolute hell, the worst of George's whole life. He continued to move his legs very slowly backwards and forwards in a slow-motion walking action. He found that by doing so it kept his circulation going and that managed to retain some feeling down in his lower limbs. The wind was like an icy cut-throat razor scraping across his face and scalp, as the survivors rose up on the crest of each wave. It physically hurt, but as more of the water was splashed over his head, he was again surprised at how comparatively warm it felt. It was also decidedly warmer down in the trough between the waves. Looking around at the drawn saturated faces, it did not look any of them was faring as well as him. Then he realised that he must look very similar. One man opposite him in the circle seemed to be asleep.

Perhaps a sleep might help? No, if I sleep, I will not be moving my legs and that will make me even colder.

After another hour, in order to bolster morale, they took it in turns to relating their life history. Each man told the others of where he came from, his early boyhood life, and of those in his family. They outlined their service career, and how many children he had produced. Some of them told some funny stories of their wedding day, while others told jokes about their mother-in-law. Many of the older hands listed the ships that they had served on, describing all the places in the world that they had visited. The older hands spoke for longer, because they had achieved more in their lives, and from the look on their faces, it was obvious that they also took some pride in those achievements. When it came to George's turn, he told them of his Island home, and of his meeting with Gladys on the ferry. He considered telling of that terrible day out on Pleinmont Point, but thought better of it. He was also going to mention the night out at the 'Dog and Duck', but again thought better of it, because embarrassingly he would have to tell them that he had been under punishment during his short career.

"How old are you, son?" said the Engine Room Chief.

"Eighteen, Chief," replied George.

"You can tell there's a bloody war on, can't you?" said the older man to nobody in particular. "Before this lot started, you had to have been in the navy at least four years before you even got considered for boats. Now they're taking sprogs. I bet he's still got nappy rash. He ain't even old enough to drink."

George felt embarrassed. It had not been his choice to become a submariner. He felt a sudden bitter resentment towards the older man.

"He's old enough to die for his country, just as you are Chief," said Lieutenant Nolan. "That makes us all equals out here."

George took some pride in those words.

"Sir, it's Bryant. I think he's dead."

The voice came from the figure bobbing next to the sleeping man.

Lieutenant Nolan swam across the gap in the circle, his face grimacing with the pain from his leg. He reached the limp figure bobbing in the water.

"I'm afraid you're right Rogers, he's had it. We'll untie him and say a prayer together. Then we will remove his lifejacket and just let him just drift away from us. The sea will be his grave. His lifejacket might be useful to us. What was his name?"

"Bryant, sir. He was the cook for this trip."

George looked hard at the sleeping man. Was it the same chap who had provided him with that welcome sandwich, which in turn had given him the impetus to seek some fresh air? He suddenly felt a tremendous sadness flood through his body.

Lieutenant Nolan addressed everyone in the group, "OK men, we've lost Bryant due to the cold. I know that we all feel drowsy. I do myself, but Bryant has made the mistake of actually falling asleep. Once your body relaxes, it quickly loses its inner heat, and hypothermia sets in. We must all stay together and try to keep ourselves awake, or any of us could be the next to follow him. Do anything you must to keep yourselves awake. Try having a quiz by asking questions and giving answers. A rescue boat should arrive to pick us up by the morning. If you feel yourself drifting off, get the person next to you to talk to you. Do anything you must to stay alert and remain awake."

Three more men died during that terrible night, each of them succumbing to hypothermia. One of them being the Engine Room Chief that had been so disparaging towards George. Despite his resentment, George could not help but feel very sorry for him. He had told them that he had a wife and four children. This war didn't only claim direct casualties. The death of the Chief plagued him for many hours. before he himself was beginning to feel drowsy, so he turned and began to talk to the man on his right. From his response, George could see the man was having the same problems. As he looked around, he realised that all of the remaining six survivors now looked to be in pretty bad shape, each man looked to be nearing the end of his personal endurance. They were all fully aware that it would not be long before it would their turn to be untied and cast adrift.

As traces the sky on the eastern horizon showed the first sign of dawn, it began to reveal broken clouds, and a sea state that had moderated considerably. Thankfully the storm seemed to be abating. For the survivors, the new day brought a fresh hope of rescue, but on the dawn roll call it was discovered that two more men had died. The survivors said a prayer, before they tried to untie the bonds that held them, but the constant pressure had tightened them beyond their ability to undo the knot. So, the life-jackets were eased off of them and had they were cast adrift. The wind had shifted around to the west and had decreased in its ferocity, the icy edge had definitely disappeared, but was not exactly warm.

As light entered his world, the first conscious thought on George's mind was his stomach. He felt absolutely ravenous, and his thoughts began to imagine fried eggs, bacon and a cup of hot sweet tea. His tongue licked his salt-encrusted lips, the sudden sharpness on his tongue wiping away the fantasy.

As he looked around at the others, suddenly feeling a little embarrassed, realising that the rest of the men were looking at him. He could see from their faces that they all looked haggard and drawn, but he must look just as horrible. Their doleful eyes were red-rimmed, seeming to have sunken back into the darkened sockets. Their pallid skin was smeared with black oil, with the lank strands of hair plastered flat against their skulls, giving them a skeletal appearance. George raised his eyes upwards towards the breaks in the clouds where gulls were circling like vultures, watching and waiting. He had seen the way these greedy birds fought over the scraps at Haslar Creek. He shuddered.

Amazingly Lieutenant Nolan was still alive, and was still trying to rally his men and keep up moral. George thought of what terrible pain he must be in with that ugly leg wound. He felt a great deal of admiration for the man, who had not once thought of himself. He had managed to survive, despite the agony that he must have endured during their night of purgatory. Maybe it had been that constant pain that had kept his mind focused!

"I am sure that it won't be long now, men. They will have realised that something has gone terribly wrong when we failed to return to harbour last night. The alarm button at the base will have been pressed long ago. I should think that every available destroyer and patrol vessel that is available will all be on their way out at this very moment and will begin searching for us. We have to do everything we can to stay alive."

If his statement had been a prayer, then no sooner was it spoken, than it was answered. Watson, one of the on-watch stokers who had been in the Engine Room when George had been so ill, suddenly spotted the top mast of an armed trawler. He began yelling. His dirty cracked face suddenly came alive with excitement, at the imminent prospect of being rescue. All four of those left alive were now waving, screaming at the top of their voices with the realisation that they were going to live. The mast of the small craft was clearly visible as it rose up on the waves, and less than ten minutes later it was manoeuvring around to recover them.

The exuberance of their shouting and waving drained them all of the last vestiges of physical strength. George had not realised just how drained of energy his body had become. He could hardly move his legs anymore as the rescue craft approached. He realised that he would probably have died today, had this trawler not appeared. This bright day would have been his last on earth, and despite his indifference towards religion, he offered up a silent prayer of thanks.

He did not have the strength to swim towards the rope ladder that dangled down the side of the trawler. On the deck, a heaving line was thrown in his direction by a seaman. George managed to grab hold of it, and held on as he was hauled in towards the ship's side. It took every single ounce of his remaining strength in trying to heave himself up that rope ladder.

His other two companions had already managed to get aboard, and were being handed a blanket to get warm. A canvas sling, fitted on to the end of a hoist, was being readied to bring Lt Nolan aboard. Once it had been thrown to him, he managed manoeuvre it over his shoulders, and raised a thumb. The winch-man then hoisted him up, and he was helped down onto a stretcher. Finally, George managed to flop onto the deck, where the hands helped him to stand, but he swayed unsteadily as everything went black, utterly exhausted.

****

George found himself in semi-darkness when he finally awoke. His first sensation was of being warm – and that felt wonderful. Although he still felt very weak, the sleep had cleared his head and he was now able to think clearly. Not trying to move initially, he lay still, enjoying the moment as he tried to analyse where he was.

The night ordeal came back immediately, and as a result he began to check his body for any damage. First, he started to move his arms and his legs, and as he did so, he felt the comforting smoothness of warm starched linen against his skin. This was certainly not his bed in the inboard mess at the base. Perhaps he was in hospital, he mused.

Turning his head carefully from left to right, he could see regimental lines of beds, and became aware of the strong smells of carbolic and starch. This gave him heart, as it appeared that nothing was wrong with his sense of smell. It has got to be a hospital! He had never been in a hospital before, but something told him that this was one.

Taking a deep breath, George forced himself up onto his elbows, and in doing so, managed to bang his head against the metal head-frame. His yell of pain brought a nurse scurrying out of an office at the end of the ward.

"Are you all right?" she asked, plumping up his pillows and fussing around him, "You lads have been through a lot you know."

'You don't have to tell me,' thought George.

His mind flashed back to the face of Fred Chapman, as he was handing him the life-jacket, followed by the images of some of the others who had perished. More faces slowly filed through his consciousness. He remembered the cook carrying the tray of sandwiches, and now his body was somewhere in the English Channel. It was strange to think that the rest of the *C301*'s crew were now lying within the confines of that metal coffin under fifty fathoms, and here he was, nice and warm, lying in bed with clean ironed sheets.

"Where am I? Is this a hospital?" he asked.

"You are at the Royal Naval Hospital Haslar, in Gosport," she replied. "You have been asleep for nearly thirty-six hours. Can I get you something?"

"Is there anything to eat?" he asked, feeling as if he could devour a horse. "I'm so hungry, and I have eaten for so long."

"You're supposed to wait until breakfast," she said. "Matron is very strict."

"Oh please, I'm starving," George begged. "If I have been here thirty-six hours, then I haven't had anything to eat anything for nearly two days."

"Well I'll check with the Duty Matron to see if I can rustle you up something to keep you going. If she says it's OK, I'll have a look in the kitchen and see what I can find." She bustled away, leaving George to the quietness of the ward once more.

He knew exactly where the RNH Haslar was. He had seen its tall brick facade every day as he had attended his submarine training at Fort Blockhouse. It lay further a little further up Haslar Creek from Fort Blockhouse. Their instructor had told them that when the hospital had been built in the mid-eighteenth century, it had been the largest brick building to be found in the whole of Europe. It was a small irrelevant piece of useless information that had stuck in his brain.

The imminent prospect of food had set George's stomach rumbling in anticipation. Nevertheless, it was nearly three quarters of an hour before the nurse reappeared carrying a tray. Although it was only two boiled eggs, a chunk of cheese, with toasted bread and butter and a glass of milk, it tasted better than any meal that George had ever eaten.

Strangely enough, the last thing that he had eaten had been those two pieces of bread that had helped to relieve his sea-sickness enough for him to venture forward. If he had not eaten that bread, he would probably be lying in the engine room of C301. Fate was a strange thing! Or was it just luck that he was still alive.

The nurse had sat with him on the edge of his bed, and she spoon-fed most of it to him. Food had never tasted so good, and he savoured each mouthful with a loving relish, rolling it around his mouth to prolong the experience before swallowing. After just a few mouthfuls he could feel his body responding to the sustenance.

The following afternoon an unexpected event occurred. Firstly, he received an unexpected visitor. It was Gladys, and when she had walked into the ward his jaw had dropped open in surprise. When she saw him, she rushed forward and leaned over his bed to kiss his cheek.

"Are you alright, George my darling? I read in last evening's paper about your rescue yesterday morning, and I came straight over here today, once I had found out where you had been taken. You have not been wounded, have you?"

Before he had time to reply, she shamelessly covered his face with kisses, and her hand stroked his brow tenderly. George immediately felt a stirring in his body – it was something that always seemed to happen whenever he was near her. At least it was another good sign that he was making a good recovery. Reaching out, he grasped her hand and pressed it to his lips, before he slowly related the story of what had happened. Her eyes filled with tears, and she shuddered involuntarily.

"The casualty list was in paper," she said. "Poor Lt. Nolan has had to have his leg amputated below the knee. You were actually mentioned in the story, George. How you helped him get off the ship."

"It's called a boat, Gladys."

She ignored the minor distinction, staying with him for over forty minutes until the matron came in and shooed out all the visitors prior to the Surgeon's early evening rounds. Vows of love were quickly exchanged, before she backed out of the ward, waving and blowing yet more kisses until the doors finally closed on her.

Once alone, the matron walked slowly down the ward with her hands held firmly behind her back. She was a rather large woman, and the posture had accentuated her already overlarge large breasts.

"Listen, men, we have a ward inspection about to take place. Surgeon Captain Oliphant will be leading a team of very high-ranking officials, who will be here assessing the capacity of this hospital to handle more war casualties. When they enter, I will call you all to attention. Those of you that can sit up, you will do so with your arms folded. All those who cannot sit up, are to lie to attention on your beds. Is that clear?"

'I don't believe what I'm hearing,' thought George. 'Lie to attention!'

She was every bit the Amazon General, giving her troops a morale-boosting talk before a big battle. There was a sudden burst of laughter from George's left. All eyes turned towards the source. A small slate board above the bed bore the name Ordinary Seaman O'Rourk. A pimply-faced youth sat there with his arms folded above his head. He looked extremely stupid, and the laughter from the other patients was infectious. The laughter was immediately curtailed by the stern staring Valkyrie in her starched uniform.

"Ordinary Seaman O'Rourk, if you persist in acting the idiot, then I will make your stay with us one you will never forget. That goes for anyone else who thinks that he is funny. After I have finished with you O'Rourke, you will all be praying to get back to your ship."

Looking somewhat sheepish, O'Rourk lowered his arms, but there was still an impish smirk on his face as Matron turned and started to walk back down the ward. Behind her back O'Rourk stuck up two fingers at her. Everyone had to turn their heads away to stifle their guffaws. Those lying down, pulled their bedclothes up over their head, their counterpanes could be seen vibrating as they silently shook with laughter. A somewhat indignant matron strode off in a huff.

George realised that it was the first time that had laughed since sailing on *C301*. He suddenly felt a pang of guilt. Why should he be here laughing, when all those others were dead?

Less than two minutes later the doors swung open to reveal a group of white jacketed doctors followed by several other men in civilian attire.

"B Ward – 'shun!" barked the Matron, as her words reverberated around the walls. She marched in and the procession of men filed in behind her.

Strangely enough, everyone in the room reacted instinctively, just how the matron had ordered – all eyes instinctively flicked to O'Rourk, to see if he had obeyed – but like the rest, he was sitting to attention.

At the fore was a naval officer dressed in a full naval uniform, with four gold rings on his arm that were interspersed with red ones denoting his profession being a naval surgeon. He in turn was followed by a doctor in the white jacket and several official looking gentlemen in Whitehall style civilian clothing. They all wore black jackets, with dark grey pin striped trousers, stiffly starched winged collars and sporting a collection of school ties. They were immediately christened the Whitehall Cavalry by some wag, whispering from the next bed to George.

The procession all stopped at the first bed, nearest to the entrance door. It was on the far side of the ward from George, so he was able to observe everything that was taking place. The Surgeon Captain was informed of the occupant by name, rank, and then informed of the man's condition by the matron.

"Hardwell – Stoker First Class – Severe haemorrhoids, sir."

"How are feeling today, Hardwell? A bit sore, but a lot better I expect. Has he had his bowels open today, matron?"

"Yes, sir."

"Was it painful, Hardwell?"

"Agony, sir."

"Good, Good – I expect you're looking forward to getting back to sea as soon as possible, no doubt," smiled the Captain.

The man gave a thin-lipped smile and nodded. "Yes, sir."

The crowd looked at each other, and at an unseen prompt, they all moved along to the next bed and the performance was repeated.

"Wilson – Leading Telegraphist – Broken tibia, sir."

"Hello, Wilson, how's the leg feeling today? A lot better, I expect. Has he started to get about yet, matron?"

"Yes, sir – by using crutches."

"Good, Good – We will get you back to sea as soon as we can, Wilson. No doubt you're itching to do your bit?"

Wilson also nodded dutifully, fully aware of the expected response. "Yes, sir."

On they went, and George was beginning to feel apprehension, the closer they got. Slowly he tested his neck by moving his head up and down, hoping that he would be able to nod at the right moment. Before he realised it, they had reached the end of his bed.

"Torode – Ordinary Seaman – Hypothermia and exposure, sir," said the matron.

"Ah, Torode, I am sorry to hear about the loss of your shipmates. Only four of you picked up from the whole of *C301* it seems. Hit a mine, I'm informed. Damned hard luck, I must say. The Channel is absolutely littered with the bloody things. We have also been informed of your heroism by your Commanding Officer, Lt. Nolan. Unfortunately, I had to remove his leg yesterday – more is the pity. We need more men like him these days. Seems you risked your own life, to get him away from the sinking vessel. So, it gives me great pleasure to inform you that you have been 'Mentioned in Dispatches' to his Majesty the King. I present to you a copy of the citation," he said, holding the paper he had just been handed in his left hand, his right hand extended out towards George.

George was taken completely by surprise, as everything in his mind had been geared to nodding his head at the right moment.

"Well done, my boy, keep up the good work," said the Captain, still proffering out his hand.

There was a pregnant silence, as the matron's eyes rolled from side to side, silently trying to tell him to shake the Captain's hand. George thought that she was having a seizure, before her hidden message registered. He reached out and shook it very firmly and taking the rolled sheet from the Captain with his other hand. A small, but polite round of applause broke out from the Whitehall Cavalry.

"We need more men like you at sea in times like these. Well done, Torode."

There was another small round of applause. For George, it was one of the most embarrassing moments of his life, and he was relieved when the party had moved on to the next bed. He for one would just be very glad to regain his health and get back to sea to escape from this madhouse.

Chapter Six

Gibraltar

George Torode was drafted to join *HMS E11* in early March of 1915, almost seven weeks following the tragic incident aboard *HMS C301*. Altogether he had spent a total of eight days recovering from that terrible ordeal in Royal Naval Hospital Haslar, and since his release for duty, he had been languishing in the Spare Crew of Fort Blockhouse. All of the submarine squadrons have a Spare Crew, whereby any submarine having a crewman falling sick, or one needing to stay ashore for personal or family reasons, he can be replaced immediately from the pool of men of all ranks and specialisations within the Spare Crew.

During that period George had put to sea twice. The first time was to replace a seaman whose wife had been taken ill just prior to one of the new E Class boats, *HMS E10* who sailing from Fort Blockhouse. For George it had involved a short time aboard – a simple overnight surface passage up the Channel from Gosport to the port of Dover. Once berthed there, the submarine was going to load supplies before proceeding out on offensive patrol along the Belgian and Dutch coasts, and on into the Heligoland Bight. As soon as the submarine had secured to the quayside, the seaman that George had relieved was standing on the dockside waiting for them to arrive. His wife was in hospital, and out of danger, so he had managed to travel down on the overnight train. George was told to grab his kit bag, and immediately issued with a rail warrant to get back to Fort Blockhouse. He watched the boat sail later that evening before walking to the railway station.

The following day, the 18th of January 1915, *HMS E10* had been reported lost with all hands just eleven hours after leaving Dover. Like *C301*, she had been unlucky to hit a mine whilst submerged, just an hour after making her first dive. Her escort destroyer had actually witnessed the explosion, but despite carrying out an extensive search, they were no survivors.

George was absolutely devastated by the news, which he received the day after his return to Fort Blockhouse. In his short time aboard *E10*, he had got to know many of the crew by sight, and he had made a couple of good friends. He was also very well aware that he was extremely lucky to be alive through the wife of the man who he had relived rallying, had she not, then he may well have been kept ashore. It would then have been George would have sailed on that disastrous patrol. Fate is a fickle companion during wartime. You are either lucky, or you are dead!

When he had been aboard *C301* and she had hit her mine, fortunately she had been on the surface, even then just four members of her compliment had survived the ordeal – but there would have been no chance of any escape from a submarine hitting a mine whilst dived. It was just the way of things in these terrible times. Every serviceman today was living the lottery of survival. George thought that he was being cynical at first, but after the *E10* incident, he liked to think that he was simply becoming pragmatic about his chances of surviving. If your number was up – there was absolutely nothing that you could do about it. After hearing the terrible news, George had resolved to stop worrying about the perils of war, because if he was destined to die – then quite simply – he would die! He determined there and then that he would simply do his very best at all times while he was serving, and just hope that he was lucky enough to come through the conflict in one piece.

His second deployment from the Spare Crew was when he had been detailed to be part of a steaming crew, manning a rather rusty old B Class boat. It was leaving Fort Blockhouse on a surface passage, going around Lands' End, before heading up to Birkenhead for a refit at the Cammell-Laird shipyard. The boat was nearly ten years old, and recently had begun to suffer several temperamental breakdowns.

Luckily the sea conditions had been favourable and they eventually managed to sail on the evening tide. The total voyage was programmed to take them three days, which was interspersed by a stopover night in Devonport Dockyard to refuel. Whilst the stokers had been engaged in topping up her tanks, George had been permitted to go ashore.

Plymouth was a pleasant city, and the numbers of sailors patronising the pubs in Union Street certainly equalled those in Queen Street and Commercial Road in Portsmouth, but George had returned to the boat early. He had become very wary of drinking too much, and he didn't want to develop a habit after his infamous night-out in Portsmouth.

Once the old B Class boat had finally been finally been delivered safely to the Cammell Laird Shipyard, the steaming crew were sent back to Gosport by train. When he had arrived at Fort Blockhouse, there was a drafting order waiting for him. When he had read the destination, it had excited him. He was to join *HMS E11*, which was a sister boat to the ill-fated *HMS E10,* and although his voyage aboard her had ended so tragically, it had served to show him what a good design these newer E Class boats were. They were some of the latest units in submarine design technology to enter service. *HMS E11* was currently berthed down on the pier in Haslar Creek, and his orders were to join her without delay.

****

A gathering depression hung over southern Britain, as a stiff north-westerly wind freshened as the small flotilla had sailed from Portsmouth. It consisted of *HMS E11*, in company with two other submarines of the same class, namely *HMS E14* and *HMS E15*, along with their depot ship *HMS Adamant*.

HMS E11 was commanded by Lieutenant Commander Martin Dunbar-Nasmith, along with Guy D'Orly-Hughes as his First Lieutenant, he was expected to achieve great things during the conflict. Nobody would reveal where they were headed.

As the flotilla made their way westward down the English Channel on the surface, *E11*'s crew of thirty had quickly settled down into their watch system. Beneath the overcast cloud and moderate sea conditions, the three submarines were positioned in line astern of their Depot Ship.

HMS Adamant was a small ship, a rather sporty looking steam yacht, complete with a curved clipper bow, which gave her more the appearance of a racer at Cowes, rather than a submarine depot ship. She was only 190 feet in length, and had a long white bowsprit sticking out over the water at the bow. There were two tall masts, one forward and one aft, with a tall thin funnel sticking up in between. She was manned by a crew of just sixty-three.

The two other submarines in the flotilla were quite literally the newest boats in the fleet. *HMS E14* being commanded by Lieutenant Commander Edward Courtney Boyle, and in *HMS E15* she was commanded by Lieutenant Commander Theodore Stuart Brodie. The latter commanding officer was known affectionately throughout the submarine service as *Dummy Head*. This appellation was used to differentiate him from his twin brother, Charles Gordon Brodie, who was also a submariner and known in the Trade as *War Head*. These strange nick-names referred to the two types of heads that can be fitted to a torpedo. One was for practice shots – hence the dummy-head, when the weapon could be recovered after its run and used again, and the other type of head being used as a weapon of war and packed with explosive – hence war-head. Both men were held in high esteem and very well respected be their peers, and had spent their whole careers together in the submarine service. So, when Dummy Head had been appointed to a command without his brother being given a boat, the news had been received with some surprise throughout the Trade. Instead of being given a submarine command, War-Head had been appointed to the Operational Staff of the Flag Officer Submarines, Mediterranean Fleet

There were rumours were running riot that a new front was being developed in the eastern Mediterranean, and many great things were expected of both of these experienced men.

The speculation that something new was afoot in the eastern Med had been running high for some time at Fort Blockhouse. During most of February and into the early part of March, the battle-ships and battle-cruisers of the Mediterranean Fleet were reported to have been attempting to force a passage through the Dardanelles, in an attempt to gain entry into the Sea of Marmara to attack Constantinople.

On March 18th 1915 the Allied Fleet had attacked the Turkish gun batteries guarding the narrow waterway, which had replied with equal gusto resulting in heavy loss of life for our own forces. The individual commanders of the British warships appeared to be too worried about their own careers, rather than show any aggressive resolve to carry the fight. Their fears of failure came before determination, and as a result of dithering the Turkish army had had been given plenty of warning of their intentions. This had allowed them adequate time to install heavy armaments, and to prepare their defences by the laying of mine fields and underwater obstructions in the waterway. As a direct consequence the Allied timidity, the battleship's *HMS Irresistible*, *HMS Ocean* and *HMS Bouvet* had been sunk. The French Navy, as part of this allied force, had also suffered casualties when the *FNS Gaulois* and *FNS Suffren* had both been badly damaged. The heavy cruiser *HMS Inflexible* had also taken some heavy punishment, and as a result was immediately ordered to return to Malta to effect repairs.

The force had been attempting to activate a plan to open up a second eastern front, thus forcing the enemy fight two armies. Victory would mean taking Turkey out of the war, and being able to supply the beleaguered Russian Army. The idea had been a very good one, but the implementation was leaving a lot to be desired. In these initial weeks, the whole operation had just been a total disaster. The repercussions for lack of ambition shown by the allied forces was still being felt at home, and the Turkish defences that guarded the Dardanelles remained intact and were as strong as ever. From now onwards, it was not going to be easy to break through, and there was a swing in thinking towards using submarines to make the initial incursions.

In early March, just prior to George joining *E11* at Fort Blockhouse, the rumours were running rife onboard that the Mediterranean area was where he would be heading with his new appointment. Having heard the talk and read the newspapers about the Dardanelles, it had caused him to visit the base library and borrow an atlas, just to become aware of the geographical location. If the mighty battle-ships were unable to breach such a narrow waterway, then it would not take too much guessing as to what type of patrols they would be undertaking.

On the morning that he joined *E11*, he found that his estimation generally matched the opinion among the crew, and those of the men on the other boats that now formed the small Flotilla. Everything pointed to the fact that the next target of the Allies attention was going to be Turkey.

Those two German cruisers, the Goeben and Breslau, who had caused so much trouble for the Royal Navy prior to the outbreak of hostilities, were still reported to be holed up in Constantinople. Intelligence reports stated that they had been making sorties up into the Black Sea to bombard the Russian forces around the port of Sevastopol in the Crimea. Many of the crew thought that they might well be used to help to repulse the Allied penetration of the Dardanelles. Should they ever be successful in forcing their way back out into the Mediterranean, it would certainly cause the Mediterranean Fleet a lot of problems in trying to track and destroy them, and with the losses they had just suffered on their initial penetration, it would place a great deal of pressure on the remaining units.

Having failed to make the penetration by sea, the tacticians had quickly decided that by the capturing of the whole Gallipoli Peninsula, it would allow the allied forces the chance to bombard the Turkish gun batteries directly from across the waterway, and thus leave the door wide open for the warships to sail through. Preparations to land an army invasion force were already well under way.

A newspaper report came in, just prior to *HMS E11* sailing, saying that more British bombardments had taken place on the Turkish positions in preparation for the landing the troops on the Peninsula, which was expected to take place in the very near future. However, logistically things were moving far too slowly, and once again it was giving the Turks the time to prepare their defences on the peninsula against any such landings. Things did not bode well.

Very early on in 1915, Winston Churchill's extremely radical plan for directly attacking Constantinople had been granted approval. By taking Turkey out of the war, it would leave a clear path for the Allies to supply the beleaguered Russian Army from the south, and therefore give them the equipment to attack the German army from the east with much more vigour. Once the enemy was forced to engage the Allies on two fronts, it should almost certainly shorten the war. Unfortunately, due to the lack of expedience shown by the Allied naval forces, the whole plan was beginning to unravel, and they were handing the advantage to the Turkish defenders.

George had joined *HMS E11* only three days before she was due to sail. He had felt quite nervous when he had arrived aboard, and knew that he did not have too much time to settle in. He immediately experienced some intimidation from his crew mates, all of them being older. They naturally regarded him with a certain amount of suspicion, because although he had just passed his course and had not had any real wartime sea experience aboard a submarine. There were some whispered remarks about his age, so he had not been surprised him when he discovered that he was the youngest member of the crew. He wouldn't be nineteen for another month or so. Although he had passed his submarine training exam with flying colours, and despite him being involved in the *C301* incident, he knew that he could not boast of any actual sea experience, other than those two trips whilst in the Spare Crew. He was also very well aware that he still had a lot to learn on these newer types of submarine, and was under no allusions that the whole of the crew would be constantly watching his every move until he proved his competence. These boats were much longer and had internal bulkheads. They were fitted with two diesel engines and boasted many more torpedo tubes.

Aboard any submarine, just one man's lack of knowledge could be enough to kill them all. All of the crews within the Trade made it their own responsibility to ensure that any newcomers knew their boat inside out. It was a form of self-preservation they employed, ensuring a better than average chance of survival. Enemy action through mines and anti-submarine action by surface forces had to be faced together, and a weak link would decrease their chances of coming through.

Although George's exploit aboard *C301*, once it had become common knowledge on the boat, had given him a little prestige, he knew that there would still be hidden eyes watching him. He felt a little at a loss during those first few days, because the internal construction of this newer class of boat was completely different from the older B & C Classes on which he had completed his training. He could hardly count that passage down to Dover aboard *E10*, because that had been conducted entirely on the surface. It knew he would have to fully acquaint himself with every system aboard, and had to do it very quickly. Prior to sailing, he had spent all his spare time locating the various pieces of equipment, and asking his new crew mates a thousand and one different questions about the operation of this equipment. He had to prove his worth to them, and only then would he be accepted as a full member of the boat. Seeing his determination to learn, the whole crew were only too willing to assist him with instruction. The quicker he learned, then the less they would have to worry and watch over him.

After sailing from Gosport, the Flotilla's surfaced passage took them westward towards the south-west approaches. That first twelve hours had gone without incident. The channel mists were cold, wet, and clinging, reducing their visibility, but on their second night at sea and there was a fair sea running, as rollers came in from the deep-water Atlantic hitting them on the starboard bow. The mists quickly disappeared leaving clear moonlit skies, but the uncomfortable motion was causing the boat to roll unevenly as they made their way around the Ile d'Ouessant. After steadying on the south westerly course for crossing of the Bay of Biscay, the rolling increased significantly, which made life aboard quite uncomfortable. George remembered that night of hell aboard *C301* – thinking that anything was better than a repetition of that purgatory. Although uncomfortable, he found that he could manage the steady motion quite well. He was pleasantly surprised that did not feel sea-sick, and reasoned that he had been cured by that baptism of fire back at the beginning of January.

During his off-watch time, George continued with his exploration of the systems through-out the boat. He quickly acquainted himself with all of the fittings, and he could already feel a greater acceptance from the crew regarding his attitude.

The surface passage was going well until they had reached the mid-point of the crossing of the Bay, when, for no apparent reason, both of *E11*'s main diesel engines began spluttering, and then one coughed so badly that it came to a complete halt, with the other having to have its revolutions reduced. The whole flotilla was forced to slow down, while an inspection took place before any repairs could be carried out.

George watched attentively as the engine room mechanics toiled over the two Vickers eight-cylinder engines, trying to trace the fault. Headed by the engineer, Chief Petty Officer Jupp, they eventually they managed to get both of the engines restarted, but not without some difficulty. During the remainder of the crossing of the Bay, both of the engines continued to give the engineers a great deal of trouble. Obviously, there was something seriously wrong! The pistons were continually misfiring, and the Engine Room staff spent all of the following night trying to trace the source of the problem. As the problem was affecting both engines, it was then suggested that there had to be some form of fuel contamination. The problem was finally diagnosed as a sea-water ingress that had penetrated into the external diesel fuel oil tank.

To give the E class submarines a longer range, much of the extra fuel that was required, was stored in the external saddle tanks. These were positioned between the main ballast tanks that provided the buoyancy of the boat. When contaminated with seawater, diesel fuel became emulsified, and it was this that was causing the engines to cough and run erratically.

As a direct result of the engine fuel malfunction, the port engine began making a faint grinding noise. Chief Jupp was fearful that the irregular running from the contaminated fuel may have damaged the drive shaft, but they would have to make it to Gibraltar to be able to investigate the problem fully.

To test their theory, the engineers switched over from the external tanks to the fuel that was stored in an internal tank. Both engines were started once again and the problem was immediately alleviated with both running smoothly. It had proved the contamination theory, but unfortunately, in solving one problem, it had created another. The single internal tank was much smaller, and its much-reduced capacity would seriously affect the submarines effective range. To remedy the first problem, all of the contaminated diesel oil would have to be removed at Gibraltar, and then the ingress problem fixed before they could be refuelled. The important question now was – could they make it to Gibraltar on the scant internal fuel supply?

After carrying out some hasty calculations, it was assessed that the internal tank contained just enough fuel for them to reach Gibraltar. Once they berthed, it should be simple enough to fix the ingress problem. Despite this annoying hiccup, the remainder of the voyage went well. All along the coast of Portugal the incessant rolling was put up with by the cheerful resolve of the British submariners, as their engines continued to run smoothly.

During the morning watch of the following day, it found the flotilla negotiating the dog-leg corner at Cape St Vincent, as they turned south east, to make their way towards the Straits of Gibraltar. All the way down from Corunna the sun had shone, and as that morning wore on, so it continued. After leaving the cold murky conditions of the English Channel, the sunshine was very welcome, but the continuous brightness of the day soon started to make the conditions below quite uncomfortable. For a start the internal temperatures began to soar. To relieve his men from their sweaty purgatory, the captain permitted three men at a time aloft for a smoke, and to enjoy the light breezes for fifteen minutes apiece. Although they were all sweaty, the crew thought these conditions preferable to the damp chilly conditions they had left behind.

Up on the conning tower, acting as look-out, George Torode was feeling a twinge of excitement, because when he looked through his binoculars, he could faintly make out the coast of Portugal, far off on their port side. Besides having often seen the coast of France from Guernsey, and of course the coast of England when he first arrived on the ferry to join up, this was the first sighting of any foreign land that he had ever seen. It had been so misty on that day he had arrived in Dover aboard *E10*, that when he had tried to locate the French coast, it had been impossible. Even now in the sunshine, all that was visible were the crests of a line of hills, the image slightly distorted by a heat haze mirage. To George, to able to feel the warmth of the sun against his skin, and to have these soft zephyrs combing his hair, it felt like paradise.

Another eight hours elapsed, and George was again taking his turn as look-out when he got his first sight of the Continent of Africa, as the small Flotilla were getting ever closer to the Straits of Gibraltar. In the pink hues of the evening light, he could see the faintest of jagged grey outlines rising above the shimmering indistinct horizon. The Spanish coast could be seen quite clearly now, lying off to port. Seagulls flew in station, escorting the flotilla by positioning their self just above and behind the line of ships. Occasionally one would bank away and dive into the water, emerging moments later with a something wriggling in its bill. Above, the sky was completely clear of cloud and George was sure that the sea was deeper blue than he had ever seen before. His mounting excitement knew no bounds, and he was now thankful that he had insisted on joining the navy that day in Smith Street. He felt a wholehearted sympathy for those thousands of poor soldiers stuck in those muddy trenches on the western front in that cloudy inclement weather they had left behind. It may even be raining in Belgium? His lungs drew in a deep breath of ozone. Yes indeed, he was glad of his decision to join the navy, as the setting sun painted the western horizon into a palette of reds and orange.

That evening, the captain informed the crew that they would be slowing down to make their entry into Gibraltar harbour early the following morning. George had found it hard to sleep, so excited by the prospect of what was to come, he arose early to volunteer for an extra period as look-out. The early morning air was much cooler than he thought it would be ,and the sun was only just rising above the African Atlas Mountains. George watched enthralled as a school of porpoises jumped in and out of the water off on their starboard side. He scanned the jagged rocks of Africa, which were now less than ten miles distant, much more defined with a small amount of cloud hovering over the tallest crests. George was enjoying every second of being aloft, but just half an hour later he was relieved by the submarine's signalman, Telegraphist George Plowman. He told him to go below, and get some breakfast before they entered harbour.

Breakfast was provided by the last of the eggs they had brought with them from Gosport, hard boiled with a thick slice of bread and butter. The bread had just started to show patches of blue mould, and the butter was beginning to develop a light covering of furry hairs. A pinch or two removed the mould, and a quick scrape with the blade of a knife found the butter as good as new. If they had remained at sea tomorrow, then those blue patches in the bread would have turned green, and it would have been inedible. There would be fresh provisions waiting on the dockside in Gibraltar.

It was another two hours before the Coxswain finally ordered the casing party aloft to prepare the submarine berthing ropes to enter harbour. Dressed in his casing rig, which consisted of a white closed knit roll neck submarine sweater over navy blue bellbottoms, George climbed back up through the conning tower hatch to retrieve those ropes from their free-flooding stowages underneath the external casing. As he emerged from the confines of the boat, he was immediately stunned by the staggering splendour of the Rock of Gibraltar, slightly shadowed, but still awesome in the full glare of the morning light. He had never seen anything like it in his whole life. As he toiled at his task, he noticed the tiny black dots of vegetation that speckled the steep slopes. There were several walls that ran vertically up and down, as well laterally, dividing off huge sections like giant gardens. In stark contrast, down at sea level, there were the orange / red terracotta tiled roof-tops of the town that ran up towards the northern edge of the narrow peninsular that joined it to Spain.

Ahead of them, the depot ship and the other two submarines had begun to swing around to port, to head up into Algeciras Bay, still in line ahead. George could not help but keep turning his head, not wanting to miss one moment of the inspring spectacle.

The steep escarpment of the Rock rose up high above the dockyard moles, which were visible along the urbanised shore-line. There were some taller dwellings adorning those lower slopes, with more of the sparse dark scrub-like vegetation high above. There were crenulated walls that could be seen, and a road could just be discerned zigzagging up the slope towards them. Most of these old fortifications dated from the Moorish occupation, which were more prominent at the northern end of the giant rock. Up along the crest, George could see the hair-like aerials of the brand-new radio station, whose glass windows were reflecting the sun. Radio was a brand-new form of communication, that was only just being introduced into the navy. A set had been fitted into the newer E Class boats and *E11* was carrying a Radio Operator from the Signal School for this deployment. He was not a qualified submariner, and had been told in no uncertain terms that he was to learn – and learn very quickly.

On the gentler southern slopes, George spotted some large gun emplacements, which he could be see had their barrels pointing directly out into the Strait. Obviously, they guarded any break-out or break-in of the Mediterranean. The Straits themselves were only twelve miles across at this point, and were constantly being patrolled by smaller warships who guarded the gaps in the freshly laid mine-fields, and anti-submarine boom nets designed to deter any possible incursion by U-boats.

Up to the north, at the top of the bay lay the white-washed houses of the small town of La Linea de la Conception, contrasting greatly against the dry dusty scrub covered hillside on which it stood.

With the berthing ropes laid out in readiness, George now could concentrate his attention on the town itself. The orange-red terracotta roof tiles nestled at the base of the Rock, cut a bloody gash in its pale flesh. The dwellings rose up the first inclines until they reached the sheer sides of the cliff. The main part of the town itself lay behind the far fringes of the Naval Dockyard, which seemed to fill this western shore-line. In the glare of the sun, the concrete and stone buildings stood out proudly in Victorian grey granite – a mini Portsmouth Dockyard, with the jibs of cranes standing up high above the sea wall. A giant inverted V showed the presence of a pair of sheer-legs, that rose high over the dockyard buildings. Sheer-legs were something that George had learned of during his seamanship training. They were a form of heavy lifting crane that could pivot inwards or outwards on their base by the use of huge block and tackles. This huge pair must be at least eighty feet high, he thought, and instead of using blocks and tackles, there would be winch operated steel wire cables.

As the submarine got closer to the dockyard buildings, George realised that they did not look any different to those of Portsmouth, Chatham, or Plymouth. Not that he had been to Chatham. These had the same brick and stone walls, complete with slate roofs. Little tank engines were plying their way to and fro, with white puffs of steam thrusting skyward as they hauled lines of wagons. He could see that there was an almost exact replica of the Semaphore Tower in Portsmouth Dockyard, that stands down on the South Railway Jetty. Everything looked so reassuringly familiar.

The casing party of *HMS E11* were stood at attention, as the submarine passed through the narrow gap between the stone moles, that formed the harbour entrance. All along the mole there stood more large calibre gun mountings, with their barrels raised upwards, like the jibs of the dockyard cranes.

The shrill monotone blast of George Plowman's bosun's call saluted the Admirals Flag, flying from the mast-head on the Semaphore Tower, as the bow of *E11* swung slowly round to starboard. Martin Dunbar-Naismith was lining up the boat as she headed down the harbour towards a gigantic pair of steel sheer-legs. They were leaning outwards over the edge of the granite stone quayside. Directly beneath them lay the sleek grey lines of a large three funnel cruiser.

George could see that beyond her, at the southern end of the harbour, were the unmistakable tripod masts of one of the latest fast battle-cruisers, although the ship itself was invisible as it rested down in the bowels of the dry dock. He could see the huge black caisson that marked the entrance of the largest dry dock in the Mediterranean. The huge warship had been dry docked to undergo repairs. The harbour walls and the berths along the inner side of the mole were lined with Light Cruisers and Destroyers. Lighters and auxiliary tenders were busily unloading their holds, trying to fulfil the constant demands from the warships. There was a French cruiser that had two torpedo boat destroyers lying alongside her. In the centre of the harbour were two whalers from one of the larger vessels, who were having pulling practice near the caisson. The whole place was a vibrant hive of activity.

The main engines were unable to go astern. In order for the captain to carry out the complicated manoeuvres of berthing the submarine, the Motor / Generators had a clutch on each side to disconnect them from the main engines, so that the forward or reverse options could then be achieved on the main motors. To carry this out, there was a Star Clutch. So, once the main engines had been disconnected and stopped, the main batteries could then supply the power to the electrically driven main motors, which were connected to the propeller shafts by the means of a tail clutch, which enabled them to run both ahead or astern.

On the surface both clutches were usually engaged, allowing both engines to drive the propellers directly through the shaft with both clutches engaged. The order to disengage the star clutch was also given, whenever there was a serious problem on the main engines. The port star clutch came out quite easily, but the Artificer Mechanic who was in charge of the Engine Room, was unable to disengage the starboard star clutch. Finally, by using all his strength, combined with the physical assistance of two stokers, the three men finally manage to disengage the clutch. It was all very worrying, because whilst out on patrol, the ability to carry out a fast crash dive would be seriously impaired if that clutch could not be disengaged quickly. The smooth operation of both clutches was an absolute essential in a combat area, to enable the electric motors to drive them beneath the waves in less than a minute. Every one of the lives of the crew would depend on it! It was another problem to add to that of the contaminated fuel. Both would have to be looked at, and these were things that was going to take time.

As the submarine approached her assigned berth, the casing party were ordered to fall out, and be ready to bring *E11* alongside. Heaving lines snaked out across the water towards the group of waiting dockyard personnel. By employing a couple of reverse bursts on the electric motors, Martin Naismith managed to swing the stern of *E11* expertly alongside the granite wall. The berthing lines were quickly made fast to the raised bollards.

HMS E14 and *E15* were already tied up, nestling alongside the depot ship, which was berthed against the quayside just forward of *E11*. Neither of the other boats had experienced any difficulties during the southern passage. That was the reason why *E11* had been assigned her own berth on the harbour wall, and not included with them alongside the mother-ship.

A team of dockyard workers were already waiting for *E11*'s gangway to be set in place, before they could begin the unloading of her contaminated fuel. The Engine Room department were going have extremely long day, and if it called for it, a long night of investigative work. Now on top of that, they also had to try and find out what was wrong with the defective star clutch.

The casing party were stood down, but George stayed aloft breathing in the ambiance of the place. The morning air actually felt warm, despite the time of year and the hour of the day. It was nearly ten o'clock. The older members of the crew stood together by the conning tower, having a smoke. George sidled up to them, hoping to be included in the friendly banter that was being exchanged. He was well aware that he had fairly done well on his first entry into harbour, and had not made any errors, but none the less he was totally ignored! Trying not to feel despondent, he went below. As he was about to go through the hatch, the sharp tone of a steam whistle made his head turn, and he spotted a small train puffing along the dockside, dragging a clattering line of empty fueling bowsers in readiness to remove *E11*'s contaminated fuel. A flatbed truck also arrived at the gangway, laden with a number of flexible rubber hoses.

The Coxswain appeared at the hatch and ordered the stokers to start rigging the hose lines from the boat over to the awaiting railway bowsers. It was going to take a long time for them to get rid of their contaminated fuel. Above them, the sky was cloudless, and the sun's strength foretold a hot sweaty afternoon was in store for the crew.

In the late afternoon, as the heat of the day began to fade, the Coxswain allowed the seamen to stand down when the last of the bowser tanker trucks had finally been filled to capacity? Feeling hot and sweaty, George went below, and grabbing his towel, he headed for the depot ship to wash off the smell of diesel and get himself clean.

Considering their reputation of not being clean, Submariners always carried a towel, which they used to wrap around their necks when going aloft on the surface during rough weather. This not only kept them warm by sealing in their body warmth, but also prevented much of the water going down their necks. It was also that same towel that was used whenever the chance of a wash presented itself. Unfortunately, there was nobody aboard the boat who carried any soap or toilet gear. These would be provided on the Depot Ship.

The men of *E11* who were not involved with investigation into the star clutch problem, were issued with hammocks to enable them to sleep in the relative comfort of the depot-ship. Just to sleep in clean bedding after a wash was the ultimate in luxury for any submariner.

The following morning, as the crew had gathered aboard *E11* for orders for their working day, high above them a *Levante* cloud smothered the peak of the Rock like a dark grey cotton wool blanket. It was blocking the rays of the rising sun, and casting cold shadows over the western side of the Rock. Strangely, out in the Bay the early morning sunshine was as bright as the previous day, as indeed was the glittering city of Algeciras over on the far Spanish shore. It seemed strange how the cloud managed to anchor itself to the top ridge, and just stay there. Down on the harbour wall, within the shadows, the crew of *E11* experienced their final taste of winter's icy fingers in the chilly morning air. The older hands informed George that the hovering cloud would lift by the time that the rum ration was issued, and that the town would be basking in sunshine by the time they ate their mid-day meal. The crew had also been told, that providing all the storing and preparation for the next leg of their transit to Malta was completed, shore leave would be granted that afternoon for anyone who was not part of the duty watch. However, the problem with the star clutch still remained unresolved, and as a consequence several unfortunate stokers were going to be required to work that afternoon.

The provision stores duly arrived on the back of a flat-bed truck, and by lunchtime everything had been stowed below. The work of clearing up the boat had also been completed. George felt the sun against his skin as he wiped the sweat from his brow, and looking up at the peak, sure enough the *Levante* had disappeared. Looking around him, he could see that the whole dockyard was now bathed in sunshine. With the exception of the Engine Room department, who still had to load the new fuel, the boat was in all respects ready to sail, but then the Engineer appeared. He had just been told that there was no diesel fuel oil available in the dockyard. With all of the contaminated fuel removed and their external tanks now empty, apparently there was nothing here to fill them. The submarines weight was a lot less without the fuel in her saddle tanks, which left *E11* riding higher in the water than normal.

The dockyard officials had had countless meetings with *E11*'s officers, and her Captain's frustration was evident for everyone to see. Martin Naismith went over to the Depot Ship for another strategy meeting. He did however, before he left, grant afternoon shore leave until 1800 that evening. By then he said that he should know more on their situation, and that he would give them an update address to the crew at that time.

Martin Dunbar-Naismith was a superstitious man, and as a result he would not be partaking of the pleasures of Gibraltar. This was due to a self-imposed pledge by him of abstaining from alcohol and tobacco until he had sunk an enemy warship. It was a silly thing to have done, something that had happened well before the last Christmas, after *E11* had conducted several fruitless and frustrating patrols in out in the North Sea. His pledge had been made more in the hope that it would happen sooner, rather than later. He was certainly hoping that in this coming year he would be able to show just what he and his crew were really capable of, although these latest defects were hampering that ambition.

George, whilst talking to other members of the crew, had learned of another tragedy that had happened last February. *E11* had been berthed on the south wall within the harbour at Great Yarmouth. One of the crew, a Petty Officer Albert George Hodder had gone ashore to get some food. When he returned, he slipped off the gang plank, falling headlong into the fast-flowing tidal water without anyone spotting the accident. He was later recovered alive by a fishing vessel, but died from hypothermia on the fourth of that month. His body was taken back to his Dorset home for burial. So far *E11* had not covered herself in glory during this war, but if their captain had anything to do with it – that was about to change.

Today was the second day of April 1915, the day after April Fool's Day. The whole Royal Navy knew that anyone stupid enough to act the fool during these troubled times would not survive very long. George Torode stretched his arms above his head in the sunshine, drawing every muscle to the extreme – it had been a hard morning's work. The sound of the bosun's call made a shrill two-tone series of notes. It always preceded an announcement by the Coxswain. In this case it was that rum was being issued.

Up Spirits – Stand Fast The Holy Ghost.

George was not quite old enough to draw his tot of grog, the lower age limit being twenty-one. The Coxswain was a large rounded man by the name of Chief Petty Officer Oliver Dowell, and as George was the only UA (Under Age for rum) member of the crew, he had made a personal decision that if he was old enough to serve his country and risk his life as a crew member, then he old enough for a tot. He had issued him a watered-down version every day ever since he had joined the boat. Due to his age and inexperience, George was also relegated to being the last in the queue, as there were a lot of unwritten protocols about the issuing of rum. He did not mind joining the back of the queue, as he was given a full glass of the warm brown liquid.

Today it was being issued on the casing, as the temperatures below were very uncomfortable. After the crew had drank theirs, George finally reached the rum fanny (a small metal bucket) and was handed a glass. He quickly downed the fiery brew, before going below to grab his towel to head off along the quay for the Depot Ship. They would supply him a lump of carbolic soap, with which he would remove most of his body odour, and hopefully eradicate the diesel impregnation that remained imprinted in his skin. All of the crew kept their kit aboard the Depot Ship to prevent it being impregnated by the diesel fumes. He was quite excited as he had decided that after he was clean, he was going to get dressed in his uniform, and go ashore to explore the delights of Gibraltar.

Mid-afternoon found him walking down Main Street in the town. His eyes were agog, as he experienced the wonders of this new alien world. Hs senses seemed to explode with every new sight, smell and sound of the place. Gibraltar was so very different from anywhere or anything else he had ever experienced during his whole life. He had been a little disappointed that England had not been that different from Guernsey, but this was a totally new experience. Here there was a composite blend of North Africa, Spain, along with the British influenced architecture providing a cosmopolitan mix. The Moorish influence was prevalent with many of the traders, who wore loose turbans, flowing kaftans and some even sported the red inverted flowerpot Fez. A taste of Spain could be found in the dingy bodegas, and the open markets where tanned moustachioed men in short-sleeved shirts, flirted with beautiful full skirted raven-haired women. Ebony skinned Africans were bedecked in their brightly coloured robes. Gold and silver trinkets stood out boldly against their dark skin. Public eating houses and restaurants vied with each other over who could produce the most mouth-watering aromatic smells. A host of unintelligible languages filled his ears. He immediately recognised French, as it was widely spoken on Guernsey, and he was fairly fluent, but there was another tongue that was prevalent from which he could detect the odd familiar word, which he assumed to be Spanish. The Africans spoke an unintelligible tongue, which had an equally unintelligible name. Naval uniforms abounded. The French sailors stood out with the red pom-poms on top of their white caps. There were also many soldiers with various shades of khaki that denoted the regiment they belonged to. It was they who manned the Rock's defences. The whole place was a kaleidoscope of wonder. It seemed to him that he was standing at the cross-roads between the two continents, and there was so much to see before he had to return for the captain's address.

As he walked along the narrow-shaded confines of Main Street, Arab traders rushed out from their shops to block his path, pleading for him to come in and buy their wonderful bargains. George had already watched the same thing happen to other sailors, further back along the street. One sailor was drawn into a shop with promises of unbeatable and fantastic bargains. The trader then began to raise the price upwards, by adding another article as a dual purchase. The sailor was told that it was at a price that only a fool could refuse, but he was obviously a man of experience because he started to haggle over the price – trying to beat the Moroccan businessman ever lower. George watched the whole process with interest. There was much gesturing, with the puffing out of cheeks, and the shaking of heads in false indignation. Each man's gestures were being exaggerated beyond the natural. Finally, the seaman had left the shop with four articles, each one being beautifully wrapped. The sailor wore an expression denoting that he believed that he had got one over on the African merchant, but George quickly doubted that to be the case, because he saw the trader give a derisive smile to a colleague, as the navy man had left his premises. Seeing this exchange made George think that he now knew how things were done here, and he felt that he would like to buy something for Gladys, but felt a little nervous about having to haggle the over price. He knew that the transaction process was not going to be easy. Maybe he would try later when he had more chance to observe the procedure again!

Main Street was awash with the off-duty crews from the warships that filled the harbour. The thoroughfare was a sea of blue serge, crested by wavelets of white canvas caps. The British style public houses and bars, vied with the bodegas, with both doing a roaring trade.

George had stepped ashore with George Plowman the signalman, and with Albert Lohden the radio telegraphist, who was being carried to man the brand-new radio transmitter and receiver that had very recently been fitted to *E11*. Both of these older men had visited the Rock several times before during their careers. They gave George the benefit of their wisdom, before he finally he decided to go in and negotiated a purchase. A beautiful gold and silver thread tasselled shawl had taken his eye. It would look absolutely splendid wrapped around Gladys' shoulders. After a somewhat disastrous attempt at haggling, George bought it for a price that he thought was a little steep, and afterwards realised that his desire to buy her something exotic had outweighed his prudence. None the less he paid the money, and as he had emerged from the open frontage of the shop, Albert Lohden began to lick his lips.

"What about a pint?" he suggested. "The old UV is just down a bit further, just beyond Casement Square."

Within the white ceramic tiled halls of the Universal Bar, or the UV as the navy affectionately referred to it, there was a heaving mass of British sailors. An immediate eclectic mix of aromas assailed their nostrils as on entry. Yeasty hops blended with olive oil and garlic, with the ever-present stench of tobacco smoke. Every one of the large circular tables was filled to overflowing, each accommodating three times the number for which it had been designed.

A sudden ear-piercing blast from a muted trumpet made George jump, it was the more alarming when he realised where it came from. Looking up he noticed the keel of a small clinker-built dinghy that was suspended from the ceiling on four slim wires. The hull was painted white, and the keel hovered some ten feet above the red tiled floor. Sat inside the boat was a quartet of musicians dressed in Spanish style clothes. There were two guitarists, a violinist, and a trumpet player, all dressed in the same grey tight-fitting suits, similar to those that George had seen in town. By sitting up there, the musicians felt relatively safe from the drunken attention of their customers below. They began their repertoire with an unrecognisable Spanish flamenco, which was totally ignored by the navy.

The three men stood near to the entrance, there being to spaces available at any of the tables. George Plowman managed to fight his way to the bar, finally returning after ten long minutes with three pints of foaming bitter. Each of the men took a long draught, each giving an appreciative aaah, before setting the glass down on a near-by window sill. They all agreed that it was good beer and was well worth waiting for. For George it was the best pint of beer he had ever tasted and for George it was certainly the very first drink since that terrible night at the 'Dog and Duck' in Queens Street. The beer they had dispensed there was absolutely foul. This was much tastier, and he took another appreciative mouthful.

The band was now playing Bizet's March of the Toreadors. It was an evocative piece where George could imagine a bull fighter entering the corrida. With each trumpet flourish, there erupted a loud – Ole – from the audience below. The crowd of sailors that filled one of the tables were from the large battle-cruiser in the dry dock. They had been shouting raucous derisive remarks up at the band. Requests for them to play the latest tunes and music hall favourites had been totally ignored so far, and they were becoming frustrated. The Iberian quartet simply carried on with another traditional Spanish number. Eventually the sailors' frustration boiled over, and they began to sing their own songs very loudly, as they tried to drown out the band. The Iberian themed tune was vaguely recognisable to George, but not so the lyrics.

Lady of Spain you're a Spaniard
Dhobi my White Front and Lanyard
Then get hold of my halyard
And pull it till somebody comes – Ole!

Sitting at the next table, not to be outdone, the crew from one of the destroyers immediately began to sing a different tune. The men from the battle-cruiser were just finishing theirs, and immediately replied with another well-known favourite. The result was an overpowering wall of noise that made it impossible for anyone to hold any normal conversation. Loud applause and much jeering greeted the end of each song. Above it all, unabashed, the four-piece band above continue to play their own chosen piece. More shouts for a change of music fell on deaf, or intentionally not listening, ears. Maybe it was a language problem! So, the crewmen from a cruiser sprang into action. From amongst the destroyer crew, a lone seaman, who was in an advanced stage of intoxication was pushed up onto the centre of their table, where he slowly began to remove pieces of his uniform, to the accompanying song being sung by his shipmates.

This old hat of mine
Has seen some stormy weather
So, I'll take off my hat and I'll throw it away
Cos it's seen some stormy weather

His cap flew across the bar like a white discus, smashing into a shelf of empty clean glasses. Broken shards dropped down from the ledge in a crystal waterfall. He continued.

This old jacket of mine
Has seen some stormy weather
So, I'll take it off and throw it away
Cos it's seen some stormy weather.

The man's jacket then sailed into the air, to the cheers of his rapidly growing audience. On its trajectory, the blade of an overhead rotary-fan caught the garment and hurled it towards the door where it landed on the head of a Petty Officer, who had just walked into the bar. A huge chorus of laughter erupted. More sailors were entering the bar, and began using the fallen jacket as a door-mat.

Not to be outdone, the crew of the large battle-cruiser took up the challenge. Their all male chorus commenced another song to the tune of the Mexican Hat Dance, but with the two songs being sung at the same time the noise was deafening.

My sister Belinda
Pissed out of the window
All over my brand-new sombrero
Said I, you fat twat
You've pissed on my hat
You have pissed on my brand-new sombrero.

The head barman of the establishment was risking life and limb when he had the audacity to demand that they all stop singing. Without further ado, he was bodily lifted aloft by three burly matelots and passed across the heads of the crowd. His terrified protests went unheeded, as he was physically thrown out through the door of his own hostelry. He landed close to what remained of the wet discarded jacket, and limped away, heading towards the naval patrol headquarters.

The actual owner of the Universal Bar was a small man with a pencilled moustache, who was now angrily jumping up and down behind the bar. He was waving his arms, appealing for quiet and calm, but his protestations were nowhere as forceful those of his barman had been – he having no wish to follow him out into the street. His efforts went totally unheeded as the combined clientele united in with one more loud rendition. The frustrated owner disappeared into a back room as the song was taken up by the crew from a Plymouth based destroyer.

Half a pound of sugar and rice
Makes lovely clacker
Just enough for you and me
Gawd bugger Janner
Oh 'ow 'appy us will be
When us gets to the west country
Where the oggies grow on trees
Gawd bugger Janner
You make fast
Kiss my arse
Make fast the dinghy.
You make fast
Kiss my arse
Make fast the dinghy
And we'll all go back to Oggieland
To Oggieland – to Oggieland
And we'll all go back to Oggieland
Where they can't tell sugar from
Tissue paper – tissue paper
Marmalade, or jam.

The remaining glasses on the shelves reverberated as the song ended in a crescendo of cheers.

Albert Lohden had to shout to make himself heard, as he explained to George that the Oggieland referred to, was the West of England, mainly Somerset, Devon and Cornwall where a tasty meat and potato turnover pasty was called an Oggie.

"I wonder when we'll all be going home," said George, but his voice was drowned in the surrounding clamour.

The disrobing sailor on the far table, was now down to his long johns. He kept stumbling backwards as he tried to remove them, but helping hands pushed him back up. All the other songs had now ceased as his final verse of the disrobing song began. The attention of the whole room now became centred on the lurching semi-naked figure standing unsteadily on the table. He finally managed to remove the last garment, and his beer drenched underwear followed the rest of his uniform. He finally stood up fully naked in just his boots with his arms out-stretched before being unceremoniously drenched by the contents of most of the sailors' glasses. Much of the liquid missed him, and either hit the musical crew of the dinghy overhead, or those of the audience standing immediately opposite. Up in their suspended boat, the forlorn musicians sat on the thwarts, dripping in misery, looking as if he had just survived the ravages of a force ten gale. The victory cheers from below did little to raise their spirits, and none of them dared to descend from their sanctuary. Immediately underneath the boat an empty circle formed, as all the waste beer that had been thrown up there began to drain out of the small plug-hole in the bottom of the boat. A hundred pairs of feet splashed through the small lake that had quickly formed on the tiled floor, as half the men began crowding around the bar to replenish their empty glasses.

The three Submariners didn't stay for a second pint, prudently deciding that it was time to leave the surface navy to their afternoon of sport, as they headed out of the door. Stepping out into the afternoon sunshine, they were confronted by several more men who were intent on entering the UV.

Behind them, they could hear the beginnings of another song being bellowed from within the confines. The three Submariners began to walk back through the archway, heading into Casement Square, meaning to go on towards Main Street. They had not gone thirty yards when they saw a squad of the Naval Patrolmen double marching down the road, with their truncheons drawn. They were followed by the head barman, holding a towel to his bloodied fore-head. As the squad reached the entrance of the UV, orders were barked and the column broke and rushed towards the doorway. The narrow entrance forced them to queue to enter. Uniformed men suddenly began to emerge from every opening. Some flying, or jumping out from the side windows, running anywhere for all they were worth – anything to escape the Crushers' truncheons.

"Good job we left when we did," said Albert, as he turned and watched the unfolding spectacle with macabre interest.

More sailors started to appear out into the roadway from the main door, having been ejected with some force from the bar. Many were holding their heads and some had blood running down their faces. Others were staggering drunkenly about the road. Some of them were still singing. Then the bleached white torso of the naked sailor appeared, wearing just his boots. He staggered bewildered into the sunshine, seemingly unaware of his state of nudity.

George thought that he looked absolutely stupid, standing there completely nude in the middle of the road. The drunken man turned around several times before falling over backwards. A crowd of the local people had gathered to watch the spectacle. Women were giggling behind their hands. Men gesticulated at the man with broad grins.

The loud throaty roar of an engine heralded the arrival of a Naval Patrol truck. Nicknamed the Blue Mariah, it fought its way through the rapidly expanding crowd, screeching to a halt just yards from the melee. It disgorged yet more patrolmen, who immediately started to gather up the drunken miscreants like nautical shepherds. Within minutes the street was clear, and as if crowing in victory, the truck's gearbox crunched its gears before driving off. As it went past the three submariners, they noticed that the back was well guarded by patrolmen, making sure that no one tried to escape, or simply fell out. All was suddenly quiet and peaceful in the road once more. George felt very relieved that they had left the bar when they did. He became aware of the perils of the demon drink once more.

"Shall we go back to the boat now? We've got to be back by six o'clock for the skipper's little speech. We can eat on the Depot Ship afterwards, and if the Skipper grants shore leave tonight, we can come ashore again," said George Plowman.

"Or shall we stay ashore until just before six, and then we can have another couple of pints?" Albert suggested, licking his lips in anticipation. George thought that it might be a bit chancy to leave getting back so late.

"You mustn't mind this slob, George. Albert ain't in the *Trade* like you and me. He's been attached to us from the new wireless signal school," said the signalman. "He don't 'ave the same commitment that we have. You an' me will head back now."

George was feeling really pleased that the older submariner had referred to him as an equal. He was also glad that they were going back now, as he wanted to get his newly bought present safely put away in his bag on the Depot Ship. The shawl had cost a bit more than he had anticipated, but he was glad that he had bought it.

They got back to *E11* within thirty minutes. News of the star clutch was still not good. The mechanics had not been able to find the fault, and despite many attempts to make a repair all had all so far failed. As a consequence, shore leave for the whole Engine Room branch had been cancelled indefinitely.

The latest rumour was that they were going on to Malta, and that to do so they would transfer some of the remaining fuel in the tanks of *E14* and *E15* into their own internal tank. Someone had made the calculation that the tank held enough fuel that would get them to Malta, but not much further. It had been discovered that they were going to need a docking to repair the leakage problem in the external tanks. It had also been said that they would sail in company with the flotilla the following night, which allow them the time they needed to transfer the fuel. Apparently, some advanced plans had been made for them to make all of the repairs once they reached Valetta harbour.

For George this was music to his ears, and the main reason that he had wanted to joined the navy. To travel far and wide, visiting these foreign climes. Sure, there was still a war to fight, but that was no reason why one couldn't make the most of it. He had relished this afternoon's visit to Gibraltar, and the thought that he could soon be adding Malta to his ever-growing list of visited places, made him feel very happy.

At 1755, Coxswain Dowell ordered everyone up onto the quayside to await the Captain's address. The First Lieutenant, Lieutenant Guy d'Oyly-Hughes RN, a tall well-built Ulsterman, stood patiently waiting for the Coxswain to form the crew into three ranks. He was the second in command, and it was his responsibility to make sure that the boat was in all respects ready for war. This included the training of the men. Once the crew were all in three ranks, he informed them of the latest situation as he knew it. He presented an imposing figure. A career officer, who was obviously going to use his time in *E11* as a springboard to climb up the ladder of success within the Royal Navy. His voice surprised George, who had always thought of the Irish as having a slow, rather soft lilting brogue. Guy d'Oyly-Hughes spoke with the fast abrasive twang of the north, but he possessed the ability to make every word sound sincere and meaningful.

He started by giving them a moral boosting talk in an attempt to keep up the men's spirits, suggesting that their boat was destined to achieve great things and that if they all did their job to their best ability then they would all have a share in that glory. As George stood there listening to him, he was reminded of a swash-buckling hero out of some Magnet adventure story. Pirates on the Spanish Main! That seemed rather apt, as standing here, he could see the coast of Spain just across the bay. So far in his career, with the exception of the Dog and Duck episode, this war really had been a great adventure, and certainly not one to be missed.

The First Lieutenant further embellished his words by making them feel that they living in the greatest and most exciting time of their lives. Living at a time with world changes events taking place. He ended by making each man feel special, emphasising what they all could achieve together, and that their combined efforts could really help to determine the outcome of the war. Every one of them knew that it was only a pep talk, but when Lieutenant d'Oyly-Hughes did it, it better than most. Once he had finished, none of the men was able to deny the fact that he felt lifted.

Standing beside Guy d'Oyly-Hughes was the only other officer serving aboard *E11*, Lieutenant Robert Brown RNR. He took no part in the actual day to day running of the submarine, mainly acting as the boat's navigator both above and below the water. His duties also included the encryption and decryption of all radio messages received and sent. Although he was only twenty-eight years of age, he held a Merchant Navy Master Mariners ticket. Before the war he had been working with Alfred Holt's Blue Funnel Line, but when hostilities broke out, he had volunteered for naval service with the RN. On enlistment he had been considered to be too old to embark on a full-time career within the Royal Navy, but none the less his undoubted navigational talents had been quickly recognised and it was thought that he would be more suited to run the chart room of a battleship. Unfortunately, with his civilian maritime status of Master Mariner, the merchant naval rank placed him higher than most of the general career officers aboard any large capital ship, and within the elitist snobbish atmosphere of the officers' wardroom, that might have proved to be a considerable embarrassment. So, he had been hidden away within the submarine service. He was a short thick set chap with an oval smiling face, auburn hair and eyes that held you with a mischievous air. He was a mild-mannered man, always exuding a sense of calm, even when the situation was at its most tense – a thoroughly good chap to have beside you in any war. His easy-going nature had been forged within the merchant marine service, far removed from the rigid discipline of the RN, which resulted in him having a very easy going and relaxed attitude towards all forms of authority within the senior service. His no frills attitude made him very popular with the crew, who regarded him as one of their own. That is not to say that he was easy to take advantage of, because anyone who transgressed the rules, received equal short measure from him as they would from the captain.

Lt. d'Oyly-Hughes was finishing off his talk.

"As you have no doubt heard, there is no diesel fuel oil available here at Gibraltar. *E14* will therefore be transferring some of the reserve fuel in her saddle tanks over into our internal tanks. This should provide us with just enough fuel to get us to Malta. The external tanks will also undergo another overhaul once we get there, before any more fuel is loaded into them. The star clutch is still very stiff, and the drive shaft is doubtful, but we are hoping to have them both fully stripped down and repaired at Valetta…"

It was at this point that the First Lieutenant was very rudely interrupted by someone in the ranks expelling wind so loudly that it caused each man looked alarmingly at his neighbour. Nobody seemed to be aware of the culprit's identity – and nobody was going to own up. Sniggers turned to guffaws of laughter, as their olfactory senses were assailed by the spread of the methane laden air. Whispered comments began.

"Who the fuck has just died...?"

"Somebody call for a vet..."

"Everybody check their underwear for lumps... We'll soon find the bastard then."

"Whoever created that needs pulling through with a Christmas tree..."

More laughter erupted.

"Stop talking in the ranks," bellowed the Coxswain, Chief Petty Officer Oliver Dowell. "If I catch the phantom farter then he will wish that he had never been born."

From that moment on the legend of the *E11* Phantom Farter was born. Just as the men became quiet, so the Captain, Lieutenant Commander Martin Dunbar Naismith RN, came walking down the quayside from the direction of their Depot Ship. Spotting him, Guy d'Oyly-Hughes called the ship's company to attention.

Turning, he saluted his commanding officer and reported that the crew were ready for his address. Naismith returned the salute, thanked him and asked him to stand the men at ease. Once they were more relaxed, he raised his voice as he began talking.

"As the First Lieutenant has probably already told you, we are having trouble getting fuel, but with *E14*'s help we should make it to Malta on a direct surface passage. A bit of bad news is that there may well be a problem with the drive shaft on our port engine. They have ordered another to be sent out to Malta, where the dockyard will replace it. The star clutch should also be quickly sorted out once we are in Valetta, and once these two problems are fixed, it will enable us to join the rest of the Mediterranean Fleet at the new anchorage within the natural harbour on the Island of Murdos. Although we have this problem with the port dive shaft, thankfully the port engine can still be run, so we will therefore be making the passage along with *Adamant,* and our two companions. I do not envisage anything standing in our way. Unlike in previous patrols, I promise you that *E11* is going to make a name for her-self on this deployment."

Each of the crew, with the exception of George, knew exactly what their CO was talking about. *HMS E11* had been launched on the 23rd of April 1914 and ever since Naismith had first driven *E11* out of the Glasgow shipbuilding fitting out yard on the 14th of September 1914, a catalogue of misfortunes had afflicted the boat. As the submarine had manoeuvred within the tidal basin of the dockyard in which she had been built, she hit a low hanging chain that badly damaged one of her periscopes. It put their schedule back for another week. Then once they got to sea and were on the surface during her first patrol in the North Sea, they were bombed by a German Zeppelin airship while they were trying to rescue the pilot of a flying boat, who had run out of fuel and been forced to land on the water after attacking the Zeppelin Sheds at Cuxhaven. They had narrowly escaped being hit. On another patrol, Naismith had managed to get *E11* into the type of firing position that every submarine captain wants. He had found himself right in the midst of the German High Seas Fleet, who was in the process of running back to their base, after one of their infrequent sorties to bombard the north east coast of England. Nasmith had seized his chance, and had carried out a classic firing set up, discharging all of his torpedoes. Unfortunately, every single one of the weapons had malfunctioned, either by missing the target, or by failing to explode on contact. The torpedo tracks were spotted by the Germans, and in the counter-attack they were very lucky to get away without being detected. Then last October three submarines, one of which was *E11*, had been ordered up into the Kattegat with orders to penetrate through the Great Sound and get into the Baltic Sea to carry out aggressive missions in support of the Russian forces. Lieutenant Max Horton in *HMS E1,* and Lieutenant Noel Laurence in *HMS E9* had both made it through successfully, but when Naismith attempted to take *E11* through, he had fallen behind due to engine problems. By the time repairs had been made, the defenders had been alerted by the first two submarines getting through, and were lying in wait for him. Realising that it would be impossible, he was eventually forced to retire and return home after very nearly being sunk by the hunting German destroyers. Since then the recent reports of the exploits of the havoc being created by Horton and Laurence from their base at Revel in Estonia, was creating headlines in the national newspapers. Both men were in the process of creating a submarine legend.

All of these missed chances had frustrated the crew of *E11*, but to a man like Naismith, whose whole naval career had developed with the embryonic submarine service, it was the ultimate twist of fate. It had been at that time that he had made his vow that he would abstain from cigarettes and alcohol until he had actually torpedoed and sunk an enemy warship. He continued with his address.

"We are sailing in company with *HMS Adamant, E14* and *E15*, very late tomorrow night. I have to tell you that this information is secret and therefore is not to be repeated to anyone. As we will have some free time on our hands tomorrow morning, I intend to practice several of the drills that may be required to know on our forthcoming patrols. It will also give some of you a last chance for some relaxation ashore tonight. This could be your last spell of shore leave for some time, so I urge you to take advantage of it. Enjoy yourself, but I do not want to see anybody as a defaulter at my table in the morning, so go out and have a good time, but in moderation." He turned to the Coxswain and ordered, "Leave from now until 0700. The submarine is under sailing orders."

Lieutenant d'Oyly-Hughes called the men to attention, as Naismith headed back towards the Depot Ship. They were then dismissed and all the men headed for the *Adamant* to rig their hammocks, and to have a meal before going ashore. Only the duty watch and some of the stokers remained on board.

The steak and kidney pie that was served up by the cook of the mess was a luxury. It was something that they were unable to re-produce within the cramped confines of their boat. With just the single hotplate to cook on, it seriously limited what could be made at sea. Aboard any submarine, once the fresh provisions had started to go bad, they would have to revert to tinned food. After the meagre rations that they had to endure on the run down from Portsmouth, this meal was ambrosia. George took his full plate, and sat down at a table with a mixed group of the *E11*'s crew. The food was delicious, and the general conversation was one of speculation and optimism. George listened intently, still eager to be fully accepted as part of the crew, he asked one of the stokers a question.

"What are the real chances of fixing the star clutch?"

The stoker turned to George, a sneer distorting his grimy face.

"Look, I don't know why they are sending us kids as crew members these days. I just hope that you've brought enough nappies for your first real patrol, because you'll probably fill them all by the end of the first day."

There were sniggers of laughter from the rest of the men sat at the table. The stoker looked around, smiling smugly at his audience. George immediately recognised that he had reached a crisis point that was going to affect his standing amongst the crew. To back down now would demote him to a nondescript, and he would end up being the lowest of the low in the pecking order. He certainly did not want to become an object of derision and suffer the brunt of many cruel jibes in the future. Slowly he slowly laid down his knife and fork.

He turned equally slowly towards the stoker and said, "Yes I've brought enough. I'll even lend you one to mop up your teeth."

Without warning his right arm flashed around like a scimitar in a sweeping arc with his fist clenched. The punch caught the unprepared man just below his nose. Its force carried George's fist upwards and into the man's right eye socket. Blood burst from the stoker's nostrils as he fell backwards off the bench seat. He crashed to the deck with his plate of food landing across his chest. George stood over him, ready to deliver more. The rest of the men sitting at the table were quick to react. Fighting in the navy was a punishable offence and they all rose to their feet, standing between the two antagonists. Slowly, with help, the stoker was helped to his feet. His finger-tips began probing his face for damage. His eyes flicked up speculatively towards George. There was a pregnant pause while the men waited to see the next turn of events. Then slowly the stoker gave a painful looking smile, and offered his hand out to George.

"You've got a strong arm there, lad. I wish I had found out how strong in some other way. I'm sorry for what I said. I was well out of order."

George reached forward and shook his hand, as he smiled back, inwardly glad that the conflict was not going to escalate. There was a general consensus of approval that honour on both sides had been satisfied. George helped the stoker clean the mess from his clothes.

"Basil Partridge," said the stoker, introducing himself. "I know your first name is George, but I don't know your surname."

"Torode," replied George. "George Torode."

Basil was one of only three stokers who were not required to begin the transfer of the fuel from E.14 external tanks into *E11*'s internal tanks. So that night the two went ashore together to sample more of the delights that Gibraltar had to offer.

After several beers in a few of the bars and public houses on Main Street, they ended up in a dance-hall cum night club cum beer cellar cum brothel called the Winter Gardens. It lay up in the higher reaches of the town. The place was packed with the crews of the visiting warship, and the noise was deafening. Tobacco smoke filled the air, creating a hovering gossamer haze that veiled the proceedings. The interior was dimly lit by flickering oil lamps, which condemned the far corners to shadow, making them appear to be in permanent darkness. A single suspended lantern illuminated a raised platform that formed the stage. It consisted of a series of planks that had placed across some upturned beer crates. A swaying mass of drunken men stood in expectantly in front of it. There had recently been a number of appearances by a scantily clad exotic dancer. Another was expected shortly, programmed by the management to ensure that the place remained full. Each performance from the women, at least George thought that they were women, evoked a chorus of lewd suggestions from a hundred drunken throats. Not one of the inebriates appeared capable of carrying out the services that he was offering. Each performance lasted no more than a couple of minutes, as any extension would be seriously prejudicial to the sale of beer. A rather miserable looking three-piece band was providing the musical accompaniment. Between the girls' performances, they also provided the music to dance. A group of local Gibraltar women, most of whom were old enough to be the sailors' mothers, were being fought over as dancing partners.

There was also another form of entertainment taking place, which consisted of a series of brawls and bar room fights. Each bout was rather like a cabaret routine in itself. Usually between two combatants, but occasionally there would be a group fight. To keep the peace members of the Royal Naval Patrol stood outside the establishment, and they were called in periodically as each new affray commenced. By the time they had reached the scene of the conflict, one or more of the combatants lay on the floor nursing a bruised and bloodied face. The Crushers would then simply bundle the pugilists unceremoniously outside, to taken away to the Naval Base detention quarters, where they would be booked in and incarcerated for the night. Each unfortunate could expect to feel the wrath of his commanding officer the following day. When the submariners had arrived, watching these fracas had initially been rather amusing, but George thought that the drunken antics of the Navy at play soon became a little bit tiresome.

After half an hour he began to find that the whole spectacle to be rather pathetic, but he could understand why these men got so drunk. Many of them were just like him, were in their late teens, and desperate to taste life, each of them knowing that tomorrow they could be dead or horribly maimed. A direct hit on a turret magazine would result in the whole gun crew being blown to smithereens, or a direct hit from a shell in an engine room, could subject men to being scalded beyond recognition as human beings, dying from the super-heated steam erupting from the ruptured turbine supply pipes. Any fractured steam pipes would peel flesh from the bone and boil a body in seconds. Flying shrapnel could disfigure, or hideously mutilated a man within a fraction of a second. The alternative of drowning in an oil covered sea, seemed pleasant by comparison. When these men drank them-self into an alcoholic oblivion, it provided a brief escape from the horrors that they may have to face in the near future.

George thought back to that night in the cold waters of the English Channel, just after *C301* had sunk. The image of that poor man impaled on the spike flashed into his mind. To die either in the water, or inside that metal tube was a horrible death – but then, there are no good deaths in wartime. He knew that he had been very lucky to survive that night. Poor old Fred Chapman had gone down with the boat. The only way anyone was going to survive this war is by sheer luck. If one had luck on his side, then you would come through almost anything that the enemy could throw at him. Was that the secret of life – fate – luck – being in the right place at the right time? He shuddered.

"I've had enough of this Basil and to tell you the truth I shall be glad to get back to sea," said George.

"I know just what you mean George, let's get out of here," replied the stoker.

Outside the air felt cool and clean. The moon and stars shone down from a cloudless sky, lighting their way down through the maze of narrow alleyways that led them back down towards Main Street. In the shadowy confines of the buildings, it was still very dark with just the occasional oil lamp aglow, lighting the louvered windows. As they passed a small recessed entrance that led into an apartment block, George noted that it was filled by the dim figure of a sailor urinating against a closed doorway. He was obviously a sailor, because George could clearly make out the three white stripes that edged his blue jean collar, as he leaned against the shadowed portal. Why on earth did he have to do that? thought, George. The residents here would be angry tomorrow morning. There were plenty of other places – the gardens – the harbour – even in the gutter – anywhere but where he was. As they went past, each of them had to step over the rivulet of urine that was running down the stone pathway.

When they finally reached the main thoroughfare, the oil street-lamps that lit their way were being extinguished by a lamp lighter. There were a couple of late-night drinking holes that were still open. These were the Spanish style bodegas, that were affectionately known in the navy as Boiled Oil Shops, after the thick sweet fortified Malaga wine that they sold. Boiled oil was used in the navy to preserve the jute hearts of wire ropes. The faint strands of a song, accompanied by an acoustic guitar, could be heard coming from one of these establishments. It sounded nothing like those raucous crudities that were being sung earlier that afternoon at the UV, but consisted of a rather beautiful lilting lullaby. They stopped to listen, but both men avoided the temptation of entering.

Once firmly back on Main Street itself, they came across a small cafe that was still open, which was still serving hot drinks and food to the stragglers, as they made their way back to their ships. Basil and George each bought a mug of soup and a lump of crusty bread. Beef Broth. It tasted good. They started talking.

Basil told him that he had been on the boat since it had first been commissioned in the Clyde-side shipyard. He described in some detail to George their exploits and the many frustrations they had encountered in the North Sea. In turn, George told him of his adventure aboard *C301* and of the night that he thought he was going to die. Both men tucked into their food. Basil broke the silence with a question that George had not expected.

"Are you married, George?"

He had never even thought of being married before leaving Guernsey. He had never been old enough for a start, but now having now met Gladys he realised that he would like to be, and would like to have children.

"No, not yet Bas, but I've a mind to be, once we get home and this war is over."

"Got a girlfriend at home, then?"

"Yes, well sort of. The trouble is that I come from Guernsey, and she lives down in Southsea."

"Blimey, mate. I don't want to appear to be a pessimist, but you'll be very lucky to find her there waiting for you once we get home from this little trip. There are thousands of men in Pompey and they're all looking for female company. She'll be whisked off by some young officer before you know it. You mark my words."

George gave a laugh of disbelief. "No way mate – she loves me. She told me so, and said she will wait for me."

He had tried to make his voice sound confident, but Basil's words had opened up the possibility of something that had never occurred to him – infidelity. The seeds of doubt had been sown.

The cafe was still doing a good trade when they finally departed and as they emerged from the doorway, George had to step back quickly as a sailor vomited right in front of him. The spectacle was enough to put them both off any more beer, so they set off at a good pace, arriving back at the dockyard gates and showing their identification, they were allowed to pass through.

The Victorian architecture of the dockyard workshops was stark, which in the monochromic rays of the moonlight made it look even colder than it actually was. The beer they had imbibed made both men wary of the many obstacles and trip hazards that abounded, carefully watching their footsteps. There were a number of railway tracks embedded in the roadway, and some of the point systems presented a number of unseen holes.

Eventually they arrived at the quayside, where the depot ship and the submarines were berthed. A hundred yards from the brow they walked into the bright lights of *HMS Adamant*'s bright upper deck illumination. These electric lights were so much brighter than the old oil lamps that were still being used ashore. Slightly blinded by their glare, they suddenly heard the throaty roar of a fast revving car engine. Realising that there was a motor car behind them and approaching at speed, they both stepped aside, fading back into the shadows of a dockside workshop.

An open topped coupe sped past, with laughter and squeals of delight emanating from the rear seats of the vehicle. The two men watch it speed down the quayside and screech to a halt at the bottom of *Adamant*'s gangway, which was just thirty to forty yards from where they both stood.

Two officers emerged from the front of the vehicle, and with exaggerated gestures of chivalry, they opened the rear doors to allow the young ladies the room to get out.

There was something about one of the men that disturbed George.

Arm in arm the group huddled together, before staggering rather unsteadily up the gangway of the depot ship. There were more whoops of delight. George didn't know them from Adam and thought that they would all be off to the Wardroom for some late-night drinks. Just then one of the officers stopped and turned to faced him for a second in the full glare of one of the gangway lights. A sudden chill went through George. He had only seen the man for a second in time, but it been enough to recognise him. It was Arthur Collenette.

Chapter Seven

Malta

The passage from Gibraltar to Malta was going well, but *E11*'s rapidly dwindling fuel supply was causing concern to everybody aboard. The boat's Engineer Chief Engine Room Artificer Arthur Jupp, has been nursing *E11*'s two diesels by continuously adjusting the revolutions to make them achieve their most efficient consumption. He has not left the engine room other than to use the toilet. He did not have far to go as the toilets on *E11*, which consisted of several tall buckets, were situated behind those same engines. The oxygen hungry pistons, drawing air down the conning tower, was also removing the smell. The contents were thrown over the side every night. Since they had sailed from Gibraltar, Jupp had sat in the gap of the hatch in the water-tight bulkhead, and had remained in this oily space both day and night. The E Class submarines were the first boats in the RN to have water-tight divisions.

Outwardly he exuded confidence, telling everyone that the boat would easily make the journey between the two ports. He would nod his head sagely, as the internal tanks were plumb dipped to measure their contents on the hour, but once the results were announced, his brow would furrow, revealing his inner concerns.

"If things continue as they are, and the weather remains good, we should make Malta with no difficulty," this was his enigmatic reply to the persistent enquiries from both officers and the men.

It was developing into a hot brilliant day aloft, and far off on their starboard beam, the mountains of Africa rose high above the southern horizon in the early morning air. Fluffy white cotton wool clouds seemed to skip along the horizon of the sea all around, while a fresh stillness in the air made it feel peaceful, like the onset of a typical English summer's day. Standing on the deck at the back of bridge as the upper helmsman, George Torode was reminded of that infamous day that as he had made himself ready to go gull nesting. The upper helm position provided a good chance for him to stand aloft in the cool air. He had removed his shirt, and could feel the sun rays caressing the skin on his back.

As the morning wore on, the further east they travelled, the warmer it seemed to become. The Alborean Basin is nearly always like an oven in mid-summer, but even now in the early spring, it could be unbearably hot. As the temperatures climbed, so did the humidity within the hot noisy fume laden conditions inside the boat, which the men quickly found decidedly uncomfortable? Just them sitting doing nothing would cause rivulets of perspiration to run down their skin of their back, like condensation down a window pane. The least attempt at work, resulted in their clothes soaking in sweat. The only relief for them was to walk into the control room and stand beneath the open conning tower hatch. The force of the air being sucked down the tower by the diesels was as cooling as a cold shower of rain. There was always a queue by the internal water-tight bulkhead hatch to obtain a few moments relief from the purgatory to be found up in the forward accommodation space. The First Lieutenant had granted the men a small dispensation in that they could spend the whole day without their shirts.

Naismith was quick in realising the problem, and established a routine that allowed two or three of the crew at a time up onto the bridge for fresh air and a smoke. He was fastidious in changing them around every fifteen minutes to make sure that he gave each man a fair break, albeit for a short while. Then, just as the men's bodies were beginning stop sweating, and feel somewhat normal once again, they were sent back down into the humid hell that was enough to try anybody's patience to the extreme.

Sitting up on the bridge on watch, it was much more comfortable. The boat's speed through the water provided a light breeze, that kept the static temperature down. Suffice to say that there was no shortage of volunteers to do an extra watch as helmsman, or to act as a second look-out. Even those who were off watch were volunteering to do an extra stint. Standing aloft in the sun, with one's shirt off, was the ultimate luxury.

They had sailed in formation, with *HMS Adamant* leading *E14* and *E15* and *E11* bringing up the rear, and this remained their formation. Naismith was glad of his decision not to remain in Gibraltar and to push on for Malta. Back in Gibraltar he had actually been given the dubious choice of either waiting there for a tanker from England to arrive, or loading some of *E14*'s spare fuel, and carrying on to Malta. It had been suggested that whilst he waited in Gibraltar, the star clutch could be completely stripped down, and the necessary repairs made. He could see the logic of this, but thinking back to all the previous frustrations of *E11*'s early patrols, it had made him all the more determined to press on towards where the action was taking place. He became adamant that he would not be left behind again, and if he had anything to do with it, he would always decide to press on. None the less he had been tempted to remain to ensure that the star clutch was properly fixed, feeling more than a little guilty that he was missing the chance of a successful repair, but out here at sea and breathing in the fresh air, Martin Naismith's spirits had soared. Surely by the laws of averages, ill fate was not going to cheat him again!

It got even hotter as the morning sun soared towards its zenith. As lunchtime approached, George was enjoying his precious fifteen minutes aloft. He had not started smoking yet, and unfairly all those that did resented him going aloft, but he stood his ground, arguing that he had just as much right to fresh air as any smoker. The smokers were forced to back down, and in winning his point George could feel a new respect from his crewmates. He did not like any confrontation, but he hated being intimidated more.

As he stood there a pod of pilot whales could be seen off to port. As those aloft watched them, there were some envious remarks about them having total freedom within the coolness of the water. The steam-like spouted exhalations from their blow holes stood out clearly against the smooth blue surface of the Mediterranean. Just after midday, the heat haze that was inhibiting views of the Africa continent was still shimmering off to starboard, making the distant mountains appear distorted, like a water mirage. High above them were the faintest wisps of mare tail clouds, which provided the only contrast in a clear Wedgwood sky. Standing there George felt truly alive, but his fifteen minutes passed all too quickly, and he was quickly replaced by the next three eager men.

On their first night at sea they had been amazed to sight the navigation lights of several transiting ships, and it was repeated on the second night. None of the vessels were being escorted. Back at home, following the early losses from U-boat attacks during the first three months of the war, most ships were now being protected by a naval escort. After six months of war, it came as a shock to see ships still displaying their upper deck lighting, as the black-out system had been employed in home waters since last August.

Thankfully, so far in this war there had not been any sign of any U-Boat activity here in the Mediterranean. The defensive patrols guarding the Straits of Gibraltar had been doing a magnificent job, there was no other entry by sea. The only other entry was the Suez Canal, which was held and controlled by the Allied forces.

On that first night, looking above their heads, the sky was a diamond studded sable mantle. A faint glowing slash across the sky clearly showed the Milky Way, which appeared magnificent with the lack of any moon. On their second night there appeared the merest slither of a crescent, as the new moon made an appearance in the early hours, just before dawn. The surface of the water was so smooth that the brighter stars and planets were reflected in its mirror surface. Shooting stars dashed hither and thither, keeping the watch-keepers both alert and amused. The wake of the vessels ahead sparkled as twinkling flashes of phosphorescent light darted just below the surface. If one tried to imagine life without the throb from the diesel engines, everything would be satisfyingly perfect. In the cool night air everything felt so normal, making it hard to believe that there was a war on.

When Lt. Robert Brown arrived on the bridge to take a star fix, he would point out the major points of light to anybody who was interested, but most crew members were more interested in their pipes and tobacco.

"That bright one up there is the planet Jupiter, and if you look carefully through your binoculars you may well see some of its moons appearing as very tiny faint dots of light close within its vicinity. Over there is the bright star Vega, which lies in the constellation of Cygnus. That large rectangle group of stars up there is the constellation of Orion, and standing off the lower left corner is the star Sirius, known as the Dog Star. That is the brightest star in the heavens. Some of the planets are brighter – Venus for instance. By me taking a measurement of the angle of certain stars, relative to the horizon here on Earth with my sextant, I then also note the exact time and from that information I can transfix a line onto a chart to plot our position. By repeating it with fix on another star, where those two lines cross will be where we are on the planet."

There was never a lack of volunteers to carry his precious instrument aloft, or to write down his measurement figures into the star notebook. Lt Brown possessed the charisma of a favourite teacher at school, and made the subject of astronomy fascinating to anyone who listened. After taking in all of the information, George would spend some of his time as the look-out trying to locate, and recognise the stars and constellations. Then he would realise that he was spending too much time looking at them, feeling guilty in not keeping a good look-out for any of the enemy.

On the evening of the fourth of April 1915, George reported the faint loom of light fanning up from the southern horizon, which Robert Brown confirmed as the position of the City of Algiers. The Captain appeared on the bridge, and he looked through his binoculars.

"Don't the French realise that they are providing a bright visual signpost to any enemy vessel? If a U-Boat ever did manage to get into the Mediterranean, that light would provide a beacon that would present them with easy prey."

Navigationally, things aboard *E11* were going as planned and the engines were managing to keep them on station with the rest of the flotilla.

By the morning of the sixth of April, everyone was quick to notice a distinct change in the weather. Conditions quickly began to deteriorate, as a deep depression formed over the western half of the Mediterranean. The wind freshened, and veered around to the north. The sea surface changed from a flat azure blue, to a turquoise grey, that quickly became interspersed by patches of white as the surface was whipped up into a foam by the strengthening winds. To the crew of *E11*, this was a much more familiar scenario, much like the conditions of the English Channel and the North Sea. The big plus from the change in conditions was that the oppressive temperatures inside the boat had dropped, which made things much more comfortable below. It came at a price however, as the worsening sea state quickly turned the once smooth surface into moderate waves of eight to ten feet in height that made *E11* begin to roll as the northerly wind force of the storm was hitting her port beam. Walls of water spray started crashing into the conning tower, soaking the watch-keepers. Although the coolness was welcomed at first, after just an hour of the buffeting, the bridge watch-keepers were forced to don oilskins.

This newly damp air was being sucked down below by the never-ending demand of the engines, and very soon the conditions within the boat had gone from one extreme to another. Instead of the humid sweaty sauna, there was now a cool moist cloying dew that soaked everyone and everything.

As the sea conditions grew steadily worse, so Martin Naismith became more concerned, because he was reluctantly forced to increase engine revolutions to maintain station with the rest of the flotilla. Down in the engine room, Chief Jupp tried to reassure him that he was still quietly confident that they would make it to Malta with their rapidly dwindling fuel supply, but everybody aboard knew that it was going to be close.

Just as darkness was beginning to descend that same night, the look-outs caught their first glimpse of the distant cliffs that lie on the western coast of Malta. Being under British control, the Island was operating a total blackout at night, so they had been very fortunate to make the landfall before darkness fell. This enforced black-out showed the huge gulf in thinking between the authorities of Algiers, and those here in Malta. At least in Malta, there was someone who was aware that there was a war taking place.

It was nearly midnight when the small convoy finally reach the outer limits off the entrance into Grand Harbour, only to find that the Harbour Authorities had shut the gate in the boom defences. At least the Royal Navy did not share the complacency of the French along the North African coast, but this created a problem for *E11*! With her fuel almost exhausted, the prospect of having to patrol outside the harbour defences all night was very concerning. If they ran out of fuel then Martin Naismith could envisage the embarrassing scenario of having to be towed into harbour by a tug the following morning, so he decided to ask permission for *E11* to separate from the group and seek shelter. Having received the OK from the Flotilla leader, he drove *E11* around into the small inlet at Marsa Scala. It was just a few miles along the coast, and the submarine slowly made its way into the tiny haven. They secured to a buoy to provide them with shelter for the night, and shut down the engines to save what meagre fuel supply was left for their entry.

As dawn broke on the morning of the seventh of April, *E11* was ready and waiting at the line of buoys that marked the position of the anti-submarine nets. A local tug, belching black smoke from her tall cigarette funnel, appeared from the confines of Valetta harbour, and quickly attached a line to the line of buoys supporting the submerged wire netting. As soon as the boom was drawn open, a local fishing vessel appeared, sailing boldly out of the harbour. Her bow cut into the swell, sending up spray in a white V formation. She was felucca rigged, and her great triangular white sail clapped loudly as the wind caught the canvas, speeding her on like an albatross riding the Atlantic Trades.

Above them, the greyness of cloud indicated that the depression had not fully dissipated, and the choppy uncomfortable sea conditions bore testimony to this fact. The small harbour tug could be seen rising and falling on the swell. Being stopped in the water also caused *E11* bob about like a cork float. The flotilla finally got the order to enter harbour, and with both of her fuel gauges just touching zero, *E11* finally managed to make her way into the harbour at Valetta.

For generations of sailors of the Royal Navy Grand Harbour has always been an impressive sight, but it was especially so for those of the crew who had never visited the Maltese capital before. For George Torode standing on the casing of *E11*, it was mind bogglingly beautiful. Off to their starboard side stood the towering ramparts of Fort St Elmo, sheer sand coloured walls, standing formidable like a cliff, and before he had time to fully appreciate it, another massive stone fort appeared off to port. This must be one of the most protected harbours in the world, he thought.

The boat had easily slipped through the second boom at the inner entrance. However, for Martin Naismith, who had been here many times before, the harbour immediately took on the guise of prison bars that may well encapsulate his command for some considerable time. His one wish was that the repairs would be completed as quickly and successfully as possible, but with a mounting defect list, he was becoming ever more concerned that *E11* would be detained here when the others sailed for the new Allied base at the Island of Murdos in the Aegean Sea.

Another very serious Engine Room defect had been reported during the night, after they had shut down the engines and had tied to the buoy. This time the port motor generator armature that had earthed, which along with the original fault of the problematic star clutch, placed them with two major defects that had to be fixed before they could enter the war. The star clutch had stiffened up so badly, that it now required the combined strength of two burly Artificers to disengage it.

HMS E11 moved slowly and silently through the harbour narrows on her main motors, and emerged into the widening expanse of the inner harbour as the casing party were called to attention. A lone Royal Marine bugler replied to the still whistle of Signalman Plowman's bosun's call in saluting the flag of C in C Mediterranean. The bugler could just be seen over to port, standing atop the imposing battlements of Fort *St Angelo*, where in days of long ago the Knights of St John had fought off the might of the Ottoman Empire. During the Victorian years this fort had been taken over by the Royal Navy, and it was now home to the Commander in Chief of the Mediterranean Fleet.

Lying in the creek below the western walls of the fort, stood the old wooden hulk of a man o' war from the Nelson era, *HMS Egmont*, which had been converted to act as a depot ship to smaller ships and submarines. She provided her charges with both accommodation and supplies. As the submarine approached, from the bridge of *E11* the old wooden hulk looked resplendent covered in a series of gleaming white awnings, from which her masts and yards stood out conspicuously. Her wooden sides were painted matt white with the contrast of black squares where her gun-ports had once been positioned. There was a series of long wooden pontoons that had been placed along her outboard side. The other two submarines were ahead, and already making their approach to tie up alongside.

HMS Adamant had already berthed alongside the stone quayside, just ahead of the hulk. *E11* began her long swing round to port, to begin her final approach. As she did so, Naismith was being forced to thread his way through a host of small naval craft, and a swarm of the unpredictable capricious dghaisas. An empty Admiral's barge ran up their starboard side, the whiteness of its holystoned decks and gleaming brass work were matched by the resplendent colours of the garishly painted Maltese gondolier style rowing boats. The oarsmen of these local craft stood amidships, and pushed their oars in the manner of a Venetian gondolier, to make frustratingly slow progress through the water.

"I wish these bloody pedestrians would get out of the way," fumed Martin Naismith impatiently, as he had to give another series of orders to avoid running one down.

All around the harbour there were several other warships of varying sizes, some berthed alongside, while others were riding at buoys. In the largest dry dock, the upper superstructure of the battle cruiser *HMS Inflexible* was just visible, the tops of her funnels still standing tall over the local houses. She was undergoing repairs after sustaining heavy damage from a mine during the initial attacks on the Dardanelles forts and gun batteries in mid-March.

George had heard many descriptions of this naval bastion of the Mediterranean, but none came remotely near to actually seeing the sheer grandeur of the place. It was stunningly beautiful. Not that he had any past experience to compare it with, apart from Gibraltar.

After securing themselves on the outboard side of *HMS E15*, George joined his fellow members of the casing party, as they lit up their pipes. He was pleasantly pleased to note that this time he was not shunned, and was actually brought into the conversation. His hard work and dedication to learn the operational systems had certainly been appreciated.

Naismith's fears of being held up in Malta were well founded, because after an electrical inspection he was told that *E11* would need a completely new armature for the port motor generator and therefore they definitely would not be able to sail with the rest of the group for Murdos. The very best estimations by the base staff could give him was a full fortnight for all repairs to be carried out. It could well be longer.

The Star Clutch had also been thoroughly inspected by the base engineers, and their combined opinion was that there was a hairline fracture on the port intermediate shaft. This caused the shaft to expand as it revolved at high speed, centrifuge force caused the crack to open in a whip effect, which in turn caused it to grind heavily into its own bearing. As it had become fractionally wider, it accounted for the difficulty in trying to disengage it. There were no spares of the right size available here in Malta; and therefore, a whole new casting would have to be sent out from Portsmouth. That alone would take between ten days to two weeks before it arrived, and once it did arrive it would still have to be milled down before the dockyard staff could fit it in place. That would cost them at least another day or two.

To make matters worse, the inboard accommodation in Fort *St Angelo* and that aboard *HMS Egmont* itself were both filled to capacity. As the crew of *E11* could certainly not be expected to live aboard their tiny craft while these heavy repairs were being carried out, it was decided that there was nothing that could be done but to billet the men ashore, and hand *HMS E11* over into the hands of the dockyard.

Shore accommodation was quickly arranged and the crew was divided into two shore Pensions, which were located on the far side of *St Angelo* Creek, just opposite to where *HMS Egmont* was berthed. These Maltese dwelling houses were limited in the number of rooms that they had available, but by squeezing four men into each double room, the whole crew could be successfully accommodated. The officers could be accommodated in Fort *St Angelo* itself. For the men it would be very cramped for everybody, but they were used to being confined, and just to have a bed would be an absolute luxury, compared with normal life aboard *E11*.

Both pensions were accessible by a road that runs around the edge of *St Angelo* Creek. The buildings formed part of a terrace that faced out on to the water, being built against the near vertical cliff cum part stone rampart wall that rose high behind them. Both were now bathed in shadow, as the sun had passed its noon rendezvous. Each of the dwellings were three storeys high, but quite narrow in width. Their exterior had been rendered in a cream coloured cement, which served to give them a bright clean appearance, although the render had fallen away in places to reveal the red brickwork beneath. Black wrought iron balconies adorned the windows of the upper floors. They had been built quite recently as part of the new road system that linked Fort *St Angelo* with the Creek road around to the dockyard.

Coxswain Oliver Dowell detailed the crew off into the various bedrooms. George was glad to have been billeted with Basil Partridge, George Plowman the signalman and Albert Lohden the telegraphist. Their room, like all the rest, was plain. Spartan was the word that Albert had used. White distempered walls were decorated by a single crucifix, which had been fixed to the wall above the wash stand. The wash stand was the only piece of furniture in the room besides the two hard mattress double beds. A pair of French doors opened out onto a tiny balcony that overlooked the creek. Leaving these doors open at night allowed cool zephyrs to enter the room to keep them cool and comfortable. Another useful feature of this particular room, from the occupant's point of view, was the fact that it was located right next door to the proprietor's private lounge, which in an enterprising spirit, the owner had hastily converted into a bar. There were twelve men here sharing the three rooms that he had available. Their Pension was called the Porto Bella. Whilst just next door, the rest of the crew were billeted in the slightly larger Star of Bethlehem. For the duration of their stay in Malta, these two establishments would be known by the crew as the Port and Starboard houses.

The owner of the Porto Bella was a short, thin, and rather frail looking man, with a face revealing his Mediterranean heritage. He stood just over five feet tall and had thinning dark hair which receded high above each eyebrow. The lack of hair on his head contrasted greatly with the huge black bushy moustache that burst from beneath his nose. His dark tanned complexion made his teeth seem whiter than actually were – a feature of which he was obviously proud, because he showed them off to good effect by constantly smiling at everyone.

The four Stokers, who occupied the top floor room above George, said that he also had a terrible case of flatulence, which they could hear every night through the wall, adjoining his bedroom. Like most of the Maltese people, he was extremely shrewd with his money, hence the hastily constructed bar which appeared to have no determined closing time. He served mainly bottled beers and a selection of liquorice flavoured spirit drinks. He told them that he was trying to get hold of a hand-pump, so that they could enjoy draught beer straight from the barrel. After their first night at the Porto Bella the crew had nick-named the proprietor Horlicks. It was a name given to him because he was a Malt who served them drinks that put them to sleep!

It was Horlicks' brother in law who ran the Star of Bethlehem, but he was not seen very often, and obviously was not as entrepreneurial as Horlicks. There were no drinks available in his establishment. Most of the more senior members in the crew had been billeted in the Starboard house, but every night they made the pilgrimage next door to use the bar in the Port House.

What Horlicks lacked in physique, his voluptuous wife more than compensated for. She was a huge round woman of some fifteen stones in weight, towering over him in both in height and girth. She was always dressed in the black attire, as worn by most of the Maltese married women. The couple reminded George of the Jack Sprat and his wife from the children's nursery rhyme. Although he could just about make himself understood by his British clients, Horlicks unique version of English gave them all a headache when attempting to translate his rather rapid verbal delivery. His spoken sentences were confusingly jumbled, as when George and his companions had first arrived carrying their kit-bags, they were greeted by him.

"Hello for yua and for your friends, hello too. English fellas OK. Queen Victoria, bloody fine chap. God save the King! Best room for yua and yua and yua and yua. Thersa plenty a booze for everybody."

He had led them up the stairs to show them where they would be staying.

"Bloody fine room – yes. Itsa shit hot – no?"

He was heard to repeat the same sentence when showing the next four men to the room above.

'We can't all have the best room,' thought George, as he made his way out onto the balcony, enjoying the view across the Creek, where he could see *E11* standing out against the white painted side of *HMS Egmont*.

Horlicks was always accompanied by a mangy Jack Russell named Fido – a sullen looking beast, that seemed to remain glued to his right heel. This flea-bitten mutt was, none the less, adopted by the crew as *E11*'s mascot. Many of the men fed it titbits from food they had purposely brought back from *HMS Egmont*, where the crew were taking their meals.

The second evening in the shore accommodation turned into a riotous party that would provide a talking point on the boat for many months to come. The beer never stopped flowing from the newly installed hand pump that Horlicks had produced with a flourish, before clamping it to his dining table. Two barrels of beer were delivered in a horse and cart, and the crew helped the drayman to carry them up to the first floor. Several crates of bottled beer were stacked underneath the table, just in case the pump should breakdown. An old piano had also materialised in the bar, and as Basil Partridge was fairly proficient in playing the instrument, it proved to be great entertainment. Three women appeared at the party, none of whom anybody could remember inviting, who became competed for with unparalleled verve for dancing, despite the fact they were old enough to be the sailors' grandmothers.

Horlicks looked to be a very happy man that night. His newly constructed bar was packed to capacity, and all of his boys were drinking themselves into oblivion. His brother in law in the Star of Bethlehem next door, never boasted so much as a glass of lemonade, which made him even happier.

The next day Horlicks had to go out, and get three more barrels of beer. The barrels had both run dry, and the supply of bottles had been seriously depleted before the night finally ended. Many of the crew believed that they could see pound note signs, instead of the usual iris. in each of his eyes.

In the days that followed, his lounge was packed to capacity on most nights after work. Horlicks had cannily reduced the price of a pint against those in the nearest bars, this retaining his growing fortune.

Fido became a great favourite with almost everyone. Having often been fed by the crew, the dog would come rummaging round the room clearing up sandwich crusts, and any remnants of half-eaten pies that Horlicks' wife produced from her kitchen. Everyone petted the animal, despite its rather doubtful looking moth-eaten coat. The popularity of his dog made Horlicks very happy. He could see his fortune being made before his eyes, and the popularity of both he and his dog knew no bounds.

That was until the night when Fido strayed away from Horlicks' heel late in the evening, going off on a scavenging sortie of the bar. As usual he was fairly successful, that was until he reached the table of Chief Engineer Arthur Jupp. The Chief was sitting at a table with two of his Artificers, when Fido threaded his way through the engineer's legs. Nobody knew exactly what had happened, but there was a sudden yelping, followed by some muttered oaths. The dog had immediately scampered back to the safety of Horlicks' heel, with its tail between its legs. That was when Horlicks produced a comment for which he would always be remembered. He marched over to Chief Jupp's table, standing with his hands on his hips, and looking him straight in the eye.

"Hey yua," he demanded of Jupp. "Why for you kicka my dog and call him fuck off, when yua know ees namesa Fido?"

From that point on, the whole crew started doing impressions of Horlicks. The following morning, even the Coxswain called the work parties to attention by using Horlicks unique version of English.

"Hey yua lot. Standa widda feet together. Arms atta the sides, and shutta upa your faces."

Rumour had it that they might be in Malta for a whole month.

****

George Torode had spent the morning painting, working hard on the casing of the submarine. *E11* had been moved to the inner berth alongside the old warship, due to the fact that *E14* and *E15* had moved to tie alongside the stone quay behind *Adamant*, as the flotilla was preparing for their imminent departure to Murdos. He

156

had enjoyed being out in the sunshine, working without his shirt, feeling the solar rays against his skin. Submariners are prone to developing sores and rashes, due to the constant impregnation of diesel oil into their skin. This, combined with a distinct lack of vitamin D from the sun light, caused them to become pale, and a lot of skin afflictions failed to heal. So, this provided a good chance to get more sunshine, which was something that seemed to heal most of the problems from which many suffered.

Lunchtime quickly came and went as Grand Harbour shimmered in the afternoon heat. It reminded George a little of home, and the balmy summers of his boyhood. Since he had joined the service, his body had quickly developed into manhood. His shoulder muscles and biceps had become muscular and well formed, along with a solid torso. His chest had sprouted a few hairs, of which he felt quite proud, and he had never felt healthier in his life than he did right at that moment. He scratched at an irritation under his arm.

Despite all the uncertainty regarding the repairs, there were many rumours abounding amongst the crew. The most probable one was that the *Adamant* would be sailing with *E14* and *E15* very soon, and that *E11* would be staying behind until every one of her major repairs could be completed. That sounded quite plausible, as the new armature and replacement intermediate shaft for the star clutch had not yet arrived from Portsmouth. It did not worry George too much, as he loved working in the sunshine here in Malta. If they were at sea, he would be stuck below most of the time. The sweaty humid conditions transiting from Gibraltar, had given him a good indication of what he could expect once they got into the Aegean Sea. By being here, it also kept them out of the main area of conflict. He was not a coward, but if they were not actually engaged in the fighting, then there was not much chance of getting killed. In these days of uncertainty, sometimes ill fate became a firm friend, but it would be inevitable that their situation would eventually change, and then destiny might have something else in store for him.

He was just finishing his work for the day, and was conducting the process for cleaning his brushes with turpentine, and wiping dry them on a piece of rag. As he stood up and looked back along the casing he had just painted, it shone, looking splendid in its new dark blue livery. The Coxswain had directed him earlier that morning, in exactly the right colour that he wanted George to use. It was supposed to camouflage them, make them hard to see at twilight, and when at periscope depth. Inwardly, he felt that he had done a good job, and he stood back once more to fully survey his efforts, checking for any patches that he may have missed. He thought that this shade of blue made *E11* look just that little more menacing, so he considered it to be a worthwhile job.

He laid the cleaned brushes down on the paint drum, and carried the lot back towards the paint store aboard the *Egmont*. Returning back to the casing of *E11*, he began clearing away the dirty rags that he had used to mop up any spillages. He bundled them all together, ready to be tossed into the waste bin on the quayside as he went ashore. Once he was satisfied that all was in order, he decided to go to the washroom on the wooden hulk to get cleaned up. He re-crossed the gangway onto *Egmont,* and as he was about to climb the wooden ladder that led to the upper deck, a Sub Lieutenant, dressed in his spotlessly white uniform came skipping down the steps. It was Arthur Collenette. George recognised him before Arthur had even noticed him. He stood his ground, blocking his route, and forcing him stop on a step, and to face him. As their eyes met, he could see initial bewilderment instantly turn to fear. Recognition flashed through his eyes, as George stared straight back at him, saying nothing at first. Arthur took a step back up the ladder.

"Hello Arthur! Fancy seeing you here in Malta? Still running away from your friends?" his tone was deliberately derisive.

Arthur's face had drained of colour, his eyebrows arched in alarm, and his eyes were wide with shock. He stared at George in disbelief, his lower jaw started to quiver as he fought for something to say. Not finding any words, his eyes darted quickly right and left for a means of escape, but he remained trapped near the bottom of the ladder. Trying to regain some composure, he brushed at some imaginary piece of dirt on his immaculate white uniform. Hesitatingly he replied.

"Er – Hello, George – fancy seeing you here. We're just about to sail off to Imbros. What are you doing here?"

"I'm on the *E11* – over there," he said, gesturing towards the submarine. Then, as if he were greeting a long-lost friend, he said, "It's been a long time, hasn't it, Arthur?"

"Er – er – Yes," he mumbled. Beads of sweat were breaking out on his fore-head – George noted that he was feeling decidedly uncomfortable.

Despite his inward anger, George had to choke down a guffaw, as he watched Arthur in complete disarray. He looked as if he were about to have an apoplectic fit. His face had turned a beetroot red, and sweat patches bloomed through the thin white drill material of his uniform. He began coughing and clearing his throat in a nervous manner.

"Yes – well – er – I can't stop and chat unfortunately – work to be done – a war to fight – excuse me please – good luck and goodbye, George."

George did not move, and so Arthur was forced to squeeze his way past. He finally broke free, and headed down the deck of the *Egmont* towards her gangway, heading to the quay. On the quayside he turned and rushed off towards *HMS Adamant*, which was berthed just astern. As Arthur headed away, George noticed that there was a dark smudge of blue paint down the leg of his white uniform. He smiled, feeling no guilt. Arthur would not escape justice. One day there would come a reckoning. His ship might be heading away very shortly, but although *E11* would be delayed here in Malta for some time, eventually they would end up at the same place.

The Islands of Imbros and Murdos had been chosen as the main anchorages for the Fleet during their attempt to force a passage through the Dardanelles. That was where *Adamant* and the two other E Class boats were heading, and it would be where *E11* would eventually be heading as well once all of her repairs had been completed.

The unexpected meeting with Arthur had darkened George's mood. After cleaning up, the Coxswain had piped Secure and the men who were not staying aboard for duty watch gradually appeared from their workplaces to form into a squad in readiness to be marched around to their accommodation. As they marched along, an image of Matthew Marquand kept flashing into George's mind and he heard himself repeating his promise to him on that fateful day. Some of his crew-mates looked at him strangely, as he stared fixedly ahead muttering to himself. Inside there was an anger coursing through his veins and it would take some time before it would dissipate. George now knew where Arthur was. Nobody can hide from justice for ever. He would bide his time and wait for the opportunity to obtain justice for Matthew. A promise was a promise after all and he was in no doubt that he would not be found wanting. Deep in his heart he knew that he could never resort to murder, but there were plenty of other ways of repaying a debt. His opportunity would come!

Later that evening George lay on his bed in the Porto Bella with his eyes closed. He had just finished having a cool luxurious bath in tepid water. It had only been a tin bath, but it was the only tub that the Porto Bella possessed. On request Horlicks' wife had provided him with some scented soap. Removing the sweat and grime from his day of labour had left his body feeling re-invigorated. A soft breeze wafted through in through the doors, making him feel comfortably relaxed. With his arms folded behind his head, he thought back to earlier that afternoon and his meeting with Arthur. His smile widened at the corners as he remembered the shocked look on Arthur's face. It had been a mixture of total surprise and absolute terror. He had made some tentative enquiries on the depot ship just after their arrival here and apparently Arthur is a Seaman Sub Lieutenant serving aboard *HMS Adamant*. He was a surface sailor, who was just two months out of the Britannia Royal Naval College at Dartmouth. His job on-board was the officer in charge of the ship's small boats. George had learned from the Quartermaster standing at the brow of *Egmont* that Arthur had been sent over from the *Adamant* to collect intelligence reports prior to her sailing tomorrow.

There was a knock on the bedroom door. "Hurry up, George," Basil Partridge's voice came through the woodwork.

"It's OK mate, the door is open. Where are we off to tonight?"

The door opened and the stoker entered. "Cor! Who smells like my mum's handbag?"

George smiled. "It feels good to be clean, Baz. Where are we off to tonight?"

"We'll take a dghaisa across the harbour to the Post Office Steps. It's only a short climb from there up to the Kingsway in town. Tonight, I am going to show you the delights of Strait Street – better known to His Majesty's Navy as The Gut."

George had heard the name mentioned before by other members of the crew.

"Why is it called The Gut?" he asked.

"Probably because it stands on a hillside, and runs downward like a gutter. I don't really know to tell the truth George, but it's a damn good night out. One you'll never forget – you mark my words."

****

The water lapped gently at the bow of the small rowboat, as the Maltese oarsman standing in the centre, leaned into each stroke. Their progress across the harbour was painfully slow, but it was a beautiful evening, with the sun lying low in an orange, yellow, and red western horizon. Above were traces of wispy cloud was edged in a pastel pink. Within the harbour the water shimmered like a mirror, reflecting the whole glorious spectacle that was Valetta. Their craft passed slowly beneath the bow of a destroyer, that was moored mid-harbour to a buoy, before gliding silently onwards towards the stone landing steps. As they bumped alongside, George craned his neck up at the towering city walls. They were really were high.

Once their small craft had been secured at the Post Office steps, they paid the ferryman, and headed the short distance towards the stone stairway that headed upwards into the heights of Valetta town itself. The stone stairway was wide, with one side was lined with cafes, bars, and homes. An old lady dressed in the standard black, sat on a wooden chair outside of her door enjoying the cooling effect of the evening shadows. She gave George a toothless smile, and he had waved back.

By the time they reached the top, both men were panting from the exertion. They were greeted by a large church that stood in the middle of huge flat tree filled expanse. There were a number of roadways threading amongst the foliage, which were filled with horse drawn carriages. George had quickly learned that the Maltese people loved their churches – there seemed to be one located on every corner. These ornamental gardens were filled with large crowds of people, who were milling about on the roadways that surrounded the stone building. The two men stopped at the kerbside to allow a horse drawn carriage to slowly clip-clop by.

Having quickly regained their wind, the two sailors made their way over towards the Piazza San Gorg, where there were many more people. As he began to look about, George became aware that there were an inordinate number of family groups walking about. Looking left and right – the roadway was awash with more of them. Everyone seemed to be simply walking up and down the main thoroughfare. There was no motorised vehicular traffic, save a few horse-drawn Gharries, which the local Landaus are called. Sweethearts strolled hand in hand, with an ever-attentive duenna a few paces behind. Husband and wife pairs walked with their children. Other people simply walked alone. People were nodding politely to each other, men raised their hats and pleasantries were exchanged. The one thing that they all had in common was the fact that they everyone was dressed in their Sunday best clothes. The men were mostly attired in their rather sombre grey three-piece suits, but they were outshone by their women bedecked in beautiful full-length dresses. The old fashion styles were wonderful, but sadly most of the colours were rather drab, but trimmed with lace. The sheer volume of people gave the place a carnival atmosphere.

George was very curious, and turned to ask Basil for an answer!

"It is because they pack in work quite early over here – because of the heat. They have an afternoon siesta. Then between five and six in the evening the shop-keepers go back to work, the rest all wake up, and get dressed to show off their sons and daughters to prospective suitors. If two of the youngsters like each other, then their respective families make all the arrangements, and the two are allowed the go out together under escort."

Basil pointed out a young couple with a chaperone in tow.

"It's also a good excuse to meet old friends and have a chat."

"It all seems a bit Victorian, doesn't it? Why can't the two youngsters arrange to go out together by themselves?"

"Because the father rules the roost over here, not unlike at home, and that's the way things are done," replied Basil. "The whole population are left footers, and like all of the Catholics, they have very strict views on that sort of thing."

George had heard the expression before, and knew that left footer was a navy term for people of the Roman Catholic faith. As they walked through the throng, George started regarding the Maltese people through newly enlightened eyes.

It was not long before the two sailors had move away from the main road, and started to leave the mass of people behind. They walked along towards the end of a narrow street, where almost immediately it made a sharp right turn. Basil and George found themselves standing at the top of a fairly steep hill, with a stepped narrow lane going down towards some buildings. They rose up on either side, many with boards declaring their occupation of being a bar. The Malata Bar and the Blue Peter Bar signs were large and stood out boldly. There were lots of oil lamps lighting up the area in various colours. George stood staring down at the glitz filled thoroughfare in amazement. It was a very narrow path, with the light from the pubs and bars splashing out across the rather dangerous looking steps. The vacant space between the pubs seethed with a mass of British sailors, in various stages of sobriety. Further down he could see some females dressed in bright alluring attire, as they moved amongst the men. Down here the women wore their hemlines much shorter than those who were parading up in the town. Their make-up was heavily accentuated, and their hair coiffured in elaborate outlandish styles. As the two men began their descent, they began to approach the first of the bars, which George noticed bore the dubious name of 'Dirty Dicks'. Unexpectedly a young girl dashed out from the shadowy interior, grabbed George's cap, and disappeared straight back in through the door.

"Oi – give that back," he shouted, as the girl disappeared. Turning to tell Basil, he saw him grinning and slowly shaking his head. "She nicked my cap, Baz!"

It was then that George noticed that Basil had already removed his cap, and was carrying it in his hand.

"Well, we'd better go in and get it back then, 'adden't we? Don't worry George, it's just their way of getting you into their bar – and she's just succeeded ain't she? It is one of the oldest tricks in the book. I suppose that I should have warned you."

So, they entered the portals of Dirty Dick's establishment. It was a dim smoky room that stank of stale beer and cheap perfume. The hard floor was a dirty, and bare of any coverings. Groups of men in naval uniformed were sat at the four tables that filled one end. Waitresses were working extremely hard to keep their glasses replenished. There were other women hovering around the tables, but George quickly guessed that from past experience that these women were not there to take orders. Some of the older women wore such gross make up, that they reminded George of an Aunt Sally at traveling fairground. Scotch Annie sprang into his mind. Oh, how he regretted that night.

"Are those ladies, prostitutes, Baz?" he asked to confirm his suspicions.

"You catch on quick don't you, George?" smiled the Stoker. "There are no flies on you, that is for sure. Your cap is over there, at the end of the bar. The girl with the red dress has it."

George followed his friend's direction, and quickly spotted the erstwhile thief. She was an impish-looking girl, rather attractive, with jet-black curly hair. George drew a deep breath, nodded his determination at Basil before setting off along the bar in her direction. As he approached, she turned her back and pretended to be busy. George stood behind her and tapped her on the shoulder.

"Can I have my cap back please?" asked George in a firm, but determinedly polite tone.

Getting absolutely no response, he repeated his request. There was still acknowledgement, so he grabbed her shoulder and spun her round to face him.

"Hey – whata ya think yua doin'?" she whined indignantly, her eyes flashing a fiery challenge.

"Sorry – er… er. I just want my cap back, please," persisted the resolute George.

"OK, I give yua eet. First, yua tell me yua name," her pouting smile was tantalising.

Feeling a little embarrassed, he told her that his name was George, but he was having trouble trying to ignore the obvious invitation in those dark eyes.

"Yua very young, sailor boy!" she giggled, seemingly delighted by her assessment.

George waited patiently while she had her fun.

"Yua very pretty too," she cooed, running her fingers against the smoothness of the black silk of his uniform. "Have yua had a girlfriend, Georgio? Yua sleep with a girl – yes?"

George blushed a deep scarlet. His mouth opened and shut, but no words emerged. He just didn't know what to say.

"If yua want yua 'at," she said. "It'sa upa ina my room. I take yua up and we get eet – OK?"

George was under the impression that she had his hat somewhere here, in the bar. He looked at her suspiciously. What were her real intentions? All he wanted was to get his cap back, and not seeing any alternative he nodded – anything for a quiet life – at least that should lead to the recovery of his cap.

If the Crushers caught him ashore without his cap, he could well end up in the detention cells for the night, so as George could see no other way of retrieving it – he nodded his head. She took his hand and led him over towards an alcove staircase. Feeling slightly embarrassed, he looked back to see if anyone had noticed their departure. They certainly had! A loud cheer erupted from the group of sailors standing over at the bar, and sitting at the tables. As he started to climb the stairs – he quickly looked over towards Basil, who was shaking his head and grinning from ear to ear.

The sound of her shoes on the bare wood steps within the enclosed stairway sounded like the beat of a drum. He followed her up, with the hem of her short skirt swishing just above his head, and his eyes caught a glimpse of the top of her thighs.

At the top there was a moth-eaten mat on the floor, and George followed the girl along a cluttered dusty corridor. Doors led off to the left and right. All were firmly closed. They edged their way past a sleeping dog, that lay curled up on a blanket. It eyed their approach without moving its head. George carefully stepped over it – it still did not move. Reaching the final door, the girl opened it and went in. George reached the door, and stood guardedly at the entrance – waiting. The girl reached out and grabbed his hand, pulling him into the room, and moving past him she shut the door behind him. It was a small cell of a room, that almost completely filled by a bed. Through the window, George could see in the first-floor window of the establishment across the road had a garishly coloured red light, which lit the room.

"My name itsa Maria. Yua like me – no!" the lips were pouting once again, her eyes daring him to say, no.

"Yes, you're very pretty," he stammered, knowing that it was always best to be honest. "Can I have my cap now – please?"

"Yes, yua can 'ave yua 'at – but only if yua give Maria a leetle kiss first," she taunted. "I think yua very preety sailor boy."

George blushed again. He had never been called pretty before – not even by his mother, and he had never had an offer like this in his whole life. His mind flicked back to the diminutive barmaid from the 'Dog and Duck', and he shuddered as he remembered seeing the real Doris on that terrible morning.

Looking back at Maria once again – he had to admit that she really was very pretty. He stood there with his arms at his sides, feeling extremely awkward and not knowing what to do next. Maria solved his problem by picking up and sliding his arms over her shoulders, and then up around his neck. Her fingers began stroking the nape of his neck, before sliding up to firmly grab his head. He felt unsure as she slowly drew his lips down towards hers. Raising herself on tiptoe, she kissed him, mashing her lips against his. Her tongue tip probed between his teeth, and sliding around his own tongue. He could feel the softness of her body, as she ground it against him. His eyes closed naturally any resistance disappeared. Her touch was electrifying, and he could feel her fingertips go back to caressing the nape of his neck. It was tantalising – electric. He had never been kissed like that before. Her lips moved hungrily over his once more, when suddenly his eyes flicked opened wide in alarm, as she bit his lip. The intensity of conflicting emotions mounted, her tongue flicking, darting, searching! She ground her hips against him – thrusting. To George's embarrassment, once again he found that he had developed a tremendous erection. His manhood strained against the confines of flap of his bell-bottomed trousers. One of her hands reached down, and firmly caressed the bulge. He gave an involuntary moan. She broke away from him. He stood there, wanting her back, panting for her.

"Yua want Maria, sailor-boy?" she had her hands on her hips, her head cocked enquiringly to one side.

George realised that his head was nodding. This was without any doubt the most exciting thing that had ever happened to him, and he certainly wanted more. She slowly walked around him, and turned the key in the lock. Spinning round, she looked at George from beneath her lowered brows, her wet tongue licking her lips.

"Is this yua first time, Georgio?"

George nodded.

"Donta worry. Yua a cherry boy. Maria, she will be good for yua. I make yua first time very good, OK!"

She expertly divested George from his uniform. She knew exactly how to unbutton the trouser flap; remove his silk without it unravelling; and how to take off the lanyard without getting it tangled up in the beckets and tapes. More amazingly she knew how the tapes of his blue jean collar were secured around his waist. George was astounded by her skill – it had taken Leading Seaman Andrew nearly three weeks to teach him these intricacies.

Finally, he stood naked, standing there in just his socks. He was feeling very self-conscious about his erection, as she slowly knelt down before him. She looked up at him, smiling, as both of her hands grasped his manhood tightly. His eyes closed as a wave of pure pleasure enveloped his body. Her firm grasp felt so good. At that moment there was absolutely nothing he would not have done for her as she moved her hands slowly up and down. Then all movement ceased, and he let out an involuntary groan of disappointment. Her fingers then began to squeeze, then release as she began to knead his flesh. George's senses began to explode, as he felt the warm wet softness of her mouth close around him.

Basil watched as George reappeared from the alcove at the bottom of the stairs. He had his cap perched jauntily on the back of his head, set like a crown of victory laurels. The stupid smile on his face plainly self-explanatory. There was another muted cheer from the sailors in the bar. He looked around and caught sight of Basil, and headed in his direction. The stoker noticed that the bottom of George's white front was sticking out from his trouser flap. When George arrived, there was a foaming pint of bitter waiting on the bar for him.

"Get that down your neck, George," said Basil. "I'm glad to see that you've got your cap back."

George drank down half the bitter in three huge gulps. Basil began to smile.

"Your white front is sticking out of your trouser flap."

Looking down, George quickly adjusted his dress. Blushing profusely as he re-buttoned himself.

"If that silly grin gets any bigger, George, your face is going to fall in half," laughed Basil.

George blushed again, and gave a school-boy giggle. Basil guffawed and tentatively he joined in with his friend's mirth. Both men found it infectious and were soon both roaring with laughter. Feeling the need to explain his absence, George tried to tell Basil what had gone on without actually resorting to the sordid details.

"She took me up to her room to get my cap," he said, hoping that would suffice.

Basil continued laughing.

"We talked for a while," ventured George, feeling that he had to say more.

Basil was still laughing. He was now rocking to and fro and tears welled in his eyes. Slightly annoyed now, George wanted to end his explanation.

"Now I'm back, and she's still up there."

Basil was holding his sides now and gasping for breath.

"All right," said George. "I admit it – I went with her. Is that what you wanted to hear?"

Basil was hysterical. George did not think it was that funny.

"She only charged me five bob, as it was my firs... er, er. She was very good about the money," hoping that would put paid to Basil's loss of control. But it didn't. Basil was busting his sides.

"OK, what's so funny about it?" he demanded, slightly annoyed.

Basil took several deep breaths, as he tried to compose himself. He relapsed twice, before he was able to speak.

"It's not what you've been doing George – it's your cap. All the trouble you took to get it back, and you've put it on back to front. You look really stupid."

****

The following morning Naismith and d'Oyly-Hughes stood looking out across the harbour from the top of the stone steps of Fort *St Angelo* pier head. Both men were desperately trying to hide their bitter disappointment at being left behind by the flotilla. They stood watching the departure of *HMS Adamant* as she sailed off in company with *HMS E14* and *HMS E15* in line ahead.

Inside, Naismith was seething with frustration, but had to admit that the three vessels made a splendid sight as they manoeuvred had into line, before heading for the buoys marking the entrance defensive boom.

Both of submarines would now beat him to the chance of making the first full penetration of the Dardanelles, he thought. Just as he had been beaten when he had tried his penetration of the Baltic, it looked like fate had decreed that he was going to be the last in once more.

Both of the submarine casing parties looked very smart from where he stood, lined up in their white sweaters and bellbottoms trousers. He could see Boyle and Brodie on the bridge of their respective conning towers, guiding their boats into their allotted position, along with the white caps of their navigators, helmsmen, and signalmen. Oh, how he wished that he were out there with them. He removed his own cap and waved it in a wide arc above his head.

"Doesn't seem fair, does it, sir?" said d'Oyly-Hughes.

As they watched the last boat heading out through the boom, they were suddenly joined by another submariner, Lieutenant Henry HG Stoker, who was the captain of the Australian 'E' Class boat, HMAS AE2, which was also undergoing some minor repairs here at Malta. Having transferred to the Royal Australian Navy, he had immediately been appointed as the captain to the second of that nation's new submarine fleet. Already being in the Mediterranean when this campaign began, he had been lucky enough to have beaten them all to the scene of the action, but his boat had sustained some slight damage after hitting the rocks at Sangrada Point, standing near the entrance to the British base in Murdos Harbour on the island of Lemnos.

Henry Hugh Gordon Stoker was a good-looking Irishman, who was very popular throughout the Trade, but he had lost a good deal of that popularity, especially with the Admiral, when he had to appear before him to explain his latest misfortune. Like Naismith, he desperately wanted to be first through the Dardanelles, and to have the chance to threaten harbour at Constantinople. Then again, that was the ambition of every submarine CO – each of them wanted the same thing.

"Hello Henry," said Naismith.

"Hello Martin," he replied. "We have both been left behind it seems."

"Yes, but I think that you may well be on your way before I am. I am still awaiting some parts to arrive from England."

So, the three disconsolate men stood there, their inner frustrations forming a common bond, but for the present there was nothing that any of them could do about it.

****

Through his persistent badgering, Martin Naismith managed to browbeat the repair staff aboard *Egmont* to arrange for his early departure from Malta. Some of the major defects had indeed been repaired, but he had pleaded for the replacement shaft for the defective Star Clutch to be sent straight onwards to Murdos Harbour, to be fitted there. When it eventually arrived there, it could then be milled and fitted in place by the engineers aboard the Repair Ship *HMS Reliance*. The old shaft had already been removed, and milled once more, before being temporarily refitted. Thankfully its operation was a little easier, having already been tested – but it was still much stiffer than it should be, and would hamper any crash dive.

All the leakage problems they had experienced in their external fuel tanks had finally been fixed after a short docking, and they had already been refuelled to total capacity. The defective armature had eventually arrived from Portsmouth, and that too had been replaced that very afternoon. He argued that the last problem could be fitted in Murdos, and the offices of the C in C Mediterranean granted his request.

Martin Naismith informed his men of *E11* that they would be sailing the following morning at first light.

The sudden news of their immanent departure came as a severe shock to Horlicks, who became genuinely distraught at the prospect of losing his cash cow so soon. Watery tears were seen forming in his eyes when he had been informed. He repeated a thousand times that he was sorry to see them go, but everyone was very well aware that his only regret was that his new fount of wealth was about to run dry. None the less a farewell party was hastily arranged for that evening. In a completely uncharacteristic gesture Horlicks declared that all the first drinks of the evening would be on the house.

By two o'clock the following morning his lounge looked like the remnants of a battle on the Flanders front line. There were inert bodies lying everywhere. The place stank of stale beer, recently expelled methane, and overflowing ashtrays. As the walking wounded staggered off to bed, Horlicks had stood at the doorway to wish them all goodbye and good luck.

At four o'clock that same morning the crew were roused from their short slumber, and told to get themselves and their kit down to the boat as Harbour Stations would at piped at six o'clock. Trying to wake some of the crew had been like trying to raise Lazarus from the dead. Most of the men looked like zombies, with vacant eyes and unshaven faces, dehydrated throats, and sandpaper tongues. Without exception, everyone had a hangover that went beyond the expectancy of survival, but surprisingly there had been no one who arrived late. Horlicks had stayed awake, and he walked along to the quayside to see them off.

"Goodbye for yua and for yua. For yua all – Bona Fortuna Eengleeshmen! God save the King!"

As threatened, Harbour Stations were duly piped right on six o'clock. The exit of *HMS E11* from Grand Harbour went without a hitch, and after passing through the boom, the Star Clutch was easily engaged prior to both diesels being started. They ran up without any mishap. It was comforting to know that at least most of the defects seemed to have been repaired satisfactorily. So far so good!

The arrival of dawn began to dispel the shadowy outline of the Island, as they headed off on a north-north-easterly course towards the Italian island of Sicily.

All went well, and on sighting Cape Passaro on the south east corner of that Island, they hugged the coastline up towards the toe of Italy. The air was fresh and clear, and it felt good to be back at sea again. Headaches slowly began to fade as untainted ozone cleansed their lungs. Copious mugs of tea gradually diluted the alcoholic.

Far away on the distant western horizon, the bridge watch-keepers could just make out the faint outline of Mount Etna, complete with a soft white plume adorning its flattened cone. Soon they made a turn to starboard, onto a more easterly course, and they soon found themselves heading out across the Ionian Sea.

The following day was the sixteenth of April, and the weather had deteriorated overnight, with steel grey clouds replacing those limpid blue skies. A long swell had developed, and the wave height increased significantly, reminding many of the crew more of the Atlantic more than the Mediterranean. Despite the uneasy motion, the port intermediate shaft still held firm.

Their next landfall was the island of Kithira, just to the south of the Greek mainland, and navigating their way through the Kithirai Channel, *HMS E11* turned to port to head north east towards the thousands of islands that littered the Aegean Sea. Thankfully the sea conditions began to ease as they began to head north.

As dawn chased away the night on the eighteenth of April, *HMS E11* finally arrived off the island of Murdos. From the bridge it looked slightly larger than many of the islands they had passed the day before, but certainly not any different in shape. The rounded, almost bare scrubby hills reflected gold in the early morning light. The island, like so many others in the Aegean, was the summit of a semi-submerged volcano, with its horse-shoe shaped harbour formed from the lopsided inclination of the crater rim. Naturally protected, it had been chosen as the main logistical base for the Allied combined force of mainly British and French ships gathered there for the next thrust against the Dardanelles.

As *HMS E11* began her approach, a French destroyer came speeding out like an ocean greyhound to investigate them. Her tricolour was stood out straight as a board in the fresh breeze, and she made a splendid sight. Following an exchange of identities, they were given permission to enter harbour at 0700.

Right on time, Martin Naismith steered his tiny submarine around Sangara Point, the exact same spot where Lieutenant Henry Stoker had damaged HMAS AE2 earlier in the month, and lined himself up to enter the harbour. They immediately began passing several French transports, anchored in the outer roads. Once inside the great, almost circular inner harbour that looked like a Roman amphitheatre with a watery arena packed tight with every imaginable type of ship. The combined smoke emanating from their funnels drifted lazily upwards, a representation of the thermal activity from this dormant cone.

As lookout, George Torode closely scanned each of the vessels with his binoculars. He counted at least ten battleships and battle-cruisers. There were vessels from every one of the allied navies, some well represented, others not so.

The French flagship Suffren was anchored close to the five funnelled Russian cruiser Askold. The old French battleship was a pre-Dreadnought, having been built in the July of 1899, heavily armed with four twelve-inch guns mounted in two main turrets. She also had six smaller turrets, each mounting a single six-point four-inch gun. Four other similar guns were mounted in her beam turrets. The Russian cruiser Askold had been purchased from Britain in 1900, being the former *HMS Glory IV*. She also boasted twelve six-inch guns. Unfortunately, most of the Russian Navy had been lost back in 1902 in the Battle of the Tsu Shima Straits during its ill-fated war against the Japanese. The Askold was one of the few remaining capital ships remaining within the Russian Western Fleet.

As they proceeded further into the harbour the British flagship, *HMS Queen Elizabeth*, looked resplendent. She was one of the newer capital ships here, having only been launched less than eighteen months earlier in October of 1913. She boasted eight fifteen-inch guns mounted in four turrets. Sixteen six-inch guns provided her secondary armament, with twelve of them being mounted in the forward superstructure and four aft. The Admirals pennant fluttered from her masthead. George gave up trying to count the number of other cruisers and the massed destroyers that formed the rest of this magnificent fleet.

Beside the warships, there were a huge number of troop ships, all filled to the brim with khaki hordes who now lined the guardrails to watch their entry with a bored indifference. Three hospital ships stood out in stark contrast in their white livery, with a huge red cross emblazoned on each side. They stood waiting patiently at anchor for the inevitable flood of business following the assault, which these soldiers were due to take part in the near future.

Several unfamiliar depot ships tended to every type of warship known unto Neptune. Their charges were tucked safely alongside, like feeding piglets to a sow. Tenders, tugs, lighters, and small boats littered any vacant space between the basking static hulls.

The wind blowing across the Aegean Sea was being forced up over the top of the Island cone, leaving the combined smoke from a hundred funnels trapped inside, which created a choking atmosphere here inside the harbour. This produced a veiled hazy cauldron, which sent the temperatures soaring like a steamy coal-laden sauna.

The surface of the water within harbour was peppered with hundreds of small islands of flotsam, each covered by several varieties of sea birds. George noted that there were even the carcasses of dead horses and mules bobbing amongst the smashed shards of wooden crates and rotting heaps of dumped vegetables, that looked like congealed pond weed. The lack of any air currents had stranded this dumped rubbish from the hundred trapped ships. Flashes of sunlight reflected from the glass of hundreds of bobbing empty bottles in the water, seemingly everywhere. The waste from a hundred galleys brought swarms of squawking gulls, as they fought and squabbled over the discarded bounty. Add to that the combined discharge of ten thousand human beings waste, it blessed the whole place a vile stench.

On the far hillside, rising up beyond the northern shore of the harbour, stood a city of white bell tents. A thousand pales of smoke rose up from a thousand campfires, as the field breakfasts were being prepared. Clouds of dust mingled with the smoke as thousands of men were drilled and exercised on the open expanse. The whole allied might within the Mediterranean had met here at this crossroad, before going onward to fight the Turk. To George, as he observed it through his binoculars, it looked like the crossroads to hell.

He was relieved by Signalman, and he below to get ready for his casing duties.

Down below, inside the boat, the men were closed up at their respective Harbour Stations. The diesel engines had been stopped, and the sudden loss of the cooling air being drawn down the conning tower quickly sent the internal temperature soaring, exacerbated by the radiant heat emanating from the hot two diesels. Things were beginning to get uncomfortable once again, which when mixed with the smell of dirty water and the diesel fuel oil, made many of the men look forward to getting alongside. They were looking forward to when they could climb up the ladder, and get out into the sunshine.

Suddenly there was a more prevailing smell that invaded all of their senses. The ominous odour was instantly recognisable as it began to permeate every nook and cranny within Control Room area of the boat. At first quizzical faces sniffed the air suspiciously, but soon faces contorted into disbelief as the frightening realisation dawned on everyone. Whistles of disgust, accompanied a few titters of laughter, as each man searched for the culprit. There was nobody who brave enough to own up.

"It's the phantom farter."

"Whoever it is, he should have been smothered at birth."

"Look for a man growing a tail growing out of his trousers."

"Take deep breaths lads – our lungs can soon filter it out."

Coxswain Dowell's stern voice called for order, but as the stench reached him, even he had to admit that there was a just cause for complaint. Someone here on-board had a serious problem with his bowels, and if he ever got hold of the perpetrator, he vowed to all that listened that he would send him to the *Adamant* Sick Bay for a cold-water enema.

HMS E11 slowly threaded her way through the anchored ships, heading towards her depot ship *HMS Adamant*. Her sleek yacht lines made her easily recognisable, and the Signalman spotted her over on the north eastern fringe of the anchored fleet. He reported his sighting to Naismith, who raised his own glasses to survey the area. There was a single dark shape secured alongside, but as *E11* approached, neither *E14* nor *E15* were anywhere to be seen. He became filled with disappointment in the knowledge that they were probably attempting to force a passage through the Dardanelles.

The Second Coxswain steered *HMS E11* expertly alongside, under Naismith's watchful eye. Soon the heaving lines were flying across the gap to the waiting crew of yet another E class boat, and *E11* was tied safely alongside. Martin Naismith took a deep breath of relief, and turned to Guy doyly-Hughes.

"We finally made it Number One."

"Yes sir, but I am sure that you will have noticed that neither *E14* or *E15* are present. It looks like we have been beaten at the post."

Naismith slowly nodded his head and became rather glum. Then his face brightened.

"Fall out of Harbour Stations Number One. Let the men up top for a five-minute smoke before you get them working down below."

He saluted, and then leaned over the voice-pipe.

"Fall out Harbour Stations below Coxswain. A five-minute smoke for all the men on the casing before the hands are turned to."

Chapter Eight

Murdos

As soon as Martin Naismith had crossed the two narrow gangways, one linking E11 to the other boat, and the second to their mother ship, he climbed up the Mediterranean Ladder, and arriving in front of the welcoming officers he immediately sensed an awkwardness – it very obviously there was something badly amiss. Commander Somerville, the Captain of the *Adamant*, wore a worried furrowed brow as he conducted him straight down into his cabin. Once within its confines he turned, looking tired and forlorn, inviting Naismith to have a cup of coffee. After making polite small talk, he seemed to be searching for the right words to say what was so very obviously on his mind. Martin Naismith could plainly see from his demeanour that he was ill at ease. The ensuing silence became more than a little awkward while the Commander composed himself.

He began the conversation by asking how *E11*'s voyage had been. Naismith told him how smoothly his boat had managed the passage, and then fearing the worst, he enquired after *E14* and *E15*. The senior officer's face immediately looked relieved that the question had been broached. The awkwardness had been broken.

"Edward Courtney and *E14* are out on their pre-entry preparation exercises, but we are all extremely worried about Theodore Brodie in *E15*. He was given the first chance at penetrating the narrows, and E15 sailed for the Marmara two nights ago. That was late on the evening of the sixteenth. I have the very sad duty of informing you Martin, that his crippled boat has just been sighted by one of our spotter planes. She has run aground, and looks to be in a pretty perilous situation. The observer of the aircraft said the she had been badly shot up on a mud-bank near Kephez Point. She could have been purposely beached just below Fort Dardanos after being struck several times by the guns, and is now lying directly below those gun batteries. We are unable to get near her. The best scenario I can imagine is that Dummy-Head and his crew are all now prisoners of war. Otherwise I hate to think of how many casualties they may have suffered."

His eyes flicked up towards Naismith, before he continued.

"By a strange coincidence it was Brodie's brother War-Head, who actually made the first sighting of her. He and the pilot, Commander Sampson, were on a sortie trying to plot *E15*'s passage through the Dardanelles in an attempt to chart her course and note any problems that she might encounter during the initial transit. Three planes went up, two to act in a diversionary capacity by dropping bombs on the gun batteries, while Samson and Brodie in the third, carried out their close observation.

Samson ensured that he stayed at a high altitude, and at a safe distance, so as not to alert the Turks to *E15*'s presence. Brodie reported that they had her in sight as she dived at about 0400 yesterday, and that was his last sighting of her, until he spotted her on the mudbank, aground at 0645. She was being fired upon by the Turkish gun battery, and he observed several of the shells had actually hit. He watched as the crew abandoned ship just after she had been beached. Some of them were killed by the shelling as they ran for the higher ground. Brodie then observed the Turkish army arrive, and all the survivors were rounded up and taken prisoner."

"Do we know how many casualties they sustained, sir?" asked Naismith, obviously shocked.

"We don't know for sure yet, but if she was hit as badly as Brodie says she was, then there are bound to be quite a few," replied the Commander. "He saw several of the crew killed by the Turkish shell fire."

"What is going to happen about *E15*, sir? We certainly can't leave her for the Turks to take to Constantinople, and hand over to their German allies."

"No, of course not Martin! We sent *HMS B11*, with Norman Holbrook in command, right up to her position to try and put a torpedo into her that same afternoon. We obviously did not want the Turks getting hold of one of our latest E Class boats," he continued. "War Head, begged to go along on the trip, you can imagine how worried he is about his brother? Holbrook managed with great difficulty to get his boat into a firing position, and did eventually manage to fire a torpedo, but unfortunately it hit one of the Turkish tug-boats that had crossed his firing line just at the wrong moment. Already the Turks have several auxiliary vessels up there trying to pull her off the mud. Later that same evening Sampson's aeroplanes also tried to drop bombs on her, but very stiff anti-aircraft fire prevented them from getting close enough to achieve a hit of any significance. There were certainly no direct hits observed. Then later that night two destroyers, the *Scorpion* and *Grampus*, were sent racing in and got within half a mile of her, but their gun crews were completely blinded by the shore search-lights. They were reluctantly forced to retire under heavy fire from the gun batteries. Yesterday morning Holbrook took *B11* in for a second attempt, but he hasn't returned as yet. He is the most experienced submarine captain that we have out here, but we must assume that he has probably failed. After lunch today *HMS Triumph* and *Majestic*, along with a destroyer escort will steam up past Kum Kale and use their big guns to fire at *E15* at a range of about six miles. Sampson's spotter planes will hopefully be able to direct their fire onto the target."

"Let me have a go sir, my boat will make it I am sure, given the chance?" interrupted Naismith.

The Commander shook his head firmly. "Don't be a bloody fool, Martin. If you are truly honest with yourself you know as well as I do that *E11* is still in a bad way at the moment. If your crank shaft should fail while you were up there, you'd be very lucky to get back here in one piece. It's hard enough for boats with no defects to get anywhere near her – so I'm sorry Martin, the answer is no!"

Seeing his disappointment, Somerville added. "Norman Holbrook had a hell of time with *B11* just before Christmas, when he won his VC. He had to negotiate five rows of mines before he could get his boat close enough to the Turkish battleship Mesudiye to be able to sink her. He only just managed to get back, as his battery power was on the edge of dying out. It is no picnic up there, Martin. Your boat has to be top shape, or there is no way that you will succeed in getting through."

"How soon will it be before my spares gets here, sir? How long before we can sail?" asked the disappointed submariner.

"I have arranged for you and your engineer to go over to the Repair Ship in my barge this afternoon. The captain of the *Reliance* is Engineering Captain Humphries, and he will be able to give you the very latest news," said the Commander.

Having nothing more to say, the two men parted company.

****

Captain Humphries welcomed Martin Naismith and his Engineer Chief Petty Officer Arthur Jupp aboard the Repair Ship *HMS Reliance* and took both of the men down into his day cabin. The *Reliance* was an ex-liner named the Knight Companion, that at the start of the war had been converted into a heavy repair ship – a huge floating mechanical workshop, complete with heavy cranes. Being an ex-liner, the Captain's quarters were vast and sumptuous to the extreme, complete with all the luxuries that one would expect on such a ship.

"My staff are working on a top priority job at this present moment in time. They are converting the old Collier, the River Clyde, into a troop landing ship. Apparently, the next plan in the campaign is to land troops on the Gallipoli Peninsula in the very near future," said the elderly engineer, conversationally.

"But what about *E11*'s repairs, sir?" interjected Naismith.

"Yes, Yes, I'm coming to that next. I have arranged for my engineers to be ready to lift and strip out your port shaft and flywheel. In preparation for this Chief Jupp – I want you and your men to remove all the engine casing and fittings and to carefully remove the pressure hull plates situated directly above the Engine Room. Then you will have to dismantle the whole of your port engine before my own men can get to work and take out the shaft. We will still have to turn and mill the new casting on the main lathe before we can fit it. The intermediate replacement shaft for the star clutch can be fitted at the same time. On completion of the fitting of both of these replacement shafts, the whole engine will need to be rebuilt as a joint effort. A test run will have to take place on the engine, and providing that goes well, the hull-plates will need to be replaced and sealed. Then you will need to conduct a series of dives, which will be needed to check the integrity of the refitted pressure hull plates. Full diving depth must be achieved. I must emphasise that this program will only be possible if everything goes to plan, and there are no unforeseen problems that crop up."

Martin Naismith did not realise just how large the problem of the engine was, and he could now see that it was going to be an extremely big job. To do it all in one of the Royal Dockyards, with all the proper facilities that are available there would be a daunting task, but to do it out here in the northern Aegean Sea with the limited resources, they were hoping for a miracle. Two miracles if it was to be completed on time. The whole of the crew would be required to assist the Engineers. Naismith knew he had no choice, and nodded in agreement to the plan; then turned enquiringly to his Engine Room Chief for confirmation.

"Does that sound OK to you, Chief?" he asked.

"Yes sir – I'll start to get it organised at once," said Jupp.

"My men have a programmed run line for the work needed to be completed on time and our very best estimation is that by working flat out day and night, it will take all of us approximately three weeks from start to finish," said Captain Humphries. "That is if everything goes well, and there are no hiccups."

Naismith let go a frustrated exhalation.

He would push for two weeks from his own men, but he knew he was asking the impossible from these overworked engineers' aboard *HMS Reliance*. The problems of *HMS E11* was simply another job to them, one of many that every Captain wanted finished yesterday.

The two submariners left the *Reliance*, but instead of going straight back over to the *Adamant*, Naismith ordered the barge to change course to head across the harbour to pay a social call on an old friend, Lieutenant Commander Pownal, who was the Captain of the depot ship *HMS Hindu Kush*. After dropping him off, Chief Jupp continued the journey back to *E11*.

The heat was oppressive within the harbour; the giant steel hulls seemed to act as giant cast iron radiators. Their huge draught created a series of baffle plates, that served to prevent surface water movement within the enclosed harbour. Without that circulating current, very little breeze could access the crater to cool the place. It also made the massive rafts of debris and waste that were lying stagnant, turn into stinking putrid piles that attracted clouds of flies, which added to the general unpleasantness. Dante's Inferno was quoted on a daily basis – and ever more waste was being added to the harbour on a daily basis.

The *Hindu Kush* was the submarine depot ship and headquarters for the staff of submarine operations here within the Aegean area. She also acted as the base for the five ageing 'B' Class submarines, and to three of the newer French boats. This squadron was being employed to watch the enemy ports, and to provide an effective blockade to the entrance to the Dardanelles. All sea trade up to Constantinople from the Mediterranean had no alternative but to go through the Dardanelles, before transiting across the Sea of Marmara. A paranoia existed through-out the more high-ranking staff that the German warships, Goeben and Breslau, would attempt a break-out sortie into the Mediterranean from Constantinople. So, this squadron was being employed to prevent such a scenario from happening.

Martin Naismith climbed aboard to see his friend, but the Lieutenant Commander Pownal had little more information that he could pass on, except for a written first-hand report of *B11*'s previous expedition up into the Narrows. He handed it to Naismith, who read it with great interest.

The Narrows was a point in the transit through the Dardanelles where it did indeed narrow alarmingly, but it also where the channel turned right almost ninety degrees. This strategic area was also the furthest point south that the Turkish navy had ventured since the commencement of the confrontation. It was of course guarded by a whole series of gun batteries and search-lights, all positioned high up on the cliffs over-looking the area. This section posed the greatest danger for any submarine trying to force a passage through into the Sea of Marmara.

Four months before, Lieutenant Commander Holbrook had won the first submarine naval Victoria Cross of the war by taking *B11* twelve miles up the Dardanelles into Sari Siglar Bay, where he found and torpedoed the Turkish battleship Messoudieh. She sank almost immediately, despite being protected by five rows of mines. A significant achievement as she had been the pride of the Turkish

Navy. *HMS B11* had been specially selected for the mission because she had recently been fitted with one of the latest submarine batteries, but despite them being longer-lasting, Holbrook had returned after nine hours dived with her power almost totally exhausted. He came back with tales of strong unpredictable currents, especially over on the European side of the channel. In the time that had elapsed since then, other boats had also experienced difficulties with these strange unpredictable tide-rips, which had resulted in submerged groundings and loss of control. The French submarine Saphir had been lost off Nagara Point, which intelligence suggested had probably been due to these tidal phenomena. It also pointed to the probable cause of *E15*'s tragic end.

When he had finished reading, Martin Naismith found the report somewhat disturbing. There were number of questions that began building up in his mind, as he handed the paper back to Pownal. The Lieutenant Commander then handed him a second written report. Last month, a trawler had discovered a line of buoys that supported a submerged anti-submarine net off the Suandere River. When she had gone in and attempted, with the assistance of a destroyer, to tow it away the net, they had both been driven off by shell fire from the shore batteries. So, it proved that submarine nets were now being used by the Turk. Along with the mine-fields, dangerous currents, it was another problem to be dealt with on any penetration.

"You might get some more up to date information if you go over and have a word with *Warhead* on the Flagship. Since his brother's boat ran aground, he has been making the hazards of the Dardanelles his own personal vocation. He personally has made a number of flights over the region, and has managed to draw the position of every Turkish defensive measure that is observable from the air on to the Admiralty chart of the area. He has also plotted every reported underwater hazard reported by ship and submarine incursions. He'll be over on the Flagship with Commodore Keyes. If anybody can help you, then it's got to be him. It is a bloody shame about his brother, because *Dummy-head* was certainly no fool. He is a bloody good, one of our best submarine commanders, and yet even he has been caught out by these strange currents. Do try and learn from the mistakes of others, Martin." Shaking hands with Naismith, he added, "Jolly nice to see you again, old friend. Good luck when you finally get your chance to have your own crack at Johnnie Turk."

Later that same afternoon, Norman Holbrook returned to the harbour in *HMS B11*. He reported that a low-lying mist had made it impossible for him to see *HMS E15* on the mud, so he was unable to attack her. The sortie made by the two battleships, *Triumph* and *Majestic* had also taken place that afternoon, but that too had proved to be a complete failure. Bad communications between the spotter planes and the big guns failed to achieve a single hit.

Later that night, as a direct result of all these thwarted efforts, a dare-devil team of volunteers manned two motorised picket boats from one of the battleships. They crept in under cover of darkness and attacked *HMS E15* with torpedoes that they launched from dropping gear. After an initial two misses, they did manage to achieve a direct hit just forward of the conning tower with their third weapon. It proved to be enough to prevent *E15* being towed away. The raid had been led by Lieutenant Commander Robinson, who was immediately promoted to Commander on his return, and given the DSO to go with his VC, which he had won earlier in the year.

****

On the morning of the twentieth of April, Martin Naismith went over to the battleship *HMS Queen Elizabeth* to visit Warhead, the surviving Brodie twin. A welcome strong breeze had suddenly developed, and the surface of the harbour had become quite choppy. The trapped heat had dissipated to everyone's relief, and with it thankfully, went most of the stench which was making everyone's lives an abject misery.

Charles Brodie was waiting to meet him on the quarter-deck of the battleship, as Martin Naismith was piped aboard. Despite their mutual high regard within the Trade, it was the first time that the two men had actually met each other, although Martin had met his brother several times before at Fort Blockhouse, and of course, had often spoken to him several times during the transit from Portsmouth. He could not help but stare in amazement at the uncanny resemblance between the two men.

After the two men arrived down in his huge cabin, Charles Brodie turned and immediately dispelled any possible unease that there might have existed regarding speculation of his brother's fate.

"Martin, some people are finding it difficult to talk about *E15* at this moment in time. They are obviously trying to spare my feelings about my brother's fate, no doubt. We have got to put all of that aside, and attempt to analyse the actual cause of the disaster that afflicted *E15*, so that yours, and other boats will not end up in the same predicament. You must see, that by us learning and overcoming these problems, my poor brother's loss will not have been in vain? Once everybody is aware of the dangers of these damned current's, he will not have died in vain! Indeed, he will go down in history as having been the path-finder who saved many lives. It is not so painful to talk about him now – quite the contrary now that it's been confirmed."

"Do you mean that you've had some news?" interrupted Martin.

"Yes, this morning, with the arrival of this Turkish newspaper – Roger Keyes gave it to me a couple of hours ago," he said, handing Naismith a copy of the local journal.

A translation of the article, concerning the *E15* incident, was attached to the paper with a paper clip. Martin read the relevant sections aloud.

"The Captain and three of his crew were killed outright by a direct hit on the conning tower… six other crew members were asphyxiated by chlorine gas… they were all buried on the beach with full military honours… the Captain had very pale skin."

Quietly and respectfully, Martin folded the news-sheet and handed it back to Charles, murmuring his condolences, sympathy and regrets. He thanked him and continued.

"At first I couldn't take it in. It felt like half of me had died. I always had a feeling inwardly that he was all right – still alive – that he had just been taken as a prisoner of war – but with this news I suppose that he is alright now – because he is now with the Lord, Martin."

He went over to a drawer, which had been built into the bulkhead at the end of his bunk, and withdrew a folder.

"Commodore Keyes called a conference here, while you were stuck in Malta. He had previously asked me to collect all information, intelligence, or even hearsay,

175

that I could find out about the temperature changes and tidal conditions here within the Straits. There is no information in the Admiralty Pilot, so I'm afraid there was very little that I could add to this fairly recent map, which has been supplied by our intelligence chaps, which I believe to be quite comprehensive."

He opened the folder, extracting a map and spreading it out across the table between them, he began pointing to a series of red dots and continued.

"This map is marked with all the known minefields, as you see. Norman Holbrook has conducted the most sorties up there, and he has already confirmed them. Edward Courtney Boyle is currently carrying out sea trials and practicing his crash dives in readiness of making his attempt. Just how Norman and his crew must have felt negotiating those mine-fields is truly horrifying to comprehend. Norman said that he could hear the mines mooring wires scraping down the ballast tanks. It must have filled them all with terror. Once Norman had made it through, he did strike it lucky with the Turkish battleship being anchored right in front of him. I have read his report – it was a classic set up and firing. After enduring that hell, he deserved his Victoria Cross ten times over."

Brodie then pointed to series of larger dots marked on the chart.

"The Turkish shore batteries lining the Narrows are here and here, marked by these larger red dots. We have even pin-pointed the position of the shore-based torpedo tubes, which are marked here and here with the purple ink. The green dots you can see are the searchlight positions, and as you will note, most of them are stationed adjacent to the guns. You can take this copy back to your boat and study it. Please note down anything that you may think will help you, and get your Number One and Navigator to transcribe all this information onto your own charts. I don't mean to sound pessimistic Martin, but please return this copy to me before you sail. It's the only one that I have at the moment. I will hopefully be able to add more information to it in the near future, once a boat actually makes it into the Marmara."

He went over to the drawer again, and pulled another set of papers from a second folder.

"We acquired this information from French sources," he said, handing another folded map to Martin. "It's a sketch map of the Straits that was produced by the German manufacturers, Krupps. It seems that the Germans had been trying extremely hard to sell the Turkish Navy one of their latest U-boats, and this information was a part of the package that was supplied to them. As you can see from the writing at the bottom, it claims that their dived submarine would have been able to up reach as far as Nagara Point, where the Turkish capital ships are usually holed up for the purposes of defence as they lie under the cover of several gun batteries. You had better take this as well and make sure that you study it carefully," he said, pushing it across the table to Martin. "Bring it back with the other chart, once you have copied down all of the information."

Martin studied the map carefully, and as he did so, Charles Brodie pointed over his shoulder and continued speaking.

"You will note that the German's claim a battery endurance of 13 hours at a dived speed of 4.5 knots, giving them a range of about 60 miles submerged," Brodie sighed. "Unfortunately, that was the only piece of information that I could to offer the conference. That is, with the one exception of a legendary story that I have heard… It is an old local legend that tells the tale of an expendable eunuch from the Sultan's household, who fell out of favour and was consequently strangled. His body was tied up in the customary weighted sack and dropped into the Dardanelles. Just when they thought that the unfortunate man would be well on his way down stream, heading towards the Mediterranean, he turned up again right under the walls of the Seraglio. If this story has any truth in it, then it suggests that there are some rather strange tidal phenomenon taking place here within the Dardanelles, don't you think? Maybe there is a strong undertow, that as yet we know nothing about?"

Martin nodded his head, still studying all the information that had just placed before him. He inwardly felt very pleased, because all of this information would greatly enhance his chances of success, once he was given the go ahead to penetrate the channel. He made a mental note to get Guy d'Oyly-Hughes to copying all of this information onto every relevant chart aboard *E11*, as soon as he returned to the boat.

"Of course, the Krupps information is easily the most important. At the recent conference, using these figures, we were all trying to calculate the amount of endurance a British 'E' class boat's battery could produce, given that a current of x strength at 90 feet at a speed of four knots. Roger Keyes had interrupted my calculations by saying… *to hell with algebra Warhead, can an E boat make it or not?"*

"Somerville was the first to say no, as did Pownall, and Boyle from *E14* – and unfortunately, without any categorical information at hand, so did I. The one solitary yes, came rather shyly from my brother. Keyes immediately jumped to his feet, declaring that he would be the first to give it a try. Two days later *E15* sailed, and I was aboard with them up as far as Tenedos. where I was landed via a ships boat from her escort, and I made my way straight over to the Naval Air Command flying boats that we have established at Tenedos.

Just as soon as it was light enough, I went up in a sea-plane to monitor the progress of *E15*. I was absolutely determined to note down every single aspect of their entry, passage, and what I hoped would be their arrival out into the Sea of Marmara. It was a beautiful cloudless morning, enough to give me absolutely breath-taking views of the whole Peninsula, and Straits themselves. Although it was still pretty dark, we did manage to observe *E15* diving, but then of course we lost sight of her. After an hour in the air we had return to Tenedos to refuel, but we took off again immediately afterwards. It could only have been around fifty to sixty minutes later when we arrived back on station, and as we flew across the white sandy beach below Kephez Point I spotted a slim grey pencil shaped object lying at right angles to the shoreline. It had a smaller black line coming away from it at an oblique angle. I then realised that I was looking at *E15,* and the thin black line was oily smoke that was coming out of her conning tower. A Turkish torpedo boat was already close by in the area, attempting to make an investigative landing. So, at some time during that sixty minutes that we had spent refuelling, my brother had either been hit by gunfire, or had met something that had caused his boat to ground in such a manner. It must have been adverse tides that caused him either to run up onto the mud, or forced his boat to come shallow. You can imagine that as soon as *E15* broke the surface, the Turkish gun batteries would have opened up immediately. The only outcome was total catastrophe, so we must discover more about these capricious tidal streams through the Dardanelles, Martin."

There was silence for a few moments before Brodie got up and went over to stare out of the scuttle. Finally, turning to Naismith and continued.

"Unfortunately, at this moment in time we just do not know what exactly happened to my brother, Martin. The night before he sailed, I sat down with him, and together we plotted the course he was going to take through the Dardanelles. I now think that we did not make enough allowances for these terrible underwater eddies, and the unknown cross currents that exist in this extremely hazardous waterway. The Admiralty charts of this area only tell us what is happening to the currents on the surface. We have to discover what goes on underneath. Remember the story of the eunuch, Martin?" He paused, and looked enquiringly at him, "That is about all I can tell you. Have you got any other questions that you would like to ask me?"

"Didn't our own Admiralty hydrographic record have that sort of information recorded before the war?"

"Apparently not! As I said there is no tidal information in the Pilot for this area. There are topographical drawings of the features of both shorelines, and very little else. I had already sent signals asking for everything that the Admiralty may hold on the Dardanelles before we arrived here, and I am afraid that this is all that I was given."

"Have the trawler mine-sweepers managed to get any fresh info? After all, they operate as far up as any vessel is able to get inside the Straits."

"If they discover anything new, they are under strict orders to report it back to us as soon as possible. So, we know as much as they do at this moment in time. I will arrange a flight for you in the next few days, so that you can go up and see what you are going to have to contend with at first hand. The Dardanelles is probably the most difficult and well defended waterway in the world today."

They talked a while longer. Charles Brodie described in more detail the various efforts that had been taken to try and sink *E15*, or at least to wreck her, and make her totally unusable. He did expand a little on the tidal current problems that he had experienced, when he had gone up in B6, explaining in some detail just how the boat had very nearly ended up on that very same sandbank as his unfortunate brother, saying the crew all felt the loss of control, as their boat was being forced across the channel. He reiterated on how well Norman Holbrook had done in taking *B11* up so far, saying that Martin might well have a word with him, which he should find beneficial.

"*HMS B11* had negotiated those same currents that *E15* attempted to get through unsuccessfully. It could just possibly a matter of timing. Norman may just have caught the tide at the right time, and therefore missed being pushed over onto that beach. It could be that my brother went at a later time, and had caught a different tide. That is very probably why he came a cropper. It would certainly be worth checking out the times, against the tides on both of those relevant days. Maybe you can work out the best time to make a penetration!"

Martin asked a few more questions to clarify some particular points, so that, when he had to face the same ordeal, he would not be making the same mistake. With that the meeting ended, and Martin said his goodbyes and returned to across the harbour back to *E11*.

The Commander-in-Chief Mediterranean Admiral John Michael de Robeck would need a great deal of convincing after the *E15* episode, before he was going to send another submarine operation into the Dardanelles. On the twenty-third of April however, Saint George's Day, HMAS AE2 with Lieutenant Henry Stoker still in command, had recently returned from Malta, and was being quickly stored. She had been given the second opportunity to attempt a penetration of the Straits.

Martin Naismith was livid that the Irishman's boat had been chosen over his own, but pragmatically he was aware that his command was still nowhere near ready. Lieutenant Henry Stoker had suffered another minor accident with his hydroplanes, just after starting out for the Straits, and he immediately brought AE2 back to Tenedos, where some hurried repairs were carried out. He sailed again in the early hours of twenty-fifth of April. His Rules of Engagement had been added to, and they now included him attacking the vessels that were dropping mines in the Narrows off Chanak, a new defensive measure that was being taken by the Turks, designed to protect their battleships.

The extensive preparations being taken for the troop landing operations near the mouth of the Dardanelles at Cape Helles, saw many vessels in the water around his craft, but Henry Stoker skilfully negotiated his way through them in the darkness. As she sailed off into the darkness, it was the last that was to be seen of HMAS AE2.

Still lying alongside her depot ship *HMS Adamant*, *E11* was patiently awaiting the arrival of her new shaft from Britain. Her bored crew sat in frustrated impotence. There was only so much maintenance that could be carried out without repetition. Every piece of equipment aboard the boat had been greased three times, all the internal brass hand-valves, hydroplane and steering wheels shone like a mirror, and there was not a spot rust to be found anywhere above the waterline. All of their diesel fuel had been unloaded into a lighter, where it would be held until they were ready to reload it. Being much lighter now, the submarine had risen higher out of the water – at least a full twelve inches. This freeboard would allow the Engine Room staff to safely remove the bolted plates of the pressure hull, directly above the Engine Room when the time came. The port main engine had already been completely stripped down, and dismantled as far as it could be – exposing the length of the troublesome drive shaft. The next difficult job was to fully remove the external casing directly above the Engine Room. Three separate sections had eventually been lifted off by the crane, and were now standing on the deck of *Adamant*, as did every sectional part of their port engine. The pressure hull plate bolts had then been removed, before being temporarily replaced to just finger tight so they would be ready to be quickly be removed again at short notice. Everything that could be done had been done, and now everybody sat twiddling their thumbs. Each of them knew that once the new shaft did arrive from Britain, and once it had been milled and was ready to be fitted, the real work would then begin. Following the successful fitting of the new shaft, the replacement of everything would finally mean that *E11* would at last be ready to have her chance of getting into the Marmara. Just at this moment in time, the waiting was very frustrating.

Despite keeping his eyes peeled, since arriving here, George Torode had not managed to spot Arthur Collenette aboard *HMS Adamant*. Whenever his duties had taken him over onto the *Adamant*, he made it a point to watch out for him. He did not know if he had been transferred, or if he was just keeping his head down. After making a few enquiries he had eventually found out that Arthur had been assigned to take charge of the launches that were attached to the old collier, River Clyde. These were the small craft that would be landing the troops ashore during the invasion of the Gallipoli peninsula. If Arthur was going to be exposed to the Turkish defensive fire, then just maybe a Turkish bullet would be enough to fulfil George's pledge to Matthew.

The next day was the twenty fourth of April, and all around them most of the ships in the harbour were preparing for sea. The hive of activity made it blatantly obvious that some large-scale operation was about to take place. Huge billows of smoke began erupting from all of the funnels as the furnaces were fired up, creating the acrid stench of ignited coal, oil and carbon dioxide, within the confined harbour.

Outside of the harbour, in the Aegean Sea itself, the surface had been choppy over the past two or three days, but at least it had brought with it the welcome breeze that had cooled down the anchorage. However, today the wind had dropped and the sea was calm once more, reforming its mirror like surface. These were the conditions that the Intelligence Staff had been waiting for, and they had given the order for the troop landings to take place later in the day. As the morning brightened, three of the largest transports, each of which carried battalions of troops, headed off towards Cape Helles, and Morto Bay. These ships in turn were followed out of harbour by the cruiser *HMS Euryalus*, who was flying the flag of Rear Admiral Rosslyn Erskine Admiral Wemyss. The next to follow was the battle-cruiser *HMS Implacable,* and then the battleship *HMS Cornwallis*. It was a magnificent and glorious procession of the nation's fire power.

More troops were cheering from the smaller vessels that were still awaiting their turn to leave the harbour, and the reverberation of their combined voices could be heard echoing off the surrounding slopes. It really was a great adventure.

The next to follow them out to sea was the converted collier River Clyde, the ship that Captain Humphries and his men from *HMS Reliance* had worked so hard in converting her into a landing vessel. George watched her make her way out towards the entrance, in the certain knowledge that Arthur must be aboard her somewhere. The great battleship *HMS Queen Elizabeth* followed later that afternoon, flying the flag of Vice Admiral John Michael de Robeck and also carrying General Sir Ian Hamilton, and his complete General Staff.

It was plainly obvious to anyone watching that the landings were now going ahead, as one by one the great ships in the harbour weighed anchor to join the majestic cavalcade. This parade went on for three days, ships after ship leaving the harbour, until by the end of the third day the harbour lay almost empty, leaving just the submarine depot ships, along with the expectant three hospital ships, with just a few store and repair ships. There were still at least a hundred smaller auxiliary vessels which included lighters, barges, tugs and tenders, with just a couple of defending destroyers. The great armada was on its way. The long-awaited invasion of the Gallipoli Peninsula was actually taking place. What a truly glorious adventure it all was!

During the next three days, colliers, oil tankers and store supply ships, were the only new ships to arrive. The crew's expectation rose with the arrival of every new supply ship, only to end in disappointment.

****

Lieutenant Henry Stoker of HMAS AE2 became the first Allied submarine commander to fully penetrate the Dardanelles, and survive to reach the Sea of Marmara beyond. That wonderful news arrived late on twenty fifth of April, the very same day that the Allies actually landed the first troops on the beaches at Cape Helles. Both events were very encouraging, raising everybody's moral, and were considered to be good omens!

Lieutenant Stoker reported back by means of the newly fitted radio signalling equipment that his boat had made it through the narrows, and had already managed to torpedo a Turkish gunboat on the way. The jubilation aboard the Flagship was such, that the Admiral ordered Edward Courtney Boyle in *HMS E14* start to store his boat, and make it ready to make his penetration.

HMS E14 was fuelled, stored, and torpedoes loaded in readiness, and just as soon as the task was completed, *E14* was immediately despatched to emulate the Irishman's success. She sailed very early on the morning of the twenty-seventh. Edward Courtney Boyle radioed back later that same day that he too had made it into the Marmara. Things seemed to be going remarkably well for the Allies. Maybe this was the turning point that would herald a change in the Allies fortunes!

Despite all of this good news being received, this was still an extremely boring time for George and the rest of the crew of *E11*. Everything that could be prepared had been prepared, and there was very little for any of them to do. Nobody wanted to swim in the fetid water of the anchorage, to do so would be a risk to life. So some boats were arranged to take those not required for duty ashore, and to land them onto the bare scrubby hillside so recently vacated by the thousands of soldiers. There they found a football pitch that had been carefully marked out, and cleared of the larger stones. A game was quickly arranged between the seamen verses the rest. It was good for them all to get some good physical exercise, and everybody enjoyed themselves until it was time to return.

To Martin Naismith, although he was glad that his friend had made it safely through, this was another case of history repeating itself. This whole episode had been an almost exact replication of the events when he had tried to follow Max Horton and Noel Lawrence into the Baltic Sea. They were still there, causing havoc to the German supplies of iron ore from Sweden. Where on earth was that spare shaft?

Then came a sudden and unexpected twist of fate that rammed home to him that he still had a very big part to play in this theatre. The loss of AE2 was announced on thirtieth of April, just five days after she had sailed. So far there had not been any reports of survivors. Then to make matters worse, the French submarine Joule, under the command of Lieutenant Vaisseau du Petit-Thouars, had been sunk with all hands while attempting a penetration of the Narrows on that same day. The loss of two boats in one day was weighing heavily in everybody's thoughts.

Meanwhile aboard *HMS E11*, life was becoming a humid hell. With everything having been removed from the Engine Room, there was now an unusual abundance of space, but during the day the sun heated the exposed pressure hull plates, causing them to radiate the heat down into the boat. It felt like they were all sitting inside a kettle, and the boat's interior felt like a sweat-box. The crew were very thankful to be sleeping in hammocks aboard *HMS Adamant*, where, with the open scuttles, it was just that little bit cooler than in the submarine's interior.

One bright thing occurred the very same day as the loss of the two Allied submarines, and that had been when their new shaft finally arrived at Murdos on the latest merchantman. The ship that was carrying it entered the harbour and immediately secured alongside the *Reliance*. The ships cranes then got to work

181

transferring the spare part, along with other ancillary equipment, onto the deck of the huge vessel.

Just as soon as the long shaft had been transferred onto the Repair Ship, *HMS E11* was moved across the harbour by a tug. She was firmly secured alongside, and the work of replacing the shaft began. With the cold move across the harbour came a complete change of mood: the crew's morale soared at the imminent prospect of action. There grew a new-found determination from every member to get the job as fast as they could. The Engine Room staff, aided by the rest of the crew, would all be working non-stop for the next two days.

The seamen were more than willing to give the engineers a hand, but were told they would only be called on if needed, and were to make sure that the rest of the boat was in all respects fit to sail.

On the ballast tanks, with the hull being so high out of the water, there was a line of sun-baked seaweed clinging to them. It was if it had been welded there, standing out as white against the blue paintwork. They looked rusty, despite George's effort in Malta. It was a known fact that any seaweed that was attached to the hull caused drag, slowing their speed through the water, and that it would have to be removed before repainting. A clean hull meant less drag ,and therefore was more efficient transit. That meant place less strain on the battery power needed to drive the propellers, which would increase their range and make all the difference in trying to penetrate the Dardanelles. The job would need to be completed before the weight of the new shaft and the engine rebuild caused the submarine to sink lower in the water once more. George Torode was given the task.

There were Engineers crawling all over the after end of the boat, just as soon as the Engine Room plates had been lifted off by the crane aboard the repair ship. It left a great gaping hole aft of the conning tower, exposing the power heart of the boat. Looking down into the void one could see the two 8-cylinder Vickers diesel engines that were surrounded by hundreds of pipes, exhaust gas trunking, and a spaghetti madhouse of electrical cables. The piston heads and casings in the port engine had been removed, along with the pistons themselves. The skeletal base of the engine, along with the old damaged shaft now lay bare, as if mechanical surgery was about to be performed on a giant automaton on the operation table. The looming jib of the crane panned to and fro from the *Reliance*'s well deck, removing the last pieces of machinery from around the port shaft. Then the removal of the old port shaft from its bearings was finally about to take place. This was also the engine that drove the damaged drive shaft of the troublesome Star Clutch. By the use of this clutch, the engine could be engaged to drive the port propeller, or be disengaged to allow the port main motor to drive the propeller. On the after part of the port motor was a Tail Clutch which was engaged during all drive modes, but disengaged when using the engine to drive the motor to act as a generator to charge the battery. With good luck and hard work, all of their current problems should soon be fixed.

****

George Torode went over the gangway onto the *Reliance,* and by using some heaving lines, he managed to tow a wooden pontoon around to the outboard side of *E11*. He then secured one line to the forward casing bollards, and the other to the stern of the boat. He was quick to realise that had been given one of the better assignments on board today, as he was able to remove his shirt, to work in the open-air sunshine. All around him the artificers, stokers, and mechanics were hard at work dressed in oil-soaked overalls, and sweating profusely. Their nemesis was the hot exposed metal of the pressure hole radiating the heat, because the harbour itself had definitely become cooler – due to the absence of the fleet. This had allowed a fresh breeze to enter the cauldron, and its rejuvenating effect was very welcome, but working inside this mechanical oven was very hard indeed.

During the past couple of days George had been asking a few casual questions about Arthur, as he and the rest of the crew were sleeping aboard *Adamant*. He had found out that Arthur had been definitely been detailed as one of the leading the coxswains in the small troop landing craft that were attached to the River Clyde. Apparently, that meant that he had to steer one of the lead boats in the assault on the beach. Today there had been some initial reports of the landings, and the expected victory seemed to be far from achievable, because Johnnie Turk was putting up some stern resistance. Those cutters and whalers were rowed ashore, but as they neared the beach, they came under heavy shell fire. Reports stated that several boats had been hit, causing many casualties. So, at this very moment, Arthur would be landing the troops on those beaches of the Gallipoli Peninsula under that heavy fire. George was glad that he had been forced into the forefront of the action. He pitied anyone aboard Arthur's craft, because in knowing that he was a natural coward, they would probably be in more danger from him, than they would from the Turk. He knew that Arthur would certainly never have volunteered for the task. He smiled to himself as he began his work on the tanks.

****

Basil Partridge was lying uncomfortably on his back in the port side of the Engine Room wing bilge, directly beneath the star clutch assembly, his body squeezed tightly in beside the engine fuel pump. He was straining to remove the retaining bolts from the housing plate. The diesel filled air lacked oxygen, which made him inhale a heady mix of the fumes from the oil and stagnant bilge water. The physical exertion of just trying to breath caused him to pant profusely, as his muscles strained with his spanner. The thermometer dangling over the motor revealed that it was a sticky 102 degrees. Oily water swirled around his midriff, mixing with the sweat that was running down his greasy face. Above him on the deck plates, Chief Jupp strode about like a conductor in front of his orchestra. He was shouting orders, pointing his finger, inspecting work, and lending a hand where needed. A man in his element and definitely the only man aboard with sufficient mechanical knowledge to complete this very difficult task they were all undertaking.

****

The signalman George Plowman also had a simple job. He was sitting up in the sunshine at the back of the conning tower, just behind the periscope standards, busy sewing Inglefield clips on to the new white ensigns that had just arrived from the latest supply vessel. Like George, he too had his shirt off, and he was using a sail-maker's leather palm and needle with the dexterity of an embroiderer.

At the after end of the Control Room, Albert Lohden sat wedged in behind the large imposing metallic box, that formed the basis of the radio transmitter / receiver. He was all fingers and thumbs as he tried to fit a new electrical valve component into this recently installed new piece of equipment. Albert was one of the fore-runners called radio telegraphists that had emerged within the Royal Navy, following the introduction of wireless radio as a new means of communication. This brand-new technology had only been at sea for two years, following its invention by Guglielmo Marconi who had received the Nobel Prize for Physics in 1909 for his achievement. Although the Royal Navy Signal School had tried to make the training course as comprehensive as possible, Albert had found the concepts extremely challenging and difficult to grasp. He was wishing now that he had remained as a simple Signalman. Semaphore was not that difficult. Instead of all of this electrical paraphernalia, it just involved two hand held flags. Although the Morse code had been fairly easy to learn, and the operation of the equipment was quite straight forward, he found learning the internal electronics of a transmitter a considerable challenge – and if he were to be honest, they still remained a bit of a mystery. Even now he still needed to revert to his hand manual to help him locate the defective valve, despite all of his recent training. If he ever lost this book and was forced to work without it, he felt unsure that he would be able to finish the job successfully. He was very hot being crammed into the tiny compartment, with the thermometer that hung from a hook above his head showing over one hundred degrees Fahrenheit. His sweat-soaked shirt was clinging to his back, and it felt a lot hotter than a hundred degrees. He had joined the navy to see the world. If he had not volunteered for the wireless course, he would not be here now. Oh, how he hated serving in submarines.

In the Royal Navy of 1915 there had, so far, been no qualified submariner's who had been trained in the new technology of wireless telegraphy, and as a consequence, wireless qualified surface sailors were being sent to the boats on temporary attachment to man the newly installed equipment. Unfortunately, these men did not possess any knowledge of the Trade, and were therefore considered as passengers by the crew.

It had certainly not been Albert's choice to be attached to *HMS E11*, being a man who had never enjoyed responsibility, he had been wishing for a posting to a battlewagon, where they would be several operators under the authority of a Chief Petty Officer, who would be there to take all the responsibility from his shoulders. On a big ship he would not even be noticed.

The radio shack in *E11* was only five feet square, and most of its interior was filled by bulky units of this new technology. He sat at a small wooden stool, that was placed under a narrow shelf that a Morse key had been secured to, which served as his working desk for sending messages. He had to wedge his body between the transmitter and the receiver to operate the Morse key. Being above average size, it was only just big enough to allow him to squeeze in and sit down. A larger man would have had great difficulty. The next job on his list was to fit the bridge aerial leads into the receiver – now where has that bloody manual gone?

In the wardroom Guy d'Oyly-Hughes and Robert Brown were pawing over a series of Admiralty charts that covered the whole of the Dardanelles, and the Sea of Marmara up as far as Constantinople. They lay strewn across the tiny table, with others folded neatly on the bunk behind them. From the intelligence information that the Captain had received aboard the Flagship, they were plotting the positions of all the known minefields, anti-submarine nets, plus any known submerged wrecks within the Dardanelles. On the shoreline, either side of the Straits, they had already drawn in the main gun batteries and searchlight positions. Despite working in open-necked shirts with their sleeves rolled up, the room was hot and tacky. The swirl of their cigarette smoke drifted up from the ashtray, as they sifted through the latest signals, and read the written reports for all the information from any previous incursions into the Strait by all vessels. Robert relayed the data to Guy, who transcribed the relevant information onto the chart.

Up in the fore-ends, the Torpedo-men were overhauling the torpedo firing reservoirs, and carrying out other essential maintenance on the torpedo tubes themselves. High pressure air hoses hissed as each cylinder was charged; grease guns clanked as working parts were lubricated and oiled. Incongruously, another man was sat in the corner peeling potatoes for the midday meal. After all, they still needed to eat! Being away from the galley aboard Adamant, they had use of the one here on the *Reliance*, but they had to prepare the food for the ships cooks to cook it for them.

****

At long last, Martin Naismith was starting to feel some relief that this difficult job was going well, which would bring his attempt of a penetration that much closer. A touch of pride went through him as he walked around the boat to inspect the progress that was being achieved by his crew. He often liked to watch his men at their work, feeling happy that there were no malingerers amongst them. Every one of them seemed to give their all. He knew that with men like these, he would be able to accomplish the impossible. Each of them was an expert in his own trade, and had more than healthy knowledge of everyone else's job. They would need to be good, because any mistake where they were heading could prove to be fatal to them all, and from the previous attempts, there would be no second chances. The Turkish forces were proving to be diligent, resourceful, and determined adversaries. The charred remains of *HMS E15* bore testimony to that. He needed his men to give him one hundred and ten per cent, to make sure of that they were all going to survive that dangerous passage. No matter how good they were, he was also well aware that lady luck would have a very big say in who lived and who died – and there was still the problem of those dangerous tidal currents to be solved!

At the end of April an intelligence report stated that the German cruiser Goeben was reported to have come out of its hideaway in Constantinople, and had sailed down into the Sea of Marmara to attack Allied transports located over on the Mediterranean side of the Gallipoli Peninsula. Her intention was to fire her eleven-inch shells right over the peninsula by using spotters ashore to direct their fire. However, the Germans then received intelligence that the battleship *HMS Queen Elizabeth* was present, and so Admiral Souchon had quickly abandoned this idea, and had prudently retired back towards the Turkish capital. The news of this sortie had spread like wildfire around the submarine crews, and everyone was eager for the chance to go up and torpedo her.

Even by working in shifts, twenty-four hours a day, it had still taken them nine days to remove the damaged shaft. In the meantime, the newly delivered shaft had already been milled in readiness to be fitted by the heavy workshop crew aboard *Reliance*. There would now be a brief respite while the new shaft was brought out from the internal workshop, and be finally made ready for insertion into the port engine of *E11*.

Later that morning, the men not directly employed on the work were taken ashore for exercise. Having just finished his assignment on the ballast tanks, George was amongst the group that jumped into a small boat and landed on the deserted northern slopes once more. They made their way up the gentle incline towards the now deserted camp sites, where they rediscovered the football pitch and a match was hastily organised. The competition was Seamen verses The Rest. The Rest included the Torpedo-men and Signalmen. Everyone put their all into the game, and soon a rising dust storm rose above the melees as each tackle was made, so much so that at one stage the dust made it difficult to see the goal. An enjoyable day was had by all, with the Seamen finally winning 23 – 9. The large deficit was mainly due to the fact that the seamen had an extra man. They all slept ashore that night, in a tent which they had brought with them from the depot ship, and a fire was built within a discarded camp stove to provide a cook-up on the beach.

The experience reminded George of the time that he, Matthew, and Arthur had all spent a night camped out on the edge of the Saumarez Estate on Guernsey. That seemed long ago now, and far so removed from an Island in the Aegean Sea. It almost seemed as if it had been part of another lifetime. He recalled that that camping adventure had taken place only three weeks before the cliff-top episode, when poor Matthew had fallen. Just thinking about it caused an anger rise within him at the injustice of it all. The image of Arthur running off along the cliff path, and seeing Matthew's face there in front of him crying out – "Make sure Arthur gets what's coming to him."

****

Martin Naismith went by launch across to the island of Tenedos. It was a fairly small island compared with Murdos, and he was landed at the tiny harbour's stone pier that was dominated by a derelict medieval castle. The tiny haven was packed with mine-sweeping trawlers. As he walked ashore the sun disappeared behind a dark cloud, and a light misty rain suddenly enshrouded the Island, seriously reducing the visibility. In the wet atmosphere, the group of wooden vessels looked like a local fishing fleet from any Scottish port on the North Sea. Instead of nets, these vessels carried the huge reels of serrated cutting wire. The Paravanes were a new fitting, but the Kite's and Otter Boards were more or less the same pieces of equipment as used on any fishing trawler.

As he walked towards the hastily constructed air-field, he was met by Commander Samson of the Royal Naval Air Service. He was in command of the Squadron of Airco DH2 bi-planes fitted with floats that were based here on the Island. There were also five of the latest Bristol Scout fighters. A wooden hanger had been constructed by the carpenters from the *Reliance* to serve as a workshop for the aircraft. The airstrip itself was a flat dusty stretch, that had been cleared of all the larger stones. Some of the largest stones had been painted white and laid at intervals along the edges, to mark the limits of the strip. A tall mast had been erected near the hanger, flying a wind-sock to give wind direction to the pilots when landing. There was also a cleared launching ramp that led down to the water's edge, from where the float planes could be put into the water, or hauled ashore.

Commander Sampson's headquarters was a commandeered farmhouse, which had a large white ensign flying from another newly erected mast standing over the barn. The barn itself had been converted to act as the spare parts store, and it was also where all the removable sea-plane floats were kept.

The flight he was about to embark on had been arranged for him by *Warhead* and had been specifically planned so he could personally scout the Narrows, and assess for himself the hazards that he may encounter there. The two-seater Farman bi-plane looked decidedly flimsy, but he thought that it was probably safe enough. When he climbed in the observer's seat, he was handed a machine gun by the pilot, Lieutenant Bell-Davis.

"It's just a precaution, sir – in case we should bump into a Hun fighter," he announced. "There are several units of them out here, attached to the Turks. Load up and let rip a short burst across the strip towards those trees over there."

Martin duly followed his instructions, and fired off a few rounds across the airstrip, happy to note that the weapon worked well. He had never had to actually use one in earnest before. Bell-Davis then gave the thumbs up to a mechanic, who gave the propeller a flick, and suddenly the engine fired up with a staccato burst of piston explosions. After allowing the engine to warm up, Bell-Davis taxied the flimsy aircraft out towards the end of the strip.

Although the bigger stones might have been removed, there were still plenty of medium sized ones left, because the aeroplane rocked and bumped its way towards the end of the runway before eventually spinning around. The engine note rose higher into a deafening roar, then even higher towards the scream of a banshee before Bell-Davis released the brake. They suddenly shot forward. Within a very short space of time they quickly climbing up towards the low cloud base. Martin's knuckles were white as he held onto the sides of the aircraft.

Once aloft he was hoping it would be clear enough for him to be able to spot the exact position of the mine-fields, and also be able to locate the lines of buoys that marked the recently installed anti-submarine nets. His hopes were quickly dashed however, because after they had climbed above the rain cloud the weather suddenly cleared which caused a blinding glare of sunshine to be reflected off the rippling water. He could see nothing but a dazzling sunlight.

They flew along the channel and he soon found that there were some vital pieces of information that he was able to glean, mainly the exact position and the structural architecture of the many lighthouses that lined this waterway. He asked Bell-Davis to make some low passes, and he was able to make quick sketches in his notebook of each of them. That information alone might prove to be invaluable, if he were ever to become lost navigationally.

As the light started to fail, he was rewarded with one of the most exciting sights of his life – the shining serenity of the Sea of Marmara, lying far off to the north as it spread out before them.

HMS E14 is there right now, he thought, and if I have anything to do with it, so will I be very shortly. As they crossed the waterway for the last time, his thoughts dwelt on the handsome Irishman, Henry Stoker, and his ill-fated command HMAS AE2. His loss just went to show how many more dangers still exist, even after one had negotiated all of these perils in the narrows. The latest reported intelligence now confirmed that he and his crew had been rescued, and that they all were now being held as prisoners of war, but their boat was down in the depths somewhere, along with the whole crew of the French boat Joule. Along with the loss of *E15*, trying to make it into the Marmara had cost the allies three boats – so far.

Flying back across the Peninsula, Martin could see fleets of ships, no more than just a series of pin-pricks on the silver sea, lying far away to the south west, but the newly landed army's battle lines were quite clear, even from this height. He was a little shocked when he realised just how little of the Peninsula the Allies were actually holding. Although the flight had not provided him with a great deal of new information, it had left him in no doubt as to the real dangers that lay ahead for *E11* and his crew.

On the morning of the tenth of May, the new shaft was ready for lowering into *E11*. The best estimate for completion was two days just to lower it down into position, and once it was finally installed in position, the port engine had then to be rebuilt around it. When everything was back together, an initial trial run was going to be needed, and when satisfied that everything was working correctly, then the engine room hull plates would have to be refitted to restore the boat back to its former water-tight integrity. After that, the casing fitments would have to be re-installed in place to provide the stream lining over the many external pipes and protrusions. Even after all that, there would be the storing of supplies, then spare parts to be brought down, plus the loading of torpedoes and fresh watering. Re-fueling was still to be completed before she would be ready to carry out her tests on the engine. Following that they would need to conduct a series of test dives down to their full diving depth to test her water-tight integrity. The list of jobs seemed never ending, and everybody was working flat out to get them done.

Eventually the engine was finally rebuilt, and a fueling lighter came alongside to fill one of *E11*'s tanks. Any more might cause the boat to sink dangerously low in the water, and with the pressure plates still removed, it might pose unnecessary problems. Several initial tests were run on the new engine shaft, starting at low revolutions. Then more runs were conducted to prove the newly refitted intermediate shaft replacement of the star clutch. The engines themselves were then retested by running them up to full speed. This was followed by carrying out a series of In Clutch and Out Clutch routines. It was repeated again and again until Naismith was finally satisfied that everything moved freely.

Another day passed and the Engine Room was almost back to normal. The hull plates were being readied to be replaced. The watertight integrity would have to be checked before the casing fairings were refitted. The stack of jobs seemed endless.

Finally, on the twelfth of May, *E11* was declared to be mechanically ready for sea.

It had been George Torode's nineteenth birthday the day before, on the eleventh of May, but due to the heavy workload there had been no time for any kind of celebration. He had spent most of it helping to fit the bolts that held down the external casing. At the rum issue, a few of his closest friends had given him *sippers* of their tot as a birthday present.

A tug arrived that very morning and took *E11* back across the harbour, berthing her back alongside *HMS Adamant*. No sooner than tying up, she had to be prepared to receive her full load of torpedoes. The navies E Class submarines were fitted with five torpedo tubes, each of which would receive one weapon, and there would be another five spares for re-loads. George was hauled in to lend a hand in guiding the long cylinders down through the narrow torpedo loading hatch.

While this was being done, all of the mechanical spares for the engines were being reloaded. As the final torpedo went down there was, no break for anyone, as the victualing provisions for their patrol had to be taken down and hidden away. As the stokers finished loading their spares, they were immediately employed in filling the fresh water tanks. Once this was completed an oil barge arrived alongside carrying all of their diesel oil to fill all, both internal and external, tanks. At the same time as all this was taking place, Martin Naismith ordered that both engines to be run, and both of the batteries to be fully charged. For the first time in many weeks the crew listened to the sweet sound of their own running diesels as they ran as generators. New life was being injected back into the old girl – a fresh injection of power that would provide the life-force of *E11*, something that had been absent for so long. The boat would soon become an independent living entity once more.

Whilst all of this work was being carried out, Martin Naismith had been on board the *Reliance* in an attempt to get a deck gun fitted to the forward casing, but he was told repeatedly that there were none available. In his opinion a deck gun would be just as useful as another complete reload of torpedoes. He had insisted that it be put down on record that he would definitely require one for his second patrol, making sure that the signal was made out, and he oversaw his official request dispatched in the out-going mail for approval by higher authority.

Once everything had been loaded, the crew were then employed scrubbing out the inside of the boat, dispelling all of the grimy foot-prints and dirty hand-marks left by the herds of oily engineers from the Repair Ship. Slowly but surely the boat was brought back into shape. The passageways were cleaned, paintwork scrubbed, and then re-scrubbed. Brass work was re-polished, and all of the bilges were pumped empty. Once dry, they were cleaned and also repainted. Afterwards every one of the suction filters were cleaned. Auxiliary machinery was stripped down, and any worn components replaced. The main propulsion switchboard gleamed with bright new copper contact breakers. During this time all of the hatches had remained open, to allow any faint breeze to be blown down through the boat, which gradually served to remove the foul stench of diesel oil that all submarines seem to retain in their deepest recesses.

Naismith was very aware just how hard his men had worked, and the following morning he sailed out into the open Aegean Sea to carry out tests on the engine shaft under actual sea-going conditions. Gradually the revolutions were increased and then the clutch was operated with each increase to prove that it still worked OK at each higher speed. Eventually the revolutions were wound up towards their maximum. The shaft and clutch held firm and any last doubts in Martin Naismith's mind were finally dispelled – mechanically they were ready.

"She's running sweet as a nut sir, much better than the old one," declared Chief Jupp.

"Well done Chief. You and your men have done one hell of a good job. Please give them all my sincerest thanks. All we need to prove now, is that she doesn't leak."

The sun bore down unmercifully as they approached their diving position. The recently refitted hull plates would have to be tested down to their full diving depth, as well as every other valve opening, and hull gland. Diving Stations were ordered to make the boat ready to go below the waves. Once they were submerged, besides checking the plates, every hull valve would also have to be worked, opened and shut systematically. Guy d'Oyly-Hughes, accompanied by Chief Jupp, went through the boat checking every valve and fitting was in the correct position for diving. This would convert *E11* being from a submarine on the surface, into a submarine that was ready to dive.

Finally, everything was ready. Martin Naismith then ordered both of the star clutches to be removed, secretly keeping his fingers crossed behind his back. They were both disengaged easily.

"Both clutches are out, sir," was the shout up the tower from the Control Room.

Martin Naismith breathed a sigh of relief, turning to tell George Torode to secure the upper helm, and climb down the tower hatch. Martin then took a last look around, and satisfying himself that there were no other vessels in sight other than their safety ship, which lay half a mile off their port beam, he made his way below. As he reached the Control Room deck, one of the seamen dashed up the ladder to secure the clips on the upper hatch. Adjusting his eyes to the dimness of the interior, he heard the voice of the seaman on the ladder above his head, as he reported the hatch shut and clipped.

"Slow ahead on both Main Motors – Open and flood 1,2,5,6,7 and number 8 main Kingston's," ordered Naismith.

Numbers 3 and 4 tanks were full of diesel oil. Stokers reached for respective hydraulic handles, and the hand-wheels that controlled the Kingston valves, giving confirmation that they were open to Guy d'Oyly-Hughes, who was the trimming officer. These giant Kingston valves were positioned at the bottom of each ballast tank and were now open for the sea water to flood in, but the air pressure inside prevented it from happening. Overhead, on top of those same ballast tanks, seaman unscrewed the main vent valves hand-wheels, which allowed this pressurised air to escape.

"Open main vents," he ordered.

The loud hissing roar from this escaping air was deafening. Slowly the noise faded, only to be replaced by the gurgling of agitated water as it rose ever higher against the hull inside the tanks. Under this extra weight of water, the boat slowly began to lose its buoyancy, gradually settling deeper in the water, but then it stopped – and the depth gauge needles flickered at six feet and stayed there.

"How's the bubble?" asked Martin Naismith, referring to the spirit bubble of the clinometer that indicated the angle of pitch the submarine was taking on.

"Three degrees by the stern, sir."

"Flood the auxiliary tank," he ordered.

Both of the needles on the depth gauge flickered, and then started to move downwards again.

"How is she now, Coxswain?" he bellowed.

"We are horizontal at ten feet, sir."

"Take her down to twenty feet. Close all main vents," ordered the Captain.

The submarine's positive buoyancy had now been sufficiently reduced to allow the Coxswain and the Second Coxswain to spin their brass wheels which operated the hydroplanes, or horizontal rudders, with which they controlled the boats depth. Coxswain Dowell operated the after planes, whilst the Second Coxswain operated the fore planes. At twenty feet the conning tower was just awash.

"Up periscope," ordered Naismith.

The periscope hydraulic ram hissed, and the hoisting wires rumbled on their metal guide wheels as the hooded lens was forced up clear of the surface water. Grasping the control handles, Naismith circled slowly around the periscope well from which it had just emerged, with his eye glued to the single viewer. Scanning the full horizon sector by sector, he noted the position of the trawler standing by as their safety number.

"Down periscope."

The tube slid down, disappearing back into the deep well in the Control Room deck.

Guy d'Oyly-Hughes and Chief Jupp then went through the boat, carefully inspecting each compartment for leaks. Valve by valve, every hull gland, was individually checked. In the Engine Room they checked every single bolt that held the steel hull plate in place, for any sign of a leak. There were none.

Stage by stage the submarine went down, twenty feet at a time, all the way down to one hundred and twenty feet, repeating the same sequence each time. She was pronounced sound after the final check at maximum diving depth, and they quickly returned up to periscope depth. Martin Naismith was a very happy man. His boat was finally fully fit and ready to engage the enemy.

"Shut main vents," he ordered. The louds thumps reverberated through the boat as the tanks were sealed off.

"Surface," he ordered.

High pressure air screamed from the tooled brass manifold, along the pressurised pipes, and into the top of each of the main ballast tanks. This time the top main vents had been shut, but the Kingston valves remained open. The pressurised air quickly massed at the top of each tank, forcing the seawater downward and out through these flood holes in the bottom of the tanks. Positive buoyancy was re-created in the vessel once more.

Shut 1,2,5,6,7 and 8 Kinston valves," he ordered.

Martin Naismith climbed the conning tower ladder up to the bridge. Below, both Guy d'Oyly-Hughes and Coxswain Dowell breathed a satisfied sigh of relief.

George Torode was ordered aloft to the upper helm, opening up the pressure to be able to take over control of the main rudder from the lower helmsman below, in steering the boat. They proceeded to make their way back towards *HMS Adamant*, where the final top up of fresh water and stores were made. The crew were then informed that the submarine would sail the following day for the island of Imbros. The penetration was on!

****

It was at this time that the submarine superiority enjoyed by the Allies within the Mediterranean was abruptly brought to a halt. Unbeknown to them, the Germans had secretly been transporting pre-constructed units of a U-boat's pressure hull down from the Krupps construction yards in Northern Germany, transporting them overland by train to be shipped down the River Danube by barge. Each of these units was then transported overland by rail to the port of Pola, on the Austrian coast along the northern Adriatic Sea. In the Dockyard there, during the latter half of 1914, and during the first four months of 1915, these sections were re-assembled until finally the complete U-boat was fitted out and launched. All of the stores and weapons for

191

the boat had been transported down in the same manner. Work had already begun on the construction of a second unit. Once the initial sea trials of this first unit had been completed, she had been pronounced seaworthy and her captain Lieutenant Otto von Hersing sailed the prototype, the U-21, down through the relatively quiet waters of the Adriatic. This would the first U-boat that had been able to breach the blockade at the Straits of Gibraltar. From this point forwards there would be submarines opposing each other in the Mediterranean, which for some time the Allies had considered as their own private lake. On reaching the Ionian Sea, Otto von Hersing brought U-21 around to port, heading eastward as he began his search for targets.

****

Firmly entrenched on the southern tip of the Gallipoli Peninsula, the Allied Army had managed to establish a small bridge-head, but at the cost of a great many casualties. The dogged Turkish army fought valiantly to dislodge them, attacking the Allied lines continuously for three days without respite. This action, which took place on the first, second and third of May was later to become known as the Battle of Krithia. Counter attacks by the Allies were then equally repulsed on the sixth, seventh and eighth of May. A stalemate ensued, as both armies began to dig in to form trench systems that were now so prevalent on the Western Front.

****

The highest point of land on the whole Peninsula was Achi Baba, which dominated the whole area of the south-eastern peninsula, and it still remained in Turkish hands. From this vantage point, the Turkish spotters were able to direct their heavy guns to rain shells down on the beleaguered Allied troops. Despite several bombardments from the allied battleships, they had failed to dislodge these troublesome Turkish gun-layers. However, this massive fire-power did have the effect of causing the enemy to pull back some of their heavy artillery out of sight from the capital ships, to leave just the spotters, who continued to direct them. The Turkish generals quickly learned not to expose their troops to this demoralising fire from the Allied artillery, and they cunningly pushed their trench lines so close to those of the Allies, that any further bombardment would have cause casualties on both sides. Supplying the front lines quickly became a logistical nightmare which caused many shortages of ammunition – a headache both for the Turk and Allies alike.

****

The losses at sea continued to mount with the sinking of *HMS Goliath* by a Turkish torpedo boat, near the entrance to the Dardanelles, which caused a heavy toll in lives. On the fourteenth of May, Admiral de Robeck transferred his flag to the battleship *HMS Lord Nelson*, while his former head-quarters, *HMS Queen Elizabeth*, sailed back to join the Home Fleet in England.

****

When it was reported to Commodore Keyes that *HMS E11* was in all respects ready for sea, he gave the order that on the next radio contact with Edward Courtney Boyle in *E14* in the Sea of Marmara, that she was to return from his patrol with immediate effect. He told Martin Naismith to be patient and await her arrival, and to use the interim period to get his crew to the peak of readiness.

So, Martin took them out and used the time to practice crash dives, rapid surfacing, and every emergency procedure in the book. They used an anchored trawler to come alongside to carry out their boarding party drills. Martin Naismith and Guy d'Oyly-Hughes tried to recreated every problem that they could expect to encounter on their forthcoming patrol. During this period, Naismith demonstrated to his men how well their craft handled, by giving them full confidence in the reliability of their boat. He purposely took *E11* down beyond the maximum limit of her depth gauges, levelling off at two hundred feet. He could not help but notice the fear in the eyes of his men, as the First Lieutenant and Chief Jupp had searched nervously through the boat for any leaks, but save for a small trickle on one of the new rivet bolts in the hull-plates above the engines, she held firm. It was a relieved crew that brought her back to periscope depth. As the men became more proficient at their individual trade, personal confidence in their own ability climbed. Morale for their forthcoming patrol was extremely high.

****

George Torode had been assigned the 'Diving' and 'Action Station' of Control Room Messenger, which involved him standing alongside Petty Officer Green, who stood at the lower helm steering position. If by any chance during an action Petty Officer Green should be injured, or lose consciousness, George would immediately take over steering the boat. His main job however, was to run and relay messages to the various parts of the boat, where the crew were closed up at their stations. He felt strangely pleased with this duty, as from where he was standing, he had a grand-stand view of all the action that would be taking place within the Control Room. It was rather like having the best seat in the theatre.

****

Despite receiving many birthday good wishes from his crewmates, the main highlight of George's birthday was, by a lucky coincidence, a letter from Gladys. It had been written two weeks before. As he carried the precious letter down from the depot ship mail office, he tried to recall his previous birthday. Last year at home there had been many cards wishing him well, which he had placed up along the mantelpiece. This year there were no cards from home, and certainly no celebration – he would have given anything to have another party with trifle and custard that his mother always made by way of a celebratory treat. Out here serving in a theatre of war, birthdays seemed to lose all meaning, and all that anybody really wished for as a present, was to live to see their next birthday.

He sat himself down on one of the reload torpedoes in the fore-ends of the boat and tore open the envelope. Gladys related the latest news from home, and had also enclosed a recent photograph. To George she looked more beautiful than ever. As he studied her face, he realised with a shock that he had almost forgotten what she looked like. That would never happen again, not now that he had a likeness of her, and he decided that he would fix the photograph inside his cap, so that she would always be close to him.

****

The following day, during the next series practice dives the men were ordered to exchange positions. Stokers were to be seen steering the boat. Engine room artificers were operating the hydroplanes. Seamen went aft and attended to the electrical switchboards, which were normally operated by the Torpedo-men. The signalman was sent aft to the Engine Room to start the diesel engines. On the next watch, they would swap round again, until everyone was proficient with each man's job on the vessel.

The only one exempt was Albert Lohden, the telegraphist. Being a part of the surface navy, he could not be trusted with the undersea world operations, despite the fact that he risked his life just the same as the rest of them did. George was sent down to the motor room switchboard to gain experience in the operation of the main breaker and field switches. These controlled the power from the batteries, that was directed onto the electric drive motors, which in turn, drove the propeller whilst dived. He felt a thrill as he turned the field hand wheel, and could feel the boats propellers responding to his touch. The only component in the boat that none of the submariners attempted was the radio equipment – because nobody knew anything about what was involved – so that was left entirely to the radio operator. Although wireless radio was an alien science, most of the crew knew the Morse code.

The final test that Naismith demanded from his crew was that they operate the boat in almost total darkness. By breaking the internal power supplies from the battery, it not only meant that every light would go out, but it also would mean the loss of hydraulics, and along with all the normal jobs that the machinery normally moved would suddenly have to be operated manually by using only the back-up emergency hydraulic systems. These were operated by a hand-pump. In the resultant pitch darkness, the only discernible light came down through the periscope eyepiece, and by the time the submarine had reached 90 feet this too had disappeared. Working the hand pump continuously was physically exhausting work, and the men often had to swap positions. Two minutes of hard pumping quickly had the fittest of individuals panting for breath. Their muscles forced oil pressure to along the supply lines to move the hydroplane rams that operated the rudder and hydroplanes. It was a painfully slow, step by step task, but provided a very primitive form of control. It was a very frightening experience, and was where their knowledge of being in the Trade was most essential. All unnecessary machinery, including the one and only ventilation fan, had been shut down when the power had been switched off. Suddenly there was an eerie silence, and this alone, coupled with the total darkness was quite unnerving. The sound of rippling eddies of water could be heard passing over the external hull projections, which seemed amplified out of all proportion. It was so dark that George could not even discern the outline of Petty Officer Green, although he was standing right next to him. It was like being totally blind. The compass illumination had gone, and it was only after one's eyes grew accustomed to the dark that they could they faintly discern the white needle and numbers on the depth gauge. Everyone was told to stay at their positions and simply carry out any job they were ordered to do. The sound of their breathing was the only indication of the presence of other people around the Control Room.

Naismith possessed a calm reassuring quality that inspired complete trust from his men. He was one of those people who would push himself to the limit, leading his men from the front, in the full knowledge that his crew would be right there behind him. In the past, he had been known to quickly reject men who had been drafted to *E11* who did not measure up to his high standards. The crew knew that they were a select, elite band, hand-picked, and by being so, they form a professional team which made them all feel proud. Their faith in Naismith was complete, because they knew that he was able to do any man's job himself, and they all trusted him utterly. He was their best chance of surviving this conflict. If he were to order them to go through the gates of hell, there would be no questions as to why! They would do their best to get him there as fast as they could. Once he was satisfied that all the systems could be managed without the use of power, Naismith brought the boat back up to periscope depth. The spot of light suddenly reappeared at the periscope's eyepiece, lighting up his face. Finally, they surfaced.

The very next day they moved from *HMS Adamant* to lay alongside the destroyer *HMS Grasshopper*, who was anchored over at Cape Kephalo. Both of the submarine diesels were left running to charge the batteries up to their absolute maximum capacity. They were going to need every last ampere hour of power available. George vaguely remembered seeing some of this destroyer's crew in the Dog and Duck in Portsmouth on that night of shame, but he did not recognise any of them.

Martin Naismith had told his men to relax for the day, write letters home, and to get as much rest as possible. After all their hard work the crew were only too glad to have a day off, and most of them spent it swimming over the side. They had also been told to lie out in the sun, get a tan, as they might not be seeing much solar radiation for some time. They were often called sun dodgers by the surface navy. They all knew that with the uncertainties of what lay ahead of them they would not be able to write again for some time. George wrote a ten-page marathon of a letter to Gladys, thanking her for the photograph, and declaring his never-ending love for her. He ended it by telling her not to worry about him. When he had finished, he just hoped that his words sounded more convincing than some of the nagging doubts that he felt inside. His fears about Gladys being pursued by persistent suitors had been somewhat quelled by her recent letter, and he hoped that his words in this epistle would do the same for her. Try as he might to forget it, he was still feeling guilty about the girl in Malta. The fact that he had been unfaithful so easily had played on his mind ever since, and he knew that he had broken an undeclared trust between the two of them. It was strange feeling of guilt, because at the same time he also felt very glad that it had happened, and was completely sure that he did not love Gladys any the less because of it. He would not care if he never saw that Maltese girl again, but it had been his first sexual experience, and for that reason alone he knew that he would always remember her. He just wished that it could have been with Gladys. It was so easy to blame the war, and use it as an excuse for a lot of things.

After placing his finished letter on the Coxswains bunk ready to be posted, George decided to go up and have a swim. Everyone was swimming either naked, or near naked, so he stripped to his passion killers and climbed the conning tower ladder. The top of the casing was littered with members of the crew in various stages of damp undress, all enjoying the pleasant weather. George sought out his friend

Basil, and dragged him away from his sunbathing to go diving over the side of the boat. Once they were in the water, they decided to explore the various underwater fittings that he had recently been painting. They began by simply duck-diving down the side of the ballast tanks, but then gradually they went much deeper. By them holding their breath, they swam down under the stern and found themselves gliding between the propeller shafts, and then moving in and around the three metal blades on each shaft. The rudder and hydroplanes proved to be ideal to hang onto, until they were forced to the surface, with their lungs bursting for air.

"This is bloody good fun, Baz," gasped George, as they trod water.

"Yeah," said the stoker. "Let's go down again, and this time I'll try and swim right under the keel and see if I can come up on the other side. Are you game?"

"Yes mate. We'll have to be careful that we don't come up under the wooden pontoon that is between us and the *Grasshopper*," warned George.

Basil nodded, and they both took a great lung-full of air, duck-diving below the surface. The water was crystal clear, and each rivet and bolt became plainly visible. Below the boat, the sun's rays failed to penetrate more than forty feet before the darkness of the deeper water absorbed them. George kicked his legs hard, sending himself down, down, swallowing hard to clear the increased pressure on his eardrums. On nearing the keel, he turned and looked back up towards the surface, watching the kaleidoscopic spectrum of sunbeams flickering as they pierced the rippled surface. Through the hull he could clearly hear the throb of the diesel engines, and was surprised when he heard the footsteps of someone walking along the deck-plates inside the boat. Basil arrived at his elbow and gave him a thumb's up sign. They glided along the keel before he pointed skywards, leading the way up the other side of the boat to the small gap between the two warships. They laughed at each other as they broke surface, with water running in torrents from their hair. Looking up at the towering grey sides of the destroyer, they saw two heads looking down enviously at their antics from the guard-rails.

"Ain't yu submariners got nuffin' betta ter do than go swimmin'?" shouted one of the sweaty surface sailors.

"Why – would you like to sail with us on our next patrol then, mate?" shouted Basil in reply.

The two sailors gave them the 'rather you than me' look, that George had seen often before. The two heads disappeared, much to the amusement of the two submariners.

Chapter Nine

The Penetration

Down in the clammy Wardroom of *HMS E11*, Martin Naismith had been sitting trying to work out the reason why so many submarines were finding the navigation of the Dardanelles so difficult. Why for instance had both *HMS E15* and *HMS B11* been pushed right across the channel, resulting in such deadly consequence for Theodore Brodie and his crew?

Guy d'Oyly-Hughes and Robert Brown were pouring over the charts that were spread across the chart table in the Control Room, as Martin pondered over the significant dangers that he and his men were going to faced. He began trying to match all the known facts against the unknown questions. One would naturally expect the submarine battery endurance to be a decisive factor, or mine-fields and other man-made hazards within the narrows to be the most dangerous things, but nearly every one of the fatalities so far had fallen foul of these natural hazards that they had unexpectedly encountered within this waterway. So therefore, it was these natural dangers must present the greater threat to their survival other than anything the Turks could devise, and he was very well aware that he had very little time to find the answer before they sailed.

From all of the Admiralty Pilotage Manuals available, along with every chart he could find of the area, and with all of the information shown to him, Martin knew that there was nothing obviously unusual. From his knowledge of tidal geography, he knew that there were some known phenomena that occurred in certain waterways around the world. He began searching through every expedition report into the narrows that he could find, thinking that they might finally come up with, what was at least would be a logical answer. When he had recently questioned Charles Brodie about his experience in *B11*, he had told him that the boat had been physically carried laterally across the channel, and almost dumped onto the mud shoal. He also said that initially they had been at periscope depth, when for some unknown reason, they had been unable to dive deeper than 40 feet. Then after the boat was carried across the channel, just as they thought that it would dump them on the shoal, it felt as if the boat was falling through space, as it went straight down to 90 feet. The exact opposite was then experienced by Norman Holbrook, who had then they had found it very difficult to come shallow again – but for some unexplained reason they also found that they could not go deeper than ninety feet either. It had been like they were stuck at that depth, and there were some unknown phenomena that was preventing them going deeper. Therefore, that depth of ninety feet must be a pivotal factor in what was occurring within the channel, and it must have a lot to do with all the other strange events that was taking place. Having listened intently to Brodie's account, and by him recalling his school geography lessons, it gave him a clue for further speculation. The physical mechanics of any broad fast flowing river that meets a sudden bend creates a series of forces that are known phenomena.

1. The river flow travels faster on the outside of a bend or curve, than it does on the inside due to centrifugal forces, and this excessive speed tends to cause water to ride up the outer bank.
2. This rising water, in trying to find its own level, then rolls over towards the inner side of the bend, causing a surface cross current.
3. This movement therefore produces an upward current on the outer side of the rivers curve, and a downward current on the inside, which then serves to increase the cross surface current effect.
4. Along with the forward motion of the water, a corkscrew action takes place in the direction of flow.
5. This clockwise, or anti-clockwise movement is determined by the direction in which the bend occurs. For instance, a right-hand bend will cause a clockwise corkscrew in the direction of flow, while a left-hand bend will cause an anti-clockwise motion.

Martin Naismith sat back astonished, suddenly realising that he had found the answer. He felt like someone had opened the curtains in a darkened room, but then he realised that this known theory would only partly explain why *B11* started off on the outer side of the bend at Kephez Point, and could not get below 40 feet. That failure to dive deeper had almost certainly had been due to the up-flow of the current on that outer side – it was the only logical explanation! This same synopsis would also explain why she was carried bodily right across the channel by the surface cross current and was almost thrown onto that shoal. That same scenario would also apply to what had happened to *E15*, but unluckily for her, she had become stuck fast on the mud of the inner bank. As a direct consequence she had met her fate at the hands of the Turkish gun batteries. *B11* on the other hand, had luckily managed to slide off the shoal and once off, she had experienced the falling effect caused by the downward flow on the inner curve of the river which would have naturally taken them deep. That all seemed to add up nicely, but what Naismith had not yet worked out was what forces had held *B11* at 90 feet, and prevented her from going any deeper. There was one more unexplained thing. Just what was that strange phenomena occurring at ninety feet? Obviously, that downward current would explain the difficulty they had trying to come shallow, but there was something else down there that was playing a pivotal role. There was a mystery force of some description lying down at ninety feet!

The more that he thought about this geographical hypothesis, the more certain he was that his theory answered most of the known enigmas that had been experienced by the Allied submarines. In his attempt at trying to explain the unknown factor, he had come up with an as yet unproven theory. As with the story of the eunuch in the weighted sack, which had unexpectedly returned to the point at which he was dumped into the water, something very similar could be happening down at ninety feet. Despite the fact that the surface current was heading south from the Black Sea, carrying down fresh water down through the Sea of Marmara and the Dardanelles into the Mediterranean, Martin figured that there was a strong possibility that this surface current may be riding over another, as yet unknown submerged current – two completely independent currents, one above the other. The salt water of the Mediterranean meeting the colder down-flow currents of much fresher water from the Black Sea and the Sea of Marmara might be the cause of such an effect? The only way that these two such large masses of water could pass each other was by one riding over the other, otherwise it would result in extreme turbulence. Could it be that the magical depth of ninety feet was where these two currents passed each other? Due to the corkscrew effect of the upper layer, it would be impossible for them to pass each other laterally. If it did so, then violent eddies and whirlpools would occur as the two currents fought for supremacy. Another known physical fact is that fresh water is lighter than salt water, and therefore a boat with a trim calculated for salt water will certainly have underwater control problems once it sails into fresher water. This theory would provide an explanation as to why *HMS B11* fell from the shoal, but could not get below 90 feet. It was because she fell through fresh water, and then had hit the undercurrent of sea water. He sat back, and gave a sigh of satisfaction. Could it all be as simple as that?

It was the only logical explanation that he could come up with, and just maybe it would be this conjecture that would provide the answers that would protect *E11* and her crew. If his theory did prove to be correct, then logically the depth where the two currents met would have to be somewhere around 90 feet. That figure should remain fairly constant, from here at the mouth of the Dardanelle's, right up through to the Bosporus, and into the Black Sea beyond. He was also very well aware that this was all pure speculation, and that there would be only one way of proving it. It was a pity that he had to stake his, and the lives of his crew in doing that. Poor *B11* and *E15* had gone into those hellish waters like blind-folded guinea-pigs, and both had suffered the consequences. Maybe the lessons learned from their misfortune would provide the help he needed for him to make *E11*'s entry successful! Hopefully Edward Boyle, in *E14*, would yield yet more information for him, when he returned from his current patrol – he was due back this evening.

He went out to the chart table, and began to explain his theories to his two fellow officers. Both listened intently, and both seemed very impressed, agreeing with the basic principles of his theory. Armed with these new thoughts, the three of them moved back into the wardroom, bringing the relevant charts with them. Using his new hypothesis, they started noting where the bends occurred during their transit, and tried re-plotting their intended course through these perilous hazards, along the whole course of the Dardanelles. It occurred to Naismith that there had been other submarine captains who had recently perished in these dangerous waters, who must have sat in their own wardrooms, just as he and his fellows were doing right now, studying all the available information to them and laying off much the same courses. They must have felt just as confident as he did right at this moment. Their excitement at the coming adventure must have been the equal to his, and yet all of their planning had ended in their destruction. The only navigational difference that Naismith could offer that would be different from theirs, was to keep as close as possible to the European side of the channel to avoid the corkscrew effect, and in doing so he hope that it will be enough to stop him being rolled over towards the Asian bank. When they made their entry, and took the initial dive, it would certainly be worth going straight down to ninety feet to test his two current theories. Unfortunately, all of these theories had to be proven, and to verify this one he would be risking everything, but by him knowing the truth about the phenomena, it would allow him to make the right corrections before those forces could affect the boat. So, it would allow him to remain totally flexible in all of his decisions in going forward, and that would hopefully be enough to carry them all safely through the other obvious dangers.

There was one other serious source of concern that Martin was faced with, and that was the battery endurance of *E11*. The first eight miles of the Straits should be navigable on the surface at night in reasonable safety by using their main engines. There were known to be some Turkish mobile gun batteries along this stretch on the Asiatic shore, but fortunately there were only two searchlights. He was pretty confident that he could continue charging his batteries right up until the point when he would be forced to dive. Then, once dived, those last and most dangerous twelve miles would have to be made submerged. It was also along this stretch where the most of the Turkish heavy-gun batteries were located, and there were several more powerful search-light positions dotted along this section of the Asiatic shore. By calculating for known head-on tidal streams, and the known currents that would mean a passage of nearly twenty hours underwater. The most economical dived cruising speed of *E11* is three knots, and he became more than little worried when he noted on the charts that there were a series of adverse currents of up to four knots around Nagara Point, right down to the narrows at Kalid Bahr and the Chanak area. This would mean that he would be forced to increase his speed up to seven knots to maintain his Dead Reckoning, and as a direct consequence of this would very rapidly exhaust his battery power. The only logical answer to the problem was to make this part of the penetration on the surface at night, a distance of approximately four miles. This would also enable him to recharge *E11*'s batteries at the same time, but it would also place him directly under the Turkish guns, and if one of those search-lights detected their presence, *E11*'s life expectancy could be measured in a matter of minutes. Despite a thorough search of the charts, there was nowhere along that whole stretch of the Dardanelle's where he would be out of range of the enemy's guns. It was certainly a testament to the Turkish Army's defensive planning. His only hope lay in stealth, and by him using the intelligence that Charles Brodie had given him. Any useful data that Edward Boyle would be bringing back was going to be extremely useful, and would naturally be an added bonus.

While he was considering this, another thought occurred to him. The Krupps map that Brodie had shown him suggested that contrary to the Admiralty information, the currents were actually much weaker than stated by as much as one knot against him in this particularly dangerous four-mile sector. If this proved to be true, then he should be able to make the dived transit without too much difficulty. With so much conflicting and ambiguous information, Martin decided that he was going to keep an open mind, and let all eventualities they met dictate his course of action. It was good to have all of this information, but he knew that Lady Luck would be playing an even bigger part in the eventual outcome.

There was a knock on the wardroom door. It was a messenger, sent from the radio office aboard *HMS Grasshopper* carrying the latest Intelligence Report. It stated that the Turks had been sighted dumping large metal obstructions, including an old iron bridge, into the main channel off Nagara Point. This fact, coupled with the obvious dangers from mines and anti-submarine nets would present him with the single most difficult voyage that he had ever undertaken. It was definitely going to be much more difficult than his attempt to breach the defences at the Narrows near Copenhagen, when he had tried to enter the Baltic Sea – where he had been forced to retreat. Despite the presence of the enemy guns, he decided that he would surface as often as he possibly could, not only to charge his batteries and firmly establish his position, but also to rejuvenate the air within the submarine which would get quite foul very quickly. So, between the three of them they laid off several courses on the chart that allowed for both a surface passage, and another one dived. He also allowed for both shallow and deep transits, above and below ninety feet – just in case his theory proved itself. He was very well aware that his plans were a bit of a hit and miss affair, but at least they provided him with a flexible course of actions for any eventualities.

There was another knock at the door. It was a messenger from *HMS Grasshopper* to say that there was a picket boat alongside, waiting to take him across to the Flagship to attend a debriefing, and to dine with the Admiral.

Debriefing! Of course, that must mean that Edward Boyle in *E14* had arrived back from the Marmara! He just hoped that Edward would have some of the answers to some of his questions. Quickly changing into his mess undress uniform, he tried to brush off the many stains and grease marks on the fabric. The acrid smell of diesel had impregnated the material, but there was nothing that he could do about it. Everybody, and everything aboard *E11* smelled the same. Before he went, Naismith reminded Guy d'Oyly-Hughes not to overcharge the batteries, and to be ready in all respects to sail just as soon as he returned. At least he hoped that tonight they would finally be getting their sailing orders. The crew had certainly worked hard enough to get them.

Aboard *HMS Lord Nelson*, as he knocked on the door of the Admiral's cabin, he entered to find Edward Courtney Boyle, the Captain of *HMS E14*, sitting with Admiral de John Robeck himself. Roger Keyes, Charles Brodie and an assortment of the Admiral's Staff Officers were also sat around the table listening to him with interest. Martin quickly noticed that Edward Boyle was the only man in the room whose uniform was in a worse state than his own. Except for the paleness of his skin, and a distinct redness around his eyes, there was nothing to indicate the tremendous strain that his friend had recently been subjected to. He had just driven his boat through the most dangerous waters on the planet, and the tiredness and fatigue on the man's face made Martin Naismith feel rather selfish, as he thought of how many question's he had lined up for him. The trouble was this tired looking man could hold the key between his own success and possible failure.

Bidding the Admiral good evening, and passing his congratulations across the table to Edward for the successful completion of his patrol, Martin sat down.

Almost immediately Edward Boyle began his patrol report. He spoke with a dreamy, somewhat poetic quality to his voice, which sounded as if he had just returned from the moon. He exuded an air of detachment, as he started to describe his experiences in the Marmara. He began by relating the amount of surface traffic that he had witnessed, detailing their size and the observed loads that were being taken over the water to reinforce the Turkish Army on the peninsula.

From his account, it had seemed to have been a somewhat frustrating patrol. He stated that he had managed to torpedo two Turkish transports. One of them was very large, but he could not confirm that it had actually sunk. He had also hit another supply ship, but his torpedo had failed to explode. In fact, he had experienced several problems with his torpedoes, some had failed to run and others had not detonated on impact. Martin noted down this fact, trying to think how he could get his men to overcome the problem.

Edward Boyle gave little mention to the entrance and exit strategies that he had employed, preferring to dwell on the enemy activity in the Sea of Marmara. He said that he had kept his rendezvous with HMAS AE2, and had actually spoken with Henry Stoker himself for a quarter of an hour. He said that the Irishman in AE2 had also experiencing trouble with defective torpedoes. He had arranged to rendezvous with Stoker again the next day, but that meeting had never happened. He looked stunned when they informed him of AE2's fate. During his transit back to Cape Kephalo, Edward said that he had had an excellent chance to sink the Turkish battleship Turgut Reiss, but unfortunately, he had no torpedoes left, except for a defective one that had a broken air supply pipe. Altogether he had had a frustrating patrol.

Naismith felt some sympathy for the man, realising that it had obviously been a patrol of so many nearly moments, but very few definite achievements. The torpedo problem sounded the most worrying!

While Charles Brodie was getting Edward Boyle's report typed up, Naismith took the chance to question *E14*'s captain closely about his navigation of the Dardanelle's.

What were the strengths of the current at various points, and at what depths?

Where did he manage to recharge his batteries?

How observant were the Turk gun batteries?

What leading marks were visible through the periscope for navigation at night?

How much warship traffic was there?

Did he meet any of the new anti-submarine obstructions that had been reported?

These questions and many others needed to be answered.

Poor Edward Boyle did his level best, but he was somewhat vague about many of the important factors that Martin had hoped he would be able to clarify. He was just pressing a point, when he was interrupted.

"Are you ready to sail, Martin?" asked Commodore Keyes.

"Yes sir, in all respects. The batteries are being fully charged as we speak," he replied.

Keyes looked up the table towards the Admiral, who gave an imperceptible nod.

"Then you're going in tonight, Martin. You will sail at 0100. Collect your patrol orders from my office before you catch the boat back over to *E11*. I think I speak for the Admiral and his Staff when I say good luck and good hunting."

There were murmurs of Hear-Here from all of the Staff Officers.

'At long last,' thought Naismith. The thrill of the moment coursed through his veins, and after so many disappointments and a forbidding series of serious defects, he savoured it to the full.

The Admiral and his Staff had other business to attend to, so Brodie, Boyle, and Naismith withdrew to Brodie's cabin to continue their discussion. Brodie and Naismith were elated by the information that Boyle had brought back about the significant sea traffic in the Marmara. The various problems with the torpedoes were more than a little worrying, and Martin had already decided that he would get his torpedo-men to thoroughly check over each and every weapon that they carried aboard. As their meeting drew to a close, the three of them were again summoned by the Admiral, and ushered into his private suite. The great man sat imposingly at the head of the table, with his dinner guests on either side.

Admiral de Robeck was a rugged, dominating individual, looking resplendent in his mess undress uniform. He greeted them cordially and offered them a glass of sherry. Besides Commodore Roger Keyes being there, who was the commander of all submarine operations out here in the Gallipoli campaign, there sat Sir Ian Hamilton, the commander of all the Allied land forces, and his Chief of Staff, General Braithwaite. Admiral Wemyss was also present. He was in charge of all the logistical support, and also formed the principal liaison between the Army and Navy. It was he who had been the initial architect in organising the establishment of the harbour base here at Murdos, which had allowed the Allies the time to amass men and equipment prior to the landings.

Martin Naismith was then made privy to all of the latest developments ashore. The Turks had been furiously attacking the Allied beach positions during the night of seventeenth of May. They had eventually been repulsed, but not without heavy casualties. The overall picture of the war in the eastern half of Europe was not good, and was giving everyone some cause for concern. Hundreds of miles to the north of here, the Russian Army was in disarray, and apparently in full retreat. It was therefore becoming more and more urgent for them to force the Dardanelles in order to relieve that pressure. Then much needed weapons and supplies could be transported to up the Russians via the Bosphorus and Black, Sea to the ports in the Crimea.

In the latest news from home, he was given an up-to-date on the latest political confrontation between Winston Churchill, who was the First Lord of the Admiralty, and Lord Jacky Fisher, the First Sea Lord. From the very beginning, it had been Churchill who had initially come up with this plan to try and force a passage through the Dardanelles and enter into the Marmara using the Navy's big ships. Once they had got through, the city of Constantinople would be at their mercy, and therefore the unhindered access through the Bosporus would be assured. He had persuaded Lord Kitchener to make eighty thousand men available, so that Turkey could be forced out of the war to make Germany to fight on two fronts. It had been Fisher who had stated that the operation needed troops ashore, to back up the naval attack. Had Admiral Carden's attacks on the forts during February and March been pursued with more verve and vigour, then the Allied armed forces would now be standing on the Galata Bridge in Constantinople. His timidity had permitted the Turks the time to build up their defences, and in doing so they had done a damned good job. Trying to breech the narrows with big warships was now a virtual impossibility, and that was why twenty-nine thousand men had been landed at Cape Helles and Gaga Tepe. The main intention was to capture the whole peninsula, and from there they could eliminate the gun batteries on the Asian shore to give access to the fleet. Unfortunately, the time that it had taken to amass such a force had again given the Turks yet more time to prepare for their arrival, and it was now going to be an extremely hard task to dislodge them. The enemy had the advantage of having all the high ground, and the strategic strong points. A situation that must be extremely worrying for Sir Ian Hamilton. He had appealed to Churchill for more land reinforcements, and had stated that his guns were getting increasingly short of ammunition. Like on the Western Front, it was settling down to be a long hard fight.

After dinner, they had drunk *The King*, and Edward Boyle was urged once more to relate again his exploits in the Marmara. Roger Keyes was more excited than anybody, absolutely delighted with the success of his patrol. Wemyss smiled across the table at Brodie, as if to assure him that they were not forgetting that it was his brother who had paved the way in his ill-fated *E15*.

During the after-dinner conversation, Naismith asked Keyes if there was any new intelligence on the German Cruiser Goeben, but was disappointed to learn that she had last been spotted shelling Allied positions from long range on seventh of May. The very latest intelligence stated that she had been taken through the Bosporus into the Black Sea to be used against the Russian positions. Martin's disappointment was quickly turned to delight when he learned that the two main Turkish battleships were to be regarded as priority targets. Their forward gun turrets had been removed and had been replaced by giant howitzers that could send a 16" shell over the hills onto the Allied held beaches. The destruction of these battleships would mean a much-improved chance of success for the Allied troops on the Peninsula.

"I am sending *E14* off to Malta for a rest and refit, so I will want you to remain up there until she gets back, Martin. Is there anything else you want to know before you leave?"

"No thank you, sir. Lieutenant Commander Boyle has kindly furnished me with all the latest information about the channel. I am hoping that from his account my own transit might prove to be somewhat easier than I had originally anticipated," he replied.

"Well then – go and run amok in the Marmara Martin!"

Keyes took him up to the Admiral, who shook his hand and wished him good luck. The whole assembly responded with a small cheer of encouragement, before Naismith left the great cabin to return to his boat.

****

At 0110 on the nineteenth of May 1915, *HMS E11* cast off her lines from the destroyer *HMS Grasshopper,* to move silently out of the tiny harbour of Cape Kephalo. Charles Brodie was standing on the Quarter-deck of the Flagship, and although he could not actually see her, he certainly heard the sound of her diesels start up through the blackness of the night. She was on her way out. The moon was low, hidden behind a substantial cloud base, but he did manage to catch a brief glimpse of E11 as she threaded her way amongst the ghostly shapes lying at anchor, but then he quickly lost sight of her in the cloaking veil of the night.

Everything was extremely quiet aboard *E11* until her diesels fired up. Astern of her the *Grasshopper* came dashing out of the tiny harbour like the lean ocean sprinter that she was. She was providing their armed escort up until the moment they dived, or until E11 ordered her to depart.

Standing up on the bridge was Guy d'Oyly-Hughes, Robert Brown, and Martin Naismith, each watching the ghostly glow of the moon through the cloud, as it slowly set into a calm sea. With its disappearance the night went totally black, with just the faintest of stars showing through the occasional gaps in the clouds. There was a gentle off shore breeze, but its force was lighter than Martin had hoped for. Ideally, if it had it been a little stronger, it would have whipped up and unsettled the surface of the water at the entrance to the Straits. Choppy water would have hidden their wake, and broken up any silhouette that they might produce. Once they were dived further up the channel, it would also have provided cover for their raised periscope. The barometer was forecasting fine weather for the foreseeable future, which did not bode well for *E11*'s attempts to remain hidden.

The boat still had ten miles to go before their great adventure would begin, but from the bridge they could already see the searchlights flashing at Kum Kale over on the Asiatic side, probing the darkness near to the wide approaches to the Dardanelles. The quietness up on the bridge was only disturbed by the steady throb rising up the conning tower hatch from the diesels. Behind them the diesel exhaust fumes billowed a ghostly grey across the water-line. There was the incessant swish from the water riding up onto the saddle tanks, more a loud whisper than a disturbance. Looking astern, in their wake there were faint flashes from a phosphorescent glow, and Naismith hoped that it would not be visible to the Turks up on the heights on the Asian shore.

The combination of these gentle sounds was not enough to mask the crackle of distant gunfire. There was obviously something big happening over on the peninsula. Unlike underwater, noise travels relatively slowly through the air, and the continuous thunderous roars, staccato of gun fire flashes, and the threatening rumble of explosions, gave the bridge watch-keepers a good idea of what was happening ashore. A sudden flash lit up the darkness, followed a few seconds later by the low growling thud. Blood red balls of light flared like summer flowers, before dying away. Several more followed, covering a much wider area, like the flickering embers of some satanic forge that had been given new life by the bellows. The closer *E11* closed to the shoreline, the more defined the explosions became, and it was not long before they could hear the single crack reports of individual rifle fire, and occasionally the clatter of machine-guns. The odour of cordite and death drifted on the breeze.

George Torode stood at the upper helm, just behind the officers. Petty Officer Green, who normally steered the boat in and out of harbour, was below, ready at the dived helm – in case they were forced to crash dive. Standing beside George was George Plowman, the Signalman, who carried a dimmed blinkered signal lamp in his hand.

The flesh-consuming fires and incessant explosions ashore were obviously taking place around the Allied trench positions. George shuddered at the thought of being on the receiving end of that hell. The whole macabre spectacle provided an of evilness compared with the relative peacefulness over on the eastern shore. Suddenly there was very loud explosion, which momentarily illuminated the rocky shoreline, making every man jump in surprise.

Using the very dimly lit compass in front of him, George Torode was being very careful to keep the boat steady on course. Peering out through the darkness, he could now faintly make out the line of white cliffs that formed the headland over at Cape Helles. Two pale plumes of smoke were rising from one of the crests. Cooking fires! The vertical plumes stood out eerily white in the blackness, like ghostly sentinels guarding the entrance to Hades. That simile appeared to be very apt considering where they were heading.

The Dardanelles were guarded on both sides by search-lights, which were positioned high up on the hillsides. The Kum Kale search light probed the darkness over towards the east. The second light was not evident, but there were more of them that could be seen further up the straits on both sides of the channel. Their pencil beams were probing the waters like the white sticks of the blind.

George counted three beams to starboard on the Asian side, and five to port on the European side. The original light that had been sighted at Kum Kale appeared to be much the bigger and brighter now, its beam suddenly flashed over their heads, illuminating the three towering white cliffs at Cape Helles.

Somewhere over in the direction of Kum Kale on the Turkish mainland, lay the ruins of the ancient city of Troy. Before the Trojan War, it had been the city that guarded the entrance to this ancient waterway they were about to penetrate. Homer's Iliad tells of the Greek invasion, and eventual victory, expounding on the terrible carnage that it took to achieve, and its bloody aftermath. Humans never seem to learn the lessons of history, because during the millennia that have followed very little seemed to have changed in this region. Here was man fighting man once again. Ahead of them, the white wake from *Grasshopper* distorted the placid water in the faint starlight. Her ghostly outline could just be made out in the darkness.

"Scary ain't it, George?" whispered the Signalman.

"Yeah it is George. I would hate to be over there in those trenches with those poor sods. The Pongo's are taking a terrible pounding by all account – Cor! Look at that, will you."

As he spoke, yet another shell landed, lighting up the whole hillside like a roman candle.

"Just think – every time one of those shells goes off, there is some poor sod is gettin' 'imself killed," said the Signalman.

"Cheerful chap, aren't you," said George.

The area all around them was suddenly lit up as if it were day as a Very Light ignited up in the sky. It hung in the air off to port, lighting up the topographical profile of the whole Peninsula. Surely it would illuminate them, and they would be spotted?

"Quiet you two," Lieutenant Brown ordered, as he bent over the compass and took bearings of the illuminated cliffs.

"Bearings, sir. Cape Helles bears 035 degrees. Kum Kale bears 128 degrees."

"Very good," replied Martin Naismith. "Slow ahead together, revolutions 150."

They were approaching a position that was exactly midway between the two rocky sentinels guarding either side of the entrance of the Dardanelles, and he purposely slowed down to diminish the effect of their wake, which would make them less visible from the shore. However, ahead of them was glowing whiteness showing the stern of *Grasshopper*, which was alarmingly evident.

Then suddenly a big shape loomed ahead, and a swift series of orders brought the boat quickly around to starboard to avoid the towering mass of an unlit battleship. They watched as its bulk as it passed close down their port side, before altering course directly back towards the entrance.

'Here we go,' thought George and as he spun the wheel, he sent up a silent prayer. The bow swung around to port, before he steadied on the new course.

At 0245, *HMS E11* was successfully passing between Cape Helles and Kum Kale.

"Read the log," Naismith reminded Brown. "We will be using DR from this point onward."

If there proved to be a lack of navigation marks in the darkness, they would have to rely heavily on accurate Dead Reckoning. Dead Reckoning is a predetermined course and speed drawn on to the chart that incorporates all of the tidal streams to show where they should be at any given time. With nothing else to rely on, the log would be their only indication as to how far they had travelled into the narrows.

The boat slid slowly past the ruined fortress at Seddul Bahr, *the Barrier of the Sea*, which was now in British hands.

At 0310 they had reached the line of Allied trawlers, who lay quietly in the water guarding the Straits. They were there to give an early warning of any outbound sortie by the enemy. This provided the Allies with the time to move the vulnerable transports and supply ships at the beach-head, and to send in the blockading heavy warships in to meet them. Not one of these tiny vessels was displaying any lights. Each lay there eerily silent like the Marie Celeste – abandoned ghost ships.

Four miles further on, and they passed between two more spectral outlines, one of which luckily turned out to be patrolling Allied destroyer. It was very unnerving, as George Plowman had not seen the vessel until the very last minute, as it dashed past them at speed. It had been a close thing.

The dangerous encounter shook Martin Naismith, and he entertained the idea of getting more lookouts up from below, but then quickly dismissed it. More men aloft would delay any crash dive as they attempted to scramble down the hatch. It could make all the difference to them escaping an attack.

"Keep your eyes peeled, Signalman – I want a bit more warning of any unlit ships," said Naismith over his shoulder.

"Aye-aye, sir," said George Plowman, but he suddenly leapt into action as he saw the flicker of a signal lamp ahead of them. It was a light signal being transmitted from the *Grasshopper*. He returned a couple of acknowledgement clicks on his own signal lamp, before he said quietly to his captain.

"*Grasshopper* is turning to starboard, sir – they wish us Bon Voyage and God Speed."

They all turned to watch the splendid sight of the Royal Navy destroyer under helm at speed, her sharp bow slicing through the surface water to send up two white chevrons high against the lofty sides of her fo'c'sle. She flashed past them, heading back down the channel towards the entrance. *HMS E11* was now further up the channel than any other Allied vessel, and very much on her own.

"We'll dive in about an hour, Number One," said Naismith down the tower to Guy d'Oyly-Hughes, who had gone down and was now standing ready below. "Sooner if we're spotted."

Guy d'Oyly-Hughes replied that he was ready and waiting to take charge after any crash dive.

The rumbling sound of their diesels seemed to reverberate back at them off of the hills on each side of the channel, but the further they could travel on the surface using these engines, then the less expenditure on the battery there would be once they dived. Martin Naismith dare not go to the silent drive until it was absolutely necessary. An extra quarter of an hour of battery power might make all the difference between them making it through into the Sea of Marmara, or catastrophe.

Listening to the sound of the diesels, George thought how loud they sounded. Standing up on top of the bridge it was very spooky knowing that the Turks were out there somewhere in the darkness, and that they would also be listening.

If I can hear them – then surely, they must hear them too – they couldn't all be deaf!

George expected a search-light to suddenly be switched on and fix on them at any second, that would quickly be followed by a barrage of fire from one of the gun positions. There were plenty of search-lights about, but for some unexplained reason they all seemed to sweep directly over them. It appeared that the beams were being aimed at the beaches on the far shore, and fortunately that caused them to pass over the top over *E11*. He reckoned that there was probably a greater risk from the European shore, where our own Army was being pinned down. If the British artillery saw the silhouette of their conning tower, which would be clearly visible against the search-light's glow coming from the Asian shore, then an alert gunner, positioned behind the trenches, might well open up on them. Hopefully they had all been briefed of their entry tonight!

Martin Naismith had read and memorised the features along this shore from the drawings in the Admiralty Pilot and Sailing Directions. Catching a glimpse of a slight dip in the line of hills that had been semi-illuminated by the search-lights, he quickly recognised the area as being the mouth of the Suandere River. This was the same area where Edward Boyle had reported that he had been fired on. Every extra half mile they could make on the surface from now onwards would be important, but he had already decided to dive a little sooner than Boyle had, because just five miles ahead of them was the huge and very powerful search-light at Kephez Point. It was already plainly visible from this distance, its beam touching them momentarily, as it swept across their bearing. As they closed, the chances of detection increased with every turn of their propellers.

At 0350 they were abreast with the hill-top named Achi Baba, having come right around the peninsula. Over towards the east, above the Asian horizon, the sky was just beginning to show the first hint of dawn, that almost imperceptible change from black to indigo that heralds the new day. What was going to happen to them today!

Martin Naismith yelled down for Petty Officer Green to engage his steering position, and ordered the course for him to steer. George was then told to disengage and lock off the top helmsman position. On completion, he was ordered below to act as the messenger, and to back up Petty Officer Green on the control room steering position. It would not be long now before they dived. The navigator, Lieutenant Brown, followed him down the hatch.

"Diving Stations," called Naismith, down from the tower. "Stop both main engines."

He then sent George Plowman below.

The Coxswain and Second Coxswain stood ready at the brass hand-wheels of the fore and after hydroplanes controls.

George Torode stood beside the third brass hand-wheel, that was the control for the rudder.

The stokers, who manned the diving and blowing panel, were busy shutting down the one and only ventilation fan. They checked the water-tight bulkhead flap valve was shut and secure, and then checked that the high-pressure air was opened to the blowing panel manifold.

In the engine room Chief Jupp was struggling with the star clutch, trying to disconnect the diesels from the driving shaft. Typically, this was the first time that it had showed any sign of a problem following its recent repair. The two diesels rumbled to a halt, causing the internal temperature within the boat to rise as the hot piston head casings radiated the heat. Thankfully the clutch was finally disengaged.

Naismith sat on the open hatch coaming, with his feet dangling down onto the ladder. He took a final look around. Everything was strangely silent, now that the diesels had stopped. The stillness of early morning was edged by the faintest hint of a breeze. The only sound was the splish-splash of small wavelets hitting the ballast tanks, as *E11* slowed to a virtual stop.

"The submarine is in all respects ready for diving, sir. Both engine clutches out. Both diesels are stopped and secure," d'Oyly-Hughes whispered his report up the conning tower.

Naismith looked down at the stop watch. It had taken 38 seconds from giving the order, and he felt that all the evolutions and drills that they had undertaken over the past few days were now starting to pay dividends. An emergency crash dive of 38 seconds would certainly be good enough to evade an enemy destroyer.

Looking ahead he visualised the course that he must take, knowing that he would be blind once they were underwater. Here we go, he thought. Taking a last deep breath of the fresh clean air, he descended the ladder. Stoker First Class Wheeler, one of the diving panel watch-keepers, climbed the short distance up the ladder and secured the retaining clips on the hatch. All eyes now followed Naismith's movements. It was he who held their fate in whatever judgements he would make. He stood with legs astride, looking like a surgeon about to perform a delicate operation at a medical academy, with all of his students avidly watching him from their observation seats.

"We're about a mile off the European shore, Achi Baba is abeam to port," he said to Brown, who duly noted the information onto the chart.

"All is ready, sir," d'Oyly-Hughes reported.

"Slow ahead on the motors – flood main ballast tanks."

He stood listening to his orders being repeated. At fifteen feet they caught the trim of the boat, and once he was satisfied, he ordered her to be taken down to 30 feet. At this depth they were totally invisible to anyone on either shore and completely hidden from the inquisitive search-lights. Everything now, hung on his and Lieutenant Brown's navigational skills.

"Up periscope."

Wheeler pulled the lever upwards, to send the long tube hissing up from its circular well in the deck – wire ropes rattled over the guide wheels of the hydraulic press as they hauled the viewing lens up to eye level. Naismith quickly scanned all round, but it was difficult to see anything, as the glare of a search-light immediately destroyed his night vision. Deciding to wait a couple of minutes before trying again, and realising that he was roughly at the same place where *B11* had been unable to get below forty feet. He knew that he would have to be extremely careful from this point onward. Those killer cross currents had to be countered immediately. Maybe this was a good time to test his theory of there being one water layer above the other!

"Take her down to eighty feet," he ordered, sending the periscope back down into its well. "Flood the forward auxiliary tank."

HMS E11 slid down to the ordered depth without any difficulty – much to his surprise. He knew that *B11* had been on the outer side of the channel, whilst *E11* was in the middle. So far so good! They were totally blind now, and he realised that he would have to fumble his way blindly onward towards Kephez Point.

The biggest threat ahead of them now was the mine-fields, and there was no way of avoiding them, so they would be forced to make the transit. They advanced slowly at three knots, not only to conserve their battery life, but also to avoid jarring or trapping any of the mine mooring wires, should they be unlucky enough to brush against one. This next section of the penetration was going to take some time, and he decided to stand some of the men down from their positions, and just leave four diving hands closed up. The next half an hour it was going to test of everyone's nerves, and the more rest that his men got, then the better they would perform.

George Torode was one of those sent forward. He was initially glad to be away from the high-tension atmosphere of the control room, but as soon as he reached the mess space, he quickly found that in being away from the action, the silence and inactivity got on his nerves. It was more of a worry doing nothing, than being involved in the nerve centre.

After ten minutes he made his way back down the passageway, and asked permission to relieve Petty Officer Green on the helm. His request was refused as it was going to be a long night, and everyone would need their share of rest, so he went back and tried to snuggle down atop the sack of cotton waste, but he knew that sleep would be impossible!

A small amount of the battery power was permitted to be used to boil some water on the hot-plate. The closed-up watch-keepers were then served with steaming mugs of kai, a naval thick sweet chocolate drink that both warmed them and kept them all alert. Not that anyone had the remotest chance of getting any sleep while they were negotiating this mine-field. Cupping the drink in both hands, the men sipped the contents to the sound of contented aahs. Naismith had reckoned on the drink being a morale booster during this, probably the tensest, of their whole passage. Having everyone still would also keep the temperature down, and by them resting it helped to conserve the oxygen supply within the boat. That would enable the men to think more efficiently.

George lay half asleep, half awake, just off of the main passageway. Everyone was fearful of what they were about to attempt. The excitement of the moment made each minute seem more like an hour. He was only too aware of the danger they were in, and the adrenalin that was racing through his blood stream, ensuring that any relaxation was impossible. Whilst they had been alongside the depot ship, he had listened to the stories and rumours that abounded, such as how *E15* had copped a packet, having run aground after experiencing strong currents. By all accounts she had been hit several times by the Turkish guns, killing six of her crew, while others had died from chlorine gas escaping from her battery. George remembered how he had experienced the effects of that same gas on that terrible night he was aboard *HMS C301*. Quite a few more of the crew of *E15* had been killed apparently in the mud, as they tried to stumble ashore, and the few that had survived had been taken prisoner of war. He remembered talking to one of the seamen from *E15* while they were in Malta. They had chatted for over half an hour, when he told him that his home was in Southsea, not that far from where Gladys lived. Now he was either dead, or incarcerated in some Turkish prisoner of war camp. When he had learned about *E15*, it had made George realise once more just how chancy the fortunes of war were. Your life could depend on one small human error, or a piece of faulty equipment, or even an unforeseen act of God, like a strong tidal current. Maybe it would be a freak current, sudden fog, or simply being spotted on the surface that would destroy them, but he was still confident that nothing bad was going to happen to them, because their skipper was the best there is at his job. Not just good – the very best! George had learned so much since joining *E11,* and most of that knowledge had come from the skipper. When he had passed his submarine knowledge exam, the skipper had been the first to shake his hand and congratulate him. He had felt at that moment that he had been fully accepted into a very exclusive club. Everything was going to be just fine – he just knew it!

Martin Naismith was the epitome of calm in the control room, continually casting his eye about, watching their course, speed and depth. His mind working overtime, as he tried to calculate where they were in relation to the hazards of the channel. Trusting his first lieutenant to take charge of the trim, his eyes none the less flicked over to make sure that the boat was running on an even keel. He had no means of assessing the external tidal current, and he knew that they would have to rely heavily on good educated guesses. Dead Reckoning would play an important part in those estimations from now. So far all had gone well, it had been very quiet with the boat operating smoothly. No sign of any mines so far!

Just as it seemed that nothing could go wrong, there came a loud clang from the forward end of the boat. Those crew members of the crew who had actually managed to drift off to sleep were awake in an instant. Everyone's ears strained, as they listened in hushed anticipation, their eyes wide with fear and apprehension. Beads of sweat began to run down their fore-heads, and sweat gushed from their backs and armpits to soak their clothes.

The mooring wire of a mine could be heard as it scraped and scratched its way down the port side of the hull. There was a distinct rasping metallic noise as it brushed its way along the ballast tanks. Every eye and ear following its progress aft, each man willing it not to hit a snag anywhere, which would haul it down to hit them. Tongues licked at dried lips. Every nerve was waiting for the explosion. Please God, let it break free! George's heartbeat raced and his breathing became short gasps. Looking about him, he could see his fear mirrored in the faces of his all of his friends.

"Stop port. Midships the wheel," Naismith said in a quiet calm clear voice, hoping that the starboard propeller would be enough to swing the stern away from the lethal obstruction.

Petty Officer Green expertly swung the wheel as ordered to centre the rudder.

"Let the stern swing clear naturally."

George found himself sweating profusely, noting that the back of his shirt had plastered itself to his skin. He remembered that terrible explosion on *C301* and the look of surprise on the face of the man impaled on the spike. Maybe it was his turn now? Those dead crewmen lying on the bottom of the English Channel might have been the lucky ones, the terrors of this war were all over for them.

Looking about him, he stared down towards the engine room, wondering just how he had ended up here within this steel shell. It really was the most surreal of environments. At this same time last year, he remembered that he had gone for his first swim in Fermaine Bay. Why did he sign up?

Realising that his breathing had shortened in frequency, he knew that he was very afraid. If that mine were to explode, like that other one had on C-301, nobody would stand a chance of escape down here at eighty feet – it would be curtains for them all. On that terrible night he had just been fortunate that *C301* had been on the surface, and even then, only four of the crew had managed to survive. With *E11* dived so deep she would fill with water in a fraction of a second. It would be very naive to think that anyone would manage to reach the surface alive.

Trying to divert his thoughts away from the danger, he began to look around at the other men at their posts, wondering what they were all thinking. Were they as scared as he was? Although most were sweating as much, most expressions remained steely impassive.

His mind flicked back to Guernsey once more, and to the lush green of the fields and trees. His mind then flicked to the crystal-clear water running from the stone culvert in front of his house. To the earthy smell of the farms at ploughing – and the sound of the church bells rolling across the parish fields on a Sunday morning – horses and cattle in fields full of daisies and buttercups – it all seemed so very remote. If he were to die out here tonight, it would be a terrible blow for his mother – he knew that she would miss him terribly – but he felt sad that she would never know what had really happened to him. Then he thought of his Gladys, and wondered what her reaction would be if anything untoward were to happen to him. She would never bear the children that he had hoped they would have together. Then Basil's words echoed back through his brain. No – she would never betray him. He was sure of that. It would have been good to have gotten even with Arthur Collenette, and he earnestly hoped that some Turkish sniper had already done the job for him. Then he suddenly he became conscious of the absolute silence all around him, and he was brought him back to the present. There were murmurs. Everyone around him was saying that they had passed clear of the danger. Then, as if to tease them, the wire gave another loud slap against the after tanks, as it continued on its journey.

Guy d'Oyly-Hughes placed his cup of kai down very gently on the bench he was sitting on, as if the slightest noise or vibration might detonate the mine.

You could have heard a pin drop at that moment, as every single pair of eyes tried to penetrate the one-inch-thick steel of the pressure hull to locate the source of their torment. The wire should have passed clear, but it could have snagged itself on the port propeller guard, and was being dragged down onto them? Many prayers were being said in that instant, and maybe they were answered, because the wire finally snapped away with a loud twang, and they all felt the slight jolt as the boat sprang free from its tether. The sighs of relief were audible throughout the boat.

"Plot the position of that mine on the chart, Navigator. We don't want to meet the same chap on the way back, do we?" ordered Naismith, speaking to Robert Brown at the chart. Getting back on course was now a priority, and he ordered, "Slow ahead together – starboard ten."

The frightened mood within the boat lifted temporarily. That mooring wire scraping down their side had been the first indication that they had actually entered the minefield, but over the next minutes there were more wires that scrapped down the side of the hull, and every one of them cut into their nerves. Every time it happened Martin Naismith would stop the port or starboard propeller as before, to prevent the mine being dragged down onto them. It was understandably very quiet within the boat during these periods. Every ear strained to detect any new wires as they initially touched the hull. The only internal mechanical noises came from the faint hum of the motors, the gurgling swish of hydraulics moving along the pipes, and a slight rattle from the steering gear.

In the forward tube-space, the torpedo-men had positioned themselves up between the two torpedo tubes with their ears pressed against the hull, ready to report the next contact. The air in the boat was starting to get very humid, but the smell that crept surreptitiously through the boat at that moment was unmistakable. Everyone knew that it was not emanating from the metal sewage buckets, situated behind the diesels. It wasn't from the stagnant water being disturbed down in the bilges. The Phantom Farter had struck again. Somehow that terrible smell served to alleviate the oppressive tension that they were all under, and everyone just burst into a spontaneous bout of laughter. It was like a relief valve lifting the trapped pressure within a tank as the dreadful stink invaded every nook and nostril. The stench, although terrible, brought home to each of men enduring the terrifying surreal existence, something that was real – a tangible link with normality. It was as if they had woken during a nightmare, and suddenly there was an old friend there who made you feel safe. The perpetrator remained anonymous – nobody cared.

After a period of ten minutes without hearing any more of the mine mooring wires, Martin Naismith went to the chart, and by using the intelligence giving the extent of the mine-field, he calculated that they had negotiated the danger and decided to risk coming up to periscope depth to establish their position. He was a little worried because according to his DR estimation for their transit through that minefield, he had assumed that they would not be clear for at least another five minutes, but the ensuing silence gave him a very good indication that they had passed through the danger. It was unfortunate that the transit through the minefield had to be made at all, but he had been faced by the simple choice of this transit, or the even greater risk of running aground. With less than an hour of darkness left before dawn light, Martin didn't want to be left high and dry like *E15* when the sun rose over those hills on the Asian side of the channel.

At 0450 he ordered Diving Stations once more in readiness to return from 80 to 30 feet. The men quickly manned their stations.

"Upward bubble, keep30 feet – Pump auxiliary," he ordered.

The depth gauge started to rise – 70 feet, 69, 68, 67, 66 feet – then it dropped back suddenly to 70 feet once more.

"She's 'eavy sir," said Coxswain Dowell, swinging the after hydroplanes wheel as he struggled to keep her at seventy feet.

"How's the bubble?"

"Horizontal, sir."

"Number One, go forward and find out what's wrong," said Martin Naismith to Guy d'Oyly-Hughes. "I'm certainly not going to blow the tanks here."

George stood listening, as this new danger had suddenly presented itself. Would this nightmare never end? The First Lieutenant returned within the minute.

"I can't find a thing wrong, sir. The auxiliary tank has certainly been pumped. There's nothing to account for the negative buoyancy, unless we have sprung a leak somewhere."

"Put both planes hard arise – full ahead together – don't let her come shallow Coxswain," ordered Naismith.

At great expense to the battery endurance, the boat's speed increased, forcing the boat to slowly rise – 65 feet, 60, 50, 40 feet.

Naismith slowed the boat.

"Hold her at 30 feet – don't let her surface."

"Aye, aye, sir – 34 feet, 30, 28 feet, 26, 25."

As the boat came shallow, George found that his knees were bending involuntarily, wishing the craft would go deeper. Was the boat going to break surface? The Turkish gun batteries would open up immediately should they do so.

"Hold her, men!" coaxed Naismith. It was said more as a prayer than an order. The planes-men sweated at their brass wheels, spinning them from rise to dive, trying to counteract this strange behaviour of their boat.

"She's coming back, sir," replied the coxswain. "28 feet, 29, 30 feet, sir."

"Well done Coxswain – up periscope."

Wheeler did his job. Naismith ordered it lowered slightly, to keep the hooded lens just above the waterline. Dawn was clearly breaking, and Naismith saw a perfect silhouette of the Asian shore, but suddenly he was almost blinded by the glare of a search-light. He stepped back blinking rapidly, before he returned to the eye piece to complete his all-round look.

"Down periscope – take her down to 75 feet – flood the auxiliary – stand by the blows."

Naismith crossed over to the chart table and leaned across it, speaking quietly to Robert Brown.

"Kephez Point search-light is abeam to starboard."

"What? But it can't be yet, sir," said Brown incredulously. "According to our DR on the chart, that should not take place for at least another hour, and I have just checked the log. It shows that we have only been making four knots through the water and the tidal information states that there has been a two to four knot current against us."

"Yes, but that's on the surface Bob – but down at eighty feet there is evidently next to no current, or maybe it is actually flowing in the opposite direction and pushing us along?"

Robert Brown still looked sceptical.

"Could it possibly be another search-light, sir?"

"What other one? There are only three on the Asiatic side that we know of. There is Kum Kale, which we passed on the way in. There is Erenkoy, which we are nowhere near yet. So, this has to be Kephez, doesn't it? We are much too close to the shore, though."

An idea came to Brown at that moment, his face lit up with sudden realisation.

"Perhaps while we were coming up to periscope depth, the boat was being forced over towards the Asiatic shore, just as Brodie was in *E15*. That would also explain why we had difficulty coming shallow just now – we were caught in the down current on the bend."

He reached over and got busy with his dividers, parallel ruler, and pencil.

"If we're half a mile off the search-light now, by coming around to a new course 048 degrees we should clear Kalid Bahr and pass Chanak," he said triumphantly.

Impressed, Naismith quickly checked his findings, because at that point the channel turned through nearly 90 degrees to port, towards Kalid Bahr, the *Key of the Sea*, which was on the European side. At the same time the channel narrowed between Kalid Bahr and Chanak to less than a mile. As Guy d'Oyly Hughes came over to stand beside the captain, Martin turned to him excitedly, explaining the theory that he and the navigator had just discovered.

"We're off Kephez Point already Number One! At this rate we won't even have to surface in the Straits at all to recharge the batteries. I am now pretty certain that below forty feet there's an underlying current of cold sea water, confirming my theory why the boat acted heavy for no reason. There is fresh water on the top layer, as you would expect from all those rivers like the Danube that run down into the Black Sea, and with us being too close to the inside of the bend we met the downward current, which is the reason that it was so hard for us to come shallow earlier. The fresh water layer rides faster on top of the slower salt layer below. That's got to be the answer to all these strange depth changes that we've all been experiencing. By us going below the upper fast fresh water current that is against us at two knots, and being down in the salt-water under-current which is travelling with us, we have made fantastic progress."

Not six feet away, George was listening to the conversation with great interest. He did not quite understand what was actually being said, but from the excitement being displayed by the officers, it made him feel more confident than he had for over an hour. The excited enthusiasm in the captain's voice indicated that he thought everything was going well. That was enough.

Naismith brought the boat around on to the new heading that the navigator had suggested. At this depth there was no absolutely fear of being stranded, as there was plenty of water above them, and any cross currents were taking place in the layer above. Unexpected and uncharted shallows started to appear, as their keel scraped along the bottom on more than one occasion. The boat juddered each time, quickly followed by a loud sandy hiss that echoed through the hull. As the boat straightened on to its new heading, Martin Naismith realised that they were in the Reach, which was the area of open water to be found directly below Chanak. The water here was deep, and they were safe enough for the present. He ordered George Torode to the helm to give Petty Officer Green a break.

At 0600 Naismith brought *E11* back up to 30 feet once more. This time, with no downward current, they had no problems in coming up and Naismith quickly checked his position relative to the new course. The early morning light was much brighter now, but within a minute his periscope being raised, it had been spotted by the eagle eyed look-outs on the Turkish gun batteries, and they were promptly fired on. The loud metallic explosions reverberated against the pressure hull, as the shells detonated as they hit the water. They became absolutely deafening. It was like being on the inside of a bell being struck by a sledge-hammer. The crew flinched with every explosion, as the shock wave slammed against the hull.

"We are through the Narrows, and I clearly saw Nagara Point. Port 10 steer – 355 degrees," said Naismith as he lowered the periscope.

George obeyed the order.

They stayed at thirty feet for another ten minutes before he attempted another look. Above them the morning light was considerably brighter now, almost full daylight. When he did come up, he quickly spotted three destroyers, who had obviously been sent out to search for them. The Turkish guns opened fire almost as soon as his periscope had appeared, but in that brief moment before the guns opened up, Martin's heart jumped. He had a clear view of two Turkish battleships carrying out manoeuvres in the direction of Nagara Point. The thrill of expectation shot through him – it was much more than he had dared to hope for.

"Down periscope – man the bow tubes – keep me steady at thirty feet."

The hunt was on and the thrill of the chase manifested within every man on board, dispelling every fear they may have had. This was the reason that they had made the terrifying journey. It was their bread and butter, and what *E11* had been specifically designed to do. After the horrors of the mine-field, they could now look forward to some real action.

Guy d'Oyly-Hughes and the torpedo-men hurried forward. It would be hard to find a more difficult place than the confines of The Narrows for a submarine to carry out an attack, but that was not going to stop Martin Naismith. He addressed his crew.

"Men, I have just seen two Turkish battleships – which I am pretty certain were the Turgut Riess and the Herredin Barbarossa, bearing 020 degrees, range two miles, steering course 230 degrees. Standby both bow tubes, set all the torpedoes to run deep – that will be enough to do maximum damage to any battleship. Standby both beam tubes – set those torpedoes to both run shallow – just in case we have to fire at their escorts."

Everyone became attentive to the task in hand. George's heart began to beat with excitement, because here he was helping his skipper to torpedo an enemy battleship! He remembered back to the end of last September, when he had read the account of how the U-9 who had sunk three British cruisers in one morning. Hopefully he was going to be part of a British crew that was going to do the same thing. He shifted his position in front of the helm, fully concentrating on the compass in front of him. The approaching action served to raise everyone's spirits, eradicating all the fear of that terrifying passage through the mine-field.

"Flood all tubes," ordered Naismith. "Open the drains and vents. Open high-pressure air onto the fore trim line."

There was a loud hissing as the high-pressure air was forced forward into the trimming tanks, which then forced the water up into the torpedo tubes. ERA Brooker turned the handles of the valves on the air manifold in the Control Room.

"The tubes are full, sir," came the cry from the forward end of the boat.

There was a fresh rush of compressed air amidships, blasting from the torpedo tube vents as the beam tubes were also flooded.

"Both beam tubes are flooded, sir."

"Open both bow caps," said Naismith.

In the forward torpedo space, Guy d'Oyly-Hughes ordered that each tube equalising valve be opened, matching the internal pressure within each tube with the external sea pressure. This had to be completed before the bow caps could be opened. Once the two pressures were matched, then each torpedo tube bow-cap could be opened by pulling a hydraulic lever. Everyone could hear the dull thud as each bow cap folded back to expose the explosive tip of the deadly weapon housed within.

"Bow caps open," shouted d'Oyly-Hughes along the passageway.

"Charge all firing tanks," ordered Naismith.

The charging of each firing reservoir took a couple of minutes. When this pressure was finally released directly behind each torpedo, it would force the weapon out of the tube. This was being carried out on both the bow tubes and the beam tubes.

"Bow tubes ready, sir."

"Beam tubes ready, sir."

Martin Naismith increased speed. Although it would seriously drain the battery, he knew that he had to get himself into a good firing position. Then suddenly they could all hear the thud, thud, thud of a destroyer's propellers as she passed very close by as she hunted for them, like a spaniel charging through the undergrowth to flush out the quarry. The sound began to fade as the range opened and then it was gone as

216

quickly as it had appeared. On the wheel, George counted the rhythmic thundering beat over an interval of one minute by using the chart table chronometer second hand as a reference. If the skipper knew the revolutions of the vessel over one minute, it would give him a better idea of her speed.

"She's doing 115 rpm, sir, I just counted the beat of her prop," he called to the captain.

"Well done Torode," replied the captain, pleasantly surprised that his crew were thinking on their feet. He tried to match her parameters to a similar sized British destroyer, and then to use the same revolutions per knot to calculate the speed.

"Navigator, check the revolutions per knot of a River Class destroyer."

Robert Brown reached down and got the reference book from the cupboard under the chart table. Flicking through the pages of information, he suddenly stopped.

"Twelve, sir."

'That gives her a speed of about nine and a half knots,' thought Naismith and that certainly tallies with the size of her bow wave. It had long been a theory of his that a target's speed could be fairly accurately assessed visually by the size of her bow wave as she cut through the water. By counting the revolutions, it would definitely confirm it. He decided that he would get young Torode to do that again.

Risking another quick look through the periscope, every hope he ever had suddenly plummeted as he saw the two battleships turning away. They were running scared, heading north, up the channel away from them and making smoke as they went. He was more than a little disappointed, but figured that as they were heading off in the same direction as *E11*, then he may as well slowly follow them. They may just decide to turn and come back down.

He now was faced with a very difficult navigational manoeuvre that was approaching. Nagara Point, which lay straight ahead, involved a very sharp turn to starboard. Beside the hazardous currents that existed, there might well be underwater obstructions around this vicinity, and he remembered a recent report stating that the Turks had thrown an old iron girder bridge into The Narrows near here.

He saw that there were two enemy destroyers who were standing off Nagara Point, presumably hoping that the submarine would be caught in the swirling current and possibly get into trouble. Martin was still giving navigation his top priority, and he had purposely moved *E11* over towards the European shore, almost running into Khelia Bay itself, before finally making his sharp turn towards the east.

After transiting at periscope depth for ten minutes he finally raised the periscope to reveal that they were now well above Nagara Point. Almost immediately more shots rained down on him as soon as he had raised the lens clear of the water. Clang – clang – clang! Satan the blacksmith was at work with his hammer again, and using *E11* as his anvil. Tall white spray columns of water rose all around them, like the trunks of silver birch. He reluctantly lowered his link with the outside world, allowing *E11* to continue onwards, still harbouring the hope that the battleships would be stopped somewhere ahead of him.

The next time he checked however, his disappointment was absolute, because somehow the two battleships had doubled back, and had slipped past him. Both of the mighty vessels were now well astern of him. He spotted them rounding Nagara Point at high speed. As his priority order was to break into the Marmara, he decided to admit defeat on this occasion, knowing that he did not have enough battery power to pursue them. Hopefully they would meet again.

The whole crew had been riding the wave of expectation, only to have all their hopes come crashing down on to the beach of disappointment. The torpedo-men had to close the bow and beam tube caps, before draining each tube. There was an air of gloom and despondency among them, which was only natural. The talk was of what might have been.

At least *HMS E11* had passed the most dangerous section of the voyage, as they were through the Narrows. This final stretch should be comparatively easy, just so long as their battery held out. The increases in speed on the way up had exhausted the precious power at an alarming rate. At frequent intervals Guy d'Oyly-Hughes got one of the torpedo-men to check the battery density of the electrolyte in pilot cells by using a hydrometer, and report their findings, which he had logged.

George was relieved at the wheel by Petty Officer Green, giving him the chance to go forward and relax. They had only been dived for just over three hours, but it seemed more like three days.

Naismith felt wary as he came shallow once more, uncertain of the currents in this area, but he wanted to check his course and position. The first time he raised the periscope something strange happened. The force of the current whipped against the raised mast, causing a wake that moved away from the boat at an acute angle. His first impression was that they had snagged something and they were towing it. Then he thought that it may be the effect of the cross current phenomena. Whatever the reason, it was going to give away their position to any alert Turkish gunner. The second time he raised the periscope a little higher to take fixing bearings it had gone.

Ahead of him there was a light-house over on the European side. It had a white painted iron framework, and stood on the rounded hill to port of the channel. Another solid stone light-house stood opposite, over on the Asiatic shore, which appeared to be actually rising out of the water. He recognised them both immediately, having seen them from the air on his flying reconnaissance, when he had recorded their details.

"Standby bearings. Karakova Burnu bears 043 degrees: Kudjuk Burnu bears 096 degrees – down periscope."

Robert Brown quickly plotted the two bearings on to the chart. They were much further up the channel than they thought, albeit a little over towards the European side. Naismith sighed with relief, as with the uncertainty of their DR predictions, there was now no mistaking their true position.

The channel began to narrowed once more, and through the periscope he managed to identify the village of Bergaz, with its domed mosque that sprouted three tall minarets.

At 0930 Naismith raised the periscope once more. The strange oblique wake was there once again, streaming off at an angle from the boat. He came to the conclusion that it was the surface current that was taking a different course to the main current that was surrounded the hull down at thirty feet. It was prevalent on every bend, and it certainly backed up his theory of one current sliding across another. So far on this penetration that theory had worked very much in his favour. It would also help other boats in the future.

It was not long before the town of Gallipoli itself came into view. It lay over on the European side, and lends its name to the whole of the Peninsula on which it stands. Through the periscope it looked like a pile of white blocks which had been strewn haphazardly across a lush green hillside. There certainly seemed to be no evidence of any civic planning to the town.

After an all-round sweep, he noticed there were a number of trawlers up ahead who were operating in pairs, and appeared to be towing wire sweeps between them. He quickly took some final bearings before going deep to ninety feet to pass below the Gallipoli mine-field. This time they were lucky, as there were no scraping wires, much to everyone's relief.

An hour later and the air in the boat was becoming foul. The men off watch slept, or read quietly if there was a light was available. Those on duty moved as little as possible, as the depleted oxygen levels caused anyone using any effort to pant for breath. Their clothes were soaked through with sweat, the sodden material sticking to them like a second skin. Everyone's hair felt lank, damp, and very greasy. Moisture condensed on the cold steel of the inner pressure hull, dripping down incessantly on everyone and everything. The deck was quite wet – in fact everything was wet. There were even small brown puddles appearing within the base of the bulbous glass of the electric light bulbs, which cast dim eerie shadows. Smoking was an impossibility, as any Lucifer match, or even a petrol lighter failed to ignite due to the seriously reduced level of oxygen. Even the prevailing smell of diesel oil had been offset by the acrid sour stench emanating from the batteries, but it was exacerbated by the overpowering foul odour of excrement, emanating from the un-emptied sanitary buckets, which were still standing in a line behind the engines. These were their toilet facilities when deep, and were emptied on surfacing each evening, when they charged the batteries. The buckets were a necessity, because the submarine heads could not be used below thirty feet, because the effluence went straight out into the sea. Each time they went deep, there emerged from the internal trim tanks a grey mist that began to rise up through the vents like a London smog, quickly filling the compartment. Things above on the surface were much quieter.

At 1330, according to their Dead Reckoning, they should have reached the end of the Straits at the point where the waterway actually opened out into the Sea of Marmara. Naismith brought *E11* up to fifty feet, and reduced the speed to two knots. Everyone listened for the sound of any propellers, but there was nothing heard. He brought the boat up to twenty feet and raised the periscope into brilliant sunshine. There were no enemy ships in sight, but was amazed to find that they had travelled so far out into the Sea of Marmara that it was difficult to see any land. The Asiatic shore was over five miles away, while over on the European side it was three miles distant. He came around to port and steered for the European side where it was much shallower, and then took the boat down to rest on the sea bed at a depth of fifty feet. Not wanting to surface yet, as Edward Boyle had reported the presence of coast watchers, who would quickly report their position, and alert any shipping. He remembered the main problem that Edward Boyle had stated that he had experienced with *E14*, was being continually harassed by patrol craft. The coastal watchers were very probably the cause. Everybody was stood down, with just one or two remaining in each compartment to watch the depth gauge, and be ready for any unforeseen problem.

Once the crew had all settled, the Coxswain issued the daily ration of rum. It was received enthusiastically, a well-earned light respite at the end of a very stressful day. George was beginning to enjoy his small issue of rum. To give it its official title, it was Grog. Two parts water, to one part of West Indies rum. On the first occasion that he had received an issue, its fiery taste had taken his breath away, his eyes had streamed as he coughed and panted to regain the air in his lungs. It had caused great amusement amongst his mess-mates. The spirit served to ease away all the nervous tension that they had all been under since they left the protection of *HMS Grasshopper* nearly twelve hours before.

Then with very little to do, everyone managed to get some sleep. While they slept Guy d'Oyly-Hughes and Chief Jupp went through the boat to check that they had not sustained any damage from the shelling on the way up. They also wanted to make sure that they had sustained no damage from bouncing off the sea bed just after the first mine-field. Giving the all clear, they too went and turned in.

At 2100 that evening, Martin Naismith assessed that it would be dark enough for them to attempt to surface. God knows that they needed to. The ashen grey faces of his men, along with their gasping attempts at breathing, made it all too obvious that fresh air was badly needed inside the boat. Everything was soaked in condensation, men, decks, and equipment. He just hoped that their low battery would have settled enough to produce the power to operate the motors. Walking into the control room he ordered the men to close up at their stations very slowly, as he was afraid that any sudden movements might cause a heart injury, due to the lack of oxygen in their blood-stream. Once they were all in position, he ordered the water to be slowly blown from the tanks, until the boat achieved a more positive buoyancy. Slowly the submarine rose off the seabed and slowly ascended to thirty feet.

"Up periscope," he croaked, not recognising his own voice.

There was nothing around them but the same hills that he had seen when they had gone deep, which were now faintly illuminated in bright moonlight. There was the odd pin-point of light dotted the hill-side here and there. He brought the boat up until the conning tower was just clear of the surface. Climbing up the ladder, he partially released the retaining clips of the upper hatch and getting a good hold on the ladder with his free hand as he did so. He did not want to be shot out of the tower by the sudden escape of the excess pressure in the boat that had been caused by the venting the torpedo tubes firing reservoirs. As he eased the clips, there was a loud howling hiss as the excess air was vented out through the small gap between the upper lid, and the hatch coaming. He waited patiently until it had all vented out through the crack, waiting until it had disappeared. The crew had to hold their noses and blow through their sinus, or swallow quickly to relieve the sudden change in pressure on their eardrums.

Lieutenant Robert Brown stood at the chart table watching the barometer for when the interior pressure equalised to equal that with the air outside. He yelled the information up to his captain. The hatch clips were then released and Naismith stepped rather giddily out into the fresh air. Below the hatch a group of men stood ready to breath in the fresh air, but after them breathing the foul air for so long, it made everyone's head swim. The men began coughing under the sudden influx of so much fresh ozone. Most of them felt nauseous, but the effects passed quickly, and after half a dozen good deep breaths, their minds cleared and their energy levels returned, as oxygen charged blood rushed through their veins. Their skin colour gradually began to regain its glow.

Around them the sea was a dead calm as Martin Naismith stood up on the bridge, where over towards the west the glow of the setting moon reflected on its surface. Guy d'Oyly-Hughes came up and joined him. George Torode was ordered aloft to act as look-out. There was an almost total silence, it was so complete that they could hear the sound of a yapping dog barking somewhere over on the European shore. George Plowman was also ordered up as the second lookout – it was widely reputed that he had the best eyes on the boat. George was ordered to stand at the top of the hatch as there was another task that had to be completed.

"Form a human chain up the tower and ditch the Engine Room sanitary buckets over the side. We have enough trouble living with the Phantom Farter, without adding to our misery," chuckled Martin. "We can charge the battery now, Number One. Start with 500 in series, but be ready to break off at any moment, as we may have to dive quickly."

George grabbed each bucket as it appeared, tipping it straight over the side of the conning tower. The smell of each made him retch, as the contents splattered down onto the tanks, some of the excrement remained there. The smell was truly awful. Finally, the last one was tipped over just as the diesels were started, which quickly refreshed the air throughout the whole boat. The rush of air also began to dry out the internal dampness and condensation. Men took turns to stand under the down draught coming down the conning tower hatch to allow their own clothes to dry out. The rest of the crew began to turn in where ever a space could be found, and generally everyone was feeling much more comfortable, relieved that they had arrived in the Sea of Marmara in one piece.

"Rig the wireless radio mast," ordered Naismith.

Albert Lohden came up to the bridge, lugging the mast, aerial, and leads. George Plowman was replaced by George Torode, and he moved over to the hatch to assist him. Between them, the two men should soon finish the task.

Their assigned radio contact for this patrol was the destroyer *HMS Jed*, which was lying anchored over on the Mediterranean side of the peninsula, only thirty miles across the hills as the crow flies from their present position. She was going to be permanently stationed off Bulair, in the Gulf of Xeros, just to relay *E11*'s signals. Any intelligence reports of major importance that was gained by *E11*, could then be immediately relayed directly to the Flagship.

Suddenly everything had to be abandoned when Plowman reported hearing a ship's engine coming from somewhere astern of them. The wireless mast was rapidly dismantled, passed down the hatch, before they plunged beneath the waves once more. A destroyer was bearing down on them from the north.

"Thirty feet," ordered Naismith.

The intruder kept to her course, and the sound of her twin propellers were heard by the crew as she passed close overhead. Naismith passed over the chance of an easy kill in favour of not revealing his presence.

Fifteen minutes later, *E11* cautiously surfaced once more and continued undisturbed with her attempt to make contact with *HMS Jed*. Naismith urgently wanted to report their safe arrival in the Sea of Marmara. Communication contact with *Jed* however was not established, and Martin was aware that it would cause some consternation amongst the submarine staff back at Murdos.

After an hour their battery had been charged enough for them to proceed further into the Marmara on the surface. At 0030 they sighted another destroyer, probably the same one that was patrolling the area. This time its silhouette was clearly displayed against the setting moonlit sea. They dived again. Surfacing after just ten minutes, they continued with their passage.

They tried several more times during the night to contact *Jed*, but received no answer. So, they moved to a position that was only fifteen miles from her as the crow flies across the peninsula, but again they received no acknowledgement that the transmission had been received. Naismith began to get anxious, as he knew there would be a growing concern for their safety by those aboard the Flagship. He wanted to let them know that they had successfully negotiated the hazards of the Dardanelles, and were now safely ensconced here in the Marmara. He began to wonder if the was defect in the equipment. It was at that moment that he realised that he had no knowledge of how this newly fitted equipment worked. It was probably the only thing aboard the boat about which he was ignorant.

At 0400 it was getting light enough for *E11* to be spotted, so with their batteries now being fully charged, Naismith decided to dive. Despite the many efforts throughout the night they still hadn't made contact with *Jed*, so *E11* began her first full day dived as she began to reconnoitre the western end of the Marmara.

Chapter Ten

The Sea of Marmara

The Sea of Marmara was formed way back in prehistory by a deep crack in the Earth's crust, caused by a split in the tectonic plates that divide Europe and Asia. This crack is a very long one, that runs north to south all the way down through the Black Sea into the Bosphorus itself, and onward through the Sea of Marmara before continuing down through the Dardanelles and into the Aegean Sea. The visual presence of so many extinct volcanoes in the Aegean Sea bear witness to the ancient seismic activity of this area. A further extension of the same crack also becomes visible down through the Red Sea, and onward attempting to sever the Horn of Africa via the Great Rift Valley of East Africa. In the distant future, this will eventually isolate the Horn of Africa from the rest of the African continent.

The northern section of the crack was filled with water some two and a half million years ago to form the Black Sea, and the melt waters at the end of the ice age breeched the land plug to form the Bosphorus and to fill, what is now, the Sea of Marmara. Both of these seas lie directly over this fault line. The Sea of Marmara is 46 miles from north to south, and 110 miles wide at the broadest point. It was named from the Greek word for marble – Marmaros, which is still quarried on its south-western shore. It is connected to the Black Sea at its northern tip by a narrow waterway known since ancient times as the Bosporus. To the south the Dardanelles connect it to the Aegean Sea. This has been the main crossing point from Asia into Europe since prehistoric man first left the African continent and ventured into the world.

These waterways have witnessed Egyptian galleys, Venetian galleons, and Greek caiques. There have been the dhows and feluccas of the Arab traders, vying with Roman triremes and biremes, each coming here to seek the smooth stone, so sought after to build palaces and temples of their cities. A major centre of trade between east and west – where the spices and silks of the orient were brought for trading to the markets of the occidental.

The jewel in the crown of this whole region is the City of Constantinople, to give it its Roman name, or Stamboul as it is known locally in Turkish. This great city of Constantine was once the capital of the Byzantine Empire, and is now a major city within the Ottoman Empire. Being built along both sides of the Bosphorus, it is almost totally surrounded by mountains. Within its confines lies the main hub of the Turkish war machine, and its port is the central distribution point in supplying the Turkish army defending the Gallipoli Peninsula. To get those supplies to the

Gallipoli Peninsula involves a lot of shipping to carry the cargoes the sixty miles south across the Sea of Marmara. Other than going by ship, the only alternative method is via a single railway track that runs all the way around the Marmara. It is a long tedious journey of nearly six hundred miles. A dirt road system does exist, but it is a hazardous journey, and much longer than by rail.

It was to disrupt and sever the nautical supply routes that *HMS E14* and now *HMS E11*, along with the ill-fated Joule, Saphir, *E15* and AE2 had all been sent on their perilous journey up through the Dardanelles. If they could seriously jeopardise the Turkish supply route, it would cause their army to gradually become isolated, and to be slowly be starved of both food and ammunition. The Allied troops on that new beach-head needed all the help they could get.

As the first dawn light replaced the blackness of the night, *HMS E11* began her first day of patrolling the Marmara. After their failure to make contact with *HMS Jed*, Martin Naismith had decided to remain on the surface and head eastward, back towards the entrance to the Dardanelles. On finding nothing of interest, they carried on towards Marmara Island, sighting it as the sun rose up from behind its cragged outline. The further east they travelled, they noticed how the colour of the water became lighter, changing from the dark blue to a pale purplish green, and finally to a pale aquamarine as the seabed shelved. The charts indicated that seabed became shallower on this eastern side of this inland sea. There was still nothing in sight!

Martin Naismith decided to set up a patrol line between this island, and the rocky headland of Kodja Burnu over on the European shore, a distance of some 20 miles. Any vessel heading into, or emerging from the Dardanelles could then easily be intercepted. They sighted nothing during that first morning, in complete contrast to Edward Boyle's description of this area bustling with sea traffic. The whole area seemed to be uncannily deserted.

At about noon, they spotted a column of smoke rising from a headland over on the European side. Ten minutes later there was another plume sighted a few miles further on, and yet another beyond that. Naismith remembered Edward Boyle's words that the enemy lit these beacons to warn their ships about the presence of a submarine in the Marmara. It was plainly obvious that it had to be *E11*'s presence that was causing this alarm, and the reason why they had not sighted any ships in the area that morning. As he scanned the shore-line through his binoculars, the smoke beacons made him think that a very similar scene must have greeted the Spanish Armada as they sighted the south coast of England in 1588. The beacons had been spaced about every twenty to thirty miles. Inwardly he felt proud of the fact that his tiny little boat, although not having found any targets as yet, was already disrupting the Turkish supply lines. It seemed that nobody was going to attempt a passage, so he decided to leave his patrol line and head along the coast to see what lay in the anchorage of Rodosto. This coastal town lay eight miles beyond Kodja Burnu, towards the west. He was hungry for a target and he could sense that his crew were getting a little impatient for some action too. The strain of that long nerve-jangling passage needed a reward; maybe it would be waiting for them at Rodosto!

Those men who were off watch, had breakfasted on porridge, a thick glutinous lump of rolled oats mixed with condensed milk and heavily sweetened by a spoonful of black treacle. The men usually held their plates under their chins and simply shovelled the pulpy oat mash into their hungry mouths. It was certainly a nice change to have something hot, because usually the rations consisted of a corned beef sandwich, if there was any bread that had not turned mouldy after the musty dampness of the transit. They would be transferring over to tinned ships biscuits tomorrow, if all of the bread had indeed gone mouldy. A favourite was tinned cheese – known to the crew as periscope cheese. When it was removed from the round can, it looked like a segment of a periscope tube. This morning, having porridge was a rare hot treat, which only occurred when the submarine's battery was fully charged, due to the power-draining hotplate used to produce it. It was used to cook when the battery permitted, which was not that often.

A surface transit usually ensured that the batteries were always fully charged, because the diesels main drive shaft drove straight through the motor generators via the star clutch, before running on through a second tail clutch to drive the propellers. Thus, the motor / generator was acting as a generator and constantly producing a strong charge that was fed directly into the battery. This was known as a running charge. By disconnecting the clutch between the diesel and motor generator it could then assume the role of being an electric motor to drive the boat through the rear tail clutch to the propellers. This was the method used when dived, or manoeuvring on the surface. By isolating the tail clutch, the diesel engine drove directly the generator, which produced a much faster charging rate, called a standing charge.

"This porridge tastes bloody good," said Able Seaman Baxter.

"Anything tastes bloody good to you, Bagsy," said Marne, one of the torpedo-men. "You were probably born in a trough, and we all know that pigs ain't that fussy."

"If anybody wants to leave some, then I will be only too glad to dispose of it for them," he offered by way of a reply.

"I rest my case," said Maine.

Radio Operator Albert Lohden entered the mess area, waving his arms for silence.

"You lot had all better hurry up and get breakfast cleaned away, because the skipper will want Diving Stations in about ten minutes."

Ten minutes later they dived submarine to make their way in towards the objective at the Rostodo anchorage unobserved. Martin was hoping that all the shipping that their presence had deterred from entering the Dardanelles, may well be holed up there. A light breeze had sprung up, which was flicking the sea surface up into small ripple's, that reflected the sun's rays in a blinding effect. However, this sea condition was going to work to their advantage as they approached the town, and even though they were only a mile from the shore, Martin Naismith was fairly confident that their periscope would not be spotted. Disappointingly, on arrival the anchorage was completely empty, with only a few fishing boats pulled up onto the stony beach.

Moving in even closer, he began to use the high-power magnification lens on the search periscope, using it as a pair of binoculars to scan the waterfront. The town was quite an impressive area of urbanisation, stretching nearly a mile from one end to the other. The houses, warehouses, and mosques, complete with their white marble minarets, staggered up the gentle slope of the hillside beyond the harbour wharf. Olive groves were interspersed with cypress trees, forming a natural division between individual plots. He could clearly see people walking along the streets, and a group of young girls sitting on a bench on the promenade. The older women were wearing the traditional white blouses with dark skirts. There was a large group of dark suited men, who were stood around the front of the mosque.

"What day is it," he asked Robert Brown, over on the chart table.

"It's Friday, sir," he replied.

'They must be going in to Friday prayers,' thought Martin.

There was little vehicular traffic, just the occasional horse drawn cart. He continued his slow sweep along the coastline. Then, on the road leading into the town from the west, tramped a seemingly endless column of Turkish infantry with their rifles at the slope. They were creating huge clouds of dust that drifted slowly out across the sea. He could see that each soldier was carrying a large heavy looking back-pack. The column was being led by an officer on horse-back. This line of troops was followed by another dust cloud, which was being created by lines and lines of heavily laden mules. These animals, in turn, were followed by yet more marching infantry. Behind them, and at a slightly higher elevation, he could see a train that was pulling a series of heavily laden flatbed wagons, with strange shapes that were covered by tarpaulins. Martin could make out the barrels of field artillery sticking out from some of the covers. Great thrusts of steam puffed from the steam engine, which reflected silvery white in the sunlight. It irked Martin to see so much enemy activity, and yet be totally impotent to do anything about it. If only he had been fitted with a deck gun.

"Why haven't we got a gun?" he groaned to anyone who was listening.

With them having a gun, they would be able to create absolute havoc ashore, disrupting these supplies and the men from getting to the front. An effective action against these troops could delay them by as much as a day, and the destruction of that train would seriously hamper their war effort. He wished that he had pressed his case for the fitting of one much harder before they had sailed from Malta. He made a mental note to ensure that one was fitted before their next patrol.

Somewhat frustrated, he turned the boat about and headed *E11* back out to sea, surfacing twelve miles from land. From this position he was able to survey a long stretch of the coast, but frustratingly there were still no ships in sight.

For the next hour the submarine lay stopped in the water, with both of her diesels running to fully re-charge the batteries. In the middle of the day the sun beat down causing the internal temperatures to soar. The lack of targets was causing some concern amongst the crew, and as it was so quiet that Martin decided to allow the men Hands to Bathe over the side. Three lucky seamen at a time were allowed to throw off their sweat encrusted clothes, to plunge naked into the crystal-clear water. The Coxswain noted each of their names, and allowed each of them just ten minutes before recalling them back aboard.

"Come in number three, your time is up," shouted some wag.

As the first three men went below, so the next three were allowed up onto the casing for their ten minutes respite from the sticky conditions in which they were forced to live. Everyone had a turn, including the officers, and from the general chatter and high spirits, everyone appeared to feel much the happier for having done so. The swimming lasted throughout that afternoon. The cooling bathe had refreshed them all and when Naismith went below, he was greeted by some friendly banter, indicating that morale was high. As he walked forward, he heard a wind-up portable gramophone playing a music-hall favourite. The clatter of crockery and utensils was a portent that the evening meal would soon be ready. The mess tables were slung up above his head in the passageway, which when unclipped could be lowered down into useful readiness. The cook of the day was preparing the last of the fresh meat and vegetables they had brought with them. Some of the potatoes had already started to turn bad, and some had already been thrown overboard. The last loaves of bread had gone blue with mould, but the enterprising cook had managed to pinch out enough of the blue lumps to be able to mash the remainder into a doughy paste, which he then had rolled out to form the crust of a corned beef pie. Tomorrow there would be nothing left of their fresh supplies. It would all be beyond redemption, and they could all look forward to canned food from then onwards, certainly until they got back from the patrol.

****

The next day there was great excitement when they sighted and stopped a sailing vessel, which was carrying a cargo of logs. Its cargo was not considered as war contraband, but they did manage to commandeer four chickens that were crammed into a wicker crate near the galley, which were taken below and made most welcome by the cook for that evening's meal. Fresh meat is always preferable to any of the canned delicacies. The tinned food could be used another day.

Later that day, a bank of cloud filled the sky, and a heavy mist formed. This prevented them from finding a target, so at 2000 that evening Naismith turned south in an attempt to make contact with *HMS Jed*. He knew that there would be great deal of consternation aboard the flagship regarding their safety.

Albert Lohden, along with George Plowman to help him, had spent the whole day overhauling his wireless set to check for any faults. Albert could find nothing wrong with the equipment, and had meticulously gone through his manual, following the instructions of every page to check out every piece of the equipment.

Martin Naismith was becoming more than a little angry at not being able to contact the Command, and he knew that Commodore Keyes and Charles Brodie, would be beginning to assume that they had been lost. Having no cause to doubt the equipment, Martin began to suspect that Lohden was the culprit for them being unable to transmit, but restrained himself from directly laying the blame at his door. The fault may well lie with *HMS Jed*, but he somehow doubted it. His greatest frustration was the fact that he had no knowledge of this new technology and therefore was completely unable to repair a wireless transmitter himself. This technology had only been in the service for two years, and was only just being installed in newer vessels emerging from the ship-yards. He liked to pride himself that he knew as much about the submarine engines, torpedoes, electrical equipment, and all the other systems that made up *E11* as any other member of his crew, realising too late that this was a serious omission in his knowledge. He had already determined that he would be rectified this upon their return to Murdos. He considered his ignorance was a failure in his duty to his crew, in that he hadn't have foreseen this problem. Lohden seemed a decent enough fellow, but he wasn't a submariner like the rest of his men. Having been drafted aboard as their radio operator from the newly established RN Signal School, he stood alone aboard *E11* in not knowing the intimate workings of their craft. He lacked that unifying commitment that those in the Trade displayed, only being trained as an operator in the new art of radiotelegraphy communications within the surface fleet. In Naismith's way of thinking Lohden belonged to a different navy, and by him not being a member of the Trade, he therefore may have different loyalties. His next assignment might well be to a battleship or a destroyer, or maybe even to a shore station depending on where his somewhat doubtful skills would be required in the future. The man had failed to demonstrate to Martin that he had full confidence with his equipment, and he always seemed to be consulting the operating manual in the office. A submariner never needs to do this, because he is familiar with all equipment's aboard his boat. Since he had been aboard *E11*, he had never had the submariner's deftness of movement through the passageways of the boat. The rest of the men scurried about like rats, getting into holes and spaces that seemed humanly impossible. They rushed along passageways that were festooned with hazardous metal valve hand-wheels and skull cracking protrusions, their heads automatically bobbing one way, then the other – even in the dark – in their eagerness to get to their Diving or Action Station. Lohden on the other hand swaggered about like an American cowboy, when he walked. He never seemed to be in a hurry, or display any expediency. The seemingly never-ending array of bruises that festooned his fore-head bore testament to the fact that he had been extremely slow to learn where these dangerous overhead projections were located.

The sailors of the surface navy were never made to learn the construction and equipment's of their vessel, as the underwater navy were. There was no one else aboard *E11* who was sported a sign of any contusion, and his mess-mates could sense that he was different from them. The most noticeable thing about him was the fact that he always appeared to be a lot cleaner than they did. The lack of water they were able to carry made the liquid a precious commodity. Most of the crew preferred to drink their allowance, and never bothered to wash. Today of course, with a swim, it had been an exception. Throughout the patrol each man remained in the same clothes that they had sailed in. Day and night – asleep and awake. Lohden had brought a huge amount of clean kit with him. He would appear for his watch dressed in his working rig that had been ironed with crisp creases, while the uniform of the other men was a pair of sweat soaked overalls. The surface navy just had different priorities than they did in the Trade. After all, this man was subjected to the same water rationing as the rest of the men, and if he chose to keep himself clean with his issue and not drink it, then that was entirely up to him. It did however create a degree of resentment, because the excessive amount of kit he had brought was taking up precious space that could have been used to keep extra rations, he seemed unable to see why he was the butt of so many cruel remarks.

Never the less, despite his inadequacies, Martin Naismith's decided that his assessment of this man's doubtful skill was quite unfair, and felt he must not allow himself to be prejudiced in his appraisal, as he may well be the victim of a, as yet unknown, defect.

At 0300 on the twenty-second of May *E11* had been navigated to within range of *HMS Jed* once more. Once more the wireless mast was passed up through the conning tower and erected on the bridge. The tall aerial leads were plugged into the water-tight sockets positioned on the bridge deck, and Telegraphist Lohden then tried in vain to make contact with the fleet for the next three hours. He sat squeezed into his tiny radio shack, fruitlessly tapping away on his Morse key.

Signalman Plowman and George Torode were standing together keeping a good look-out watch up on the bridge. As the two of them stood aloft in the cool night air under a glitter of stars, it was hard to believe the carnage that was taking place only 20 to 30 miles to the south of them.

"The skipper was beginning to get frustrated, what with the lack of targets, and with us not being able to contact the base. It's really appears to be getting to him," George Plowman commented. "I wonder where he'll take us tomorrow."

"I don't know, but I trust the skipper's judgement. He's bloody good at his job. There's no messin' about with him. Wherever he takes us, I'll go with him," replied the young man from Guernsey.

"I agree, mate. At least with him, we've got a better than average chance of seein' this war through, and gettin' 'ome in one piece at the end of it," said the Signalman. "I know that my missus would find life very hard without me."

"We didn't make it all the way up the Dardanelle's just to get caught napping here in the Marmara itself! It'll be good to get this patrol out of the way though, cos maybe they'll send us home once we've done our bit?"

"There is a fat chance of that happening before this peninsula has been secured."

"I think I'd like to get married once we get home," said George suddenly, with a boyish enthusiasm. It just seemed to him at this moment in time, that his future definitely did lay with Gladys. He just hoped her feelings towards him had not changed.

Signalman Plowman smiled to himself. "Good luck mate."

After another hour the attempt at trying to make contact with *HMS Jed* was abandoned for the night. During the rest of the night the batteries were fully charged.

All the next day Martin Naismith brought *E11* around to head north east once more, making their way up towards the city of Constantinople to carry out an initial reconnaissance. When they arrived five miles south of the city, there was disappointment at not sighting any shipping either entering or leaving, but they quickly managed to ascertain the general topography of the harbour approaches. From the lines of buoys, they could see, it became obvious that anti-submarine nets were being employed. There may well be a mine-filed as well.

With the distinct lack of shipping in the Marmara, it appeared that *E11* had the whole of this Inland Sea for their own use. Later that afternoon Naismith decided to surface early at 1600. As the tanks were blowing, they had to crash dive immediately when a destroyer suddenly appeared out of nowhere, immediately turning towards to attack them. They stayed deep, and once the enemy ship given up, they watched as it disappeared back over the horizon.

After ten minutes they surfaced once more, carrying on towards this crossroads of the east, propelling on just one of the diesel engines, the other engine being used for a standing charge to keep their batteries fully charged. Despite waiting outside the entrance to the port, no traffic was observed. Why was it so quiet?

At 0300 on Sunday the twenty-third of May, the towering mass of Oxia Island, which reached up to some 300 feet in height, loomed up out of the darkness. Coming around to port at periscope depth, Martin steadied back on to their northerly heading. He noted that the Island may provide them with a hiding place between future visits to the approaches to Constantinople.

The atmosphere aboard the boat had an edge of excitement, because they all knew that they were going in to get close to their goal today. Martin Naismith had given the crew a briefing of his intentions. As the morning light began to divide the horizon into sea and sky, they were greeted by the awesome spectacle of the fabled city that stretched out before them in a great semi-circle. The Constantinople foreshore showed a series of ancient fortifications, huge warehouses, and the funnels of some large ships standing at the piers. Great domes and minarets seemed to jostle for position with the jibs of cranes in an attempt to catch the first rays of the early morning sun. They lay just five miles to the south of the entrance into the Bosphorus, but there was still the nets and mine-field to be determined before they could get anywhere near the port area.

A sloop rigged sailing ship passed slowly ahead of them, so they surfaced, ran in alongside and boarded her. They had not been aboard her five minutes when the lookout reported a steamer approaching from the west, apparently inbound for Constantinople. Quickly recovering their boarding party, they dived and attempted to head her off, but unfortunately, she had already spotted them and was running at full speed towards the shelter of the harbour. Being much faster, the vessel managed to reach safety long before *E11* could get into a position to make an attack. She was a very large ship, standing high out of the water with three tall masts, with one fat squat funnel, and sporting a curved clipper bow. It was highly probable that she was a troopship returning empty, after delivering her cargo of men to reinforce the Turkish army on the peninsula.

There was a frustrated snort from Martin as he saw the ship beginning to pass through the boom in the harbour defences, but then realised that her escape would not be a complete waste of time. Martin began calling out the vessel's course and position to Robert Brown over on the chart-table. This enabled the navigator to plot every one of the courses that she took as she evaded the mine-fields, to get safely into the harbour – it was good information that may come in very helpful in the future. A tug was observed as it towed back the line of buoys, making a gap in the submarine defence net. They then managed to note the exact location of where the boom defences were positioned, knowing that for them to pass through, they would have to follow a ship in. There was nothing else in sight.

So being frustrated once more they turned around and concentrated their attention back towards the sailing vessel, which while they had been occupied, had tried to get under way again. They stopped her once more, and it was d'Oyly-Hughes this time who led the boarding party. They made a thorough search for any contraband. George Torode and George Plowman were acting as lookouts on the bridge while the operation took place.

George was scanning his binoculars slowly along the shoreline of the distant City. The great rounded domes of the mosques stood out high above the rooftops, like soap bubbles on a bowl of water. The whole horizon above the cityscape wore a dirty haze of pollution that lingered over the rooftops, probably the combination of the smoke from ten thousand breakfast fires being lit. George had read countless stories of the Crusaders and their battles with the Saracen in this part of the world. This place was once a main base for the Christian forces, before the Ottoman Empire conquered it. Genghis Khan and his Tartar hoards had made their entry into Europe right here. Alexander the Great had begun his conquest of the Middle East and India from this very spot. The very name of Constantinople conjured romantic thoughts, and now here he was standing less ten miles from the place. He was realising another of his ambitions, because visiting places like this had been one of his main reasons for wanting to join the navy. To be able to see such places of mystery and legend was the fulfilment of a dream. His ambition had been fuelled by reading about the exploits of the great explorers searching for new lands, or pirates, corsairs, and the buccaneers of the West Indies raiding Spanish treasure ships. Here aboard *E11*, we are not so very different from those pirates, he thought. We are here to plunder or sink whatever the Turks puts to sea. We are robbing this sailing boat right now – that is if there is anything aboard her that we can rob.

As his glasses scanned the harbour entrance once again – he stopped suddenly as his eye caught – something unfamiliar. That small strange shape, it wasn't like the rest of the shore buildings – it was moving – it looked more like a small ship – it was a warship!

"Small warship coming out of the harbour entrance, sir," he shouted, with his arm pointing to the position.

Once more they quickly recovered the boarding party. There was a look of relief from her master, as they had scrambled back onto the casing, serving to show how the fortunes of war moved to and fro. Martin Naismith manoeuvred himself away from the sailing vessel and dived immediately. After closing up at Action Stations, he conned the submarine into a position to be able to make a firing shot.

"Steer 063 degrees – half ahead together."

The crew had quickly closed up at their assigned places and a tense excitement was running high. Would this be their first kill?

George Torode was no exception. He could feel his heart pounding within his chest. Standing in his usual position beside Petty Officer Green at the helm, he could feel the earnest expectation for success.

"Flood bow tubes."

They could all hear the familiar hiss of the compressed air, as it forced the water out of the trimming tank and up into the torpedo tube.

"Charge the firing tanks."

Everyone was eager to assist in this task and there was determined activity taking place throughout the whole boat.

"Bow tubes ready, sir," said Guy d'Oyly-Hughes.

"All positions stand by."

Naismith cautiously raised the periscope. It turned out to be a Turkish gunboat, and to his surprise it had not come out to chase them – but amazingly a group of men appeared on the fo'c'sle and prepared to drop anchor. Maybe that merchantman they had chased had reported seeing them, and this chap had been sent out to act as a deterrent? He could clearly see the fo'c'sle party preparing the cable on deck in readiness for dropping their anchor. Then suddenly everybody heard the thunderous rumble of anchor cable through the hull, as their anchor plunged down to the sea-bed. Once the vessel had made itself secure, the Turkish sailors disappeared below.

As Naismith watched, there seemed to be very little activity aboard. The only sign of life was when the head of a look-out appeared up on the vessel's bridge. Martin thought that his assessment of it was acting as guard-ship to the city entrance had probably been right?

"Bring her to 20 feet, Coxswain. Make sure we don't break surface."

Nearer and nearer they crept, like a cat stalking a mouse – 800 yards, 700 yards. Naismith aligned himself directly at the target and placed the vessel right in the centre of the cross wire in the periscope lens. At this short range he shouldn't miss, provided the torpedoes ran true!

"Standby starboard tube......... Fire!"

There was a clatter, followed by a loud thud that jolted the whole boat as the torpedo was physically pushed out of its tube by the compressed air. As soon as it had departed, there immediately followed a draught of cool air that blew through the boat, as the compressed discharge air was vented back inboard, and almost immediately, followed by a violent hissing as a certain amount of water was also allowed to flood into the tanks to replace the weight of the departed weapon. As the boat lurched uncertainly, the Coxswain and the Second Coxswain spun their wheels, fighting to keep control. The seconds were counted down before there was a sudden dull boom – and a spontaneous cheer came from every mouth aboard.

"Got her! Got the bastard! Take that Turk!"

Naismith ignored all of the jubilation around him, keeping the periscope trained on his victim, he became somewhat mesmerised watching the effect of his first torpedo hit on an enemy warship. He noted that the torpedo had hit the gunboat full amidships. It was good to know that the torpedo had ran true before water and debris had shot up into the air and caused the ship to list over to starboard almost immediately.

A smile of satisfaction creased the corners of his mouth as he watched many of the Turkish sailors appearing from hatches. He continued to watch them, and had to give them their due, because they were not going for the life-boat, but heading towards the gun rather than abandoning ship. A flicker of admiration went through him, as he knew that the vessel was obviously sinking, but they were obviously going to fight till the end. The barrel of the gun was being trained around, and it pointed directly at the periscope lens. There was a puff of smoke and a bright flash appeared as the gun-crew got off the first round. An echoing metallic clang on the submarine's hull told them that the shell had exploded somewhere in the water just astern of them. Naismith couldn't help but feel some respect, as the vessel was literally sinking under their feet, and yet they were still preparing the weapon to fire another round. Another flash came from the muzzle, and suddenly everything went black. Seawater came flooding down the inside of the periscope. The Turks had hit them with their dying shot! He realised that there was only the lower lens glass that was holding back the pressure of sea water from flooding down into the boat. Chiding himself for being so complacent, Martin quickly gave the next order.

"Down periscope," he shouted – luckily nothing happened.

"Periscopes jammed, sir," said Wheeler.

The top of the periscope was sticking out of the water indicating their position. If he went deep now, the lower lens might blow in under the increased pressure and yet he had to get it below the surface.

"Take her down to 30 feet – hard a starboard – half ahead."

He knew that he had to quickly open the range, even though there were no more sounds of gunfire coming from the small warship. Raising the second periscope, he immediately saw the gunboat was sinking by the bow. It had only taken five minutes from when she had been hit. He could clearly see the name on her stern, as it rose higher and higher, before following the bow downward on its final journey – 'Pelenk-i-Dria'. Feeling somewhat humbled by the brave audacity of the Turkish gun crew, and experiencing a lot of personal guilt about the damage to their periscope, Naismith abandoned his proposed second reconnaissance of Constantinople.

As they increased the distance from the sinking, he became very angry with himself for his complacency and underestimation his enemy. It had cost them a vital piece of equipment. He conned *E11* out into the relative safety of the open sea, fully expecting a swarm of destroyers to come out after him like a swarm of angry hornets – but fortunately none appeared.

After a safe period of being submerged, and with nothing heard overhead, *E11* surfaced to inspect the damage to her eyepiece. The boat's two Artificers went up to the bridge and quickly found that the six-pounder shell had passed right through the upper tube of the forward periscope, almost severing it – and there was no spare aboard. It would be virtually impossible to replace it out here away from the *Hindu Kush*, so it was decided that temporary repairs would have to be carried out to make it safe, and to prevent any chance of flooding.

After consulting Admiralty Marmara Sailing Directions and the Admiralty Pilot for this area, Naismith decided to retire to the island of Kalolimno, which stood off the Gulf of Mudania. According to the Pilot it was inhabited entirely by Greeks. Although they were not exactly allied to the British cause, the Greeks certainly bore no love for the Turks.

As they arrived, they could see that the island was long and narrow, with hills that rose up to form strange conical peaks. The penned drawing of the silhouette within the manual reminded Naismith of the raised back spines of a Stegosaurus. Looking through his binoculars as they approached, he could see several tiny farms and hamlets, with just one small harbour which would certainly not be big enough to host a warship of any size. They carried out a quick reconnoitre of the tiny harbour which revealed the presence of a couple of fishing vessels at anchor there. However, after his recent humiliation, Martin was being extra cautious, and carefully circled the island once again. Satisfied that all was clear he surfaced and then anchored *E11* in about ten fathoms of water off the western shore.

Chief Jupp and his two assistants came up to the bridge to begin the repairs, each of them looking every bit the oil-covered artisans of the deep that they were. With the Engine Room chief were ERA Brooker and Stoker Wheeler. Extra lookouts were posted to scan every sector of the horizon. The top tube section of the periscope would have to be unscrewed, and the empty hole would then have to be plugged securely enough to be able it to withstand the water pressure at their maximum diving depth. For the rest of the patrol they would have to rely solely on their second, larger search periscope. The damaged one had been their attack periscope, which had a thinner head and only possessed one eyepiece, so that very little of it showed above the water. It had certainly been a lucky shot by the Turkish gun-crew to have actually hit it. The search periscope was the larger of the two, and had two optical lens' giving greater magnification. To contain these extra optic's, it was fixed into a thicker tube, and as a result more would show more above the surface, but it also had the advantage of having a greater field of vision. Fortunately, an attack could be carried out by using either periscope. Martin knew that he would just have to be much more careful when using the larger one in the future.

The men's muscles flexed and contorted, as the artificer's strained on the rope windlass. Their biceps bulged as they pressed against the wooden stave they were using as a lever. One of the men moved the other two aside, giving a mighty roar as he very slowly swiveled the tube on its very fine screw thread. ERA (Engine Room Artificer) Booker was probably the strongest man on the boat. For that very reason he had been the obvious choice, in the absence of having the correct tools on-board for the specific task of unscrewing the damaged head. He was working under Chief Jupp's direction, with young Stoker Wheeler acting as his assistant. After two hours of sweat and strain, the damaged section had finally been removed. It was a very tight thread indeed, and it had seemed to be an endless task of continuously turning the top section anti-clockwise before it finally came away.

With the top of the periscope removed, the submarine was now at its most vulnerable, with a large hole that now prevented them from diving. Once the top had been removed, a thick round wooden bung was hammered into the hole and held securely in place by using a screw clamp. This temporary fix would serve to withstand the water pressure at one hundred and twenty feet, and at the very least it made the damaged periscope seaworthy. The engineers began to clear away their equipment.

Inside the boat the rest of the crew were kept usefully employed by carrying out minor repairs, and cleaning the compartments. Albert Lohden, the telegraphist had been ordered to strip down and check every component of his radio transmitter and receiver yet again. Naismith planned to make another attempt at contacting *HMS Jed* later that night.

When all tasks had been completed, Guy d'Oyly-Hughes inspected the boat as part of the normal Sunday sea routine. He was pleasantly surprised to find everything in a very clean order. The men had worked extremely hard, but although the boat was clean, every man looked filthy.

On completion of the inspection Martin Naismith ordered the hands to a prayer service in the forward torpedo space, but as the men filed in, he could sense that there something was different in their general demeanour. Their normal complacent attitude had been replaced by one of amusement and concealed excitement. Secretive smiles were being exchanged. They had just sunk their first warship he knew, but it had been at the cost of one of *E11*'s two eyes. Losing it would stack the odds against them, and he wondered what they were up to.

The crew obviously did not view their predicament in the same light. For them, a long-held jinx had just been lifted from *HMS E11*. It was something that had plagued the boat since her emergence from the builder's yard. All those frustrating, fruitless patrols in the North Sea, and the ignominy of the thwarted attempt to enter the Baltic had suddenly been lifted from their shoulders. All the mechanical setbacks they had suffered since leaving Portsmouth no longer mattered.

As the service finished, Martin Naismith passed amongst them, trying to discover the cause of this strange mood his men were in. All he saw were big beaming smiles on their faces, and when he enquired as to the reason, they would simply shrug their shoulders in reply. It was as if they were keeping something from him – hiding something and being very mischievous about it. He was puzzled – he did not quite understand what it was.

Finally, he dismissed the men and made his way aft, walking down the passageway towards the wardroom. When he drew back the green curtain that divided the officer's private space from the passageway, there on the table lay an uncapped bottle of beer, and an open box of cigars. Suddenly everything made sense. He remembered the vow that he had made all those months before, stating that he would not touch drink or light up a smoke until he had sunk an enemy warship. Guy d'Oyly-Hughes picked up the bottle and poured him a glass of the beer. As he took a sip, a great cheer went up from the men, and he then drank half of it down. Stepping into the passageway, he raised his glass to them.

"Thank you. I have a wonderful crew. Here's to us all!" he said, holding the beer aloft, before draining the glass.

The rest of that Sunday afternoon was spent swimming around the boat and having the chance to take some welcome physical exercise on the casing. Most of the men swam naked, but a few dived in wearing their clothes in an attempt to wash them clean of the sweat. It was when they emerged from the water that they stripped off, spreading out their garments on the hot metal of the casing, letting them dry in the sun in a matter of minutes. It certainly got rid of the smelly body odour that became encrusted within the material.

George and Basil took to diving off of the conning tower, repeating their earlier fun alongside the *Grasshopper* just prior to sailing. Each man dived deep down the side of the ballast tanks, right under the keel and appeared up the other side of the boat. The water was so clear, that they could actually see the bottom sixty feet below them. They were joined by some of the other members of the crew, intent on matching them, but few could equal their prowess.

In this rare moment of free time Guy d'Oyly-Hughes sat on the casing watching them. Under his arm he had gathered some pieces of wood from packing crates that had once held the fresh vegetables, along with some old used tin cans. For a reason known only to him, he was intent on constructing a raft. Once he had finished, he launched it off the ballast tanks and proudly watched as it floated perfectly. He instructed one of the crew who was swimming by, to attempt to stand on it, but it had flipped over, sending the sailor headlong into the water – to the great amusement of all. However, their amusement was short lived when a warning cry from one of the conning-tower look-outs sent them all scurrying back down the hatch.

"Ship bearing Green 20, sir."

Martin Naismith climbed out of the water, wearing nothing but his birthday suit. He went straight up to the bridge to where he had left his pair of cricketing trousers hanging over the compass. There would be no time to carry out a test on the repair on the periscope. They would just have to pray that it held.

"Everybody below – break the charge – Diving Stations!"

As the last man disappeared down the hatch, Guy d'Oyly-Hughes shouted up from below.

"Both engine star clutches out – both tail clutches in – the submarine is opened up for diving."

Robert Brown took charge of winding in the thirty fathoms of wire that they had used to moor submarine, which had a small mushroom-shaped anchor that could be raised and lowered from within the boat, even whilst dived. Robert ensured that all was secure before following the men below.

Scanning the approaching vessel through his binoculars, Naismith decided that she was too small to waste a torpedo on. As they had not been spotted, he would simply dive until she passed clear – and that is what he did.

Dinner that night consisted of Hard Tack Hash, which had been made from tins of bully beef mashed and mixed with crumbled ship's biscuits. The addition of some chopped onions was made to the glutinous mixture. After another good mashing together, it was patted into fritters and fried on the hotplate whilst the battery was being charged. It was Spartan fare, but everyone ate hungrily, and enjoyed every mouthful.

Everyone managed to grab some sleep that night, whilst the submarine remained within the lee of the Island. This period of relaxation came as a welcome change to the pressures of their daily routine. Their tiredness that night was probably caused by all of the unaccustomed fresh air and exercise.

Later that evening *E11* silently left the shelter of the island, heading off towards the radio billet at the western end of the Marmara. Trying to contact *HMS Jed* had now become a top priority, particularly after the loss of one of their two periscopes. Martin Naismith was secretly hoping that Commander Samson would be able to fly them out a replacement headpiece for the periscope, using one of his sea-planes.

That night, the wind dropped, and a billion stars glittered in the cloudless sky. Martin decided to take the First Watch from 8pm until midnight. The battery was fully charged, so they were running very slowly on their motors. Everyone aboard was feeling reinvigorated – fully refreshed. The boat had been trimmed right down with absolute minimal buoyancy. The helmsman was steering from the lower position, with the boat completely prepared to dive within seconds in any emergency. The Coxswain and Second Coxswain were standing idly by at their respective hydroplane hand-wheels – just in case.

Alone on the bridge, Martin was enjoying the solitude, feeling alert and ready for anything that fate could throw at him. The night air felt fresh and he was hoping that on this occasion they would be able to pass their report. There was a light cool breeze blowing through his hair, and caressing his skin, a rare pleasure.

Approaching his rendezvous point with *Jed*, Martin called down for Albert Lohden come up and to rig his aerial. Leaning over the faint light of the bridge binnacle, he rechecked the signal that he had composed for transmission. He could hear the grunts and groans from the tower as the Telegraphist struggled to pass the electrical leads, up towards George Plowman. The aerial itself was secured into its bracket on the bridge by means of two wing nut clamps. Then the electrical leads were then attached, and the plugs pushed into a water-tight connector located on the deck. They were ready to try again. Naismith handed Lohden the signal, as both communicators went below to the radio shack.

"Ready to begin transmitting, sir," Guy d'Oyly-Hughes shouted up, relaying Lohden's message.

"Carry on," called back Naismith, from his lofty perch.

Martin Naismith was still very unsure that his message would be passed and his trust in his Telegraphist's ability was diminishing with each failure. He had no qualms regarding his confidence in the rest of his crew, but they were men in the Trade, like himself.

After fifteen minutes, contact had still not been established. He knew that *HMS Jed* was only just on the other side of the peninsula in the Gulf of Xeros, which was no more than fifteen miles away from their present position. Lohden had stripped down the radio transmitter several times since their arrival in the Marmara, in trying to trace the fault. So, if the transmitter was OK, then the fault must either be with *Jed*, or there must be some other cause for the fault within the extraneous pieces of equipment.

Martin still bitterly regretted not having had even the most basic instruction in the art of radio telegraphy. He had desperately wanted to take a course before being given command of *HMS E11*, having learned that the wireless was to be fitted. Unfortunately, the advent of the war had prevented it. In his mind's eye he tried to trace the electrical system, attempting to analyse where the problem could lay. In assuming that the fault lay within *E11,* and not with *Jed,* and also knowing that the fault was not in the transmitter or receiver, then logically it had to lie somewhere between the radio shack and this aerial. So therefore, it must be either in the aerial itself, or possibly in those connection sockets for electrical leads. There could be a break in the continuity of the wire within the rubber leads, which was a fairly reasonable hypothesis, considering that they were also unable to receive any messages. The leads from the aerial had to be plugged into a water-tight fitting in the deck here on the bridge, and Naismith's eyes were drawn down to the water-tight socket. He decided that would definitely be the next point of Lohden's investigation. This problem had been the only thorn in their side since sailing, and as a result they had been totally isolated since their departure from *Grasshopper*. The Submarine Staff Officers must now be assuming that *E11* had been lost.

After another failure from the radio shack, he decided to he would retire and order the Telegraphist to thoroughly check these electrical leads, and the dry connection water-tight plugs before making another attempt during the early hours of the morning. He called Lohden up to the bridge to unrig the aerial.

"Trace and check all of the external fittings from your equipment right up to the aerial, Lohden. Give particular attention to your aerial connections, and the electrical leads themselves – especially inspect the area around the aerial water-tight plug connections up here on the bridge. We must locate this problem," he said to him, as he unscrewed the clamps.

At 0200 on the twenty-fourth of May, *E11* came within range of *HMS Jed* once more. Edging ever closer over towards the shore as he dared, Martin Naismith finally pinpointed their position by using the mountain peaks of Elia Tepe and Mal Tepe further westward. Lohden was instructed to send the same signal as before. Naismith had stayed on the bridge, but after handing the watch over to Lieutenant Robert Brown and bidding him good night, he went below. He had only been sat down in the wardroom for ten minutes when there came a knock at the curtained doorway, and Lohden's head appeared at the entrance.

"I've made contact with *HMS Jed*, sir."

Naismith was absolutely stunned. He couldn't believe his ears!

"Are you sure, Lohden? This is great news! Was the reception clear?" he asked, smiling incredulously.

"Yes sir," answered the Telegraphist, his chest swelling with pride.

"Did you finally manage to trace the fault?"

The Telegraphist's chest began to collapse, folding inward, as if it had been punctured. "I – er, that is we, Plowman and myself – we found a defect, sir. It was in the aerial connection plugs up on the bridge," replied the man.

"Do you mean in OUR aerial connection plugs, Lohden?"

"Yes sir, er – you see, there's this oil cup fitted where the aerial leads come in through the pressure hull, sir – it should have been full of oil to provide the wires with complete insulation, but it was empty – and it was that which was causing it to short circuit, sir. It was earthing the transmission straight into the water – I'm very sorry, sir."

Naismith was silent, while he digested the information. Then his face paled with anger.

"Tell the First Lieutenant I want to see him now," he seethed at the man in the doorway.

As soon as Guy appeared, the captain ordered him to clear the lower deck and to muster the entire crew in the control room immediately. Despite the early hour, within one minute his crew were amassed, standing bleary-eye, scratching at unknown irritations, all looked slightly bewildered.

Martin Dunbar Naismith emerged from the wardroom with a doleful Lohden trailing behind. He stopped and indicated for Lohden to stand beside him. The Telegraphist looked downcast and very nervous. He ordered Guy d'Oyly-Hughes to call the men to attention. He then addressed them all very succinctly and deliberately.

"I have called you all together to bring to light an incident whereby one lone individual can be responsible for the destruction of all of us. I consider a man in this category more deserving of the death penalty than any poor shell-shocked soldier whose mind has been stunned by explosions and who as a result walks away from his place of duty. Personally, I think that I could forgive the man who succumbs to the ravages of an abused mind. However, the man who accepts the responsibility for a post of major importance in being a part of a wartime crew, owes it to his shipmates to be fully conversant in his professional knowledge. This man here must have known that he was not fully capable of meeting any emergency that might have arisen, and therefore he is a menace to his ship-mates and a traitor to his cause."

Albert Lohden stood there, a picture of abject misery, but Martin Naismith did not spare the rod on himself either.

"I am ashamed to admit that, that due to my own inefficiency, I was unable to tell this man how to make the correct effective repair. Therefore, now that the repair has been made, let this be an end to the whole sorry affair and may we all learn a lesson from it because it is all of us who are at fault here. We all need to learn the layout of this new radio system – and when we get back, I will make sure that we all do. This must never be allowed to happen again."

The men were then dismissed and nothing more was ever said about the incident. Following his public rebuke Albert Lohden became a model member of the crew from then onwards. He strove hard to learn the basic rudiments of being a submariner, and his whole attitude towards life aboard *E11* became more Trade-like. For the rest of the patrol, such was his zeal that he very seldom left the confines of his tiny radio shack. As they walked by, the crew would see him crammed into its darkened confines, with his face occasionally lit by the occasional arcing blue flashes that were still being produced by the damaged aerial.

For what remained of that night Martin Naismith stayed with Lohden in the radio shack while the periscope defect report was sent through. After four days without news, he was also eager to learn of the latest intelligence. Several reports came back, the most serious being that *B11*, while patrolling off Smyrna had sighted a U-boat on the surface – the first one to be seen in the Mediterranean. When Naismith had enquired how the land operations were progressing, the reply simply stated that – Heavy fighting continues.

****

At 0600 that morning the submarine remained on the surface, when the lookout sighted smoke on the horizon. Martin Naismith immediately set full revolutions and set off in pursuit. Whoever it was, they were going too fast for *E11* to catch, but at least it was an indication that ships were beginning to move in the Marmara once again.

Then at 1000 they sighted a small steamer approaching from the east, heading straight for them. This time Martin was not going to take chances and dived the submarine before he was spotted and as soon as they reached periscope depth. He began studying the vessel carefully through the one remaining periscope. Her freeboard was considerably lower in the water than normal, indicating that she was carrying a heavy cargo. A careful study of her upper-works revealed that she did not appear to be armed. Swinging the submarine around in a semi-circle as she passed, he surfaced the boat on her port quarter. Climbing up the conning tower to the bridge with a megaphone, Martin shouted across for her to stop, by using the little of Turkish language that he knew. The vessel's master seemed to take no notice, and totally ignored him. He began to alter his course, turning his vessel away from the submarine.

"Rifle and ammunition to the bridge, at the rush," shouted Naismith down the tower.

George Torode clambered up, clutching the Lee-Enfield .303, complete with a canvas bag slung over his shoulder filled with loaded clip magazines.

"Right young Torode, load five rounds if you please. I want you to fire the rounds through the bridge windows of that ship."

"Aye-aye, sir," he replied.

George quickly loaded and levelled the weapon, aiming directly towards the vessel's bridge. Aligning on the fore-sight on the central window, he held his breath while he squeezed the trigger slowly. The recoil slammed the butt into his shoulder. The smashed glass showed a jagged black star, standing out against the sunlight reflecting from its surface.

"Good shot lad – and another four if you please," said Naismith, looking through his binoculars.

George took out four more windows with the same determined precision. Naismith increased the revolutions to overhaul her. Picking up the megaphone, he placed the mouthpiece against his lips.

"Stop!" he shouted, again.

They obviously understood what was expected of them, because panic began to erupt on board the vessel. No doubt they fully expected a torpedo to follow this first act of aggression. The ship's captain left the bridge of his vessel, while it was still proceeding at half speed. Some of his crew desperately began trying to lower a lifeboat, but a distinct lack of expertise caused it to capsize. Dangling by its falls, it was ripped away from the davit as soon as it touched the water. It had been the size of the ships own bow-wash that had flipped it over, and all of its occupants were thrown into the sea. Had the captain slowed down, then they may well have had a successful launch. Then a lot more men suddenly appeared on deck dressed in sandy uniforms, and proceeded to lower a second lifeboat, but that too quickly followed the fate as the first. Some of them began panicking, while others seemed so afraid that they simply hurled themselves into the sea.

Looking back, George could see that the vessel's wake was strewn with bobbing heads and waving arms. Naismith steered *E11* over towards the first lifeboat and called down for Guy d'Oyly-Hughes and two seamen to come up and right it with grappling hooks. The evolution took them just a few minutes and once righted, he left the swimming Turks to get aboard and bale it out, so that they could rescue their other comrades in the water. Using his engines, with both clutches connected directly into the propeller shafts, he ordered maximum revolutions and set off in pursuit of the steamer.

George felt excited, really alive as he stood aloft in the warm breeze of the morning. He was still clutching the rifle in his hands, and could feel the power of the steel craft throbbing beneath his feet as the diesels thrust them along at full power. They steadily began to overhaul their quarry once more. As they slowly drew up alongside once more, one of the wing passageway cabin doors swung open and out steeped a man dressed in a lightweight light brown chequered knickerbocker suit. Strolling over towards the rail, his open jacket revealed a dapper white waistcoat. On his feet he wore a pair of bright yellow leather calf length Cuban heeled boots. The man leaned nonchalantly on rail, lit a cigar and shouted across to Naismith in English – albeit with a North American accent.

"Good morning, captain. I'm very pleased to meet you," he called.

"A good day, sir. Will you please go and tell the crew to stop their engines," Naismith shouted back, somewhat perplexed by this unexpected turn of events.

The American flicked his cigar overboard, turned and disappeared through the bridge wing door, and within the next minute the vessel's engines began to slow down. As he appeared back out on deck again, George was simply amazed at the man's appearance. He had never seen anyone dressed so garishly.

"What ship is that?" shouted Naismith – using the megaphone.

"She is the Nagara out of Constantinople – bound for Chanak – carrying Turkish marines."

Armed men came up through the conning tower, and stood behind Guy d'Oyly-Hughes, ready to act as boarding party.

"Any war contraband aboard?" shouted Naismith to the American.

The American made much of the moment. Reaching inside his jacket he extracted a leather wallet from an inside pocket. He flipped the top open and removed another cigar – making much of lighting it before replying.

"Well," he drawled. "I'm not too sure – I haven't really examined the cargo."

Impatiently, Naismith steered the submarine's bows close to the steamer to enable d'Oyly-Hughes and his men to leap aboard. An initial search revealed a six-inch gun barrel lashed to the deck under a tarpaulin, and in the fore-hold there was a six-inch mounting and several twelve-pounder pedestals. In the after-hold they found it to be full of boxed six-inch shells, and stacked on top were large drums marked Krupp, displaying a logo made up of three interlocking circles. These contained the brass cartridge cases for the big fifteen-inch guns based ashore, that were shelling our troops. Guy d'Oyly-Hughes went back on deck and shouted his report across to Naismith.

"Right. We'll blow her up. Set charges low down against the side in the after-hold. Collect the ship's papers, along with all of the captain's documents and bring any charts they have with you when you come back aboard."

While the charges were being set, Guy sought out the flamboyantly dressed American and asked him his business on the ship.

"I am Mister Raymond Gram-Swing of the Chicago Herald, sir," he said with an outstretched hand. "I am here to report on the war."

He shook hands and shouted across to his captain. "He's a newspaper man, sir – a Mr Gram-Swing."

The man leaned over the rail and shouted.

"I want your story, captain. The whole of America will want to read about this! How many submarines do you have in the Marmara?"

"Eleven," Naismith laughed. "You can be sure that you will get plenty of stories, Mr Swing. We're sinking every Turkish vessel that we come across, with the exception of hospital ships of course. Incidentally, did you know that there was war contraband aboard?"

"The United States are strictly neutral in this conflict, sir," he replied with a smile.

"Well, tell the crew over there to get off as quickly as possible, as their ship is about to be blown up, and I earnestly suggest that you get yourself off at the same time, sir."

On the far side of the vessel the crew had already began lowering one of the remaining life-boats. They were more successful this time, as the ship had eventually stopped in the water.

"Goodbye, captain – and I hope to see you again someday!" said the reporter with a wave of his hand.

George was still amazed at the man's attire. He leaned forward, and asked a question that had been troubling him.

"Is that man one of those homosexual men, sir?"

"No – he's just an American, Torode. Now you keep an eye on the vessel should any of the troops appear bearing weapons. If they do you are to shoot them dead – is that clear?"

"Yes sir," replied George, rather hoping that nobody came up on deck.

Having just ignited the fuses to the charges, Guy d'Oyly-Hughes came running aboard with young Torpedo-man Baxter just behind him. Once they were aboard, the submarine went full astern on her motors and watched as the last ship's lifeboat slowly pulled clear of the doomed vessel. While they were waiting for the four-minute fuses to run down, Plowman, who was the look-out, called out to them,

"Ship approaching from the east, sir."

Naismith spun about, turning his gaze to where Plowman was indicating and studied the second vessel through his binoculars. She was still some distance off, but he could that see she too was also heavily laden, and was roughly the same size as the one they were dealing with right now.

When the explosion came, it took them all by surprise with its ferocity. A column of smoke and flame shot skywards, throwing debris in every direction. The after section of the hull burst open like the skin of a tomato in the oven, and water could be seen flooding in. The ship started to heel over almost immediately, starting to go down quickly by the stern, which lifted her bows high into the air for a few seconds before she slid beneath the waves and disappeared from sight. There was just a foaming maelstrom to mark her resting place. Beyond the disturbed water the surviving lifeboat drifted aimlessly.

Before the smoke had cleared over the Nagara's grave, *E11* had dived once more and was stalking her next quarry. However, not surprisingly, this ship had observed the fate of the Nagara, and had immediately turned to head for the nearest port – namely Rodosto. Abandoning any further attempt at concealment, Naismith surfaced the boat, and set off in pursuit on main engines at full revolutions. The distance between the two of them slowly decreased. All the while, the steamer was sounding long alarmed blasts on her siren, and they could see from the thick black acrid smoke belching from her funnel that her engineers were trying to force another half knot from her. Soon it became evident that she was going to make Rodosto before *E11* could catch her, but Martin Naismith was not going to be put off by that. He knew that he would still be able to attack her in the port. As they neared the town, there was a lot of activity taking place along the foreshore. Hundreds of spectators had heard the blasts of the ship's siren, and had come down to the waterfront to watch the unfolding drama just beyond the limits of their harbour. On the stone pier, reaching out from waterfront, stood a number of Turkish troops. Others could be seen running along it to join them. *E11*'s look-outs immediately began scanning the shore-line to make sure that there was no artillery being prepared. The steamer entered the port, a huge white froth of water at her stern as went full astern, just as her bow reached the end of the pier. As she nestled alongside, a gangway was hastily thrown across the gap, and the crew immediately began abandoning their ship – running up the pier into the mass of the approaching troops who had come to defend her.

"How deep is it there?" enquired Naismith of Robert Brown.

"Barely six fathoms, sir," he replied.

"That's just enough – slow ahead together – flood bow tubes and charge firing tanks," he said, giving the now familiar orders.

He pressed the klaxon twice, sending *E11* sliding gently down beneath the surface of the sea, and just a minute later her bow was nudging its way along the sandy bottom as they neared the harbour bar at the entrance. The submarine inched its way slowly forward, her keel scraping along the sandy uneven seabed. Naismith wanted to be sure that he would be close enough to ensure a hit, but the water started to become so shallow, that a considerable section of the periscope began show above the surface. At a distance of 1000 yards from the jetty he was ready.

"Standby bow tube – standby – fire!"

The torpedo was sent on its way, and everyone waited and waited – the silence became overpowering as each man wished for the explosion. The great thunderous report was the shock wave hit the hull with such force that it sent the boat into a rocking motion. Naismith raised the periscope and watched as the whole ship became engulfed in smoke and flames. Almost as soon as he lowered the periscope, there was a second explosion that was ten times louder than the first, temporarily deafening everybody aboard. It was easily the loudest explosion that any of them had ever heard. Naismith tentatively chanced another look at his victim, but there was nothing remaining but smoke and falling debris. The ship had completely disintegrated, taking with it the end of the pier and all of the defending troops that were on it. A quick scan along the waterfront revealed an awful lot of major damage. Some of the taller larger buildings had been semi-demolished by the blast. He also realised at that moment that there must be a great many civilian casualties. The scene of so much destruction shocked him, but his boat and the safety of his men became the first priority as he set about manoeuvring his boat to get out of the danger zone.

"Slow astern both," he ordered. "That ship must have been full of explosives. She has been blown to smithereens. There must hundreds of casualties along that water-front. I noticed that there were a lot of people along there just seconds before I fired."

HMS E11 backed off slowly, away from the shallows and out towards the deeper water, scraping along the bottom once more as she went. Still watching through the periscope, Naismith saw that other troops trying to bring up artillery, and making preparations in readiness to fire their weapons. He heard a rifle bullet clang against the exposed periscope tube. He lowered it immediately, not wanting a reoccurrence of their encounter with the gunboat. As soon as they were out of range of the guns, he surfaced the boat to inspect the periscope tube for any damage. Luckily the bullet had lodged in the lower brass section and was easily extracted. Had it penetrated the upper, more vulnerable section, then they would now have been in serious trouble.

"Two torpedoes fired, and three ships sunk. That is a jolly good day's work, sir," said Guy d'Oyly-Hughes to his captain.

He smiled ruefully, "I am just very sorry that so many civilians have probably been killed. I know that we have to sink everything the Turks put to sea, but it always comes hard when innocent people get in the way."

He turned towards Robert Brown, who was leaning on the chart table.

"Lay off a course for Constantinople, Robert. We'd better get in there while we still have one eye to see with."

Chapter Eleven

Constantinople

At 0630 on Tuesday the twenty-fifth of May 1915, *HMS E11* was abreast of Oxia Island once more, after making a surfaced night passage over the Marmara from its western communication position. Ahead of them the sun had just risen above the distant snow-capped mountains on the Turkish mainland. The early morning rays created a spectrum of colour, evaporating the shadows from the Oxian rock faces. Beyond the island lay several smaller islands, many covered with lush pine, with thrusting spears of Cyprus. All around them there were more smaller rocky islets, littering the approaches towards the harbour at Constantinople.

George was standing his watch on the bridge as look out. He was experiencing the same strange thrill of anticipation that he experienced when they had attacked the Turkish gunboat. Today was going to be different however! Today they were going to attempt a penetration into the main part of the largest harbour in the whole of Turkey. Today they were going to attack Constantinople.

Martin Naismith had been given the top priority of attacking the German cruiser Goeben, and her attendant light cruiser Breslau, by the Submarine Staff back at Murdos. He was just hoping, that by some stroke of luck they would be in port, but the latest intelligence reports positioned them up in the Black Sea. The report had stated that they were being used to bombard the Russian positions around the ports of the Crimea, and Naismith hoped that fate might just be on his side in that they may have returned early. The German's lucky escape from the Royal Navy back in those nervous days just before the outbreak of the war had been reported worldwide, causing the service a lot of embarrassment. Those two ships remained a permanent reminder that Germany's had out-foxed the British, and their destruction would come as a devastating blow to Teutonic moral. At the same time, it would also give everyone involved in this perilous endeavour who were engaged in taking the Peninsula a tremendous boost.

Standing in the fresh morning air, George could not help but wonder what fate had in store for them today. For that matter what was going to be *E11* fate? Would they all still be here to see the stars tonight? The dangers that lay ahead were only too obvious, with more minefields, submarine nets, narrow waterways, heavy surface traffic, and perilous unknown tidal streams. Destiny's dice were heavily loaded against them once more, but the thrill of their proposed adventure was more than compensated for the dangers. One summer, back on Guernsey, he remembered playing at pirates with Matt and Arthur on the wreck of an old ketch that became exposed at low tide in Rocquaine Bay. The wooden skeletal remains provided them the imaginary transport to take them off to the most exotic ports in the world. He recalled that Constantinople had been one of their destinations on those fantasy voyages. His boyhood now seemed so long ago, and Guernsey so very far away, but he could still recall the feeling of elation every time they pretended to sail the wreck into a foreign port. He was experiencing that same feeling right now. Maybe it was just pride; the pride in being part of this small elite unit that gives them the feeling of invincibility! They were indeed a totally isolated – like a band of pirates – operating completely independently behind the enemy lines, using their initiative and sheer ingenuity to survive. George felt extremely proud to be here, just as the Elizabethan seaman of old must have felt a similar pride in attacking the Spanish treasure ships – although there could have been an element of personal avarice attached to those early enterprises. Just as the Spanish had feared those old rovers, so they were going to cause fear and mayhem here within the Turkish heartland.

His analogy that they were like a band of pirates was true, not only in their actions, but also in their dress. Because of the constant heat, many of the crew had discarded their naval uniform, wearing all kinds of casual civilian clothes that they had taken from some of the small vessels they had boarded. Naismith himself had deviated from his oil stained cricket trousers, to wear an old pair of white uniform shorts. Nearly all the crew wore sandals instead of boots. Various designs of shorts and shirts in a myriad of colours were being worn to save their uniforms for when they returned back to their depot ship. Overalls were still being worn by the stokers on watch in the Engine Room, as wearing shorts increased the danger of being burnt on the hot metal of the engines. One of the crew had seized a pair of the Turkish bulbous balloon-like pantaloons, and provided the crew with great amusement as he paraded them through the boat. Another, sported a pair of brightly coloured Turkish slippers, complete with curled up toes. This unconventional attire had become known throughout the boat aptly enough as *Pirate Rig*.

Martin Naismith had been quick to emphasise that this change of attire would only be permitted whilst they were on patrol, and just as soon as they made the passage back, then they would all be required to revert back to the normal uniform dress regulations that was employed by the rest of the service. He could see that by relaxing the dress code, it gave his men greater purpose, and made their lives that bit more comfortable in the lighter attire.

Standing just ahead of George, at the front of the bridge Martin Naismith turned as he standing above the conning tower upper hatch, and ordered him below. The captain took a final look all around, taking a last deep breath of fresh air, before he too descended the ladder. The upper lid was thumped shut onto its rubber seating, sealing off the natural freshness of the outside world. The retaining clips were engaged, and *E11* quickly dived down to periscope depth. Standing at the periscope Martin immediately brought the boat around on to a northerly heading, straight up towards the cityscape. When he had been on the bridge, he had noted that there was a light morning breeze which was whipping the sea surface enough to produce a very fine spray, which he now hoped would serve to hide his periscope. Unfortunately, this hope quickly turned to despair, because on his first sweep the same spray produced droplets on the lens glass, distorting his vision. Naismith was annoyed at being forced to continually dip the exposed glass lens below the water to wash it clear. Slowly the submarine made its approach towards the city as it grew out of the horizon.

An hour passed, and another look through the periscope saw the city in all of its majesty. Every one of the buildings appeared golden and bright in the radiance of the morning sun. Although he knew that there was a breeze up there on the surface, Naismith could see that the air was sparkling and clear.

He brought the submarine around onto a new course to head up towards the outer limits of the harbour defence nets, and was happy to note that the effect of the spray had decreased significantly. As he moved his lens across the sprawl of red terracotta rooftops, he could see some of the magnificent domed buildings, bursting up like the rounded humped backs of a pod of whales breaching the ceramic surface. They were all accompanied by the pointed needle-like minarets thrusting skyward, each showing the protruding concentric balconies, bulging like the rings on a bamboo cane.

In the waterway he could just make out the steam ferries, belching out huge clouds of black smoke as they plied their way between the European and Asian shores, but was disappointed that there were no ships in sight entering or leaving the port.

Then on the next look he spotted a group of fishing boats, appearing from nowhere at the far end of the line of buoys that marked the entrance. With the submarine being on the outside of the harbour defences, he badly needed a vessel to enter or leave, so that he could take advantage and slip through the opening of the booms. He could see a possible problem, as this capricious fleet of fishing boats and dhows, were obviously just beginning their working day. He would wait for a larger one, but there was the mine-field to get through first.

He went over and stood beside Robert Brown at the chart table. Together, by using the vital information they had gleaned from observations of the entry of the large vessel during their previous reconnaissance, Martin decided that he would go deep and negotiate his way in through the minefield. Going down to eighty feet, he steered straight towards the boom. Fortunately, this time there were no contacts with any of the mooring wires, and on returning back to periscope depth, he immediately noticed that the small vessels were passing through the boom. He was just too late! Then he spotted that it was being held open for the approach of a rusty tug-boat, that was belching thick black smoke. It was the opportunity that he wanted. Then he realised that it was the vessel that operated the opening and closing of the boom nets, not coming out, but was intent on shutting the boom. He did not have much time.

Taking his chance, Naismith increased speed and went deep once more, gliding *E11* straight through the opening left by the departing flotilla. Standing in the control room, there was a smile of satisfaction on his face, giving every man confidence that the perilous journey was going well. A renewed determination filled them all as the submarine headed straight towards the narrow harbour entrance. Two miles from the gap, he slowed the boat and decided to wait and see if anything of significance would present him with a target.

By 1200 they remained undetected, and were less than a mile from the entrance. Through the periscope he could see the large square Marmara Tower that stood over on the foreshore to the north of them. It would be just another three more miles further before they reached Seraglio Point, the sharp corner that guarded the approach to the golden horn. Martin Naismith steered *HMS E11* over towards the European shoreline at this point.

The stiff breeze they had experienced outside the harbour had now completely disappeared, and the glass of the raised periscope lens remained clear and dry. The coastal road, that runs from the fish harbour at Kumkapi, around the headland tip, before heading up towards Seraglio Point, was now clearly visible. Martin Naismith began to describe everything that he could see, sharing his visual experience with his men. Looking through the double eyepiece, he could see people walking with a purpose. Some were pushing carts, while others rode on bicycles, or donkeys, and very occasionally a motorised vehicle would thread its way through the general throng. Along this waterfront, there were many small brightly painted craft bobbing restlessly at their buoys, or anchor lines, in this lively sea.

"Flood tubes," ordered Naismith, although there were no targets in sight at the moment, he felt that as they were nearing the harbour entrance, it would be as well to be prepared.

Keeping *E11* a mile distant from the western shore, and leaving himself just enough room to pass around the Seraglio Bank, he altered course slightly to port when the dome of St Sophia was bearing due north. He was now heading indirectly in towards the harbour mouth, with its prominent white lighthouse clear on their port bow, as they finally entered into the lower reaches of the Bosphorus itself.

As the harbour mouth became clearer, so the waterway itself suddenly began to narrow. The continents of Europe and Asia now lay just one mile apart. Martin had already seen that over on their starboard bow lay the big Haidar Pasha port terminus and docks. Just to the north of the port lay the old town of Scutari. He scanned back to the port area. There were long lines of cranes, canted obliquely at the piers, and beyond them several tall grain elevators providing a semi-industrial scene. He noted at the quaysides were the masts and funnels of many merchant vessels of all shapes and sizes. He watched as the crane jibs traversed to and fro, filling their holds. A short distance away, finer on his starboard bow, standing mid-channel on a small rocky island, was the unmistakable solid square cube landmark of the Leander's Tower. This was a good time to take a navigational fix!

Passing his bearing of the Tower, taken from the periscope, over to Robert Brown on the chart table, he quickly spun the optics around to align on Seraglio Point. Both bearings were quickly plotted and Robert Brown declared that they were safely in the middle of the channel.

On hearing the name of Leander, George remembered Mr Jeffries at school telling the class of a story from a book of Greek Legends. He had related the tale of the unfortunate Leander, who had drowned in the Hellespont in his attempt to swim over to meet his true love, Hero. To him it felt amazing that he was right here in the very same stretch of water where that legend had been created. Was it too soon to hope that they were going to make a legend of their own!

With their entry into the Bosphorus itself, the single ventilation fan had been shut down, and within the boat the atmosphere was becoming hot and humid. With the lack of any movement of air, the uncomfortable conditions were being exacerbated by the heat produced by the bodies of the crew. This increasing heat quickly initiated the condensation process, where the hot air met the relative coolness of the pressure hull, creating moisture droplets. Sweat began pouring down faces, and exuded from every inch of their bodies. Their clothes quickly became sodden, sticking to their skin in a wet embrace. The moisture drops began to fall from the cold pressure-hull like a summer shower, making the deck wet. There was no escaping the purgatory for anyone. Unable to get away from the conditions, submariners quickly learn that by sitting still the symptoms of their irritation will gradually ease. It does not go away, but is borne with a stoical resolve. Most simply tried to ignore it, knowing that it was part of the Trade. Somebody remarked that as the air was so hot and steamy, it exactly matched where they were – because Turkey was famous for its steam baths. The titters of laughter served to ease the tension.

Another quick look through the periscope revealed that over on the European shore, just a quarter of a mile away on their port side, stood the upper ramparts of the imposing walls guarding the Topkapi Palace. This was the Sultan of the Ottoman Empire's main residence. The building itself stood high on the promontory that directly overlooked Seraglio Point. Just beyond, he could clearly see the great dome of the Hagia Sophia – one of the most famous churches in Christendom, and now a mosque under Ottoman control.

Martin Naismith started describing its features to anyone who listened, when suddenly the bow of the submarine was pushed hard over to starboard by some unseen phenomena. Eyebrows lifted, and a surprised expression filled every face. Were they going to be pushed over onto a mud shoal?

Staying at twenty feet to avoid the dangerous deep currents, Martin carefully brought the boat back around to port, as they glided on past the shallow spit at Seraglio Point, and actually entered the main part of the harbour of Constantinople itself. Immediately after rounding the point, Martin could see the masonry arches of the Galata Bridge directly ahead of him. Although uniform in design, he knew that the centre section could be removed to allow ships in and out of the Turkish naval port beyond. The bridge parapet was adorned by hundreds of fishermen, their rods sticking up like the hairs on a caterpillar. As he scanned the bridge, he felt a pang of disappointment, because he could see that the removable sections of the bridge were clearly set in place to allow the road traffic to pass over the structure, which made it impossible for him to proceed any further. Martin knew that there would be rich pickings in there, but with a frustrated grunt he brought *E11* around to starboard. While they were making their turn, he carefully scanned each of the masts of the warships protruding above the bridge structure, but was unable to identify any as being of cruiser size or heavier. Certain of the fact, he would make a radio report tonight that there was no sign of the two German ships. He thought that most of the Turkish capital ships must be employed in the Black Sea against the Russians, or could be found somewhere down in south in the Dardanelles! He remembered that there were two battleships down there for sure.

Another recheck confirmed that the German cruisers were definitely not at home – so he decided to proceed onward to seek a new target, and suppressing his disappointment, he conned the boat northward up the waterway in search of a target.

As the boat continued around to starboard, so the harbour traffic in this area increased dramatically, as this was one of the main ferry port terminals of the city. Martin suddenly realised that he faced the constant danger of being run down. Many of the larger ferries berthed at the quayside here, with their tall funnels belching black smoke, they were casting off their lines without any warning, swinging straight out towards the centre of the harbour. Over on the quayside Martin could see the smoke from the many cooking fires, as vendors cooked fish rolls for sale to the passengers.

Raising the periscope was becoming increasingly hazardous, and was seriously adding to their chance of being detected. More ferryboats would suddenly appear out of nowhere, each filled to the gunwales with passengers, and passing far too close for comfort.

On this next look, Martin could see that out in the middle of the waterway there were a number of tugs towing several large barges strung out in long lines. They were all linked as they headed south towards the mouth. He lowered the mast quickly as the mosquito buzzing of fast motor launch was heard speeding past.

The next time Naismith chanced to raise the periscope, he found himself looking directly into the face of the captain of a passing Arab dhow. The master mariner was standing imposingly at the stern, with his legs apart, wearing wide red bulbous pantaloons. His dark navy jacket was with worn without a shirt, and he had his arms folded across his chest. Naismith could see from his surprised expression that he had spotted the periscope. His mouth had dropped open in sheer astonishment, and he began to rub his eyes in disbelief. Martin did not give him a second chance, a swirl of water was all the man would see when his gaze returned to the spot!

The next time he raised the periscope, they were just astern of a Turkish Admiral's barge, which they had heard passing close overhead. The flag pennant was fluttering quite clearly on the stern, as its bearing opened.

With a slight lull in the surface traffic, Naismith took a quick series of fixing bearings to check his position before lowering the periscope once again. He left it down for a distance of a quarter of a mile before chancing his next look. After all they were in the heartland of their enemy. It was an opportunity would be very difficult to repeat, and he became determined to find a target to attack, something that would really create an impact here.

On his next look he spotted a warship ahead.

"Yes!" he shouted excitedly.

Everyone's eyes turned towards their captain expectantly. Their ears strained, wanting to hear a description of what he had just witnessed – excitement began to mount. Martin brought *E11* around to port.

"There is a cruiser at anchor – bearing 028 degrees – distance 500 yards. Standby to open bow caps! I'm going to close him – full fields – watch your depth Coxswain."

The torpedo-man working at the motor switchboard increased the field switch to give maximum resistance across the armatures, slowing the drive motors.

Martin was hoping that it was one of the German cruisers, but then as he scanned her decks, his excitement was punctured by disappointment.

"Hold everything," he declared. "I can see her flag – she's a bloody American. Trust the Yanks to get in the way. Down periscope – keep 30 feet – steady as she goes. She must be here on a courtesy visit. How the bloody hell did she get through the Dardanelles, I would like to know?"

The air of anticipation around him burst like a balloon. As they closed the vessel, he could see that she was the *USS Scorpion*.

A thought came to him. She must simply be trapped here, as the Dardanelle's have been declared a war zone, and any transit would be out of the question, not even by a neutral warship.

Giving the cruiser a wide berth, he took *E11* along a line of buoys, as they drew closer towards the centre section of the Bosphorus. All the way Naismith was continuing his search for the German cruiser Goeben, but apart from the American cruiser, there were no other warships in sight. Failing to find his intended target, he steered *E11* around to port to head over towards Pera, a suburb of Constantinople, on the northern side of the Golden Horn part of the European shore.

As they got nearer, he noted that there were several vessels moored on the quayside there, and he immediately selected a large troop transport that was tied up directly in front of the Topkhana Arsenal – which formed part of the main Turkish Army Barracks and Stores Depot. There were a number of smaller vessels lying just ahead of her, and he thought that he might be able to fire a torpedo amongst them, and also hit the trooper with a left and right shot.

He began his set up, however just at the moment of he was about to fire, without any warning, the bow of the submarine veered off to starboard. Realising that this area was where the main current of the Bosphorus met a counter current coming down from the Black Sea to create a great deal of turbulence, he steered *E11* out of the trouble area.

In these restricted waters there was not a lot of room to manoeuvre, and Petty Officer Green was struggling on the helm to maintain his course. Once the eddying effect had passed, and taking note of this recent phenomena, Martin quickly carried another set up to recalculate his aim at the larger vessel . He fired his port bow tube. The whole of the submarine shuddered as the compressed air forced the torpedo out from its launcher, despatching it off on its deadly mission.

In the fore-ends, standing at the bow tubes, the torpedo-men could hear the high-pitched whirr of the Brotherhood three-cylinder compressed air driven engine as it started up and drive the weapon forward, quickly accelerating up towards forty knots.

Watching its wake through his periscope, Naismith was suddenly horrified as the torpedo's track suddenly veered off at a right angle, before it leapt completely out of the water. The weapon crashed back down with a huge splash, and disappeared beneath the surface.

"Capsized gyro," he snarled, quickly rechecking his alignment on the target. "Standby the starboard tube – Fire."

He watched the track of the second torpedo as it headed directly out towards the large transport. It would be at least fifty seconds before impact. Safety first, and he began an all-round sweep. He was just completing it when he noticed the track of another torpedo that was heading straight towards him. Instinctively he shouted.

"Full ahead both! 75 feet – Flood the Auxiliary Tank! Take her down as quick as you can Coxswain. That rogue torpedo has circled and is heading right for us."

Every member of the crew could hear the torpedo as it sped close overhead, only to circle once more before heading off over in the direction of the Galata Bridge. They eventually heard it explode somewhere over there.

Seconds later there was a much heavier second explosion, as the second torpedo struck the large Troop Carrier berthed at the Arsenal Quay. Naismith was longing to come shallow to be able to observe the effects of his shot, but he was not entirely sure that the torpedo that had so narrowly missed them was their own rogue. It could just possible that it was one that had been fired from the shore based German Brennan tubes, that the Turks were reported to possess as part of the city defences.

If it was one of these weapons, then he knew that they were wire guided from the shore, and could be physically directed straight onto their target. Deciding to stay deep, he issued some orders.

"Hard a port – Slow ahead both – Hold her at 75 feet – Navigator set a course back towards the southern entrance."

Suddenly there was the booming sound of gunfire – it came from every direction – all around them. It was like standing under a constantly rumbling thunder cloud. They had certainly disturbed a hornet's nest.

Every gun that protected the city must be firing at any ripple in the water.

George felt his shoulders instinctively retract with each close explosion, the adrenaline flooding through his veins made every action sharp and decisive. He felt elated at having been part of a successful strike at the Turkish heartland, but there was a twinge of disappointment that there were no warships to be had. He just could imagine the chaos taking place within the city above. There must be absolute panic up there, after being hit by a hidden, unknown attacker. As a parallax, he thought of the consternation caused if a U-boat were to go up the River Thames into the Pool of London and torpedo a ship.

Then suddenly, without any warning, the deck began to incline downward beneath their feet, despite both of the hydroplane operators taking correcting actions. Both men were spinning their hand wheels, fighting desperately to ease the angle, but it continued to increase.

After a few minutes of terror, the angle began to reverse, and then I was the bow that rose, as the stern went down alarmingly. Guy d'Oyly-Hughes desperately tried to compensate, ordering water to be flooded into the forward tanks – but before Stoker Wheeler could carry out the order, the boat gave another huge lurch, rolling first to port, and then to starboard. It was as if some powerful giant paddle was stirring the waters around them into a maelstrom. No matter what they did, the elements were in total control. Then suddenly the submarine went completely out of control, and both the planes-men panicked as they tried to prevent the conning tower from breaking the surface. What had actually happened was that the very strong current that was being funnelled down through the Bosphorus from the Black Sea, was suddenly confronted by a multitude of counter currents coming at an angle from the Golden Horn, which met up just beyond Seraglio Point to create these whirling eddies. In this area there was also the seaward influx, flowing inward from the Marmara, which was enough confusion to create this vortex of tide rips. It felt as if the boat was on a joy ride at the fair, as *E11* rose sharply, before diving ever deeper. Trying to fight these unpredictable events, was like a cowboy trying to tame a bucking bronco. The boat's head would swing around rapidly, before suddenly rushing back the other way. On the helm Petty Officer Green found it impossible to predict the next movement. In his attempts to keep control. the submarine actually turned three full circles whilst being in the grip of these strong tidal forces. They were simply at the mercy of these natural phenomena. Time seemed to lose its meaning, in their efforts to maintain equilibrium. Then all of a sudden, the thunder of the guns began to fade, and as the external noises slowly abated, so the boat movements began to calm, and the violent movements eased. Martin did not want to risk showing a mast, so he went over to the chart table.

"Have you any idea at all where we are, Robert?" he asked the navigator.

Lieutenant Brown had been hunched over the chart, between frequently checking the log, trying to ascertain exactly where they had ended up. He had just applied the latest information to his best DR estimate – it made no sense what so ever. In answer to the captain's question, he could only shake his head. It was like playing a game of blind man's bluff – only it was them who were the ones who were giddy and blindfolded. They had little clue as to where they were. He looked up at the clock.

"I can only give you a very approximate guess, sir," he replied. "I have no idea how far that current carried us. I am just hoping that we do not get funnelled towards the Golden Horn area. I think that we should be somewhere just to the north of Seraglio Point, heading out towards the harbour mouth."

"I hope so too, Bob," he replied.

It was nearly half an hour since the torpedo explosion, and the gunfire from the shore batteries had completely ceased. As the quiet became apparent, it was about this time that they managed to fully regain control of their craft. Still deep and only knowing by their compass in what direction they were pointing, they had absolutely no idea how far the current had carried them. The cessation of the gunfire probably meant that patrol vessels were now out searching for them, and they had the nasty habit of dangling nasty little explosive charges at the end of dragged lines that exploded on contact. He knew that he had to establish his position, but said, "We will wait another twenty minutes."

Everyone sat still in an uneasy silence, sweat still exuding from every pore. The air had become very stale, and their breathing became laboured. Each second seemed a minute, and every minute a lifetime. Their jangled nerves reacted to every anomaly – highly tuned to meet the unknown. Therefore, the faint change in the air quality they were breathing was quickly noted. It was strange how the perpetrator always seemed to wait for these moments of crisis. Maybe it was simply a nervous reaction that caused the miscreant to discharge his unwelcome cargo. This time, due to the tenseness of moment, it was not welcome and the foul stench caused great annoyance.

"If I catch the dirty bastard who keeps releasing himself, I'm going to impale him on the end of a torpedo," said Coxswain Dowell loudly from the after hydroplanes hand-wheel.

Every pair of eyes searched other faces for some sign of guilt, but the culprit was not about to give his secret away. He must be already aware that he had far too much to answer for.

Twenty minutes later there was another violent rocking motion, as *E11* went out of control once more. They were actually pushed down so deep that they scraped the along the bottom, as they could hear the keel scratching its way along the seabed. Re-established some control, Naismith decided that he had to come shallow to establish their position.

"Full ahead both – Keep 30 feet."

The periscope broke surface, Naismith completed an all-round look to make sure the boat was not in danger before breathing a sigh of relief. They had thankfully missed the entrance to the Golden Horn, and were back in mid-channel, still heading down towards the entrance. Even better, the bow was pointing in the right direction!

"Standby bearings – Dome of Hagia Sophia bears 306 degrees, Chamlija Tepe bears 069 degrees – Plot those quickly."

Robert Brown marked them down on the chart, and breathed a sigh of relief.

"We're well clear of any danger, sir, and in the centre of the channel."

"Good – Robert take us out through the plotted course, and then steer south west – Inform me when we're approaching the mine-field – fall out from Action Stations."

The tension evaporated as the men left their stations, and they made their way back to their respective messes. During the next hour the Navigator managed to con *E11* clear of the Turkish capital without any further difficulty.

The transit of both the mine-field, and passing through the submarine net went without incident, and by 1530 that afternoon they were lying deep within the Marmara, completely out of sight of land. Naismith surfaced the boat, and quickly announced Hands to Bathe. After all of the tension of the day, it was just what everybody had been dreaming of. They all had a turn, and it acted like a release valve, a welcome way of venting off all the nervous strain that they had been subjected to. The cooling waters not only washed away the sweat and the grime from their bodies, but many of the crew were beginning to develop nasty red rashes, a direct result of the sweaty humid diesel laden atmosphere they were forced to endure, and the seawater seemed to eased their discomfort. Most of the men jumped over the side in the clothes they had been wearing all day in order to wash away the salty sweat encrusted in the material. They quickly dried in the afternoon sunshine, and soon their world began to feel normal once again.

That evening Martin Naismith took the First Watch up on the bridge. He knew what a strain his men had had to endure, and decided that tomorrow he would take a full day of rest. After finding a safe area he would give the crew a Make and Mend. In the Navy this term stemmed originally from a day set aside to give sailors in Victorian times the opportunity to make new, or mend their old clothes. In more recent times it had become the Navy's term for some time off from their official duties.

He steered the submarine back towards anchorage at Oxia Island, and the following morning the men were turned to cleaning out the boat, which had become increasingly foul. On completion Martin Naismith had carried out an inspection accompanied by Guy d'Oyly-Hughes. It was intended to be a semi-formal walk through the boat, and the two officers had spent a good deal of the time chatting to the men, raising their spirits and morale.

When they reached fore-ends, where the reload torpedoes were stowed in securing racks, looking at the long sleek weapons gave Naismith an idea, following the near miss of the rogue weapon that had suddenly turned of them and very nearly put an end to their penetration. He began thinking how to make sure that each and every weapon would perform correctly.

On completion of the inspection of that compartment, he ordered that a barrel of fresh water, that had been relieved from the ship they had sunk with explosives, be used by the men to be available for them to wash their clothes thoroughly. Hands to Bathe was piped once again. Naismith took the watch on the bridge, watching his men relaxing. He called Guy d'Oyly-Hughes up to share his thoughts.

"I've been thinking about that weapon that we lost yesterday to a toppled gyro, Guy. We go through such immense risk and significant dangers to get these torpedoes up here. Each one must be worth its weight in gold. What about if we were to reset the sinking mechanism, so that if one should miss, or the weapon should develop a problem, or possibly fail to explode, then the torpedo will float to the surface at the end of its run? Then once the target has passed clear, it will be a simple case of us going to over to pick it up. We can easily reset the detonator on the warhead to make it safe. Then all we have to do is simply rig the portable davit, and hoist it back on-board. Once we have it back below it can then be overhauled and reconditioned before it's recharged, so then we can use it again. That way every one of the weapons that we bring up here will be used to good effect! Any weapon that is lost is one wasted needlessly."

Guy d'Oyly-Hughes nodded his head, absorbing what Martin had just said. It had sounded simple enough, and he wondered why he hadn't thought of the logical idea himself. However, being a stickler for the rules, he thought that he should remind his captain of the official submarine standing orders.

"The torpedoes are designed to sink, sir, so that other surface vessels won't accidentally run into them."

Naismith smiled ingeniously.

"Yes Guy, that is all very well in normal peace time – but we are at war. So, if we are going to pick up these weapons, that rule will not apply – will it? Even if we can't pick it up, the only vessels in this area that could run into them are those of our enemy. So that will save us all a lot of trouble of having to aim and fire the wretched thing again. Don't worry, I will take the full responsibility for any mishaps."

So, Martin Naismith instigated a new order that henceforth all the torpedoes should be set to float after their run. That meant that every torpedo was going to be a hit from now onwards, be it on its first firing, its second, or if necessary, even the third firing.

After having talked to his men earlier that morning, the general consensus of opinion was that they should have some sort of a celebration, following their successful attack on Constantinople, and so he ordered the cook to try and produce a decent hot lunchtime meal for everybody. There was no shortage of volunteers to lend a hand in the task. Tins of bully beef were opened, and the white fat was carefully scraped off the top of each can. Several packets of ships biscuits were then pummelled into a powder in a metal bowl, and the fat was added to the mix. This was kneaded together to produce a rough coarse dough which was then rolled out flat, using an empty bottle. The metal baking tins trays were lined with this rather sticky pastry. Then each case was filled with the mashed tinned meat, which in turn had been mixed some bottles of a Yorkshire Relish mixture. This culinary masterpiece was then covered with another layer of the pastry. The meat pies were baked one at a time in the tiny electric oven. This was the first time on this patrol that the oven had actually been used, because it uses so much battery power. As they were anchored with engines constantly charging the batteries, this time it did not matter. When each pie emerged, the heavenly smell set everyone's taste buds drooling in anticipation. It proved to be a very tasty meal, although it took some time to scrape some of the hard-baked pasty away from the surface of the trays afterwards.

After lunch there was another session of Hands to Bathe, which was particularly refreshing in the shimmering heat of the early afternoon. Once everyone was had taken their exercise, the men relaxed on the casing, getting as much sun as they could before their skin turned red. Everyone's spirits rose, and many of their fearful doubts about surviving out here in the Marmara were quickly lifted. The change in the mood in the crew was plainly visible, as everybody seemed to be talking at once, bandying jokes, and singing popular ditties.

Lieutenant d'Oyly-Hughes, along with two of the men, began building another raft from some of the scraps that were due to be jettisoned. It was another small square affair, but this time it had the loom of an oar sticking up through the middle. An old tobacco tin had been formed around the top to make it look like the hooded lens of a periscope. It soon became the object of some amusement for the onlookers. When Martin Naismith came down and joined Robert Brown, who was staring at the creation as he stroked his chin thoughtfully, he was informed of the navigator's conclusions.

"I think Guy has made us a new periscope, sir."

Guy d'Oyly-Hughes heard the remark and looked up at them from the ballast tanks.

"Do you really want to know why I built it, Bob?"

Robert shrugged his shoulders. "Is it to give our friend the Turks a target to practice his ramming techniques?" he guessed.

The intelligent guess surprised the First Lieutenant. "Well – Yes, in a way. Ah, but while he is busy trying to ram it, what do you think that we'll be doing?"

"Watching from a safe distance and splitting our sides laughing," said Robert confidently, through guffaws of laughter.

"Maybe you would Robert, but I'd be trying to torpedo him!"

Robert's laughter suddenly ceased and Naismith leaned forward to get a better view of his Number One's new toy.

"Aircraft bearing green two zero," the cry from the bridge look out, sent everyone scurrying below.

"Come on men. Clear the casing – Diving Stations," roared Naismith.

The naked men in the water scrambled up onto the tanks, snatching up their clothes from the deck and half jumping and half falling down through the hatch in their hurry to get below.

"Tail clutches are in – Engine clutches out," someone screamed from the Engine Room.

"All hatches shut," was another shouted report.

Naismith now stood alone on the bridge as the aircraft made its run in towards him. He had a distinct disregard for the Turkish pilot's accuracy in bombing. Taking off his hat, he waved it in a long arc above his head, before stepping down into the hatch.

"Open main vents – Flood auxiliary – Half ahead both – Take her down to 30 feet," said Naismith, not pausing for breath, as he gave the string of orders.

Despite Martin's scepticism the following loud bang was uncomfortably close, and was followed by two more in quick succession.

"That's his lot," said Naismith to no one in particular.

He surfaced the boat once more, confident that the aeroplane would now be impotent. Stepping up onto the bridge once again, the aircraft was nowhere to be seen. Putting his binoculars to his eyes, he quickly scanned the horizon. Then his heart stopped in his mouth, as he saw a periscope less than half a mile away. At that very second, just as he was about to give the order to crash dive when he remembered Guy d'Oyly-Hughes' newly made raft, and his face broke into a smile.

"He probably aimed at my raft, sir – that's what saved us," said the First Lieutenant, once he had joined him on the bridge.

"That's probably why he got so close, and damned nearly hit us you mean," smiled Naismith.

None the less he ordered the toy periscope to be recovered because it intrigued him, and he manoeuvred around to pick it up. Once it was taken back on board, he set a course over towards their signalling position to report their attack on Constantinople back to base.

Later that evening, Naismith and d'Oyly-Hughes sat in the wardroom together mulling over the charts, and carefully going over their past operations. The rhythmic buzz from the transmitter in the radio shack had become a welcome sound, providing them with a direct link to their base. It was a very long report, which detailed the sinking of the Nagara, and of the ammunition ship alongside the pier at Rodosto. It also included a description of their triumph at Constantinople.

An hour passed, then two, and still the Morse code was being tapped out on Lohden's transmitter key. He was still having great difficulty with the set, but with his new conscientious attitude towards his job he persevered. Impatiently, Naismith made his way up onto the bridge and joined Robert Brown, who was the Officer of the Watch.

The wind had got up causing the sea to splash up against the ballast tanks, causing a fine spray to dampen any exposed skin. The lookouts were Plowman and Torode, who were both finding it difficult to maintain their night vision because the dampness of the air coated the lens of their binoculars. Just above them the aerial continued to spark, lighting up the moisture laden atmosphere with tiny blue arcing flashes. The flickering was not only destroying the night vision of the lookouts, but it would obviously be observable from some distance, which may attract any curious observer. Naismith sent Brown down to see how Lohden was getting on.

"Tell him to speed things up," he added as the navigator's head disappeared down the hatch.

It would be absolutely ironic if they were to be caught on the surface, with both lookouts blinded, just as they were reporting their successes. He sent Plowman down to get a towel to clean the glasses. Two minutes later the navigator reappeared, with Plowman just behind him.

"He's just finished, sir – the signal has finally been sent. Apparently, *Jed* has one reply for us and Lohden's waiting for it now."

"That will have to keep until next time," said Naismith anxiously. "Take down the wireless mast."

He kept Brown and one lookout on the bridge with him, sending Plowman below as he steered the submarine away from their communications position, turning to head out into the central Marmara.

By 0100 on the twenty-seventh of May, they noticed voluminous clouds forming grey patches overhead against the black sky. Another half an hour and the moon peeked up above the distant mountains, illuminating the sea with a silvery monochromic sheen. With the fresh chilled breeze, it was one of those eerie nights that gave one an uneasy feeling, which was not helped by having their own presence exposed for all to see.

"Red two zero, sir – something's moving," whispered George Torode, from his position behind the captain.

Before Naismith could raise his binoculars to his eyes, Lieutenant Brown's body moved suddenly.

"It's a ship – right ahead, sir!"

More like two ships, and as Naismith raised his binoculars towards the new report as the moon suddenly disappeared behind a cloud, causing visual contact to disappear.

"Time 0140," Brown noted in his notebook.

"Port 30," ordered Naismith.

The boat swung around in a wide semicircle as he reversed his course, trying to stay ahead of the unidentified vessel.

"Flood main ballast," he ordered down the voice pipe.

The roar from the top of the tanks caused the boat to gradually lose buoyancy.

"Stop flooding."

The casing was just awash, with just the conning tower showing just above the surface.

"Depth 6 feet sir – boat is level and in trim."

"Go below Robert, as I will want full records of this attack. Oh, and send the First Lieutenant to the bridge, if you please."

HMS E11 was lying low in the water now, and she would be very difficult for anyone to spot. The faint mercurial shapes behind were slowly overhauling them, and finally they came back into view. As each shape was being assessed, it clearly broke into two vessels, as both gradually overhauled them from astern.

Eventually the two officers and the lookout managed to identify three distinct ship shapes through the darkness. The two outer ones were definitely destroyer sized vessels. The one in the centre was still indistinct, but appeared to be much larger than the other two. In the solitude of the bridge an excited anticipation was escalating.

Relaying the constant bearings of all three vessels down to Robert Brown, produced an accurate course and speed set up on all of them. They loomed larger and larger out of the eerie shadow-scape of an unseen horizon. None of the ships were showing any lights, when all of a sudden, the clouds parted enough to allow a shaft of moonlight to illuminate the group, like a spot lamp on a theatrical stage.

"It's a bloody battleship, sir – It's the Barbarossa, the one we saw on the way up," said Guy d'Oyly-Hughes excitedly.

"We won't be able to see a damned thing through the periscope in this weird light, so I intend to carry out a surface attack. If we submerge and let the destroyers go by, we will not have time to re-surface before we lose her, as she's travelling too fast for me to catch. Brown reckons that they are doing twelve knots. Our only chance is to let the two escorts overtake us, and then close in and quickly fire at the Barbarossa before we're spotted. We will dive directly after firing. Guy, go below, I want everyone geared up and in tip top readiness for this. Bring all tubes up to the firing condition."

The First Lieutenant was just about to go through the hatch, when the captain called again.

"Tell the Motor Room switchboard operators that I will want full power as we manoeuvre in for the shot. We will need a rapid increase in speed as we line up to fire, and then we'll revert back to full fields once more. Send the Navigator back up, I will need his expertise here, and put the Leading Torpedo-man on the firing set up gear. Put Plowman on the wheel, flood and equalise both of the bow tubes in readiness. Torode I want you to keep a good eye on those two destroyers. I want to know immediately if you see any alteration of course by either of them."

George was now able to see the great vessel quite clearly, which looked very similar to many of the late Victorian battleships, many of which were still in service within the Royal Navy. Her tripod mast's and funnels rose high above the pyramid shape of her squat superstructure. She looked like a low-lying island heading towards them. He could just make out the white 'V' of her bow wave, as she cut through the water, as he turned his attention towards the escorts.

"Port ten," the captain ordered.

George heard George Plowman's voice repeat the order up the voice-pipe.

Barbarossa had been right astern of them, as Naismith edged *E11* slightly away from her track, over towards one of the destroyers that was escorting her. He chose to go towards the landward side in the hope that the shadows from the shore horizon would hide his silhouette. When satisfied with his position, he slowed down to reduce the whiteness of their wake, and allow the three enemy ships overtake him.

"Bow tubes ready, sir."

Brown was still taking bearings, working out courses and speeds, allowing for the deflection angle that they would need to point and fire their weapons.

"What water have we got below us, Robert?" asked Naismith.

He consulted the folded chart that he had stuffed in his old great coat pocket.

"Forty-five fathoms, sir," he replied.

Martin gave a grunt of approval. That was plenty of room.

They were almost abreast of the Turkish destroyer, lying out on Barbarossa's starboard beam, when she zigzagged away from them.

Speaking quietly to both Lieutenant Brown, and the lookout, Naismith said, "I'm going to turn in for my firing course now. Keep your eyes glued on that other destroyer Torode, and tell me the second she alters course."

Leaning over the hatch, he called down.

"Group up – Full power – Starboard ten… Steady – keep on that course – Full fields. We should be able to fire in approximately one minute… Keep her steady now! Standby… Standby."

George saw the angle on the destroyer suddenly begin to change, its triangular silhouette narrowing as it spun around to port.

"The destroyer is swinging around to port, sir! Altering towards us… steadying up… heading straight at us, sir… she is increasing speed – range three hundred yards."

"Get below," screamed Naismith, then leapt down the hatch himself. "Group up – Full ahead together – 50 feet – Take her down quickly!"

As he slammed the hatch shut, Naismith caught a quick glimpse of the destroyer's sharp bows, complete with a tall V' of spray streaming away in each direction, chiseling full ahead towards them. The one aim of her captain was to use that chisel as a ram to split *E11*'s hull wide open. The submarine shot down at an oblique angle, just before the thunderous roar of the destroyer propellers churned overhead, the thrashing blades thumping through the water just feet above the conning tower.

"One hundred and ninety revolutions sir," called George, checking his beat with the navigation chronometer.

"She means business, I'm afraid," said Naismith. "she was going flat out trying to ram us. Steady her at 50 feet – Shut bow caps – Drain the tubes."

The disappointment in his voice was unmistakable. Barbarossa had got away by the skin of her teeth, yet again.

"Bad luck sir, that must have been a very close decision," said Guy d'Oyly-Hughes, returning from the forward torpedo space.

"Yes – I was about to fire when that bloody Turkish destroyer turned and came straight at us. Well spotted by the way, Torode," he said to the young Guernsey-man, standing behind the First Lieutenant. Then returning his attention back to his second in command he said, "I only needed another thirty seconds and she would be down here – where we are now."

The crew were listening to their conversation from their positions, each man feeling equally deflated at being denied a kill.

"Never mind, it is a fairly small sea, and we are bound to meet her again! I've got Barbarossa written on one of those torpedoes up at the front end, and I'm going to make sure that I deliver it to her right amidships."

The murmurs of approval from his men, showed that his little display of bravado had their blessing. However casual his remark might have appeared, it was something that he truly believed, a feeling that destiny had marked him down to be the destroyer of that particular Turkish battleship.

Everything went very quiet above them. He doubted that the destroyer would have been detached from her escorting duty to search for a dived submarine in the moonlight. Not wanting to take any chances after the near miss, he kept *E11* deep for the rest of a clammy night.

They surfaced at dawn the following day into a deserted calm sea. The craggy outline of Marmara Island was silhouetted once more against the rising sun. Patrolling slowly eastwards and charging their batteries they passed the Island, but kept well out of sight of main coastal land areas. The crew were employed on cleaning the boat once more, while the torpedo-men began overhauling each of the torpedoes in turn.

It was not until 1700 that same evening, that they sighted anything. It was a small steamer with the sleek fine lines of a yacht, that was heading straight towards them, apparently unperturbed by the submarine's presence. She was making a good speed, and never changed her course. Naismith climbed the conning tower ladder up to the bridge.

"We'll stay on the surface and stop her," he announced.

When her range was approximately half a mile, a small puff of smoke suddenly appeared from her fo'c'sle. The booming report of the small gun reached them a second later as the shell landed only a hundred yards ahead of the submarine bow.

"She's a bloody 'Q' ship – Diving Stations – Everybody below – Flood auxiliary – Trim for diving."

Down below, the raucous throaty blast of the klaxon sent everybody tumbling as they tried to get to their feet. Men ran to close the ventilators, turn the Kingston valve handles that let the seawater into the ballast tanks and rotated the hydroplane wheels into the dive positions. In the Engine Room the ERA's were fighting to shut down the diesels and disconnect the engine's star clutches; then they had to reconnect the tail clutches from the electric motor to the propellers, which had been disengaged to charge the battery. The on-watch stoker was struggling to shut the great engine exhaust vent; Chief Jupp, on seeing the peril of the dangerous situation dashed over and lent his muscles to those of the man. After what seemed an age, the vent securing handle slowly moved, just as Guy d'Oyly-Hughes poked his head through the water-tight door and shouted impatiently.

"When are we bloody well going to be ready to dive?"

"When you bloody well keep your nose out of my Engine Room!" Jupp snarled, completely losing his temper and knowing full well the future consequences of doing so.

A second later the vent clunked shut.

"Shut off for diving," d'Oyly-Hughes' voice carried through the boat.

The yacht fired once more, her aim thankfully not improving, and the shell fell short by eighty yards. Naismith noted that their aim for line was very good, but quite poor for distance. That Turkish gun-layer would be getting a roasting from his CO. He didn't fancy waiting to see how their third round fared, so on hearing the First Lieutenant's report, he headed for the hatch.

"Full ahead together – Take her down to 30 feet."

Out of danger now, he brought the submarine around, and headed once more back towards their signalling position.

The signals they received that evening were quickly decoded by Robert Brown. The radio equipment was proving to be so inefficient that it had literally taken hours to receive the reports. However, they did contain some surprising information detailing the panic that they had caused by their attack on Constantinople. The ship that they had torpedoed was the *Stamboul*, which had been towed across the harbour in an effort to keep her afloat, but she had sunk at Harem Iskelessi, where her upper-works could still be seen above the water. Their other torpedo, which had gone astray, had struck the Custom's House Quay. The two explosions, and heavy gunfire from the gun batteries at Kassim Pasha on the hills above Hagia Sophia, had caused total panic amongst the population, who thought they were about to be invaded by the whole Allied Fleet. Shops had closed, and a rumour abounded that the Sultan and his Ministers would be moving across to the Asian side of the city. Troop's, who were in the process of embarking in four transports, were quickly landed back onto the quay and many of the ships failed to sail. An intercepted signal stated that all troops, guns and supplies would now have to be sent by rail and road until further orders. It was satisfying to know that their second torpedo had run true and sunk the Stamboul. She must have been towed over to Harem Iskelessi, as she was actually sinking when he had lowered the periscope. Where she lay now was over on the Asiatic side of the Bosphorus, opposite the wharf where they had actually torpedoed her. Another piece of less happy news stated that their new attack periscope top-piece was not available, and would have to be ordered out from England.

****

At 0630 on the morning of the twenty-eighth of May, they were on the surface once more, having just completed another communications marathon with *HMS Jed*. It was a fine morning with a mirror flat sea. The air was clear and the horizon definition pristine. The visibility was calculated to be out as far as twelve to fifteen miles from the top of the conning tower. Straight after a breakfast of porridge, some thin wisps of smoke were sighted far off, appearing just over the horizon to the north of them. Naismith came up to the bridge, and waited until the superstructure of five merchant vessels, along with their destroyer escort, appeared above the curvature of the Earth, as they zig-zagged down towards them.

He dived the boat immediately, long before there was any danger of *E11* being sighted by the enemy. Looking at them through the only periscope, Naismith identified a convoy of one large merchantman accompanied by four smaller ones, with a lone Turkish destroyer acting as their escort. The warship was leading the small group by at least one mile. He allowed them to close, placing himself in a good position to fire at the largest of the ships.

At 0715 Naismith went deep, to passed under the destroyer escort, allowing the warship to go right overhead before rising very slowly to twenty feet, as he did not want to cause any spray from the periscope on such a calm surface. Edging himself into a position to attack the large merchant vessel, he fired one torpedo from the port bow tube.

There was a forty second delay before there was a tremendous explosion as the weapon hit her aft on the port side. A resounding cheer was echoed throughout the boat. By now the escorting destroyer was some way off to the south, so Naismith had the luxury of watching the effect of his work through the periscope, relaying a narrative of what he saw to the crew.

"Smoke and flames are shooting up into the sky… She's settling down deeper in the water aft… she's starting to heel over to starboard… She is going down by the stern… faster now… Her bow's lifting right out of the water… it's going down fast now… the water looks like it's boiling… she's down, sliding fast now… She's gone!"

From the torpedo striking to the bow disappearing below the waves had only taken just over a minute. The alerted destroyer had turned back towards them, increasing her speed and having probably seen their periscope she started firing her forward guns.

"Down periscope – Take her down to 80 feet," ordered Naismith.

HMS E11 went down very slowly, finally straightening until her decks were level once more.

"On depth 70 feet sir," said the Coxswain, after a pause.

"The depth ordered was 80 feet, Coxswain," said Naismith.

"I know, sir, but we can't get any lower. Something is preventing us."

"Naismith brought the boat ten feet shallower, before dipping her bow once more in an attempt to get deeper. Again, submarine levelled itself off and remained stuck at seventy feet, refusing all attempts to go below it. Both the Coxswain and Second Coxswain who were standing at their hydroplane controls looking puzzled and slightly uneasy. This was no time to mess about with uncertainties, especially with an enemy destroyer searching for them overhead."

"Hydroplane wheels back to zero," snapped Naismith, taking charge of the situation.

The two men obeyed, and the boat remained statically level at seventy feet. Naismith pondered the problem for a moment. This could only be one of those temperature layer problems that he had calculated might exist before they had left Murdos prior to the patrol? Perhaps this was an area where there was a layer of warm water, that was lying over a patch of much colder water, like oil floating on water to form a distinct boundary between the two liquids! The submarine would become heavier in the warmer water, and easily go down until it met the colder water. When that happened, the submarine would have become lighter and they would have needed to take on a lot more ballast to be able to go any deeper. The same effect has been known to occur at river mouths elsewhere in the world, where fresh water rode out onto salt water, again giving a two layered effect. Whether this was the case here or not, he was not absolutely certain. Maybe it was the fresh water coming down from the Black Sea via the Bosphorus, emerging out into the Marmara to ride over the colder saltiness coming up from the Dardanelles. Naismith decided to experiment with his supposition and use this new effect to their advantage. He gently allowed *E11* to rest on this layer, very much like sitting on the bottom of the seabed itself, and found to his satisfaction that his theory was proved. After a safe interval he brought the boat up to thirty feet and raised the periscope. He could still see the destroyer, dashing to and fro like a spaniel hunting through the bushes, searching for them vigorously in the wake of the convoy. The rest of the smaller merchantmen were disappearing over the horizon, leaving him with no alternative but to break off the action.

HMS E11 had four torpedoes remaining and Naismith was now confident that each one would register a sunken ship. That last convoy had come from the direction of Constantinople, yet *Jed*'s last appraisal signal had stated that all the traffic from there had ceased, and that everything was being sent by rail and road. Once the boat was back on the surface, he decided that they would head northwards once more to find out exactly what was going on.

By 1130 the day had turned very warm and a heat haze had developed which created a mirage effect, totally obscuring the horizon all about. Lying just off Oxia Island, where they could monitor all activity on the main sea approaches to Constantinople, they lay stopped in the water.

Half an hour later, a medium sized ship was sighted passing out through the harbour defences. She set a course that seemed to be taking her southward towards Panderma, and was certainly of a size that was worth a torpedo. *E11* dived at 1230 and Martin immediately began to stalk her, creeping towards her track to position the boat in a good firing position. As the submarine closed, Naismith could see that her decks were crowded with troops. Inwardly he was slightly annoyed that only three days after his attack on the Stamboul, the Turks had resumed using the port once more. To look on the brighter side, there was going to be a lot more targets.

At 1345 the target was just 1000 yards away, and Naismith completed his set up and fired a torpedo from the starboard beam tube. He watched the track as it headed straight towards the vessel's bridge. As he watched and waited, he experienced an uneasy feeling of guilt. Seeing the track of the torpedo heading straight towards the target, he also saw the men moving about on the decks and knew that soon they would all be struggling for their lives. His conscience fought with the ethics of killing his fellow human beings, but qualified his decision to fire by thinking that these same troops could be killing Allied soldiers in the trenches on the Gallipoli Peninsula tomorrow. This thought quickly dispelled any doubts that he harboured.

Then the first of two strange things happened in quick succession. The first was there was no explosion at the predicted time, and the second was that the ship stopped her engines and drifted to a halt. What the hell had happened? Had the torpedo failed to explode, but caused enough damage to stop her? Should he fire another torpedo? The smoke from her funnel curled idly upwards into the blue sky, occasionally interrupted by a small belch of white as she let off steam. After a few minutes her engines started up once more, and she altered her course on to a new heading that would bring her even closer to *E11*. He watched her as she drew level and suddenly his eyes opened wide in shock.

"My God!" said Naismith at the periscope eyepiece, before turning to the First Lieutenant, he invited him to have a look. Guy d'Oyly-Hughes studied the vessel before he too whistled in amazement.

"Good job you missed, sir," he said.

"The mass of people on that deck were not troops, but women and children." Taking the periscope back he said, "But I didn't miss her Number One, our torpedo passed directly underneath her. The depth setting must have been wrong."

"I am sure that Torpedo-man Baxter set ten feet on that weapon sir, I stood behind and watched him do it, and I will vouch for it. If it ran deep, then there has to be a defect on the weapon itself," said Guy.

"Well, we will soon find out," said Naismith. "Because once this ship gets out of the way, we are going to surface and go over and pick the bloody thing up!"

When the ship had finally disappeared over the horizon haze, they surfaced and quickly found their erstwhile weapon bobbing in the water at the end of its track. British submarines do not carry a small boat, and so it was Naismith himself who stripped off. He made his way onto the casing, from where he dived into the water with a specialised spanner tied by a cord around his neck.

On the bridge, Guy d'Oyly-Hughes prudently ordered slow astern, backing off to lay some distance away from the bobbing weapon – just in case. If the weapon were to explode, at least the boat would not suffer any damage. As Martin swam alongside the torpedo, he could see that it had indeed struck the ship, as one side of the warhead was crumpled on one side, but for some as yet undiscovered reason, it had failed to explode.

When a torpedo is fired, it remains initially safe as it leaves the tube, and it will not explode for the first forty-five yards of its run. The head is fitted with a small propeller, so that as it travels forward through the water the propeller winds down a protective sleeve to expose the firing pin, which is only one sixteenth of an inch away from a mercury detonator. The slightest impact should complete the circuit and cause it to explode. This meant that inside this damaged warhead casing of the torpedo there was an exposed detonator that Martin now had to make safe before any recovery could begin. He was fully aware of the delicate stage that the torpedo had reached, and it was with a pounding heart that he climbed up onto the weapon to begin the hazardous work of de-activating the fuse. Sitting on top of 320lb of volatile Trotyl did little to boost his confidence.

As he sat on an eighteen-inch steel tube in the middle of the open sea, it evoked a vision of The Boy on a Dolphin, an illustration from a book of Greek Myths that he had read as a boy. He took great care not to let his legs and feet dangle down too far towards the contra-rotating propellers. Sometimes during practice firings, a recovered torpedo would retain a pocket of compressed air which, when knocked or tilted, could cause the blades to rotate for a second or two. If that happened here, it would be enough to cripple him for life. He would fix those propellers after the fuse in the warhead was made safe. His heart was pounding like a drum as he manoeuvred himself around into position. The danger of having his legs shredded, with the possibility of the warhead going off, was enough to get anyone's heart pounding.

As he began work, he could feel the sun's rays tickling the skin on his back. If he was going to die here today, then God had picked lovely weather for it to happen. Very carefully, using the special spanner, he unscrewed the firing pin and loosened the mercury detonator assembly. A small wavelet splashed up against the weapon, nearly knocking the tool out of his hand, making him thankful for the lanyard that tied it around his neck. Once the firing assembly was completely free, he slowly withdrew it from the warhead, and was able to make it completely safe as he wound down the sleeve by turning the propeller until it fully covered the trigger. Finally, it was safe at last.

Taking a deep breath of relief, he then slid himself backwards along the cylindrical casing of the weapon and pushed forward the starting tripping lever. He knew that this would stop any compressed air that might have been left within the reservoir. When the torpedo is fired this lever hits a projection fitted to the top of the torpedo tube and this lever is forced fully backwards. This releases the compressed air contained within the reservoir in the weapon into a reducing valve, which brings the pressure down to a working pressure, which is then fed into the three-cylinder diesel engine. Even now, the smallest amount of air trapped within the engine cylinders could cause it to suddenly cough and make the contra-rotating propellers kick, which would act as a giant food mixer. Not fancying his feet and legs being turned into mince, Martin worked very carefully. Once he ensured that the weapon was completely safe, he waved his arm, beckoning the boat to make its approach.

On the bridge Guy d'Oyly-Hughes conned *E11* back towards him rather cautiously. A heaving line was thrown out to Martin, which he tied around the waist at the mid-section of the weapon. Then he swam back over to the boat, carrying the firing mechanism with him. Once back on board he went straight up to the bridge, and expertly brought the submarine alongside the torpedo.

A swan neck derrick had already been rigged into its bracket on the forward section of the casing. Lying on the casing in readiness was the metal bellyband, with a brass wheel fitted on each side. It was attached on the end of a hoisting wire that ran through a lifting block and tackle attached to the derrick. This band had hinged sections which opened to allow the metal band to be wrapped around the weapon. Once this band had been secured in place around the torpedo air cylinder by two of the torpedo-men lying prone on the ballast tanks, the weapon was then ready to be raised up on the wire hoist. A set of torpedo loading rails had been rigged on the casing to enable the crew to pass the weapon back down through the Torpedo Loading Hatch. The torpedo was winched up out of the water, carefully turned inboard by twisting the derrick, and then lowered down onto the rigged deck rails. These rails curved downwards, running all the way through the loading hatch, and down into the for-end stowage compartment. The bellyband's two small brass wheels fitted exactly into the rails, as it was lowered down into the interior of the boat, where it was placed on wooden blocks in the centre of the compartment. The rails and derrick were quickly unrigged, and passed below. Then the hatch was secured, and work began below of the torpedo's refurbishment.

Once below the weapon underwent a full inspection, before being parted into segments, section by section. The damaged warhead explosive was carefully unpacked through the access plate, and ERA Brooker's strength was used once again to hammer the phosphor bronze casing back into its original shape. In the engine compartment of the weapon, on checking the depth setting, it certainly had been set at ten feet, exactly as stated by the First Lieutenant.

Why then had it failed to explode?

Maybe it had hit the vessel very deep, and had glanced off to pass underneath. Looking at the dent, surely a collision of such magnitude would have been enough to cause the detonation? Martin Naismith was just glad that it had malfunctioned, because God had been looking out over those women and children! This weapon is more than capable of sending a 10,000-ton vessel to the bottom with just the slightest bump. The thought of all those women and children being blown to bits, or drowning, sent a shiver of horror down his spine. Guy d'Oyly-Hughes came up with the best explanation.

"I think that it's because this is the torpedo that fate has designated for sinking Barbarossa, sir." With that, the incident was not spoken of again during the patrol.

Later that night they stopped a sailing vessel, and boarded her. They relieved her of chickens, eggs, butter, cigarettes, dried fruit and three large baskets of ripe cherries. Guy d'Oyly-Hughes also purloined several pieces of likely looking timber, to satisfy his new craze for building rafts. As there had been no weapons of war being carried by the vessel, they had let her carry on her way. That evening everyone dined most royally.

So, the submarine war patrol continued, sighting new vessels, gathering fresh information, and continually evading detection. A daily routine revolving around them charging their batteries, enjoying the cooling breeze through the boat as it supplied the oxygen hungry diesels, followed by long hot sweaty hours of being dived, as they either stalked another of their prey, or carried out a reconnaissance. The constant strain of being hunted and having to keep a continual look out, knowing that the slightest mistake could mean death for them all was beginning to etched into the men's faces. To ease the stress, Naismith often allowed a session of Hands to Bathe, where they were allowed to wash their clothes, knowing that it was good for both morale, and their health.

During each period of relaxation Guy d'Oyly-Hughes duly used the quiet time to build the modified design to his raft, now capable of being dismantled and stowed below. In many of sea-trials that he carried out, he found that they were able to support a weight of a 20lb without the fear of capsizing. His mania for building rafts was not completely without foundation. He had long harboured the idea of swimming ashore with such a raft, to carry out a sabotage operation, either to blow up a railway-bridge, or at the least to destroy a section of the rail track. To do so he would need to get the explosives ashore – hence the raft. Now that the enemy were using the rail network more and more through *E11*'s continual presence, the case for this taking kind of action was starting to gain some credence. Unbeknownst to him, Martin Naismith was also giving the same idea some serious consideration. There had never been a submarine-delivered covert landing to his knowledge, so a successful raid might lead to further missions, and ever more ambitious attacks in the future. It was certainly worth consideration, especially as they were not fitted with a deck gun.

It was also during this quiet period that Chief Jupp was brought up before the captain as a defaulter. His outburst in the Engine Room against an officer, had been witnessed by several of the junior ratings, and naval regulations were adamant in stipulating that such a misdemeanour should not go unpunished. Under Naval Law,

Martin Naismith had no option but to demote him to the rank of Second Engineer, but in having no other choice, and more especially nobody else to replace him, he was then forced to advance ERA Brooker to the position of First Engineer. He added the proviso that Booker would work under the supervision of Jupp, and take his advice. It was the only way that Martin could satisfy the Navy's strict structure of punishment, without losing one of the best submarine engineers in the Trade. Jupp's punishment would be in the form of a reduction in pay, coupled with the lesser rank, yet his prestige and authority aboard would remain intact. In a year from now, his case would be reviewed, and he would then be promoted back to First Engineer.

At dawn, on Monday the thirty-first of May, they were dived once more off the port of Panderma. Despite the devastating destruction caused by the ship exploding, Naismith had rather enjoyed the attack on the vessel at Rodosto. The thrill of the chase in that very shallow water had finally culminated in a kill. He had not known that the vessel had been packed with ammunition, for him it had been an adrenaline laden high. Thinking of the number of people that must have been killed as a result of his action had sickened him, but he took comfort from the fact that most of them had been troops who were being sent to the front lines to kill our own men. After all, this was war, and it was a case of kill or be killed. Yet he still felt guilt when he remembered sighting all those civilians close by, just before that devastation. He considered his primary purpose for being out here was to sink ships, and their cargoes, not to kill fellow seamen or innocent civilians. He was also aware of the propaganda value of the attack, because the destruction had been achieved in front of witnesses, where the reported losses would not be swayed, or minimised by the Turkish government's propaganda machine.

"Large liner bearing 210 degrees at anchor – distance five miles – Standby bow tubes."

The response, throughout the boat was electric and immediate. Life on a submarine could be described as 99% utter boredom, interspersed by 1% of the most intense action found anywhere. The routine patrol life was, on the whole, very mundane and boring. That one per cent of intense action was like a drug for the crew, an injected thrill that lasted them through the inevitable dreary, sweaty, damp inactivity, until the next period of action.

"Bow tubes loaded."

Panderma was a fair-size town, quaintly situated on a hillside overlooking a small bay on the south side of the Marmara. A white mosque with a single minaret stood at its apex, and was the only real distinguishable landmark when viewed from the sea. Beyond it, there was a gap in the hills that marked the spot where the railway from Smyrna entered the town from the north.

On the slopes of the hillside above the town, there were literary hundreds of regimented canvas tents, denoting the presence of a military encampment. He could see row upon row of the light-coloured bell tents, standing out against the greenness of the grassy slope. To Naismith, this suggested that they would have lookouts posted, with the strong possibility of them having some artillery pieces already placed in position, and knew that he would need to be very wary to this possibility. As the submarine drew closer to the coast, Naismith spotted several small craft plying between the jetty and the anchored liner. Each of the boats looked to be full of soldiers who were being ferried out to the liner from the shore. They were embarking troops to be transported around the peninsula, probably to the town of

Gallipoli. That meant that the maximum number of internal hatch doors aboard the ship would all be open, which would make her easier to sink. We couldn't have timed it better, he thought to himself.

"Set torpedoes to run deep, it will cause maximum damage."

He let Guy d'Oyly-Hughes and Robert Brown have a quick look at their intended victim. Robert Brown went over to the cupboard beneath the chart table to consult his reference books. He quickly identified her as one of the latest vessels from the German Rickmer Line.

At 0920 they were within range, and Martin fired the port bow tube at the unsuspecting target. The torpedo struck the ship amidships on her port side. It made an exceptionally loud noise as it detonated, due mainly to the shallowness of the water within the bay. The force of the explosion physically lifted the ship in the water, before she settled back and started to quickly list over to port. Almost immediately she started to settle deeper in the water, as the increasing list quickly showed the width of her decks. He could see men scrambling here and there, trying to prevent themselves from sliding down the steep incline.

The small craft re-appeared, scurrying around her as it began to evacuate the troops that they had boarded. A bossy little tug came steaming out of the port with the obvious intention of towing the sinking vessel into shallow water for either salvage or repair. Small puffs of steam appeared at her funnel, and Naismith could almost hear the repeated blasts of her steam whistle as she tried to attract the attention of the Master of the stricken vessel. She passed under the liner's bows, quickly managing to get a line aboard. Seamen appeared on the fo'c'sle of the troopship, and could be seen slipping the anchor as soon as the tow line was made fast. White water thrashed at the stern of the tug as she struggled to pull the vessel in towards the beach. It would be a race against time, as the liner was now settling lower and lower in the water. Naismith could have easily finished her off with a second shot, but he only had three torpedoes left. She was obviously badly damaged, and although she may be salvageable, it would take the Turks months to make effective repairs, during which time she would be out of service. To remain here any longer would be chancing their luck, so he turned *E11* out of Panderma Bay and spent the rest of the day quietly on the surface charging their batteries. By having fully charged batteries it gave them a greater chance of escaping any threat or danger.

That night, Guy d'Oyly-Hughes ambition to attack the railway became less of a dream when *E11* was surfaced near the northern shore of the Marmara, close by the ancient Byzantine castle of Eski Iskelessi. He and the captain were standing on the bridge listening to a steam locomotive that was puffing along the single-track line at a distance of just under half a mile. Sometimes they could actually see the violent red sparks dancing from its braking shoes as it rounded the bends, before being forced to negotiate a viaduct that took the line across a deep V shaped chine cutting into the hillside. From this point it was nearly six hundred miles to reach Panderma via Smyrna by rail, but it was less than sixty miles by sea. Scutari lay some thirty miles over to the northwest. Running in close to the shore, they were at one point only four hundred yards from the beach, as Guy pointed to the spot he had previously mentioned to his captain as a possible raiding point. The viaduct was just crying out to be blown up.

"If only we had a deck gun," mused Naismith once more. "From here it would provide the gun crew with a fantastic training opportunity."

Watching the progress of the steam train, the two officers were alone on the bridge, with just George Torode standing behind them as the lookout. As the train ran across the iron viaduct, the rhythmic rumble changed to a lighter clatter. Staring through their binoculars they could make out the faint glow of a lamp in the window of the guard's caboose. The two officers were joined on the bridge by Robert Brown, who was due to relieve the First Lieutenant on watch. The Signalman arrived at the same time to relieve George Torode.

"This is obviously the place to land, sir," said the First Lieutenant.

"How much water do we have below us here, navigator?" asked Naismith.

"Thirty-five fathoms, sir. It remains pretty deep until about fifty yards from the shore before it quickly shelves up to that stony beach," he replied.

"You won't be able to do it all alone, Number One. You'll have to take a good swimmer with you. He could push the raft ashore for you, and then help you to carry the charges up to the viaduct. That would leave you fresh to set the charges, when you reach the railway line. After you fire the fuses, you can both swim back to the boat. Who do you think would fit the bill of being your swimmer?"

Guy d'Oyly-Hughes said that he would give it some thought, and went below to formulate his plans. Being thirty miles from Constantinople, it would be that much harder for the Turks to affect a repair. Just the logistics of supplying the repair materials would keep the line out of action for some time. The Turks would then have no alternative but to carry everything by sea, which would provide *E11* with more targets. Once he had gone below, Brown spoke,

"Surely that bridge will be well guarded, sir?" he protested. "Guy may be killed or captured. I don't want to speak out of turn, but he's needed much more here on board. Anyway, why take the risk and effort to blow up a railway line that they can probably be fixed within thirty-six hours?"

"Agreed Robert, but think of all the repercussions it would create! Another unexpected setback like that would destroy the Turks morale, and cause a great deal of consternation in high places! If we had two boats up here in the Marmara, one could carry out the sabotage, while the other guarded the approaches to Constantinople, because while the railway is out of action, they will have no option but to transport everything by sea. It would force them to divert more men and resources to guard every bridge and viaduct along the whole six hundred miles of track. That would keep a lot of enemy soldiers away from the front lines on the peninsula. If we can disrupt enemy supplies by both sea and rail, then we might well see a quicker end to this campaign. An army cannot fight without good logistical support. Anyway, I think that Guy will have a good chance of carrying it off and getting back in one piece, otherwise I wouldn't even consider sending him."

The following morning whilst dived they did another full reconnaissance of the target area through the periscope. It was certainly a very beautiful stretch of the countryside which was mountainous, with deep tree filled valleys. The lower slopes had been cleared and cultivated, mainly to orchards of apple, almond, with what looked like varieties of Prunus. High above the tree line, the snow-clad peaks stood proudly like white capped sentinels, majestic against a clear blue sky. There were many small hamlets lying close to the shoreline, some had small fishing boats pulled up on to the shingle beach. Several had cattle pastures of lush green meadows surrounding them. A line of rocky cliffs stood as a backdrop to this blissful pastoral scene, where wispy, wind-blown waterfalls cascaded down the slopes into unseen pools.

They searched all the possible anchorages and inlets for enemy patrol craft that might be located along this stretch, but found them all to be deserted, so they headed back towards the area they had initially selected for the beach raid. When they were opposite the viaduct once more, Guy d'Oyly-Hughes took over the periscope and started to make a series of detailed drawings of the three stone columns that supported the span of the viaduct. He then, using the magnified viewer, and drew details of the connecting iron box girder construction. Another sketch of the general area showed the main patches of shrubbery, and the scrubby undergrowth below it, noting down all the possible paths and tracks that might be a way up the slope, which may also provide a good escape route if required. When he was finally satisfied, the submarine turned away from the area to await nightfall. Guy was sitting in the wardroom when Naismith entered.

"Well, who have you chosen to help you, Number One?" he asked.

"I was thinking of that young seaman – Torode, sir. Although he is still quite young and inexperienced, he's strong, keen, and an extremely good swimmer."

Naismith remembered seeing him swimming under the boat when they had their day off. He had also proved himself a good shot with a gun recently, the captain recalled.

"I agree that he's a bit young, but a good choice none the less – go and ask him to come and see me will you, please Guy?"

He disappeared into the passageway. A minute later, the young seaman's head appeared at the curtain.

"Did you want to see me, sir?" he asked nervously.

"Come in, Torode – I want a word."

George entered nervously, as he had never been invited into the officer's mess before. Naismith looked up at him.

"It was your birthday recently, I believe?" he asked him.

"Yes sir – May the eleventh – I was nineteen."

"I was particularly impressed by the way that you concentrated your mind to passing your submarine knowledge exam after you joined us at Portsmouth. I have also noted that you are a strong swimmer. I know that you're still considered to be a youngster by the service, but I want to ask you to volunteer for man's job tonight. It's rather a dangerous mission Torode, and you don't have to do it of course, but I think that you're a good candidate to go. Tonight, the First Lieutenant is going to swim ashore and attempt to blow up the railway line that we saw through the periscope this morning. I would like for you to go with him. If you accept the task then your job will be to push one of his rafts laden with explosives ashore for him, cover him with a revolver while he fires the charges, and then you both return together. If you agree to volunteer, I'll be landing you in approximately one hour. What do you say?"

George couldn't believe his ears. It was everything that he had ever dreamed about. It was the chance to show his true worth. It would show Gladys that he was the man for her, and he so wanted her to be proud of him!

"You can count on me, sir," he said with a youthful exuberance.

Chapter Twelve

Saboteur

The sea water still retained a residue of the sun's energy. Its velvet smoothness felt wonderful around George Torode's legs, as if silky fingers were lightly caressing his skin. He was swimming in the nude, using a slow strong side-stroke, while pushing the home-made raft ahead of him. He had decided to use this stroke, as it made good steady progress over a long period, and did not to disturb the surface water unduly. The First Lieutenant swimming alongside him was employing a breast stroke.

Securely tied to the top of the sturdy raft was a pair of his newly washed overalls. They had been rolled tightly around his gym shoes. Another similar bundle contained the clothes of the First Lieutenant. After being tied together both sets of clothing had been wrapped in an oilskin cloth, which had been sewn together using some of the signalman's bees-waxed sail-maker's twine to ensure that the package was virtually waterproof. Lying directly beneath the bundle was a large square box that had been similarly wrapped. There was also a smaller package. The larger of the two contained two 14lb demolition charges, complete with firing fuses, and two boxes of Lucifer matches. The smaller package contained a Webley service revolver with ammunition, a folded map with two pencils, and a small hand-held compass. There was an eighteen-inch sharpened bayonet tied to the top of one of the slats. This was easily the best raft that the First Lieutenant had built so far, and it easily supported the deadly cargo. Pushing it through the water wasn't too arduous a task, and George was managing to keep up a good steady stroke.

Guy d'Oyly-Hughes, was also swimming nude, fully alert to all around him, as he made each leisurely stroke.

The submarine had already disappeared behind them, melting silently into the blackness of the night. When she had eventually dived beneath the surface, it had amazed George at just how loud the air venting from the tanks had sounded. It had been the first time that he had experienced that submarine operation from an external point of view. The cacophony had only lasted for about twenty seconds before it was replaced by total silence. George just hoped that if there were any sentries ashore, they had not heard it. All was eerily quiet now, just the gentle ripples in water as each stroke was completed.

Alongside him, George could hear the officer's shallow rhythmic breathing as he swam. The light from newly risen moon struck the mountaintops, giving a silver border to their silhouette. Up near the railway there was a rocky cliff that plummeted down into the shadows of dark vegetation.

"Not far now, Torode," whispered the officer.

George panted a short reply, before giving the raft another heave forward. The swirling eddies and ripples in the water sounded louder! Then George realised that it was the water lapping on to a stony beach.

"The beach is just ahead of you," whispered D'Oyly-Hughes.

No sooner had he spoken than George's toes dug into the shingle of the shelving seabed. Staggering slightly, he found his foothold and stood up. Leaning down, he grabbed the raft in both hands, guiding it up towards the water's edge. The water ran from his naked body as he emerged from the sea.

Guy doyly-Hughes held up his hand for him to stop, his head turning left and right, his eyes searching for any signs of danger along the expanse of the beach. George suddenly felt cold as the night air brushed against his wet skin, and he started to shiver. He needed to get dressed in his overalls and gym shoes.

Between them the two men lifted the raft out of the water, and carried it high above the tide mark. The stones hurt their feet, as they made their way into a patch of dry tamarisk scrub. Using the bayonet, George cut the packages open, before both men quickly donned their clothes and footwear. Feeling warmer and being shod, they then lifted the fragile raft once more, removed the packages, and hid the raft from view. Kneeling down, they both began stacking the various articles out on the stony ground.

George reached over and picked up the Webley pistol, carefully loading it with six rounds from the box. He emptied what was left of the ammunition from the box into his side pocket. Placing the looped land-yard around his neck, he stuffed the weapon into the other free pocket, and patted it confidently. He then picked up one of the local hand drawn area maps and slid it into his breast pocket, along with a pencil. He passed the other across to Guy, who had picked up the compass. George slid the bayonet through a belt loop on his overalls, and stood up.

"Ready?" enquired the officer.

George nodded. They picked up the charges and the box of fuses. George followed him inland as they wound their way through the mass of tamarisk trees towards the pines that stood inland. As they were forced to brush the sharp spindly branches aside, some sprang back causing scratches. George found that the foliage was soft enough, but he quickly learned to avoid the wood. Prudently, he allowed the officer to move further ahead, and followed behind at a safer distance. After leaving the stony shore line they both started to feel hard rocky stones beneath their feet, that stabbed up hard into the arches. Some were quite large, and they both took care to look out for the more hazardous ones – but it was very dark. They started to climb the hillside that rose up towards the railway track. The higher they climbed, so they felt the effects of the cooling onshore breeze blowing in off the Marmara. George followed the First Lieutenant faithfully.

It is strange, he thought, here I am in the middle of enemy territory and I don't feel the least bit scared – certainly no different than from walking around the streets of Malta. Far from feeling afraid, he found that he was actually enjoying the adventure – and that is what it was, he decided – a great big adventure. He felt very proud to have been asked to take part in this mission. This was real action, fighting the war on the front line, and he felt that he was really doing his bit for King and Country. If the First Lieutenant and he were to be careful, and take no risks, this should all be over and done within the hour. None the less he very well aware that tonight would not be without its dangers.

The fact that he was a member of *E11*'s crew, which was probably ten times more hazardous than any other single combat unit taking part in this theatre of war, didn't seem to register with him. To him, just being the member of the submarine crew was his normal daily routine, and he enjoyed the comradeship and bonhomie of his mates. Doing this on the other hand, was pure adrenalin filled excitement.

Quite soon, they emerged from the scrubby vegetation and undergrowth where the climb became steeper. Up ahead of them, beyond the pine trees, they could see the cliff top on which ran the railway. Before they knew it, they were making their way amongst trees trunks, and could immediately feel the cushioning effect under their feet from the carpet of brown pine-needles. Winding their way through the trunks, they climbed ever higher. Then base of the cliff loomed, and Guy called a halt for a breather, before they tackled the challenging climb.

It was indeed a steep climb ahead. The First Lieutenant went up first and then George passed up the two packs of explosives. Repeating the manoeuvre, they gradually scaled the cliff, taking another well-earned breather when they stepped onto the railway track. A minute later they began making their way along the track towards the viaduct. The air was still up here, cool, but hardly a breeze.

The First Lieutenant stopped, and handed George his package.

"Here take this Torode. I will keep the fuse wire and detonators with me. You can easily manage the two packages on the level ground, I am sure. When I get to the girder section of the viaduct, leave the two charges with me and make your way back down to the base of the central stone column. I am going to make my way out over the bridge until I am directly above you, and place the charges. You stay hidden, and I will make a quick reconnoitre to make sure we will not be disturbed. I will set the detonators and then lower the fuse wire down to you before I come down and join you. The we will light the fuse, and make our way back down to the beach together. By the time it goes off we will be back at the raft. All we have to do then is use it to swim out, and get picked by the boat. Any questions?"

"No sir," he replied, taking hold the second charge.

The two were quite heavy as he followed the First Lieutenant towards the viaduct. It felt good to be back on firm level ground. The structure came into view in the moonlight, stretching out to infinity across the chine. He could see a small stream below cascading down, the water flashing white as it tumbled over the rocky bed.

On reaching the viaduct Guy raised his hand for him to stop, and he placed the charges on the ground, breathing heavily. That was not so much fun!

Looking about, the silver steel expanse of the Marmara stretched out before him. Somewhere out there below the surface was *E11*. The skipper may well be looking at him right now through the periscope! Out here on the bridge the breeze reappeared which was welcome as he realised that he was sweating. Between him and the shore-line lay black bobbling clumps of vegetation. It surprised him that the distance to the water's edge was only three hundred yards.

"It is all clear. I could not see any sentries. I will be able to lay the charges and fit the fuses. You start to make your way down to the central pillar and I will join you when they are set. The we will light the fuse, and can make a dash back to the landing point. There will be fifteen minutes before they go off. Any questions?"

George whisper no. He shivered, and began to feel cold. The breeze felt stronger and he shivered again. The thrill of this adventure was fading.

He made his way back down the cliff, and arriving he sat down, land leaned back against the stone column. Above, he could hear the First Lieutenant panting as he placed the charges one at a time. He eased the revolver from his pocket, holding it ready for use – just in case. This was getting exciting!

All went quiet above, and he was suddenly startled when the First Lieutenant emerged out of the darkness. His voice came in a whisper.

"There are two sentries up there. They just walked out onto the viaduct from the far side. I did not see them when I made my first reconnoitre. We are going to have to take them out before we can fire these charges. They will see them otherwise. Do you think that you can do that, Torode?"

George gulped. It was something he had often asked himself. Could he kill a man? Then he quickly realised that this mission would fail if he did not. He nodded his head, hoping that he would not let the Jimmy down.

"Good. I knew that I could rely on you. I will use the bayonet, and you can pick up a large rock to use. Pick a big one, and smash the man over the head. Do not use the revolver unless you really have to. If there are other soldiers around, the sound will alert them. Once we take these two out, then we will quickly fire the fuses, and run like hell back to the landing point. Any questions."

George shook his head. His heart was thumping, and his mouth was full of saliva. He was not looking forward to this bit.

Arriving back up on the railway tracks, they both stopped to catch their breath.

Guy d'Oyly-Hughes led the way towards the viaduct. As they walked, George reached down, and wrapped his finger around the trigger of his pistol, with his thumb resting on the cocking lever in readiness.

They reached the edge of the viaduct and began searching the darkness for the soldiers. Both felt secure in the shadow of the cutting into the cliff. It was George who first spotted the two sentries sitting on a section of the box girder nearest to them. Both men had their backs towards him. They were smoking, and he could just hear their voices. He could feel his heart was beating faster. This bit of the adventure was quite scary, not the fun he had been expecting. He tried to steel himself as he was going to have to kill someone in cold blood. Could he do it? If he didn't, they may well kill, him and this mission would end in failure, or if they both survived then they would be taken captive. If they were taken prisoner, then they would probably be shot – because they were out of uniform, and would be classed as spies. Kill, or be killed – that was the law of this war. He took a deep breath. A new resolved went through him and he steeled himself once more – telling himself mentally that he could carry out the task. After all, he had killed that rabbit that his uncle had only wounded with his shot gun, the day they had gone out shooting on Guernsey. After the act, he remembered that he did not feel good about himself.

Guy brandished the bayonet, indicating for George to pick up one of the large stones that lay beside the track. George gulped. It would have been a lot easier with the gun. He just hoped that the man would be facing the other way when he hit him. Reaching down, he groped around the area by his feet, his hand finally grasping hold of a fair-sized lump of rock – half the size of a rugby ball. Picking it up, he showed it to the officer for approval.

"That will do fine – now be as quiet as you can. Remember, you are going to take out that nearest sentry on the right, and I will move past you and kill the furthest one on the left – OK? Let's go," whispered Guy d'Oyly-Hughes.

All about them was eerily quiet, except for the faint rustle of the trees that stood up from the cliff edge to seaward. Standing deep in shadow, they knew that they would have the advantage of surprise, but it was too quiet! They were going to have to be very careful.

What had happened to the voices?

Edging themselves slowly forward, both men suddenly froze as the fiery spluttering of a Vesta match burst into life, no less than thirty feet from where they were standing. The glare lit a face briefly in its fiery glow, as a man drew hard on his cigarette. His companion appeared out of the darkness, stretching his head forward to share the flame, and light his own smoke. His presence provided the confirmation that there were still just two sentries.

"Just two," mouthed Guy, holding up two fingers, and closing to George's ear, he whispered. "Be very quiet, and be very careful where you are treading."

George realised that he was now feeling quite scared, because his heart was thumping like a bass drum, but knew that there was no time to dwell on it. This must be how Pongo's feel, just before hearing the whistle that orders them over the top, he thought. Maybe it was a bit like having butterflies before going on stage, just before the curtain goes up. At least those army boys had rifles and bayonets, he thought, looking down doubtfully at the rock he was holding.

They both began to edge their way along the rock face of the cutting, inching slowly through the shadows towards their quarry. Ten feet to go! The soldiers had resumed their sitting position, and had turned away.

George suddenly stubbed his toe on a large nail that held the rail in place, which hurt like hell, but he managed to suppressed a yell of pain through clenched teeth. Unfortunately, some loose stones that had been used to bed in the sleepers of the track, rattled from under his feet.

"Shit," he hissed.

Pressing themselves instinctively against the rock, both men held their breath. The two sentries ahead were either deaf, or completely oblivious to sounds of the night, as neither showed any reaction. Neither moved from their sitting position on one of the rails. On the next look, both were visible, the glowing tips of their cigarettes plainly marking their position.

At a distance of just under eight feet, Guy's arm stopped George's progress. Holding up the bayonet in his right hand, the officer mouthed the words – ONE – TWO – THREE. Both the submariners stepped forward, before breaking into a run at the unsuspecting soldiers. At a distance of five feet, one of the sentries sensed that something was happening, but before he could stand George had brought his rock down with a thudding crack onto the man's skull. His half-turned face wore a look of surprised terror, his eyes glaring wide in alarm, as they glazed over into unconsciousness and he fell. As he fell George could see huge rivulets of blood covering his face, as he collapsed to the ground.

The second sentry had also begun to rise, but before he stood fully erect Guy brought his bayonet up to enter his rib cage just under his left shoulder blade. He forced it deeper into the man's heart. He died almost instantly, without so much as whimper. Both of the Turkish soldiers lay prone, near to where they had just been sitting.

"Good lad, you did well Torode – now I want you to stand guard here, just in case one of these blighters decides to wake up, and raise the alarm. I'm going to set the fuses, and then I will light them here. As soon as I have finished, we will be on our way back to the beach. OK?"

George nodded, raising his thumb. He certainly did not feel like a good lad. In fact, he felt quite sickened by what he had just done. Were they both dead? He could not really see – they were not moving – it was too dark. They were just two lumps on the edge of the track.

Guy d'Oyly-Hughes disappeared into the night as he moved out towards the centre of the bridge. George moved closer to the lumps and looked down at the two bodies. There was no apparent sign of life, and as if to prove it he reached out with his foot and pushed hard on the back of the sentry that the First lieutenant had stabbed. The body had simply rolled over, and from the wide eyed blankness of the man's expression, he could see that he was definitely dead. He remembered that rabbit he had killed, it had eyes that had looked like that. Feeling quite nervous, he levelled the revolver at the other body – just in case. He leaned over and peered closer over the barrel of his pistol. The back of the man's head and hair was sticky wet with blood, he could smell the hot metallic odour – it was horrible. He was lying face down – thankfully. No, despite what the First Lieutenant had said, he didn't feel that he had done well at all, and he just hoped that he would never have to do that again.

After standing for five minutes on his own, the moon had risen much higher above the crested skyline to the east, its silvery light gave some definition to the two bodies. George looked up at the welcome distraction, realising too late that the glowing orb was destroying his night vision. When he turned his head away, it was like being blind! He tried staring into darkness over towards the west, and after a minute, he tried refocusing on the two dead Turks. One of them had huge leather boots on his feet, which stretched out across the rails. They were the biggest boots that he had ever seen, and he wondered what size they were! Neither of the bodies had moved. Just as well – he did not want to have to hit the man over the head again. After a while, he felt a bit silly pointing the revolver at dead Turks. He released the cocking lever, and replaced the weapon back into his pocket. Then he went over picked up one of the sentry's rifles, ejecting the round that was in the barrel, and removing the magazine clip, which he tossed away. He saw the First Lieutenant in the moonlight, with just his head showing above the box girder and he placed the charges.

The ever-rising moon began to reveal more of the area, but George squinted, as he still could not see the far end of the bridge. He hoped that nobody else suddenly appeared. The lunar glow blanked many of the stars, as George was left standing there with the two bodies at his feet. He shuddered. The adventure was becoming a bit of a scary nightmare. Come on, sir!

If anything were to happen to the Jimmy tonight, then how on earth would he get back? The boat was due to pick them up at 0100, but the Jimmy had the only watch – he also had the compass. He realised that he would just have to guess the time, because if he got it wrong, then he would be left holding on to the raft for ages.

He took another looked at the bodies lying before him – although dead, they both looked quite frightening. Even in knowing that they could not hurt him, he still felt unnerved by their presence, longing for all this to be all over with. It would be better once they were swimming back towards *E11* from the recovery point. Despite all the dangers he faced by being one of the crew, he knew that by being aboard *E11* he was as safe as he could be in this warzone. He definitely would never swap jobs with one of those pongo's in the trenches. Looking back down at the two men once more, he could see the cry of protest frozen on the man's lips. His companion lay very still face down, and George could now see the dark patch of blood on the rock he had used. There was one thing that he was very sure of, and that was that he would never hit the man over the head with the rock ever again – even if he were to wake up. That sound had been sickening. He stood up, checking along the length of the railway in both directions – just in case there was a train! There was no sign of the Jimmy. Where bloody hell was he?

Then the wind dropped, and the night air suddenly became comfortably warmer, as he stood there in his overalls. Despite his initial misgivings, George started to feel a little better about the situation. His overalls were dry, but they stank to high heaven. It wasn't body odour, but starch. These were brand new he realised. It felt good to be in dry clothes, and to be standing comfortably in the clean fresh air. It raised his spirits. That was the only problem with being on the boat – the hot humid smelly atmosphere. Yes, it would not be long now – all he had to do was to wait until the Jimmy returned, and then they would be on their way back to the boat.

A draught of cooler air then blew along the track from the east, which caused him to shiver once more, and he hunched his shoulders. The invasion of cold air caused him to want to relieve himself. He tried to resist the urge by hopping from one foot to the other, but it was no use, he had to go.

He crossed back over the tracks towards the rock face from where they had emerged, undid the buttons at the front of his overalls and breathed a sigh as his urine began to splash against the stones – it was such a relief. As he was about to finish, he heard a faint metallic click behind him. It was the click of a trigger? Spinning around, George ducked down instinctively onto one of his knees, just in time to avoid the rifle mounted bayonet skimming an inch over his shoulder – the sharp flat blade just missing his neck. The sudden shock of the attack took his breath away, a flash through his mind recalled that he had taken out the ammunition from both rifles, but he had forgotten to remove the bayonets! The stock of the weapon banged against his ear, and he heard the blade ping as it snapped against the rock-face – such was the force of the lunge. His evasive manoeuvre had forced the revolver out from his pocket, and he could feel it dangling loosely on the end of its lanyard, somewhere down by his right knee as he stood erect and grabbed the rifle stock. Using every ounce of strength, he pushed it away from him, turning fully to face his adversary. The soldier was grunting with effort, and moving his hands down the barrel to swing his rifle around as a club. George could see the mixture hatred and pain embedded in the Turk's eyes. The dried blood in his matted hair and on his face made for a frighteningly, gruesome picture. Obviously, he was the one that he had hit over the head with the rock. How on earth…? He had definitely looked dead – knowing that he should have made absolutely sure. George's heart was pounding like a reciprocating engine, as he prepared to face this new threat to his life. The soldier drew back the weapon, preparing to swing, but George didn't give him time to complete the manoeuvre. He sprang forward, getting hold of the gun halfway down the stock with his left hand, whilst desperately fumbled for the revolver with his right. The rifle was wrenched to and fro, as each man fought for supremacy. The Turk thrust the weapon forward once more, hoping to break George's grasp. He staggered backwards, but managed to keep hold of the rifle. Suddenly the soldier gave another stronger lunge forward, which this time worked to George's advantage, as he stepped aside making the Turk's momentum carry him past and loose his grip. George managed to grab the man around the neck with his left arm – applying a strangle hold by using every bit of strength that he possessed. George's right hand continued groping for the revolver, his fingers splayed, frantically seeking the pistol grip. His fingers suddenly found the lanyard, and gripping it, he jerked it upwards to find the weapon jump up into his hand. His thumb flicked off the safety, and bringing it swiftly round, he stuck the barrel under the Turk's chin and pulled the trigger. The top of the man's head exploded in a fountain of blood and brains, spraying into George's face. His enemy collapsed like a pole-axed steer, collapsing into a crumpled heap at his feet – any life-force gone forever. George took a deep breath, knowing that this time that the man was definitely dead.

He stood there for a full minute panting for breath, his mind struggling to regain full control of his stunned emotions. The sweat poured down his face, and he could feel his body trembling. Slowly he calmed – his irregular breathing gradually regaining a steady rhythm. Taking several long deep inhalations, he released them hissing out through his teeth. As he did so he felt his mouth rapidly filled with saliva, and despite desperately swallowing, the bile laden vomit came rushing up from his stomach, gushing out of his mouth to cover his victim. As his eyes opened, George looked down at the Turk, seeing the gaping hole in the top of the man's skull. He felt nauseous, and he vomited again, but managed to turn away, because he didn't want to cover the soldier for a second time. Guy d'Oyly-Hughes came dashing back from the centre of the viaduct, just as George was finishing.

"What the hell happened?" he demanded.

George wiped his mouth with his sleeve. His eyes were still watering, as he pointed to the dead man at his feet.

"He tried to kill me," he said hoarsely.

The officer looked down at the body dispassionately.

"Come on, the charges are set, and the fuses are lit. We have fifteen minutes. Come on Torode, that shot will have woken every Turk between here and Constantinople. They will be coming to investigate before you have a chance to think. We will make our way down to the shore-line and get the raft. Then swim out for the rendezvous. Follow me."

George let him lead off, and followed. He felt so much better after being sick, and much happier that they were on their way back to the boat.

The descent of the cliff was not as easy as the climb. They made slow progress, but they eventually made it back to the natural ridge near the base of the columns. As they began to move downhill through the scrubby vegetation, they heard shouts behind them. Sure enough, the shot had definitely attracted somebody's attention. The First Lieutenant and George ducked down, using the sparse clumps of shrubbery to hide. Looking back up to the viaduct, two heads were silhouetted against the moonlight. George could hear the questioning tone in their voices, as they peered down. He took a sight on one of them with the pistol – just in case! Then they spotted him, but before the soldiers managed to give the alarm, George squeezed off the first round. The explosion from the pistol shattered the stillness of the night. A hideous yell of pain turned into a scream of terror, as one of the soldiers toppled over the edge of the viaduct. His flailing twisting form plummeted down, hitting the ground with a sickening thud just a hundred and fifty yards from where they stood. A vision of Matthew falling to his death flashed through George's mind in that instant. He looked for the other soldier, but he had disappeared.

"OK – let's get out of here," whispered, Guy.

Both sailors made a dash for the beach. It was another one hundred and fifty yards to the water's edge. Half skidding down the slope, they headed towards cover of the tamarisk trees on beach beyond. Their forward momentum increased as the slope steepened. Then came the sound of first rifle shots, but neither man stopped to investigate. Guy turned left towards where the pines trees stood, in an attempt to seek some quick cover. The sharp cracks of the rifles quickly turned into a fusillade. The whizzing zing of bullets buzzed around their ears, as they ran headlong down the slope towards the trees. Puffs of dust burst around their feet, as the shooters aim got more accurate. George began to zig-zag. The last thing that he remembered was running at top speed, and his foot hitting something immovable. There was an explosion of pain, before he was sent flying, and everything going black. He had landed on his head and shoulder, knocking the wind from him, and causing him to lose consciousness. His inert body continued rolling down through the twisted undergrowth. Over and over he went, until finally coming to an abrupt halt in the middle of a thick clump of shrubbery. He was just twenty yards short of the trees, with the shoreline just beyond.

Guy d'Oyly-Hughes had already reached the trees, and continued his headlong rush through them onto the beach. Reaching the water-line he started sprinting towards the hiding place, where they had left the raft. Quickly spotting the mound of vegetation, he pulled away the pieces of tamarisk. It was only then that he realised that Torode was not with him. He looked back down the beach, but he was nowhere to be seen. Had he been hit? Should he go back? Then he could see what looked like the whole Turkish army beginning to descend down the slope, and heading towards him. There was absolutely no choice for him to make, he'd have to swim for it – albeit alone. Throwing the fragile raft ahead of him, he waded out into the Marmara and launched himself after it. He could hear the babble of chatter from the soldiers behind him, but did not stop to see their progress. Spouts of water began spouting off the surface not twenty feet away. His legs kicked faster, trying not to make a splash and reveal his position. He was praying that the darkness would eventually hide him, if he didn't disturb the water. A couple more waterspouts appeared further away, until at last, they finally stopped. Maybe they had given up – or had hopefully lost sight of him? At least he had made his get away! What on earth had happened to young Torode – had he taken a bullet?

****

Consciousness slowly returned, and George's first impression was that his head hurt, and had he gone blind? It was so dark. As he tried to move, he heard himself groan with the effort, and gave up. There was a terrible pain in his left ankle, and so he remained still.

The scrambled nerve cells in his brain began to clear. He found it quite frightening being surrounded by all this vegetation, and the air was filled with dust. Where in hell was he? Then the dam burst, and it all came flooding back. Panic gripped him. Where was the Jimmy? Had he missed the rendezvous with the boat? The realisation of his very dangerous predicament suddenly became very clear. He was afraid, and genuinely uncertain as to what to do next. Wanting to ascertain exactly where he was, he opened his eyes once again, blinking to make sure that they were open. At first, he could not see a thing. He turned his head – there and there – still nothing but darkness. *I am not blind – am I?* No, directly above he just made out the pin-points of light – stars. He started to move, but the cloying vegetation made the initial attempt a failure. Was he lying in a bush?

Reaching out with his hand, he could feel the wooden sharpness of the sprigs and twigs – another quick search with his outstretched arm, confirmed that he was indeed lying in the middle of a bush. He lay back, and could hear some rifle fire in the distance, but it quickly ceased and everything went quiet.

The faint sound of lapping waves broke the silence – so he was near the beach? He and the Jimmy had been running for the beach. The Turks had been chasing them. He heard some more shots way off to his left – then they stopped once more. Beginning to run his hands over his body, he checked for any wounds or abrasions. Then there was the sound of voices, making him catch his breath in fear. His found the lanyard around his neck and followed it along until he found the hard handle of his revolver. Gripping it gave him doubtful reassurance. Listening out for the voices, his senses strained, trying to glean every clue as to what was going on around him. Suddenly three pairs of booted feet passed by as they slid and scrambled down the slope, less than a yard from where his head lay. One of them was carrying a swinging lantern. The light danced about like a giddy firefly. The dust nearly caused him to cough, but he held his breath until his chest had settled.

Another pair of legs dashed past wearing putties up to their knees. The soldier he had killed up on the viaduct with the gun flashed into his mind. These were the Turks, who had been chasing them. More shots were being fired further down the slope. Where was the Jimmy? Were they shooting at him?

Two more pairs of leather boots slithered by, churning up more clouds of the choking dust, scrambling on down the slope. The shooting stopped again, and someone began shouting. Everyone seemed to be heading down towards the beach. Lifting his head slightly, he tried to peer out through the foliage, needing to establish just what his situation was, but he could see absolutely nothing. Then he parted some of the bush. and through it he could make out the line of wet shingle, glinting faintly in the moonlight. Against that shimmer, he could make out the vague shapes of the soldiers standing along the waterline, and could see the one carrying the lantern join them. They all seemed to be milling about at the bottom of the slope.

More shouting erupted, and quick look revealed the soldiers beginning to fan out, forming into a long line directly below him. They looked like a line of pheasant beaters, and he realised who they were trying to drive from cover. His heart started to beat faster, as they began to start their ascent of the slope, up towards where he lay. He knew that it would not take them long to find him. A great fear gripped him, because if they continued, they were definitely going to find him. He had killed that sentry, and that would mean him facing a firing squad. If he tried to move, he would be seen, and if he stayed here, he would be found. They were no more than twenty-

279

five feet from where he lay. Should he run for it, or lie completely still? Running would only result in him being shot. He started to dither, trying not to panic.

A massive thudding jolt shook the ground beneath him like an earthquake. The great shudder of the shock-wave was instantaneously, and only just preceded the loudest explosion that he had ever heard – seeming far louder than any torpedo explosion. It made him jerk in terror of the unknown, and his body instinctively curled into the foetal position, with his arms covering his head. After the initial shock, George knew that it was their explosives detonating. If that bridge fell this way, then he was lying just below it on this slope. He felt his body trembling with fear, knowing that if it did fall, he had no protection beneath this thin layer of vegetation in which he was lying. Then came what sounded like a rain shower, except it was not rain, it was huge lumps of brick and stone debris. Some larger ones thudded into the ground close by. Then he heard a scream! To add to his terror there came an eerie distorted howl, filling the night air. It was the groan of twisted metal – being bent grotesquely out of shape.

George lay terrified until the shower began to fade away, but immediately there came more heavy thuds as huge pieces of metal fell from the top of the viaduct. Gigantic sections of the box girder were bouncing and rolling down the slop. A whirling, spinning section of metal spun down past George, killing a Turkish soldier standing less than ten feet away. It happened so fast that the man did not have time to scream. Then the air filled with another intimidating rumble, as the whole box girder structure came crashing down. Several more lethal pieces of metal came cart-wheeling down the slope. George chanced a fearful glance up the hillside in time to see one of the stone columns collapsing. It toppled towards him before smashing into a thousand deadly missiles. With it came spaghetti strands of metal rails which were left dangling from either end of the void. Stones came thundering down, hitting the hillside and creating an explosion of dust. Instinctively covering his head once more, he closed his eyes and prayed. The choking thick dust cloud billowed and filled his vision, covering everything and everybody. More hideous screams erupted through the veiled curtain, some suddenly cut short, others unnaturally high. The central structure was down, and large stones continued to bounce past like Yorkers at Lords. Suddenly a relative calmness settled over the area, nobody could see a foot in front of them, but it all went quiet.

Most of those soldier's, who had come up the hillside from the waterline, had fled back down in panic, wading out into the water in an attempt to save themselves. Realising that he was fairly safe for the present, George sat up, looked all about, surprised to find him-self alone. Taking immediate advantage of the mayhem he rose, and headed for the tamarisk trees near the beach. As he started to move his left ankle gave way and he stumbled, but knowing that this chaos was not going to last for long, this would be his only chance of getting to some point of safety. Painfully he limped down towards the beach, arriving the tamarisk trees. On his way down, he passed within three feet of some of the soldiers, who didn't even give him a second look. Each man was unrecognisable as his uniform, face, hair and clothes were all completely smothered in dust. George could only assume that he must look the same. He managed to work his way over towards the trees and finally, with some relief, he staggered into their midst. Although the pain was excruciating, he managed to make his way through them in the concealing darkness, heading back eastward towards the landing beach.

If the Jimmy had made his escape, then he realised that the raft would probably not be there. If it was still there, then that shooting he heard would probably have done for him. On arrival he was proved correct, it was gone, and not hesitating he simply turned towards the water and waded straight in.

The water soon took his weight, and the pain eased from his ankle, although he found that he was unable to use it to propel himself through the water. He swam using the same sidestroke, slow and easy, gradually putting some distance between himself and the shore. After five minutes he chanced a backward glance. He could still see the huge cloud of smoke and dust rising high above the viaduct area, but was unable to assess any details of the damage – but he had a good idea that the Turks would not be using it for some time.

He recalled the Jimmy's words. He said that they would be picked up half a mile from the shore at 0100. It was going to be difficult for him to judge the distance, and he had absolutely no idea of what time it was. Maybe the Jimmy is somewhere just ahead of him, waiting for the boat!

Having been knocked unconscious, he tried to remember the sequence of events in order to get an idea of the time. The detonation must have taken place roughly ten to fifteen minutes after they had fired the fuses – so the Jimmy could not be too far ahead of him. That meant that he was only knocked out for a short while. He was just praying that he would be able to assess the distance from shore fairly accurately, and that *E11* would be there to pick him up.

As he swam, he felt such a relief to be away from all of the danger, but he knew that he would feel even better once he was safely back aboard. The ache in his foot felt a lot more comfortable in the coolness of the water, and he could move it a little easier. His pounding headache had also gone.

The definition of the shore-line slowly faded from view, and he noticed that the water was feeling decidedly cooler than it had been on the inward journey. Behind him, he could still hear shouts and screams echoing across the water. He looked back once more and found that the moonlight lit up the huge cloud of dust, making it stand out like a giant mushroom against the darkness of the hillside. He must be just about a thousand yards from the shore! Looking all around, there was no sign of the First Lieutenant, and knew that he dare not chance calling out.

After another ten minutes he began to shiver. He was getting cold and could feel the muscles in his legs beginning to tire with the continual action of treading water. The downward drag in the water from his wet heavy overalls, was beginning to impede his ability to stay afloat, and knew that unless the boat were appeared fairly soon, that he would have no alternative but to head back to the shore.

Another ten minutes passed, and he could feel himself getting really tired. The downward drag from his sodden clothes was sapping his remaining strength. All around him there was stillness. Just then something unnerving occurred, when he suddenly felt that he was not alone. Alarm! His senses sharpened on an extremely frightening experience. There was a vibration in the water, he could feel it through his whole body. It gradually grew stronger, followed by a loud hissing noise, which he instantly recognised. His spirits soared, because he knew that it was caused by compressed air. His strength and determination returned and his eyes began searching the darkness for *E11*, very aware that he dare not risk shouting out, just in case the Turk heard him and fired on the boat. He started swimming as fast as he could towards the direction of the noise, looking through the darkness when he could just make out the faint outline of the submarine. It was some way off, but despite his weariness, he put on a spurt towards safety.

After two minutes he realised that it was further away than he first thought as he had to stop for a breather. Then, to his great anguish, he saw white water thrashing at the stern of the boat, and it started to move away from him. He stared after it in disbelief. They couldn't leave him here! He tried to convince himself that they must be manoeuvring around to pick him up. They had to be. He knew it would be useless him trying to catch up with the boat, and having no other option, he decided to remain where he was.

After five minutes there was no sign of the boat. His strength was waning fast. Another five minutes passed, and he was forced to accept the fact that he had been left behind. He started to feel very angry.

Bastards, he thought. At least they could have made a token search for him. However, after a moment, he had the sense to realise he was wasting his energy here by treading water – they were not going to come back. One of the bottom legs of his overalls had slipped down, and was covering over his plimsoll. He was beginning to find it very difficult to kick that leg to gain any propulsion. Luckily it was his left, and although his ankle was recovering well, he realised that he was going to need every bit of his remaining strength just to make it back to the shore. He set up a slow but determined rhythm, and as he did so his anger began to cool. After all he could not really blame them. They had no idea that he was there, and they were risking their lives by being on the surface so close to the shore.

What the bloody hell was he going to do now? He felt cold, alone, and very afraid for his future prospects. His despair was complete when he finally waded his way ashore. He still could hear the Turks further up the beach, shouting to each other. Shivering, and trying to gather his wits together, he knew that he that he would have to make some sort an escape plan. First things first. He was going to have to find somewhere, close where he could dry out while he formulated a way forward. Things could not be worse.

He walked up into the tamarisk, and then onward through them into the pines, where he found a thicket with some shrubbery that he did not recognise. It was green, with large leaves which would hide him. For the moment, that would be enough. He sat down heavily, his wet clothes became covered with pine needles. After an hour his clothes became a little dryer, and he felt more comfortable. He was beginning to know the meaning of the word despair.

He tried to think of what he could do, remembering at the briefing that the skipper said that he would bring *E11* back after twenty-four hours, and attempt another pick-up should anything go wrong. Maybe that would be his best option. He would have to keep out of the way until then of course. The trouble was that he had no idea of the time, and trying to guess midnight was not easy. If he got it wrong, he could be swimming around for hours. What if they missed him again? Leaning back against a tree, mentally he tried to run through all the information that he had gleaned about this part of the world. He had seen the Admiralty chart in the wardroom at the briefing, although much of what had been said meant very little to him, he knew in which direction Constantinople lay, but the Allied lines were over a hundred miles away, across the Marmara, then over on the south side of the Gallipoli Peninsula. It was impossible for him to swim anywhere near that distance, so obviously if he was going to get back, he would need a ship to take him across, or alternatively he would have to travel the six hundred miles overland by train. Either way trying to get to the Peninsula, through enemy territory, with having none of the language, was not going to be easy?

In assuming that the trains would be heavily manned by the Turkish military, his capture would be inevitable, but he thought that it might just be possible for him to stow-away aboard a ship. All the ships were in the capital. Scutari was the main port of Constantinople. He remembered the skipper saying that it lay somewhere to the east of the city, a place where most of the Turkish logistics for the conflict was loaded for transport over the Marmara. So, there must be lots of ships at Scutari, and luckily, he knew in which direction Constantinople lay.

When they started off on this mission and were swimming towards the shore, he remembered the Jimmy saying that they were about thirty miles from Constantinople. If he could just manage to get there, then it might just possibly for him to find a ship. Maybe he could creep aboard at night! If he managed to get back to the Peninsula, he knew that he would still have to make his way through the enemy lines, because the Turkish army had Allies surrounded. His chances of success were terrible, at the best. Despondent, he laid back, trying to rest while his clothes dried. He had plenty of time in which to think.

Anyway, all being good, he would first try and make the rendezvous with *E11* tomorrow night. But what if he missed her again?

First things first – if he had to – how was he going to get to Constantinople? Walking was probably the only logical thing that immediately came to mind. Thirty miles would take him at least a couple of days, maybe three – especially with his ankle as it was. He would have to move at night, and lay up during the day. So, if he had to walk, then what did he need to know? He knew that he had to head west, and that was about all. If Scutari had been to starboard as they had entered the Bosporus, obviously he would arrive there first, before he reached the city itself.

For now, I am going to have to stay here and hide until all this fuss dies down, he thought. He shivered in his despair, suddenly going on full alert on hearing some voices close by. He flattened himself on the pine needles, and they pricked him terribly. After a couple of minutes, he pushed himself up and tried to peer through the foliage. Silhouetted in the reflected moon gleam on the sea surface, he could see a line of soldiers. He watched them as they made their way eastward. They may be back at any time. This was not good. Were they looking for him?

After fifteen minutes he decided that he could be discovered here, and knew that he had to find somewhere safer. Then he heard more voices that grew out of the darkness. This time they made their way up into the trees, and he could hear them talking to each other. It sounded like they were searching for him. Maybe trying to stay here to make the rendezvous was too dangerous, and not such a good idea. He tried to think of his next move as the voices began to fade.

Maybe he should just try to get to Scutari! At least he would have the railway to show him the way, but knew that he would have to be very careful. There was no better plan that he could think of, so he decided to use the cover of this darkness to climb further up the hillside. If he could make his way up to somewhere near that cliff, it would put him just below the railway without being seen, and then at night maybe he could navigate his way west from there. It was the best idea that he could come up with.

So, he set off. Staying within the confines of the pine trees it took some time before he reached the base of the rock face. His ankle was very painful, and son arrival he managed to find a small depression in amongst a thick stand of pine trunks. Squatting down, he slumped back dejectedly against the bark of a tree, with his head in his hands. His utter despair was complete, and the tears of frustration welled up into his eyes. He had no money, no food, and only the clothes that he stood up in. He was not wearing any official uniform, and if he were to be captured, he would probably be tried for spying. The penalty for that was the firing squad. Then, with a sudden flash of realisation, he remembered – THE MAP!

His fingers reached into the breast pocket of his overalls where he could feel the wet, folded piece of paper. Carefully trying to pull it out, he stopped, realising that it was so wet that it would tear. To get it out, he would firstly he would have to remove his overalls, then extract it very carefully. It would have to dry before he could attempt to unfold it. Undressing quickly, he hung his overalls over a low bush. Very gently, with his fore-finger and thumb he extracted the map, and spread it out on a bed of pine needles. He placed a stone at each corner to prevent it being blown away.

There were no more sounds coming from the soldiers and he decided to settle down for the night. He guessed that it must be somewhere around two o'clock in the morning. It was cold, and he was naked, so he found a sheltering rock and curled up into a ball at its base, hugging his own body in an effort to gain some warmth. He closed his eyes, hoping for oblivion from this nightmare.

Chapter Thirteen

Alone in a Strange Land

Was he dreaming? He was woken by what sounded like a steam whistle. Last night he had witnessed the destruction of the viaduct with his own eyes. Surely a train could not have been able to cross there? The Turks could never have repaired it so quickly. Making a quick decision, he decided that he would go and investigate, but first he had to get dressed. It was very early in the morning. Still fairly dark, the dawn light was no more than a splash of pastel shades in the eastern sky.

How he was missing life aboard the submarine, missing his crewmates, and earnestly wishing that he was there right now. Strangely he missed the comforting sounds, followed by the awful smells of Baxter passing wind. He always swore that he was not the phantom farter. Even the ever-pervading stench of diesel that accompanied his every waking thought. A thick dollop of porridge, with a spoonful of jam for breakfast. That last thought made him realise just how hungry he was.

Shaking the sleep from his head, he awoke fully, finding himself naked. The events of the last few hours came flooding back into his mind. Firstly, he felt elated that he and the Jimmy had blown up the viaduct last night? Then he remembered the steam whistle – they had, hadn't they? He recalled that bits of that falling bridge had nearly killed him. So how could that train...? The whistle noise that he had heard had been unmistakable, and now he could hear the whoosh – whoosh – whoosh of escaping steam from a stationary engine, and judging from the intensity of the noise it was quite close.

After brushing away the pine needles from his body, he dressed quickly. His ankle was painful, but he found that he could walk on it with just a slight limp. The stiff drill material of his overalls remained damp, but he ignored it, to make his way towards the edge of the pines. From cover, he peered out through the branches, up to where the viaduct had once stood, and he was very relieved to see a great big gaping hole. The half of the central column was missing.

The train that he had heard, was standing over on the far western side of the chine. A black monster emitting clouds of steam. It must have just arrived from Scutari with a repair squad, he surmised. He could see that it was loaded with all manner of materials on the flatbed wagons behind the engine. There were a lot of men milling around the area. If it had indeed arrived from Scutari, then logically, it would eventually have to return, as it obviously could not proceed further. If he just could manage to get himself aboard somehow, it may provide him with a ride back towards the port area of the Capital, saving him days of walking. He went back to get the map.

As he walked through the trees, he looked eastwards towards the sun rising above the distant mountain peaks that lined the horizon, but then realised that there was a thin grey line of low-lying cloud dividing the sky from the sea giving one the impression that the day may well be colder than usual. Shivering, George carefully picked up the map and spread it out, fully aware of how vital its information was going to be to him. As he studied it, he could see where last night's landing point had been marked, and on this scale, it looked just a few miles down the coast to reach Scutari, but it was probably a very long way. Unfortunately, there was no attached scale to be able to judge distance. The railway lines around the Marmara had been clearly marked. One ran west from Constantinople towards Uzun Keupri, and Dedeagatch, before going down to the Mediterranean coast. If he took that route it would still leave him with over fifty miles to get back to the Allies lines. The other rail line ran eastward from Scutari for a hundred miles before turning south, and then continued for another three hundred and fifty miles towards Smyrna. It then headed back northwest to Panderma on the southern shore of the Marmara. From there, it was still over fifty miles by sea to reach the Gallipoli Peninsula. He realised that route was not possible, as the destruction of the viaduct prevented trains from using it. After last night's attack there would be nothing using this line until it was repaired. That left the option of stowing away aboard a ship heading for the peninsula. To do that he had to get to Scutari. He tried to endorse this by reasoning that if he could get a vessel heading for the Peninsula, he would have a decent chance of walking overland towards the Allied lines. He had not yet a clue as to how he would be able to pass through the Turkish army lines, but he would have to face that situation once he was there – he needed to take things one step at a time.

He carefully folded the map back into its original creases, and replaced it back in his top breast pocket. Rising warily, he headed back up the steep slope towards the bottom of the cliff. On arrival he continued to use cover to observe what was happening.

He could clearly see the train on the far side of the crippled viaduct. It was a huge 2-4-2 engine that had been employed to deliver and push a flatbed crane into position, along with other two flatbed wagons were behind the engine, loaded with rails and lengths of wood. They were obviously going to leave the crane here to lift the materials into place for the repair, he thought. They are certainly wasting no time. He could see that a working party had already started to unload and stack these materials, and he watched them for fifteen minutes, before scanning the general area below the track, trying to work out a route to that engine without attracting any attention.

The unloading looked to be going well, and a lot of the repair materials had been stacked in neat piles beside the line. Wooden beams and metal girders were already being carried out along the track towards the viaduct. He could see from the small amount of materials that were lying there, that it would not be anywhere near enough to complete a full repair. At least another load or two would be required. It was a single line track, so therefore this train would probably be leaving soon and heading back to Scutari to collect the next load. He made up his mind there and then that he would try and get aboard before it left – but there was a problem! He still had get across to the other side of the chine to reach that train, and that involved crossing two hundred yards of open ground with nothing to use as cover in broad daylight.

Then he looked down towards the area just above the beach and something caught his eye. He noticed that two workmen and two soldiers were carrying the bodies of the dead, who had been killed last night. Patiently he watched them as the bearers negotiated the steep terrain, eventually climbing up the far embankment to reach the train. The bodies were slung unceremoniously onto the back of one of the newly empty flatbed wagons. He could see that more bodies were being carried up the slope from the same general area below the viaduct, and in all he counted nine dead. Over by the train, the labourers of the work-force were still stacking the materials and more importantly he noted that they were dressed in a varied assortment of clothing. A bold plan began to form in George's mind, which might just work. If he did not try, he realised that he would eventually end up being captured.

He made his way down towards the first rise up from the beach, using the thick vegetation there as cover. Slowly he worked his way over towards a small stream that ran down the centre of the chine. Just thirty yards from where he was hiding there were several men who were scouring the tangled undergrowth, searching for any more bodies!

Taking a dep breath, and feeling terribly vulnerable, George stood up, and walked determinedly out towards the stream, moving left and right through the clumps of scrubby vegetation copying the actions of the other men. He kept his head down, as if he too were searching the ground for bodies. Gradually he edged his way across the water, and made his way over towards the far side of the chine. The paranoia of someone challenging him was his constant companion. On reaching the steep slope, he made his way upwards towards the train. Nobody had turned a hair, but it was a terrible feeling – the expectation that someone would shout – challenge him. Trying to remain unobtrusive, he dared not looked around and check. As he neared the top, he headed straight into the small stand of pines that stood just below the embankment on which the train track lay.

Once within the shaded protection, he let out a huge sigh of relief, allowing his breath to return before making his way carefully under the stretched low pine branches. Tentatively he began to clamber up the edge of the scrubby embankment towards the railway track level to check the situation near the train. A few workmen were in the process of unloading the last of the materials, and he noticed that the steam crane wagon had been uncoupled, and had been pushed into a position from where it could be brought into action. The steam boiler had obviously been flashed up, as he could see a thin plume of smoke rising from the small chimney fitted in the roof of the cab. He could see that the crane would soon be lifting off the last of the five metre lengths of angle iron girders, and swinging them around to place them over near the viaduct. George realised that he didn't have time to dither, he tried to figure out how he was going to get aboard.

After ten minutes the crane was in use, and as its jib swung around, away from his position, every one of the labourer's heads turned with it. Seeing his chance and throwing caution to the wind, George stepped out from his cover and went straight across the embankment, and ducking down under the coupling, he made his way between the two flatbed wagons. Standing fully erect, he could see the line of dead bodies, lying on the furthest one. After another quick check along the line towards the viaduct, he climbed up on the wagon. His nose wrinkled in disgust as he saw that some of the terribly mutilations, but did not hesitate as he laid himself face down amongst them. The metallic stench of dried blood was overpowering, and flies were buzzing, crawling all over the corpses. He wretched twice, trying hard not to throw up, forcing himself to lie as still as possible. Eventually he had to bring his arm around and bury his face the material on his sleeve, using it as a filter to evade the sickening stench.

It could had only been lying there for a few minutes, but it seemed to have been a lifetime, before he heard some of the labourers puffing nearby. There were grunts followed by another body being thrown across his legs. The sun was rising ever higher, and he could feel its rays beginning to heat the deck of the flatbed.

It was with some relief that twenty-five minutes later the train whistled blasted out. It was a precursor to the train slowly moving off, which was just in time, as George was on the point of vomiting from the putrid reek emanating from the bodies. Still he forced himself to remain absolutely still, sensing that the train seemed to be crawling along at a frustratingly slow speed. He waited. Then George could hear the voices of men. They grew louder as the train approached them – and then he heard them fade as the wagon passed them by. With the forward motion came a welcome breeze, which also eradicated most of the stench. Lying still for so long was very difficult. Itches needed scratching, and his muscles ached, needing to be moved to facilitate blood-flow, and with trying to cope with the obnoxious smell had was hell on earth. However, the train speed soon began to pick up, and before too long it was rattling along at a goodly pace. The forward motion increased the breeze, and he lifted his head for the first time. The clickety-clack rhythm soon freshened the air and George could begin to breathe more freely. He noticed that his overalls were dry.

Having spent the best part of three quarters of an hour staring at the crushed khaki puttied leg of one of the dead Turks, he chanced raising his head higher for a good look around. He immediately noted that the engine was facing the opposite way to the direction of travel. It was in reverse gear, pushing the two flatbed wagons ahead of it along the track. The flatbed crane unit that had been at the front end of the train, had been left back at the viaduct. A good inspection of the train revealed that the coal tender blocked the driver's view of him. The driver would have to physically lean out to one side to be able to catch sight of him. If he stayed in the centre of the flatbed wagon, then he would remain hidden. Things were looking good – so far!

He got himself up, relieved to be moving away from the stinking corpses and standing erect, he stretched every muscle. He sat on the back edge of the wagon, nearest to the engine, and let his feet dangle, knowing that he would be safe here.

Looking about at the countryside that was flashing by, he was pleasantly surprised at how peacefully rural and quiet everything seemed to be. Turkey was beautiful, and nothing like he imagined it to be. Once the railway track began to move inland, away from the coast, he could see a series of lush fields lining the route, many green, others growing cereal crops, and cattle grazing in the verdant meadows. Small herds of goats, and flocks of chickens were dotted around the farm buildings, while in the background, the hills receded towards the north. It was strange – he had always imagined Turkey to be dry, dusty place. Probably an impression that had been formed by the scant features of the surrounding hillsides within the island harbour at Murdos, before they had sailed on this patrol.

An hour quickly passed, and George began to notice that the farms were becoming more frequent. Small villages began to flash by, and then a small town, as the outermost limits of the city beckoned. This build-up of the urban sprawl warned him that the train was not too far from its destination.

George had not been idle, using the time to think carefully about his next move. He knew that he could not stay aboard this train. If he stayed on here all the way into the city, he would surely be caught when soldiers came to remove the bodies. He was worried that he may stand out in a crowd. For a start he was wearing navy blue overalls and gym shoes, albeit very dirty gym shoes, and he didn't speak a word of the Turkish language. So, he decided that he would have to make a jump for it from the train, the next time it slowed for a bend. Then, hopefully he could rough up his overalls to make him look more of a common labourer, but he had a deep fear stirring in his stomach about all of the unknowns that he had yet to face.

Admitting to himself that things had gone well so far, complacency was not an option, because he knew that he would need all of his wits and ingenuity to survive whatever fate had in store.

The train began to slow and he knew that he did not have a choice but to take advantage, and get off while he could. So, he made his way over to the edge of the flatbed, climbing down onto one of the iron steps of the wagon on the outside of the bend. Hopefully the driver would be hanging out on the inside of the bend watching his train. With his feet on the bottom rung, he was only three feet from the stones that bedded the sleepers into of the track. Leaning out, he quickly made sure that nobody back in the engine cab was looking his way before he gazed ahead. The bend was coming up and he noticed that there was a line of trees forming an avenue that lined the track. Then he noticed another line of trees running at right angles, and George thought that this may be a cross road intersection. He was pretty sure that the engine driver would be leaning out of his cab on the inner side of the curve, so being here on this side, he was hoping that he would not be spotted.

The bend loomed. He readied himself, hearing the squeal from the brakes as the train slowed down. The passing frequency of the telegraph poles decreased and George readied himself. If he misjudged his leap, he could injure himself severely. The train began to negotiate the bend, and he launched himself off the step. His body tumbled over and over before crashing to a stop at the bottom of a dry ditch.

"Oooof," he groaned, as the air was knocked out of him. Gasping for breath, he rose, and quickly checked himself for injury – but found none. There was a pain in his right shoulder when he had rolled over a rock, and his ankle still hurt a little from last night, but he could walk on it reasonably well. Having regained his breath, he looked for the train – the driver and fireman were still hidden within the confines of their cab, and had not appeared to have noticed his departure. Ducking down into the waist high grass he watched it getting smaller until it became distorted in the mirage of heat haze rising from the track. Brushing the dust from his overalls, he coughed and spat some grit from his mouth. Looking around, he found him-self standing by the row of trees, and moved into the shade for cover, which would allow him to make a quick reconnoitre of the area. He knelt down to hide himself between the trees, feeling that this first stage of his plan had gone rather well.

Above him the sky was now the deepest blue, cloudless except for a dirty haze on the horizon hovering over the direction of the city – or at least where he assumed the city to be. Just across the rail track, far in the distance, he could make out the Sea of Marmara stretching out like a shining mirror. A pinpoint of white revealed the sail of an Arab dhow, that was slowly tacking its way up towards Constantinople. Somewhere out there was *E11*, George thought to himself ruefully, wishing they would magically appear and rescue him.

Turning his attention back towards the problems that he faced, he noticed that beyond the avenue of trees, there lay a few ramshackle houses, clustered around the small domed roof of a tiny mosque. George took his time in assessing the situation. He knew that there were small villages in Britain, where agriculture composed the prime industry. They were usually positioned at a crossroads, or at river crossing. Looking ahead he could see that this small hamlet had gathered itself around this railway as it was crossed by a dusty road. Maybe they made their living by maintaining the track, or supplying locally grown produce that could be taken directly into the city market by train? Using the cover of the trees, he crept closer to the buildings, the whole place appeared to be deserted, bar a few scrawny chickens, pecking desultorily in the grass, and an old ginger dog that lay sprawled across a doorway, lazily watching his progress.

George's heart began to pound. Would that dog bark a warning? He watched as it strained to get up to its feet, before plodding across towards the shade of a water butt, before collapsing and lowering its head back down onto its paws. Beyond the houses, far out in a field, George could just make out the figures of two men and one women toiling on this land.

Had they all left the house and gone to work?

At the back of the houses, he could see laundry fluttering limply like flags, hanging on a line. Another good check – there was definitely no sign of human life.

Continuing to use the trees as cover, he selected one of the houses, that was displaying more washing than most. It also had a well-stocked vegetable patch. A thought of his own back in Guernsey came into vision.

After another goodly period of observation, he finally satisfied himself that it was safe. Dashing up to one of the poles, he reached up and removed a shirt, and a pair of trousers. Stuffing them under his arm, he bent down to uproot some of the growing carrots, before dashing back to his hiding place. Rolling up the garments into a ball, he tucked them inside his overalls. While he waited to make sure that it was still clear, he began brushing the dirt off of the carrots, before he began chewing them.

Having got this far, he decided that his next goal was to reach the city, and following that, he would try and find a boat. At least it was a basic plan, and with these two aims in mind, George began to trek along the edge of the rails in the direction that the train had disappeared. There were no other rail systems, just the single track, so he reckoned that it had to lead to the city. He tried to keep close to the line of trees that ran parallel with the rails, using the shade to keep cool, and to conceal his presence.

It really was a lovely day, but George seemed unaware of the weather as the morning turned to afternoon. The ever-present paranoia – the feeling of being discovered – made him check everything. He found himself diving for cover for the least reason. On one occasion a seagull cawed high above him, and rising out of the ditch, he felt embarrassed and quite stupid.

Another half a mile, and he approached another small lane that crossed the railway track. There was no human presence for as far as he could see, but George noted that there was a ramshackle railway workman's hut near the intersection. He drew the revolver from his waistband, and keeping low, he made his approach. Scanning the lane in both directions, both were clear – in fact this whole country seemed to be deserted – which was just as well.

Crossing the dusty lane, he tentatively approached the hut. It was a flimsy wooden structure, designed to hold the tools of the track repair gangs. The door was bolted and padlocked, but a loose board at the back afforded him entry. A grime-encrusted glass window provided little light to the interior. He began to search for anything that would aid his cause, and was quickly rewarded by the discovery of a workman's discarded jacket. It was a very shabby jacket, and it took a good shake to remove the insects who had taken up residence. With the trousers and shirt from the washing line, it would give him less conspicuous clothes, rather than wearing his submarine overalls.

He quickly changed, enjoying the feel of the freshly laundered linen against the skin on his back, but once he had donned the jacket, it soon became dirty. The trousers were old but fairly clean. They were a little wide around the waist. George undid the knot in the lanyard from the revolver, looped it through the belt beckets and tied it around his hips. Using some black greasy compound that he found in one of the pots in the corner of the shack, he used it to darken his gym shoes. Finally satisfied that they looked like an old pair of shoes, he covered the sticky grease in dust. He hung his overalls on the peg where the jacket had been, but as he turned to leave, he remembered the map and went back and removed it from the breast pocket. Looking fondly at his overalls, he was happy that he had made a fair exchange, so it was not a robbery. Feeling less conspicuous, George started feeling more confident about facing whatever lay ahead, as he set out once more.

Half an hour later found George walking at a steady pace along a dusty unmade road that he was hoping led towards the port of Scutari. It was approaching mid to late afternoon, and the heat of the day was as just beginning to ease. He had left the railway track behind, and taken to a road after noticing a small signpost that was positioned not far from the hut. The sign had a direction inscription in both Turkish and Greek. Even with his total lack of both languages, he could translate the letters on the sign as Scutari.

Soon he reached the fringes of suburbia spilling out from the City, having engulfed some of the peripheral country villages and hamlets. He walked onward, trying to appear as unobtrusive as possible, keeping his head bowed. He began to had pass local people and felt somewhat comforted by the fact that they had shown no interest in him whatsoever. His confidence began to return.

By five o'clock he had reached the edge of the town of Scutari itself, where he was met by a blend of east and west, which reminded him a little of the back streets of Gibraltar with its mixture of Moorish bazaars and modern shops. Looking about him, he could see that everything here was a lot shabbier than in Gibraltar. The shop signs were mainly in Turkish, but there were others that used the Cyrillic alphabet. He had no idea what sort of establishment he was passing until he was near enough to see inside, or was able to smell the products on offer. He noticed that one of the signs was in Arabic, with its unintelligible squiggly writing. Another proprietor had a distinctive Slavic appearance, and George thought that he may be Russian, or at least from one of the Black Sea states. It certainly seemed to be a cosmopolitan kind of a place, which he hoped would serve his purpose well.

Soon he found himself walking through the main streets, experiencing the vibrant hustle and bustle of daily life in this suburb of the Turkish capital. The whole place was generally filthy, with huge piles of rotting garbage heaped at the edge of many of the roads. The occasional avalanche caused a blockage in the drainage channels, resulting in wide smelly pools that stretched across the thoroughfare. There was an oily scum floating on the liquid morass, which seemed to attract thousands of flies, and George was forced to negotiate these buzzing hoards to be able to continue with his journey.

He felt the general amiable mayhem of a market atmosphere, as traders fought for custom of those passing their shops and stalls. Most of the shop frontages opened directly out onto the street, and many had their wares for sale on display on the fore-court, outside. One shop had huge carpets hanging down

from wooden frames that jutted out at right angles from the walls, displaying the intricate designs. Another was selling a gold coloured metal, that George thought might be brass – or maybe even a copper alloy – that had been crafted into various utensils. They were not the kind of utensils that George was used to. They came in every size and shape, all covered with a fine tooled engraving. He could only guess at some being coffee pots, but other shapes defied any explanation. Passing one shop, he could see the owner sitting at a work-bench using his thin engraving chisel and small hammer to create the most wonderful patterns on these metal items. Next door, in the very next shop, chickens squawked from woven basket cages, and goats bleated pitifully from their rope tether. Down a side alleyway there were cattle tied to a post. From the river of blood flowing out from a gutter in the alleyway, George surmised that it was an abattoir. As he walked past one of the animals, it raised its tail and splattered a load of smelly wetness onto the cobbles. Somebody laughed at his misfortune, but George hurried on. He was immediately hit by a terrible stench, and searching for the source he spotted piles of guts and offal, in a stinking heap. The flies were here as well, and looking back towards the tethered animals, he realised that they were waiting their turn.

Horses and donkeys, some pulling heavily loaded carts passed him, and to George's amazement he actually saw a line of camels carrying huge bundles of firewood faggots, stacked high on their backs. He never seen a camel before, and he stood in awe watching them go past, amazed by how their long necks swayed in time with their gentle gait, before smelling the trail of a sweaty pungent aroma that seemed to drift in their wake.

A steam lorry blasted a series of toots at the animals, and the people that were blocking its path. There seemed to be people everywhere.

George was trying to remember his lessons from school, when Mister Jeffries had taught them about the Crimean War. He was sure that it was here at Scutari that Florence Nightingale had established her hospital for the wounded from that war, but he never imagined then that one day he would actually be here.

People here were dressed in both the eastern and western styles, but generally they mostly wore shabby looking clothing – just like him. Many were clad in the loose flowing robes, or kaftans with a striped patterned material that reminded

George of the mattress on his bed at home. Baggy trousers with a bolero jacket seemed the order of the day for the men, and full skirts worn down to the ankle, with a headscarf for the women. Many of them sported other varieties of headdress: there were Turk phakeolis, Jewish kappots, Arab qalifeh, Afghan pakol, Balkan kalpaks, or the more common fez. In a complete contrast, businessmen walked past him dressed in immaculately tailored three-piece suits, complete with homburg hats, and spats over the their highly polished shoes. A group of old men sat at one of the tables outside a coffee shop playing backgammon. They were each wearing old black two-piece suits with open neck white shirts, smoking foul-smelling cigarettes. They contrasted greatly with the peasant population in their dirty rural working clothes, having spent the morning at their labour, or having come straight into town to sell their produce fresh from the fields.

Interspersed amongst the populace there were the uniforms of every kind and colour. The khaki of the Army, dark blue for the Navy, black for the Police, grey for Postmen and the sandy brown worn by the Civil Militia. Peaked caps vied with the conical headwear of the soldiers.

The smells of the coffee and sweetmeats aroused George's latent hunger, and he realised just how thirsty he was. He had enjoyed the carrots he had stolen, which had also served to quell some of his thirst, but these invasive aromas were enough to send his taste buds into overdrive. The rising steam from the samovars billowed out from the cafe windows, and he looked longingly at the displays of aromatic, spicy foods being prepared at the pavement stalls. There were strange confectionaries such as nougat, and lokum, filled with nuts and fruit peel, covered with a fine powdery sugar on the display trays. Sweet desert pastries such as baklava were dripping with honey and pistachio nuts. Almond cookies were still hot from the oven, and smelled heavenly. George looked up to find a shopkeeper eying him suspiciously, as he looked at his mouth-watering wares. Most of these vendors looked to be an eagle-eyed bunch, and George knew that he did not dare chance stealing anything. If he were caught it would be catastrophic.

It was getting late in the afternoon, and the house shadows had lengthened, dark against the pastel sunlit gable wall as he walked by – evening beckoned. Another mile found George climbing a steep road, where he passed a newspaper seller who was obviously shouting out the latest headlines. He paused to try and learn of any new developments. It was very frustrating not being able to understand what everybody was saying. Even with his fluency in French, it was not enough, he could not understand a thing of what was being said.

Momentarily distracted, he stepped off the pavement just as a handcart rattled by. Being heavily laden with vegetables and fruit, the old man pushing hit a kerbstone in his effort to avoid him, narrowly missing his foot. The toothless owner shook his fist, swearing loudly at him. Sometimes gestures were enough to bring translation, but those all around were turning and starting to take notice. George waved and made gestures of apology as he turned away from the danger of being discovered. He was quick to spot that the old man had not noticed that a some of his fruit had rolled off his cart into the gutter. Nobody had bothered to pick them up, as the gutter was full of filth. After the man and his cart had carried on up the hill, George returned and retrieve the bounty, placing them inside his shirt. He followed the handcart up the hill, keeping at a safe distance from the old man. Near the top of the climb he came upon a public drinking fountain beside the road, where he carefully washed the fruit and wiped them on his shirt. After quenching his thirst, he began to eat his fill.

****

From the top of this hill, George was afforded the most magnificent view overlooking the majestic harbour area of the city. Almost straight across the water from where he stood, he could see the Topkapi Palace, the Sultan's residence, standing up on the promontory above Seraglio Point. He remembered the skipper taking a fix from there. Down to the right of it he could see the ferry terminal quays that had several smoky ferries berthed. That has got to be the Golden Horn, and beyond that must be the Galata Bridge, he surmised. He could see the forest of ships masts that the skipper had described, lying on the far side of the bridge. To the right, a hill rose up steeply, where he could clearly see the tall round Galata Tower, standing half way up. All around that area in front of the bridge, the water traffic was chaotic as the boats vied to get alongside at the passenger terminals. It made him wonder how *E11* had ever managed to miss being run down by so many of them. Turning to look southward, he was afforded a view down towards the docks, where there were many small boats bobbing at their moorings. The wharfs along the waterfront were crammed to capacity with every size and shape of merchant vessel. He could see the jibs of the cranes, continually swinging in and out in an effort to load them. George turned around and directed his attention northwards, taking in the breath-taking spectacle of the Bosporus stretching out towards the entrance to the Black Sea. He could now clearly see that the city stood on both banks, with the roof-tops interrupted by domes and minarets along the Constantine skyline. Tall-funnelled ferries were belching black smoke as they plied across the waterway, transporting the populace between the two Continents. The waterway was dotted with literally hundreds of tiny craft, most using gondolier rowing action, very similar to that used in Malta. So far – so good.

How time flies. Amazingly it had only been a week ago that *E11* had entered this magnificent harbour? He had seen the Admiralty chart, and had heard the captain describing this scene from the periscope, but now actually seeing it for real, it just seemed amazing. From the descriptions, and what he had gleaned from the chart, he managed to identify some of the places. Over there, further to the right of the Galata Bridge, would be the Arsenal Quay where they had torpedoed the troopship. That large group of buildings there must be part of the barracks, he surmised. Returning his gaze towards Scutari, he could see the wreck of a ship near the Harem Iskelessi. She was lying hull down in the water, with just her superstructure showing. That must be the very ship, the *Stamboul*, he had learned the name from the intelligence signal they had received. The port of Haidar Pasha, where most of the logistics destined for the peninsula was being loaded, lay just beyond. A smoky haze hovered above the hoard of masts and funnels that were berthed down there.

That is obviously where I've got to head for, if I'm ever going to get a boat across the Marmara, George determined.

Not having been challenged so far, his confidence was growing, and was increasing with every step he took. He chided himself, because he did not want to be over confident, but was relieved that he had blended well into the populace so well. Realising that he was going to have to take some risky decisions soon, he determined that he would try to use maximum caution with every decision because there would be no second chances. He had heard the adage that the best place to hide was in a crowd, and so far, it was proving to be true. Nevertheless, he felt his heart miss a beat with every new uniform that he saw. He began to walk the down the hill, through the crowded streets towards the docks, and the journey was thankfully uninteresting, and uneventful.

On reaching the outskirts of the port gates, the amount of vehicular traffic had increased significantly. Long queues formed, waiting to enter, where the combined exhaust gases had built up to decrease the visibility. There were lines of trucks, all seemed to be loaded with every commodity, from bales of hay to heavy munitions. The people around the entrance were being pushed back, forced to one side and crowding the pavements. A file of marching troops threaded their way through this human morass, with their rifles at the slope. A clear path opened, as the people moved back to get out of their way. As George stood and watched them, he thought back to his training days in Portsmouth, thinking that these recruits looked to be a rather scruffy bunch. Knowing that Leading Seaman Andrews would have had a thing or two to say about their ability to march. They seemed to amble, rather than actually march. An officer riding on a white charger bumped into George, sending him staggering over into the gutter. A snarl of unintelligible abuse poured from gritted teeth. George didn't need an interpreter for what he said, and scrambled to get out of his way.

As he reached the port area, the houses suddenly became into warehouses, and the shops turned into workshops. There was a long straight road that led straight down to the quays at Haidar Pasha itself. All along it was packed with stevedores and dockworkers, spreading out as far as the eye could see. George followed the soldiers through the gates, keeping to one side, as he headed towards the berthed ships.

On reaching the waterfront, the towering metal sides of each ship rose before him, standing high above the quayside like steel cliffs. As he looked down the line it was hard to see a gap. Gang planks slanted upwards as long crocodiles of stevedores could be seen carrying sacks, crates and boxes from the warehouses, disappearing in through square holes in the side of ships. The cranes swung in arcs, the jibs moving up and down, as they deposited deck cargoes aboard. A single, much taller crane, was effortlessly lifting heavy artillery pieces high into the air, swinging each across to the decks, and down into the open holds. On the quayside small steam trains tooted warnings, people could be seen diving aside as it moved up and down the dockside, dragging a retinue of shabby trucks, clanking and rumbling along behind. Above the harbour, a chorus of seabirds produced a raucous overture towards this hive of human endeavour.

George stopped and stood to one side to take it all in, letting the industry passed him by. It was time to assess what he was going to do next. Thankfully he had made here in one piece, to the place that he needed to be to stow himself aboard a ship heading to the Peninsula – but how the hell was he going to get aboard one? Which one would be heading to a convenient port on the Peninsula? He guessed that most of them would be heading in that general direction, but how was he going to find out which one for sure? It would be no good him landing in Gallipoli, as that would be full of the Turkish military. He decided that the only way was to stand here unobtrusively and observe. Then hopefully he might learn more of what was taking place.

So, standing in the darkening shadows, over on one side of the roadway, with his back against the brickwork of a dockside storehouse, he let the hustle and bustle pass him by, quietly watching the hectic scenes unfold before him, hoping to discover something that would provide him a clue that would enable him to formulate a new plan of action. He stood there for over an hour and a quarter, and the twilight had turned into night, when suddenly he noticed a pile of boxes on the back of a slow-moving truck. It provided the hint that he needed. He could read the black-stencilled word GALIBOLU on each of the wooden crates.

He remembered helping Lieutenant Brown amend his charts, just before they left Murdos. Galibolu was written in brackets on the Peninsula itself, under the word Gallipoli. It must be the local Turk name for Gallipoli!

He pushed himself off the wall, and ambled along the edge of the road, keeping pace with the vehicle through the mayhem of activity. Finally, it stopped at the gangway of a small steamer bearing the name of *Pearl of Petra*, which was registered in Athens. It was Greek owned!

A team of dock stevedores stood nearby, waiting to unload the boxes. George went over and stood in the scant protection of an alleyway directly opposite. Under the floodlights that lit the dockside, he could see that already a gang of men who were filing up the gangway, each sweating profusely under the huge weight of a sack of coal on his shoulders. The procession was slowly filling the bunkers of the steamer. Over the next hour, there were two more trucks that arrived, each loaded with similar marked crates to the first. Once the coaling had finished the men began unloading the trucks.

A loud burst of orders behind him made George spin around. A Turk army officer was yelling and gesticulating at a group of marching soldiers, dressed in dusty khaki uniforms. The raggedy file made its way down the quayside, scuffing to an untimely halt at the gangway of the ship just ahead of the Pearl of Petra. George moved himself back into the shadows of the alleyway to watch. A clatter of rifle butts echoed off the stone quayside, as they lowered their weapons. He had already made his decision, deciding that he would attempt to get aboard the Pearl of Petra, but obviously not now with these soldiers about to embark.

Arc lights flooded the quayside as work continued without pause. After the soldiers had disappeared aboard the ship, he had watched it sail. The bunkering of the ship opposite him was continuing and he considered walking out, picking up a sack of coal and simply walking up the gangway, but he had no knowledge of the internal layout of the vessel, and someone would very likely ask him questions. He decided to try again later, maybe in the early hours of tomorrow morning.

Having nothing else to do, he turned back up the hill towards Scutari. Despite eating those three apples, he was feeling ravenously hungry and very much in need of a decent meal. The tightness in his stomach was aggravated as he passed by shops once more with the pervading smell of sizzling kebabs and onions, hissing invitingly on open charcoal grill fires. These odours tortured his mind and the constant with the omnipresent smell of the strong Turkish coffee on the air.

It was getting late, but the place was still a hive of activity. As he made his way through the crowded thoroughfare, began he began to silently contemplate his next move. Suddenly he heard a lot of shouting ahead of him, and he craned his neck to see what was occurring. He could hear screams of determination, injustice, and outraged yells, knowing that he did not need to be able to speak Turkish to understand that somebody was being mistreated. Standing up on tip-toe, he tried to look for the cause of the disturbance, and spotted heads bobbing and weaving in and out amongst the crowd. Someone was running to evade capture, and he could hear the shrill tones of police whistles being blown. Behind, he could see the light sandy coloured conical hats of the Civil Militia, pursuing their quarry. Someone was definitely being chased! People began to stop to observe the unfolding spectacle, before stepping back to avoid a collision with the fugitive and soldiers. Arms and clenched fists were being raised and waved, along with cries of indignant anger. Who was being chased!

George prudently stepped to one side in preparation to get out of the way. He was standing under a stucco arch, that led off into a murky cluttered alleyway, from where he could watch what happened without hinderance. Fifty yards away, and he could see the caps of the Civil Militia were in hot pursuit, as the escapee had almost reached the point where he stood.

Whatever made him do it, he could not explain afterwards, but he reached out and grabbed the jacket of the fugitive, dragging him over into the alleyway. To his utter amazement, found himself staring at a young, wild-eyed girl. Instantaneously, both of them realised their predicament, and together they dashed down into the alley. George began pulling down empty wooden crates, that were stacked against a wall, to block the narrow passage behind them. It was quite dark as they dashed along its confines, George gradually drew the girl away from the rabble, swimming and kicking his way through billowing sheets of newspaper, broken bottles, and rotting vegetation, as they ran into a second adjoining alley.

At the next corner George stopped to see if they were still being followed, letting go a sigh of relief as he saw it was clear. There was no sign of the militia! Not saying a word, the two continued onward at a fast walking pace, but he noticed that the girl was now leading the way. Panting and gasping, they eventually emerged out into a small open courtyard, standing back off the alleyway, which they accessed via a gap between the walls. It revealed a tall four storey block of dwellings. Looking up at each, he noted that they had rusting cast iron balconies, which extended out above their heads. He could see a child's face through the railings of one, curiously watching their arrival. A washing line stretched from that balcony, right across the gap to the adjacent block. It was heavily laden with laundry. Above them the first stars could be seen through the wafting linen sheets, as they walked past the communal water pump.

The girl appeared to know exactly where she was, and breaking free from George's clasp, she headed for one of the ironwork staircases, beckoning for him to follow. There was a large oil lamp that hung down between the blocks, its light making their negotiation of steps easier. They climbed two floors, before walking along a landing towards a dingy door sporting some flaking paintwork. She produced a key and entered. Once inside, they both sat down at a bare table, slowly regaining their breath.

As their composure returned, each looked up at the other at the same time. George looked at her grimy face in the dimness, realising for the first time, that she was quite pretty. She certainly did not look like the common fugitive, that was his first impression. Why was she wearing trousers? The whiteness of her teeth flashed against her tanned skin, as she studied at him. She removed her hat, releasing a mass of Titian curl's that cascaded down across her shoulders. It was obvious that she had deliberately dressed herself as a boy, but why? He could see that her eyes were studying him, before an inquisitive eyebrow arched upwards. Her lips pouted, and he could see her face filling with a hundred questions. Had he made a mistake in helping her?

She spoke rapidly in Turkish, apparently asking him the first of those questions.

Seeing his look of utter bewilderment, she repeated the question more slowly. Again, George's lack of response created confused lines across her brow.

She tried another tongue, only to obtain an equally incomprehensible expression.

"You speaka te Eeengleesh maybe?" she enquired tentatively.

Seeing George's immediate response, she smiled, and continued.

"My name ees Mina Papandross – me Hellenic – how you say? – er – Greek."

George reached over the table, and shook her hand politely.

"How do you do. My name is George Torode."

"George – Georgios, that ees a good Greek name also. Your second name, that is Eeengleesh also?"

"No, it's from Guernsey. That's in the Channel Isles, near the coast of France. Iles du Manche, the French call them."

She looked him over, trying to work out who he was and what he was doing here.

"But you are Eeengleesh – not French – Yes?"

"Yes of course," said George, wondering how anyone could mistake a Guernsey-man for a Frenchman!

"Well, Georgios, thank you for your helping of me – they are all pigs in the militia – they are like the wild animals."

"What did you do to make them chase you?" asked George, curiously.

"Never mind that! Who are you? A soldier, maybe, who ees fighting in Gallipoli perhaps?"

"A sailor," he confessed. "I'm trying to get back to the war."

"How you do that? Is your ship here?" she enquired.

"No. I was going to try to get aboard a ship down at the docks. I saw one down there earlier today. She's bound for Gallipoli and I think that she will be sailing soon."

"You not get on ship now – too many soldiers watch – you wait for me to fix – I will help you – just like you help Mina – OK?"

Her smile was gorgeous.

George nodded, smiling his thanks.

"You are hungry – Yes?" she asked. "I fix some food."

It was the answer to all of George's prayers. "Yes please," he said.

Chapter Fourteen

Mina

The taste of the thin vegetable broth was heavenly, especially supplemented by a huge slab of unleavened bread, easily bettering any dish that he had ever eaten. George gorged himself, eventually accepting three helpings, before his appetite was sated. The girl made some coffee while he was eating, and whilst they drank it, he could feel the fear and tension of the last thirty-six hours beginning to evaporate. He finally felt safe! Stretching out his legs, he leaned back in his chair, letting his eyes scan the room. It was remarkably unprepossessing, and very basically furnished. Other than the table and chairs, there was an iron stove, the embers of which she had used to make the meal, but were now smouldering towards extinction. A stone slab jutted from the wall under the single window, with an earthenware bowl sat atop. In the corner stood a large unmade bed. The white-washed plastered walls flaked, showing signs of decay, with small sections having fallen away to reveal the red bricks beneath. Although the building was old, he could see that she had done her best to make it look cosy. The girl finished her coffee.

He helped Mina to clear away the remnants of the meal, and they sat down together to talk. The flow of conversation was somewhat stunted, due to the mutual language problem. She possessed some stuttering English, and she managed to explain that she was the daughter of a wealthy Greek merchant who ran a small fleet of ships and dhow's that were based here at Constantinople. She told him that her father had recently discovered that she was having an affair with the Turkish captain of one of his ships, which to his eyes had been the greatest insult that she could have dealt him. The age-old animosity between the Greeks and Turks may have been bridged in business, but where blood and family were concerned, it was as strong as ever. During the resultant argument, Mina had declared that she could no longer live at home, and had stormed out of the house and taken this room down here near the docks. Although her father still supported her financially, she made little contact with him. Through a lucky twist of fate George discovered that the Pearl of Petra was actually one of her father's ships. Maybe her skipper was the object of her desire? George said a silent prayer of thanks for having been led here.

Then their conversation turned towards George, and he immediately felt uneasy. He found her questioning extremely awkward, initially trying to pretend that he did not understand what she was asking.

"Yua maybe a deserter from the navy?" she enquired, staring him straight in the eye.

"Er – no, not exactly," stammered George, unable to return her look. "I fell overboard from my ship, and I managed to swim ashore. Now I'm trying to get back to re-join the Allies, near Cape Helles."

He decided that it wasn't that much of a lie, as he actually had swum ashore from his ship – although it had been voluntarily. She thought for a moment. Her eyebrow suddenly arched.

"I think maybe you tell Mina the big whopper lies," she said. "No Engleesh ships come into Dardanelles."

He felt very uncomfortable, disliking having to lie to her, but he couldn't tell her about the raid on the viaduct, or that he was a member of the crew of *E11* for that matter. After the submarine attack on Constantinople, the Turks would like nothing better than to get their hands on one of the perpetrators. He could imagine the propaganda that Turkey would enjoy if his face was splashed across the newspapers of the world's press. Even if he were to be captured before he could make it back to the Allies, he knew that he had to pretend that he was just an ordinary sailor who had simply got lost.

"You gota be plenty good at the swimming, Georgios – Tell Mina how far you swim from your ship?"

"Two miles, or so," lied George.

She walked behind him and tweaked his ear.

"Ow," he yelled.

"Then how you get to Constantinople? You can swim maybe a hundred kilometres – That ees like Leander swimming over the Bosphorus to meet his Hero over one hundred times. There are no Engleesh ships in the Sea of Marmara – only submarines."

Her face suddenly lit up with the realisation.

"Ah – Submarine! My father had one of his ships stopped by the Engleesh submarine, but it just stole some chickens and other foods. Another one attacked the city last week – a very big ship was sunk. Are you from a submarine, Georgios?"

He didn't know why he nodded. She was a very astute girl, and she seemed to be able to see through every lie that he had just told. It seemed pointless trying to continue the pretence.

"Ah ha, Mina is right;" she clapped her hands in delight.

He suddenly felt a terrible vulnerability, and he watched her to see if she would make some kind of an excuse to leave. Would she report him to the authorities? Would she betray him?

"So why you lie to Mina? I pretty smart girl you know. You cannot hide any story from me."

"I know, and I am sorry. I just need to get back to the Gallipoli peninsula, and I thought that you might hand me over to the militia if you knew who I was."

"Yua bloody stupid, Georgios. You save me from the militia. They would arrest me. If not for yua, I would be in prison cell. Those pigs are not nice to women prisoners, Georgios."

He could feel himself being re-appraised as her eyes began to search for the things that they had obviously missed earlier. She made a few murmuring sounds, as if she were coming to a decision. Her next words shook George.

"You wanta come with Mina? We go and ask my father to get you on Pearl of Petra, yes?"

It was everything he could have ever wished for, the answer to all his prayers. "Yes please," he replied thankfully. "Yes, I would like that very much."

****

It was quite dark, except for a quarter moon, with a thin cloud cover masking most of the stars. Despite the lack of light there were a lot of people out and about. George had not a clue what the time was, but reckoned that it must be well past ten o'clock. Before they had left the apartment, Mina told George to stand back, and let her do all the talking whenever she needed to. She said for him to act as if he were her brother, and to just say nothing. They had received several strange looks, mainly because in a male orientated society like that of Turkey, to let a woman take charge of things – like the buying of tickets for the ferry, and the tram – it was very unusual. So is allowing a woman walk beside the man, although in Constantinople it is not as uncommon as in the rest of the country. The Greek influence sees to that.

As they walked down towards the ferry terminal, they found that it was as busy as ever. Mina got around any suspicions at the ticket booth by flirting unashamedly. George tried to remain remote and unobtrusive, but found it difficult. They took one of the ferries directly across the Bosporus towards the Galata Bridge terminal, where as George stepped onto the quay-side, he actually encountered the fish roll vendors that the skipper had described during their attack of the city. He watched the fillets being grilled over a fire, before being inserted into small bread rolls. They turned right from the terminal and headed towards the bridge, and it was not long before they approached the arch of the Galata Bridge. It was a wide walkway and George's eyes turned left, searching the Golden Horn for any warships, but he found it far too dark to see anything. On the bridge, he noticed hundreds of men ling the balustrade on either side. Most were fishermen, interspersed by shoe-shine boys. Descending the slope on the far side, he could see a steep hillside looming ahead. Standing tall half way up the hill, George could see the lofty roundness of the Galata Tower with its low pointed conical roof. Climbing up the steep road took them an age, far longer than he had first assumed. Panting heavily, the two of them eventually reached the top, where George was amazed to find another, completely separate part of the city. A long road ran north along the ridge of the hill. Another a mile of walking along the shop lined streets, and they arrived at her father's house without any setbacks. Through-out the journey Mina appeared to be confidence personified, but it had been a nerve-wracking experience for him. To have men gesticulating, and gabbling away in front of him, in a language that he couldn't understand, was quite frightening. Knowing that he could easily have been arrested, he did not know what to do, or how to react! One man had taken offence at his apparent refusal to reply to his question, and became quite aggressive, even raising his fists to offer violence. George's hand reached across towards the inside his dishevelled jacket for his revolver. Mina's hand stayed the movement, and calmed the situation by giving the man a reassuring smile, and a long explanation. Her soft gabbled words quickly altered the man's expression, as he nodded his head in an understanding manner, and smiled sympathetically, finally coming over to pat George on the shoulder. George stood perplexed, not having a clue as to what excuse she had used to cover his refusal to answer. Everyone around them all seemed to be nodding and showing a lot of understanding, as they looked at him with expressions of kindness, and some with, what could only be

301

described as pity, even backing out of the way to allow him to pass. He did not know what he had done, but whatever it was it had worked. Just thankful for the opportunity to get away from the awkward situation, George strode off behind Mina, but curiosity got the better of him.

"Mina! What did you say to those men back there at the ferry terminal?"

She smiled. "I just tell them that I am your sister, and that you are an idiot. That you have no brains, and I have to look after you."

"Thank you very much," said George, feeling that his pride had been dented.

She laughed unashamedly.

Her father's house turned out to be a huge mansion. After turning off the hill-top road it lay at the end of a long driveway with tall slender cypress forming an avenue up to the house. As they walked up the drive George was amazed to see several white marble statues standing in the grounds. Most depicting classical heroes, but the white marble made them stand out like ghosts in the darkness. Through the shadowy darkness he could just make out some topiary bushes that lined the immaculate lawns, with the occasion cedar tree providing an isolated splendour. Around the borders there were a forest of shrubs, which during the daylight would obviously provide both spectacle and privacy. Ahead of them, the huge white façade stood out starkly. In his encyclopaedia at home he had seen pictures of the Acropolis, and although this was much smaller, the four Ionic pillars were none the less impressive, supporting a neo-Greco portico. This stood out in stark contrast to the poverty and filth they had passed on their way here. It was an oasis of tranquil opulence.

Mina headed straight up to the front door, and hammered on the brass knocker. A minute later an imperious looking butler appeared, wearing a dark navy suit with gold piping, sporting a red tasselled fez. George could see that he was of eastern European appearance, with heavily oiled hair, with pock marked skin on his face and neck. He sported a huge bushy moustache, which completely masked his mouth. His eyes widened in surprise as he recognised Mina, and bowing low, he admitted them both. Mina said something to him, as he closed the door behind them.

The inside of the large entrance hall it was equally impressive, with smaller tall slender Ionic columns, standing up from a black and white chequered marbled floor, supporting a mezzanine level at the far end. He felt the faintest wisps of an untraceable breeze, that made the room feel wonderfully cool. Giant family portraits hung in a procession along the walls, peering down disdainfully at any arrivals. Overhead, a rotary fan spun silently. The source of the breeze!

They followed the servant up a grand curving staircase, which led off to one side of the hallway up to the mezzanine landing. It was edged with an ornate gilded interlaced ironwork, which was surmounted by a polished dark wooden banister. As the butler led them slowly upward, the sharp click-click of his metal-heeled shoes echoed off the walls, like the rhythmic tick of a grandfather clock. They arrived on to a red carpeted landing that looked down over the hallway where they had first entered. A short distance along the carpet they halted before a pair of tall doors, and the butler disappeared inside, leaving them standing alone.

"Your father seems to be doing quite well!" whispered George, smiling at her.

"He owns three other houses like this one in other Turkish ports, and two more in Greece," she replied nonchalantly.

The butler reappeared, and ushered then into a grandiose reception room. Once through the door, George stared about the cavernous room in awe. Hanging high on the walls were more paintings, mainly landscapes this time, although to his left there was a portrait of a man and woman, staring at him in silent judgement. Persian carpets were strewn liberally about the floor. Desks and cabinets lined the walls, and at the far end was one of the largest fireplaces that George had ever seen, thinking that it would need half of the trees growing on the Sausmarez Manor Estate on Guernsey to keep it going for one just one winter. It was empty now of course, with a forged ironwork basket that looked strangely small within the vacant hearth. The settees and chaise-lounges that were positioned around its immediate vicinity seemed to be made of some luxurious gold brocade. Each liberally adorned with tasseled cushions.

A disarming silence descended once the butler had closed the doors behind them, to disappear about his duties. The room appeared to be deserted, until the emergence of a figure, who rose silently out of a high winged back chair, near the fireplace.

Alexandros Spiros Papandross cut an imposing figure, as he turned to meet them. He was dressed in an immaculately hand tailored grey lounge suit, white silk shirt, and crocodile shoes. Standing over six feet tall, with his hair greying at the temples, he looked maturely distinguished. He walked directly over towards his daughter.

"What brings you here, my daughter? And who is this young man with you?" he enquired, using his native Greek.

His voice was surprisingly soft for a man of his build, and his eyes flicked over George, trying to assess something beyond his dishevelled appearance. George felt self-conscious under his gaze, and not understanding a word of what was being said, he looked down with some embarrassment at his grime encrusted gym shoes.

"Father, this is Georgios Torode. He is English. Today he helped me to escape from the Civil Militia. It happened earlier this evening, and now he desperately needs your help," Mina replied in Greek.

"Would it be too much to ask why the Civil Militia was chasing you, Mina?" her father asked, with both of his eyebrows arched.

George could immediately see the family resemblance.

"It was just because I was attending a meeting that supported Armenian and Kurdish independence. The Militia were sent in to break it up, and to arrest the leaders. We tried to stop them," she replied.

"You always were the militant activist, Mina – never content to mind your own business, you always want to play the major role in any civil disobedience. You obviously see yourself as an integral part of the new rebellious generation that seems to be forever looking for a cause to support. You will get yourself into terrible trouble by pursuing such a course of action, and there may soon come a time when I will be unable to help you."

"I am my father's daughter. You told me that you did very much the same thing when you were my age, father."

She went on to tell him of what she had managed to learn from the English sailor. As he listened, Mina's father turned to look at George in a different light. When she had finished, he walked over to him, and offered his hand. The man had a vice like handshake, which made George wince, and to his surprise he also spoke perfect English.

"I want to express my sincere thanks to you, young man. This wayward daughter is my only child. She is capricious to the point of distraction, but still my only child. She tells me that I can be of service to you?"

"Yes sir!" George replied, thankful to regain control of his hand.

"You are from the British submarine that attacked this city just a few days ago, are you not?"

"Yes sir," George admitted, knowing that he was in too deep now for any further pretence.

"After your submarine spared one of my ship a week ago, I am only too willing to show my gratitude. What is it that I can do for you?"

"I urgently need to take passage aboard one of your steamers, sir – The Pearl of Petra. Mina tells me that she is sailing tomorrow night for Gallipoli. I have to get back to the Allied lines, so that I can re-join my submarine," said George. "To do so I have to cross the Sea of Marmara."

Alexandros moved slowly across to the fireplace, and stood silently pondering George's request. After a minute he appeared to have come to a decision, pulling a tasselled bell-cord that was made from the same red material as the cushions on his chair. The door opened almost immediately, revealing the obsequious butler standing framed in the entrance. Papandross spoke in Turkish to him, and the door closed.

"Come, sit down both of you. I have ordered some coffee and cognac. I would like to ask you some questions," he said, putting his arm around George's shoulder and leading him towards the seating area around the fireplace.

They talked together for over an hour. George sipped the brandy carefully, enjoying its smooth fiery warmth that seemed to permeate through to every muscle in his body. The Greek merchant asked him some very difficult questions about the submarine, and its activities over the past weeks. Without deliberately lying, and trying very hard not to give away any strategic information, George did his best to answer.

"Tell me, Georgios, why did your Capitan choose to spare my sailing yacht, especially after he has sunk so many other ships?" he asked, pouring him another drink.

"I do remember that incident, sir," George replied. "It was because she was not carrying any war contraband, and therefore was not tactically important to the situation on the peninsula. We only sink the vessels that pose a direct threat to our forces. Our orders are to sink any ship that carries Turkish logistical supplies to the peninsula. Your vessel was only carrying segments of marble, which would obviously not be used against our forces. However, we did make good use of the chickens and eggs that she was carrying."

"Ah yes, her master told me that was all that you took. As far as I am concerned you are most welcome to whatever you want in the way of supplies. These Turkish swine are now refusing to ensure my vessels, so I am being ordered to send out my ships out to face the possibility of being sunk, without any guarantee of recompense. They will only pay the normal rate for transportation, yet they expect me to accept that gamble every time one of my ships sails. They demand that I carry whatever they order. If I were to lose one of my boats, then it would obviously cost me a great deal of money," he pondered what George had said for a moment and then continued. "So, if my vessels do not carry any war supplies, then your submarines will not sink them? Is that correct?"

304

George nodded with his mouth full of brandy, and he swallowed it too quickly, causing him to momentarily gasp.

"Yes, sir," he said in a hoarse whisper – the brandy was delicious. "That is the policy of our boats at the moment. Are you a supporter of the Allied cause, sir?"

"The trouble with any war young man, is that one is expected to take sides. Here am I caught right in the middle of this conflict with my business interests very much at risk. I simply want to be able to continue conducting my business without any external hindrance. The sooner that it's all over, then the better it will be for me commercially. The Turks cannot win against the Allies, although they are preventing them from reaching their objective. So, it has become a stale-mate! If I am forced to side with anyone, then I suppose it would have to be with the Allies. The Turks has never been a friend to Greece, and were it not for the fact that my money is tied up in these waters, I would return to my own country tomorrow. Forgive me for saying so, but your countrymen are just as greedy for the control of world trade as the German's are. In my eyes, this imperial greed is being tested to destruction on the battlefields of Europe. One side is no better than the other, while the whole of Europe tears itself to pieces. There will be no winners at the end of this war – as every nation will be on the edge of bankruptcy – not just financially, but in the loss of their youth. The world has never witnessed such unimaginable casualties. If any good does result, it will be in the form of a more even distribution of power throughout the world. Imperialism is on the point of dying. I think that the days of the British and the German Empires will diminish when the true cost of this conflict becomes apparent. These Turks, who have finally brought an end to the Ottoman Empire, have been foolish enough to side with the Austrians and the Germans. They do so because they think that it will be they who will grow fat from this conflict. They have been offered many incentives to ally themselves to the Austro-Hungarian Empire in the past, but have never taken it up. Turks have always been a mercenary people who will work with the one who pays the most. To tell the truth they are human parasites who sit on the edge of a conflict attempting to grab everything that they can from the fray. So, they force me to transport all their food supplies for nothing, and they say that my service will be rewarded once the Allies have been defeated. They are swine – they remove all my profits and try to squeeze me out of business. I must be thankful that they supply the coal and oil for my vessels, otherwise I would certainly be bankrupt. There has never been any love between us. The Greek and the Turks have been opposite cultures ever since the days of the Trojan War. Now the German influence has become the driving force, and I have found that they are equally as bad. They endorse all of the bad decisions made by the Turks with a rod of iron. The Germans have no time for Greece, so together they force me to side with the Allies. At least your Lord Byron fought for Greece in our war of independence against the Turks during the early 1800s."

"Will you help me to get back to the Allied lines please, sir?" George said, aware that his own reasoning was beginning to become a little confused, following the liberal amounts of brandy that he had consumed. He took another sip to try and steady his thoughts.

"I will write a personal letter to the captain of the Pearl of Petra, which you can deliver to him personally. Make sure that you give it to him alone. Do not let it fall into anyone else's hands, or we will both be in big trouble. If you are unable to deliver it then destroy it. Do you understand?"

George nodded, trying to concentrate hard on what the man was saying. Everything was becoming confused.

"Wotsch the Captains name, schir?" said George to the empty space where the Greek had been sitting.

George winced, as Mina's elbow struck him in the ribs.

"Do not drink so fast, you get drunk!" she whispered.

George remembered that night in the Dog and Duck in Queens Street. He did not want a re-occurrence of that to happen. He tried to look for Mr Papandross.

Alexandros Papandross had crossed the room, and sitting at a desk writing a letter set over in an alcove. Finishing, he neatly folded the paper and placed it into an envelope. He stuck the edge with a dab of paste and sealed the flap with wax. Standing up, he crossed over to where George sat and handed it to him.

"Guard this with your life sailor. Failure to do so, and we are both lost men."

Taking it, George placed it in his pocket.

"Thank you very much schir, I'll make schure that they know of your kindnesch, when I get back," George held out his hand, ready for the firm grip this time. "I will do my best to ensure that my captain knows which vessels form part of your fleet. I am sure that he will sh-pare them."

"Take care, Englishman," said the Greek, as he shook it.

"Georgios, we go now," said Mina. "You need some fresh air. Come, up you get."

Looking up at her father, she smiled a message of thanks, as she helped an unsteady George over towards the door. George tried to wave to him over his shoulder, but Mina was already ushering him through the open door.

The journey back to Mina's room went rather quickly for George. Everything was a bit of a blur, but just a few things remained in his memory. Like him bumping into a donkey. Mina said that the animal had tried desperately to get out of his way as he had staggered down the road, but somehow, he had managed to walk into it. To make matters worse he had almost been knocked down by an omnibus. Mina had breathed a long sigh of relief when she had eventually arrived back at her apartment. Drunkenness was rarely seen in any Islamic country, and she feared that they would be arrested. Within the confines of her room, the last thing that George remembered was falling backwards onto the bed. It was very late and his weary body finally succumbed to the sapping tiredness of the last thirty-four hours. The heady effects of the brandy had torn away the last shreds of self-defence.

When he awoke, George immediately became startled. It was that fear of waking and not realising where he was. His head hurt and his tongue was very dry, but the full reality of his predicament eventually dawned. He moved to sit up and quickly realised that he wasn't wearing any clothes, immediately covering himself with the sheet. He could not remember getting undressed? Indeed, his memory of the latter part of their journey back was distinctly vague. As he stretched his muscles under the smoothness of the linen sheet, his hand touched something warm and soft. Further exploration revealed silky skin that covered the unmistakable curves of a woman – a naked woman!

"You too restless Georgios," said Mina's voice, in the darkness of the early hour. "You only sleep for an hour."

Shooting into the upright position, George stared, trying to focus on the figure lying at his side.

"But – but – that is – well you're not wearing any… – that is, you are unclothed, completely naked," he stammered.

She tittered and slid closer to him, enjoying his embarrassment. He coughed nervously, moving backwards towards the edge of the bed. Her girlish giggle became very suggestive, and her searching hands left little to the imagination. To his surprise, his response was immediate, as his manhood sprang to attention under the girl's playful manipulations.

"Ah mmm," she murmured in appreciation, as she caressed him.

He groaned, falling backwards onto the pillow, his mind spinning, but begging her to continue. The sheet domed as her body rose up, looming over his, her knees straddling his stomach. Rising up on her thighs, she reached down with her hands, groping, grasping him and guiding him towards the inevitable harbour. Holding him in place, she slowly lowered herself. She moaned in ecstasy as she felt him penetrate her, thrusting stiffly. Finally, she was sitting fully on the top of his thighs. George could stand the teasing no longer and reached up and grasping her waist, he raised her once more until he felt himself almost leave her. Then holding her firmly in that position, he thrust his hips up against the back of her thighs. Her gasp was loud and repeated with every push from his pelvis. Mina's legs parted involuntarily, wider as his rhythm increased. As she climaxed, her body stiffened, every muscle stretching. George couldn't help himself as he followed her almost immediately. They both held the moment for several seconds, before she collapsed onto him, her head burrowing into his shoulder. Panting their appreciation of each other they lay spent, side by side. Slowly their breathing returned to normal. She craned her neck and kissed him on the cheek, before rolling away from him.

"That was good Georgios, I think maybe we both need that very much – yes!"

"Yes Mina, I think that we both needed each other more than we realised," said George, his voice deep and soft in his post coital bliss.

"You don't forget your Mina, Georgios. When war is over, you come back and find me – yes!"

He nodded his head. After what they had both just experienced George didn't know how he would manage it, but he knew that he would certainly try to come back one day. As he thought about his home, it brought back the memories of his journey through this war so far. A rush of guilt flooded through him as his mind suddenly remembered Gladys. How on earth would he explain Mina to her? They were just two desperate people finding comfort in each other, but he had just done the one thing that he hoped that she would never do to him. His feeling of guilt immediately manifested into shame, knowing that he had cheated on the woman he had told that he loved. Did he still love her? After all, if it were not for the photographic image tucked into his cap back on-board *E11*, he was not sure that he would have remembered her features – what she looked like. Mina was just as pretty as Gladys!

The euphoria of their lovemaking faded quickly into a depression of regret for George. Why did he have to feel like this when what had just happened had been so good? It had been the most fantastic event of his life. Mina's voice disturbed his thinking.

"You have to go now, Georgios – the Pearl of Petra leaves at five. We only have just over one hour. Come get dressed – I will take you down to the docks. The captain is a Greek named Raftopopulos. He might be a Greek, but he is not a man to be trusted. Like all Greeks, he bears no love for the Turks, but he is a natural rogue by nature. Do not tell him anything about how we met – just give him my father's letter, and stay out of his way until you arrive at Gallipoli. When you get there, get off the ship as soon as you can – you understand? If there is a reward out for you, then he may just try and claim it when you land."

George nodded once more, then stood up and pulled on his dirty trousers that she had folded over a chair. A match flickered briefly, before light blossomed into a warm glow as the wick ignited in the oil lamp on the table. The walls were bathed in soft silhouettes, elongating the shadows of their bodies.

He was aware of Mina behind him, who was also dressing hurriedly. He turned to face her, and saw that her eyes were wet with tears. Feeling an enormous tenderness for her, he found himself shackled by the moral dilemma that was doing battle in his conscience. He wanted desperately to take her in his arms, while knowing that in doing so he would only be compounding the wrong. Suddenly he gave in to his emotions, reaching for her, holding her tightly against him. encircling her yielding body with his strong arms. How could a man promise love and devotion to one girl, and yet find such absolute pleasure and complete compatibility with another?

"You not forget your Mina!" she murmured against his chest.

"No, I won't ever forget you Mina," he answered truthfully, completely sure that he meant every word.

She went over to a chest of drawers and picked out a bright square of red. Crossing to George she twisted it into a long length and tied it around his neck.

"There," she said. "Now you will have something of Mina's."

Their parting kiss was long and tender. Finally parting, she led him out of the small apartment, down the darkened staircase, and back out through the courtyard. The early morning stillness was only exceeded by the darkness in the courtyard. He walked blindly into a sheet that was hanging from one of the washing lines stretching across the yard. His flailing arms swept it aside. Feeling somewhat embarrassed, he followed Mina's sure steps, and they eventually emerged back into the street where they had first met.

Had it really just been just the day before! It was with amazement when he realised that he had only known Mina for ten hours, and yet so much had happened. She had made such an impression on him. He watched her walking in front of him and his heart felt full.

They turned down towards the docks and along the long road from where they could see the spot-lights on the illuminated quays. On arrival they were met by an industrial amount of human activity, despite the early hour. It was obviously a twenty-four schedule being employed here, because it was just as busy as when he was last here. Stevedores were busy loading ships, picking up sacks and boxes from the back of truck's and rail cars. The heavier loads were being embarked using the cranes. George could hear a herd of mules braying incessantly from a corral located behind one of the administration buildings.

They quickly found the Pearl of Petra. She was lying low in the water, being fully laden and obviously being readied for sea. Her hatches looked to be well battened down. A group of the dock workers stood idly by the quayside bollards, awaiting the signal to cast off her securing lines. There was no human traffic moving up or down her gangway, suggested her immanent departure. High above them, her decks were stacked high with crates, each covered by canvas tarpaulins. More crates lay aft of the mid-ship bridge superstructure with its tall single funnel.

The loud voice a megaphone-initiated movement from the men on the fo'c'sle. George looked up to see a shadowy figure with a white cap standing out on the bridge wing. More seamen could be seen walking along the wing passageway, making their way down towards the stern. Two more men waited by the gangway, in readiness to raise it. All noise diminished in readiness for the ship's departure. Realising that they were short of time, Mina turned to George.

"Come Georgios, I will take you straight up to Raftopopulos' cabin now. They are just about to leave. Then I will have to go – OK!"

He nodded, leaned forward and kissed her cheek. Something inside him did not want her to go, but knew that he must leave her. As they emerged from the shadow of the warehouse, the shrill neigh of a horse made them both turn their heads. Sharp orders were bellowed through the darkness and there was a loud clattering of horse's hooves and boots on the cobbled quayside. Then from the corner of the warehouse came a Turkish army officer, riding a white charger. He was wearing a kalpak fur hat and held a sabre in his hand. George remembered him from the previous day, it was he who had arrogantly knocked him into the gutter. A squad of soldiers appeared, all running out in an attempt to block off the entrance to the quayside beyond the warehouse. Spinning around, the two of them saw the same thing happening at the other end of the berth. They were trapped here, between the warehouse and the ships side! There was no escape.

Then, out through the darkness, came smartly dressed figure, who walked out into the glare of spot-light. George thought he recognised him. There was something familiar about the way he walked, and as the man turned his face towards them, a huge bushy moustache was revealed – it was the very distinctive figure of Mister Papandross' butler. He moved over and stood beside the officer seated on the horse, as if seeking his protection.

"We have been betrayed!" cried Mina. Glaring with wild eyes at the cringing butler, she screamed abuse at him, her face contorting with hate and revulsion.

"Vromia (Filth)!" she screamed.

Ignoring her outburst, the officer shouted at them.

Turning to George, a seething Mina interpreted the order.

"They are telling us to surrender, Georgios."

George's hand reached inside his jacket for the revolver, determined that they would not be caught, he was determined to go down fighting. Attracted by the spectacle unfolding on the jetty, the sailors aboard the Pearl of Petra had stopped their work, and were now leaning over the guard-rails to watch the action unfolding below. A berating megaphone voice from the bridge sent them scurrying back to their stations. The same voice bellowed at the men waiting beside the berthing ropes down on the quayside. The securing lines went slack and were lifted off from the bollards and thrown hastily into the water. A steam winch rumbled into action as it wound in the ropes in through the fairleads. The heavy hinged gangway slowly began to jerk upwards off the quayside, as the two seamen sweated on a block and tackle. George stood there dithering, not knowing what to do next. It was Mina who had the answer.

"Run for the ladder, Georgios. It's our only hope," shouted Mina, already leading the way out towards the ship.

He didn't need telling twice, covering the short distance in ten long strides. Ahead of him, Mina leapt onto the gangway as it continued to rise upwards, with George immediately behind her. His hand pushed her up towards safety of the wing passageway. He had to heave himself up, and on standing he turned with his gun raised, ready to cover Mina as she struggled upward. On the quayside, the troops were already sliding back the bolts of their rifles, loading bullets into the breech, and bring their weapons up to bear.

Two well directed shots from George's gun sent them all diving for cover, and the officer on the white charger moved back behind the warehouse wall, but at the other end of the quayside the soldiers were taking action. They began to send a hail of bullets peppering the ship's paintwork all around them. Then the soldiers who had just taken cover became heartened, and started to re-emerge, before they too began to fire at the fugitives. George shot one through the head, and he collapsed dead. Unseen by George, another soldier stepped out from behind a crate and took deliberate aim. The shot zipped by George's head, but it struck Mina in her neck. George heard her cry as he returned the fire of the soldier. The soldier was thrown backwards, a blue-black hole above his right eye socket. George turned as Mina's body fell down towards him, and he caught her instinctively. Carrying her in his arms, he leapt up the now near horizontal gangway steps. Her dead weight strained every ounce of his strength, but he made it to the safety behind the metal side screens of the wing passageway, collapsing down onto the deck behind their protection. He dragged Mina's lifeless form into the safe haven. Bullets ricocheted all around him, and then he saw the two of the sailors cowering beside him. One still held the end of the lime that had just secured to a cleat. He looked down at Mina, who was now lying in his arms, her eyes wide with fear at the realisation of what had just happened. George was panting from all of the effort. He did not want her to die – they had only just met. What could he do to save her? He reached up and pulled the silk scarf that she had given to him from his neck, and tied it around the wound to stem the blood.

A quick check revealed that the end of the gangway was over twelve feet clear of the quayside. At least those soldiers would not be able to follow them for the present. He looked down at Mina once again, seeing that her upper body was sticky wet with blood. A pulsing redness was still oozing from a gaping hole in her neck. Her eyes opened, staring and wide. He made soothing tones, telling her that everything would be OK. She searched his face for any signs that would tell if she was going to die. Trying desperately to prevent the unfolding inevitability from reflecting in his eyes, George reassured her again. Stroking her face tenderly, and whispering that they were safe and that all would be well.

"It's OK. We're safe now. Hang on, my love. We'll find you a doctor. There's bound to be one on board."

Beneath them the whole ship shuddered, as the great propeller churned the water, slowly edging the ship away from the dockside wall, and inching out towards the mid-channel. The shooting became sporadic as the soldiers realised that they had lost their quarry. George felt Mina's hand grasp his sleeve and pull him towards her. He leaned closer, and could hear the gurgle as blood began to block her windpipe.

"I love you, Georgios," she said hoarsely.

"I love you too, Mina," he said softly, stroking the strands of hair from her face, knowing that he meant every single word.

Her body jerked, a convulsive spasm shuddered through her whole being, and then she went limp. The grasp of her hand fell from his arm. There was one final, long gurgling exhalation, before nothing. The blood flow had ceased. He could see that the fear had gone from her eyes, and he gently closed the lids, before laying her body down on the deck. Finally, he gave way to the tears that fear had held in check, and sobbed for this beautiful girl who had just been so cruelly taken from him.

In his grief his mind recalled another pointless death, so many years ago, as an image of Matthew's face increased his misery. This beautiful girl, so full of life, such fun to be with, now lay dead. Her youthful spirit would never rise again. He had known her for such a short time, yet he felt that he had known her forever.

One of the seamen edged nervously towards him, fearful of being hit by any of the last stray bullets. He spoke to George in Turkish, pointing towards the water-tight door. He helped him carry Mina there, and once inside, the metal door was slammed shut. The man secured it with huge metallic hinged clips. They laid Mina's body to one side in the passageway. He was safe – but at what a cost! Picking up the bloodstained scarf, George looked down at Mina one last time, and retied it around his own neck. It was cold from the wetness of her blood, as he turned to go and find Captain Raftopopulos. Moving along the passageway, he was suddenly confronted by several seamen blocking his path.

"I want to see your captain," he demanded.

They looked nervous, their looking beyond at the body.

Getting no response, he said firmly, "Cap-i-tan."

The word evoked a reaction. One of the men gestured for him to follow, and led him up three metal ladders to the bridge. It was very dark as he raised his leading leg up over the hatch combing that led onto the bridge. The area was lit by two small oil lamps positioned directly above the binnacle, where three men stood. The one standing, had his hand grasping the wheel, who was obviously the helmsman. The other two wore dishevelled officer's uniforms. The taller was taking bearings and plotting them on the chart, and logically George took him to be the navigator. The remaining man stood in the centre of the bridge. George greeted the captain, and presented him with the letter from Mina's father. To George's great relief, he spoke English, and seemed to be totally aware of what had just happened. He showed some sympathy to his plight, and conducted George into his cabin, positioned behind the bridge itself. Inside he opened a cabinet, and poured them both a large glass of brandy.

"One of my seamen tells me that there is a body of a young lady lying on the cross-deck passageway. Is it that of Mr Papandross' daughter?"

George nodded, the sudden welling of emotion making it impossible for him to speak. He was amazed at the captain's near perfect English and impeccable manners, nothing like the picture that Mina had painted of him. Now it was the captain's turn to go quiet, his mind seeming to wander off on a flight of fancy. He coughed when he realised that George was looking at him curiously.

"Mina was a precocious young lady, a beautiful free spirit that no one could tame. I too, will miss her. Do not worry about her my friend, I will take care of this matter, and I will see to it personally that her body is returned to her father."

He sighed heavily, as if realising he must set aside his own feelings for the time being, and read the letter.

"My boss asks me to help you in any way that I can. We are due to arrive at Gallipoli at nine o'clock tomorrow morning, and no doubt there will be a reception committee waiting to arrest you on the quayside. As I presume you do not want that to happen, I have a suggestion to make. If I were to slow my ship down as we approach the entrance to the Dardanelles, you can slip over the stern and swim over to the European shore. I will then proceed on into the harbour at Gallipoli, and report that you jumped overboard badly wounded, rather than face capture. I will show them the body of Miss Papandross, and explain that she died from her injuries before you left the ship. You will appreciate that I have to live with these people, and cannot afford to be implicated in this incident."

George nodded his agreement to the plan, and showed his gratitude by shaking the man's hand. He knew now why Mina had been so touchy about the captain. It would seem that there had been some sort of relationship between them, which had left Mina harbouring a grudge against him. Maybe she did not want George to find out about their affair!

Raftopopulos had shown him every consideration, ordering a decent meal, and a comfortable bunk for the night. His old blood-stained jacket was taken from him and thrown over the side, replaced by a seaman's navy-blue reefer jacket.

Unfortunately, due to the traumatic events of the last hours, George was unable to sleep. He lay awake thinking of what he could have done different that would have prevented Mina's death, before he finally succumbed to oblivion. At five thirty the following morning, a Quartermaster appeared at the cabin door to make sure that he was awake.

"Capitan – want – you," said the man, his finger pointing at George, and then up towards the bridge overhead.

George dressed quickly. The newer jacket was a pleasure to put on after the dusty old jacket. He made his way up the metal ladder to the bridge. The early morning sun was bursting in through the glass, and as he looked through the pane, he could see the outline of a dark area of land off to starboard, standing out in shaded splendour.

Raftopopulos was standing there, conning his vessel in towards the centre of the narrowing channel that lay directly ahead. It was George's first view of the bridge of such a large ship, and in daylight its height above the water took him aback for a second. On board *E11*, the conning platform was never more than eight to ten feet above the surface of the sea. The gnawing horrors of the previous night remained an imprinted nightmare, but they slowly melted away from his thoughts as he looked out on the clear warm day. He just wished that Mina could have been there to see it!

"Good morning, young man. I hope you managed to get some rest, for you have some very difficult decisions ahead of you. In five minutes, I will slow down in order for you to jump over the stern, but before that I want you to have a look at my chart, then at least you will have an idea of where you are heading once you reach the shore."

The Greek took him over to the chart table and pointed out their present position, and then showed him where the Allied lines were. He showed him exactly the point that he should swim for. It was a distance of nearly a mile. That was not going to be easy.

"When you jump overboard, you must do so from the stern rail in order for you to miss the blades of the propeller. When I see you wave from the water, I will increase my speed, and continue my approach towards Gallipoli. I wish you luck in your attempt to get back to your ship."

The captain held out his hand. There was an honest compassion showing in the man's deep brown eyes.

"Thank you, captain, for all your help," said George, feeling slightly at a loss for right words, but returning the handshake warmly. "Please look after Mina's body. Tell her father that I am so very sorry for her loss."

A seaman conducted him down through the ship towards the stern. On arrival, he handed George a cork-filled life jacket, which he took, but did not put on. He knew that if he wore it as he jumped, he may well injure himself. The collar of the life jacket around his neck would act like a hangman's noose, as his body plunged down into the water. He had read accounts about this from the newspaper reports of the sinking of the Titanic out in the Atlantic just over three years beforehand. Several of the bodies, that had later been recovered from those icy water, had broken necks as a direct result of wearing lifejacket's when they had leapt into the sea. Therefore, he decided he would carry his when he made the jump, as it would provide a good buoyancy aid once he was in the water.

The seaman left him, and he turned to look out over the transom rail. Behind the ship, he could see several gulls flying in formation over the turbulent wake. He could hear the occasional grumble of thunder, which puzzled him at first, with there not being a visible cloud in the sky. Then he realised that it was coming from the front lines down at Cape Helles. It seemed ironic that he would soon be heading in that direction. Clambering up onto the rail, he waited for the ship to slow. During that short time, he cast his gaze westward, over towards his destination – the European shore. He saw the tops of the dry rolling hills, broken by hedgerows, fields, sparse pastures, interrupted by the occasional farm, looking dryer, but much like the countryside back home. He longingly wished it were Guernsey, his Island home seemed so far away, and totally unobtainable right at that moment.

The steady rhythm of the reciprocating engines began to decrease in frequency, the throbbing sound dying away. Looking forwards up towards the bridge, he saw the captain appear out on the starboard bridge wing and wave his arm at him. Not waiting to assess the danger, he turned with his foot on the top rail, hovering there a second or two before stepping out into nothing as he made his jump. He closed his eyes as he plummeted downwards, seemingly being in the air for an inordinately long time, and feeling the wind rushing upwards past his face. Feeling a little disoriented, he opened his eyes to enquire what was actually taking place, just as his feet hit the water. The life jacket was forcefully ripped out of his hand. The shocking coldness of the water engulfed his senses as icy daggers attacked his once comfortable areas. The liquid clinging viscosity immediately slowed his descent, and he could feel his body begin to rise back towards the surface. His eyes were still open, and all around him he could see the clouds of sparkling bubbles. Everything was so quiet and muffled, save for that slow steady drumbeat of the engine. He kicked his legs vigorously to aid his ascent, and as his head broke through the surface, he sucked in a huge lungful of air. Having the oxygen to ensure his survival, his eyes started searching for the cork life-jacket. Twisting himself around in the water before he saw it lying nearby. A couple of determined sidestrokes, and he reached out and grabbed it, hugging it close for immediate support. Looking up towards at the towering mass of the receding ship, he waved to the lone figure on the bridge wing, receiving a final answering wave. There was a puff of smoke from the funnel, rising like a ball of cotton wool into the blue expanse, before the thudding vibration from the propeller could be felt through the water as the propeller increased revolutions. Soon the vessel was on its way, heading off southward towards Gallipoli, and George began to feel very alone. At least he had made it over here to the correct side of the Sea of Marmara, but at such a terrible price, feeling the loss of Mina once again, and wishing she was here with him.

Holding the cork float tightly with both hands, George began kicking his legs hard, heading directly for the shore. The distance he had to cover was only just under a mile, but he steadily reduced the distance.

Eventually his feet scraped the hardness of the stony beach, and he staggered, as he tried to rise under the weight of water that filled his jacket pockets. Finally gaining his balance, he waded ashore with water pouring from his clothing. His newly acquired reefer jacket had sagged badly out of shape. The material of his thin linen shirt clung wetly to his skin, as he walked up towards the water's edge. Almost in panic he reached up and touched the red scarf around his neck – it was still there. It was all he had that belonged to Mina. At least his gym shoes allowed him to walk over the stones more easily. He smiled when he looked down at them – the water had washed away much of the engrained grime, and some of the white canvas was showing once again.

Looking up at the hillside before as he stood on the beach, he noted that this whole area seemed to be devoid of habitation, and he walked a short way inland before finding a bush under which to quickly hide the cork life-jacket. Looking out across the channel, he checked the position of the sun, judging the time would be approximately seven o'clock.

He set off, heading up a hill in a direction that he assessed as being the most direct route towards the Allied lines. On reaching the first rise, he looked out over towards a small copse of trees, knowing that it would provide the perfect hiding place while he dried out. As he headed towards it, he began to think about his next course of action. As he was now fairly confident as to what direction to take, he began to think about what he should do if he met a lot of military activity? He had heard the heavy gun-fire after all, but decided that he would have to deal with all eventualities as he met them.

Finally, he reached the shelter of the trees. The sun's rays were quite strong as he settled down on the dry grass at the edge of the small copse. Unfolding his precious map, he laid it out on the grass to dry, carefully placing a stone at each corner. This was the second time that it had been soaked. He quickly undressed and hung his clothes over the small lower branches of a tree, so they would not been seen from a distance, but decided to keep his trousers on. The soft grass looked inviting, and stretching out he luxuriated in the warmth of the solar rays. It felt good to be alive, and he experienced a flash of excitement go through him as he realised that he was now about ten miles from safety. As he looked up at the wetness of his new jacket hanging forlornly on the branch, it suddenly reminded him of his old one that had been heavily stained with Mina's blood.

Was that only last night?

He knew at that moment that the memory of Mina's death would remain with him forever. Her spirit would now always be a part of who he was. As his mind drifted from one problem to the next, he gradually found his consciousness drifting away, and he lay there in a dreamlike state, halfway between a deep sleep and semi-consciousness.

His senses were suddenly alerted as he heard the sound of girlish laughter. Had it been real, or had it been part of a dream? His eyes swept the area which looked to be deserted. Surely there couldn't be anyone around here, as he would have heard them approaching? There it was again!

He was fully awake and he leapt up and assumed a crouching position, his hand reaching for his gun. His eyes scanned the immediate area as he crouched low under the lower branches of the tree. From this shelter he peered out, up towards the top of the hillside. There was nothing in sight along the crest, and when he checked downhill in the direction that he had arrived from, it was also vacant of any human life.

The hairs on the back of his neck prickled. Holding his revolver, he spun around, levelling and cocking the weapon at the same time. Less than fifty yards away he saw two young girls holding hands, staring at him curiously. They were smiling, but when they saw the gun in his hand, their eyes became wide and frightened. Looking past them, and then left and right, he breathed a sigh of relief when he saw that they were alone. He slowly released the hammer, lowered the gun, and standing up. The two girls had turned and were headed off for an unknown destination. He watched them disappear before he stood fully upright. Walking up to where they had been standing, he could see a track leading towards the line of a hill, from where a thin pale of smoke rose. He knew that it would not be long before someone would be heading up here to investigate the stranger on the hill who was holding a gun. Grabbing the rest of his clothes and the map, he quickly dressed, and continued uphill at a steady pace. He eventually reached the crest and looked backwards over the ground he had covered, relieved to find that there was nobody was in sight. His dented confidence slowly began to grow once more.

Walking along the ridge, he finally reached the highest point of the hill from where he was afforded a wonderful panorama. He could clearly see both of the headlands marking the northern entrance of the Dardanelles, realising that it was from down there that he had swam ashore. Then by fully turning, he could just see the faintest glint of the Aegean, far over towards the south west. He also realised that less than ten miles towards the west of him lay the Gulf of Xeros, where *HMS Jed* had taken station to send and receive signals from *E11* whilst she was on patrol. He started to consider the possibility of him heading over there, and to trying to swim out to her – but he quickly dismissed the notion as a complete impossibility. The area in between still lay in Turkish hands, and so he knew that he would have to make the long trek down the spine of the peninsula, heading towards where the Allies had landed at Cape Helles.

He still had absolutely no idea about how he was going to get through the Turkish lines, but once he got to that particular stage of the journey, then he was hoping that he would be able to re-appraise the situation and find a logical answer. Until then he would just have to take his chances, as and when they presented themselves.

This backbone of hills ran along the centre of the peninsula from the north-north-east down to the south-south-west. From the top of this ridge George could see only the bluest of blue skies, with thin small wisps of the purest white clouds and once he re-commenced his journey, he became filled with determination and hope.

After a while George found that he was quite enjoying walking through the Turkish countryside, and although he could still hear those distant rumbles of gunfire, the sun was shining, wild flowers abounded, and birds were singing. He was pleasantly surprised at just how grassy these hills were. Down at Cape Helles the Allied troops were reporting that the terrain there was barren, dry, and dusty. It could be a direct result of the continual bombardment taking place down there, but was more likely to be the warmer Mediterranean influence. The topography of Murdos was much the same, but up here it was hard to believe that there was even a war taking place.

The sun became exceptionally hot around mid-day, but there was a gentle south-westerly breeze blowing in off the Aegean, which made George feel quite comfortable as he strode purposefully along. The solar rays were bothersome against his head however as he did not have a cap, so he opened up and used the map to cover his head to keep off the direct rays.

Passing along hedge lined lanes that seemed to be filled with the continual buzz of insects, it reminded him of walking the lanes of Guernsey. Far off to the south-west, he could even see some cattle grazing far below him on the lower pastures, but these Turkish beasts did not look capable of producing the same creamy milk like that of the Guernsey cows. Another rumble of explosions focused his mind – they seemed much louder, and strangely out of place on such a fine day. On the positive side, despite his trepidation, the explosions made him realise that at least he was heading in the right direction.

As he continued on his way his thoughts turned to Gladys, and he tried to imagine what she might be doing today. Would the weather in Southsea be as nice as it was here? He knew that one of the first things that he had do on his return to the safety of the Allied lines, was to write a long letter to her. So much had happened to him since his last one! Obviously, he would not mention Mina, because no matter how much he tried to justify their relationship, Gladys would never understand. Then he realised that he was going to have to lie to her, because yesterday would always remain one of the greatest things that had ever to happen in his life? It would always be something that would be unmentioned between them, a dark secret never to be revealed, even if they were ever to get married. As he realised that it was something that he was going to have to think about very seriously, Gladys faded from his thoughts.

He was hoping that if all went well, he would be back at his base by this time tomorrow. If he did manage to do that, it would be strange, because he would arrive there before *E11* returned from her present patrol. He smiled to himself, as he imagined the looks of amazement on the faces of his crew-mate's when they saw him standing on the depot ship, as they made their approach to come alongside.

As his head began to clear the next rise, George instinctively threw himself flat on the ground. Not two hundred yards away was a gravel track that was filled with lines and lines of marching Turkish troops. Keeping his head down, he cursed himself for being a day dreaming fool. Trying hard to crawl backwards he realised that he had dropped his guard, and had allowed complacency to replace alertness. He should have noticed the dust thrown up by those hundreds of pairs of boots, or at least heard the crunch of their heels on the stony path. His heart was pounding in his chest, not daring to breathe for fear of giving himself away. Had he been seen? He heard some shouts.

A minute passed, and then another. Perhaps they had not seen him – oh God – please don't let them find me! Not after going through so much. After another minute his confidence began to return. The lack of response was enough for him to think about raising his head, and he had just started the movement, when the sound to his right brought a new stab of fear.

The loud bark of a Turkish voice came somewhere behind him, making him realise that he had indeed been noticed – and he had in fact been well and truly trapped by his own stupidity. Raising his head, he saw that he was completely surrounded by soldiers, each of them pointing a Mauser rifle straight at him. Again, the barking of more Turkish babble, and George resignedly raised his hands and stood up.

Two soldiers, more boys than men, rushed forward, quickly confiscating his revolver, and removing his precious map. His hands were securely bound behind his back, and he was shoved forward, down towards the column of troops on the dusty track.

On arrival he became an object of curiosity, as he was dragged before a Turkish officer sitting astride a big bay mare. He sneered down at him and shouted a question at him in Turkish. To George it was just gibberish. The officer let forth a loud snort of frustration, and for his ignorance of the language, George received a kick in the chest from the rider, which sent him reeling backwards. Hauling the reins around the horse's neck, the Turkish officer cantered off towards the front of the column.

A sergeant assigned four young soldiers to guard George, and as the column began to move off, his bodyguard delighted in pushing forward with the butts of their rifles. One hitting him much harder than necessary.

After half an hour of walking, the Turks thought it funny to take it in turns to prod him, and try to kick his ankles away in an attempt to trip him up. With his hands tied behind his back, he fell easily, which resulted in howls of laughter. If he faltered or lagged behind, he received more thumps from a rifle butt. Other Turkish soldiers came running up, curious to have a look at one of their enemy, many contemptuously spitting at him before returning back to their place in the column. His face and shoulders quickly became spattered with spittle, as more of the Turkish soldiers delighted in using him for target practice. This purgatory continued all the way down the southern hillside below the ridge that faced out towards the Aegean.

Another hour went by, and far ahead of the line George could see that they were headed towards a large encampment, which lay spread out across the hillside, halfway below the slope that they were now descending. It looked like a small town of canvas tents sprawled across the hillside. Smoke hung above the encampment like a dark cloud.

As they neared, George noted that a small mosque stood at the centre of the tented community, adjacent to some ruined farm buildings. The mosque had a circular domed roof with a single thin minaret. A white flag pole had been fixed to it, to which huge giant red flag hung, with a white crescent and star, moving languidly from the lack of breeze. A heat haze, filled with dust, hovered above the tent city, mixing with the smoke from the hundred cooking fires that he had seen earlier. A sharp bugle blast disrupted the steady rhythm of marching feet, and several squads of men could be seen running, assembling into lines at the entrance to the camp.

Looking about him, George surmised that this was probably one of the main Turkish rear base camps containing reserve troops, as they prepared to take their turn up in the front line. He tried to count the number of tents, but quickly gave up. There were simply hundreds of them, maybe even five hundred to a thousand! He tried to work out with an average of ten men per tent, that there must be somewhere around five thousand troops based here. Things were certainly not looking good for the Allies!

The column suddenly halted just outside the encampment, as two sentries challenged their progress. There was an exchange of words, and they were eventually allowed to pass. More orders were shouted, relayed by the growling, gruff voices of the NCO's. Groups of troops broke away from the main column, leading their heavily laden mules over towards the far extent of the encampment. George guessed that the mules were carrying yet more tents, that would be used to house these newly arrived troops. The remainder of the column were marched forward and then ordered to align themselves into two huge groups in front of the stone mosque.

There was a rounded brick arch entrance into the mosque. A wooden wall had been built across the opening, into which a small door had been inserted. Once the troops had finally finished arranging themselves, there came another blast from the bugle! A minute later the small door opened to reveal a moustachioed Turkish Officer, dressed in a navy-blue uniform. Each shoulder was adorned by large ornate epaulettes, that seemed to drip gold down each sleeve. Instead of a cap, he was wearing a red fez, and from the kaleidoscopic array of the medal ribbons across his chest. George assumed that he must be the Command Officer of this encampment.

The unseen bugler blasted a few more unrecognisable bars, announcing his presence. Orders were barked, and everyone around him sprang to attention. The Turkish General took a deep breath, sucking in his paunch of a stomach, before producing a lazy salute. The bugle sounded again and the whole assembly relaxed. Then the officer on the bay horse dismounted, and approached him. More salutes, more handshakes, and pats on the back were exchanged before they turned and disappeared together into the mosque. The soldiers were all stood at ease.

George quickly became an object of great curiosity to the many young soldiers from the camp, who were on their way to fight against the infidel, because he was the first of his kind that they had ever seen. Every one of them appeared to be very keen to catch a glimpse of their foe, and he started to feel a little like an exhibit at a zoo.

An NCO appeared after twenty minutes. He yelled at the young soldiers, who all scampered back into line. He held a revolver in his right hand as he strode straight towards George, and began pointing over towards the mosque, indicating for him to walk there. Four of the soldiers were detailed as an escort, one of whom gave him a whack from the butt of a rifle for no apparent reason.

As he began to move forward, there came loud shouts of alarm, and a complete panic suddenly broke out. It was George's turn to be curious, and he turned his head left and right, looking for the cause. The young soldier's broke ranks, shouting excitedly as they prepared their weapons, each loading ammunition into the breech. Several of them were pointing up towards the sky, when a throaty roar of a petrol engine erupted above as a spotter bi-plane passed low over the mosque. Flickering yellow flashes appeared from the observer's position at the front of the aircraft, immediately followed by the loud staccato clatter of a Lewis gun. Spouts of dust appeared in the dust just beyond the mosque, as several screams pierced the mayhem.

Looking up George saw the red white and blue roundels on the wings – it was British! The faces of the pilot and his observer were less than a hundred feet away, as the aircraft flashed overhead. He watched as the observer lifted a small hand-held bomb and drop it over the side of the aircraft. It fell, exploding less than two hundred yards from where he stood. A great fiery mushroom threw bodies into the air, as the force of the blast hit George, causing him to stagger backwards. Through the smoke he saw a damaged old barn. Bricks and debris were flying everywhere, he heard more hideous screams. Scanning the area, he saw several inert figures lying on the ground, others were writhing in agony. Oh, if only that plane could have picked him up!

Suddenly he was grasped by the shoulders, and pushed roughly forward before being forced through the small entrance door of the mosque. George thought that if the aircraft were to return and drop another bomb, that he would rather have remained outside, than be in here. Inside, there was a hollow echo to voices as the soldiers as they shouted at him. After marching in the heat of the afternoon sun, the interior had a welcome coolness. The sudden lack of light caused him to squint through the murk. It was also very quiet, the only audible sound coming from the tapping of a type-writer, hidden somewhere behind a series of canvas screens that seemed to fill the inside.

In the centre of the circular nave area, he saw that it had been partitioned off by ropes, that had been strung between the stone pillars. Sheets of canvas hung from the ropes, to provide open topped office rooms for use by the General's staff.

Looking through the dimness, George noticed that the only source of light came in some thin slits, that were set high into the dome. The yellow glow of several oil lamps was fanned upwards from behind the canvas screens. A sudden flutter of wings revealed a pigeon that was using one of the slits as an entrance. Surely it must leak when it rains, he surmised.

Two young officers came up with their pistols drawn, and grabbed hold of George's arms. The guards were dismissed, and they force marched him down past the canvas partitions towards a wooden door, that was set in a stone wall. Two armed sentries stood guard the portal. Inside he could see the fat General sat behind a desk, reading through a sheaf of documents. It was strange because outside it was the late afternoon, yet here inside the mosque, it needed a huge oil lamp to light his desk. An infantry officer was standing at his right hand. George was unceremoniously pushed in front of the General, and made to stand at attention. After what seemed an eternity, the General finally raised his eyes and looked imperiously up, his penetrating eyes made him feel extremely uncomfortable. It was as if he were trying to see right into his mind, and read his innermost thoughts.

"Who are you?" he demanded, in heavily accented English.

George remembered the lecture that the Coxswain, Chief Petty Officer Dowell, had given the crew concerning being captured.

"George Torode – Ordinary Seaman of the Royal Navy – K21770."

The scratching of a pen on paper to George's left made him turn. A soldier was writing down his words, as he spoke them.

"That is very commendable, young man," said the Turk, his voice melting into a friendlier tone. "You say you are a British seaman, but you wear civilian clothes.

What ship are you from, and how did you come to be ashore this far up the peninsula?"

George remembered the same conversation with Mina!

"I'm off a destroyer, sir – I fell overboard, and was lucky enough to swim ashore."

The General's mouth creased into an expression of frustration.

"Then why were you carrying an officer's revolver, and a map of this area? Surely you do not walk about the decks of a destroyer with such things? How did you come to be wearing the jacket of the Turkish merchant marine?"

The General's voice rose higher with each question, ending almost in an accusing scream. 'Oh shit,' thought George, 'how do I get out of this?'

"Er – when I swam ashore, sir – there were bodies lying on the beach. One was an English officer, and I borrowed his gun, seeing that he had no more need for it. The jacket came off a civilian casualty. I was getting cold, you see," George wondered how he had thought of all that so quickly.

The General listened attentively, and for a second George thought that he may have swallowed the story. He was wrong.

"You seem to be very clever at finding convenient corpses, especially ones that are well dressed. How fortunate you are that they were laden with specialist equipment just at the right moment. Perhaps you are just as good at creating these corpses, like the two soldiers that you shot in Constantinople last night. We received a signal to say that you may be heading in our direction. How did you manage to get off the ship that you escaped in? They found the body of your girlfriend aboard her, as soon as she docked this morning at Gallipoli."

George was taken aback. How on earth did they know all that? He had no alternative story, so he had to continue with the bluff.

"I don't know what you're talking about, sir. It was just as I have said, falling overboard from my ship, and finding those bodies. My ship was *HMS Grasshopper*. Check it out, and you will see that I am not lying."

The loud thump of the Generals fist on the table made George jump.

"Do not take me for a fool, young man. You are a saboteur, or a spy, perhaps both and you have been caught. I am sure that you are very aware of the penalty for such activities in times of war. Unless you co-operate fully with me, you will be shot at sunset tonight. I am going to give you a short period to think very carefully about your future before you decide on your next course of action – because your life will depend on what you say when you return here. I urge you take advantage of my offer, and not to throw your life away. Take him away."

The armed officers grabbed his arms and marched him out of the room, back along the canvassed aisle towards another wooden door, situated right at the back of the mosque. He was thrown into a dark, windowless room, landing heavily on his shoulder, as he crashed into besoms and buckets in the corner. The door was slammed shut and bolted – the inside it was cramped and very dark. Probably a cleaning store, he thought.

Fear began to invade his thoughts as he lay on the bare stone floor, his eyes adjusting to the lack of light as he tried to regain his composure. With his hands tied behind his back, he wriggled himself up into a sitting position and leaned back against a wall. After some effort, he managed to stand upright, and thirty-five minutes later he managed to saw through the cords that bound his wrists together by rubbing them against the rusted rim of one of the buckets. He ran his hands over his sore wrists, as he began to reflect on the predicament that he now faced – well aware that he was in real bad trouble. It was no good chiding himself again for being so complacent, it was what was going to happen over the next few hours that mattered. The idea to try and escape crossed his mind.

He began checking around the cell, but it revealed nothing, there was only the one entrance and that had been securely locked and bolted from the outside. His mouth was dry, as he had not had a drink for a very long time. How on Earth was he going to get out of this? Would he get out of this?

Two and a half hours later, he was duly collected and marched back to the General's office. He stood once more before the table, feeling the pangs of real fear, knowing that if he got this wrong, he could be facing a firing squad in just a few hours. If this did not go well, then this could be the last day of his life! There would be no tomorrow.

The General looked up, and began his questioning once again. His voice was warm and paternal.

"I do not want to have to order your death, young man. You have now had some time to think about your situation Ordinary Seaman George Torode. Yes, we know that you are one of the murderers from the British submarine that has been plaguing our coasts. We know that you were one of the saboteurs responsible for the destruction of the railway viaduct fifty kilometres east of Scutari, were you not? You managed to kill many of our soldiers there as well. The only way you are going to save yourself from the firing squad is by given your fullest co-operation. Refusal will bring your death. What do you say? Come – you are a young man – certainly far too young to die. You want to live to see your family again. Just a little co-operation will mean that you will see an end to this war and return home – you must want that, do you not?"

George was dumbfounded. How the bloody hell had they found out that he was a submariner? He had only told Mina and her father about his being from *E11*. How on earth did they manage to link him to the viaduct? Nobody else knew about that! Taking his silence as a sign of possible acceptance, the General continued in his friendly sounding manner.

"We are not asking you to betray your comrades. We just need some information on your submarine operational movements. Your friends will not be sunk. We will just put in place more defensive measures, so that they will not be able to sink our ships. That is fair – is it not. By co-operating with us, you will not only be saving yourself, but you will also be working with an old friend of yours."

Old friend? George gave the General a puzzled look.

The loud click of the door latch made him turn his head, and his mouth dropped open in utter amazement.

"Hello, George," said Arthur Collenette.

Chapter Fifteen

Betrayal

The sight of his fellow Guernsey-man left George dumbfounded, and confused beyond measure. Questions began to queue in his mind. How on earth had Arthur got here? What the hell was he doing walking about so freely amongst the enemy? Was he going to be exchanged for Turkish prisoners of war? Maybe I would be part of any exchange? No – the General had said I would be co-operating with an old friend. George was nonplussed! Did that mean that Arthur was already co-operating? The more he searched for answers, the more his mind grew suspicious. Something was terribly wrong here. George had first-hand experience of just how Arthur's evil mind worked. He had to admit to himself that he was desperately in need of a friend at this moment in time – because he had never felt so alone – but he also knew that that Arthur Collenette was not a friend he could trust.

Allowing no time for any explanations, he was forcibly taken from of the Generals office and placed in one of the canvas rooms. His two guards forced him to sit down at a rickety wooden chair in front of a small table. Arthur followed him in, and sat down directly opposite across the table. He certainly did not appear as afraid of his presence, as he been that day aboard *HMS Egremont* in Malta. Arthur appeared confident, obviously assured in having the upper hand. How George hated his smug self-righteousness expression etched across his face.

George looked up at the domed roof high above him, as he tried to think of a simple logical explanation for his presence here.

Despite his external confidence, Arthur coughed nervously. George decided that he would listen to what Arthur had to say, but then it dawned on him as to where the Turks had received all of the detailed information that they had on him. Any lies that he made henceforth was going to be vetted by Arthur. He stared at him, noting Arthur's increasing uneasiness, and he decided that he was going to have to provide some good answers as to why he was here with the enemy. Everything he said from now onwards had to be carefully chosen if he had any chance of surviving tonight.

Arthur coughed again, before starting to speak. He was obviously under the supervision of one of the armed Turkish officers, who was fluent in English. George began feeling very scared.

"It's good to see you again, George. It's been quite a while since Malta," Arthur's voice still sounded nervous.

He seemed to be trying to recreate something between them that never existed. Maybe he had told the Turks that they were friends! Any friendship that existed had died that day long ago on the cliffs at Pleinmont Point. From the tone in Arthur's voice, George became convinced that he was about to lie, even though he had hardly said anything. Maybe it was an instinct, or it was something that he had learned over the years he had known him. Like that time that he had known instinctively that it had been Arthur who had killed his step-father. George knew from old not to trust him. He knew that everything he was about to say to him was going to be a lie.

He sat there, looking across the table, studying Arthur, and saw that he was dressed in the uniform of a Turkish navy officer. Had they loaned him the clothes because his own had perished? He could see that Arthur was starting to find the encounter more and more difficult – a fact that pleased him greatly. He went for the jugular.

"More to the point Arthur – what are you doing here? You look very smart by the way, and you seem to have made quite a few new friends. How exactly did you get here, and why are you wearing our enemy's uniform?" said George, finding it hard to disguise the contempt he had for him.

Arthur began answering him, hesitatingly.

"When the landings began on the twenty fifth of April, I was attached to one of the troop landing barges that were operating from the HMS River Clyde. It was my job to take loads of soldiers from the landing ship to land them on the beach, and then collect up any wounded and ferry them back to the hospital ship. Then it was back to the River Clyde to pick up more soldiers. It was terrible George, because the Turks were thoroughly prepared in the defences, and were waiting for us. It was absolute carnage – a complete slaughter-house. They were dug into well planned positions, and had machine guns firing directly at each barge as it discharged its men. There were hundreds killed and wounded before they made it on to the beach. There must have been thousands cut down on that first day alone. Only the smallest of beach-heads was finally established. There was very little cover for them, and our men became trapped on that beach. On May the second, I was running another contingent of troops ashore when my own craft came under heavy mortar fire. All of the other small landing boats began zig-zagging, taking avoiding action. I began to do the same, when an almost direct hit on my craft killed at least three of the soldiers outright, and left us badly holed. We immediately started taking on water, and I had the rest of the landing party bailing for all they were worth. It was no good, we were sinking, and so I turned the craft and made for the nearest point of land. The tide must have carried us westward, and we landed just beyond our beach-head on the Turk side of the line. Almost from the moment we touched the beach, we immediately we came under heavy rifle fire. Several more of the soldiers from my boat were killed. The boat had had it, and we had nowhere else to go. So, we managed to find some shelter behind a small dune. Behind us, in the water, there were several of the badly wounded clinging to anything that floated. We watched them as they were picked off by Turkish snipers. Almost as soon as we had arrived, they mounted an attack and charged our position. We were completely overrun, and I was captured along with the seven other survivors. We were the only ones to make it from the whole boatload of thirty-six."

"Only seven?" enquired George sceptically.

"Yes. It was terrible," Arthur looked at him for sympathy, but finding none, he continued, "It was the worst experience of my life, George. Hand to hand fighting with bayonets. They were far too strong for us, we didn't stand a chance."

"Where were you during all this fighting, Arthur?"

"Well, I was invited to fight by the sergeant, but I could not find a gun. As I was a sailor, I was told to stay where I was and keep my head down while they fought off the attack, but they weren't lucky enough, and failed to repel them. We became trapped, surrounded and as I was the only officer left, the soldiers asked me what they should do. I simply said – Surrender."

"So, while the troops with you fought to the bitter end, you stayed out of the way in the relative safety of a sand-dune. Twenty-nine men died just to allow you to wave a white handkerchief and walk into captivity."

"It wasn't like that George, honest it wasn't. There was nobody else left. It was pointless trying to put up further resistance, or we would have all been killed."

George's snort of derision brought forth another guilty look from Arthur.

"So where are those other six soldiers now, the other who were captured with you?"

"They are also dead, as you will be if you don't do exactly as they say. The only reason they didn't shoot me was because I agreed to give them a little information. Nothing that would be of any real use to them, you understand. I have told them nothing that they probably did not know already. If I hadn't, I too would be lying at the bottom of a ditch."

"Do you mean to tell me that those six soldiers have all been executed?"

"Yes," said Arthur, in a rather matter of fact tone.

Looking at him, George could see there wasn't the least sign of remorse, regret, or shame for his actions. He sat there, genuinely believing that he had done the logical thing.

"So, you sold them out as well, Arthur, just as you sold out Matt that day on Pleinmont Point. You sold us out to save your own skin when the going got tough. You're not only a coward and a murderer – now you're a traitor, too."

"At least I'm alive, George Torode! You won't be this evening, unless you give them the information that they are asking for. You've only got about half an hour to decide. Get off your high horse and think about yourself for once. What good are you to anyone, if you are dead?"

"It's something to do with a thing that you know nothing about, Arthur. It's a thing called self-respect! If I'm about to be shot, then at least I'll go to my maker with a clean conscience, and I will be able to rest easy in my grave. There will only be one place that you'll be going Arthur Collenette and I'm just sorry that I won't be the one to send you there."

"George, don't be a fool. They have asked me to offer you this one last chance. Listen to reason. They will spare your life, if you just answer a few simple questions. This will be your last chance to live. Think of your family!"

"I am thinking of my family, Arthur – that is why I can't do it."

George looked across the table at Arthur, feeling nothing but contempt for the pathetic figure sat there. Disgust quickly became loathing, which fermented and fumed inside of him, like the molten magma below the Earth's crust. He could feel a lump of hatred rising in his throat when he thought about those six men that Arthur had betrayed. Why was this maggot still alive? So many good soldiers were laying down their lives at Cape Helles to help end this terrible war, and here is Arthur, collaborating with the enemy as if it was the most normal thing in the world. Suddenly the injustice of it all welled up inside of him and his reason snapped.

George launched himself at Arthur. The table went flying and chairs crashed across the floor as he lunged and grabbed him by the throat. Arthur screamed in terrified panic. The pair fell backwards ripping the canvas partitioning screen from its rope support. Arthur's eyes bulged wide, as he fought desperately to remove George's hands from his windpipe. His face began to turn red and then purple, but George's vice-like grip only increased the pressure. Arthur's legs were kicking about violently, in a forlorn attempt to find a purchase that would enable him to throw George off, but the room started to dim before him.

Arthur was only saved by the appearance of three soldiers, who had been summoned by the Turkish officer. One stunned George, with a thump from the end of a rifle butt to the back of his head. He collapsed senseless onto Arthur, before being dragged to his feet by the other two, and held securely. The third man now had his rifle pointed directly at George's head. The blow had caused George to momentarily black out, and as he attempted to keep his balance his mind fought to regain certainly. He could feel the warm sticky flow of blood running down his neck.

Slowly his faculties returned, and he looked up to see Arthur's face directly in front of him, his contorted facial features spitting hatred. It was easily the evillest expression that George had ever seen – when a distant memory came back to him. He had seen that same look once before. It had been a long time ago when Arthur had been in one of his rages, and was ranting on about his Stepfather. It had been shortly after that tirade that the poor man's body had been found lying on the Vale Road. Arthur's voice was hoarse, a hissing venom.

"OK, have it your own way George. You'll be dead in less than thirty minutes from now. There are some people in this world who just can't be helped, but no one can say that I didn't try. You should have listened to me, George."

It dawned on George at that moment that Arthur was insane. He was the devil incarnate. Not human being at all, but an entity of pure evil that needed to be destroyed. Arthur really did believe that he was doing the right thing. Despite the tight grip on his arms by his two guards, George lunged again, trying to get at him, but his arms were quickly twisted painfully up behind his back. He gave in, with a frustrated snort. Taking several deep breaths, he willed his body to relax. The only emotion that he felt then was one of utter contempt for this piece of shit standing before him. He was impotent, and his guards quickly frog-marched him back to his cell.

Lying on the stone floor once mire, George was incensed by the unfairness of it all – the fact that Arthur would be alive, when he was almost certainly was going to die tonight. Despite of all the terrible things that he had done, Arthur would survive, and that was so unfair. An inner rage seethed through his veins.

He remained sitting very still with his back against the stone wall for a long time, desperately trying to think of anything that would save him. Here, within the darkness in his confinement, he knew that it must be getting close to the evening outside. What had fate in store for him? Was he actually going to be taken out and shot – or was it another of Arthur's ploys to get him to comply? If he was actually going to be shot, as according to Arthur's last outburst, he didn't have very long left. Thirty minutes, he had said. That surely must have passed by now. Was he about to die? Surely it can't just end like this! Then it suddenly occurred to him that he might not see the sun rise tomorrow morning. If he was going to die, then he wouldn't even be here to see the moon rise later tonight. Life would simply go on the same without him in it. Rather than sit here and wait to die, he decided to try something.

Just then he heard a tiny scratching noise in the corner, which made him turn his head. He just caught sight of a rat's tail as it vanished into a small crevice, at the base of the wall.

Bon chance mon brave, he thought. At least you have found a way out of here. He stared at the small hole where the rodent had been. Just maybe!

Before he could rise and investigate where it had gone, he heard the crunching sound of boots on the stone floor outside his cell. The sharp clunk of the bolts being drawn back was followed by the rattle of a key in the lock. He could feel the stab of real fear going through his body – was this it? The heavy wooden door was suddenly thrown open. The Turkish officer, who had sat behind Arthur, was framed in the doorway.

"Come," he beckoned.

Outside there was an escort of soldiers, standing there with to their bayonets fitted into the barrel of their Mauser rifles. He was marched back to the Generals office once more and to his surprise, he was provided with a chair. Two of the guards stood at his shoulders. The General smiled patiently, and when he spoke, he sounded more like a father giving an errant son some well-intentioned advice, than an interrogator.

"As you may have seen from your friend's treatment, we have looked after him, and if you were to co-operate, then it would mean that we can also be your friends too. It is such a waste of one's life to have to die for a cause that is already lost. Your Allied friends are completely pinned down on the beaches of Cape Helles. They have absolutely no chance of breaking out. For you all, the war is lost."

George said nothing.

The General looked at him curiously. He had been surprised when he had been told of George's attack on Arthur. He wanted to know what the cause!

"What is the problem between you and Arthur Collenette? There seems to be a lot of bad blood between you. What is it?"

George remained silent.

"He has been very co-operative, and as a consequence he has been treated very well since his capture. He has been given a woman. You could have one too, if you are sensible. Once this campaign is finally over you would be included in an exchange of prisoners for our own men. No one need ever have to know that you helped us. You would be able to see your mother and father again, your wife, or sweetheart. Take your time to think my offer over very carefully before you reply, because this will be your last chance. Will you help us?"

"Get fucked – and you're wrong. Somebody would know if I co-operate – ME!" sneered George, half rising from his chair.

Soldier's immediately grabbed him, pinning his arms, making any movement impossible.

"You are a very silly young man. Take him away!" said the General resignedly.

Back in the cell once more, George immediately crossed over to where he had seen the rat. It was a small hole and peering down at it, he could just feel a draught of fresh air funnel up through the tiny aperture, but on further investigation he found that the floor was made of stone. Trying to break it, even with a pickaxe, would take hours. He didn't have hours, and he certainly did not have a pickaxe. His spirit slumped. Trying to find a way of this situation was useless, and he realised that escape was impossible. The thought of his imminent death frightened him. He just hoped that he would be able to face the end like a man.

A mental picture of his mother and father came to him. The whole family were sitting at the meal table, and they were all telling him to be brave. Tears formed in the corners of his eyes.

Then Gladys came to mind. What would she be doing around now? She was probably sitting at home, reading a book, or playing cards with her Aunt Lucretia. She would be totally unaware that this was going to be the hour of his death. That was the one thing that he regretted more than anything – the fact that nobody would know of how, or the real reason why he died. The thought of collaboration did flicker briefly through his mind briefly – it was temptation personified to live – but he could not bring himself to do it. His desire to live was very strong, and although collaboration would guarantee him surviving the war, he had quickly discarded the option.

Maybe he could just tell them a pack of lies! It might help the Allies, especially if the Turks were to act on a fictional story, but no sooner had the idea occurred to him than he realised that it would not work. It was completely hopeless because Arthur would instantly know that he had lied, and would enjoy informing them of that fact – the traitorous bastard.

His only wish was that his Mother and Father would somehow get to learn truth, and know that he had faced death bravely. More than anything else, he wanted them to be proud of him.

Gladys would probably never know what had happened to him. His parents did not know that she existed, and she only knew that he hailed from Guernsey. So, the only way that she might learn of his death was from the casualty lists published in the national newspapers. He would likely appear as being missing in action.

Nobody but bloody Arthur Collenette would ever know the truth of what had happened to him. He could just imagine what stories that slimy snake would be telling, if he managed to get home in one piece. Just like that time on the cliffs at Pleinmont, George knew that he would end up becoming the villain of the tale. He felt a terrible frustration that he would be there to speak up for himself, and clear his name. Oh God, don't let this happen to me. In the name of Jesus deliver me from my enemy.

It seemed an eternity before the key rattled in the door once more. His eyes widened in fearful anticipation. It swung open to reveal the same squad of soldiers. The same officer pushed past them, and motioned for him to rise. Two of the soldiers came into the cell, grabbed roughly, and half dragged, half pushed him into the middle of the squad of men. His hands were retied behind his back. His breathing became short, more gasps of fear. The Turkish officer bawled some orders, and they moved off towards the main door.

Oh God, it was actually happening! It all seemed like a crazy dream, and oh how he wished that it was a nightmare, and that he would soon wake up aboard *E11* – but shortly he would not be waking up ever again!

He remembered the boyhood games they had played on Guernsey. Being captured by the Boers, and being sent to the firing squad. He remembered going home to tea afterwards. That had been a game. This was real life. This was the last walk he was ever going to make. Life of Earth would go on, but he wouldn't be here to share in it. He would be dead, and at that moment he realised just how precious one's life really is. The thought of collaboration flicked through his mind again, but he shook his head. Never! Some things had to remain a certainty.

He was still very alert, and became determined that he was not going to miss a single second of these final moments. They would not cheat him out of these last few precious minutes. In the past, he had often wondered how he would die, and what would happen at the end, where and when his death would take place, but he never thought that it would happen so quickly. The squad reached the big main doors of the mosque, and he was forced through.

Outside it was inky dark with no moon showing, but there were some stars visible through the partial cloud cover. Beyond the edge of the mosque, the hillside was lit by a thousand oil lamps, as they hung from a thousand tents. As they crossed the bare patch of open ground in front of the mosque, he cast his eyes about. The whole hillside looked beautiful, like a thousand fire-flies is their summer mating ritual. The air was fresh, clean, and cool, blowing straight in off the sea. George took a long deep breath, trying to steel himself for what was about to come. Although he felt very much alone, the fresh salty tang somehow gave him reassurance. He could not say that he wasn't afraid, because he could feel his legs trembling, threatening to give way, as if they were made of jelly. Fighting hard not to show his enemy just how afraid he really was, he felt proud that he had been a man within the Trade, and he would die knowing that he had served his country well.

It was nearly a hundred yards from the mosque entrance, before they reached the ruins of the barn that had been bombed that afternoon. There was a sick feeling in the pit of his stomach as he walked. Taking a series of deep breaths, he straightened his back, marching onward determinedly before he detected the smell of the recently burnt explosives. The acrid stench filled his senses as the squad reached the execution area far too quickly. This is it!

In front of them there was a stone wall that had formed part of an old barn, this and two other sections were all of what was left after the bomb that had been dropped from the spotter plane? He was taken over and stood against the tallest of three walls.

As George turned around, he could see that an audience of Turkish soldiers had gathered, shady spectres standing silently behind the firing squad to witness the spectacle. As he had walked towards the barn area, he had noticed the fresh earth of a line of six newly dug graves, thinking that they must belong those poor bloody soldiers that Arthur had betrayed. Each of those poor souls would have made this same journey, and each must have felt just as frightened as he did right now. He felt a sudden affinity with them, because like him, they had all made the exact same decision of non-compliance. Then his mind was sent reeling, as he caught his breathe as saw the fresh earth of seventh newly dug hole. It was obviously waiting for him. A macabre thought came to him. If there is life after death, then maybe by dying it would be rather like to joining a new ship. You were drafted from this world to join another.

As he stood there on his shaky legs, he recalled how nervous he had been when he had joined *E11,* and that first meeting with his new shipmates. If there really was an after-life, then he would soon be meeting the occupants of those mounds. Oh God, in the name of Jesus please have mercy on my soul, forgive me for all of my sins, and accept my soul into heaven!

He was manhandled into position, forcibly pushed back against the remaining brickwork. Looking up, he faced the line of the men who were about to kill him. They stood there idly smoking, leaning on their rifles, and looking rather bored. Their total disregard annoyed him, because these individuals were going to put an end to his life, and they could not give a damn. It was so disrespectful. Then in the sky high above him, there was a flash of lightening. A storm was on its way.

A Turk officer stepped forward, leaned over and began to pin a square of white material over his left breast. As he did so George's mind became filled by several conflicting emotions. At least he still had Mina's scarf tied around his neck, maybe he would see her again very soon! Then his anger returned with a vengeance at his not being unable to effect any change to what was about to happen – but as the man fiddled with the pin on his shirt, he felt another flood of fear pass through his body. There were just seconds to go. This was the last minute of his life. This was it!

The frustration at being forced to meekly stand here, and accept the fact that they were going to take his life from him was unbearable. He felt a complete and total impotence! Nobody had the right to take his life like this – nobody in this world but God. Give me a weapon to go down fighting, and I won't regret dying one little bit, but to die in such a manner as this was absolute shit.

The Turkish officer had finally finished pinning the material to his shirt, and stood up in front of him. As he stared straight at him, George could smell the cheap brandy and stale tobacco on his breath.

"Do you want a blindfold?" he asked.

George shook his head. He wanted to see and experience the beauty of this planet right up until the very last second. The Turkish officer returned to his squad.

George said another silent prayer, thanking God for his life. He thanked his mother and father for his birth, and for bringing him up so well. He asked that Gladys might be spared her grief. There was a brief flicker of comfort as he realised that he would soon be seeing Mina again, and Matthew of course. That would be good. It would not be long now.

Then all his regrets immediately disappeared, when he thought that he could see Arthur amongst the audience. The hurricane lamp hanging on the corner of the barn revealed his presence standing over there in the shadows. George saw that smug smile on his lips. At that precise moment, George experienced such an unprecedented hatred for another human. If he had a gun in his hand, he would not have bothered with any of the Turks around him – they were just the enemy doing their duty. He would shoot Arthur dead without any guilt or remorse, knowing that he was ridding the world of evil in its vilest form.

There was a faint buzzing overhead that made the firing squad stare up into the darkness of the sky. It might be that spotter plane returning, just like the one that had strafed the troops this afternoon on his arrival, but a quick check revealed nothing visible in the darkness. Even if it was the same plane, its arrival would not affect what was about to happen. It would not provide him any assistance, thought George.

The Turkish officer was shouting loudly, trying to arrange his men into a decent line. George could see that through the darkness, beyond where Arthur standing, that there were some more flashes of lightning, followed this time by a loud roll of thunder.

Lightening, he thought. A storm brewing. It's a pity I will not feel the rain on my face. Oh, how he wanted to experience that wetness.

Three more lightning flashes were followed by three more claps of thunder.

Something was wrong!

'That is strange,' thought George as he looked upward into the sky, 'these light clouds up there do not look like they are part of a thunderstorm. All of that bad weather must be out over the sea!'

The sound of the rifle bolts being operated jerked his mind back to the subject in hand. This was it. He took a long deep breath, and braced himself, waiting for the report from the guns. Suddenly he realised that he desperately needed to go to the toilet. Is this the last thought that I am going to have? Wanting a pee! Whatever – it did not matter anymore. Even at this final moment, he still had held the belief that something would happen to save him. He wondered if every victim who faced a firing squad thought the same thing. He let go the huge breath of air that he had been holding.

A loud order was yelled by the Turkish officer, and the soldiers all sprang to attention, raising their rifles.

George held his breath once again, and waited.

Another shout and they aligned their sights on the tiny piece of white material pinned over his breast.

He could not help it, but he instinctively closed his eyes, and tilted his head forward. He felt the need to urinate so very badly. Any second now and it would be all over, he thought. He wondered if it was going to hurt very much. Goodbye Mum – Goodbye Dad – Goodbye Gladys…

The first explosion was a complete surprise to everyone. It happened just over a hundred yards away as the mosque seemed to erupt into a mushrooming ball of flame and exploding debris. The blast must have killed everyone within fifty feet of the building, because it certainly knocked everybody else off their feet. Some were thrown great distances by the force, resulting in terrible injuries. George had been somewhat protected from the blast by the adjacent barn wall, which saved him from any serious injury and protected him from the flying debris. None the less its force threw him bodily against the wall.

The bodies of the firing squad, who had been standing clear of the wall, were lying all over the place, their weapons nowhere in sight. Seconds later, a series of even louder explosions began to systematically obliterate the field of fire-flies.

Everyone, everywhere, began to panic, with nobody knowing where this rain from hell was coming from. Self-preservation became the order of the day, but nobody knew which way to run, or where to seek shelter. The explosions were becoming more frequent, and a lot more indiscriminate – seemingly falling anywhere. Great mountains of earth erupted in giant columns.

George knew where they were coming from, and once he had managed to struggle to his feet, he began running for his life. He knew that there was a battleship out there somewhere out on that dark sea that it was bombarding this camp. The spotter plane that flew over this afternoon on his arrival had obviously made reports back at base about this new troop concentration.

George ran forward, as fast as he his legs could carry him, but with both of his hands tied behind his back, it was not easy to keep his balance, and he fell twice before reaching the tented encampment. He blundered blindly into several soldiers, who were running in the opposite direction, but they were more interested in saving themselves than stopping him. A huge eruption was thrown skyward off to his left, but he did not falter. Just getting away from here was the one and only thought in his mind. He ran down one of the lines of tents, taking care to hurdle over any guy ropes. There were still some lamps hanging on the surviving tents, which thankfully lit his way. Several of the other tents were ablaze.

Reaching the end of the final line of tents, not slowing at all, he ran off into total darkness. After another hundred yards, and he began to slow his pace, realising that he could seriously injure himself should he fall in the darkness. Using what starlight there was available, he turned and headed straight down the steep slope in the direction of the sea. Behind him, the violent explosions continued – and were now almost incessant – confirming that the firing ship had found the range. George did not look back.

As he descended the hillside, he felt a terrific elation. He was not going to die – he had been given a second chance – his prayers had been answered. His first instinct was to place as much distance as he could between himself and the camp. He kept up the good pace. The darkness was almost complete, so he slowed down to a fast walk.

There was one thing that kept going through his mind; it was the hope that Arthur Collenette might have been standing right beneath one of those twelve-inch one-ton shells when it landed.

Just then the slope of the hillside dropped unexpectantly and his legs had to double their pace just to keep up with the pull of gravity. He began losing his balance, feeling his body running wildly out of control, as the increasing gravity accelerated his efforts to remain standing. Suddenly he was falling, rolling over and over until he lost his senses, and everything went black.

When he awoke, it was broad daylight. The sun was shining down through the foliage that fanned the sky high above him. Everything around him was eerily silent. Then he heard the trickle of water, and the sound of twittering of birds. Checking all around, he was unable to hear or see anything else.

As he tried to sit up, there was a terrible pain in his shoulder. It felt like a stabbing knife., and he could feel the dried blood and the painful soreness above his right eye. He moved his legs – they seemed to be OK! He gave another loud prayer of thanks. Then, despite all of the pain, he managed to rise to his feet. He looked about him, checking his position to discover that he had been lying in a shallow ditch. It had tall sides, and was covered by shrubbery, which had thankfully had provided him with some cover. Another quick visual check all around, and he felt fairly safe.

His next thought was to free his hands. Forty minutes later, working through an excruciating pain barrier, he finally managed to remove the bonds from his wrists by rubbing the rope against a sharp-edged rock. He realised that his left arm had been badly sprained, broken, or maybe it was dislocated. After unbuttoning his shirt with his free hand right down to his waist, he cradled the damaged one in the opening. It provided some support and eased the pain a little.

Assessing where he was, he could see the sea between two hills ahead of him. He decided that he would try to head on towards the Allied lines along the coast, before the Turks started searching for him.

An hour later found him half-sliding, half walking, down a hillside, before he finally emerged out from the undergrowth to find himself standing on a rocky, pebbly shore-line. Walking out to the water's edge, he stared into the limpid liquid enviously. It looked shallow and clear, with the tops of several semi-submerged rocks just breaking the mirror surface further out. The gentle lapping of the water in the morning sunshine calmed his nerves for the first time since his escape. Using his free had, he splashed himself all over.

Life was truly beautiful. Having come within a whisker of losing everything, he was certain that the world possessed a beauty, he had previously taken for granted. This rocky shoreline for instance, could easily have be a replica of any of the inlets along Guernsey's west coast. He started off southwards, in the direction of the Allied lines, seeing the coast disappear into the infinity of a hazy mirage.

Using as much cover as was available, after an hour, the constant pain forced him to stop, and sitting on a rock he looked in both directions, reassured that this coastal strip was completely deserted as far as his eyes could see.

As he sat there, he could hear the sound of gunfire begin. Another battle was beginning. It was louder than yesterday, a good indication that he was heading in the right direction.

George must have walked another ten miles before he came anywhere near to any of the fighting. He was feeling extremely hungry, as he hadn't eaten a thing since the night that he and Mina had left her apartment. At least he had managed to quench his thirst from that small trickling brook that drained the upper slopes down which he had initially descended.

Just walking was causing him a great deal of pain – his head, shoulder and arm were all an absolute burning agony, but on the positive side – he was still alive. He also realised that he must be running a high temperature, his facial skin was soaking with sweat and felt hot to the touch, but he had no option but to keep going.

With the sea to his right, and the dusty hills rising steeply up to his left, the topography had become much drier, the vegetation more scrub than the lush growths he had left behind yesterday. Ahead of him, apart from a few intermittent explosions, he could now hear the faint sporadic bursts from machine gun fire, and the occasional crack of a rifle. It was obvious that he was getting closer, but he knew that if he were to try to get through during daylight, he would be committing suicide, and so he found himself a quiet shaded cove in which to hide until it got dark. There he found some thick clumps of course grass, in between which he lay down under the shade of an oleander to rest until night fell.

Once complete darkness descended, and just as last evening before the moon had risen, he set off once more along the beach, using the utmost caution, and carefully watching each foot-fall to keep as quiet as he possibly could. His senses became knife-edge alert, where the least sound caused him to duck down, and freeze. Progress was painfully slow, but with a dogged determination he forced himself to keep walking. He lost any idea of how far he had travelled, or indeed, where exactly the Turkish lines were. The thudding explosions, and sharp rifle fire were very close now, as he edged his way along the water-line. Suddenly he heard some voices through the darkness, they were quite close, and they were not speaking in English. Somehow, without realising it, he had walked right along the edge of the Turkish front line without so much as a challenge. Off to his left, in the direction of the voices, he could just make out the lightness of the sandy dunes, but could see no sign of any soldiers. He began moving again with extreme caution, taking advantage of any cover. Each short dash that he made, was carefully pre-planned to make sure that it would not leave him exposed for any long period. Little by little he made his way from one rock, or mound of sand, to the next. He could now clearly hear the sound of the enemy chattering voices, some sounding to be quite close, as others whispered softly in the night. Keep going!

Then suddenly, there was a huge explosion that lit up the whole area in monochromic splendour, and George could see several of the Turkish conical helmets sticking just clear of a trench above him. They were also keeping their heads down, and he took advantage of the moment by trudging on determinedly, keeping close to the water's edge, and using the darkness of the sea surface to hide his silhouette.

Twenty minutes later another star shell burst high over towards the north, which lit up the whole area as if it were day. He threw himself down to the rocky beach; the cold water was invasive as he forced himself to remain stock still, enduring the pain through gritted teeth. With the return of darkness, stabs of pain punched through his body as he tried to rise.

Realising that he was deep within the Turkish front lines, he became paranoid, expecting at any moment to be challenged, shot, – or be taken prisoner again. More voices were heard as he trod forward very carefully, his eyes looking up towards at another sandy rise. More heads appeared, and he could see some soldiers manning a machine gun position. The gun itself was sticking out from the top of a dune, but the actual figures were being masked by a huge clump of marram grass.

George remained crouched down, before another look confirmed that they were definitely Turkish helmets. If they were to stand up fully, they would easily spot him. He waited, hardly daring to breathe, but knew that if he didn't continue walking, he would never get back to safety. Once the moon did start to rise, he was going to be totally exposed, so he had to get clear. There was not much time left to him.

Moving very cautiously, he slowly inched his way past the helmets and apart from that one incident, he never actually saw the enemy again. How far would it be to the Allied lines?

Half an hour later, and the moon was just starting to peak above the eastern horizon, when George sensed something, or someone, moving ahead of him. With the new light rising he knew that he would be terribly exposed, so he ducked down and froze once again, because if he could see somebody moving ahead, then logically they could see him. They had! His heart began to thump like a hammer as a challenge was yelled out of the darkness.

"Who goes there, friend or foe?"

"A friend mate – a bloody knackered friend," was all George could answer.

****

George woke up in the Sick Bay aboard *HMS Adamant*, luxuriating within the feel of clean laundered linen sheets stretched on a mattress in a steel framed bunk bed. He was told that he had slept solidly for the fifteen hours since he first arrival, a sure measure of the fatigue and strain that he had been subjected to.

When he had opened his eyes, the Sick Berth Attendant had had been under orders to inform Captain Somerville, but no one was more surprised than George, when the sick bay was called to attention when the Commander of the Submarine Flotilla walked in. He was followed by a retinue of assistants, as well as Commander Charles Brodie, head of Submarine Operations on the Admirals Staff.

333

"At ease please," said the Captain, as he stepped through the hatch doorway. "Where is he please, P.O.?"

"Over there, sir," said the Senior Rating, pointing to George's bunk.

George gulped as watched them approach his bed. He looked amazed as the officers began crowding around his bunk.

"Well, Torode, you certainly seem to have been through the wars by all accounts. No pun intended, of course. We received a signal from *HMS Jed* only the day before yesterday reporting the success of Lieutenant d'Oyly-Hughes and yourself in attacking the railway viaduct in the Gulf of Ismid. Strangely enough in that same signal, you were officially reported as *Missing in Action* and here you are back with us before *E11* is due to return off her patrol. I must say that you have made it back in remarkably quick time, considering the distance that you must have covered. The Admiral has already been informed of your exploit, and quite frankly he is very impressed by your obvious ingenuity. We are not expecting *E11* back until early next week, so I want you to relax and use the time to get yourself fit again. The doctor tells me that you have suffered nothing worse than a badly sprained shoulder, plus a few minor cuts and bruises that will heal up in time. So, if you are feeling up to it young man, I would like you to give us a full account of the whole patrol from the time that you left here, the attack on Constantinople, and please include a full account of your attack on that railway viaduct. I am waiting to hear how you managed to make your way through enemy territory, and get back here in one piece. Is that OK with you?"

"Yes, sir," said George. "What is the date today, please?"

"Why, it's the fifth of June," said the Captain, with a quizzical look at George.

George nodded. The last few days had seemed like a lifetime. Taking a long deep breath, he began his account. The Captain held up his hand for him to pause and called to the Sick Berth staff to bring seats for them all. Once they were comfortable, he asked George to begin again.

"Well sir, as you know we sailed from Kephalo in the early hours of the nineteenth of May. My God, that was only just over two and a half weeks ago," he said, when he realised the length of the whole patrol. "I'm sorry, sir, it's just that it seems much longer ago than that when we sailed. I thought that we had been away nearly four weeks. Time does funny things when you are aboard. Maybe it's the same regular routine that does it? That, and all the dangers we have had to face and along with the all ships that we have boarded and sunk," George apologised.

The officers all listened attentively, eager to get a first-hand account of a patrol that had already received huge publicity in the world press. They wanted to glean any new knowledge that had not yet been relayed in the signals from *HMS Jed*.

George's telling of *E11*'s patrol was periodically interrupted by questions from Commander Brodie, and it took him nearly a full hour to relate it all. He had made sure that they were all fully aware of Arthur Collenette, and of his traitorous co-operation with the Turkish military. In him revealing Arthur's traitorous actions, he would never be able to tell any of his lies again. In George's mind it wasn't that he was telling tales, this time it was his turn to get his story in first. The only difference was that he would be telling the truth. Captain Somerville stood, obviously he had another appointment.

"I am going to leave my Sub Lieutenant here with you, Torode. I would like you to repeat your account to him, so that he can write it all down. He will type it up for the Admiral's attention. Try and be accurate as you can with the dates and times as they will be included in the official report of your journey back!"

"I would never have made it back had it not been for Mr Papandross, and his daughter Mina," said George in a matter of fact tone.

"So, you said. Is this chap in Constantinople – Papandross! He is sympathetic to the Allied cause did you say? I want you to give my Aide here, anything you can remember about him, and any details of his shipping business. Try to remember where his house is located within the city, and if possible, draw a map You said that it was his butler who betrayed you, which probably means that the Turkish security service already have him under surveillance. Rack your brain for a description of the butler! Beside the Pearl of Petra, and the sloop that *E11* stopped, can you remember the names of any other of the Papandross vessels?" said Captain Somerville. "The more information that you can remember, then the more you will help with the campaign. Anyway, we'll leave you now to get some rest, and have a quiet chat with Subby Pritchard here. There is absolutely no rush, you can take your time repeating your account. I just wanted to add my own congratulations on your quick thinking under very trying conditions in getting back here so quickly. You certainly used your initiative. Well done Torode, you did a very good job, and we're all very proud of you."

With that, most of the officers disappeared, filing out through the water-tight door and leaving him alone with the tall, gangly looking Sub Lieutenant.

"My name's Subby Pritchard," he introduced himself. "The Captain wants me to write down all that you can remember."

"Well, we had better get started then, hadn't we, sir?" said George.

****

HMS E11 was ordered to return from her patrol on the seventh of June, and after negotiating her way back through the many perilous hazards of the Dardanelle's, she emerged once more back into the Mediterranean. She had immediately headed for the small harbour over at Kephalo, after another close encounter with a mine on her way out.

George Torode was discharged from the Sick Bay very early on the eighth of June. His arm was still in a sling, and his face remained rather puffy, especially around his eye, but otherwise he felt truly rested. After reporting to Spare Crew C.O, he asked for permission to go over and meet *E11* at Kephalo. His request was granted, and he managed to cadge a lift in one of the fleet tenders that was taking out fresh supplies.

The tender's crew, once they learned that George was from the *E11*, quickly treated him some respect – such was the reputation that the tiny submarine had gained during her patrol. There was something about the deferential way in which they acted that had made George feel a little uncomfortable, but in being absent he had no idea how wide-spread the news of *E11*'s exploits had been reported around the world. The boat and the skipper, Lieutenant Commander Martin Dunbar-Naismith, had become the most famous submarine in the world.

The Sick Berth Attendant had told him that *E11* had made headlines in the national press at home as well, and in most of the major journals right around the world. George recalled the American Mr Gram-Swigg, when he had shot out the bridge windows of the ship, who was taking passage aboard. He had told them that he was a newspaper reporter. So, it was logical that was how their exploits had become world-wide news. The submarine patrols were fast becoming a legend amongst the Allied troops in the trenches, their achievements representing the only real success story in this whole bloody fiasco that was the Gallipoli campaign.

It was a perfect summer's day. The sea was flat calm, shimmering like a mirror. Overhead the sky was a cloudless azure blue, right down to the slight haze that distorted the horizon. Already it was far too hot for doing anything strenuous, and even the gulls sat coolly, floating about on the surface of the sea.

As the tender got underway, it quickly increased speed, its forward motion through the water was enough to create a welcome breeze. In the far distance on the northern horizon George could see the coastline of the Gallipoli Peninsula, but from where he stood at the bow of the craft it looked no more than a faint discolouration. It was hard to believe that over there were men dying in droves. After walking along that dangerous coast, George had an appreciation of the condition the soldiers are experiencing. All the hopes of an early success in taking the peninsula had now completely faded, and the battlefield had developed into a replica of the Western Front in Flanders. Many of the fruitless over the top charges, carried out against a hail of steel from the Turk machine guns were producing terrible losses. The lives of hundreds of good men were being wasted in attempting to gain a few precious yards of dry dusty ground.

George thought that it was terrible that anyone should have to die on such a beautiful day as this. He now had a quite different opinion of Turkey as a country, having seen a bit of it. Although these Aegean Islands that they were using as a base were the dusty tops of extinct volcanic cones, further north, the Turkish heartland was quite lush. The northern side of the Gallipoli peninsula itself was green enough, but it soon became much drier down at Cape Helles, and along its southern edges that faced the Aegean. He remembered the greenness of the country he had passed through during the train ride. The Turkish people going about their daily business came into his mind. They were not so very different – a different culture certainly, but they had all the same trials and tribulations that the British experienced in their everyday lives.

Then his mind suddenly flipped to the horror of the firing squad he had faced, and he realised that he might have never have seen this beautiful day – he shuddered. He had been within a minute or two of being shot, and buried in that freshly dug grave.

Life is nothing but fate, he decided. It is a series of personal events that clash with everybody else's personal events, culminating in extreme life or death crisis points, whereby the outcome is decided by the toss of a coin. If you pick the heads side you live, failure to do so, and you die. If you gave your everything and did your very best, then you stood a far better chance of picking the right side of the coin.

Standing up in the bow of the tender, he took a good deep breath of the fresh morning breeze. The sun's rays felt warm on his face and as the cool air brushed over his skin it prevented him from sweating. He felt so thankful to be alive, because if that salvo from the bombarding battleship had been a minute later, he would not be here. His name would just be another that was added to the ever-growing casualty list, and Arthur Collenette would have got away with being a traitor. The fact that he had reported his treachery gave him some satisfaction. It partly repaid his promise to Matthew, because justice will eventually be delivered. Silently, he said another prayer of thanks for his salvation. As he finished, he thought for a moment. Did God deliver me? Is it God who was in charge of everyone's fate? Is there even such a thing as God?

The rounded tops of small islands they were passing lay far off on the horizon, like pimples on a smooth skin, too far away to discern any distinguishing features, as they approached more that lay ahead, George pointed to the largest of them and asked the Coxswain if it was Kephalo. The Leading Seaman nodded his head from the confines of the steering housing.

"We're going to pass round that point of land over there, and the harbour is just beyond!" he replied, pointing towards his objective.

Half an hour later saw the tender entered the anchorage, and George immediately spotted the dark low shape of *E11*, tied up alongside the destroyer *HMS Grampus*. The tender was brought skilfully alongside the submarine's bow. George Plowman walked up along the forward casing to secure their bow line, and began winding it on to the forward bollards.

"Hello, George," shouted George Torode.

The signalman turned from his work, his eyes searching for the voice.

"George Torode – you old maggot! Everybody thought that you had caught a packet after the Jimmy returned alone. The skipper has you posted as missing in action. We have even had a whip round for your folks, and there are plans to sell your kit when we get back to the depot ship. We managed to get nearly two pounds and seventeen shillings and four pence between us all. Just shows you how popular you were – er – I mean, are."

They both laughed, and he jumped across the gap to join the Signalman.

A group came up from below to pass down all of the fresh stores. Basil Partridge was one of them, and he and the rest tried to shake his hand, or pat him on the back, as they set about their work. George Plowman led him down towards the conning tower.

"Stand here George, in the shade. The rest of the chaps below will be so pleased to see you, we all thought that you 'ad been killed. Even the First Lieutenant said that he thought that he saw you go down. He was absolutely certain that you 'ad been shot, and he 'as been feeling terrible at 'aving to leave you on that beach. I know that the Skipper will be pleased as well. He said that losin' you was the only blight on an otherwise perfect patrol. Pretty upset about it, he was. I think that he considered it was 'is fault that you went missin'. 'Ow the bloody hell did you manage to get back before us?"

George gave him a brief account of his adventure, explaining how he had sprained his arm, and bruised his face.

"You certainly 'ave seen some action, George. We've 'ad a high old time of it since you've been gone mate. After losin' you, the very next day we headed over to our signal slot, to reported your mission to *Jed*. As I said, you were reported as missin' in action. That sounds funny now, doesn't it?" said the signalman.

George could only smile. "Did you have any more successes, George?"

"If you remember we only had three torpedoes left, and the skipper sank another ammunition ship with one of them. There was a terrible explosion and she went down in three minutes. It was only an hour later when we chased a small steamer that tried to beach her-self on the shore over near the small town of Panidos. The skipper fired a torpedo, but it missed and despite it being set to float it still sank. The funny thing was that while we were searchin' for it, we were attacked by a troop of Turkish cavalry that appeared from over a hill. They came chargin' down towards the beach wavin' their sabres and firin' their rifles at us. We must be the only submarine in the world to be attacked by a troop of horse soldiers. They were pretty accurate too, they 'it the connin' tower a couple of times. So, the Skipper had to abandon the search for the torpedo."

"So, you actually lost that torpedo then?"

"Yes, and the skipper was jolly mad about it I can tell you. Then just after dinner, that same day, we were at periscope depth when we sighted two destroyers escorting a small two-funnel steamer. We fired at the steamer, but missed. It went right under her, the skipper reckoned. It was the same torpedo that went under that ship carryin' all those women and kids a couple of days before. Anyway, none of the ships noticed that they 'ad even been attacked, so we waited until they disappeared before surfacing and going over to pick it up yet again. We took it back onboard through the stern torpedo tube this time. It came onboard back to front, so the torpedomen 'ad to dismantle it, section by section, then turn each one around, before they could reassemble it facing' the right way, before reloadin' it in the forward tube."

"Blimey, that all happened while I was on my way to Constantinople," said George.

It was the Signalman's turn to smile. "I ain't finished yet," he carried on with his tale.

"That same day we were nearly rammed, and had to crash dive. We broke our record by taking' only sixteen seconds to get under, but in doin' so we also managed to flood the engines. So, the skipper surfaced again when it was all clear, and headed over towards *Jed* communication spot once more. "

"That must have been the night that Mina got shot, as we tried to get aboard the Pearl of Petra," said George, a sorrowful tone in his voice. "She was such a pretty girl, George."

"I'm sorry that she got killed mate, she sounds a like smashin' girl. It sounds like you certainly wouldn't be here now if it wasn't for her."

"No," said George reflectively.

Fate is such a strange thing. If he hadn't grabbed her in the street in that moment of madness, they would never have met, and she would still be alive. He may still be in Constantinople – and she would probably have been arrested. He remembered how she had given herself to him so unselfishly, and he had never experienced such tenderness for anyone before, not even for his Gladys. His mind returned back to the present.

"Did you eventually manage to use that last torpedo, George?" he asked.

"Yes, we did, the Skipper sank a large transport with it. We closed to 300 yards before he fires. It was just off the Moussa Bank near Chanak. The Skipper was hopin' that one of the Turkish battleships might be holed there, but he was out of luck. It was a fittin' end for a torpedo that had been fired twice before. The ship went down very quickly."

"Did you have any more trouble coming back through that minefield, George?"

"You would not believe it, George. We got ourselves down past Nagara Point, George, but off Kalid Bahr the boat became quite difficult to 'andle. You won't believe it mate – but we only 'ad a bloody mine snagged on the forward hydroplanes;

it was trapped there by there its moorin' wire. We had to carry the bloody thing all the way down through the other minefields, as we went past Kephez Point. As you can imagine we were all sweatin' quite a bit. Looking out through the viewing port in the conning tower, the Jimmy said that the front end of the boat looked just like a kid's hand stretched out as it held a toy balloon. We only managed to get rid of it once we got down near Cape Helles, and only then by going astern and blowin' the tanks at the same time. We actually surfaced goin' backwards. We 'ad to, otherwise the bloody thing would 'ave hit the forward casing. The manoeuvre managed to detach mooring wire though, and our escort – HMS Grampus here – was ready and waiting to hold our hand and bring us back home."

George Plowman had a habit of making the most horrifying and dangerous events seem like Sunday stroll down a country lane. Listening attentively, George Torode knew first-hand about all those dangers, and made allowances for his friend's lack of detail. If that mine had touch anywhere on the casing of the submarine, its 80lb charge would have ripped through the three-quarter inch steel plate of E11's pressure hull like a knife through butter – just as that one did when he had been aboard HMS C301 in the English Channel. To have to drag it nearly ten miles, bobbing about on the end of its wire must have been absolutely terrifying, but George knew that he would have preferred that to his terrible experience of facing that firing squad.

The stores were still being passed down through the forward torpedo loading hatch, and as the last of them disappeared, the two men finally went below, before the hatch was closed behind them. The signalman had to assist George down the near vertical ladder, but once he reached the bottom, more of his crewmates welcomed him back, many patting him on the back, not thinking of the shooting pains it caused in his shoulder. The humid sticky heat hit him like an old friend, and the familiar beads of sweat began to run down his back, soaking into his white front uniform top. His welcome home carried on as they passed through the water-tight bulkhead, and on into the passageway leading aft.

The First Lieutenant Guy d'Oyly-Hughes came out of the Wardroom to see what was causing all the commotion. His jaw dropped open in surprise. No one was more relieved to see George than he was. He had carried the guilt of George's loss since the night of their attack on the viaduct, and he immediately invited George into the Wardroom to relate his adventure and answer his queries. Martin Naismith had gone over onto the Grampus to use their washing facilities prior to them returning to the fleet base at Murdos.

"Well, you certainly have had an adventure, haven't you?" he said, once George had finished the telling. "We're moving across to Murdos later on today, and you're more than welcome to ride back with us, if your arm is up to it of course!"

George gladly accepted the lift, saying he wouldn't need his arm to act as the Control Room messenger.

"Oh, no you won't my lad. You will be riding high, up on the bridge with the captain and me. You were up there as helmsman when we left first Kephalo to enter the Dardanelles at the start of the patrol. So, it is only right for you to be up there when we return back to the Fleet anchorage. You can stand next to Plowman."

Once he had left the Wardroom, George went and retold various parts of his story to the other members of the crew, before he was interrupted by the pipe for

Special Sea Dutymen, which sent them all scurrying to their stations in readiness for leaving harbour.

He needed a bit of assistance to climb back up the conning tower ladder, it was vertical, before he eventually he emerged up on the bridge where the captain greeted him warmly, and congratulated him on his initiative in returning so quickly. Moving to the rear of the bridge, he stood beside the signalman.

After *E11* had slipped her lines from *Grampus*, her bow turned as she headed out of the harbour at Kephalo. They were cheered by every one of the small ships there that they passed. *HMS E11* had certainly become quite a celebrity. The weather was still perfect as they headed out into the wide expanse of the Aegean Sea. The breeze created once they were under way was most welcome, immediately dispelling the sultry stickiness of being below. George felt so good to be back on board. It truly felt like coming home, but it was also felt a little unnatural to be standing there in his best uniform. The throbbing steel beneath his feet made him feel secure and safe.

When they entered the anchorage within circular harbour of the Island of Murdos, every single ship, both big and small was lined from stem to stern by men waving their hats and caps. They were royally cheered into harbour by thousands of welcoming voices. The noise seemed incessant, as the raucous din echoed off the surrounding hills. The casing party were elated, enjoying every moment, as the captain manoeuvred to make his approach to come alongside *HMS Adamant*.

As the berthing ropes were being secured, George looked up at the top of the companion ladder on the Depot Ship. There was a gaggle of white uniforms waiting there, along with more gold braid than he had ever seen before. He recognised Captain Somerville straight away, along with some of his staff from his time in the sick bay. Lieutenant Commander Brodie was there too, standing next to a Commodore, who George assumed had to be Roger Keyes.

Martin Naismith left the final intricacies of securing the submarine to Guy d'Oyly-Hughes, and was ceremoniously piped off *E11*. He was then piped again, as he boarded the Depot Ship, and George watched them all up there, warmly shaking hands, all smiles before disappearing below to Captain Somerville's cabin.

"Hey George," shouted Baxter, as he walked back from the forward casing. "That little piece of talent that got shot while you were away. Did you manage to give 'er one?"

George's temper welled up inside him, but before he exploded, George Plowman stepped in to defused the situation.

"Do you know what Bagsy, your tact and diplomacy are only exceeded by your fluency in Hindustani," he said pushing him away from George.

"But – but I don't know any Hindustani," protested the bewildered torpedo-man.

"I rest my case," said the signalman.

An hour later, George Torode was summoned by a messenger to report to Captain Somerville's cabin aboard *Adamant*. He was taken down into the passageway, and told to wait outside the great cabin door. When the door opened, he was asked to enter by the Captain's Petty Officer Steward. Once inside he was immediately overawed, he had never been invited into such august company. Around the highly polished mahogany table sat many of the officers that George had only heard of by name. He could see that they had now been joined by Lieutenant d'Oyly-Hughes. All heads turned towards him as George entered, and he felt himself shrivelling under their gaze.

"Ah – come in Torode," said Naismith. "Gentlemen, may I introduce Ordinary Seaman Torode. He and my First Lieutenant carried out the successful attack on the railway viaduct near the Gulf of Ismid."

Turning to George, Martin Naismith spoke to him quietly.

"I would like you to give Commodore Keyes your personal account of what happened to you, from when you made your escape from the viaduct, right up until your return."

Standing there with all those high-ranking officers staring at him, George wished the deck would open up and swallow him. His throat became dry, he coughed nervously, but once he had begun, he found it became easier and easier.

On completion, he was closely questioned by the whole assembly. Commodore Keyes seemed particularly interested in his association with Alexandros Papandross and Captain Raftopopulos. Finally, he asked the bombshell question.

"On the next patrol that is to be undertaken by *HMS E11*, if you were to be landed somewhere near Constantinople, do you think that you could re-establish contact with these two men?"

George was absolutely stunned. It was the very last thing that he had expected to be asked. He was fairly sure that he could remember most of the way to Mina's father's house, despite him being the worse for the drink on the way back. It would simply be a case of locating the Pearl of Petra in the port area of Scutari, for him to be able to get hold of Raftopopulos.

"Yes sir, I suppose there would be no problems there, except that I can't speak a word of the Turkish language. Last time I had Mina – er... I mean I had Mr Papandross' daughter to help me, but it would be very difficult trying to get through the city alone. I am not too sure about the Captain of the Pearl of Petra though. That would all depend on where his ship was, and there is always a heavy military presence around the port area."

"If we were to make arrangements for someone to meet you who can speak the language, do you think that it would be possible?"

George knew that it would be possible. If only he knew a few words of Turkish himself then he might have been able to do it on his own, but he knew that it would be much easier having someone who could translate.

"Yes sir, that would be possible," he replied.

"Would you be willing to undertake another mission into Constantinople?"

"Yes sir," said George, feeling the warning stab of pain in his arm. It was as if it were trying to remind how it came to be hurt.

There was a general discussion around the table before he was dismissed, and he was allowed to make his way out of the cabin in order to allow the officers to continue their deliberations. Once the door had closed behind him, Commodore Roger Keyes spoke to the assembly.

"It is by sheer chance that this young man has stumbled on the possible recruitment of a reliable contact right in the middle of Constantinople. If we were to offer him safe passage for all his ships, or some monetary inducement should one of his ships be sunk inadvertently, then I feel that we may have the ideal operative working for us. Imagine the intelligence that he could supply to us. He will be privy to information on the Turkish shipping schedules, which would be a fantastic bonus for our submarines on patrol in the Marmara. They could intercept, or lie in wait for each individual target. He would also hold all of the cargo manifests for every vessel in port, and that would enable us to cherry pick the best targets. We would also have information on ships that were passing up and down through the Bosphorus. There would be itemised lists of the numbers of troops, and munitions, being embarked for the front, plus the sailing times of each transport. That young man has been through a terrible ordeal, but he is now ready to go back. I think that says a lot about our men's fighting spirit. We have an agent in Constantinople already, but he is finding it difficult to gain access to the information that we so badly need. It was he who sent the report of all the pandemonium that you created Martin, when you entered the port. So with this Greek chap in our pocket, we could treble the information coming out. We could virtually cut their supply lines to the peninsula, and isolate their whole army. This could prove to be the turning point to this campaign. I want to propose a mission into Constantinople to set up, and establish links with this new line of communication."

The idea was accepted in principal and after some minor conversations, the meeting dispersed in genial agreement. Martin Naismith was extremely happy with the outcome of his debriefing. It had been decided that *HMS E11* was to be sent back to Malta for a mini refit, and a re-paint. The latest logistic news suggested that they would be fitted a twelve-pounder quick loading gun while they were there.

Chapter Sixteen

Maltese Refit

It was the twenty-third of June 1915 and *HMS E11* was laying alongside in Malta undergoing her long-needed maintenance and repairs. The men had been billeted ashore once more in the two shore-side pensions, Port and Starboard. A grinning Horlicks, accompanied by his enormous wife – The Amazing Maria – had been waiting to meet them with open arms, now that news of their patrol had now achieved worldwide fame.

"Hello for yua – my famous friends – yua kicka the Turk arses good huh – the bar, eet ees open – tonight mya pay – free for yua. All yua beer have my house on."

Some things thankfully never change, and one of them was Horlicks wonderful interpretation of the English language. Everyone quickly settled back into their old rooms, enjoying the chance for a long relaxing bath in hot soapy water, and clean sheets on their bed.

That night gave them all a well-earned period of relaxation to let off steam, a welcome relief valve to release all of the pressures from the patrol – and what better way of doing it than to have free beer. Whilst on patrol the restricted cramped conditions afforded them absolutely no comfort. There were few bunks, and so they slept where ever they could. Existing within a steel tube filled with a diesel laden atmosphere, with no real toilet, or any washing facilities was enough to test even the strongest resolve. So, for the crew just to be able to sit in the comfort of a chair, wearing clean laundered clothes, and to be able to fully stretch their feet out was pure heaven. With the added incentive of the free beer for the night, it provided the next best thing to paradise.

Having been away from civilisation for such a long time, and having had no access to alcohol, with the exception of their daily rum ration, the free drinks quickly went straight to their heads. What was intended to be a rip-roaring night of celebration, ended up as a bit of a damp squib? The Amazing Maria never managed to get up to sing as Horlick's had promised, because most of her audience were either asleep in their chairs, or leaning across one of the tables in a semi-stupor. Many of the crew had simply retired early. The following morning there were some sore heads.

"Yua fella's need plenty a practice widda booze – all sea, no play, yua pretty dull fella's – I gotta mucha booze for yua – come back tonight – mya wife, she gonna sing for yua after work."

Every single man had to work overtime that afternoon, as the boat had to be prepared for its docking down in the harbour's dry dock. The removal of torpedoes, fuel, and various pieces of auxiliary equipment's had to be landed ashore. It was all going very well, but it required a lot of co-ordinated manpower.

Before the docking, the crew were the recipients of good news, because many of the components that had been damaged during the patrol had already arrived from England. In contacting *HMS Jed* with a requisition signal the moment that something became defective, it enabled the logistic team aboard the Flagship to order replacements immediately. The main motor armature had already arrived, and was standing in its packing crate on the dockside, waiting to replace the damaged one. The old one had already been unbolted from its mounting in readiness for being lifted out of the boat, but the Engine Room hull plates would have to be removed once more to enable a crane to remove it from the after end of the engine room. However, the twelve-pounder gun, that they hoped would be here for their next patrol, had still not arrived from England. Martin Naismith was praying that it would turn up before they were due to leave, but the logistics department of *HMS St Angelo* emphasised that there were no guarantees. Should it fail to arrive in time for their second patrol, they were promised that it would definitely be fitted for their third – should one still be required. Most of the crew were hoping that they wouldn't have to do a third patrol, but judging by the present dismal rate of progress in the Dardanelles campaign, it was looking to be more of a certainty.

Once everything aboard the submarine was ready, a dockyard tug towed the boat across the harbour towards the great dry dock, where she was swiftly installed. Standing up on the side of the huge dock, the crew had been allocated and quickly taken over, some rather shoddy dockside accommodation. The buildings were brick built, consisting of an accommodation block in which the duty personal could sleep, and a large communal dining hall with an attached galley. The main hall was utilised to eat their lunchtime meals, issue the rum ration, and to spend the hours break at lunch seeking relief from the unrepentant sun. The accommodation block contained one shower, along with a line of five wash basins, and two toilets. There were some metal framed beds for the duty crew. Those not required for duty returned each night to their shore-side accommodation.

The submarine was positioned exactly on wooden iron bound blocks that stood along the central line in the dock. Huge twelve by twelve lengths of timber were floated into place, each positioned between the ballast tanks and the dockside to stop the boat from rolling over off the keel blocks. Then the dock was pumped dry. The boat's keel then finally settled down onto the keel blocks that held the submarine four feet above the dock's stone lined bottom.

Finally, once the last of the salt water had been drained away, and the boat sat there drying in the Maltese sunshine. The hot midsummer sun bore down incessantly, quickly evaporating any water that seeped in through the seal of the huge steel caisson at the end of the dock, which held back the seawater of the harbour.

HMS E11 looked incongruous raised above the dock bottom, but it was done to allow a complete under-fitments inspection to take place. After having grounded several times, and spent several nights sitting on the seabed during the patrol, everything below the waterline was going to be inspected for damage. Much of the below surface paint-work would have been scraped off, and would need to be re-painted.

344

During her time here most of the major defects, including the split intermediate shaft, were to be repaired or replaced. The damaged periscope had quickly been changed, replacing the one that had been holed by the Turkish gunboat Pelenk-i-Dria.

After the inspection, a repaint had been ordered of the ballast tanks and all under water fittings. With the boat being in dry dock, it was a good chance to get rid of all the rust and weed growth that was prevalent below the waterline. This would improve the stream-lining efficiency of the boat through the water, saving them both fuel and battery power. The anchor cable would also have to be ranged in the dock bottom, overhauled and joining shackles greased. Internally, as all the bilges had been pumped dry before docking, they would also be given a traditional repaint. Once that lot was completed, all that would be left to do was to undock. Then it would be back to storing the boat for war once more. Just after that had been completed, they would be heading back to Murdos.

The next morning, deep down on the dock bottom, underneath the boat, there was hardly any movement of the fetid air. Standing in the shadow of the ballast tanks the two men could feel the heat emanating off the stone floor of the dock. George Torode and Able Seaman Brassington had been detailed to paint the underside of the ballast tanks, and the keel itself. Despite them working in the shade, both of the men were sweating profusely. The estimated temperature must be above a hundred, and with no moving air, the humidity soared.

Due to the injury to his arm, George was there to assist the other man. His arm was still very stiff and painful, and although it was recovering well, it certainly was not yet ready for any heavy work. Whilst Brassington was using a Long Tom to apply the paint, George was following him along behind him using a four-inch brush to fill any patches that he had missed. He had a wooden step-ladder to be able to reach up to the higher areas. Trying to apply the thick sticky paint to the base of the underside of the tanks was a little like trying to spread treacle onto the ceiling. Both men had spent the previous day with chipping hammers and scrapers, removing any flaky paintwork or rust, as they prepared the surfaces to receive this gooey dark blue paint. This underwater section would need two applications to provide a decent protective coat against future attacks of rust, and to prevent the regrowth of seaweed. George found it particularly difficult using only one hand. He had officially been placed on the Light Duties list, but he found it hard to stand by and be idle, while the rest of his shipmates were all working flat out. The coxswain had allowed him to work, but not for long periods.

"I hate this bloody paint, don't you Brassy?" said George.

The older seaman put down his Long Tom, wiping the sweat from his brow, he turned to the George.

"Yeh, it's crap," he said. "'Ow's the damaged wing now, George?"

George waved his arm about, as if to show that it was mended.

Brassington smiled. "Little birdie – with a broken wing – cannot fly – cannot sing – useless bastard."

"They called it a partial dislocation with a complex sprain, Brassy. It's healed quite quickly, but I do have to keep it in a sling for another two weeks. Since all of the external bruising has gone down, it's been OK. It's a bit hard painting with only one hand though."

Brassington changed the subject. "Yer know when yer were 'elped by that Greek girl George! Well did yer… you know… did yer give 'er one?"

"She was killed helping me get away, Brassy. So please don't speak ill of the dead," snapped George. He tried hard not to lose his temper.

"Sorry mate, there's no need to lose you rag with me. You did give 'er one, then?" said the Seaman with a leering grin.

George was just about to tell Brassy that he did not appreciate his humour, when they joined by two more seamen, who had been assigned by the coxswain to help with the painting.

Brassington sneezed, and wiped his nose with his paint-covered fingers. It left a huge blue-black smudge under his nostrils, making him look as if he had a moustache. The foursome began painting on both sides, making their way aft towards the propellers.

They were still going hard at it when the lunch break arrived. The shrill whistle of the bosun's call wailed from the dry dock accommodation, high over their heads.

"Up spirits – Stand fast the Holy Ghost! Hand's to dinner."

Everybody had noted the blue mark, but nobody bothered to say a word about Brassy's painted moustache, as they all had paint splashes dotted over their faces on stopping work. Leaving their brushes to soak in a bucket of turpentine, the men wiped off most of the paint spots from their exposed skin with a spirit-soaked rag. Then the four of them ambled across the dock bottom out into the sunshine, and made their way to the steep stone steps that led up the side of the dock wall. As they climbed Brassington began to impart more worldly philosophies that, according to him, had been hard won from his life experiences.

"Do yer know what Lads! We're like the buccaneers of old we are. Back on that last trip, we were takin' prize ships, sinkin' others, just like old Franky Drake and 'is band of bloody pirates."

"Well, you only need a beard to go with your moustache, and you'll look the part, Brassie," said one of the men.

They all laughed. Brassington looked perplexed, unaware of the existence of the smear, he didn't see the joke. The thought of the rum issue was uppermost in his mind.

At the far end of the dry dock there was the looming backdrop of a gigantic caisson. As usual, there was some seawater trickling down the sides, as only the sheer weight of the water pressure of the harbour outside, sealed it in place. That continuous spray of water served as a constant reminder that they were working 30 feet below the level of the Mediterranean.

Once the four men arrived at the top of the dry dock, George looked back down at the boat lying far below. *E11* looked small within the immensity of the giant dry dock, which had originally been built to accept the bulk of the largest battleships that were at sea. A huge gangway had been lowered down by crane, laying it halfway down the dockside to stretch across to the top of the casing to allow internal access through the conning tower, and the torpedo loading hatches. The Engine Room hull plates were being replaced, following the removal of the old defective armature from the motor generator, and the installation of the new one.

Each member of the crew took their turn at being the cook for the day. Within the dining hall there were scrubbed wooden tables and benches, and the place was swept out every day as the kitchen area was prone to being infested by a type of cockroach. They were huge flying beetles, that the older hands called *Bombay Runners*, as they scampered about the facility. They were thought to be harmless, until one ran up the wall of the mess hut and launched itself into the air, to flutter its way back down to the floor. This quickly became a more frequent event. If someone happened to be in the way there would be an inevitable collision, which would be enough to unnerve any unsuspecting sailor. So, they began to be hunted unmercifully. The lids were always kept firmly on every cooking pot, just in case their guidance system should fail. Nobody liked the idea of biting into a crunchy piece of meat – no matter how fresh.

To amuse the crew during the lunch-break, a dartboard had been nailed to the back of the entrance door of the kitchen. Consequently, it was unwise to enter without checking that a game was in progress.

Once everyone was present, the rum ration was started to be issued from a round wooden tub, with the legend God Save the King in bold brass letters screwed to the side. The Coxswain, ordered his assistant, who was known on board as the Tanky, to pour out the day's measure under his supervision. The men milled around the table expectantly, while the exact amount of rum was being poured from the stone jar into the tub to be mixed with water before it was dispensed.

"Get away from the rum tub, and form an orderly queue," shouted Coxswain Dowell. "You won't get anything until I'm happy with the line."

The men grumpily complied with the order, shuffling into a ragged file. An aroma of boiled cabbage came wafting across from the galley, which served to destroy any appetite that the men may have had!

"Who's cooking today, Swain?" asked Brassington, who was the first man in the queue.

"I'm glad that you asked that Brassington because today we have that great chef de cuisine Stoker Wheeler, who has volunteered to tickle our taste-buds for the whole of this week with his gastronomic talents," replied Dowell.

Then noticing the blue-black smudge under Brassington's nose, a big broad grin creased his face.

"Do you know that it is illegal to grow a moustache in the navy, Brassington? Admiralty Regulations state that you are entitled to grow a full set of moustache and beard, but not just one or the other. So, when you have finished work today, I want your pathetic attempt removed – do you hear me?"

Brassington had not a clue of what the coxswain was talking about. He just nodded, and said that he would. Now where was that rum?

"Wheeler is only cooking to get out of working in the Donk Shop (Engine Room). The gravy that he usually makes could be used as lubricating oil," said Torpedoman Mayne.

"He's not that bad," the Coxswain said in his defence, unable to take his eyes from the colourful wonder that was under Brassington's nose.

"The last time that he cooked, seven of us went down with diarrhoea, Coxswain," replied the same man, gloomily.

"Yeah, his corned beef fritters looked more like something that the Ten Commandments were written on – I cracked a tooth on the batter," replied Mayne.

"Well, in that case, you lucky bastards, we have a real treat in store, cos today he's creating brassica et chops de agnoo avec pummelled poms de terre," said Dowell in a pathetic attempt at a French accent.

George Torode smiled, as his French was fluent. On Guernsey, most people could speak the local version known as d'Guernesiaise, a patois of Norman French.

"Creating? Cremating it, more like!" said the sceptical Mayne. "Wots that then, Swain!"

"Yeh, what's that Froggy rubbish, when it's at 'ome then, Swain?" repeated Brassington doubtfully, his teeth appearing amazingly white under the darkness of his upper lip.

"Lamb chops with mashed spuds and cabbage," smiled the Coxswain, proud in his translation.

Then, applying his mind to the issue of rum, he said, "Right, as you are first in the queue as usual Brassington, take a glass of rum and get it down your neck."

Not needing to be told twice, Brassington picked up the standard glass tumbler, which was two thirds full with the mixture of rum and water, and began playing to the impatient, but captive audience behind him, he ran the glass under his nose in the manner of a wine connoisseur. He then assumed an upper-class accent in an attempt to imitate a gentleman sampling the stock at a St James' establishment.

"Ah – yes – it's a pretentious little Jamaican number. A cheeky distillation created by those dusky Islanders for one's delectation. It glides down the throat in a strangely presumptuous manner. Its aroma catches, nay assails one's nostrils like a hyena with halitosis. The canes were probably cut from the south; no more probably on the southwest side of the plantation with a blunt machete at around three in the afternoon on the second – no I'm wrong there – the third of June 1912... not what one would call a mature vintage."

The coxswain stepped in between him and the queue, swiftly curtailing Brassington's humour.

"Something has certainly seemed to have assailed your nostrils Brassington – wiped it off as soon as you've finished your rum. That is an order. Now get that down your neck lad, or it'll go back in the rum tub as the Kings Measure. Take another second of my precious time, and your arse will be greasing four lace-holes in my starboard boot."

The glass flashed up to the sailor's lips, and its contents were drained in three large gulps.

"It's tantalising bouquet fair rots your teeth," Brassington persisted, licking his lips.

"Piss off," said the Coxswain. "Come on Baxter you're next, come and get your neck oil."

Being the youngest member on the boat, George Torode was always last in the queue. In the hierarchy of the rum tub, rank has its privileges, and it was right that as the youngest he should be the last to be issued his tot. Any of the potent liquid that remained in the tub after the last tot had been issued was pronounced as the Kings Measure, and was emptied into a glass to be passed around to those who wanted an extra sip. A small sip was all that was allowed, and each recipient was carefully monitored by the rest of the men to make sure that it was only a sip.

Five minutes after that last glassful had been drained, the noise level in the hut had risen from the normal conversational level, to that of a cage full of parrots trying to make themselves heard above the furore on the trading floor of the Stock Exchange. Any trivial matter, no matter how menial, was being argued fervently by anyone, and even the most placid of conversations would develop into fierce debates.

The most insignificant of topic's quickly attained ardent defenders both for and against. Any lack of hunger, or reticence to sample Stoker Wheelers culinary expertise quickly disappeared, replaced by ravenous appetites that were eager for a plateful of whatever Wheeler and fate had prepared. Their expectation was quickly dampened however, when the lid was removed from the metal cooking pot. The fact that the meat it contained had once been an animal named a sheep bore no resemblance to the offering that Wheeler had produced. The unappetising looking result from his whole mornings labour left everyone speechless. On the inside the pot, the liquid surface was covered with what looked like tiny orange lily pads, which were in fact globules of fat. A white leg bone emerged above one edge, looking rather like a periscope appearing out of a stagnant pond.

The opportunist Brassington leaned across the table, attempting to remove it, hoping for an extra portion of meat. However, his greed was quickly deflated – because what he extracted was just a white bone. There was not a shred of meat attached to it. The men began to wonder where the meat had gone. As each plate received a ladle full of the contents, curious eyes began to search for anything that resembled a piece of meat. It was then debated that if one could break through the layer of carrots and fat, and to actually delve down into the morass of onions and cabbage that lay in suspended animation beneath, it might have just been possible that they might have found some tiny shreds of meat – or at least the remains of one of the hundreds of Bombay Runners who had misjudged their trajectory. Each bowlful was accompanied by a doorstop sized slice of bread. Fortunately, the doubtful stew actually did taste of meat and everyone ate heartily, during which time Wheeler received many suggestions as to how he might improve his culinary skills. These mainly involved him learning to read, so that he could follow a recipe. At one o'clock, the bosun's call played its monotonous tone once more.

"Out pipes – Hands turn to!"

Some of the gathered assembly had fallen asleep, after washing up their plates, the soporific effects of the rum had taken hold. Card schools were reluctantly abandoned, cribbage boards carefully placed away, and the pack of cards inserted back into its box. Those making use of the dart board on the back of the wooden door, were hurriedly trying to finish their game.

"Come on then – you heard the pipe – let's be having you – get your arses into gear – back to work – I am looking for a volunteer to clear a blockage in the officers heads, and the last one out of this hut will be that volunteer," said Dowell as he entered – just as a dart narrowly missed his ear.

The scramble to get out of the door sent chairs flying.

"A log jam is it, Swain?" asked Mayne. "Is it going to involve dynamite?"

"One of the officers hasn't passed a sheep by any chance, Swain?" quipped Brassington. "Cos it managed to escape from Wheeler's cooking pot."

The Coxswains eyes settled on Brassington's top lip, and any sign humour faded from his features.

"Brassington you 'aven't cleaned your lip like I told you to. That is direct disobedience of an order. I could 'ave you up at the captain's table, or you could take my punishment. What will it be?"

Knowing that he didn't really have a choice, Brassington mumbled.

"I'll take your punishment, Swain."

"Then get yourself down to the officer's heads, and give them a thorough clean. I'll be down there in half an hour, and if they aren't shiny and immaculate then you and your nose will be entered for the high jump."

The sailor vanished in the direction of the officer's accommodation block. The only thing that marked officer's quarters from that of the ratings was the addition of a pair of thin curtains that had been hung in the windows. They also boasted two of the new flushing Crapper toilets, unlike the buckets that were being used in the ratings accommodation block. Rank certainly does have its privileges.

****

The afternoon passed in sleepy indifference, mainly from the effects of the rum, but aggravated by the fierce unrelenting heat. Brassington had re-joined them beneath the tanks after his hour of extra cleaning duties. He was complaining as usual.

"I'm sure that one of their lordships must 'ave given birth to a yule log in there," he declared. "It took me ages to break it up with a big stick, and finally flush it all away. Those new toilets are fantastic though, but then the coxswain made me empty all the buckets from our own heads as well. 'Ere lads, have I got any paint under my nose? The Coxswain keeps takin' the mickey."

"There is still a faint blue smudge on your top lip, Brassy," said George, trying to be honest.

Grabbing up a rag soaked with turpentine, he rubbed it under his nose before picking up his long tom to recommence work. By mid-way through the afternoon, George and his friends had finished two thirds of their painting assignment, when something unusual occurred to break into the daily pattern of life. The bosun's call could be heard whistling up on the dockside, and it immediately attracted everybody's attention. A loud voice echoed around the dock walls.

"Do you hear there – all hands muster at the dockside galley – Standby for the Captain's address."

The painting party stopped working, lowered their brushes, and removed the cloth turbans which they had tied around their heads to protect their hair from the paint droplets. They each looked non-plus at one another; this could mean only one of two things. It was either very good news – or it was very bad news – there would be no in between.

"Wot the fuck is up now?" demanded Mayne, wiping his hands with a turpentine rag.

"I dare say we'll find out when we get up to the galley," said George.

"Do ya think we're gonna get sent back ter the Marmara?" asked Brassington.

Despite his attempt to clean the paint from his lip, there was still a faint blue smudge showing.

"Well, one thing is for certain, we will not be going anywhere without the Engine Room hull plates being fully screwed back in place, and carrying out a dive to check them down to full diving depth, Brassy. That will take at least one day," replied George. "Then they will have to check out and test all the replaced fittings. That should take another day. All we have to do after that is load stores, torpedoes, and take on fuel. That will be another two days. After that we are set to go."

The four men trudged up the stone steps, panting heavily as they finally reached the top.

"Come on you lot, get fell in with the others," shouted Coxswain Dowell impatiently.

"Wots goin' on Swain?" asked Brassington, as he shuffled passed the Senior Rating.

"When the Skipper speaks to us, we'll both know Brassington. Now get fell in and keep quiet. There's still a trace of a blue shadow on your lip."

Brassington wiped under his nose with the cuff of his overalls, creating a fresh bright blue smudge ran from one cheek to the other.

"Is that better Swain?"

Dowell shook his head in disbelief.

"See me afterwards Brassington," he said. "I think I have just found someone to peel the potatoes for tonight's meal."

HMS E11's crew of thirty stood on the dockside in three ranks, awaiting the arrival of their captain. Lieutenant d'Oyly-Hughes stood at the front, and appeared to be as ignorant as to what lay ahead, as the rest of them. Then there came the sound of a car engine, as it rounded the dockside complex, which made all heads turn expectantly.

"*E11* ships company – HALT," shouted the officer in his broad Northern Irish brogue, bringing the crew to attention.

We must look a real ragamuffin bunch of pirates in our working uniforms, with most of us covered with paint, oil, and grease. 'Maybe Brassie is right,' thought George Torode, 'maybe we are an offbeat bunch of modern-day pirates.'

It wasn't one car, but two that rounded the bricked corner of the foundry workshop. Their brake lights flashed, before they came slowly to a halt in front of the squad of men. The door of the first car opened, and out stepped Martin Naismith in an immaculate white dress uniform. He was carrying his ceremonial sword, and he looked very smart – the absolute antithesis of his crew. That in itself was odd, but as he stood smartly before them, he immediately turned his attention towards the approach of the second car. Despite them standing at attention, all eyes swiveled in that direction. Looking through the glass of the car door revealed the presence of an even more august figure. With his gold epaulettes flashing in the late afternoon sun, the Commander in Chief of the Mediterranean Fleet, Rear Admiral John Michael de Robeck climbed out from the opened rear door. His Flag Lieutenant had rushed around from the other side of the car to open it for him. Everyone thought him to be on board his flagship off Cape Helles.

Lieutenant d'Oyly-Hughes marched forward and saluted smartly, and reported to his Captain that the ships company were mustered, correct, and that everything was ready for his address. Naismith, with the Admiral standing behind him, addressed the crew.

"You are all probably wondering what is going on. The Admiral just has returned to Malta aboard a fast destroyer on naval business. He has asked me to muster you all here at short notice for his address."

He then called them all to attention.

"*HMS E11* Ship's Company – HALT!"

Turning to the Admiral, he saluted.

"*HMS E11* ship's company are ready for your address, sir!"

351

"Very good, stand them at ease please, Captain," said the Admiral.

"*HMS E11* Ship's Company – Stand at… EASE!"

The great man moved forward, his Flag Lieutenant at his elbow, who handed him a document.

"Stand easy. Good afternoon men. Can you all hear me? The men in the back rank – am I audible?"

Lieutenant Brown was standing behind the rear rank, and stated that he could hear him perfectly.

"Good," said the Admiral. "I have just received the following message from the Admiralty today, and before it is distributed throughout the fleet, I wanted you all to be the first to hear the news. It reads as follows – Following the very successful patrol by His Majesty's Submarine *E11*, it gives their Lordships much pleasure to announce that His Majesty, King George the Fifth, has conferred the award of the Victoria Cross to her Commanding Officer, Lieutenant Commander Martin Dunbar Naismith." He went on to list the successes of their patrol. He coughed as he reached the end of the first paragraph. Then continuing… "To her First Lieutenant, Lieutenant Guy d'Oyly-Hughes, and her Third Hand, Lieutenant Robert Brown, we confirm the award of the Distinguished Service Order. Again, he read the reason for their award. It was followed, to everybody's surprise, by the final paragraph. To every other member of her Ships Company we award the Distinguished Service Medal for an outstanding patrol. It is signed by His Majesty, King George the Fifth, and Their Lordships of the Admiralty."

He let the news sink in before continuing.

"Men. I want to add my own personal congratulations. Your achievements will go down in the annals of the history of the Royal Navy. Because of you, the Army ashore on the Peninsula is being given a breathing space, and the precious time they need to get the foothold to be able to push forward to take the whole of the Gallipoli Peninsula. Its capture will leave the way clear for us to breach the Dardanelles, and then to attack Constantinople itself. I am pretty certain that these awards are unique within the traditions of the service. I certainly cannot remember another case where the efforts of an entire crew have been so justly rewarded. I want you all to relax during your time here in Malta, because you will be going back shortly to continue your very important work. You will have my full support in all of your forthcoming endeavours."

Turning to Martin Naismith, he continued.

"Now Martin, I would very much like to meet your ships company personally."

Naismith moved aside, and then walked with the Admiral along the files of his men, introducing each man in turn. The Admiral shook each man's hand, having a short word with each of them. Brassington was standing to George Torode's right, and when the Admiral reached him, he stopped.

"Able Seaman Brassington," said Naismith.

"What's that black mark on your face, Brassington?" asked the Admiral.

"It's paint, sir," interrupted Coxswain Dowell, who was following the officers down the ranks. "He has been painting the keel."

"I must say that it makes you appear somewhat sinister, Brassington. A bit like Blackbeard the Pirate – what – Ha-ha!" said the Admiral, laughing at his own joke.

The rest of the officers tittered politely. Brassington looked very pleased with the Admirals comments, he was sure that he was a clever man who certainly knew what he was talking about. They moved on to reach George Torode, Naismith made the introduction.

"Ordinary Seaman Torode, sir."

"Ah, the Guernseyman, who got lost in Constantinople," said the Admiral. "You have been mentioned in dispatches once before. So, this will be your second commendation. Well done lad."

It took George aback, not only that the Admiral heard about his exploit aboard *HMS C301*, but also the fact that he knew that he came from Guernsey.

"You and Lieutenant d'Oyly-Hughes will be coming to see me before you leave for the next patrol. You are a very brave young man who has showed a lot of initiative, and I am very proud to shake your hand."

He moved on, leaving George absolutely shell shocked. Why on earth would an Admiral want to see him, he was just a lowly Ordinary Seaman?

After they passed the last man, the crew were brought up to attention while the Admiral climbed back into his car. After the car had rattled its way around the dockyard complex on its way back towards Fort *St Angelo*, the Captain addressed them all, thanking them for all of their past efforts. As he was about to head towards his car and drive off, d'Oyly-Hughes interrupted.

"Three cheers for the captain – hip-hip-hip."

"Hooray," screamed the men, and then again even louder, as it was repeated.

There wasn't a man standing there who would not have followed Martin Naismith through the gates of hell. He was very touched, and he spoke to them again before getting into the car.

"Men, this is a great day for all of us. Due to your devotion to duty, we have accomplished the virtual impossible. You have more than earned the recognition that has been bestowed on you this day, and I thank you from the bottom of my heart. I'm a very lucky Captain! Coxswain, I want you to pipe leave from now until 0600 tomorrow morning."

He got into his car and was driven away. The crew were dismissed from their ranks, and they mingled together on the dockside until the car disappeared out of sight – then the conversation erupted.

'Fancy old Nazzims gettin' the VC!'

'What about all of us gettin' the DSM, then!'

'We must be the most decorated boat in the whole bloody navy!'

"Three cheers for old Nazzims – Hip-hip…" shouted Petty Officer Green again, tossing his cap in the air.

"Hoorah," shouted the crew for all they were worth.

After the third hooray, they all continued to cheer their elation.

"You heard the Captain, Coxswain. Leave is granted from now, until 0600 tomorrow morning," said d'Oyly-Hughes.

There were yet more cheers.

****

Within the confines of the Porto Bella that night, the party that had failed to happen on that first night of their return from the patrol, actually took place. First, at Horlicks insistence, they were made to sit and listen to his wife's unequivocal version of Ave Maria. He had hired a local musical trio, consisting of a pianist, an accordion player, and a drummer. They did not seem to quiet grasp the tempo of the piece, but they more than made up for it in their enthusiasm in playing. Dominating the centre of the room stood Horlicks large wife, who he had helped up onto an orange box. The crew sat there amazed, as to how anyone could sing so off key. Horlicks was standing behind the bar, with adoration in his eyes, that were damp with emotion. His dog began to howl in time with his wife's higher notes, which received more applause than she did. Being somewhat affronted by the derisive tone of her audience, The Amazing Maria finally waddled out of the bar, her pride in tatters. Once she had disappeared, Horlicks stood on a chair, his hands held up appealing for silence.

"Hey yua – Sailorboys – shutupaya faces – my wife, shesa good – no?"

"NO," came back the instant reply from the crew.

"OK – OK – I know yua donta mean it – yua justa joke a – Eenglish humour – I know yua wanta more – but yua haveta wait – cos Horlicks, he get for yua at mucha money a dancer. Her name ees Marietta, and for yua, she dances the veils seven. Shesa very mucky girl – No toucha the bum, OK!"

Their cheers of approval made Horlicks very happy – he liked it when his boys were happy. When they were happy, they bought more beer, and that made him richer, which in turn made him even happier. Out from an adjoining room appeared the lovely Marietta. At least she must have been lovely once – which had probably been some time before her forty-fifth birthday. To call Marietta voluptuous would have been an understatement. She had more flesh than her seven veils could ever possibly cover. As she had mounted the orange box, the trio struck up an erotic tune, although the rhythm got lost somewhere between the piano and the drums. Marietta stood with her legs slightly apart and she began to gyrate her hips. This, with an occasional pirouette with a wave of her arms, appeared to be her interpretation of Salome's legendary dance. The veils, along with her excess adipose, began to vibrate in sympathy. The sailors looked on in amazement as to how she had the courage to leave the safety of the adjoining room. Soon, there was so much of Maria in motion that sections of her under-arms began to knock into the huge bulge of her melonlike breasts, causing a wet slapping sound. Her excesses of her stomach began bouncing up and down, which also slapped against her breasts. So much of her was slapping, that it put the drummer off his beat.

The sudden clash of the cymbal surprised everyone, and a great cheer went up as the first veil went up into the air and flew across the bar. It landed on Horlicks head, he grinned and held it aloft in triumph – to yet more cheers.

Tonight, they all felt happy, every worry and fear forgotten. Today's good news, combined with good friendship and companionship was all that mattered. Their families and loved ones were safely ensconced at home, and, just for this brief moment in time – they were temporarily forgotten. This was their other family – the men whom they shared all the dangers. Today there was no need to be concerned about anything, and they all needed this evening to ease their minds away from all those terrors that awaited them on their return to the Dardanelle's. If God permitted them to come back from the next patrol unscathed, then they would be only too glad to return home to their loved ones.

George Torode was sat at a table with Basil Partridge, George Plowman, and Albert Lohden. Each of the men was on his fifth pint of beer, and each was feeling nicely mellow and ready for more. They had decided on a new acronym for their newly presented medal – the DSM – not the Distinguished Service Medal, it now stood for Drink Some More.

"That Marietta's a big girl ain't she, George?" said Basil, his eyes never leaving the huge breasts of the dancer.

"A big lady," corrected George.

"Get that last mouthful down yer neck George," said the stoker, trying to imitate the Coxswain at tot time. "I'll get the next round in."

As George was draining his glass, there was another loud clash on the cymbal and the second veil flew through the air and landed on his head. Another big cheer erupted.

"You lucky bastard George," shouted Able Seaman Brassington, standing over by the beer barrel. His bleary eyes were busy devouring the excesses of the voluptuous Marietta.

George couldn't see how catching of a piece of coloured gauze should be so lucky. He gave his empty glass to Basil, who placed it on the table by the beer barrel. Soon they were all consuming the next round of drinks.

"There ain't many of them in a pound, is there George?" shouted Brassington, indicating towards Marietta's melonous breasts. "You could make yerself deaf in between those."

The band in the corner continued to play, before another clash on the cymbals came a little previous, announcing the imminent launch of another of Maria's veils. Those precious few seconds gave Brassington the chance he had been waiting for, and he moved forward into a better position to be able to catch it, but he missed, and the recipient was the Coxswain, CPO Dowell. More cheers were accompanied by many derisive remarks.

George got up to go and relieve himself, making his way down the corridor to the toilets. Standing at the long urinal wall, he let out a long sigh as the pressure on his bladder eased. He was really enjoying the evening, and as he was doing up the buttons on his trouser flap, he heard a low groan from the single WC in the corner. The door was ajar, and he pushed it fully open to find torpedo-man Mayne sitting there snoring, with his trousers nestled down around his ankles. He looked very comfortable, and so he left him there to sleep it off. As he re-entered the bar once more, he was met by another clash of the cymbals and before he knew it another square red cobweb landed on his shoulder. More cheers erupted and there was some excited clapping now. As he passed by the lop-sided grin on Brassington's face, George couldn't help but wonder why he was looking at him so enviously. He must be pissed, he thought.

"What's the matter Brassy, you look like you've lost your last shilling?" said George.

The sailor, who still exuded the smell of turpentine, despite having taken a soapy bath, was still sported flecks of the black/blue paint speckled around his neck. On closer inspection George could still see the faintest traces of the dark smudge on his top lip.

"It's alright for you George, you got your leg over when you were stuck up in Constantinople, and now you're going to dip your wick again. It ain't bloody fair!" he replied, close to tears.

"What do you mean Brassy, how am I going to get my leg over in here?" asked George incredulously.

"You've caught two of the veils now, and there's only two more to come. I ain't got a chance now."

George still hadn't a clue what he was babbling on about.

"What does it matter if I've caught two veils, Brassy?"

"Well whoever catches the most gets to take 'er back into 'er changin' room and fuck 'er."

George stared over at the lovely Marietta. He gulped. Her nearly nude figure looked quite grotesque. Great hummocks of white flesh hung from her, like the sagging bulges in a reefed sail. There was nothing George wanted less than to be stuck in a private room with Marietta. How on earth was he going to get out of this without losing face?

Turning towards the forlorn seaman sitting at the bar, who had his eyes riveted to every crevice that Marietta treated him to, the answer was suddenly very apparent.

"I tell you what I'll do Brassy, seeing as your one of my best mates. I'll let you 'ave my two veils for a glass of Ouzo, and half of your tot tomorrow."

The sailor's brow furrowed, as his alcohol-soaked brain tried to calculate the offer. He took another look at Marietta – rum or Marietta – it was going to be a hard decision for him. Rum and Able Seaman Brassington were inseparable bedfellows, kindred spirits you might say.

"That is good of yer to offa, George – But 'ow about a glassful of Ouzo and a quarter of my tot!"

"You are smooth talking bastard Brassy, and you drive a hard bargain, but seeing as it's you, old mate – done," said George rather too quickly, but breathing a secret inner sigh of relief. He just felt so glad to be rid of the responsibility of the veils as he passed them across the table to him with a wink.

"Bon chance mon brave," he said.

Two more clashes of the cymbals, and the lovely Marietta stood there in her expanded birthday suit. A very happy Brassington had managed to catch one of the last two veils. Doing a blubbery pirouette, she held up her arms, accepting the over-enthusiastic cheers and applause from her audience. Looking like a beached beluga, she awaited the lucky sailor to claim his prize. An over enthusiastic Brassington held up three veils, and Horlicks adjudged him to be the winner. His smile split his face in half, and he raised his thumb in George's direction as he left the room hand in hand with his prize, accompanied by the loudest chorus of cheers.

Horlicks suddenly appeared with a large glass of Ouzo, and placed it in front of George. "Yua friend – he buys thesa for yua."

George shared out the glass of the liquorice-flavoured spirit with his friends. The evening was warming up to be one to remember. He smiled to himself, realising that as he had taken a quarter of the tot from the man who was always first in the rum queue, a deed that would certainly advance his prestige amongst his crew-mates. Horlicks stood on the chair once more, his arms aloft.

"Shutupaya faces – yua like Marietta – no?"

"NO," came back the reply once more.

"Nowa the banda, theya play yua favoureet muzeek whila yua all drinka mucha more beer. Singa the songs ifa yua wanta."

Half an hour later Brassington emerged from the changing room to a rapturous round of applause. His dishevelled appearance made him look like he had just gone twelve rounds with the heavy weight champion of the world. George thought that in a way, maybe he had. His white front was hanging outside of his trousers, with his front trouser flap still hanging down. Milking every moment, Brassington strode around the room, waving a gigantic pair of Marietta's knickers above his head. Just then someone standing at the back of the room near the door, called the whole place to attention, as into the bar of the Porto Bella walked the First Lieutenant, Guy d'Oyly-Hughes.

"At ease men, please carry on. I've just popped in to have a word with Ordinary Seaman Torode," he said to the men standing to attention. Then seeing George, he walked across the room to his table.

The ambient conversation started up once more, but with a somewhat more respectful air.

"Good evening Torode, sorry to interrupt your fun, but I've just called in to tell you that you and I will be going to see the Admiral tomorrow morning at 1000 hours. Do not go down to the dockside in the morning. I will clear that with the Coxswain now. Stay here and get dressed into your number six uniform, and I will meet you here at 0930 – OK?"

"Yes sir, no problem," replied George. "Can I buy you a drink, sir?"

"No thanks, nice of you to offer, but I have to get back to a rather boring function in the wardroom. Looks like you're all having a whale of a time."

As the Jimmy walked back towards the exit, he was bumped into by the inebriated Brassington, who had inadvertently staggered across his path wearing Marietta's knickers over his head. The collision knocked the sailor back onto the floor, mainly due to the First Lieutenant being well over six feet tall and having the body to match.

"If you were correctly dressed Brassington, I'm sure that you wouldn't have tripped over your white front like that," he said with a smile at the corner of his mouth, betraying his false officious tone. "Maybe it was that pair of ladies underwear on your head that blinded you." Then he peered at the sailor's upper lip. "You're not trying to grow a moustache, are you Brassington? They are not allowed in the navy you know. It will have to be a full set, or nothing."

"Shorry Shir," was all he could say.

As the officer disappeared, Brassington, still sitting on his backside, stared after him in disbelief.

"'E's built like a brick shithouse. It was like I walked into a wall," was all he could say.

George drained his glass before he stood up.

"Want another, George?" asked Basil Partridge.

"No thanks Baz, if I'm going to see the Admiral tomorrow, then I'm going to try and get some shuteye. I'll need to have a clear head in the morning."

With that, he said his good nights to the rest of the revellers and left the bar.

****

At 0930 sharp, George was picked up in an official staff car from the front door of the Porto Bella. Horlicks preceded him down the steps and opened the car door for him. He now regarded George with a newfound respect. Naismith and d'Oyly-Hughes were already sitting in the back, as he climbed in beside the driver.

"Good morning Torode, you look very smart, are you alright there, sitting in the front?" said the Captain, adjusting his dress sword away of his legs.

"Did Brassington make it down to the boat OK this morning?" Guy d'Oyly-Hughes continued.

"Yes, I'm fine, thank you sir. Brassington was up and dressed on time, sir. He left the Porto Bella at the same time as the rest of them, so I assume that he made it, sir," George replied honestly.

Riding through the narrow streets of the Maltese capital during the morning was a completely new experience for George. He had only seen these thoroughfares whilst walking back to their accommodation during the late afternoon, after a hard day of work. Nearly all the walls were rendered and whitewashed, or had some pastel shade splashed over their stuccoed exterior, but most were of the plain natural orangey yellow stone. Each house seemed to blend into the next by an unseen join. The front doors opened directly out onto the street, as only the larger roads had pavements. Each opened doorway had a wooden chair filling the gap, usually with an old man or old woman sat on it, taking the first warming rays of the sun. The women, without exception, were clad in a black garb with white lace collars, and a shawl that was either around her shoulders, or over the head. Most of the older men wore three-piece suits, with either a Homburg, or a flat cap. Hand-barrows were being pushed along at a leisurely pace and a pair of laden donkeys followed their owner on the end of a slack rope. Everybody appeared to have all the time in the world. The one thing that George would always remember about Valetta was that there seemed to be a church on the corner of every cross-road in the city. These centres of religious sustenance never closed their doors, and there were always worshipers either going in or coming out. Religion was not just for Sunday's in Malta. George had quickly grown to like the Maltese people. They thought in very much the same manner that the British did. They were invariably friendly, and unlike many other ports of the Mediterranean, they would speak freely to the sailors. After all, there had been jolly jack tars visiting their island for over two hundred years. Maybe the affinity that he felt with them was because of the fact that he too was an Islander.

The car approached the main gate of *HMS St Angelo*, the navy's main shore base, and the Naval Headquarters on the island. Two sailors, dressed in full white uniforms, wearing white belts and gaiters and carrying Lee Enfield .303 rifles, stopped them at the barrier. Both Officers and George produced their Pay and Identity Books for inspection. They were waved on. The sentries sprung to attention and brought their weapons from the slope to the present, slapping their rifle butts in salute as the car passed. The near vertical ramparts of the Fort towered high above them, built in great stone blocks. A series of sloping ramps took them swiftly up towards the Staff Offices of the Admiral.

This Fort had once been the home of the Knights of St John, a religious order of medieval knight's templar, who originally ran the place as a religious hospital. They came under attack from the Ottoman hordes of Islam during their expansion in the Mediterranean, led by the Turkish Sultan Suliman. The knights mounted a heroic defence, using the bodies of their own dead comrades to block any breaches in the walls, and despite the overwhelming odds they proved to be the victors. Malta was never again troubled by the Ottomans, and it was never subjected to serve under the banner of Islam. As a consequence, the cross of St John became the national emblem on the Island flag.

At the Admirals' offices, more sentries appeared, Royal Marines this time, guarding the entrance of the Staff Offices. A smartly dressed Petty Officer saluted Martin Naismith and Guy d'Oyly-Hughes, turned and conducted them all up a carpeted staircase. The Admiral welcomed them into his office, indicating for them to sit in the three chairs that had obviously been previously positioned for the purpose. The men removed their caps, giving them to the Admirals Steward, who retired from the room with them.

"Nice to see punctuality, you're right on time. Well done. Now let's get straight down to business."

George felt decidedly uncomfortable. He wasn't used to mixing with officers, especially ones of such high rank. He shifted on the chair, trying to make his movements unobtrusive.

"I have the official report of your attack on the railway viaduct at Ismid right here in front of me, but I would like to hear your own individual versions of the attack," said the Admiral.

Martin Naismith led the account by telling of how the target was first selected, and of the reconnaissance they had carried out prior to the landing. Guy d'Oyly-Hughes then took over and told the major part of the tale, allowing George to add his comments when necessary. George told the great man about how the Turkish sentry had surprised him, and of how he had had to kill him. Then Guy explained how he had trouble igniting the demolition charge and how they both had to descend the slope at speed under fire. He then let George carry on with his part of the story. As George spoke, he gradually lost his initial nerves, as he noted how interested the Admiral appeared to be. He related right up to the point of how he managed to get to Constantinople.

"I know that you have already told your Constantinople story to various members of my Staff a hundred times young man, but I would like to hear it for myself at first hand," said the Admiral.

George coughed, to clear his throat, and began another account of his adventure. When he had finished, he noticed the Admiral looking at him, his mind obviously churning something over.

"I'm very impressed with all of you, and I want to inform you that I have mentioned you in dispatches to the Admiralty as part of *E11*'s remarkable patrol report. The VC and other decorations are a just reward for one of the most daring naval submarine patrols that has ever been conducted. I believe that this is the second time you have been mentioned in dispatches, Torode?"

"Yes, sir," said George. "On the day that I was about to complete my submarine training I was aboard *HMS C301* when she hit a mine in the Channel last January, and I helped the captain, who was badly wounded, to get away as she sank."

Turning to Naismith, the Admiral addressed him directly.

"I am sorry to inform you that unfortunately the gun that you requested to bombard similar viaducts may not arrive out from England in time Martin. Believe me when I say that I have made my displeasure known, and so initial plans have been drawn up for several more of these covert raids, similar to the one that you carried out. It is vitally important that we hamper the Turkish supply lines as much as possible. That doesn't just mean the sinking supply ships at sea, so please continue to blow up as many bridges and viaducts as you please. You have my complete support. In cutting those rail links, it will cause the Turks just as much disruption, and by the way, another attack on Constantinople would not go amiss, unless they have changed the position of the minefield. The propaganda value of your last raid there, was immense."

Turning once again towards George, he spoke very slowly and pointedly.

"As for you, young man, what I am going to say to you is classified as Top Secret, and it is not to be spoken of outside this room, do I make myself clear?"

"Yes sir," said George.

"We are very interested in Mr Papandross, the man who assisted you with your safe return. He clearly has sympathies to the Allied cause and that could be of great advantage to us. I would like you to land during the next patrol and meet our agent in Constantinople. Then he will help you to make contact with this man once again. I will give you an official letter which I want you to hand to him personally. If he decides that he would like to accept our proposals, then he should respond by giving you a letter in reply. You will then return to a pick-up rendezvous with *E11* with that letter and give it to your Captain. Do you think that you could handle that?"

"Yes sir, but the last time I had a lot of language difficulties. There was no transport into the city. I was lucky enough to have help from Mr Papandross' daughter, otherwise I think that I would have eventually been arrested."

"I know that Torode, that is why I am going to have you met by our man in Constantinople. He is totally trustworthy, and will personally make sure that nothing bad happens to you. Being of Turkish extraction himself, he speaks the language like a native. He will be instructed to take you wherever you wish to go, and to return you afterwards to the rendezvous spot."

"In that case sir, I am sure that the plan should go very smoothly."

"Good," said the Admiral, looking at Martin Naismith. "There will be another briefing before you leave Malta. I am proud of the fact that the navy are helping to bring to a timely end to the appalling casualties that we have been suffering on the peninsula."

With that the meeting was curtailed, and the three of them left the Staff Offices. Before George was allowed to make his way back to the dockyard, Naismith took him aside and spoke to him.

"Remember what the Admiral said, Torode. Don't speak about this to anyone, is that clear? That especially applies to other members of the crew."

"Yes sir," he said, saluting his two commanders, and making his way down to the pier-head to catch a service transport back to the pension.

****

After changing into his work clothes, it was nearly 1130 in the morning when he finally reached the submarine dockside complex. He made his way down towards the stone steps, to help finish painting the underside of the ballast tanks. Basil Partridge met him before he went down.

"Hello George, ow did it go get on with the Admiral? Did you enjoy your cup of tea and sticky bun?"

"I didn't stay that long, Baz," he replied, hoping he would not ask any more questions.

"Oh, by the way. I don't know if you've heard, but the deck gun arrived in port this morning. They're goin' ter fit it tomorrow while we are still in dock."

'Well at least one good thing has happened today,' thought George. Just as he was about to go down into the bottom of the dry dock, another familiar sound reached his ears, the bosun's call whistling its familiar notes?

"Up spirits, hands to dinner – Be very aware as stoker Wheeler is cooking again today."

The warning was very apt, as three of the crew had gone down with diarrhoea that morning. Apparently, the Coxswain had been in the galley all morning watching Wheeler very closely as he scrubbed the place from top to bottom. Once it was to a standard he approved of, he stood over him to check if he was doing anything that could cause an infection. George felt thankful that he was not feeling hungry, but remembered that he still had Able Seaman Brassington's debt to collect.

Chapter Seventeen

The Second Penetration

The Island of Murdos appeared ethereally through the first hints of the early morning dawn. It was no more than a discolouration on the north eastern horizon as *HMS E11* aligned herself at the entrance into the harbour. Passing through the entrance, it looked all too familiar – with the recent arrival of some large supply ships from England being the only noticeable thing that had changed within the confines. These supply ships were arriving on a daily basis, bringing everything that was needed by the task force. Food, stores, and men – they were the life-line for the invasion force. The hustle and bustle of the surface traffic was as hectic as ever. Many of the larger Allied warships remained at anchor, but some were missing, a few having suffered crippling damage, had been sent to Malta to effect repairs.

The hospital ships were the busiest of all the different types of ships. Every day there was a steady stream of casualties arriving from the peninsula, some days were worse than others. These floating medical facilities had been converted from ocean going liners, fully equipped, to the same high standard as a major shore-based hospital. Each vessel came complete with its own teams of surgeons and nursing staff. There were two of these great vessels sitting sedately at their moorings, like basking white whales in the scorching sunshine, one called the Oceanic was the sister ship of the ill-fated Titanic. Many of the minor warships were tirelessly ferrying the wounded from the beaches at Cape Helles, back here to Murdos. A third, medically equipped troopship, had been converted in order to transport the thousands of casualties back home. The sheer numbers of fatalities from the fighting ashore were beginning to match the horrifying statistics appearing on the Western Front. Many of the casualties did not just come from enemy action, but from a number of tropical diseases that were wreaking havoc in the fly infested trenches. Dysentery was killing more men than the Turkish bullets. The over stretched medical teams were working night and day in order to keep up with the influx.

As part of the standing force, the same group of depot ships remained here in the harbour. They provided continuity and succour to their charges. Their hard-working crews toiled unceasingly in their efforts to keep all of the submarines in a fighting condition and ensure that each was totally seaworthy. These dedicated back-up teams provided repair after monotonous repair. Some of the older B Class boats were continually breaking down, and it was a never-ending task in trying to keep them operational. HMS Adamant lay at anchor, awaiting her famous prodigal offspring.

The warships anchored in the harbour on the day of *HMS E11*'s arrival consisted of a couple of the older capital ships, along with three cruisers, and a number of destroyers. Countless merchant vessels filled every available space. Huge colliers and colossal oil tankers floated like sun-drenched metal islands. A shimmering heat haze could be seen rising from their sun-baked decks. Clouds of coal dust billowed, as dark clouds emerged from the holds of the colliers. The crew of the warship berthed alongside could be seen carrying bag after bag across the narrow gangways to replenish their own bunkers. Other warships stood off, awaited their turn to move in alongside to their fill own bunkers, just as soon as this one had finished.

The stores and munitions ships were all very busy. Their derricks moving to and fro to transfer their cargoes onto the tenders for distribution amongst the fleet. Other, smaller supply craft were also queuing to be filled, before they headed off towards the Allied beachhead at Cape Helles. This kaleidoscope of logistical planning set a hectic pace for everyone involved.

As *HMS E11* nosed her way into the lion's den, there was faint cheering from each of the merchant ships that they passed. They exchanged courtesies by the dipping their ensigns. Every guardrail on every warship and auxiliary quickly became crammed with people, all eager to catch a glimpse of the small submarine. *E11*'s reputation lay undiminished – she was enjoying the same world-wide celebrity as any Hollywood film star.

HMS E11 had been relieved in the Sea of Marmara at the end of her last patrol by the arrival of Lieutenant Commander Edward Courtney Boyle in *HMS E14*, who had been ordered to keep up the submarine presence to maintain the Allied threat against Turkish shipping. He was still up there now, as *E11* manoeuvred her way in towards *HMS Adamant,* with her crew stood on the upper deck. From the forward casing, the heaving lines were coiled and ready to be thrown towards the waiting the hands on the fo'c'sle of depot ship. Ratan fenders had been lowered down the ship's side to the waterline, hanging there like giant conkers on a string, to prevent the two vessels colliding heavily, which may cause scratches or damage their ballast tanks. Manilla berthing ropes were hauled up from free flooding sections below the casing of *E11,* and laid out in long lines on the top of the casing. Tied to each eye was one end of a heaving line, which would be used to haul it up towards the bollards aboard *Adamant*. The same thing was happening back aft, and the casing party sweated as they hauled in the slack ropes to bring the submarine ever closer.

Finally, the main motors had finished manoeuvring, and each line had been secured to their own individual bollard on the casing. Once she was secured alongside, a block and tackle lowered the depot ship's access companion ladder down into its position. Being hinged at right angles at the bottom, it resembled a small drawbridge, which then flopped outwards and over onto the submarine casing. After Naismith was piped off *E11*, Captain Somerville and his staff met him at the top of the steps, before all of the officers disappeared down into the bowels of the ship.

One of the first of the crew to leave the boat was Able Seaman Brassington. His destination was a visit to the naval surgeon in the depot ship's sickbay. Since leaving Malta, he had developed an exotic condition with his waterworks, following his enthusiastic encounter with the lovely Maria. Refusing to admit that he had a venereal disease, he had convinced himself that there was nothing wrong by thinking that his penis simply had developed an uncontrollable leak, rather like having diarrhoea at the back end, or as with one's nose that continuously drips with a case of influenza. Following an examination in the sick bay, he expounded this theory to the naval surgeon, who gave a snort of derision after the rather tearful examination, but he was in no doubt as to his diagnosis.

"I tell you what Brassington! You can call it a leaky willy if you want to, but until they come up with better name for it, I am going to call it Gonorrhoea!"

So, it was that the luckless Brassington was temporarily drafted away from *E11*, sent inboard to join the Spare Crew based on *Adamant*, where he joined the ranks of the great unclean. He was not alone in his , and on arrival he was issued with his own mug, knife, fork and spoon, and ordered to use only 'Rose Cottage'. This was a toilet specially laid aside for the sole use of the men suffering a similar condition such as himself! The thing that worried him most of all was that if his medical problem had not begun to clear up sufficiently before they were due to sail on the next patrol, he was going to be left behind.

"I'm not bein' replaced by some Spare Crew ranger!" he declared defiantly. "Those ignorant bastards will never be able to overhaul and refit a torpedo the way Old Nazzims likes 'em to be done. I'm essential to the skipper sinkin' those ships, I am."

The next few days aboard *E11* were spent loading spares for the engines, spares for various other machines, spares for torpedoes, spares for spares. Then they were loaded with their full outfit of torpedoes; and a full load of ammunition for their recently fitted 12 pounder gun that now stood menacingly on their fore-casing. As each load was lifted from the well deck of *Adamant* by the depot ship crane, there was a crocodile line of *E11*'s crew to strike it down below, box by box it disappeared into the innards of the boat. It was like watching a giant conjuring trick, where a bulky pile stores, almost as big as the conning tower itself, slowly disappeared down into the tiny craft?

Although *E11* looked comparatively small on the surface, most of the living space within her pressure hull actually lay below the waterline. All that remained above the waterline were the streamlining of the outer casing over the top of the ballast tanks and conning tower. Even so, on paper she was still a small craft. Everything went below into a restricted space that matched the measurement a sewer pipe, but to the trained submariner it was a cathedral of available stowage space. Tins of corned beef disappeared down into the wing bilges, hidden behind auxiliary machines, and filled the narrow spaces underneath the torpedoes. Packets of dried food, like flour, desiccated vegetables and ships biscuits, went into a store that is smaller than a broom cupboard, until it that was completely jammed full. Everything disappeared into wherever a space could be found, and the position of each item was noted down by the Coxswain. Then smoked sausages, smoked ham, salted beef, and even smoked cheeses, all wrapped in muslin cloth appeared. These could be found dangling from overhead pipes, or hung from any available protrusion away from the damp decks. Bread and bags of pies would also be hanging along the passageway bulkheads, but these would be eaten within the first week – before they started to turn green.

In the final load before sailing, more crated tinned foods would be laid along the single passageway still contained within the boxes, which allowed the crew to walk on top of them. This means of storing was known as laying a false deck. These sealed cans were a modern addition to the submarine fare, and would provide the crew with nutritious food once all of the fresh victuals were eaten, or had rotted away.

The fresh bread and pies would only be loaded at the last minute and would not last more than three days within the humid heat and dampness of the diesel laden air. Any longer than that produced a green mould that developed very quickly to make them inedible, but not to be outdone, the crew would pick out the mould affected areas and eat them, which extended the life of the bread ration to nearly five days. Butter was another victim of the mould, because after three to four days a layer of the furry mould would appear on its surface, but this could be scraped away before use without any consequence, but after five days it would begin to taste like diesel oil.

The sacks of fresh potatoes were stacked in the forward torpedo space, but these were limited to two weeks at the most, before they too became putrid. After the bread had gone, the crew would revert to ship's biscuits for their carbohydrate ration, but these were so hard they challenged even the best set of incisors. Patience and chewing mixed with saliva ensured that they filled a stomach. On patrol, the men would be faced with constant dangers day and night, so they needed good nourishing food to maintain their physical well-being.

Over the coming days, the internal navigation within the boat quickly became a good deal more hazardous to anyone but the most seasoned submariner. Due to the extra crates of food, each man had to walk through the passageway bent forward, while at the same time avoiding banging his head on the hundreds of hand-wheels, stop-cocks, or indeed the bags of suspended food.

On the well deck of the depot ship, each of the submarines alongside had its own designated area, on which a pile of stores would be placed before the crane lifted it over onto the casing of each of the boats lying alongside. It was not unknown for the less scrupulous crews to acquire some extra victuals from the other piles, when guarding eyes were diverted.

"Where are you going Able Seaman Brassington?" bawled the Coxswain, as the luckless seaman was about to make his way up the companion ladder. He had been temporarily loaned back to *E11* to help with the loading of the stores.

"I'm just off inboard to see the Doc, Coxswain," he said.

Dowell walked up to him, as he waited at the bottom of the ladder.

"Another special treatment – is it?" he enquired, with a sadistic grin.

"Yes Coxswain," he replied. "They are bloody agony."

"Well, you had better make sure that you don't come back down here empty handed Brassington," he said, giving the forlorn seaman a knowing wink.

It was sometime later that Brassington reappeared at the top of the ladder, and came charging down the companion ladder three steps at a time. On his shoulder he was carrying a large crate of tinned herrings in tomato sauce.

"Quick," he yelled to the first man in the domino chain. "Get this below as soon as you like, and tell the Coxswain that it's Acquired Stores."

The crate was quickly broken into, and its contents disappeared down the hatch. The light wooden slats of the crate were gently nudged over the side of the boat, where they mixed with the other rafts of stinking flotsam. These floating islets of debris seemed to be magnetised, as they remained tight against the ballast tanks before the reluctant current slowly moved it away towards the stern of the submarine that lay ahead of them. Each individual tin was then passed along the passageway, through the control room, onward through the engine room, past the electrical switchboard of the motor room, to finally end in the after ends. There it was quickly hidden behind one of the tool lockers near the hydraulic rams that operated the rudder. Once all the tins were down, then a large sack of potatoes was then placed in front to hide their existence.

Within five minutes, a red-faced Chief Petty Officer, who was in charge of the depot ship stores, appeared on the casing of *E11*.

"Where's your Coxswain?" he demanded of the Trot Sentry.

"I'll get him for you, Chief," said the torpedo-man Mayne. He went to the hatch and yelled down, "Tell the Coxswain that there's a Chief Jack Dusty from the depot ship on the casing to see 'im."

Jack Dusty was naval terminology for anyone controlling stores. Dowell appeared on the casing.

"One of your thieving bloody crew has just run off with a box of my Herrings In. Where the bloody hell is it?" he demanded.

"Now just a minute, I have been below checking everything that has been coming down this hatch, and I haven't seen a crate of Herrings In. If it should turn up, then I'll make sure that it is sent straight back to the *Adamant* – OK!"

He gave Dowell a sceptical look, but his eyes revealed that he wasn't satisfied.

"I'm sure it came down here," he protested.

"I do hope you're not calling me a liar," said Dowell, with an aggrieved look.

"Oh no," said the Chief.

"Good. Then to show there are no hard feelings, why don't you pop down at tot time, and I'll give you sippers. If I was you, I would go and try that boat berthed on your port side. They have a bunch of magpies in that crew. It makes me feel almost ashamed of being a submariner when this sort of thing happens."

So, the Stores Chief left feeling sorry that he had even considered that the thief could have been anyone aboard *E11*.

****

Just prior to them coming out of the dry dock in Malta, *HMS E11* had been fitted with their new 12-pounder gun, and with it came a new addition to their compliment. Petty Officer John Kirkcaldy had been drafted out from Portsmouth to the boat, to act as their new gun-layer. After a good talk about his task with the Captain and the First Lieutenant on arrival, he was ordered to select a gun crew and train them. A final list of candidates was drawn up, but none had ever carried out any gun drills. The crew had been selected mainly from the Seamen and Torpedo-men. Each man had then been assigned a position on the gun, before he set out to teach them the rudimentary drills, that they would need to know to operate the weapon. It was hard work, and it became quite boring, due to the repetitive nature of his instructions. Once they had been familiarised with the operation of the weapon, it then became a daily set of drills for them to practice. Those not selected for the gun-crew, and this was the remainder of the crew, were assigned positions to pass the ammunition from the internal magazine, up the conning tower, and then up onto the casing to the gun mounting. There had been many opportunities to practice these drills whilst they had been on the passage to Murdos. Petty Officer Kirkcaldy seemed to be fairly happy with the gun crew responses after his first week aboard. He had emphasised that some shooting practice would have to be carried out prior to them sailing on the next patrol. Both the positions of gun-layer, and gun-director could only be improved by practice. Martin Naismith also knew that they would have to practice a Gun Action Surface, and a Gun Action Crash Dive in the event of coming under attack. Everybody was feeling more confident with this new weapon aboard. It would prove invaluable in stopping the smaller vessels, and also inflicting much more damage to the rail installations ashore, without having to land another sabotage party.

****

HMS E11's officers attended a series of pre-patrol briefings. They were informed of the latest defensive deployments made by the Turk in and around the Dardanelles, and what tactics were currently being employed against the submarine menace. There were also talks from the Army, telling them of the latest developments from the front lines over on the peninsula. It wasn't good to hear such dispiriting news, but it did serve to make them more determined to try and bring about a change in the fortunes of those beleaguered troops. So far, despite the submarine successes, the chances of a successful end to this campaign seemed to be slowly ebbing away.

There was a talk by a thin framed lieutenant, with short greased hair, on how the Turkish shipping strategy had changed, along with the tactics and ports their shipping were using in the Marmara. He listed a number of them that had been granted the presence of a protective patrolling destroyer. He also pinpointed the positions of some recently installed shore batteries around those ports, and a hundred other things that might prove invaluable to them. Aerial reconnaissance were doing invaluable work.

Commander Sampson, from the Fleet Air Arm then gave a talk, accompanied by some aerial photographs showing the very latest changes in the Dardanelles defences. The positions of the reinforced shore batteries, newly laid minefields, another new anti-submarine net, and some recent blocking obstructions that had been dropped had all been added since their last patrol. The information was duly noted down by Guy d'Oyly-Hughes, and Robert Brown made notes to amend the relevant charts.

On the twenty-eighth of July, two reports were received. The first one stated that the French submarine Marriot had been caught in the new anti-submarine net just the day before, whilst being dived off Nagara Point. Somehow, she had managed to entangled herself within the wire mesh, and the French crew were unable to extricate their boat. They remained trapped underwater, totally impotent for a number of hours. Eventually, as the air began to turn stale, so they was forced to surface and surrender, and the whole crew were subsequently taken prisoner.

The second report contained somewhat better news. The Army General Staff declared that there was to be a second main beach assault. It stated that fresh troops had already been landed at Suvla Bay, and that it was hoped that this would threaten the enemy from a new direction and force him to fight on two fronts. This should take the pressure away from the Cape Helles beach-head. The majority of the soldiers comprising this new landing force were from the combined ANZAC force.

That very same day HMS E7, under the command of Lieutenant Commander Archibald Cochran, returned safely from her patrol in the Marmara. She tied up next to E11, and there was a verbal exchange of friendly banter between the two crews.

With the crews standing on their respective casings, the flow of jokes and general abuse was mainly orchestrated by Able Seaman Brassington. His incessant bragging began to make the crew of *E7* more than a little angry. They had just undergone those exact perils, and had undertaken the very same risks as *E11,* Many of them began to resent his derision. It quickly developed into a confrontational situation. Peace was quickly restored when their respective Coxswain's emerged, and ordered both of their crews below.

Lieutenant Commander Archibald Cochran of *HMS E7* had had a very successful patrol working in conjunction with Edward Courtney Boyle in *E14*, who still remained up there in the Sea of Marmara. Several stories were related down in *E11*, as the other members of each crew had had more friendly discussions with their counterparts.

With the loss of the Marriot and via the grape-vine, there was rumoured to be a huge new net had been stretched across the narrows at Nagara Point by the Turks. This provided a formidable barrier between the Asian and European shores for anyone transiting north or south. It was reported to reach right down to the seabed, as the French submarine had found out to her cost. On her way out, Cochran in *E7* reported that he had hit the wire mesh at a depth of 110 feet going at full speed. Fortunately, the impact at that speed had been enough to carry her on through. He said that the wire had parted sufficiently to allow his boat to squeeze through without difficulty. The Turks would certainly be able to repair that hole very quickly, and would probably reinforce its strength. It was just another new hazard that would have to be negotiated.

George Torode was ordered to attend a pre-patrol briefing the following morning of the thirtieth of July. It was good that the crews had all been given lockers aboard *HMS Adamant* in which to keep their kit while they were away on patrol. If they had to take everything aboard *E11* it would quickly become infested with diesel oil, the smell would make them un-useable.

George had to change into his best white uniform, and he follow Martin Naismith and Guy d'Oyly-Hughes as they made their way into the cabin of Captain Somerville.

"Come in gentleman," said the Captain to the officers, totally ignoring George. He was left standing there kicking his heels while coffee was served to his superiors. After being under the misapprehension that he too would receive a cup, any hopes were quickly dashed as the officers turned and made their way towards the conference table. George trailed along meekly behind; his deliberate annexation was making him feel angry,

As he entered the conference section, his eyes scanned the luxurious cabin. There was a dimness, caused by there not being many scuttles, enhanced by bulkheads being lined by thick polished mahogany panelling with shiny brass fitments. Inside, the air was hot and stale, but a rotary fan mounted on the deck-head, provided a welcome stirring breeze.

Already seated around the rectagonal table, were Commodore Keyes, Lieutenant Commander Charles S. Brodie, Lieutenant Commander Archibald Cochrane of *HMS E7,* and an unknown man of a middle-eastern appearance, who was dressed very smartly in western style clothes.

Captain Somerville invited the *E11* men to take a chair, this time making sure that George was also seated – not at the table itself – but just behind the officers on a chair placed against the bulkhead, well away from the table. George was beginning to feel really pissed off. Then, as Captain Somerville stood and began making the introductions, when there was a knock at the cabin door.

"Admiral's barge approaching, sir," said the Petty Officer Steward.

"Thank you, Roberts," he said reaching for his cap. "Please make yourselves comfortable gentlemen. I will only be a few minutes."

Everyone around the table looked at each other; a pregnant pause ensued, making everyone feel awkward. Eventually someone broke into their thoughts.

"Your new gun looks absolutely splendid, Martin," said Commodore Keyes, trying to ease the tension.

"Thank you, sir, I am hoping that it will prove to be invaluable on our next trip. Just as *E7*'s twelve-pounder has recently proved to be. I'm sure that we too can make a good case that every boat should be fitted with one," replied Naismith.

A chorus of bosun's calls could be heard whistling the salute up on the Quarter Deck above them, announcing the Admirals arrival. Two minutes later the door opened and Captain Somerville called everyone to attention. The Admiral strode in, heading straight for his chair at the head of the table. Once he had sat down, the rest of the assembly lowered themselves into their seats. The Admiral immediately nodded to Archibald Cochran.

"Welcome back Archie, a good patrol I hear!"

"Thank you, sir. Yes, we did rather well."

"How did you find your newly fitted gun?"

"It was absolutely invaluable, sir. It was especially good for stopping dhows and the smaller vessels, which on a couple of occasions saved us wasting a torpedo. We did quite a bit of bombarding of the enemy positions as well."

"Good – good. Well done. Please pass on my congratulations to your crew. Let's get straight down to business, gentlemen," said John de Robeck, and then looking directly across at Martin Naismith he said, "On your next patrol Martin, you will be carrying at least one extra passenger."

The Admiral turned his attention towards the man in civilian clothes. He was slightly built with strongly pronounced middle-eastern features. There was a thick moustache that matched his curly jet-black hair.

"Gentlemen, may I introduce Mr Karim al Mizri," said the Admiral. "He is the eldest son of a prominent local family, and was educated at both Eton and Oxford. Mr al Mizri has been doing invaluable work for His Majesty's Government for a number of years. Indeed, it was through the efforts of Mr al Mizri, along with the assistance of our own Mr Slade in Constantinople, that we received the first reports of your attack on that city, Martin. He was there on that day you entered the city, and actually observed the panic that your little attack caused. As a member of the Kurdish nation, his people have been subjected to unparalleled persecution by the Turks for many years, so he bears them no love. It is our intention to land Mr al Mizri, along with Ordinary Seaman Torode during the first stage of your patrol. Where is Torode?"

George timidly raised his hand. He inwardly cringed as he became the focal point of the meeting. The Admiral looked directly at him.

"Move your chair to where I can see you," he demanded. "Ordinary Seaman Torode, we want you to make contact with Mr Papandross in Constantinople. It is our hope that once a liaison has been established with that gentleman, he will be able to provide us with vital intelligence that will prove invaluable towards the war effort here in Gallipoli. You will be ably assisted in getting to his residence by Mr al Mizri."

There was a stirring around the table, as his words sank in.

"What we have to do now gentlemen, is to formulate a plan to land Mr al Mizri and Ordinary Seaman Torode somewhere on the coast that is near to Constantinople. It has to be somewhere that is convenient for Mr Slade to drive out to, and be able to pick them up. Where and when, is what we have to decide? Who would like to begin, Martin?"

Martin Naismith looked toward his First Lieutenant, and spoke for the first time.

"My Number One has already drawn up a plan to attack the Turkish railway system again, sir. Our main targets are not very far from the first viaduct that we destroyed on our last patrol. One is a bridge, about ten miles further west, which, if we succeed will prove to be much more difficult for the Turks to repair. However, it will take a much larger explosive charge to cripple it. So, if we could carry some sort of collapsible raft, or even an inflatable rubber boat which was launchable from the ballast tanks, then it would then be possible to transport the explosive ashore. This could be combined with getting Mr al Mizri and Ordinary Seaman Torode ashore at the same time. My First Lieutenant, Lieutenant d'Oyly-Hughes, will be leading the expedition and he will obviously need some assistance in carrying the heavy charges up to the bridge. If we could combine the two operations, the raid would provide the perfect diversion for them to make their entry into Constantinople. My First Lieutenant could be back on board by the time the detonators go off, and if I were to make myself visible at the same time, it would serve to divert the attention of any sentries."

The Admiral listened intently, nodding his head at the logic of the plan.

"Sounds like a sound idea to me, what do you think, Roger?"

Roger Keyes readily agreed. He was so encouraged by the sheer audacity and daring of the plan that he gave Martin his immediate full support. *E11*'s first covert landing had been the first ever attempted by a submarine, and its success opened the door for more.

"Good," said Admiral John de Robeck. "Just where exactly is this bridge? Someone get me a chart of that area."

Guy d'Oyly-Hughes reached into his briefcase and extracted the folded Admiralty chart. Opening it out across the table, it revealed the whole of the Sea of Marmara. He stood at the Admiral's shoulder, and began pointing.

"You can see the Gulf of Ismid, right over here on the top north eastern corner of the Sea, sir," he said indicating to the area. "You can also see that the railway heads eastward from Scutari along the shoreline to the first viaduct that we destroyed, which is here, sir."

The Admiral peered over at d'Oyly-Hughes' finger, his head nodding.

"We have had an intelligence report which stated that the same railway was operational again within seventy-two hours of you blowing it up," said the Admiral. "Let us hope that your next target will be harder for them to repair."

"Well, ten miles back towards Scutari, there is another small inlet, sir. It is more of a ravine type split in the cliff, where a stream cuts down between the two sides. There are two stonework pillars that take another iron girder box bridge across that divide – much like the other bridge we destroyed. If those pillars are blown sir, it could hamper the Turks for a number of weeks because they would first have to rebuild them, before they could reposition another girder box bridge. Also, it's less than twenty miles to Scutari back along the railway track, so Mr al Mizri and Ordinary Seaman Torode could be in the city within an hour of being landed. That is, providing there is a car waiting there to pick them up. As you can see from the chart sir, it's quite a big bridge, so I won't be able to carry enough explosive ashore on my own. My original plan was for Ordinary Seaman Torode and myself to swim ashore, pushing a much larger raft, as we did before. If a rubber boat were to be made available, we could take it with us on this patrol, and we would be able to load it with double the amount of explosive. It would be enough to smash those stone pillars to smithereens, sir."

The Admiral looked pleased, and smiled.

"Well I'm convinced. If it's approved by your staff Roger, then it's OK by me," he said. "Can you drum up a rubber boat for *E11*?"

Roger Keyes nodded.

"I am sure that one can be found, sir. I cannot see much wrong with the plan at the moment. I'll get my chaps to go over the finer details, and contact Mr Slade to arrange dates and times etc."

"Right gentlemen, let us now move ahead to the actual meeting with Mr Papandross. Ordinary Seaman Torode is the only one sat here who has actually met this gentleman, so it is essential that he be the one to re-establish contact. Mr al Mizri here will be on hand to get him there safely. Torode will be carrying with him an offer from us of very good terms, should he decide to assist us. It appears that he favours the Allied cause over the Turkish alliance with the Austro-Hungarian German pact. Knowing what you know about the man, do you think that he will accept this offer, Torode?"

George coughed nervously.

"Er – Yes sir, I'm sure he will. His main worry, as far as I could tell, was for the safety of his ships. He was very worried that they would be sunk, because the Turks are not guaranteeing him any remuneration. The Turkish military are making him use of his fleet to carry their lesser important logistical supplies. If we could guarantee his ships a safe passage, then I think that he would be willing to do more or less anything that we ask of him. With him having no protection or insurance from the Turks, I am doubly sure that he will want to avenge the killing of Mina – I mean Miss Papandross – his daughter, sir. I know exactly where he lives, but as I mentioned before, his butler is a traitor who reported us to the Turkish authorities. I recognised him on the quayside on the night I made my escape. I'm not sure if Mr Papandross is aware that he has a spy in his household, sir! So, all the while that he is working there, everything that takes place there will be reported to the Turkish security, and any attempt to contact Mr Papandross will definitely be reported to the Civil Militia. I would rather not go near the place until I am sure that he is not going to be there, otherwise there is a big chance of my being arrested."

"Ummm! That is a good point," said the Admiral thoughtfully. "This butler could certainly be the fly in the ointment, and he could affect the outcome of this whole operation. He will have to be disposed of before the meeting takes place. Can you handle that, Mr al Mizri?"

All eyes turned towards the suave looking man, seated next to Roger Keyes. He spoke for the first time, his voice surprisingly deep, considering his slight stature.

"If you mean can I kill him, Admiral – the answer is yes, sir. I have a number of contacts within the city on whom I can call. I could possibly do it myself. It may cost money of course, but the task itself should not be a problem. We can make it appear like a bungled robbery, so that it cannot be linked to Mr Papandross. Once this young man and I reach Constantinople itself, I will have my own car at my disposal, so we can go to my lodgings, from there I can make more definite plans to get rid of the butler. I can almost guarantee you that he will disappear the following day, and we will then be able proceed to make the contact."

George was surprised by the man's impeccable English, with hardly a trace of any accent. His facial features had shown no emotion as he made the offer to kill the butler.

"I think that I would be happier if the man disappeared without trace, but as you say the Turkish security people might just get suspicious. The botched robbery scenario might make them less suspicious!" said the Admiral.

The assembled officers nodded their agreement.

"Hopefully by the time that that the butler's body is discovered, we will have this young man back at the recovery point, awaiting to be picked up by your submarine."

"Will the butler's death compromise, Mr Papandross?"

"Not if it is made to look like a robbery, sir."

"I'll leave that to you and your team to work out Roger," said the Admiral to Roger Keyes.

"I'm sure that we can come up with a satisfactory solution, sir," replied the Commodore.

"OK, OK," said the Admiral. "That all seems to be very clear cut to me. Has anybody anything more to add?"

"Yes sir," said Guy d'Oyly-Hughes. "When exactly would you like this little event to take place?"

"I'm open to suggestions there, but I think that the sooner rather than later," said the Admiral. "I want this man on board supplying us with information as soon as possible."

Martin Naismith raised his hand.

"May I then suggest that we make it one of our first priorities, sir? I suggest within the first few days of my arrival in the Marmara, and as soon as the strategic situation allows," he said. "Then if there should be a mishap, it will give us more time to try again, and to make alternative arrangements. We are going to need to arrange a rendezvous to recover Mr al Mizri and Ordinary Seaman Torode, once the mission has been achieved."

"Mr al Mizri will be staying in Constantinople, but as you say, we will have to recover Ordinary Seaman Torode," said the Admiral. "I'll leave that side of things to you and your staff, Roger. You can liaise with Martin before he sails."

Commodore Keyes nodded again, making a note on his pad.

"There's just one other thing, Martin. You know of course, that Edward Boyle in *E14* will still be in the Marmara when you arrive, and I obviously do not need to tell you to have a good chat to Archie here, before you leave. Boyle apparently is also doing very well, so between the two of you, the Turks will not know which way to move. Just watch out for that bloody new anti-submarine net, as we don't want you going the same way as the poor old Marriot. Has anyone any questions?"

There were none.

"Well – I think that just about settles things. I wish I could stay longer Somerville, but I've another meeting with the bloody Pongoes in half an hour. Thank you, gentlemen, and good luck."

George remembered the term Pongoes, from the day that he joined up at St Peter Port. He had heard it used many times since being here in Murdos, but it seemed rather strange to hear the Admiral using the term. The men around the table stood to attention, as the Admiral left the cabin.

****

HMS E11 had finally completed her storing and taken on fuel. She had then moved from the haven at Murdos, across the Aegean to the harbour at Kephalo on the fourth of August 1915. The war was one year old today, and there was still no end in sight. The submarine lay berthed once more alongside another G Class destroyer, *HMS Greyhound* this time. She had arrived under the cover of night, to prevent any reports being passed to the Turks. She was fully loaded now, and totally ready to go.

A small rubber boat had been supplied, which was rolled up very tightly, and been stowed in the Forward Torpedo Space. When it had arrived Torpedoman Brassington had immediately claimed it as his own property, and was already using it as his bed. The crew got quite excited when they saw it, thinking that they were going to have good sport during the Hands to Bathe periods, something had proved to be so popular on the last patrol.

The other thing that they managed to bring with them at the last minute was Able Seaman Brassington. His exotic ailment had cleared up sufficiently to allow the doctor to pass him fit for sea. The Coxswain had not been amused however, as he had been informed by that same doctor that he would have to continue to administer the treatment once a day for the duration of the patrol.

"Do you know Brassington, you cause me more work than any ten others in this crew," said Dowell. "Now I have to treat your leaky willy because you can't keep your trousers buttoned up."

"Sorry Swain," said the luckless seaman, smiling.

"You do know that you could be charged with wasting good oxygen, don't you Brassington?" continued Dowell.

"Yes Swain," answered Brassington, still smiling.

"In all my time in the Andrew, and with all of the people I have met during my twenty years of service, I consider you to be the best example for the legalisation of euthanasia, Brassington?"

"What's that ooothenise… thing, Swain?" his smile had been replaced by a perplexed frown.

"I rest my case, Brassington," said the Coxswain resignedly, dismissing the man from his presence.

Karim al Mizri had embarked earlier that evening, just an hour before *E11* had slipped her lines from *Adamant*. His presence aboard immediately created a lot of curiosity and speculation, and once the crew had found out his name, he was promptly nick-named Old Misery. It proved to be an inappropriate nick-name, because the Kurd always wore a broad smile, and possessed a very good sense of humour.

After lying safely securing alongside *HMS Greyhound*, the following day was been designated as a day of relaxation for the crew of *E11*. There was a chance to swim over the side, write letters home, and visit the small canteen aboard the destroyer to purchase some last-minute luxury items. The crew had been informed that they would be sailing at 2300 that same night. Everybody wore an air of expectancy, tinged with the fear of the unknown perils that lay ahead of them. The loss of the French boat Marriot bore witness to the fact that the Turks had not been idle since they had returned from their last patrol. They would shortly be facing those very same dangers.

A TOP SECRET report stated that there had been a sighting of a German U-boat at the Golden Horn naval yard in Constantinople. It was thought to be the same submarine that had torpedoed the battleship *HMS Triumph* on the twenty-fifth of May, and had also damaged the battleship *Majestic* two days later on the twenty-seventh off Cape Helles. Intelligence stated that the U-21 had arrived in Constantinople on the fifth of June for repairs and refit. Her Commanding Officer was known through intelligence to be Lieutenant sur see Hersing!

On that afternoon prior to sailing, George Torode was sitting on the casing. He had managed to write a long letter home to his parents, and another extra-long one to his Gladys. As he wrote, he had looked around the small harbour, realising that she was so very far away – it was almost as if she existed in another world. Then he realised that she was. The war was not being fought on British soil, although the rising casualties were affecting many families. Before the last patrol, she had sent him out a small portrait photograph of herself, which he had kept safe tucked inside his cap, but for this coming patrol he had managed to buy a small frame while in Malta, in which to keep it. He had managed to wedge the frame between two pipes in a corner of the forward crew's quarters, and he would be able to see her image every day from now on. The picture had quickly been spotted by his mess-mates, which had evoked several compliments, making him feel happy. He knew that this would probably be his last chance to be able to sit in the sunshine for several weeks. When he finished his correspondence, he placed the two letters on the Coxswains bunk – they would all be collected and taken aboard the destroyer before sailing.

At 2230 the submarine went to Diving Stations, and once the boat had been converted from being a surface craft into a submersible that would be able to dive in less than a minute, the full realisation that they were commencing another patrol finally hit home to the crew. Since arriving back at Murdos everything had just been a daily routine of storing, fuelling, loading torpedoes, gun drills, but tonight was the culmination for that all of that hard work.

HMS E11 was ready to sail, and Naismith went up to the bridge and ordered Harbour Stations in readiness to slip. The casing party came up, and quickly singled up the berthing ropes. She was now simply held alongside the destroyer by just two springs, and a single breast rope forward and aft. At a signal from the bridge, all of the lines were let go, and the main motors churned up a slight disturbance at the stern. The propellers slowly forced the boat away from the warship. Looking up, there were a line of ghostly faces staring down at them from guardrails of *HMS Greyhound*. Each one of them appeared to be very content to be where he was, feeling sorry for those below them in their steel coffin, off on their way out to face God knows what.

"Standby both main engines – stop together – engage both engine clutches – engage both tail clutches."

There was only a slight delay, before the reply came that both diesels were ready to start.

"Start both main engines. Half ahead together – revolutions 360 – steer 085."

There was a rumbling cough, followed by tympanic roar as each of the engines fired up, slowly rising in volume as the revolutions were applied, and the rush of air down the conning tower quickly increased to a howling gale.

George Torode was the upper helmsman once again. Petty Officer Green was standing by the lower helm down in the control room, ready to take over should they have to dive in a hurry. George took a deep breath, steeling his mind against whatever he may have to face over the next twelve hours. He could feel an inner excitement holding his fear in check. As the increased revolutions drove the boat ever faster, the wind began to ruffle his hair, making him feel good.

They made a slow turn, and the destroyer began to melt away into the darkness astern, as their bow began swinging around towards the pencil beam search-lights at Kum Kale, standing over on the far side of the entrance at Cape Helles. The line of the hills along that Asian coastline could just be made out against the starlit sky. There was the occasional explosion that erupted over on the peninsula, a brilliant flash preceded a red glow before fading away to darkness. The flashes of artillery fire were like watching lightning out at sea, momentarily illuminating the hills in a monochromic second of time.

"It's fuckin' eerie, ain't it, George?" said George Plowman.

"I'd hate to be in those trenches. It must be hell on earth over there," replied George.

"I suppose all those Pongoes would say the same about goin' to sea in a submarine," said the Signalman philosophically, as he scanned the horizon with his binoculars, his body turning slowly as he continued to sweep around. Suddenly he stopped, his gaze settling on a bearing.

"I've got a bow wave visible at green 165 sir," he called to the two officers, standing at the front of the bridge.

"What do you make of it, Plowman?" said the captain.

"It looks like it's the *Greyhound* sir, coming to escort us in. It's definitely a destroyer. I think that she's one of ours, sir."

Naismith readied himself to dive the boat, should he have to, waiting anxiously for a better identification. There was a sigh of relief when it did indeed prove to be the *Greyhound* overhauling them. She passed up their starboard side, taking a leading position half a mile ahead. The sparkling phosphorescence of her wake was clearly visible, which made station keeping that little bit easier.

There was another flash off to port, as a star shell illuminated the hilly landscape. George remembered the star shell fired that night he had walked along the beach back the Allied lines. He remembered how it had turned darkness almost as bright as day. The iridescent light hung in the sky, like a pendant electric bulb. The sudden crackle of machine guns, followed by the snap, snap, snap of rifle fire accompanied its appearance. More artillery duels commenced, and trench mortars began to fire.

Each shell explosion was now plainly visible, and several columns of smoke rose up in quick succession, like raindrops on a puddle.

A cruiser sped past them a mile or so to starboard, heading back towards the south west. Another mile and they began passing the group of minesweeping trawlers that lay stopped in the water, all completely blacked out. George remembered them from their last entry. Cape Helles seemed to loom up very quickly, and *E11* passed around the point of land less than a mile from the shore.

"Not far now mate," whispered George Plowman, rubbing his hands together excitedly.

"Not far to what! To face those bloody killer currents that try to carry us over onto the shoals. To come up against the new strengthened submarine net that reaches down to 200 feet, or maybe having to dodge in between those mine mooring wires. Maybe you are looking forward to be fired at from the gun batteries every time that we raise our periscope. Is that what you want, George? We've lost enough boats in these waters already, and at the moment we are favourites to be the next. If you're looking forward to that mate, you need your head examined."

George Plowman looked crest fallen.

"Port ten," ordered Naismith, at the front of the bridge.

"Port ten," repeated George, swinging the wheel to apply ten degrees of port rudder. "Ten of port wheel on, sir."

"Very good," said Naismith, as he brought *E11* around Cape Helles to enter the Dardanelle's proper.

The search-lights over at Kum Kale were plainly visible as they panned out across the water ahead of them. Every time they came close, it caused George involuntarily to duck his head. He smiled to himself. It was stupid, he knew, but the next time it came around he did the same thing.

The other search-lights, further up the channel, could now be seen quite plainly, their white pencil beams probing the darkness. If they managed to locate *E11*, then all hell would break loose from the high ground up above that far shoreline? That was where the gun batteries were located, and from the practice that Johnnie Turk has been getting of late, they were pretty accurate. They travelled another three miles before *Greyhound* turned sharply to starboard, and flashed past them heading back towards Kephalo. The rising whine of her turbines could be heard quite clearly, as they raised her speed up towards twenty knots.

They were completely alone once more. If most submariners were honest, this was the way they preferred things to be – isolated – masters of their own destiny.

George's thoughts strayed from the imminent dangers around him, thinking that the nervousness he was experiencing in the pit of his stomach must be how stage actors feel on the opening night of a new play. Butterfly's, they called the trepidation of facing an audience for the first time. It was much the same for him now, because he was about play his part in another patrol, but here, he was fully aware of how the audience here would react should they detected the presence of *E11*. He shuddered – no, it was not butterfly's he was feeling, it was sheer bloody terror.

"Keep a steady course, Torode – you're two degrees off the heading."

"Sorry sir," he said, applying the corrections to the helm, knowing that he would have to concentrate better.

Standing beside Martin Naismith was Robert Brown, staring through his binoculars.

"I can just see Kephez Point, sir. It's being silhouetted by the large search-light at Chanak. Five degrees on the starboard bow range about two miles."

Naismith checked out the bearing.

"Yes, I have got it! Well done navigator. You can go below now, and take Plowman down with you. We'll be diving very shortly. Steer 051 degrees, Torode."

"051 degrees, sir," George replied.

The two other men made their way below as ordered. The howling air whistling down the conning tower increased as their bodies restricted the air flow. The noise of the diesels seemed deafening in the surrounding silence of the night. 'They must be deaf if they can't hear us,' thought George, amazed how they could not, remembering feeling the same thing on the first patrol. Once the two had disappeared below, Naismith turned to the youngest member of his crew.

"Do you have any reservations about your forthcoming mission, Torode. With Mr al Mizri's help, do you think that you can get him to the right address, OK?"

"Oh yes, sir, I'm pretty good at remembering landmarks in foreign places. I soon found my way around Valetta and Gibraltar with no problem. It was a long walk uphill – nearly a mile I would say – I remember a huge office building next to a small mosque. It led into the road where Mr Papandross houses lies. I remember the road quite distinctly. It was lined with trees, an avenue if you like. His house was about another mile down that road. It lay back in its own grounds and there were two white-washed stone pillars at the gate, each had a pyramid on top."

"It's all very well finding your way around friendly cities Torode, but Constantinople is the heartland of our enemy. If you are caught, they won't be making the same mistake twice. You were very lucky to escape on your last adventure. If they catch you again there will be no way that you will be getting back to us. I am going to fix up a rendezvous point, and give you some precise times to be picked up. If you are not there on the first pick up, I will return at the same time every two days, until we do pick you up – do you understand?"

"Yes sir," replied George. "You'll give me all that information before we go ashore, will you, sir!"

"Yes, there's no need to worry as there will be a full pre-mission briefing."

George felt somewhat reassured. He looked at his captain, standing behind the canvas screen at the front of the bridge, when something caught his eye, just to the right of Old Nazzims head. There was something moving in the water over there.

"Sir," he whispered. "Green 25 degrees, there's something moving over there."

Naismith's binoculars where up in an instant, searching the bearing.

"Secure the wheel, and get below," he snapped. Then he called down. "Steering from lower helm – Course 051 degrees – Stop both engines – Out both engine clutches – Engage both tail clutches – Slow ahead together on main motors."

George secured the upper helm, and was on his way down within ten seconds. The whole of the control room team watched his arrival.

"Take over the helm P.O.," he said to Petty Officer Green. "The heading is 051 degrees."

"What is it, Torode?" asked Guy d'Oyly-Hughes.

"There was something moving over on the starboard bow, sir," he replied.

The two blasts of the klaxon sent everybody scurrying to carry out the emergency dive. The main vents were opened, the Kingston valves opened, the giant muffler valves were still being shut as the engines were stopping. The auxiliary tank was being flooded. The Coxswain and the Second Coxswain began turning the diving planes hand wheels to operate the fore and after hydroplanes, placing them both hard to dive. Both engine clutches were quickly disconnected, to allow the switchboard operators to Group Up the main motors. The motors hummed as they drove the propellers through the tail clutch, giving them the speed necessary to take the submarine quickly under the water. Naismith's feet appeared on the ladder, followed by a loud dull clunk as he shut and clipped the conning tower hatch.

"Destroyer bearing Green 45 degrees," he said to Lieutenant Brown. "Take her down to 60 feet – steer 045 degrees. Achi Baba bearing 342 degrees – Kephez Point bearing 053 degrees. That was all I could see. Well spotted Torode."

"Was it a Turk, sir?" asked Guy d'Oyly-Hughes.

"Couldn't see what she was, but I wasn't going to wait around to find out."

"On depth – 60 feet sir."

They stayed deep for fifteen minutes. At 0110, Naismith decided that whoever it was must have passed clear.

"Bring her up Number One," said Naismith, standing by the search periscope.

"Hydroplanes five degrees to rise – Keep 30 feet – Pump auxiliary," ordered the First Lieutenant.

Stoker Wheeler, the demon chef from the Maltese dock-side accommodation, stood ready to raise the periscope as the deck tilted upwards at the bow. The planes-men used a bubble set in a slightly curved spirit level glass known as a clinometer, which had been calibrated to give the angle set on the boat. Using their hydroplane controls, the two men could set the exact amount of rise or dive they required to maintain the angle for the propellers to drive the submarine up or down. Everybody instinctively leaned their bodies towards the bow, while the boat climbed slowly up through the water.

"50 feet – 45 – 40 feet..." sang Dowell's voice, from the after-hydroplane position.

"Up periscope," ordered Naismith.

Wheeler sent the brass tube hurtling up through the water-tight gland set in the top of the pressure hull. Grabbing the two handles, Martin scanned swiftly around the horizon, breathing a sigh of relief.

"Nothing in sight, Kephez Point is coming up. I estimate that we are about one and a half miles from the start of the minefields. Lieutenant Brown, the best bearing I can get of Kephez Point is that – 074 degrees," he said. "Pay attention everybody – we are going deep now to transit through the Kephez Point minefields. Tell the Fore-Ends to listen for mooring wires. I want complete silence. Down periscope, take her down to eighty feet Number One."

Guy d'Oyly-Hughes nodded. "Eighty feet, aye, aye sir."

"Use five degrees of bow down bubble, keep eighty feet – flood auxiliary," he ordered.

The bow began to tip downwards as the motors drove the boat ever deeper into the blackness. The angle on the boat made everyone lean instinctively back towards the stern this time, and as the boat's angle levelled off, so everyone stood upright once more.

"On depth eighty feet."

"Very good – Slow ahead together."

They felt a very slight vibration, which made the boat roll imperceptibly, as a series of cross-currents tried to grab the submarine. Were they being carried across the channel on to a shoal? Naismith, following his instinct and the knowledge that he had gained from the previous patrol resisted the urge to come shallow to check their position. Beads of perspiration began to form on everyone's brow. The terror had begun.

Would they get safely through the minefield? That was the next challenge facing them. Their ears strained, but this time they were lucky, and there were no mine mooring wires heard scraping along the hull.

An hour later, all was still as the boat moved along at the slow speed setting. Miraculously the transit through the minefields had gone totally without incident. The Navigator used their Dead Reckoning position to ensure that they were well past the danger, and Naismith brought the boat up to periscope depth once more.

On arrival a quick navigation fix revealed a surprise, and everyone could hear the huge sigh of relief from the Captain. He was astonished, because they already were approaching Chanak and Kalid Bahr, the deep-water currents had carried them along like an express train once more.

"Starboard ten – Steer North," said Naismith, still using the periscope to navigate his way through the dangerous turn. "I can see the lights at Nagara Point ahead. Number One, when we go deep at the anti-submarine nets, I want you to go up in the conning tower. You can use the tower viewing ports to look ahead to warn me if we are not going to make it, or you can give me any advice should we hit a snag."

"Aye, aye, sir," said Guy, as he climbed up the steel rung ladder, and disappeared up through the lower hatch.

The conning tower was fitted with an upper and a lower hatch. When one stood inside on the rim of the lower lid, just below the closed upper hatch there were four viewing ports at eye level fitted into the forward and after, port and starboard sections of the circular tower. They were quite small, circular, and each contained a one-and-a-half-inch thick piece of glass mounted on to a rubber seating. They were originally designed to be able to carry out surface navigation in extremely severe weather, where an open hatch might prove to be prejudicial in heavy seas.

At 0305 with the submarine still at periscope depth, Naismith finally sighted the line of buoys that was supporting the new steel mesh net. They stood out as a black dotted line along the reflected silver surface of the sea from the search lights at Nagara Point.

Was that a new search-light off to starboard?

No! Naismith quickly realised that the Turks had trained a single fixed search-light permanently on to the line of buoys, that would allow observers the chance to see any significant disturbance created by a submarine trying to penetrate the barrier. It was rather like the Turks acting as the net umpire during a tennis match, with their finger resting on the wire to detect a faulty serve, because there was going to be an awfully large faulty serves when the submarine tried to burst through that net.

"I can see the nets, dead ahead, range is half a mile. Standby – we are going to try a first-time immediate penetration. Going deep now. Half ahead together. Keep 110 feet. Number One, get ready at your position. Navigator, take over the trim. Down periscope."

The boat slid swiftly down to her new depth under the increase of power. Naismith hated having to use the extra battery power, but knew that he needed the speed to try and get under, or to force a hole through the net. The battery would be exhausted that much quicker, but he had already decided to use the same method that Archie Cochrane had used in *E7*, when he had emerged from his recent patrol. Not long to go now!

"Full ahead together."

Being six feet tall, Guy d'Oyly-Hughes was standing on the top rung of the ladder, as he squatted in the cramped confines of the conning tower, looking out through the forward observation port. These four ports provided the only windows available to look out from inside the boat. Looking through the forward viewer, he could see nothing, the water ahead was very dark. Off to the right there was a lighter sector, but there was no sign of the net.

Suddenly there was a change in the intensity, as a slight flicker of light appeared from the surface, flashing as it passed overhead – the beam of a search-light was passing over them. Smaller flashes of tiny phosphorescent particles suddenly began to appear, then they would flash by on either side. Suddenly the water ahead began to lighten like an underwater dawn. He realised that it must be the fixed search-light that was illuminating the line of buoys at the surface. The new glow slowly intensified, and he began to make out the elongated shape of the forward casing, all the way up to the bow. It looked ghostly, monochromic, totally surreal under water, as mottled pools of light began to dance over the steel plates.

"Fixed search-light glow visible ahead, sir," he called down the tower.

The water assumed a strange opaqueness, when slowly the squares of steel wire mesh began to materialised through the unnatural light. Suddenly the whole net appeared just in front of the bow. At that precise moment, Guy recalled what had recently happened to the French boat Marriot, which had become entangled at this very spot, and how she had been finally been forced to surface.

"Net is dead ahead. We are just about to hit it, sir!"

"Standby everybody, brace yourselves," Naismith said aloud. The word was quickly passed through the boat. "Hold on to something firm."

As Guy d'Oyly-Hughes watched, the boat's bow ran directly into the squares, their symmetric square patterned form was violently distorted out of shape. A sudden heavy jolt was felt throughout the boat, which caused everyone to stagger forward a pace.

Were they going to get straight through – or – had they been caught? Were they going to be trapped in this steel snare? The same questions were flashing through everybody's mind. Strangely enough, the wires appeared to snap on impact, allowing the boat's bow to squeeze itself on through.

"It parted on impact sir. We're nearly through... wait, we are snagged aft, sir... no the wire is moving along the after casing... still moving... it's gone, sir – we're through!"

The running wire, that stretched from the bow to the top of the periscope standard, lifted the top of the hole neatly over all the protrusions of the forward gun mounting, the conning tower, the bridge itself, and the periscope standards. They shot through the hole before something seemed to snag at the after-end of the boat. There was a loud screeching of steel on steel, as the wire was drawn in towards the stern. Then there was a loud crack and all went silent. The boat gave a jolt of freedom, and they were completely through the hazard.

A faint cheer could be heard from the more remote compartments, as imprisoned fears escaped from dry throats in an exhalation of relief. It was 0315 and they had just passed through, what they hoped was, the most hazardous stage of the voyage.

Now they had to negotiate the sharp turn at Nagara Point in virtual darkness. Martin Naismith knew that if he were to raise the periscope, his presence would be detected almost immediately, but he needed to check his position. He raised the periscope, and very quickly took his fix. Above on the hills and cliff-tops, the fires glowed around the gun positions that lined this narrow sector. Strangely they had not been detected – maybe because it was such a dark night!

Ahead, the waterway took an almost right-angular turn, in their passage, and Martin became concerned enough to raise the periscope once more. It was very reassuring that they were not fired on immediately. It was so dark that Naismith kept the periscope up most of the way through, without a single shot being fired at them.

Disappointingly the anchorage at Nagara Point was completely empty. He had secretly harboured a hope that one of the Turkish battleships might be lurking in there. This time he was unlucky! Maybe he would be lucky on the way home! Undeterred, he checked out the second anchorage at Ak Bashi Liman and found a large transport lying there.

"Flood both bow tubes – equalise and open bow caps – Charge both firing reservoirs," he ordered, bringing the boat around to get a good firing shot.

On the periscope, he passed continual bearings to Robert Brown over on the plot.

"I make you 600 yards from the target, sir," said Brown.

"That's just about right – standby to fire the port tube – stand-by – FIRE!"

The torpedo seemed to explode within a few seconds of being fired. It was a rivet shaking detonation that was followed by a cheer from the crew.

"Good ol' Nazzims," said an unseen voice.

"We've hit her on the port side… She's listing already… My goodness, she's rolling right over… She's going down very quickly… She's going down now, by the bow. Port twenty – give me a course to continue up the passage please, Pilot."

On they went, up through the Narrows, and apart from the appearance of a Turkish destroyer doing over twenty knots, they glided past the town of Gallipoli. Unfortunately they did not encounter any other enemy traffic. The rest of the passage went completely without incident, and they eventually emerged once more in the Sea of Marmara at 0745.

Out of sight of land, they surfaced and commenced recharging their nearly exhausted batteries. Each member of the crew was given a little time up on the bridge for a smoke. After the strain of the penetration, the morning breeze felt like a breath of freedom to each of them. They were back in their old hunting ground, after a near faultless entry, they already had one sinking in the bag. Hopefully there would be many more to come, as the whole crew looked forward to wreaking more havoc in this inland sea.

Chapter Eighteen

The Gulf of Ismid

During those first two days the crew of *E11* were relishing being back in the Marmara. After travelling straight over to their communication position to send the signal that they had arrived safely to *HMS Jed*, they returned to remain on the surface at the northern end of the Dardanelles, well in sight of land. By them remaining in that position, every ship that the Turks needed to supply the Turkish Army on the peninsula, would have no option but to pass them. It caused a stir ashore, because their presence produced the familiar columns of white smoke, that could be seen rising in almost vertical columns in the still air from the distant hillsides. It was a desperate attempt by the Turks to warn any merchant shipping of their presence, but either the Turkish captains were short-sighted, or they chose to ignore them, because the sea-traffic never seemed to diminish. This indolent attitude provided *E11* with a non-stop supply of targets.

Their first victim was a large dhow, which they stopped whilst being surfaced, and using the newly installed twelve-pounder to place a shot across her bow. This gave the gun crew their first chance to put into action the long hours of practice carried out at Murdos. After manoeuvring alongside the vessel, the boarding party leapt aboard. It was quickly found that she was carrying war contraband. Naismith allowed the crew to get away in a small boat, before she was quickly despatched with a scuttling charge.

Their second victim to appear was a small transport, which they sighted just an hour later. Naismith ordered the boat to dive, and manoeuvred himself into a firing position. He watched her approach through the periscope.

"Stand-by to flood the starboard beam tube – charge reservoirs," he ordered.

The vessel came sedately onward in total ignorance of the hidden danger lying in wait for her, heading blindly for Gallipoli.

"Open outer tube door – standby to fire."

They had nine more torpedoes left, and therefore could not afford a miss. Although a miss could be picked up later, it was much easier for all concerned to achieve a first time hit. Naismith took a final set-up.

"Set-up concurs with the plot sir, giving you a deflection angle of green four-nine degrees," said Robert Brown.

Naismith set his periscope at forty-nine degrees off the starboard bow and waited for the target vessel to move slowly into his eyepiece. It appeared, and crept across lens. When its bridge centred itself on the crosswire, Martin Naismith watched its progress until the perfect moment.

"Good – come on my beauty – that's it – just a few more yards – standby tubes – fire," he said calmly.

There was a huge whoosh as the torpedo was launched, causing the deck of the boat to give a slight shudder as compressed air forced the weapon out of its tube housing. The sudden release of a ton in weight made the boat roll slightly.

"Down periscope," he ordered. He had learned his lesson about watching his victim, after his attack periscope had been damaged on the last patrol.

All went quiet as he and the men waited for the explosion. There was nothing that any of them could do to affect the outcome. The explosion was heard very shortly afterwards, and there came a faint cheer of relief throughout the boat.

"Up periscope," ordered Naismith.

The sight that greeted him was not the one that he had been expecting. After being struck by the torpedo, the explosion had caused the vessel to swing around 180 degrees, to face the direction from which it had come. She appeared to be stopped in the water. He watched and waited to see what damage he had caused, when suddenly there was a great thrashing of white foam rising up from under the stern.

"She's going astern, intending to beach herself," declared Naismith. "Gun crew get ready – standby for a gun action surface."

The men dashed here and there, some relieving others at their Diving Station. The gun crew quickly manned the conning tower, each man carrying a live round of the 12-pound ammunition under his arm in readiness for immediate action once they reached the surface. More men formed a line along the narrow passageway, creating a supply chain to feed them with more ammunition. Up inside the tower, the retaining clips from the hatch were removed, and left dangling, which left just sea water pressure holding it tightly shut. High-pressure air was slowly bled into the boat, increasing the internal atmospheric pressure within the hull, in comparison to that on the surface. This was all completed within thirty seconds. All was ready!

Guy d'Oyly-Hughes increased the submarine speed, ordering both hydroplanes hard to dive. As the boat began to take on its customary downward angle, he ordered the central main ballast tanks to be blown. High-pressure air screamed through the pipes, a loud bang reverberating against the pressure hull as it suddenly expanded inside the tanks, forcing the water out through the lower Kingston valves at the bottom of each tank. The contra-forces of the hydroplanes trying to take the boat deeper, was gradually being overtaken by the effect of the ever-increasing positive buoyancy. The boat seemed to bounce with indecision as it dithered as to whether to rise or fall. Just as the needle on the depth gauge flickered indecisively, the First Lieutenant ordered that both the hydroplanes be reversed and placed hard to rise. Now with both forces were acting in the same direction, it caused the boat rise up through the water like a cork.

The Coxswain was shouting the depth and he had to speak very quickly.

"Thirty feet – Twenty-five – Twenty feet – Fifteen…"

At fifteen feet, the First Lieutenant blew a whistle, which told the gun crew to begin trying to force the hatch open. The combination of the men pushing up on the spring-loaded hatch, aided by the increased air pressure within the hull, quickly overcame the rapidly decreasing sea pressure on the outside of the hatch. Suddenly it flew open, and a huge bubble of air was released, keeping out most of the seawater that began falling down all around the men. Within a second or two the boat was on the surface revealing a clear blue sky above.

Down below in the control room, it was like sitting beneath the Niagara Falls, as an ingress of water cascaded down onto the deck.

Above, as the boat bobbed on the surface, the gun crew were climbing out, manning the gun and loading a shell into the breach, as they trained their weapon around.

Petty Officer John Kirkcaldy, a fiery Scotsman, who had spent the past month whipping his gun crew into shape, was screaming his orders. All of his hard work was paying off as the first shot was fired in less than thirty seconds after the whistle had been blown. A column of water rose thirty feet short of the target.

Kirkcaldy made the slight adjustment on his sight, sending the next round to explode against the side of the ship. Several more followed, but despite these hits, the vessel continued to make sternway, and finally managed to run itself aground on the mud in shallow water. She became stuck fast, well and truly aground on the thick mud. Rather than waste further ammunition Naismith decided to retire, knowing full well that if the gun crew should need any more practice, they could always return to complete this ship's destruction at their leisure. He ordered a northerly heading.

During the night of the sixth of August, Naismith headed southward once again, heading over towards the entrance of the Dardanelles. From their previous experience in that area, and using the latest intelligence reports, they had learned that Turkish warships were tending to base their operations in that vicinity. Naismith badly wanted to increase his tally of military targets, and recent the increase in the numbers of escort warships based at Gallipoli suggested to him that this particular position would be his best chance of achieving his dream of meeting a battleship. It was also in this area that they had been programmed to rendezvous with *HMS E14* on the evening of the eighth of August. At 0440 on the morning of eighth, they were on the surface, sitting just off the town of Gallipoli in the darkness of the early morning.

Unknown to the crew of *E11*, the Suvla Bay beach landings were proving increasingly difficult for the Turks to defend. Despite heavy losses, the ANZAC forces had managed to make a beach-head largely due to the submarine menace seriously hampering the enemy supply lines, and intelligence suggested that they had insufficient heavy artillery and ammunition to repel these new land assaults. It was for that very reason that the battleship Harridin Barbarossa had been sent down into the Dardanelles to fire her half-ton shells right across the peninsula onto the ANZAC troops lying on the beaches of Suvla Bay.

Early that morning at first light, *HMS E11* lay on the surface charging her batteries, standing stationary in the cool air. The stars were still visible as the first hints of the dawn was just beginning to make its presence felt, low across the eastern horizon. Lounging against the periscope standard on the bridge were Lieutenant Robert Brown, and George Torode, each keeping a good look-out through their binoculars. Both men were glad to be aloft, enjoying the coolness of the early morning zephyrs. Down below the rest of the crew, who were not on watch lay peacefully asleep. Their batteries were fully charged, and the main engines had just been stopped. All was ominously quiet – expectant.

Maybe it was intuition, or that strange feeling one gets when one knows that something significant is about to happen; George Torode suddenly felt it, as he scanned the horizon with his binoculars. The moon had already set behind the peninsula, and the dawn was giving just enough light to define the two continental shores. Over towards the east George could just make out the line of the low hills between the sky and the horizon. As he scanned his binoculars along the jagged line of those distant hills, something caught his eye, and he lowered them, trying to look in that direction with his naked eye. There was nothing! He raised his glasses once more, settling on a pinpoint of light that he had seen, a single flash that was only there for the briefest fraction of a second. One moment it was there and the next it had gone. Then a vague phantom shadowy shape loomed out of the darkness, and he could just discern the outline of a ship. As he centred the glasses, a second appeared to be moving to the right, and then another. They were all blacked out, and none of them were showing navigation or steaming lights – maybe somebody aboard had been careless with a dead-light? Their ghostly outline could just be discerned against the eastern dawn glow.

"Red seven five, sir – possibly two, maybe three ships in sight," said George.

The officer casually pushed himself off his steel resting place and quickly checked out the report.

"Well spotted Torode," he said, leaning over the hatch, he shouted down. "Tell the Captain, I have two ships visual at 015 degrees – possibly warships."

Naismith was standing alongside him within thirty seconds, staring at the new arrivals through his own binoculars.

"Diving Stations," he ordered immediately.

The crew scrambled up from their slumbers, running across the crates of tinned food to their assigned positions.

Lieutenant Brown immediately went down the hatch to man the plot. The signalman, George Plowman, came up and relieved George Torode, who went below to stand beside P.O. Green.

"Submarine closed up at Diving Stations, sir," said Guy d'Oyly-Hughes.

"Very good, Number One – Bring both bow tubes to readiness – charge both reservoirs – be ready to dive at a moment's notice."

Maybe it had been wishful thinking, but as Naismith stared at the ships something in his thumping heart told him that one of them was a battleship. The size and shape of the bigger target suggested that she was indeed a very large warship, and the smaller two were probably her escorts. Focusing on the larger vessel, he could see that it had two funnels, and from general appearance it seemed to be familiar. She had one large gun turret forward of the bridge, and another aft. He gave a sharp intake of breath, as he suddenly realised that he was looking at the outline of the Harridin Barbarossa. It was either her, or her sister ship, the Turgut Reis. The Turgut Reis had recently been reported to be unseaworthy, so this is probably the Harridin Barbarossa, his old adversary – his spirit soared. This time he was not going to be denied, this time he was going to sink her.

"Get below," he ordered, and following the signalman into the tower, and he pressed the klaxon twice.

The submarine slipped silently beneath the waves, awaiting the arrival of her prey, giving Naismith the luxury of doing three set-ups before it was time to fire.

It was enough time for Robert Brown to fully establish all of the ships course and speed.

"Target is confirmed as the Turkish battleship Harridin Barbarossa, escorted by two destroyers. I intend to fire one torpedo at the battleship."

He looked over at the boat's chronometer, located above the chart table, it was 0500 exactly.

"Standby firing set-up – target bears 046 degrees – range 700 yards – I am 35 degrees on his starboard bow – his speed 15 knots."

"The plot concurs, sir – his course is 191 degrees – set the same deflection angle," said Brown.

Naismith already had the periscope set at the deflection angle, waiting for the great vessel to appear in the lens. The bow of the vessel emerged at the edge of the glass, and very slowly began its transit across the lens.

"Stand-by," Martin Naismith's voice was strangely calm.

Then the bridge of the great vessel edged its way slowly into view, and as the huge mass of the superstructure followed, it almost filling his lens. He waited until the lens centreline wire touched the centre of the bridge structure.

"Fire," he called calmly.

The torpedo was released, carrying its cargo of doom towards the unsuspecting capital ship. Keeping the periscope raised, Naismith was able to watch the wake of the torpedo as it headed off on its collision course. Gradually the target and weapon tracks merged resulting in a flash, preceding a huge column of water that rose from the amidships section of the battleship's starboard side. A massive explosion, and a hammering shock wave accompanied the spectacle a second later.

"Got her," he snapped. "I knew that one of our torpedoes had her name on it."

The crew cheered in wild enthusiasm, as their pent-up excitement finally bust, rather like a cork popping from a champagne bottle.

Martin continued to watch through the periscope, hoping to observe his victim's final moments. He became frustrated, because for a while nothing seemed to happen. The great ship just seemed to continue ploughing on through the water regardless of the grievous injury he had inflicted, seemingly unscathed by the direct hit. Naismith stood at the periscope lens spellbound. Had the damage been superficial? Maybe he should have fired two weapons! Had just the one torpedo not been insufficient? Had he allowed her to escape once again? Surely not – not after that apparently good firm hit. Then…

"She's slowing down – she's definitely stopping!" he said, any trace of disappointment quickly evaporating from his voice.

The cheering stopped, and everybody was staring towards him expectantly. Then suddenly all hell broke loose. The capital ship opened up with her secondary armaments, retaliating with everything she could fire at their very vulnerable periscope. The loud thumps of her shells quickly grew, coming ever closer to the submarine. After losing one periscope on the last patrol, Martin knew that he was not going to be able to watch what he hoped would unfold, but he continued to stare in fascination. More spraying impacts splashed across the lens, dimming his view. It was definitely too perilous to stay up.

"Flood auxiliary – keep 60 feet."

The gunfire stopped as suddenly as it had started, and after just a few minutes, Naismith's curiosity got the better of him, he couldn't resist coming back up to periscope depth for another look.

"Keep 30 feet – pump auxiliary."

It seemed an age before the boat managed to climb back the last few feet back to periscope depth. Stoker Wheeler sent the periscope up ready for Martin to get a view, just as soon as the external pressure of water had eased enough to allow the hydraulics to operate. This was the single most dangerous moment for any submarine, arriving at periscope depth when not being fully aware of the surface situation. As they arrived on periscope depth, Martin quickly did a swift all-round sweep to make sure that the two escorting destroyers would not prove to be difficult. He could not either – they were nowhere in sight. Coming back onto the target, the battleship lay with its stern pointed towards them, just over a mile to the south. Another all-round sweep of the periscope confirmed that there was definitely no sign of either of the escorting destroyers, leaving just the bulk of the battleship in view. Another check, and once he was satisfied that *E11* was absolutely safe, he trained back towards the stricken vessel.

"She has definitely slowed down, and she is starting to list to starboard. Yes – she's definitely in bloody trouble," he said excitedly.

Another loud cheer of relief from the men echoed right through the boat. Naismith watched as the bow of the great vessel slowly turned, as it tried desperately to head over towards the shore. Oh no, she's trying to beach herself, he thought, she can't get away again.

"She is definitely in trouble – it looks like she is trying to make for the nearest point of land. If she starts to make way again, we will try and put another fish into her."

As he watched there sudden came blinding flash, followed by a deep rumbling explosion from deep within the bowels of the stricken vessel. It was followed by further, louder internal explosions of varying degrees of severity, sounding like the grumbling of a summer thunder storm. Then suddenly there was another huge flash, and a tremendous shock wave that hit the hull like a blacksmith's hammer against an anvil, an indication that one of the battleship's main magazines had just gone up. Thick black smoke began to billow ominously from her forward turret. She was obvious dying internally. That huge blast had proved to be her death knell. Naismith could only stare in abject wonder, as almost in slow motion the magnificent ship rolled completely over, and went straight down taking two hundred and fifty-three of her crew with her. Naismith glanced over towards the chronometer once more. It was 0513.

****

After a breakfast of porridge with a spoonful of plum jam, the excitement of the morning quickly dissipated, and the rest of the day was spent in a fruitless hunt for more targets. There was one thing that had not dissipated, and that was the enthusiasm of Torpedoman Brassington, who did not appear to have lost any of the adrenaline high that the attack had produced.

"Three torpedoes used, three ships sunk, and one of 'um a battlewagon – and it's only our third day up 'ere. If you 'ad left me behind, I can't imagin' wot wud 'ave 'appened," he bragged.

"Well for a start, we wouldn't be likely to catch the clap off you," said the stoical Mayne.

"Yeah, and Old Nazzims had a bit to do with it as well, you know Brassy. After all, you just have to pull the firing handle," added Baxter.

"They'll probably give me another medal," he persisted.

"The only medal you will be likely to get is the VD Scar and Bar," said Mayne. George Torode walked in, carrying the evening meal on a wooden tray.

"Oim starvin'," said Brassington. "Sinking ships always makes me 'ungry."

"What we got tonight, George?" asked someone behind the brash torpedo-man.

"It's your favourite Brassy, cheesy – hammy – eggy – on a raft. This will definitely be the last of the fresh bread. All of what is left has turned a nice shade of aqua-marine," replied the Channel Islander. "So, enjoy it."

On the tray lay the thick cut squares of sliced bread, each having been covered with an equally generous slab of cheese, which in turn was topped with a slice of tinned ham, and crowned with a fried egg. Several hands reached towards the tray, groping for a portion. George Plowman took charge of the situation.

"Right, grab just one each, and get it down your necks," he said trying to do an impression of the Coxswain at tot time.

Torpedo-man Mayne looked down at his slice of bread. "Is this what they mean by having a square meal?"

It was always a favourite, and when it was George's turn to cook, it was a quick and easy way to provide a popular nutritious meal without using too much power on the hot-plate. The frying of a few eggs only took five minutes.

"I also managed to boil some water, so there's some rice pudding for duff. I've thrown in some sultanas to give it some taste," he announced.

"Oh, what a feast, cheesy – hammy – eggy, followed by Niggers in the Snow. Don't forget who nicked the eggs lads," said Brassington, between mouthfuls. "Well done George."

"I thought you nicked a box of 'Herrings In'?" said Baxter.

"I went back and nicked a box of eggs as well. I'm definitely in the Coxswain's good books I am! It was also me wot got the sack of sultana's that's in the rice puddin' tonight. A regular little tea leaf, that's me."

Nobody answered, as every mouth was already full of food, with them all eagerly looking forward to the dried fruit mixed with the rice pudding. The rice had been cooked in sweetened water, as they were unable to carry any milk. If it was not served with dried fruit, then a spoonful of a tinned fruit preserve would help with its digestion.

Later that evening, after the meal had been cleared away, George Torode was told to report to the Wardroom. Appearing at the curtained partition, he was welcomed in, and told to take a seat, which was difficult as all three were occupied. Naismith, d'Oyly-Hughes, and Mr al Mizri already filled most of the confined space.

"Good evening Torode," said Naismith, seated at the small table with a chart spread in front of him. "Come in. We're going through the plans for landing you tomorrow night."

Three empty plates held the edges of the chart down, none of them showing any left-overs from the evening meal. An ashtray, full of stubbed cigarette butts, kept the fourth corner in place. He squeezed himself in, as Mr al Mizri flattened himself against the tiny cupboard door to allow him to pass. George noticed a huge bump on the poor man's forehead. He was obviously getting used to submarine life. Negotiating the table, he finally found a space in the corner, and rested his bottom against the rim of a large valve handle. Guy d'Oyly-Hughes was finishing a cup of tea, as Martin Naismith looked up from his deliberations on the chart.

"I want to make this our one formal briefing, prior to landing the three of you tomorrow night. There are a number of things that I want to cover. There are three primary objectives that need to be discussed prior to the start of your main mission to Constantinople. Firstly, I intend to remain the surface for as little time as possible after I launch you in the rubber boat at 2300 tomorrow night, which will be the ninth of August. Secondly, you know that the target is the railway-bridge on the north shore in the Gulf of Ismid, which we intend to destroy. Thirdly, you two will assist the First Lieutenant in getting the explosives ashore, and planting them in position for him. Only when they are in place will Lieutenant d'Oyly-Hughes let you both to proceed towards your rendezvous with Mr Slade. He will then fire the charges, and paddle back in the rubber boat, whilst you both go off on your little holiday to the Turkish capital. Any questions so far?"

This had been discussed already, they were all familiar with the initial stage of the operation. Nevertheless, d'Oyly-Hughes had a question.

"What sort of time fuse do you think I should use, sir?" he enquired.

"That is going to depend on what Mr al Mizri has arranged in the way of getting to Constantinople. Mr al Mizri, can you enlighten us, please?"

The Kurd stood, and after bumping his head once more on an overhead pipe, he decided to address the briefing sitting down on the bunk.

"Yes, I do have arrangements that I hope are going to be satisfactory. They have all been cleared by the Base Staff. There will be a car waiting for us on the old road at the top of the ridge that runs almost parallel to the railway, at midnight on the ninth of August. That will give us one hour from landing to meeting the car. This car will be driven by Mr Slade, who is one of your agents based in Constantinople. He and I observed your antics when you attacked the city during your last patrol. We were standing in the Pera cemetery, looking through binoculars, and trying to count the number of merchant vessels loading at the quays there. Your attack came as a complete surprise to us, as it did to Constantinople as a whole. Hopefully Slade will be carrying a change of clothes for us both, and he will take us straight to a safe address where we can make our final plans to see Mr Papandross," he looked at the submariners, waiting for their approval.

"Well, that sounds pretty good to me, how about you Torode?" said Naismith.

"Er – Sounds good sir, anything is better than walking twenty miles. Will the letter that I am going to deliver be included in with the explosives, sir?"

"Yes, it has already been packed within the water-proofing pack. Once you get ashore the First Lieutenant will give it to you when he divides the explosives for transportation up to the bridge."

Guy d'Oyly-Hughes broke into the conversation.

"If we leave the boat at 2300, then by the time we get ashore and we carry the explosives up to the bridge, set them, it's going to be at least midnight – maybe a bit later. So, I suggest that I give you time to reach the car before I fire the fuses. If I use a fifteen-minute fuse, it will go up when we are all clear of the scene. You two should be well on your way to Constantinople."

Naismith nodded at the sense of the suggestion.

"Any comments on that?" he asked the assembly.

"Unfortunately, it is about a mile and a half from where we land, and all uphill to the closest point of the road, sir," said Mr al Mizri. "So, I suggest that the fuses are fired about thirty minutes after we leave the scene. Then, with a fifteen-minute delay, that should give us time to get clear!"

It was agreed.

"That leaves picking you up, Torode. Mr al Mizri, I take it that you can get Torode back to the landing point?" asked Naismith, pointing to the chart, looking enquiringly at Al Mizri.

"No problem, Captain," he replied.

"Good, then I will make sure that I am lying off the bridge in the Gulf of Ismid at 2300 on the tenth, eleventh and the twelfth of August. I will wait for one hour on each occasion. That will give you three chances of swimming out to the rendezvous. Let's just hope that nothing goes wrong this time and that you make it back first go!"

"Don't worry sir, I have no intention of staying any longer than is necessary," said George.

They continued on for a few more minutes, finalising the last details of the arrangements. Finally, Martin Naismith spoke.

"OK then – that seems to be about it. You will all be issued with a watch this time, which will be wrapped up with the explosives to keep dry. We will make sure that they are all synchronised before you leave. Now if there are no more questions you will have to excuse me, as we have to go and rendezvous with *E14* in half an hour. I can't wait to see the look on Edward Boyle's face when I just happen to mention that we've sunk the Harridin Barbarossa on the way over to meet him."

****

HMS E14 was clearly outlined on the surface against the western sky through the binoculars of both George Torode and George Plowman. She lay stopped in the water, fully silhouetted by the last pastel epitaph of the sun set. Edward Courtney Boyle had trimmed his submarine well down, whilst waiting to meet his relief in the Marmara. *HMS E11* was pointing directly at her, hidden by the gathering gloom of the eastern sky, which was probably the reason why they had not been spotted by *E14*.

"Signalman, using the red filter on your signal lamp; make to *E14* the following – Good evening *E14* – I am coming alongside," said Martin Naismith, his voice was very gentle, little more than a harsh whisper.

George Plowman picked up the signal lamp, and aligning it towards the stationary submarine, he began transmitting the message. The blinkered shuttering around the aperture allowed only the recipient to see the piercing flash of light. His fingers began clicking on the trigger, sending the Morse code.

"Message sent sir," said Plowman.

"Very good."

All eyes were now trained on *E14*, in anticipation of her reply. The response came quickly from a faint flickering light.

"She's sending, sir," said George Torode.

"H-E-L-L-O M-A-R-T-I-N W-E-L-C-O-M-E B-A-C-K T-O T-H-E M-A-R-M-A-R-A," spelt out the signalman. He relayed the information on to the Captain and added. "Signal ends, sir."

Martin Naismith brought *E11* around in a wide semi-circle, made his approach and stationed himself within thirty feet of *E14*.

"Keep a good all round look out," he told the two men at the back of the bridge, before turning his attention towards *E14*.

"Good evening Martin – did you have any problems coming up?" yelled Edward Boyle from the bridge of *E14*.

"Just that bloody anti-submarine net that they've strung across the narrows at Nagara Point, Edward. You have to hit it head on at full power. Have you heard about the Froggy boat, Marriot?"

"No, what happened?" replied Boyle.

"She got caught in that net just after it had been laid, and was eventually forced to surface. All of the crew were taken prisoner, and the boat was scuttled."

"I'm sorry to hear that. I met her CO just before we sailed. Have you had any luck so far, Martin?"

"Managed to sink a transport in the anchorage at Ak Bashi Liman on the way in, she went down in two minutes. How have you got on?"

Boyle took a long time listing the achievements of *E14*. They were mostly small craft, but included some larger troop transports.

"I think that we must have arrived in the lull following the mayhem that you had created on your patrol Martin, because Johnnie Turk seems to have stayed in port for a while. If he does venture out, he is always heavily escorted. We managed to sink the Pelk-i-Shevket, which was sister ship of the ship that you sank off Constantinople on your last patrol. Also got a large troop transport, she had field guns stacked all over her decks. Five other steamers and, believe it or not, thirty-two dhows." finished Boyle.

"We had a bit of luck this very morning Edward, just before we set out to meet you this evening," said Naismith, barely able to contain himself.

"Oh really! What was that Martin?"

"We've just sunk the Harridin Barbarossa, Edward!"

At first, Edward Boyle thought that he was joking, but the excitement in Naismith's voice convinced him.

"That is absolutely bloody fantastic, Martin," he said without a trace of envy. "Absolutely marvellous, congratulations. You're sure she went down!"

"Her forward magazine went up Edward, and she went down after just ten minutes."

"That is bloody wonderful news."

They spent over a quarter of an hour chatting. Edward Boyle giving Martin the latest intelligence in the Marmara, and he in return Martin gave him the latest news about the situation on the Peninsula. He told Edward of his intention to land the two men in the Gulf of Ismid, and he asked him to cover the southern end of the Marmara while he did so. He reiterated his warning about the dangers of the anti-submarine net. Just then, one of the lookouts spotted a small steamer without any lights.

"Looks like we're in luck, Edward," called Naismith across the space between the two boats.

"There is still just enough light. Let's take her on the surface, Martin. You take *E11* and attack from her starboard side, and I'll come in from the port. Your newly fitted twelve pounder will be able to do a lot more damage than I can do with my puny six pounder."

With that they parted company, each of the sinister sleek low-lying vessels melting into the enveloping darkness. The first indication that the master of the steamer had that his vessel was under attack, was when a column of water rose ten feet off his starboard bow. Bawling orders at his helmsman, he bought his craft around, heading straight for the mud on the nearest shore. Both gun crews began firing continuously. Zigzagging for all he was worth, the master managed to ground his vessel after only sustaining seven hits. Unfortunately, two of the shots had ignited his cargo, and there remained a serious danger of losing her. He knew that he was now a sitting duck, when for some reason the submarine that was doing all the damage suddenly stopped firing.

Aboard *E11*, Petty Officer Kirkcaldy was in his element, bawling orders amidst clouds of cordite, quick to berate any slowness or inefficiency. Standing behind the mounting, he made sure that the loading sequence was perfect, before he pulled the lanyard to fire his weapon. Seven of their shots had hit the steamer, and she was just about ready to give in, when suddenly the barrel mounting trunnion pin sheared on the recoil of the next firing. The whole barrel assembly jumped out of its cradle and came crashing down onto the top of the casing, In jumping out of the way to avoid his foot being crushed, Petty Officer Kirkcaldy toppled over the side into the water. It was only by the quick thinking by the rest of the gun crew that prevented the barrel from following the Scotsman into the sea. *E11* circled to pick up their man, and with their prey firmly aground, and unable to go anywhere, they retired from the scene.

A quick inspection by the Engine Room department revealed some serious damage to the mounting. The trunnion securing plate had completely sheered. This plate held the two lugs of the gun barrel firmly into its position on the mounting, and without it, the barrel was not usable. The whole gun would be totally inoperable until a repair, or until replacement, could be made and fitted. The gun crew tied the stricken barrel firmly and securely to the top of the casing.

Over on their port side *E14* continued to pummel shells into the stricken ship until she was well and truly ablaze. Satisfied that the ship was doomed, they sailed over close to their sister submarine where Martin Naismith bade Edward Boyle farewell, wishing him God Speed for his exit through the Dardanelles. Bringing *E11* around, he set off on their passage up towards the Gulf of Ismid.

There was no spare part carried aboard for repairing the sheared trunnion plate. The Chief Engineer's assessed that, despite having very limited resources on board, that they could possibly make a replacement, and if successful, they would be able to remount the barrel within two days. After a lot of consultation with Guy d'Oyly-Hughes, Martin Naismith decided that in spite of this unexpected setback, the landing would go ahead on the night as planned. For the meantime they would simply leave the barrel of the gun tied securely to the upper casing, and then try to find some secluded corner of the Marmara in which to hide *E11*, so that the repair could be carried out.

That night, during their surface transit, the sea was a flat calm. A moonless sky was lit by a billion stars, that were slashed in half by the milky way. Up in the forward end of the submarine all was quiet. The crew were relaxing, some playing cards, others sleeping, while others were just talking. Brassington was curious.

"'Ow come you're goin' on this landin' George?" asked Able Seaman Brassington, enviously.

"Because I went through Constantinople when I was making my way back to the Allied lines, Brassy," he replied, hoping that he wasn't going to be asked any awkward questions.

"So, you, an' this Mr Old Misery, are goin' ter do a bit of spyin', are yer?"

"I can't say anything about what we're going to do Brassy, so don't ask me!"

"Look George, we're in the middle of the bloody Sea of Marmara, miles from our lines, I ain't exactly going to pop ashore and tell the Turks that two naughty boys are comin' ashore termorra, now am I? So, yer might as well tell me."

"I can't Brassy, but I'll tell you all about it when I get back. How's that!"

Their conversation was overheard just down the passage, within the confines of the senior ratings quarters.

"But, but…" persisted Brassington, when the gruff voice of the Coxswain came to George's rescue.

"Brassington it's time for your treatment – and I've a strange feeling that this one is going to be very painful."

Brassington's mouth fell open. Being unable to complain, or find a reason not to attend the daily agonies that he had already undergone, Brassington left George alone, looking like a condemned man going to the gallows. Bagsy Baxter called over.

"Want a game of cribbage, George?"

'Why not,' thought George, and he sat down at the crate that they were using as a card table.

****

At 2215 on the ninth of August, *E11* was on the surface travelling eastward in the Gulf of Ismid. It was particularly, dark with the sliver thin crescent of the new moon was just peeking above the eastern horizon. There was a light breeze which made it feel colder than it actually was.

Up on the bridge, Martin Naismith conned his boat in towards their objective. They were propelling slowly on one engine, with the other being used to directly charge the battery. The tail clutch had been disconnected to allow this main engine to be run at full revolutions into the motor / generator to produce a rapid charge.

The Turkish coastline was discernible by the starlit sky, although it was impossible to make out any recognisable distinguishing features. Two flickering fires could be seen, slightly above the waterline, marking the position of Turkish sentry posts guarding the vulnerable points along the railway. At 2245, he leaned over the hatch and called down.

"Stop starboard – stop both main engines – disengage both engine clutches – engage both tail clutches – slow ahead together on main motors."

He was joined on the bridge by Guy d'Oyly-Hughes, dressed only in shorts, a khaki shirt and sandals.

"All ready below, Guy?" asked the Captain.

"Yes sir, the rubber boat and explosives are at the bottom of the Torpedo Loading Hatch. The strong-backs are being removed right now, and clips are off the hatch in readiness. Torode and Karim al Mizri are dressed the same as I am. Our little run ashore should not take too long to complete."

"Good! Don't forget to give Torode the Admiral's letter once you get ashore and unpack the explosives. Then you can get in there, set those charges, fire them and

393

get out as quick as you possibly can. If anything does go wrong, stay with the other two, and try to get back on our prearranged dates," said Naismith.

"Don't worry, sir, I'm sure none of us wants to stay any longer than is necessary."

The Captain nodded, then leaned over the hatch and shouted down.

"Port twenty – Stop Port – Steer 080 degrees," he ordered. Then turning to his First Lieutenant, he said, "Good luck Guy, get below now and standby. I'll be letting the three of you off in a few minutes."

The water was cool, but not cold. The rubber boat bobbed through the water ahead of the three men, who were swimming. It was a small craft, not big enough for all of them, and the bulky weight of the three large demolition charges made it sit deep in the water. The small boat had rope hand holds looped around its edge, and each man grasped one while kicking with his legs and paddling with his free arm. With a quick backward glance, they saw *E11* swiftly disappearing into the night, her low silhouette soon cloaking her invisible.

They had the best part of a quarter of a mile swim to reach the shore. Although there were the two others with him, George experienced the same nervous feeling of isolation, as memories of his recent adventure came flooding back. He hoped his thoughts were not trying to warn him of any unseen dangers that lay ahead. The launch had gone without a hitch. Many of the ratings had helped to pass the rubber boat up through the hatch, where it was quickly inflated. Once it was in the water, each man had patted George's back, wishing him good luck, before they went back down into the bowels of the submarine.

The rubber boat was then lowered down over the curve of the ballast tank into the sea, with its deadly cargo aboard. The three men simply slid down into the water, and hung on to it. Once they were all in place, Guy d'Oyly-Hughes had quietly called out, "Goodbye," before they had set off at a steady pace.

The faint lapping noise of the waves splashing up onto the stony beach could be heard before their feet felt the firmness of the shingle beneath their feet. Dragging the boat up the last few yards, they stood at the water's edge, as Guy tried to ascertain their bearings. The packages were removed, and the boat carried up into vegetation. Standing wetly in the night breeze, it suddenly felt cold. Guy d'Oyly-Hughes realised they would have to keep moving, and so he began to un-wrap the water-proof packages. He passed out the watches, and they all checked the time. Then he passed the letter, still wrapped in grease-proof paper, to George, who placed in his breast pocket. There were two revolvers, and Guy took one, passing the other to George. They each grabbed one of the explosive packs. All was ready.

"The target is up there, to our left," he said, pointing to the top of the incline that ran up from the beach. "We will now carry the explosives up to the base of the columns supporting the railway bridge. I have all of the fuses."

A sudden terrifying feeling of *déjà vu* overwhelmed George. For a start the location was an almost exact replica of the previous one. The cliffs were a little steeper perhaps, but there was a small stream that ran down the valley much the same. He had started out like this before, and the memory of what followed was so painful that it made him shudder. Taking several deep breaths, he became calmer.

A quarter of an hour later found each man making their way along the shore-line towards where the stream entered the Marmara. From there they intended to climb straight up along the edge of the water-course to the base of the bridge structure supports. As they walked, George looked out across the black shimmering waters of the Marmara. The horizon was undiscernible, and despite a good look, there was not a sign of the submarine, just a flat emptiness. They soon arrived at the stream.

"OK, help me get these explosives up to those two pillars, and once we have placed them and set the fuses, you can both be on your way," said d'Oyly-Hughes.

The three began the climb, and by the time that they were halfway up the steep incline, they spotted the glow of a fire. It was way off to one side of the bridge, but the flickering flames were plainly visible.

"Are they going to get in the way, sir?"

"Not if we are all very careful. Watch where you are treading, and keep low. Ready?"

George and Mr al Mizri nodded. The stream here was more forceful, more of a gentle cataract, where the waters tumbled down, splashing over rocks towards its eventual goal. As they approached the base of the left-hand pillar, the box girder railway support loomed overhead, serving to blank them from the sentry fire. It gave each of them more confidence, knowing that if they were quiet, there should be no interference. The actual fire was located over three hundred yards beyond the far side of the bridge. After placing the charges on the ground, George and Al Mizri rested while Guy d'Oyly-Hughes made an initial survey.

He re-appeared and directed them to carry each pack of explosive up behind the column. On completion he set the fuses, and turned.

"OK. Good luck you two. I shall wait here for fifteen minutes before I fire these fuses, then I will be heading back to be picked up. We shall pick you up at the appointed time, Torode. Good luck Karim, I hope everything goes well for you."

The two men made their way under the bridge and headed uphill towards the crest. George turned halfway up, noting the exact location of the sentry fire in relation to the bridge. The information may come in handy on his return.

Below them Guy d'Oyly-Hughes sat in the shadows, waiting the full fifteen minutes before he fired the three fuses. He then began make his way back to the pick-up point. On reaching the shore, he began jogging along the water-line to just a hundred yards from the rubber boat, when a flash of lightening lit up the country-side, immediately followed by an ear-splitting explosion. Echoes of the explosion reverberated off the nearby hills, but not stopping, Guy towed the boat out from the vegetation, and down into the water, launching himself he began paddling out towards the rendezvous position. Reaching the point where he assumed to be picked up. He stopped, turned around and looked back towards the direction of the bridge where he could just see the smoke. A huge pale plume of smoke rose high above the position of where the bridge had been, masking the whole area, making it impossible to ascertain the exact amount of damage.

As the other two men reached the crest of the hills, the sound of the explosion made both the men stop and turn. At that moment they were well over the ridge, so never saw any of the damage it caused, but they certainly had felt the shock wave through the soles of their feet. It made them hasten their pace. Just ahead of them lay the compacted grit road that led towards Constantinople, along which they were due to meet their contact. It had only been a mile and half mile on the chart, but it had included that steep hillside, which had proved to be particularly challenging.

George let Karim lead the way now, as he knew the spot where the car would be waiting. When they had reached the road, Karim turned and headed westward. Ten minutes later and they were still walking, when suddenly a set of headlights could be seen approaching. Taking cover in a roadside copse, they watched a lorry-load of troops go thundering past.

"We know where they're off to, don't we Karim!" said George, as they resumed their walk.

The Kurd smiled. Suddenly, there was the single flash of a car headlights, which made them both stop in their tracks. Then they flashed again. The vehicle was parked well back off the road, hidden between two small hillocks, not visible from the road traffic.

"It's OK, it's my friend Mister Slade. We ride the rest of the way in comfort," said Karim.

Chapter Nineteen

The Death of a Friend

The city of Constantinople, or Stamboul, to give it is local name, is like Rome in that it stands on seven hills. However, unlike Rome it is utterly unique in that it is the only major city in the world to sit astride two continents. It was once the Capital of the Byzantine Empire, after being founded in year of 324 AD by Constantine the Great, defender of the faith in Eastern Christendom. As the centre of the Orthodox Christian Church, it remained a Byzantium strong-hold until 1453, when it was overrun by the expanding Ottoman Empire, under the leadership of Sultan Mehmet II.

Its name came from its founder, the City of Constantine, or Constantinople. Today the influence of both cultures remains very evident within the city, a strange mixture of the Middle East, with the heavy influence of mainland Europe. Mehmet V, the present Sultan, no longer wields the unlimited power enjoyed by his predecessors. Following the military coup of 1909, the last true Sultan Abdul Mamit II had been overthrown by Enver Pasha, and Mehmet V is now nothing more than a puppet head of state. Enver Pasha, known to his people as Ataturk, had effectively become a military dictator, and is without any doubt the ruler of Turkey today. Indeed, it was Ataturk who had recently aligned the Turkish Ottoman Empire, with that of the Kaiser Wilhelm's Germany.

****

So early in the morning of tenth of August George Torode once again found himself in confines of this ancient city. He stretched his legs out languidly in the comfort of clean sheets, luxuriating in the wonderful experience of having slept in a real bed following a hot cleansing bath following his arrival. He awoke dreaming of Gladys, recalling their walk together on Southsea Common, but in his dream, they were stood amidst a sea of yellow daffodils in the early spring sunshine before going to the tea-room near the Victorian pier. George had given a waitress their order, and when the girl returned, he turned to hand her the money and found himself looking directly up into the face of Mina. The shock had been enough to disturb his peaceful slumber, causing him to wake sooner than he would have liked. There were beads of sweat on his fore-head, which he wiped away with the sheet. He closed his eyes once more, hoping to drift back into the solace of oblivion, but it was impossible – he was awake.

Lying with his eyes closed, he could hear a rhythmic tapping, which in the hierarchy of annoying noises lay somewhere between a dripping tap and Brassington's snoring. What the hell was it? Squinting through one eye, he sought the source. It turned out to be a rotating fan hanging that hung down from the ceiling, directly over his bed. The blades were turning like giant wooden scimitars, but moving so slowly that he could not detect the slightest disturbance in the air – and it certainly needed oiling. The lack of a breeze made him aware of the beads of perspiration, and brushing them away caused a slight trickle of dampness at his temples to run down his cheeks. He wondered if the perspiration was caused by the heat, or from the sudden shock from seeing Mina's face so distinctly.

Deciding that he would bathe his upper body, he got up and looked around the unfamiliar layout of the chamber. There were a pair of twin louvered doors at the single window, which he had flung wide last night to allow any breeze in to dispel the cloying humidity from this cell of a room, but right now the early morning sun was spewing heat into it. The temperature must be off the scale, he thought. His skin felt damp and tacky as he raised his head from the pillow, noting that his bed was bathed in sunlight. Obviously, that was why he felt so hot – it was like lying on the beach at noon in Fermaine Bay on Guernsey.

Looking around at the fitments, he saw that the room was sparsely furnished. Beside the bed, there was just a wooden dressing table, surmounted by a ceramic water jug and bowl. A long forgotten wooden chair filled one corner, the seat piled high with old books and papers. A wooden wardrobe was the only other piece of furniture.

He rose hoping that the jug was full of water, as the thought of a freshening wash became very appealing. There was a cracked mirror that hanging on the wall above the table, set in a dark varnished wooden frame.

'Someone is in for seven years of bad luck,' thought George.

His mouth felt terribly dry and he craved a drink, as well as a wash. He could feel sharp stubble scratch his finger-tips, as he rubbed his chin. He had not shaved since they had sailed.

From the window came the faint roar of the city below his window, and through it he could hear a faint wailing noise. It sounded like some distant music hall act, where a man dressed in a leather clad Tyrolean farmer's garb, yodelled this way through a popular song. Unfortunately, it was not that melodic however. He became curious, and crossing over to the open window he leaned out over the small balcony, and began scanning the rooftops. There was nothing untoward. Still attempting to trace the source of the strange noise, his initial reaction had been to look down, as this bedroom was on the fourth floor of a tall building. He remembered the long climb up several series of stairs on arrival last night. Then it came again, and he realised that the noise was on a level with him. His eyes centred on one of the tall thin minarets he could see sticking up through the rooftops, like a teaspoon from a cup. George grasped the iron railing lining the top edge of the balcony, leaning forward to study the structure further. Squinting, he could just make out the silhouette of a man standing within the confines of the narrow epicentral veranda, that was approximately half way up the structure. It was the first minaret that he had ever studied close. His initial thought, was that it looked like an illustration from one of the H.G. Wells novels – where the eccentric scientist and his friend travelled up to the moon in a rocket ship. He began to listen to the noise with interest. Not being able to discern any recognisable words, he thought that it sounded more like a mendicant chant than a yodel. He realised that the chap in the tower, who was making all the noise, was carrying out a very similar task to a monk by calling the faithful to worship. Despite the different creeds, trappings, and dogma, religion was religion, no matter in what the language, or country it was practiced. Everyone prayed to the same God, although known by many different names, but they worshipped in differing ways…… and yet strangely everyone thought that their particular ideology was the only right one, and that everyone else had it wrong. If he were truly honest, George was not sure that there was a god! How can a benevolent god allow all that slaughter to take place down a Cape Helles? Blinkered religious attitudes causes intolerance, he thought, and religious intolerance leads to conflict. Most of the major wars in history have been fought by self-righteous zealots defending their own particular ideology. The crusades immediately sprang into his mind.

George shook his head in bewilderment. Why can't people just practice their own version of divinity in private, and leave others to practice theirs? Even the good intentioned Christian missionaries had a lot to answer for, because in trying to convert their congregations by delivering their message of salvation, they were forcing a modern civilisation on an ethnic people who had lived very simple but successful lives for thousands of years. A way of life that had endured without trouble for hundreds of generations, and without any major troubles. In their being forced to change so quickly, many of them had lost their way, and their whole society structure crumbled. Trying to force any beliefs on to others was a bad thing, he decided.

He was fully awake now, looking out over this amazing city, his eyes filled by the sights and sounds of the Turkish capital that lay spread out before him. The breeze out on the balcony was a little fresher, but the sheer heat of the sun forced him back inside, to seek the shade.

Karim had left him to get plenty of rest, telling him that he would pick him up later this morning. He did not mention at what time, but George was feeling the need to freshen up, and began to make preparations to wash and shave. There was a bar of soap in a tray, and looking into the mirror, he hardly recognised the hairy face that was staring back. While living aboard *E11* he never ever got the chance to use a mirror, and therefore had never been aware of how the effects of a long patrol changed his appearance – and now actually seeing that change, it came as a bit of a shock.

As he studied himself, noting that his features had matured quite a lot from the peach-faced youth that had left Guernsey nearly a year ago. All of the puppy fat had gone from his cheeks, leaving a strong determined jaw-line. He was pleased with the image.

As he finished his shave and wiped his face with the towel, he looked into the mirror once more, where he could see the features of his father staring back – which logically was not a surprise. A refreshing face wash in the bowl was finished off by running his wet hands through his hair. He had washed it in the bath last night, and it having dried made it unruly. Searching through the wooden drawer under the wash-stand produced a comb, which he used to good effect Reaching down, he pulled on his trousers, and walked barefoot out to the balcony once more.

This time he enjoyed the warmth of the rays, and was cooled by the wafting air blowing in off the Bosphorus. His spirits soared. Leaning over the balcony, he looked down on the emergent city, but seeing the Constantinople in daylight evoked a strange fatalism within. This was his third visit here. God and fate had to be linked in some way – didn't it? If God has the great plan for the human race, then he must also know what is going to happen in the future.

He had been thinking about life a lot during the few quiet moments that there had been in Malta. From what he had seen of this war so far, everyone's chance of survival seemed to be controlled by fate, and as far as he was concerned God has absolutely nothing to do with it – despite what the padre would have you believe. He had been told that the Turks believe that Allah tells them how to live their lives, just as Christians think that God does the same to them. The same person had also said that Allah and God are one and the same entity. 'So, if he guides both religions, why is their conflict between them? Each of us are taught from the cradle, that if we err from the teachings and dogma of the bible – or indeed the Koran – then one is condemned to eternal punishment, while total adherence will bring the reward of eternal life in heaven – or paradise. So how does that work, when an army chaplain gets blown up by a shell in the trenches on Cape Helles, when he was standing right next to a heathen who survived? A true man of God, killed before some of the commonest soldiers who have very little or no faith. I think that God has no more to do with who lives and who dies than I do,' thought George. 'Just by being in the right or wrong place at the wrong or right time can determine if you live or die, is just a matter of fate. If I had not joined the navy that day in St Peter Port, I would now be stuck in a trench in France with the very real chance of being killed. That does not mean that being in the crew of *E11* is not without risk, but at least we are a team who have a certain degree of control on our fate.

'Certainly, we as individuals, have little say over what fate has in store for us! Nobody can predict the future. We simply obey the orders of our superiors, hoping that by doing so, we will make the difference to ensure our survival. Ours is not to reason why – ours is but to do and die, as the old saying goes.

'Could that lack of self-control be the reason why people have practiced religion from early history? In believing that a supernatural being holds your future in his hands – then by praying to him it gave the people a degree of personal control over their destiny? That does not mean that any God is the controller of one's fate because Gods are the creations of people's minds, who use them to remove the responsibility for their life's difficult decisions. Believers can then blame God or Allah for any unfortunate occurrence's in their life. A deity becomes someone on whom they can dump all of their worries and frailties. He is there to explain and provide an answer to every unknown on the planet. Both of these main religions promote a doctrine of goodliness and love, but in reality, both they are totally intolerant of each other to the point of conflict. If only each were to put into practice the teachings within their holy books, then it would serve to reduce world conflict and produce a more tolerant society.'

George's mind drifted back to his youth, and to the Church of the Holy Trinity in St Peter Port where he was baptised, and to where he was taken every Sunday without fail. The one and only time that he missed going, other than that fateful day on the cliffs, had been to Matthew's funeral service after he had been killed. Every other Sunday he remembered seeing all of those spiritually refreshed faces emerging from the doors. There were big smiles on every face. Religion must have played a big part in creating those smiles – didn't it? Were those people feeling that they had gained favour by worshipping God, and thereby keeping all the nastiness of life at bay? Or was it, pure self-righteousness on their part, smugly being seen to be doing the accepted thing within the society of their peers? The human race liked cohesion, and always looked down on those who dared to be different and stand up against what they perceive as the status quo. Anyone who challenges conventional popular thought, or rebels against an elected authority, is invariably ostracised by the majority. Mina sprang to mind. Oh, how he missed her. Oh, what a life they would have shared together!

His thoughts of Guernsey made his mind wander through the streets and contours of his home town. In his mind he walked down the High Street to its junction with Smith Street. He recalled the day that he had joined up, but as his eyes focused on the Masonic hall, the memory suddenly disappeared. He found himself looking out across the streets and rooftops of Constantinople. Although everything was so very different here, somehow everything was very much the same. Houses were houses, whatever shape or form they assumed. People might be dressed differently here, but they still went to work to earn a living, just as they did back on Guernsey, or in Portsmouth for that matter. Personal existence is the same for everyone, he thought. They are all making the best of what is available to them. Fate!

Some of the streets below him was still deep in shadows from the buildings that stood opposite. People scurried about their business along these thoroughfares. He looked up at the clear sky, feeling that this was going to be one of those days that would be alive with promise. If fate was on his side today, then he would be back aboard *E11* by the end of it.

The familiar sights, noises, and smells drifting up from below brought Mina's face to his mind once more. The last time he was here, she had been very much alive. Why did she have to die? His eyes were drawn across the water, over towards Scutari, as he tried to work out where exactly they had met, and where her apartment would have been located. Being unable to recognise anything, he realised just how much he missed her. They had only known each other for a few hours, yet with her he had found an affinity with her that he had never experienced before – which was strange, he realised, not even with Gladys. His mind wondered over what he would have done had she lived. Then he thought, if she had lived, he would have been faced by the dilemma of a choice between Gladys and her! Something inside him already knew that he would have chosen Mina! Did that mean that his feelings for Gladys were waning? Did it mean that he no longer loved, Gladys? He wondered if she was still being true to him, and was not being pursued by all and sundry, as Basil had implanted in his mind in Gibraltar. In trying to convince himself that he did still love Gladys, he realised that after Mina had been killed, it had produced so many nagging doubts. If only Mina had lived, because he knew that he still had very strong feelings for her.

Taking a more inquisitive view at the city, he noted that the house in which he now stood must be situated on a hillside. It was located on a raised elevated position relative to the Bosphorus, because he was able to see right across water over to the Asian shore. In one direction, he looked out over the city's tiled rooftops towards the four minaret's that surrounded a great majestic dome, which he assumed could only be Hagia Sophia. He looked the other way, and the sea of terracotta tiles swept away down the hill towards the water, which seemed to be full of small craft, ferries, and dhows. The last time he had viewed it had been from over on the Asian side, which was probably why it looked so different. He still thought it amazing that he should have been underwater in this harbour. The air above the water was hazy, a discolouration from excess smoke belching from the funnels of the ferries. The waterway shimmered; a dark wide scar, as if a giant sword has slashed the city in two. It was strange to think that was Asia was just over there on that far bank.

Just to the north of where he stood, a branch of the waterway curved off the main channel, arcing around to the west. Most of it was obscured from George's view by the maze of roof tiles. Beyond he recognised the large round tower half way up the hillside. He remembered climbing that hill with Mina, and passing close by. He could just make out far end of a multi-arched bridge that crossed towards the far shore below it.

'That has to be the Golden Horn,' thought George.

The bridge was packed with people, and the parapets were still crammed with fishermen with hundreds of rods stuck out like the hairs on a caterpillar. He remembered the Skipper describing it. Now, here he was looking down on it.

That bridge definitely has to be the Galata Bridge, he surmised and the Turkish Naval Dockyard lies just beyond. He remembered studying the chart of the harbour with the First Lieutenant, at their briefing. The First Lieutenant and Karim al Mizri had patiently, but methodically, gone through all the major landmarks with him. It was paying off now.

Over on that far shore beyond the Galata Bridge, was the area of Pera, where Old Nazzims had torpedoed the ship at the Arsenal quay. It seemed strange viewing it from up here, knowing that he had been below the surface just down there.

He looked at his watch. If there was time when Karim arrived, he fancied going down there just to see if the German cruisers Goeben and Breslau, were still holed up in port. Or maybe even the German U-boat U-21, that latest reports suggested was berthed here. It might prove to be useful information for the Allied Intelligence people when he got back.

Just then there came the sound of a key being inserted into the door lock mechanism? It swung open to reveal Karim al Mizri. George stared open mouthed. Gone was the dirty smelly little man dressed in the khaki tropical clothes, replaced by one of the most smartly dressed men that George had ever seen. He was immaculately attired in a sharply pressed grey silk suit. A dazzling white shirt that made his face appear even more tanned than it actually was. The grey black/striped tie was positioned perfectly, tacked in place with a diamond stud pin that glinted as the sun's rays caught it. The lighter grey hand-stitched waistcoat matched his spats, worn over gleaming black patent leather shoes. He carried matching grey gloves, a black top hat, complete with a hickory cane surmounted with a silver knob handle. Middle Eastern he maybe, but conventional he certainly was not. He would not have been out of place walking down Whitehall towards St James Palace in Parliament Square, or among the financial houses of the City of London.

"Hello George. You and I need to establish just where Mr Papandross' house is. I have a team that is ready, who are going there to take care of the butler. Then we can have the meeting. So get ready, and we will make our way over there right now."

"Yes," said George, overawed by the imposing figure before him.

"Cok Iyi – I suggest that you wear a simple light jacket, and a pair of trousers. It is going to be a warm day, and we will be gone approximately three or four hours. There are some clothes hanging in the cupboard over there."

"What does Cok Iyi mean, Karim?"

"It is Turkish, which means *very good*, George."

He nodded, feeling no sympathy for the imminent demise of Turkish butler. He was going to get what he deserved, but it felt a little strange to know that at this moment in time, the man was living his last hours. He recalled his terrible experience in front of the firing squad, which had all been because of that man. He was to blame for Mina's death, and if asked, George would have willingly carried out the deed himself. A fresh vision of the man formed in his mind, standing at the quayside with his finger pointing directly at them, like Judas Iscariot betraying Christ to the Romans.

There was a loud report, as a car engine back-fired in the street below. George's head turned involuntarily towards the noise, as he walked to the wardrobe to retrieve the jacket and trousers. As he began to dress, he wondered why Karim was dressed as he was.

"Karim! Why are you dressed so elegantly?" There, he had asked the question.

"Because I have my own business here in Constantinople George, and I am going to a meeting just as soon as we have completed our visit to Mr Papandross. I will make sure that you get back here before I go. Afterwards, I will come and collect you to get you back to your pick-up point later tonight."

"I have been thinking about us taking a walk down to the waterfront. Maybe make our way along to the Golden Horn to see what ships are in! Maybe try to find out if the two German Cruisers are there. I also want to see if the German U-boat is in port. What do you think?" said George as he donned the coat.

Karim's smile was patient.

"You remember Mr Slade, the man who drove us here last night!"

George nodded his head, remembering the half-English, half-Turkish man who had supplied the clothes that he was now wearing. He had been quite chatty as they had travelled back towards Constantinople. Once they had reached Scutari, he had driven the car straight down to the ferry terminal. They had all remained within the car, sitting patiently while he had enquired about the next ferryboat to take them across the waterway. All of the large ferries had ceased running, and so Karim had taken George across in a small private rowing ferry. Then they had walked up through the streets straight here to this safe house, while Mr Slade had simply disappeared off into the night.

"Well it is his job to gather that sort of information. He has been here doing his dangerous work for the past year, and he has several men in his team who work down there. They daily gathering lists of such information, and it is all passed back to him to collate. He then sends a weekly report to the Allies. So, although it was a very good idea George, it is something that is already well in hand. Please don't go out unless it is with either Mr Slade, or with me, because if you are caught it could prove to be very dangerous to us all."

George nodded.

With that they both left the apartment, descending the staircase down to the street below. George was amazed by the number of people that created a buzz of activity that hit him. The loud hum of an electric tram could be heard as it struggled up the slight incline, carving a passage through the populace like the bow of a ship through the water. As it passed by, George noted that the windows were filled by people on their way to work. The roadway was heaving with vehicles, carts and wagons, all trying to negotiate the press of people that filled it. Horns were being honked, and donkeys were braying in protest as they made their way down towards the ferry terminal. From there he could remember the route that he and Mina had taken.

Once they had reached the ferry terminal on the waterfront, the quayside appeared to be even more crowded than the vibrant streets they had just walked through. Smoke was billowing from the fish vendors stalls, who were selling a slice of grilled fish wrapped in a bread bun. Drinks of every description, hot and cold were on offer, as they made their way past the ferry terminal kiosk. Ahead of them lay the Galata Bridge, which was still lined with hundreds of men fishing. George looked down into the grey green oily water, hoping that those grilled fish had not been caught from down there.

George clearly remembered alighting here with Mina. Just then a car drew up beside them. It was driven by Mr. Slade, who indicated for them to get in. They drove up the steep road, where George noted the round Galata Tower looking old and formidable as they passed by. This was so much better than walking.

At the top Mr. Slade asked George for the directions as he drove along the ridge road. There were a few electric trams up here, although the main thoroughfare was nowhere near as busy as the ones below. Another mile, and he came across the intersection where he had fallen foul of the donkey. Logically his mind back tracked, and he quickly found the road that led to Mina's fathers house. It was now just a matter of another half mile up to the entrance gates of the house itself.

On arrival they did not enter immediately, driving on by, as George pointed out the place to Karim. The two columns surmounted by pyramids at the entrance were unmistakeable. Karin was hesitant.

"George," said Karim, with an expression of concern. "I did not realise just how far it was to this place. It is going to take me far too long to go all the way back down, get my team and get back up here to do the job. By the time we all get back up here, it will throw out our whole programme, and you may miss your rendezvous. So, I have been thinking as we drove here. Are willing to come with me and carry out the job now? What do you say?"

George gulped. When he had said that he would willingly have pulled the trigger himself – he didn't actually think that he really would have to do it! It had been necessary for him to kill that sentry on that first viaduct raid, because he if he had not, then he would now be dead himself. It had been self-defence. A number of doubts began to fill his mind. Was he actually capable of killing another man in cold blood? Searching for the reason to do so, he thought back. That man had been the cause of Mina's death, and George knew that he deserved everything that was coming to him – but could he actually pull the trigger himself? Karim seemed to sense his uncertainty, and guessed what he was thinking.

"Don't worry George, I will kill him. All that I need you to do is to help me carry him out of the house to a quiet place, where we can hide his body without being seen."

George could feel his pulse beginning to increase, but he knew that he could handle that situation, and nodded his agreement.

****

On the last day of his life, the butler of the Papandross household brought a fresh pot of coffee and the daily paper for his master, placing them carefully on to the table near to where he was sitting. It was nearly ten o'clock in the morning, and the sun was already hot in the sky. There came a grunted thank you, and he made a slight bow, leaving his master to breakfast alone.

Although he went through the motions of being the obedient servant, inside he felt nothing but contempt for the Greek sat at the table. He was absolutely convinced that Papandross was as much a traitor, as that slut of a daughter of his had been. For almost a year now, the Turkish security department had recruited him to spy on his employer. It had proved to be quite profitable, providing him with nearly double his salary. All that he was required to do was report back anything untoward. All had been quiet until six weeks ago, when he had admitted the daughter Mina and the escaped enemy prisoner into the house. He had carefully listened to the conversation, and had immediately taken the information to his paymasters. Much praised had been heaped on to him, and a squad of soldiers had immediately been despatched to intercept them at the docks. They had miraculously escaped, but both had deserved to be executed; they were enemies of Turkey and of Islam. The fact that they had been here asking for the Greek's help should have provided the proof needed to confirm his suspicion that this piece of Greek shit was also a traitor, but Security HQ had told him that they wanted him watched further. They told him to remain in his position, and report anything else of a subversive nature. The butler knew that the Greek would eventually make a slip, and then he then would be executed for the traitor that he was. Allah Akbah!

Alexandros Papandross sat at his table eating fresh figs and yoghurt, with a slice of hot buttered toast. He was scanning through the newspaper headlines. The loud resounding knock at his front door diverted his attention momentarily, but he ignored it, his eyes searching for news of the fighting down on the Peninsula.

The butler, noted that his master was not going to move to answer the knock, and so made his way sedately towards the entrance hall. The lazy Greek bastard, his time is coming very soon, he thought. The corners of his mouth creased into a smug, self-satisfied smile, as he remembered what he had found in his master's bureau last night. There had noted several papers and some letters that would prove beyond doubt that Papandross had been deliberately altering the manifests of his cargoes, attempting to remove anything that would endanger his ships. These altered documents were all the proof that his paymasters would need. There had also been a notation in a small notepad giving details of some bribes that had been paid to dock officials, who had endorsed his crime. These were vital war supplies, which he had purposely diverted from one of his ships and stored in his warehouses. Cargoes of non-military supplies for Gallipoli had then been loaded in their place, while his original cargo had eventually been allocated to another vessel that he did not own. The Greek was very aware that the Allied submarines did not destroy non-military cargoes. Written in the margin, there were notations naming the recipient's, and the amount of each bribe that he had paid? The butler felt very proud of himself in being able to recognise these pieces of paper for what they were. The Greek was a traitor, and he felt sure that he was going to be arrested just as soon as his spymaster had read his latest report.

On reaching the bottom of the staircase, he made his way over towards the front door. Having already spent the very early hours of this morning at Army Intelligence, he was feeling a little tired, but duty to his country came before any rest. His written report had been personally delivered to his spymasters at four thirty this morning, as he wanted to back at his duties, so as not to cause suspicion. Once the Greek was taken away, he would have this whole house to himself. He would be the master of all he surveyed. Reaching for the door-handle, he opened it, to reveal a man with his arm levelled at his head holding a gun.

Spiros Papandross was just about to pour himself another cup of coffee, when the abrupt sound of the front door slamming with unusual force made his hand jump. Some the coffee leapt over the rim of his cup, and stained the table cloth. He stood and hurried over to the door to investigate, walking out onto the landing, but looking down over the banister he saw an empty hallway and nothing amiss. Where was the butler? He called out his name – but there was no answer. What the hell was going on this morning? He was totally unaware of the two muffled thuds that came from the rear of the house, as he returned back to his coffee.

Mission accomplished, but as Karim al Mizri and George had walked back down the driveway away from the house, something that the butler had just screamed at them just before they had shot him was deeply troubling. He had had inferred that the Turkish security already knew something.

"I think that it may be more prudent for us to go right now, and for us to go and meet Mr Slade, George. I think that we both need to get as far away from here as we possibly can, just in case this house is being watched. If everything remains calm, then he can drive you back here this afternoon, and after my business meeting has been completed, we can still get you back to the rendezvous tonight. You did well back there, George. That is the fate of all traitors."

George had felt quite sick that he had watched a man die.

****

George returned to the safe house a little after midday, and Karim went off to his meeting. The ambient temperature had risen considerably, and George was hot and sweaty. Poor Karim, the clean-cut immaculate appearance of earlier that morning had been replaced by a rather dishevelled and a somewhat harassed appearance at having to dispose of the butler's body.

Karim was only gone an hour before he arrived back. He went over poured them both some of the pressed fruit juice, that still remained from breakfast, which he downed in one long draught. Regaining his breath, and cooling quickly under the fan, Karim turned to George.

"We don't have too much time George; Mr Slade will be coming for us in about fifteen minutes. He has had one of his men watching the house since we left, and there has been no trouble observed. Now that we know the address, Slade will be able to get us back there quite quickly. I feel very uneasy about the butler words however, and I do not want to spend too much time on this George. When we get there, just go in and give the letter to Papandross, get his answer, and come straight out. The risks have risen significantly and I do not want to press our luck. Get yourself ready, I'm going to change into something that is more comfortable."

After they had manhandled the butler out of the house, they had frog marched him around to the back to an outhouse, which was used by the gardeners to keep their tools. As they entered the butler started screaming something at them in

Turkish, and they quickly pushed him through the door. Once inside they threw him to the ground, and before he could recover and sit up, Karim had wrapped and old sack around the gun to prevent the sound carrying, placed it against his temple and pulled the trigger twice. The sack had prevented blood from spraying everywhere. Then George covered the body with old tarpaulins in gardener's outhouse. Karim took no part, and had stood back so as not to get any of the dust on his suit. When he had finished, Karim translated to him what the butler had screamed. He said that it would not be long before the security soldiers came and arrested Papandross. They debated whether they should they just warn him, or go back to the safe house. They both realised that they were going to have to be extremely careful. Safety first! After having a quick chat, they decided to go back to the safe house, and return later in the day. If the place was swarming with the military – the mission could then be abandoned.

Back at the apartment they waited for Mr Slade, and when he arrived, he became wary after hearing the news. He suggested that they returned in his car and survey the house from a distance. If the coast was clear, they then could go in and give Papandross the letter. They should also warn him, and make him aware of what the butler had screamed.

"I should leave straight afterwards if I were you two – just in case there is any truth to what the butler said," he suggested. "I will be waiting with the car at some distance. So, I will be able to see what is going on. Just get out as quickly as you can, and that will be the end of the mission. We can then get you back to the pick-up point George."

Mr Slade knew exactly where the house was, but when he drove up to the gates, he drove past, drawing into the side of the road two hundred yards beyond the entrance. From the car all three men scanned the place for any untoward activity. It appeared to be very quiet. The decision was made to carry on with the mission.

George and Karim then got out and walked back the short distance. By the time they reached the driveway, Slade's car had disappeared, but they knew that he would be watching from somewhere close.

"Don't worry George, Slade will not be too far away. He will be sure to keep us in sight. All you have to do now is to make contact with Mr Papandross, and get him to agree with the proposals in the letter. Once he has written a reply, then get out as quick as you can, and you will be on your way home."

The early afternoon was holding the heat of the day, but everything seemed perfectly normal as they walked up the shady tranquil tree-lined driveway. The cooling shade from the trees was welcome, as they came to the entrance.

George was feeling a little uncomfortable. Things never seemed to go smoothly. There was always a hiccup in what should have been a simple plan. Today has certainly not gone as he had expected it to.

He reached up and rapped the knocker. After a short time, he was relieved to see a short, clean cut man answer the door. Obviously, Mister Papandross has more servants, other than the butler. Karim addressed him in Turkish, and the man bowed, and invited them into the hall. The place seemed all too familiar as George walked in. They followed the man up the familiar staircase. A wave of regret swept through him as he remembered that last time that he had trod these steps, he had been following Mina. That had only been a few weeks ago, yet it now seemed more like another lifetime.

The servant said, something unintelligible and Karim replied. They were led into the same room, which appeared to be empty. The back of the winged chair that Papandross had been occupying on his last visit, still stood over near the fireplace. A leg and foot could be seen, protruding from one side, and as he approached George spoke in English, knowing of Mr Papandross linguistic capabilities.

"Good afternoon Mr Papandross, it is good of you to see me again."

A lone figure rose from the chair, standing up fully without turning. George stopped, immediately feeling that something was not right, and an uneasy stab of fear went through him. It was not Spiros Papandross, yet there was something strangely familiar.

"Who are you? Where's Mr Papandross?"

Karim's hand reached for his gun, located inside the shoulder holster that he was wearing under his jacket.

"I wouldn't do that if I were you," said the figure. The tone in the voice sent an icy chill through George.

"Arthur Collenette!"

The figure turned fully around, and there stood the man that George hated more than anyone else in the world. He was wearing the same dark blue uniform, but it was now that of a Turkish Naval Commander. There was a smug smile of satisfaction emblazoned across his face, and George could see that he was quite obviously relishing this moment. There was a crash behind them as the doors burst open, a scuffle of feet producing a squad of soldiers, who quickly formed a line along the back wall. Each soldier held a rifle pointed directly at them. Karim still had his gun in his hand, but he wasn't foolish enough to use it. He slowly lowered it to the floor.

"I can't say that it's a pleasure to see you again, George. I must say that you certainly don't seem to learn from your previous experiences, do you?"

"I can see that you've been promoted Arthur," said George, sarcastically, as he eyed the three rings on Arthur's arm. "Pity it's not in an RN uniform, eh?"

Both George and Karim were ordered through into a study, that was next door, where they were both handcuffed, before being forced to sit down in front of a green leather topped desk. A Turkish army colonel entered the room, and sat down behind the desk. He was wearing the Turkish Intelligence Corps Army uniform, and removing his cap, he laid it down on the table in front of him. A thin pencil-line moustache divided his face horizontally, accentuating his sharp chiselled features. His slick black hair was heavily oiled, revealing the onset of baldness. A pair of cold, penetrating eyes matched his aloof personality. Arthur walked in behind him and stood with his back to the door, directly behind them with four soldiers, who stood over by the far wall. Two more came in and positioned themselves directly behind each of the prisoners.

"Where is Mr Papandross?" demanded George, trying to rise from the chair.

The iron grip of a strong hand on his shoulder forced him back down into the chair.

The Colonel stood up, and slowly walked over towards the solitary window, where he turned and raised his finger to beckon George over. The pressure on George's shoulder was suddenly released.

George was wary, but rose slowly and made his way across to the window. Standing there beside the Turkish officer, he followed his gaze out through the glass. He could see that he was overlooking a brick floored stable yard. Part of the old stable-block that had obviously been converted into a garage, as there was a shiny black Rolls Royce Silver Ghost standing there, looking resplendent in the afternoon sun. Standing beneath the branches of a slender poplar growing at the end of the building, he could see a line of soldiers. They standing at ease, with their rifles held loosely at their side. A stab of fear filled George – as he remembered being in front of a firing squad. Just then, one of the garage doors opened, and from the darkened confines emerged a Turkish army officer, followed by a pathetic figure being dragged between two burly guards. He was wearing the remnants of a white shirt, and a pair of grey flannel trousers. Several patches of blood stained his shirt. The victim managed to glance up at the window. His face was a bloody mess, very badly bruised, with gore still trickling from his nose and the corner of his mouth, but George recognised him immediately. It was clearly Spiros Papandross!

He was un-ceremonially dragged over towards the wall that was standing at right angles to the garage, and was forcibly popped up against it. Fear gripped George, as he realised that the wall that was facing the line of line of soldiers, and he knew what he was witnessing. As his guards released their grip, Spiros slumped immediately, unable to support his own weight. One of the soldiers was despatched to the garage, re-emerging with a light wooden chair. Papandross was placed upon it, and his arms were tied behind his back. George's mouth went dry. It was very obvious what was going to take place.

"This is where all traitor's end up young man. It is the fate that you can expect for yourself, unless you answer the question's I am about to ask you," said the Colonel, in a very matter of fact tone. "Watch very carefully young man, because this could be you in the next hour or two!"

There came the sound of loud metallic clicks, as rifle bolts were worked, as the bullets were thrust into the breach. George's attention became riveted on the events unfolding in the yard below. The soldiers were standing to attention now. He couldn't believe what he was witnessing, as their rifles came up to the firing position.

"VAR," screamed the officer in charge of the execution squad.

The volley of shots was as one, and the front of the Papandross' shirt burst apart in an explosion of red. The force of the bullets hitting his body threw him and the chair backwards towards a faint cloud of powdered brick that erupted from the wall. The body toppled sideways off his chair, and remained inert. George could see the blossoming stain on his shirt material, expanding like a red flower that was opening in the morning light. His mouth had gone completely dry.

The guard came over and dragged George back towards the chair at the desk. A quick search of both George and Karim revealed the letter that he had brought for Mister Papandross. The Turkish officer opened the envelope, and read it with some interest, before laying it down on the desk in front of him. He then lit a foul-smelling cigarette, purposely blowing the smoke into George's face. George obligingly coughed, causing the Turk to smile, obviously pleased by the reaction.

"How did you know that we were here to meet, Mr Papandross?" asked George curiously.

"I'll be asking the questions, but since you ask, I will grant you an answer. His butler was found murdered just over an hour ago by the second agent that we have installed in this household. We have been watching the traitor Papandross for some time. The butler reported to us only last night, that he had discovered some papers to prove Mr Papandross was a traitor, and it was always our intention to pick him up today. After the body had been discovered, it became plainly obvious that something was about to unfold. So, it was simply a case of keeping out of the way, and waiting for that something to occur. Thank you for being punctual, and not keeping us waiting for too long!"

Arthur moved around the room, and went and stood behind the colonel's chair, looking very pleased with his self. George would have smashed him in the mouth, if his hands were free.

"Merhaba Al Mizri bay, we have been waiting a long time to meet you in person. Today has certainly has been a very profitable day for us."

The colonel smiled, and behind him Arthur was grinning. The navy-blue uniform he was wearing was obviously new, but he now wearing a red fez, instead of the more usual naval white peaked hat. George thought that he looked totally stupid.

"Well Al Mizri Bay, the letter states what you were going to discuss terms with the late Mr Papandross. What information were you hoping to take back to your Christian paymasters?"

Mr al Mizri sat there in total dejection, his silence was deafening. He had obviously made a determined pledge that he was not going to say anything. George could see from the look of despair in his eyes that all was lost, and so he too decided that he too would remain silent. If he was going to be executed, then he was not going to betray his country.

"Why have you come here with this murdering scum from the British submarines? Were you landed here by a submarine – is that what happened? Who is your contact here in Stamboul? Is he the man who is going to take you back to a rendezvous, once your meeting here had finished?"

Again, his questions were greeted with total silence. Arthur leaned forward and whispered to the Colonel, who eyed George and nodded. The unheard conversation continued, and suddenly the Turkish officer's eyes flicked up, fixing directly on George.

"So, it seems that you have visited Papandross bay before young man? This is certainly not your first visit to Constantinople either is it, above or below the water? Why have you dared to come back here again, after taking so much effort to get back to the British lines?"

George said nothing. His heart was pounding in his chest, but he was determined to remain resolute. If Karim could remain silent, then so could he. After several repeats to his question the Turk began to lose his patience, and his fist slammed down onto the desk.

"Do you have orders to take my friend Al Mizri bay back to your submarine? I want to know where you will be meeting your vessel."

George never answered.

"This is your last chance young man, because if I do not get some answers soon, you too will be going out to that garage wall. Do I make myself clear?"

Both men sat in their chairs. Heads bowed. Silent!

"Take them away," he said to the guards.

They were taken to a domestic cupboard, which stank heavily of floor polish and ammonia. When the sounds of the soldier's feet had died away, George dared to speak.

"What do we do now, Karim?"

"We must try to be very brave George, as I don't think that we will get out of this alive. If you have a god to whom you worship, then I suggest that you make your peace with him."

****

An hour later, and they were brought back into the study. The guards made them sit in the same chairs. The Colonel leaned back in his chair, his elbows on the arm rests with both sets of fingers locked in the form of a bridge across his chest. His cold were eyes were intimidating.

"You have had some time to think over your predicament, and I would like some answers – and I want them now. Firstly, Al Mizri bay, I want to know of any other business that you had with Papandross bay. What information were you going to receive from him? Were you sent here by the British, or the French? I assume that as the letter is written in English, it was the British who sent you. Give me the names of your other associates here in Constantinople, and their addresses? Answer now."

He patiently waited a full minute for a reply, which soon became obvious that it would not be forthcoming.

"We have just received confirmation that your gun exactly matches the calibre to the one that killed the Papandross' butler, and that it has been fired very recently. I do not need to convene a court martial to find you guilty of his murder, and the sentence for premeditated homicide is death. By talking to me you may just escape with a lesser sentence. Just give me some of the names and addresses of your co-conspirators and you will live."

Receiving no answer again, his mouth creased into an impatient grimace, before he turned to George. His voice softened.

"You are a young man, and you must have much to live for. Do not be a heroic fool like your friend here. All that I want to know is where your submarine is located, and when and where are you going to rendezvous to be picked up? Just tell me that and I will let you live."

The colonel picked up a folded dossier that lay on the desk in front of him. Flicking through the papers he looked up.

"Did you have anything to do with the explosion that destroyed the railway bridge at Ismid, only twenty kilometres east of here? Is that where you were both landed? Is that the place where you will be picked up? Just give me the date and time and you will live."

George knew that if he answered they would send a warship to patrol the gulf. He took a deep breath, but although he was feeling extremely frightened, he still said nothing. Looking sideways at Karim, he could see that all was lost by the look in his eyes. Becoming pragmatic, he realised then that he wasn't going to get away this time, and that there was not going to be a fortunate bombardment to save him. The Turks knew that had Papandross been recruited, and how he could have significantly helped to increase the tally of sinking by the Allied submarines. Their deployment was already severely hampering the supply lines to the Turkish troops on the peninsula. The best information that they might hope to extract from Karim, were the names of his fellow operatives here in Constantinople. So, if he held out, then his life would be totally irrelevant to them. He would be just another spy that they had removed from the network, and by the look on Karim's face, George could see that he was very well aware of the fact.

George felt angry that he had ended up in this situation, having worked so hard to extricate from capture on his last mission. He was now experiencing that same sick feeling in the pit of his stomach. He was also fully aware that his chance of surviving now were no better than Karim's. The only possibility of delaying the inevitable would be for him to drop a hint that he might know something about the submarine operations. He did not have to give them anything that would endanger his friends – just give an indication that he might know something. It could just be enough to give him some precious time to try and think of something.

The trouble was, of course, was that they would be able to check any information he gave with Arthur Collenette, who would be only too willing to tell them that he was lying, and that would quickly leave him in the same predicament. The only thing that George had over Arthur, that he could not contradict, was the fact that he was a submariner. He was unfamiliar with their working, and therefore he could not confidently say anything too definitive on their operational tactics. So, if he were to intimate that he may know something, it just may be enough to keep him alive for a little longer.

What on earth was he going to say? It would have to be a plausible lie that was beyond Arthur's understanding. He had absolutely nothing to lose, so might as well give it a try.

George looked up at Arthur, and could see by the look on his face that he was itching to confirm or deny anything that he said. They obviously knew who he was, and they seemed to have all the details of his last adventure contained within that file on the desk. No doubt Arthur had furnished them with that, and a lot more information. He had probably told them the name of the boat he was serving on. He knew for certain that he could not place his crew-mates in any danger, so therefore he had to be very careful about what he said.

"Where will your submarine be picking you up?" asked the colonel.

He kept silent at first, making the moment last as long as he dared, before he finally spoke.

"I will not know that until later," said George tentatively.

"So, you will know!" The Turkish officer was instantly interested, and leaned forward across the desk.

'That is the first point to me,' thought George. 'He has taken the bait.'

The Turk turned towards Arthur and whispered a question from behind his raised hand. They were in conversation for over a minute. Despite straining to hear what was being said, George could only hear some mumbled words. He felt encouragement when Arthur shrugged his shoulders. Then he watched as Arthur went across the room and made two telephone calls.

Karim looked sideways at George, his face had a quizzical expression, unsure of the game he was playing. He was sure that George would not give away any secrets or endanger his shipmates, but did not understand what was happening. George winked at him – and he watched the corners of his mouth flicker into the faintest of smiles.

"What does that mean – you will not know until later?" said the Colonel curtly.

George shifted in his seat. His brain was racing, trying to come with something that might sound plausible.

"The information will be passed to me by a courier," said George, hopefully.

The Colonel became very interested now. He seemed very relieved that one of the prisoners was starting to talk. George could see that he was ever hopeful of trapping more of Karim's contacts.

"Where will this courier contact you?"

"I can't tell you that," replied George, not wanting to make it seem that he was giving away any information too freely. He looked at the sky out of the window. The afternoon light was just starting to recede. He wondered what the time was.

"When will the courier contact you?"

The interrogation hit a dam. George knew that they expected him not to say anything – so he kept quiet – hoping that his silence would be misconstrued as his reticence not to reveal the information. He used the precious time to think of a story logical line that they might swallow. The stalemate continued for nearly half an hour.

The room felt as if it was shrinking, taking on the dimensions of a condemned cell. Unless he could create a logical storyline quickly, then his chances of ever getting out of here were nil. He could see that the Colonel's patience was beginning to wear thin, and that he was obviously getting tired of repeating himself. George was beginning to despair, when suddenly the door opened and in walked a German naval officer. His heels clicked, as he saluted the Colonel and he introduced himself. The gloomy atmosphere within the room lifted instantly.

"Lieutenant sur see Otto Hersing, at your service Colonel," he said, as he nodded his head. "I have been asked to attend you here."

George turned his head, knowing who he was. He looked up at the man who was reputed to be the captain of the U-21. His boat had emerged from the Austrian port of Pola in the Adriatic during May, and had so far sunk two allied battleships, *HMS Triumph* off Gaba Tepe and *HMS Majestic* off Cape Helles. He realised that U-21 must almost certainly must be holed up somewhere in Constantinople. She must be hidden somewhere in the Turkish Naval Yard, just up from the Galata Bridge in the Golden Horn, he thought. This was certainly going to add a new dimension to our submarine tactics in the Sea of Marmara. Were they going use the German boat to hunt for the British submarines operating in the Marmara? He immediately realised that he would have to be very careful what he said from now onwards, as any slip on his part could bring about the death of his crewmates. Arthur Collenette was standing just behind the German, his smug smile making it obvious that he was covering his lack of submarine knowledge by enlisting the help of an expert.

"This man here is Ordinary Seaman George Torode. We know that he was serving on *HMS E11* in May," said the colonel, indicating towards George.

'Arthur Collenette has obviously been talking to his friends again,' thought George.

"*HMS E11*, eh," said the German nodding, there was a degree of respect in his voice. "Zats zer boot of our gud friend Lieutenant Commander Martin Dunbar-Naismith. I must say congratulations – You did very well on your last patrol young man."

George said nothing. So, the German continued.

"So *E11* is in the Marmara again? I suppose it vas your boot that sank the Harridin Barbarossa two days ago. Vas it your boot zat also destroyed zer railway bridge in the Ismid Gulf last night?"

George still said nothing.

"What is the calibre of the new gun that you now have fitted?"

George said nothing. How on Earth did he know about the gun?

"You destroyed a steamer yesterday morning. Das report said zat zer ver two submarines, vats zer name of the udder boot?"

George's silence persisted.

"Ver do you go in zer Marmara to receive your radio signals?"

George remained defiant. The German gave a frustrated snort. He could see that he was wasting his time.

"You are a very silly young man," said the German, realising that it was obvious that he wasn't going to get any answers. Shaking his head, the German moved over to the desk to have a quiet word with the Colonel. He nodded, and the German left the room without looking at George.

All went quiet.

The Turkish Colonel stared at George, who was now beginning to feel real fear, as he wondered what would happen. From the furrowed lines of his brow, George could see that the Turk was trying to come to some decision. Was he going to live or die? Had he chosen his words well, but were they enough to challenge his curiosity enough to keep him alive!

Finally, the Colonel stood up, and spat out a series of orders. A group of soldiers appeared instantly, crashing through the doorway and grabbed hold of both George and Karim. They were very forcefully bundled out of the room, heading for the door that led out onto the landing above the entrance hall, but at the last moment they turned, heading for a different doorway. A staircase led down, and then outside through a tradesman's entrance into the stable-yard. George felt himself trembling.

Oh god is this it? Once outside, he noticed that it was the late afternoon, almost early evening. There was a strange mellow stillness in the air as the heat of the day began to dissipate. The two men were roughly dragged through a swarm of midges, that were dancing in the last of the fading sunbeams. George tried to move his head to avoid them, receiving a thump from a rifle butt to urge him forward towards the garages. Utter terror had gripped him, as he now realising that he had overplayed his hand? This was going to be his end, of that he was now certain.

He glanced back over his shoulder, to where he could see a group of faces framed in the first-floor window. As he did so, he remembered how Papandross had made exactly the same response while he was being carried to his death less than an hour before. Worse of all, he recognised the face of Arthur Collenette smiling through the glass, standing beside the Turkish Colonel.

As they drew nearer to the garages, he saw the same shoddy squad of soldiers as they began shuffling out from the stable doorway in the stable-block. Most of them were still smoking as they carried their rifles, others digging into their ammunition pouch for a round. They shuffled back into another rough line, just as they had done when Papandross had been sat on the chair, and began to load their weapons with the same casual indifference.

An order was barked, and the soldiers dropped their cigarettes as if they were burning their fingers, grinding the stubs into the brick paving with the toe of their boots. It was even the same Turkish officer who had given order to them the order to fire at Papandross. Their guards pushed them both forward against the garage wall, and backed off, leaving them there alone.

The Turkish officer approached Karim and George. One at a time, he grabbed hold of their shirts and pushed them roughly against the garage. He seemed to be enjoying the occasion.

Déjà vu! This could not be happening again. George knew all about this hellish situation only too well. The complete terror of it all had returned like a returning nightmare. His head was sweating, and from that moment onwards, the whole event took on an ethereal, dreamlike quality. Every ounce of George's fight and resistance had totally collapsed, and he hated himself for not resisting and just accepting his fate. He looked about at the layout of the garage fore-court, which made him feel more like a casual observer than the major participant of this hell.

The Turkish officer stood back and watched while one of his men pinned a white handkerchief to each of their chests, before he sauntered back to join his comrades.

Then he shouted an order to the squad. More metallic clicks of the bolt action, as the soldiers loaded a round into their barrels. The implication of the noise brought George violently back to reality to the situation in hand. His breathing reduced to a pant, and he heard himself snorting through his nose, nearly crying in frustration as his hands fought in vain against the binding metal of the handcuffs that held his wrists. This can't be happening again!

Looking up at the sky, he realised that this was going to be his last view of this world. It was getting dark, and the shadows were growing ever longer. It was no good trying to deny the fact that he wasn't terrified. He broke into sobbing gulps, noisily sucking in the air. Looking back across the stable yard one last time to see Arthur Collenette still smiling up at the window. The bastard! He took a deep breath – he had to be brave! He stood erect. Die well.

Standing beside him Karim seemed to be unusually calm, almost as if he too had resigned himself to his fate. His face was pale, his eyes watery, his whole being seemed filled with utter despair.

Another shouted order brought the firing squad to attention.

'Oh God! This is it,' thought George. 'This is really how it's all going to end.' Another screamed order, and the firing squad made ready by taking aim. George could see each of their eyes staring straight at him along the barrel of their levelled rifles, as each man took a bead. A groan from Karim made George turn his head towards him. His whole body was shaking uncontrollably from head to foot. There was a widening pool of steaming urine at his feet.

"Courage, mon brave," he heard himself say.

George took a deep breath and waited. Here we go! This was it. He held the next inhalation, waiting for the bullets to smash into his chest. God take me in your arms. Forgive me my sins. I truly repent them in the name of Jesus. Why don't they fire? He opened his eyes, and stared directly into the squad of men.

"VAR," they all fired at that same second.

The combined report from the rifles was absolutely deafening. The soldiers disappeared in a billowing cloud of smoke, which blanked their faces. George staggered, more in surprise at the noise than anything else. To his right, Karim's body flew backwards, thumping heavily against the wall. There was a loud grunt, as the wind was knocked from his shredded lungs. His body collapsed to the ground, like that of a pole-axed steer at an abattoir. George's throat had gone dry as he continued to hold his breath – awaiting the expected pain. His shoulders had instinctively tried to fold forwards, hunching across his chest in a vain attempt at self-protection. He could not hold the air in his lungs any longer, and it burst forth in short panting terrified bursts. The smell of fresh cordite filled his nostrils with his next inhalation. He coughed as the acrid fumes reached his lungs. What was the delay – get it fucking over with?

His eyes had instinctively closed as they had fired, and they were still closed now. He was afraid to open them, fearing that if he did, the Turkish officer would walk over and place a revolver to the side of his temple and pull the trigger. Nothing happened.

Had they missed me? He opened his eyes – Karim was dead – so why wasn't he? All had gone very quiet.

It was now ten seconds since they fired – why had no bullets hit him? Or had they! Was he in fact dead? Is this what death feels like? No – he could definitely hear movement. The soldier's boots began scuffing on the bricks. Had there been a jam! They could not have all missed him – could they? Had he been shot already, and he just cannot feel it? Maybe it didn't hurt when you were shot, or maybe you can't feel any pain after you die. Can you still hear normal things after death? Is this what it's like to be dead?

He began to stare about as his senses became aware that he was still standing – his legs were shaking – so he tried moving his toes – yes – he could feel them against the leather inside his shoes. Then he heard a shouted order from the Turkish officer, and realised that he was very much alive! The smoke cleared and he could see the squad lowering their weapons, ejecting the empty cartridges. Some of the soldiers were already lighting up fresh cigarettes. What the hell had happened? As if seeking reassurance that they had indeed fired the weapons, he turned to check Karim. There lay Karim's crumpled body. His lifeless, unseeing eyes were staring up at the emergent stars in the twilight heavens.

The firing squad officer detached himself from the group, and walked over towards George, whose heartbeat increased tenfold. If the bullets had all missed, was he now going administer the Coup de Grace? Is he going to put his revolver to the side of my head and blow my brains out? Maybe I am wounded, and he wants to stop my suffering, just as anybody would put down a horse with a broken leg. God accept my spirit into your embrace, said George silently. Protect me lord, in the name of Jesus, deliver me from this hell. His bladder finally failed, and his urine soaked down through his trousers. He could feel the warmth of the liquid against his thighs.

Where was that Turk? He was behind him, standing over poor Karim.

His brain tried to mentally do a search of his body, physically checking for any injuries, but as he did so several pairs of rough hands grabbed him. Filthy cigarette stained fingers dug cruelly into the flesh of his upper arms as he was hoisted up to his feet, before they began to drag him backwards across the yard. His heels scraped across the rough brick paved surface.

George had absolutely no fight left in him. He could feel every one of his muscles twitching uncontrollably as his body sagged in submission. Around him, he could hear the curses and groans from the soldiers, finding his dead weight challenging as they dragged him. There was nothing that he could do about it, so he just let them pull him wherever they wanted – there was no fight left in him.

As they were about to enter door of the house once more, his eyes looked up and he saw the stars. They were so beautiful. Worldly realisation began to return, and his mind began to clear from the fog of terror. His inner resolve began to flare, as he began be aware of what was happening to him. Where were they taking him? What were they playing at? God, how his trousers stank.

It was a strange emotion that he was experiencing at that moment, because he became angry that he had been cheated out of his own death. He could see the garage wall receding, with the crumpled figure of Karim, still lying against it. That is where he should be – over there beside him. It should all be over with now. This is not fair. They were cheating him. Why are they torturing him like this? Some of the soldiers started to lift the body as he was dragged through a doorway. His heels began banging against the edges of a bare wooden stairs, as he was hauled ever upwards. He could still hear his guards grunting under his dead weight. The wetness of the trouser material had now become noticeably cold against his legs, and the cider smell of ammonia was pungent. Their clumping footsteps sounded deafening against the bare wooden floorboards, as he was bundled along a narrow passageway and literally thrown into a small bedroom. The roughness of the wooden floor scratched his shoulder, which was still a little tender from his previous experience. He was pulled up again, and pushed back onto the bare mattress of a metal framed double bed. He was rolled over onto his stomach and released one of his hands from the handcuff. The loose handcuff was then attached to a solid metal frame of the bed. As the two burly soldiers left him, they locked the door behind them, leaving him there still shaking from fear, still unable to come to terms with those last terrible minutes.

As his body began to slowly calm down, he could feel tears pouring down his face. Reaching up with his free hand, he wiped them away, surprised to find that his face far wetter than it should be from just tears, before discovering that he was sweating profusely. Had it been from the heat, or the utter terror he had just experienced? It was then that the questions started to formulate.

Why was it that he was here, and poor Karim was lying out there?

All of his troubles should be over now, why was he being tortured like this?

That was it!

He WAS being TORTURED.

He was being tortured because the Turks thought that he may know something. His plan had worked, but he knew that he was still in a great deal of trouble.

That was the answer – the sole reason for this whole horrific pantomime taking place. He was being softened up for yet more questioning. They would let him calm down for a while, and then begin the grilling again. There might use physical torture the next time.

With the realisation of what had actually happened, he knew that he had to make an urgent plan of action prior to the coming questions. An intense inner anger quickly replaced any self-pity. He would never give away any information that would imperil his shipmates, but he needed to think of what he was going to say. If he said nothing then he would be taken out there again. He was determined not to go through that horror again. If his deception did not work, then he determined that he would die trying to fight his way out of this hell-hole, at least he would be satisfied that he had given his everything in his attempt to escape. He would go down fighting.

A strong self-determination began to fill him as the basics of a plan began to take shape. He wriggled himself over onto his back, and soon found himself panting from the effort. His eyes started to examine just how his wrist had been secured to the bed-frame. At least things were a little easier with one hand free. He lowered his head, and used the striped material of the mattress to wipe the wetness from his face.

As he rose, he heard the door behind him open and the footsteps of somebody entering the room. George slowly rolled over onto his back. At first, he could not make out the person because of the salty tears that were still stinging his eyes, but he recognised the voice as soon as the man started speaking. It was Arthur Collenette! This must be the prelude to more questioning.

"George, I am so sorry for what happened to you. Please tell them whatever they want to know, because they will really shoot you next time if you don't. It was me who saved you just now. I begged them for your life, saying that I would try and get you to give them the information that they want. Let me be your spokesman, George. Tell me all the answers, and then I will tell them. That way you won't be the traitor George and you will live. For the sake of poor Matthew, do this George."

George could not believe what he had just heard. Arthur had never cared a shit about Matthew? He had left them both to die that day on the cliffs. Arthur was evil – the devil incarnate. He was standing there in front of him now, urging him to betray his country, attempting to turn him against everything that he knew was the right thing to do. Arthur was a snivelling coward, a lapdog doing his paymasters bidding. George could feel an intense anger boiling up inside him. He looked up at Arthur, feeling such an intense hatred seething within. He recalled their schooldays, and how Arthur had stood just as he was now, trying to persuade him to play truant. He had always been bad.

Then something strange happened. It was weird, because at that moment all of his hatred melted away, and all that he could feel for his old schoolboy friend, was pity. Lying back with his head on the mattress, he developed a wry smile. Yes, that was it! That was the answer! Arthur had always been rotten all of his life – well at least from his earliest childhood. It probably wasn't his fault – he had simply been born like it – and it had grown with him. Some people are born evil. He gave another little snort of derision at the realisation.

Standing at the door, Arthur took George's smile as a gesture of acceptance, and he moved towards the bed to get closer to him.

"I'm glad that you've decided to be sensible, George. There has been too much bad blood between us. You will quickly find that you won't regret your decision. The Turks are quite generous to those who are able to see the all of the nasty things that have been committed against them. Once you see what the British and French are doing is totally wrong, then they will reward you too. They have been very good to me."

Arthur had reached the edge of the bed, and as he began to lean over George his voice becoming softer and more reassuring. Inwardly George seethed – Arthur actually believed that he was about to betray his country. His naivety was quickly dented as George's knee shot up very sharply, catching Arthur perfectly in the groin.

"Aaagh," his strangulated voice became a low agonised groan, as his eyes bulged and he collapsed forwards on to him, gasping for breath. As he fell, George quickly rolled onto his side, and brought his other knee across as hard as he could. It was a lucky strike, but his patella caught Arthur full force in his temple. He was unconscious before he hit the floor.

George had not planned the manoeuvre, it had just been an instinctive reaction, but he quickly realised that it had created the opportunity for him to get out of here. He struggled over to the edge of the bed, and reached down with his free hand to begin rummaging through Arthur's pockets for any keys. There was a bunch attached to his belt, just under his uniform jacket. After pushing up the jacket, the belt was awkward to undo, and it seemed to take an eternity, but the buckle suddenly fell apart. He quickly slid the bunch off the leather strap. Then in his haste his fingers began fumbling through them. Inserting each in turn into his handcuff, but none seemed to fit. Most handcuffs had a common key – didn't they? Oh God, please let me find it!

He realised that his hand was shaking, so he stopped, took a long deep breath and went through them again. He was more careful this time, slower and surer. More control, less speed.

Success! One of them fitted, and turning it quickly – he was suddenly free.

As quick as he could, he stripped Arthur of his uniform, and then handcuffed his hands behind his back. George donned the Turkish naval uniform as fast as he could, knowing that he had did not have the time to make any fine adjustments. Stuffing the corner of one of the pillows into Arthur's mouth, he took a deep breath to compose himself before he opened the door and stepped outside into the passageway. It was clear.

His mind struggled in confusion as he tried to think of the internal layout of the Papandross house from his last visit. Carefully locking the door behind him, he put the key in his pocket. Which way? He remembered how they had veered away from the door that led out onto the landing, and taking it he emerged out onto the landing above the main entrance hall. It was clear, and he breathed a sigh of relief, so far so good. His eyes quickly checked for any signs of life below the balcony. There was nothing he could see. Ahead of him the front door stood open. He ran his hand through his hair, as he placed the stupid looking fez onto his head. Moving along the length of the landing, he came to the top of the large staircase. Looking over the banister, down into the hall below, he faltered when he saw a fat Turkish sergeant sitting at a bureau under the stair-case. He could not stop now. Steadying his pace George knew that did not have time to dither, or to try to think of another plan. Stepping forward, trying desperately to look as confident as he could, he descended the steps. The sergeant suddenly heard his approach, looked up and leapt to his feet. Trying to draw in his portly stomach, he stood to attention and gave a smart salute.

As George returned it, he caught sight of furrows starting to materialise on the man's forehead, showing that he was having some doubts.

"Cok Iyi," said George, as he increased his pace towards the entrance, walking straight past the smiling soldier.

The man babbled something behind him, but George didn't stop. He silently said a thank you to Karim for his short lesson in the Turkish language, and continued walking straight down the drive towards the front gate. All the way down he experienced a horrible feeling of paranoia, expecting to be challenged with every step.

It was very dark outside now, and he decided to head straight for the safe house. Taking off the fez, he wiped away the fresh sweat away with the sleeve of his jacket. There were no street lights, and the thoroughfare was somewhat difficult to negotiate. His mind was desperately trying to remember the route that Slade had taken up here, as all the familiar landmarks had disappeared in the night. The one thing that was certain – he had to get as far away from this place as fast as he possibly could. Thankfully he knew which way to turn towards the road that ran along the top of the ridge. That would be a good start.

After an hour, and following several wrong turns, he finally managed to find his way back to the ferry terminal, and from there he quickly retraced his journey back up the hill to the safe house. Karim had shown him where they hid the key, so that any of his team could enter at any time. All of the way back George had feared that he would be recaptured at any moment, and he felt extremely relieved as he walked through the door. At least now he would be safe, for the present at least.

Slade arrived after another hour. He was very surprised to see George, as he had been expecting the worst. George related his experience, and told him of Karim's fate.

He nodded sympathetically, as the story of terror unfolded. Shaking his head at the news. He could see that George had obviously been through hell, but his mind was trying to estimate how the damage would affect the spy network here in Constantinople.

"Karim gave them no information? No names – no addresses?"

"He was very brave, Mr Slade. He refused to tell them anything."

'None the less this place may well be compromised already,' said Slade, and immediately realised that they would have to abandon it. He knew that he would also have to get George back to his rendezvous as quickly as possible, as by tomorrow they would smother the Gulf of Ismid with troops, or maybe a warship. Tonight, he would have a better chance of returning him safely.

"It was a miracle that you weren't recaptured, George," said Slade.

"What makes you say that?" asked George.

"Your shirt tail is hanging out under your jacket," he replied with a snigger.

That was the second time he had done that in public. He began looking down to find the tell-tale piece of clothing. Then, seeing the smile on Mr Slade's face, George realised that he was joking, and his face smiled for the first time in many hours.

****

Stepping out from the offices at Army Headquarters in Constantinople, Arthur Collenette was still smarting from the blistering tirade he had just been subjected to from the Turkish Colonel. George's escape had seriously jeopardised his credibility with the Turks, and he knew that he would have to prove himself anew to regain their favour. It was all bloody George Torode's fault; he had been the bane of his life since his childhood.

To Arthur's twisted mind, he was totally responsible for his present awkward predicament. He hated George with his whole being, and had done so since their days at school together. Arthur had always had to use his ingenuity and guile to be able to keep up with him and Matthew. Yet, almost effortlessly, George had always been that one step ahead of him in all areas, mentally as well as physically. Way back, he remembered that it had been George who had so nearly unmasked him after he had killed his stupid stepfather. Arthur had been totally confident that nobody would have linked him to the murder – yet somehow George had managed to. Thankfully he had remained silent.

His step-father had deserved everything he got. What a liar that man had been, blatantly deceiving his mother by making her believe that he could care for her better than he could. She would never have had anything to do with the bastard, had she known what a deceitful man he really was. As soon as he arrived, he immediately

420

wanted to spoil his relationship with his mother, and take away her affection. He had to die, and it had only been George who had believed that it was he who committed the act. It had taken a lot of careful planning to devise a way so that no suspicion would fall on him, and he had been quite proud of the achievement, but he still did not know how George had figured it out. He was now standing between him returning home safely, once this war was over. He was going to have to die.

Arthur smiled again as he remembered how easy the murder had been. The movements of his step father were known to him, and on the night that he had chosen, it had simply been a case of waiting on the Vale Road until he arrived. Punctuality had been one of his virtues. He was always so trusting, even obligingly turning around, as Arthur pointed to a fictitious light in the sky to expose the back of his head. His cheek muscles flickered, as he remembered smashing the spade down. The sharp metal edge had cracked through his skull as if it had been a green marrow. The man had been dead before his body had fallen down on to the road. That feeling of sheer triumph in destroying an adversary had been so exhilarating, and he felt a total vindication that had completely overwhelmed him. Making his way home afterwards, he remembered a feeling utter satisfaction, because from that moment on his mother would always put him first. She would need him now – he had made sure of that.

On the Pleinmont Point cliffs that sunny mid-morning, Matthew had deserved everything that he got. He was always the clever dick in school, and he would be alive now if he had not taken such umbrage over that silly joke about his mother? After all, it had been a simple statement of fact that everyone else on the Island were aware of. It was beyond his comprehension why he had chosen to fight. If he had saved Matthew, then everybody would have known about how he had backed away from the fight. Arthur knew that he would have been branded a coward by leaving them to their fate. Why should he have stayed – they didn't really like him anyway – he knew that. If he had not come up with that story, then the whole tale would have come out. It had been George again who had tried to convince people that it was he who had started the fracas. It was always been George who got in the way, and who made his life awkward. He had just done it again.

After his rollicking at HQ, he had been told in no uncertain terms that it would he who would lead a search to recapture George. Failure was not going to be tolerated again. He vowed that when he recaptured him, he would personally take charge of the firing squad. It would be even be more wonderful if George was only wounded by the firing squad, because then he would have to shoot the bastard dead with his revolver. His hand gently rubbed the lingering, hollow pain in his groin. That had been unforgivable. He is going to die.

As he approached his quarters, the pain, combined with his bottled resentment, was still seething inside. He knew that the escape had certainly not been his fault, and when he got his hands on that bastard he would take great pleasure in making him pay. A dog crossing his path let out a yelp out pain, as he kicked out at it in his temper.

He threw the door to his apartment wide open with a resounding crash, knocking some plaster from the inner wall. A startled scream came from the girl who had been assigned to him inside. She was a dark-haired Armenian girl, who had been forced into servitude after her village had been wiped out during one of the recent purges by the Turkish army. With their men-folk lying dead all around them, the womenfolk had little choice other than to follow their orders. The older women had been shot in front of her, and she and her friends had no option but to bow to their fate. The Army's excuse for carrying out the atrocity had been that they were hunting for nationalist insurgents. The men were probably trying to found a homeland, but in doing so it also it provided the Turks with an excuse to get rid of these troublesome ethnic nationalistic groups, and at the same time supply the officer corps with a bevy of female comforters.

The Armenians had always been a prickly thorn in the side of Turkey, ever since they had overrun their homelands to the north and east. The world had condemned their efforts to kill them off, as genocide. Over the last year, this practice had become more frequent, and by quelling the Armenian nationalists, the surviving residue was used to supply the Army with women. Fighting men need comfort.

She was cowering at the end of the settee, with her hands at her mouth to stifle her fear, her eyes betraying her terror.

"Bitch," screamed Arthur. "Get me a drink."

She darted over to the shelf and poured him a large scotch, hoping that the fiery spirit would calm his anger. Tentatively she approached him, holding out the drink at arm's length. It was sent flying as he swung his arm across his body, catching the side of her face, and knocking her to the floor. Blood trickled from the corner of her mouth, as she fought to regain her senses. Her arm was raised instinctively, to prevent further attacks.

"Pleeze Artha, no hurt me."

Looking down at the pathetic, vulnerable figure lying before him, Arthur felt a zing of sadistic sexual desire flood through him. Taking a deep breath, he slowly undid his belt, exaggerating his movements, purposely adding to the girl's distress. He delighted in the power he held over her, and he drew yet more ardour from the forlorn pleading look in the girl's eyes.

She knew what was about to happen. He had done it many times before, but it had become more frequent of late, especially when he had been drinking. His form towered over her, his legs apart, as he wrapped the leather strap slowly around his fist.

"Pleeze not hurt me. Me be good to you. You can do whatever – pleeze, no belt."

The toe of his boot brought her plea for clemency to an end, sending her sprawling across the floor towards the far wall. His eyes centred on the exposed expanse of her upper thighs, where her skirt had risen high around her hips. A sneer of lust flickered across his lips, and he wound the end of the belt tighter around his hand.

"No – no – pleeeeze," she mumbled.

He loved it when she begged for mercy. A whoosh through the air terminated in a loud thwack, as the belt bit deep into her skin. Her scream was piercing. The first blood oozed almost immediately, and the sight of the redness against her milky white skin sent Arthur into a frenzy. His arm rose and fell in quick succession, only stopping as he ran out of breath.

Her back ran red. Dropping the strap, he ran his hand slowly through the gore of her back – his heavy breathing revealing his arousal. Twisting his fingers into her hair, he pulled her body over on to her back. Frantically, he ripped the skirt from her. It was only at moments like these that he felt like a real man, standing over the snivelling girl cowering in her nakedness.

He divested himself of his clothing, roughly forcing the girl over onto her hands and knees. Then kneeling behind her he grasped her hips, and almost immediately forced himself into her. Her scream of pain only made him thrust himself deeper. Thinking only of his own need, his thrusts became more urgent. It didn't take long for him to reach his climax, holding the sobbing girl in place as the moment of relief finally claimed him. He extracted himself, letting her body sag to the floor. He had already forgotten the frail form at his feet as he left the room. She lay there in agony, unable to move. Every fibre of her being felt dirty, defiled and disgraced after being continually raped by this monster. Only her eyelids moved, to clear the tears. She knew that she would kill him one day – even if it meant her own death.

Chapter Twenty

Flight of Fancy

George sat waiting patiently at the rendezvous point, less than a mile to the east of the remnants of the bridge that he had helped destroy. He was very wary, because whilst he had been in Constantinople there had been extra sentries posted in the bridge area, but thankfully by using the cover of darkness, getting around them had not proved difficult. He was just hoping that they were not carrying out patrols along this part of the shoreline.

As he sat patiently waiting, he could feel that there was an edge to the air that made it seem distinctly colder tonight, and he gave an involuntary shudder as if to prove the fact. Sitting alone, tucked within the darkness of this clump of vegetation, he was feeling quite depressed, because he still had not come to terms with the terrible events of earlier this afternoon. The image of Karim's blood-spattered crumpled heaped body kept flicking into his mind.

Was it really just this afternoon? It seemed like a hundred years ago, but he realised that it had only been this afternoon. His mind had been physically numbed by his ordeal, so he tried to recall the sequence of the events that had unfolded. If Arthur Collenette had had anything more to do with his interrogation, he felt sure that he would now be dead, and he had thanked God a hundred times for his fortunate escape. It was strange how people reached out to God when their lives were in peril! If he had not taken that split-second opportunity, then he shuddered to think of what may have happened. One thing that he was determined to do, was to report Arthur Collenette to the Skipper when he got back. He wanted it all written down so that he would face justice at the end of this conflict. He knew that he had been so fortunate to have escaped.

George recalled the fear of walking back through the streets of Constantinople earlier this evening, dreading the moment that someone would challenge him, and cause his re-arrest. Every shadowed alleyway he passed made him stop to make sure that it clear, and that no soldiers were waiting ready to spring out and get him. He could still feel that same paranoia – even now.

When he finally reached the security of Mr Slade's safe house, he had sat alone in the bedroom for over an hour, with his body trembling uncontrollably. He realised that his emotional state of mind was in tatters, but he was physically unable to take back control. There seemed to be nothing that he could do to stop the shaking, and he hoped that it would eventually stop on its own accord. He remembered trying to lie down on the bed, but as he had closed his eyes, a rerun of the nightmare would begin all over again. So, he sat up quietly, and eventually his muscles did begin to calm down until everything gradually returned to normal – but his mind was still in turmoil. When he thought that he was coming to terms with the ordeal, his eyes suddenly fill with tears, and he found himself crying and sobbing uncontrollably. Although feeling extremely tired, his body seemed to be totally incapable of relaxation, so he decided that he would sit in a chair on the veranda, thinking that the night air might ease his tensions. Staring out across the rooftops, he was amazed at how many life changing events had taken place in the short time since having breakfast here.

It had been then that Mr Slade had arrived. He was fully aware that something had gone very wrong, and seeing that Karim was not with George, he knew it was bad. After remaining in his car outside the Papandross house for over an hour, when they had failed to reappear, he had no option but to drive off. The alarm bells in his head were ringing a grave warning, and he had immediately gone out to contact all the other members of his team, ordering them to lie low until further notice. Getting back here to the safe house was his last call, and there was a look of relief on his face when he saw George.

Slade had tried to comfort him, encouraging him to relate what had taken place. George explained how they had walked straight into the trap, and he broke down in tears as he tried to tell him of how Karim had died.

Slade's face became grim, and George could see that he was extremely worried. He politely waited to allow George to finish his account, before saying that they should get clear of this safe house as soon as possible, as its location could soon be compromised.

George watched him as he had gone from room to room, clearing out everything that may be incriminating. It made him appreciate the everyday pressures that Slade himself must be under, conducting his dangerous work here in the city. The appreciation of that fact made him feel slightly ashamed about his own fears. Slade was fighting his war right here in the middle of the enemy, and every day he was under the constant threat of being betrayed, or of being discovered by the Turkish counter espionage forces. In a strange way this realisation helped George come to terms with his own state of mind.

The two men left the house together twenty minutes later. Slade took him straight down to the ferry, where they crossed over the Bosphorus to arrive at another safe house that was located over on the Asian shore. It was just after eight o'clock in the evening when they arrived.

Mr Slade had made him comfortable, before sitting patiently, and listening to his whole story once more. He had been extremely sympathetic, writing down George's account as he listened, making notes on which Turks were there – especially noting the appearance of the German U-boat commander.

Just the retelling made George feel a whole lot better, and in doing so it had helped make things fall into place. As he finished, he began to feel the pangs of hunger. Was that a sign that the worst of his nightmare was over? It was to be expected as he had not eaten since breakfast, and he asked Slade if he could have some food. It was eight thirty in evening when they shared a simple meal together. An hour later they left the house to drive George to his rendezvous with *E11*.

They set off from the outskirts of Scutari in Slade's car, but after less than half a mile they came to a halt. The road ahead was solidly jammed at an intersection, and the situation was being controlled by a lone policeman. Sitting there the warm night air with the windows down was pleasantly comfortable and coldness that George had felt earlier had disappeared. The blockage had been caused by a convoy of trucks heading down to the docks. Once they had driven clear, it came as a surprise George how quickly Slade had managed to reach the drop off point.

It was extremely dark as they arrived, and once Slade had switched off the headlights only starlight provided any dissemination. The milky way glowed like a diamanté belt stretched across the heavens. George found it peaceful in the dark, after all the light pollution within the city.

Opening the car door, he turned to say goodbye to Mr Slade, whose creased brow clearly displayed his continuing concern for him. He had been a good friend, and George had a great deal of respect for the agent.

As he stood there, he felt how should try and explain to him how fate had played a very large part in his escape, and as he did so he realised that there was nothing that he could have done to prevent Karim's death. The one and only thing that had saved him from the same fate had been his hint that he may have some information. It had been those few words that had tipped the balance between life and death, and certainly enough to save from the firing squad. He gulped when he realised that he had been so close to dying. Had he chosen to remain silent, then he would now be lying beside Karim. He asked Slade how he managed to live with all of the pressure and constant danger every single day.

"Every man has to find his own way to fight his war, George, and in a very few cases, it can be through individual contributions that will provide the final victory. You have to remember that I was here when it all started, and after being contacted by British Intelligence, that was when my war began. You chose your war via the submarine service, and that is certainly not without its dangers. Sometimes a man's war consists of standing in a trench facing his enemy, or as in my case it is by living amongst the foe, where I try to undermine him from within. George, I agree with your thoughts that fate plays its hand in all our lives. It could well have been you who had died today, and it could have been Karim standing here recounting the very same story. It was Karim's fate that decreed that he should die today, and in a way, he had been very lucky that his death had been so quick. That Turkish Colonel who ordered his death made one bad mistake George, because he could well have ordered that he be taken to the Security HQ, where he would have been tortured to make him reveal all of our names and addresses. It takes a very strong man to remain silent when there is someone is using a blacksmith's hammer to break your bones. Even the strongest amongst us are unaware as to how much pain we can take. Talking would not have saved Karim, because they would still have killed him. Karim knew that he was going to die, and you have absolutely nothing to blame yourself for. Had he talked, then I may well have been accompanying you on your swim tonight George, because I would have had to face torture and the firing squad. So, in a way Karim gained a small victory – even in death."

Slade's words helped him, as George began to realise that he had been blaming himself for Karim's death, and he took some solace from his words. After a short silence he told Slade that he felt that he was slowly coming to terms with what had happened today. Slade reached into the glove compartment of the car and produced a bar of chocolate. He broke it in half, and shared it with George. It had tasted so good.

"George, I have here my latest report for you to carry back with you. I have also written a detailed account of what happened here today, which is also included."

He reached down behind his seat to produce a strange looking object, that immediately aroused George's curiosity. From his original appraisal, it had obviously been a round tin coffee canister, into which Slade had placed his report. The lid had been sealed with beeswax to make it watertight. Then he had clearly wound an old bicycle tyre tightly around the tin, before inflating to provide the object with positive buoyancy. It looked like a misshapen rugby ball with a hernia. George looked at it in wonder, and smiling he looked at Slade, his eyes querying the strange package.

"I agree that it's not very pretty George, but it will give you a bit of buoyancy and will save you having to tread water if the submarine is delayed for any reason. Just make sure that the contents are delivered safely to your captain, because the information that it contains is very important."

"Thanks for everything Mister Slade, stay safe," he said, closing the car door. He stood there, and watched as the tail lights disappearing down the dusty track.

Checking that all was quiet, George commenced the final part of his journey, making his way back down the hillside towards the beach. The near total darkness had given him the time to get his eyes get fully adjusted, and he found that he could see things quite well using the star-lit sky. He quickly found the stream bed that he and Karim had used to navigate during their ascent. From the hillside he could see the stars reflected on the pewter surface of the Marmara, light enough to supply a background to guide him down the hillside. There were two fires, one at each end of the bridge, but he chose to follow the stream straight down between them. He stopped for a short while near the damaged stone column, trying to make a detailed appraisal of the damage. Two pillars had lost their tops, almost down to the half way point. The box girder that carried the rails had been blown to pieces, the twisted remains lay below him, further down the hill.

Soon he was walking along the strand, with the water lapping at his feet, heading back towards the nearest point of the beach from where he was due to meet *E11*. He quickly located the spot and immediately began to hide himself amongst the vegetation, where he sat down to wait.

After half an hour he began to feel apprehensive. Remembering how the boat had missed him on his last mission, and his mind became plagued by doubts. Would the submarine arrive on time? Would he have to wait another forty-eight hours, should *E11* fail to spot him? These negative thoughts sent his spirits plummeting, and he felt very alone. He looked his watch. It was coming up for ten thirty. There was still half an hour to go before the rendezvous. Although he was feeling very tired, he knew that he could not allow himself to sleep.

It was colder here beside the water, as there was a cool wind fanned down from the hills behind him. The chill served to bring him back to full consciousness. Another shiver! George reckoned that it must be blowing down from the Black Sea – maybe from the stark bleakness of the Russian Crimea. Trying to ignore it, he decided that he could cope with a little cold – there was only another fifteen minutes before he started swimming. At that moment he was surprised when he suddenly broke down and cried once more. He was so grateful to be alive, and reasoned that his tears must be ones of relief.

The fresh feeling from the wind blowing through his hair had made him realise how precious his life really was, and how very easy it was to lose it. One minute a person was very much alive, and in the blinking of an eye, their life was extinguished. Turned off like an electrical breaker switch. Both Karim and Mina's images came to mind. Both were good people that he had become involved with – even loved – and both were now dead. Life was so fragile. You had to look after yourself, or you would suffer the consequences. He determined that he would never stop looking after himself. Taking a good deep breath of the night air, he began to feel more at one with himself.

He looked at his watch once again. It was 2240. Finally, the time had come for him to go into the water to swim out and meet *E11*. His mind tried desperately to remember the date – but for some reason he could not. It did not matter. The passage of time had lost all meaning.

The boat should be surfacing in approximately fifteen minutes, so he had better begin his swim now. He walked down the beach, wading out into the water. Bracing himself against the cold, he moved further out until the sea reached his waist. It was warmer in the water than it was out. He held the package that Slade had given to him out in front, as he launched himself forward and began kicking his legs. He could feel the inner tube supporting his weight. Then he realised that his watch was still on his wrist – it would be ruined. He didn't care – it was too late now. His swimming action was deliberately slow and easy to conserve as much energy as possible. He was silently praying that *E11* would not be late, and would surface on time. If he missed her this time, then he would have to spend the next two days in hiding on the beach with no food or water until the next time he would be picked up. Please be there!

He tried to guess the distance he had just swum, thinking that it must be approximately half a mile out from the shore, then stopped and rested. He simply held on to the inner tube to keep himself afloat, letting his legs dangled down below him.

'Good old Mr Slade,' thought George. 'This inner tube is just the thing, every bit as good as a lifejacket.'

Thinking of a lifejacket caused his mind wandered back to that night in the freezing waters of the English Channel. That night had been one of the loneliest feelings in this world, being in the water in almost total darkness and miles from land. At least when *C301* had gone down he had been in the sea with other survivors, and had the benefit of their companionship. Out here, although it was nowhere near as cold, the solitude was extremely disconcerting. With only his head showing above the surface, and the rest of his body hidden in the dark depths below, he began to feel very vulnerable. Any large marine predator could attack him with impunity! The only marine predator that he wanted to see right now was His Majesty's Submarine *E11*. He was just glad that this wasn't a shark-infested sea! There are no Nobby Clarks in the Mediterranean – at least that's what the Coxswain had told them all, but it was still very unnerving, this feeling of being totally exposed. Would the boat turn up, or would he still be floating out here as it got light? It would be so easy for them to miss him.

There was a splash in the water a few yards away. It made him jump. Was it a fish? George started to feel edgy. There must be other types of large fish about besides sharks. What about a swordfish? George wasn't so sure about them. He had eaten a swordfish steak on a night ashore in Malta. Wasn't the swordfish a kind of shark? Maybe not, but it can grow to be nearly as big as one. Torpedo-man Maine said that he and Lieutenant Brown been on the bridge when they had seen a school of pilot whales, whilst they had been on the passage from Gibraltar to Malta. Do pilot whales eat you! Some whales have got awfully big teeth.

All of his senses began to scream in alarm as he sensed something below him – that terrible feeling that he was not alone. A sixth sense that told him that there was an unseen presence that was nearby! There are no whales on the Marmara – are there? He spun himself completely around in the water in a mild panic, but there was nothing visible. Any prey must experience this same feeling of terror, in that instance before a predator makes its strike. The alarm bells rang in his head as the sea suddenly began to vibrate. He could feel a faint resonance within the water which was producing a series of tiny ripples that remained stationary on the surface. They grew in intensity, as the tonal frequency increased. Was it an earthquake? No, it had to be the boat, it just had to be!

George's heart began to pound in his chest, and his breathing became short and sharp as the adrenalin began to flood through his veins. Less than a hundred yards away from his position, the surface of the sea began to boil and froth. Then through the maelstrom rose the conning tower of the submarine, like a denizen emerging from the deep. White water was draining down from the metal tower, as she finally settled calmly on the surface. Sheer relief flooded through George as he watched the faint fiery flecks phosphorescence, as the last of the water poured from the drainage holes in her casing – it was good old *E11* – he was home! The vibration ceased, preceding the clang of the upper lid opening. The sudden sound of voices carried across the smooth surface of the water.

"Over here," shouted George. "I'm over here."

The men on the tower heard him immediately – sheer relief flooded through him – he could see them waving. He began swimming towards the boat and heard the rising excitement in their voices, as they prepared to help him. A whimper of thankful relief escaped from his throat, as his hand reached out and touched the hardness of the steel tanks. Eager welcoming hands appeared out of the blackness, each eager to help him climb up the ballast tanks. More hands began patting his back, and he heard the familiar voice of Martin Naismith calling down from the bridge.

"Welcome back Torode. How was Karim when you left him?"

George's mind immediately flashed back to the garage courtyard and the bloody gore emblazoned across Karim's shirt. He remembered that blank look of amazement on his friend's face, as if he could not believe that he had just died. Poor Karim! Realising that the others were looking at him with some curiosity, George replied to the captain's question.

"Sir – he's dead," said George, shaking his head. He broke down once more.

There was a murmuring on the bridge, seconds later Guy d'Oyly-Hughes appeared at his side.

"Come on Torode, let's get you below. We'll get you into some nice dry clothes, a mug of hot kai, and you'll soon feel a whole lot better. I'll get the Coxswain to issue you with the tot that you missed today. Then you can come down to the wardroom and have a quiet word with the captain and me – OK!"

George knew that he needed the reassuring presence of his shipmates around him, and for the first time in forty-eight hours he began to feel truly safe. His body was shaking uncontrollably, mainly from the breeze on his wet skin, but after a good rub down with a rough diesel smelling towel, it ceased. It felt so good, even though the towel was absolutely filthy.

Once he was finally dressed in dry clothes, and had a hot mug of Kai (strong sweet cocoa) thrust in his hand, he breathed more easily. The drink tasted so good, and he could feel its warmth travel all the way down inside.

A rumble from aft indicated that the engines had just started, and a draught of fresh air invaded the boat. Stoker Wheeler brought in some ships-biscuits and cheese, just in case George was hungry. He smiled as looked at the fare, but he was not hungry. His messmates were strangely quiet around him. They seemed to sense that all was not well with him. The Coxswain was the next to enter the mess-deck.

"I got special permission from the Jimmy, as you missed the rum issue today. Here you are Torode – it's purely for medicinal purposes of course. Get it down your neck, lad," he said, handing him the glass of neat rum, before retiring back to his own mess.

George smiled before he took a large gulp of the undiluted fiery liquid. Choking on the unaccustomed strength of the drink, he nevertheless appreciated the kick that it gave him. Its invasive warmth remained in his bloodstream, and suddenly he became hungry. He took a bite out of the cheese. Even that had the taste of diesel. Oh God, thank you for my deliverance, he said in silent prayer. Before he knew it, he had cleared the plate.

"Skipper wants to see yer, when yer ready George," said Brassy sticking his head around the corner of the passageway. "Cor, where'd yer get that tot of rum from?"

'Good old Brassy,' thought George. He was the salt of the earth, but he still couldn't imagine how he had managed to fancy that ugly stripper in Horlick's bar on that night in Malta.

"Thanks Brassy, it was given to me for medicinal purposes by the Coxswain. By the way," he asked mischievously with a grin, "How's your leaky willy?"

"Dried up a treat, thanks for asking George, but the Coxswain says he's gonna keep up the treatment until we get back. Oim still under stoppage of rum as well, more's the pity. Sadistic bastard, that's wot I call 'im," he said.

"I heard that Brassington," came the Coxswains voice from down the passageway. "If you want to see my birth certificate, you'll note that the name of my father is clearly visible for all to see. Now get back on watch, or you'll find out how sadistic I can be."

George slowly made his way down the passageway after Brassington had disappeared, and knocked on the wooden bulkhead beside the drawn curtain that divided the wardroom from the rest of the boat.

"Come in," said the soft Irish brogue of Guy d'Oyly-Hughes' voice.

"Ah Torode, come in man."

"It's good to have you back," said Naismith, sitting at the table.

"Good evening sir," said George.

Some room on a bunk was provided for him to sit on. It felt good and soft and smelled wonderfully of sweaty socks and stale cigarette smoke. It was great to be home. He remembered that Karim had sat here, in this exact place. He smiled as he remembered him banging his head as he stood up at the briefing, just prior to them being landed.

430

"Obviously things didn't go as planned, so when you are ready please tell us about your time ashore from when you left us," said Naismith.

It took George some time to cover all the events in their entirety. Then the two officers began to question him on particular points.

"Do you mean to tell me that the Turks actually executed Karim without a trial of any kind!" said Naismith.

"Yes sir. Once they realised that they weren't going to get any information from him. They just dragged us both out and stood us against a wall and..." George's voice trailed off. "I still can't think why they didn't shoot me too. I think they were torturing me, sir – trying to break my spirit in an effort to make me tell them everything."

"It must have been a terrible experience, Torode," said d'Oyly-Hughes, patting him gently on the shoulder.

George's throat choked up, and all he could do was nod his head.

"Tell us more about this German submariner that interrogated you – Lieutenant Otto Hersing," urged Naismith, purposely changing the subject.

"He was only there for about five minutes. He knew all about you sir, and he was aware of most of the sinking's on our last patrol. He also assumed that it was us who sank the Turkish battleship as well. I certainly didn't tell him anything, sir."

"I'm sure you didn't, Torode."

"The U-21 is in Constantinople, sir."

"That is very sobering news. We will all have to be somewhat more cautious in the future."

George told them all about Arthur Collenette being a traitor, and then his memory seemed to go blank. Maybe it was the effect of the rum!

"You did a remarkable job, and we're all very proud of you. Is this Arthur Collenette, the same man you reported at your de-briefing following your last adventure? He was a Sub-Lieutenant off the *Adamant*, you say!"

"Yes sir, he's from Guernsey, like me. We were once school friends, and I've known him most of my life."

Guy d'Oyly-Hughes was busy writing down the conversation, his pencil bobbing up and down as he tried desperately to keep up with the spoken word.

"Something will have to be done about him. Can you tell me more about the damage we inflicted on the railway bridge?" he said.

As George began to explain in detail about the damage to the bridge, he suddenly remembered the package that Slade had given to him.

"May I go and fetch something that I've brought back with me please, sir? It's from Mr Slade – he said that the information contained within is very important, and that I am to give it straight to you."

It was only a few seconds before George reappeared, handing over the still inflated package to Naismith. It had been so well sealed that it took the Captain several minutes to open it. Once he managed it, he carefully took out the rolled-up papers, unfolded them on to the table, and began to read. His eyes flicked along the lines of text. Suddenly, he stopped, and he re-read the same paragraph.

"My goodness Guy, this is dynamite. We've got to get this information back to Fleet Headquarters as soon as possible. Set a course for our communications position immediately. Tell Lohden and Plowman to rig up the communications mast as soon as we get there."

He turned again to George, "You have done exceptionally well young man, and you can be sure that I will mention that fact in my report. Off you go now and get some sleep. You'll be excused watches until the morning."

HMS E11 arrived in her radio transmitting position in the early hours of the twelfth of August 1915. George Plowman quickly rigged the aerial mast, assisted by Albert Lohden, who then went below to the transmitter in his tiny radio shack to send the report that Naismith had written on the transit. The strobotic blue flashes from the electrical arcing within the equipment were accentuated within the darkened confines of the tiny compartment. George imagined it as a recreation of the lightening experiment that gave life to the monster in Professor Frankenstein's laboratory in the Mary Shelley novel. The erratic tapping of Lohden's Morse key seemed go on for ever, as he transmitted the long signal. On completion they were ordered by their communications ship *HMS Jed* to await a reply.

Twenty minutes later, the high-pitched Morse code began rattling out of the receiver. Albert Lohden scribbled down the message on his signal pad. He was used to receiving confidential information, but it was a hard job sometimes for him to keep that information away from the rest of the crew. If he were to accidently drop a snippet of information, it would fly around the boat like a bush fire, so the officers would be immediately be aware of the source. He knew that it would be more than his job was worth to reveal anything secret. Since his chastisement he had become more accepted on-board, and he had even taken to learning the intricacies of the Trade during his off-watch time. Ripping the completed signal from the pad, he made his way up to the bridge and gave it to the captain.

Naismith read the message:

Message Reads –

1. Need Slade report at Flagship a.s.a.p.
2. Will send Commander Sampson in seaplane 121700.
3. Position 40.51N 27.08E
4. Return O/Sea Torode to Flagship for de-briefing.
5. Congratulations on sinking Harridin Barbarossa.
6. Continue patrol as ordered.
7. Good luck and good hunting.

"Get the mast down, tell the First Lieutenant and Ordinary Seaman Torode that I want to see them in the wardroom," he said to Lohden, who saluted and disappeared back down through the hatch.

****

At 1700, *HMS E11* was on the surface at the rendezvous position awaiting the arrival of the seaplane. George was standing in readiness on the bridge and despite the heat of the late afternoon he was dressed in his white woollen submarine sweater. Naismith had suggested it, after remembering how cold he had been during his reconnaissance flight over the Narrows, just prior to their first patrol. George's forthcoming flight to attend a de-briefing aboard the Flagship had been one of those secrets that had been impossible to keep from the rest of the crew. Once it had become common knowledge, he had been subjected unmerciful questioning.

"'Ow come you're so important, George? They don't give rides in aeroplanes to everyone, you know," said Brassington.

"I don't know Brassy," he replied. "They probably want a first-hand account of my trip into Constantinople."

"You get to go to more places than Scott of the Antarctic, George. We'll be bloody salutin' you next."

"You wouldn't catch me goin' up in one of them aeroplanes, they're bloody death traps," said the ever-cheerful Mayne. "They're just a bunch of wooden struts, covered in canvas, all held together by bits of string."

"You'll miss all the fun George, think of all them battlewagons that Brassy will be sinkin' while you're away!" said Baxter.

"I'm not going by choice," said George. "It's orders. I'd be staying here with all of you if I had my way."

On the bridge, it was George Plowman the port lookout, who first spotted the faint dot that appeared just above the southern horizon.

"Aircraft bearing Green 115 degrees, about 5 degrees above the horizon," he yelled.

All eyes turned towards the bearing.

"Standby at Diving Stations, and be ready to go down very quickly if this isn't Sampson," Naismith yelled down the hatch to Guy d'Oyly-Hughes.

The aircraft approached head on, until it was about a mile away, before it suddenly banked away to port, and began to circle the submarine. They could see the familiar roundels on the wingtips, as Commander Sampson waved from the cockpit.

The Airco DH2 seaplane then made its landing approach, and after splashing down on the surface, it taxied over to where the submarine lay stopped in the water. Sampson climbed out of his cockpit, got down onto one of the floats, and threw a line across to eager waiting hands standing on the ballast tanks. The bi-plane was hauled alongside and Sampson jumped across the narrow gap waving a bottle of champagne, having left the aeroplanes engine just ticking over. He climbed up onto the casing, just as Naismith and Torode began to climb down from the bridge.

"Good evening, Martin. I've only just heard about the Harridin Barbarossa – it's a tremendous boost to the morale of the troops ashore – you've become famous all over again. Congratulations," he said shaking his hand. "Here, I've brought a little celebration."

He started unwinding the wire from the cork.

"Good evening, sir – how was your flight?" said Naismith. Although he was in command of the submarine, the pilot, being a Commander in the navy, outranked him.

"The Turk threw up a bit of flak coming across the Peninsula, but none of it came too close. I'll just get the bloody cork out of this bottle, and then it will be my pleasure to drink your health."

The bottle suddenly exploded, making everyone jump. Sampson first held it out for Naismith to drink from. Then he passed it around all the other members of the crew who were on the casing. It ended back with Sampson, and he held it aloft.

"Cheers," he said, taking a long drink himself. "You all deserve it. Well done Martin," he drank again. Wiping his lips with the back of his hand he said, "What have you got for me?"

Holding out Slade's waterproof envelope towards him, Naismith beckoned George forward.

"This is the package that the Admiral is so interested in sir, and this is Ordinary Seaman Torode. He will be coming back with you."

The Commander eyed George up and down.

"Ever flown before, Torode?" he asked.

"No, sir," George replied.

"Well, put your lifejacket on. I'll get you strapped in, and you just sit back and enjoy the ride. Leave the rest to me – OK! Oh, by the way, can you operate a Lewis gun? "

George nodded doubtfully. He remembered back to when Leading Seaman Andrews had instructed the class in its intricacies one frosty morning on the Tipner shooting ranges at Portsmouth, during their basic training.

"Good – You will find one attached to the rail that goes around your seat. Let's hope that you won't have to use it. Now get yourself across the gap onto that float, and I'll show you how to get into the observer's seat."

George had heard of parachutes. They were the devices that allowed you to jump out of a damaged aeroplane, to be able to float down to earth before it crashes, and he was expecting to be wearing one for this flight. He looked concerned when he was not offered the option, so he supposed that none were carried, but thought that he would ask – just in case.

"We don't bother with those bloody things. They are big, bulky, and far too heavy. They only get in the way. You will be much more comfortable without one." The pilot motioned for George to board the plane. George gulped.

"Bye, George," yelled George Plowman, waving from the back of the bridge.

George waved as he climbed down onto the ballast tanks, before making the perilous leap over onto the nearest float of the plane. The aircraft dipped down alarmingly under his weight, so he clung on tightly to one of the struts. He could not believe how flimsy the aircraft actually was. It was just as Mayne had said – just bits of wood, wire, and fabric. There were tiny wooden spars, taught wires, and painted canvas. At least the float he was standing on appeared to be made of some sort of light thin metal.

To be leaving the solid security of *E11*'s steel pressure hull for this flimsy thing made George wish that he had been given a choice about staying aboard. Samson started shouting some instructions, which were difficult to hear above the noise of the rotary engine. Following the Commander's pointing instructions, George managed to climb up into the observer's seat. Sampson then jumped across the gap, causing the aircraft to rock alarmingly, before he climbed up into the cockpit behind him. He leaned over the edge, to point out the safety harness to George. Even after he had strapped himself in, his nervous apprehension failed to decrease. He felt his heart thumping in his chest. The few aeroplanes that he had ever seen always seemed to have the propeller at the front, but strangely this one had the engine fitted behind the pilot's cockpit, with the prop pointing backwards. He could hear it there now ticking over, giving the occasional cough in its mechanical throaty drone.

The Lewis gun that the Commander had mentioned sat before him, a retaining lanyard holding its barrel down, and the whole mounting was secured to the circular metal ring that ran right around the edge of the observer's position. It was secured on to the rail by a swivel, that allowed it to be elevated and depressed, as well as it being able to be trained through almost 300 degrees.

"Were you joking about the parachutes, sir?" George shouted back to him, still harbouring the hope that they had one discretely hidden beneath his seat.

"I told you. We don't bother with the bloody things. There is nothing to worry about. Just sit back and enjoy the ride."

The cursory remark didn't exactly reassure George, who was of the opinion that they may well prove to be very necessary, so feeling more than a little frightened, he placed the goggles over his eyes as he had been instructed to do. He couldn't see much as they quickly fogged up, so he raised them up, resting them on his forehead. The bridge of the submarine was now packed with sightseers, as Naismith had allowed several of the crew up to witness their departure.

Commander Sampson began revving the engine. The rear-mounted pushing propeller coughed, before it began to whirr faster, and it quickly masked all other sounds. Sampson accelerated the engine again, and the sudden increase in noise was absolutely deafening.

The two seamen standing on the ballast tanks pushed the front of the aircraft away from the submarine, and Sampson increased the power further as he taxied the seaplane away into open water.

Looking down between his feet, George could see the water flashing past beneath, through several small holes in the canvas where the wire braces passed through the aircrafts skin. He felt a nervous thrill as the wind blew through his hair. He experienced a frightened anticipation as he realised that this was going to be the ride of his life, albeit without a parachute!

Suddenly the engine's tone increased up to an ear-splitting roar, that caused the whole fuselage of the aircraft to rattle alarmingly. George thought that it was going to explode, as the aircraft began to accelerate across the water.

He leaned his head over the rim of the gun-rail, and could see the white splashes of foam, as the floats skipped across the surface. Equally white were George's knuckles, as he gripped the sides of his seat. The plane bucked and jolted as the floats struck each of the small waves, until it became a bone-jarring torture. The plane lifted slightly, as the aircraft skipped, then hopped twice more as it clipped the tops of the waves, before finally lifting into the air.

George opened his eyes, giving another terrified look out over the side of the aircraft. He gasped, suddenly feeling very disorientated. They must have been at least fifty feet above the water, as he watched the sea falling away beneath him. It was terrifying, and he felt his stomach churning. The plane tilted over violently to the left, and he held on tight as Sampson banked around to head south west. A tap on his shoulder made him turn, and he saw the Commander pointing downwards. Following his finger, he could just see *E11* looking very small, with her bridge packed with waving figures. George waved back excitedly as they flew over the boat, his head turning to watch them as they receded astern.

Despite his pumping heart George realised that he was actually enjoying the experience very much. The higher they climbed, the more peaceful everything seemed be, with only the deafening roar of the engine spoiling the experience. He was very glad that the captain had suggested that he wear his Submarine sweater, because it was indeed quite cold up here – certainly much colder than it had been down on that beach last night.

George assumed that the land ahead, which he could see stretching from horizon to horizon, could only be the Gallipoli Peninsula. It was funny to think that he had actually been walking down there. Above them the evening sky was heading towards twilight, more so over towards the east. He quickly tried to judge the distance from the submarine to where they were now, and was amazed as to how fast they must be travelling. It would have taken the boat at least an hour to travel the same distance.

Looking down over the side he could see the entrance to the Dardanelles, clearly visible at it stretched out below them. So, was the town of Gallipoli itself, a little further down the channel. The buildings visible as an urban discolouration against the land. As he looked down, he began to realise that this panorama looked exactly the same as it does on the Admiralty Chart. He would often look over Lieutenant Brown's shoulder, when he was laying off his courses on the plotting table. There was a ship steaming along, down the channel and he could see the V shaped wake streaming out astern. A pity, as there was no way of alerting the skipper as to its presence.

As they began their transit across the Peninsula, George began searching, trying to recognise some of the other points that he knew from the charts. He could see the high ground of Achi Baba below them, and ahead of them lay the shimmering silver glow of the Mediterranean. A few small villages dotted the bland-scape, but nothing that was vaguely familiar. From up here it all looked like pastoral farmland, but down there somewhere was the place where he had been held prisoner.

Quite suddenly the whole texture of the land below changed. The surface became darker with large sandy brown patches. It looked to be scorched, as if a blow torch had eradicated all traces of the green mantle, leaving just a speckled brown carpet. Dotted craters littered the surface, looking like those on the moon that he had seen through his binoculars at night, but this was the moonscape from hell. Then he could see a tight web of faint black jagged lines, radiating across the landscape that puzzled George at first, before he realised that they were the trench positions. Bright flashes were bursting down there on the ground, quickly followed by puffs of smoke. Someone was firing a barrage onto the enemy lines. It looked horrible, and George became so thankful that he had picked the navy on that day that he had joined up in St Peter Port.

Then all of a sudden, he could see several mushroom grey clouds bursting into life all around them, some of which were quite close to the aircraft. Each of the bursts opened like smoky grey flowers. They dotted sky off to the left of the aircraft, and others were slightly below them. More small puffs of smoke started to appear around them, but these were slightly higher than their present altitude. The Turks were firing fragmentation shells up at them.

George looked back at Sampson with a worried frown on his face. The Commander seemed oblivious to the impending danger, wearing a broad grin below his goggles, which showed the whiteness of his teeth.

Off to his right the Mediterranean Sea now shone like a mirror, gleaming in the setting sunshine. Far out on the horizon, he could just make out some of the distant islands, and he wondered which ones they were. Looking down at the coastline, George could see some smaller dots lying just offshore, which he assumed were units of the Allied Fleet. From up here they look like innocent toy boats, yet it is those toys that are probably carrying out that deadly shelling of the trenches that he saw a few minutes ago, he thought to himself.

More small puffs of cloud started appearing around the flimsy aircraft, looking like small balls of grey-black cotton wool, before they flashed past and disappeared astern. One of them burst a little closer; near enough for George to hear the faint explosion, and he could see the ignition flash from the fuse. A piece of shrapnel whizzed through the upper wing, leaving a small jagged tear. A thin shred of material started flapping like a banner in a gale. Sampson immediately sent the biplane into a side-slipping, stomach-churning dive to the right.

Caught unawares, George grimaced as he clung on to the sides of his seat once more. Had they been hit! Were they going to crash! It felt like riding in a runaway perambulator, that was rushing headlong down a hillside out of control. As a boy, he, Matthew and Arthur had been given an old one by a neighbour, and with it they had terrorised the residents of St Peter Port.

The ground came rushing up to meet them at an unnerving speed, and George had his feet braced in front of him, against one of the cross struts. He could feel the blood in his body being physically drawn down by the gravitational force as Sampson levelled off. This was worse than being at sea in a force ten gale! He decided that he was so very glad to be a sailor and not an airman, as he felt his stomach starting to rebel at the ever-changing shifts of gravity.

Achieving level flight once more, he relaxed his grip, and chanced another look out over the side. Thankfully they were not going to crash – realising that it had been an evasive manoeuvre. A few seconds later a neat line of small round holes appeared in the lower wing to his right. It looked as if it had just passed under the stabbing needle of an unthreaded sewing machine. How could those exploding shells create such a neat pattern? Then he heard something! Faintly he heard Sampson's muffled shouting from the pilot's position directly behind him, but turning his head, he couldn't make out any of the words. The officer was gesturing frantically. George released his harness, and turned right around to follow the Commander's gesticulating finger. He immediately saw another plane, off to the left of them, and slightly behind. It started banking around in order to follow them. Then George noted the black cross edged in white on each wingtip.

'Bloody hell,' thought George in amazement, 'it's a German fighter.'

He could see the pilot's brown leather helmet sitting in the cockpit, as the top of the plane tilted towards them. Following further gesticulated instructions from Commander Sampson, he could see that he was telling him to get the Lewis gun ready. Then half standing, half squatting, his fingers struggled to untether the Lewis gun. It came free, and George had to place his feet firmly against the main frame beneath him, or he realised that he might just slip through the wooden slats covering of the floor and plummet earthwards. Checking that the circular magazine was firmly fitted, he panned the gun around on its sliding rail, ready to meet the German aircraft on its next attack. His fingers wrapped around the pistol grip handle, and he reached forward to raise the back sight. Sampson had his thumb raised, and was nodding his head in approval of his actions.

The Fokker completed its turn, and was about half a mile distant. It seemed to be manoeuvring itself in readiness to make another attack from their rear. George knew that he would have to wait until the enemy aircraft came much closer, before he could fire his weapon with any hope of hitting it. Attempting to hit a moving target at this range would just be a waste of ammunition. So, he used the interim time to practice aligning the Lewis on the German aircraft, following it around until it went beyond the extreme limits of the mounting rail. As the German past astern of them, try as he might, he could not get a bead on the enemy.

His heart was pounding, half with excitement, half with fear. Commander Sampson was heading directly for the Allied lines as fast as the plane could fly, whilst keeping a wary eye on his adversary. George pointed this time, indicating that the German fighter had completed his turn, and was heading straight for them. He pointed at the gun, trying to explain in sign language the predicament of not being able to take aim. He was completely unable to bring the weapon to bear on the German aircraft.

Sampson took a quick look over his shoulder. The German was indeed right astern of them, and with its superior speed, it was closing fast. He quickly grasped the problem, because suddenly the seaplane veered thirty degrees to the right. The sharpness of the manoeuvre nearly threw George over to one side, and he had to grasp the mounting rail to steady himself! Taking another look at the German, he quickly noted that he had enough movement on his weapon to be able to take a sight. He traversed the weapon right around, and now he had the Fokker fully in his back sight. 500 yards, 400, 300, wait thought George. The words of Leading Seaman Andrews came through the mists of time – Place the target in the middle of the back sight – Hold your breath and gently squeeze the trigger. But before he could fire, the Fokker began to follow them round, and it quickly disappeared once more behind the propeller. It became impossible for him to fire. He knew that had to be aligned quicker the next time.

Sampson immediately turned thirty degrees the other way. George had already begun to traverse the Lewis back around the rail to the other side of the aircraft, and this time he stood ready and waiting for the German to come into view. It quickly appeared and at a range of just 200 yards. He could clearly see the German pilot making fine adjustments to make sure of his shot. George could see its wings dipping one way then the other, as the pilot jockeyed his fighter into the perfect firing position.

At 150 yards George began firing, trying desperately to keep the gun steady as it bucked violently on the mounting rail. It seemed to be jumping about all over the place, and looking along the barrel, he could see the line of his tracer bullets arcing away towards the enemy aircraft, realising that he was firing too low!

Again, the German followed them around and again Sampson altered to allow George to see the target. This time George had traversed the gun all the way back around, determined not to fire low this time. His next burst passed under the Fokker once more, but only just below the wheels of the aircraft. He stopped firing, made a slight adjustment to his back sight. Then letting his weapon lead the line of the German aircraft, he sent another full burst towards him. By using shorter bursts, he sprayed the plane like a fireman trying direct his jet of water onto a flaming inferno in a strong wind.

Strangely the German had still had not opened up with his machine-gun, but his wingtips were flicking up and down as he continued to adjust to his position. He was desperately trying to position them into the centre of his sights, before actually squeezing his trigger. Samson was equally determined that he was not going to allow that to happen.

Then at last the German did fire. It was a short burst of white-hot tracer, that George saw passing harmlessly through the wire rigging on the right-hand wing.

Maybe George's shots were unnerving the foe! Maybe he was an inexperienced pilot who was just learning aerial combat!

There were some more jerky corrections from Sampson, which caused George to swing the Lewis Gun around once again, before he could get another sight on the German. When the aircraft's position was relatively stable, George he let him have a longer burst, finally feeling the gun jump as it clicked on empty. From the tracer he had just fired he could see that the Fokker seemed to absorb the flying metal.

'Oh God,' thought George. 'We're in trouble now – where the hell are the spare magazines?'

After a quick panicky search of the observer's position he quickly found them. They were in a canvas satchel bag, that hung down one side of his seat. Whipping off the empty canister, he tossed it over the side, and bent down to get a fresh one. There were five spares and he stood up, and immediately had trouble trying to click the new magazine into position, fully expected the German to be firing at them by now. Still the new magazine was proving difficult to fit, and frustrated, George removed it, composed himself as Leading Seaman Andrews' instructions came back to him, as if he were standing right beside him. It clicked into position on the next attempt.

Sampson's sudden yelling made him look backwards. The gun was at last ready for action, but the German seemed to have disappeared. He quickly searched the sky on both sides before he saw it. The Fokker was some 300 feet below them, spiralling downwards with smoke pouring from the Mercedes engine. Beneath the forward canopy there was a sudden flash, and wind driven flames trailed backwards from the engine cowling like a colourful streamer in a gale. He could clearly see the pilot desperately trying to beat them back with his arms. Slowly, the German pilot gradually disappeared from view as the fire engulfed the whole mid-section of the aircraft.

George watched in transfixed horror as the macabre spectacle unfolded below him. The plane continued to spiral down and down, with its thick black tail trailing out behind. It finally disappeared in a ball of flame as it crashed into a crater near one of the Allied trench positions.

That, but for the grace of God, could have been us, he thought. I would not have wished that death on anyone.

George had learned some hard facts about aerial combat very quickly. The chief one was that in this lofty theatre of war, it was a straight-forward case of kill or be killed – but that same maxim could probably be used for any theatre of war. War, like life itself, was really just a game of chance. By carrying out your training expertly, you could possibly reduce the odds that it would be you who died. George certainly had no wish to die yet.

Looking back at the commander, his smile created an equatorial split of his face. George gave a half wave, as he re-secured the Lewis gun, and retook his seat, buckling himself in with the leather strap.

As he sat there, he realised that his hands were shaking. It was not the cold, but the adrenalin that continued to course through his veins. He began taking several deep breaths, and was glad to feel his body gradually calm. Out over the darkening blue of the Aegean Sea, he could make out the grey humps of the islands he had seen earlier, now looking like a school of whales breaching the mirror smooth surface. As they flew ever closer, heading for the largest of the group, the horseshoe shaped anchorage of Murdos was suddenly recognisable. As always, it was brimming with ships. 'Murdos,' thought a relieved George. 'We're home.'

He could see the Flagship lying down below, as Commander Sampson brought the flimsy aircraft around onto its landing approach. Down, down they went, until the surrounding hills began to blocked the horizon. The lower they went, the more deflated George felt, because if the truth were known he had really enjoyed his first flight, but he could have done without that Fokker getting in the way. On the whole, it had been one of the best and most exhilarating experiences of his life.

He hated the landing however, fearing that the plane was going to nose-dive into the harbour and send him down into the depths of the anchorage with the aircraft on top of him. His fear quickly subsided as the speed started to reduce to a taxi-like crawl. The huge towering mass of the Flagship suddenly loomed up over them, as a recovery pinnace cast off from its side, and headed out in their direction.

Sampson climbed down onto one of the floats and secured a line to enable them to be towed towards the massive bulk of the battleship. As they drew alongside a wooden pontoon, the structure of the great ship towered high above them. A crane was being panned out to retrieve the aircraft. George was told to climb down and get into the pinnace by Commander Samson. The boat then made its way over towards the companion ladder, where they disembarked and climbed upwards. On reaching the deck, Commander Samson grasped George's hand.

"Well done lad. Well done indeed," he said pumping his hand up and down. "You handled that gun very well. I am so glad that you're an expert."

"I'm no expert, sir. That's the first time I've fired one since I left training," said George.

"Well, the standard of training is certainly improving," said Sampson, pumping his hand once more.

A voice from the deck high above them, yelled down.

"Excuse me, sir. The Admiral is waiting for you in his day cabin."

"Thanks," called Sampson. "We're on our way."

George waited nervously outside the great man's door with Commander Sampson. He felt a bit conspicuous wearing only a smelly submarine sweater and his dirty diesel-soaked working trousers. His hat was long forgotten, he had left it jammed above the hydraulic pipes in the passageway of *E11*. Too late had he remembered that the photograph of Gladys in its frame that was still tucked above a trunking! The one saving grace was that the Commander was still dressed in his flying suit, and wearing his flying leather helmet, which made George feel a little easier, but he still looked much smarter than George. The door opened and the Admiral's Steward stood there wearing a look of distaste as he eyed George's dishevelled appearance.

"The Admiral will see you BOTH now," he said, unable to see how anyone in the Royal Navy could be dressed in such a slovenly dirty disgraceful fashion.

The Admiral was indeed waiting for them. With him were Commodore Roger Keyes, Lieutenant Commander Charles Brodie, Captain Somerville and several of the other submarine captains.

"Come in, gentlemen," he said. "Take a seat, won't you. Thank you for coming so quickly."

George had never been called a gentleman before. He sat down with his back bolt upright, feeling distinctly uncomfortable in such august company.

"Relax for goodness sake, Torode. We're fighting a war, not attending divisions at Whale Island." The Admiral's words were meant to ease his discomfort.

George smiled nervously, and changed his position, hoping he looked more relaxed. The Admiral spoke again.

"Did you have a good flight?"

"We were attacked by a Fokker fighter bi-plane coming over the Johnnie Turk lines sir. Young Torode here, shot him down with the Lewis gun," said Sampson.

"Well done lad," said the Admiral, obviously very impressed. "It seems that there is no end to your talents. I expect that you would both like a coffee after such a thrilling experience?"

The Petty Officer Steward begrudgingly placed two cups before them, and poured steaming black liquid into each of them. The Admiral waited until his flunky had left the cabin.

"OK. Let's begin," said Admiral de Robeck. "We received the signal reporting the sinking of the Harridin Barbarossa. That was absolutely brilliant news, good for the moral of the soldiers over there in the trenches as well. I want to hear about everything that has happened since you sailed, Torode. Firstly, did you meet up with *E14* as arranged?"

"Yes sir. We met her the night after we arrived in the Marmara. It was the evening of the that same day that we sank the battleship. As we were just about to part company a small steamer was sighted and we carried out a joint engagement against it. *E14* used her six ponder, and we used our twelve pounder. Despite being hit several times the steamer managed to beach her-self by going astern, but she was fully on fire when she hit the mud. We parted company with *E14* just afterwards, but we found another steamer the next day. The captain didn't think she was worth a torpedo, and so we attacked her once more with our gun. The trouble was, the gun mounting trunnion plate fractured, and knocked the gun-layer over the side, but fortunately the gun crew just managed to save the barrel from rolling over the side as well. The captain hoped that the Engine Room Artificer's could fix it later during the patrol. That all happened before the night that I was landed with Mr al Mizri, sir."

"These gentlemen beside are all eager to hear how *E11* got on with the new anti-submarine net at Nagara Point. Can you tell us briefly what you know?"

Trying to think clearly, George began his account.

"My job is the control room messenger, sir. So, I had a good view of the whole operation. The Captain said that the only way to get through the net, was to hit it head on at full speed. Otherwise, you will be likely to get snagged, as the French boat did. Our First Lieutenant went up into the conning tower and he watched everything from the viewing port. He said the net parted on impact, and that our riding wires carried the edges of the net up and over the gun mounting and the conning tower brilliantly. We did snag something aft however, but our forward speed snapped it, and we carried on through."

Both Keyes and Brodie were very interested in this part of the story. They kept up a barrage of questions, some of which George was unable to answer. They wanted to know the size of the wire mesh, and the points on a chart where it stretched from and to? How far it reached down under the water? George could only shrug his shoulders, or surmise on some of their enquiries.

The Admiral saw that they were asking a little too much from him, and directed them to allow George to continue.

George went on to tell them about the ship they had sunk just past Nagara Point in the Ak Bashi Liman anchorage. Then he expanded his story about the ship they had caused to run aground, after being engaged by their twelve-pounder gun. All the assembled company were smiling at him. George thought they all looked rather comical sitting there in their gold braid with their big grins.

"Tell us about the Harridin Barbarossa sinking, Torode," said the Admiral.

George composed himself, as he tried to recall the sequence of the events.

"We were patrolling the southern Marmara near the entrance of the Dardanelles, just off Gallipoli, sir. I was the look-out. It was about 0445 on the eighth of August when we spotted two possible warships heading for the channel from the central Marmara region. We thought there were three at first, but what we thought was two ships turned out to be the Harridin Barbarossa escorted by a single destroyer. The Skipper... – er sorry, I mean Lieutenant Commander Naismith, did his initial set up, and then fired one torpedo at her. It struck her starboard side near the bridge section of the hull, and at first it didn't appear to have hurt her too much. The Captain told us what happened as he watched through the periscope. He said that she had slowed, shortly before suddenly there was this terrible internal explosion from deep inside, and she slowly rolled over and went down. The Captain described it all as it happened and said that her forward magazine had blown up."

There were smiles all around the table, and there were several quips about showing the Turks who was boss. The morale in the room had visibly soared, and George realised at that moment just what the feat that *E11* had achieved really meant. If it caused this sort of reaction amongst the top brass, then it must have done wonders for those poor souls in the trenches.

"This is simply amazing, after all of the set-backs that we have suffered ashore and our recent losses amongst the Fleet itself, is feels good to have some real success at last. So, is your gun operational again!"

"Yes sir, they fixed it while I was away on the mission with Mr Karim al Mizri. They used it to sink a dhow yesterday morning before I was picked up, sir."

"Remarkable! They are all that way from their depot ship facilities, with no heavy machines to make a replacement, and yet they have repaired a piece of ordinance that would have challenged most of the mechanics on the *Hindu Kush*," said the Admiral, to the general assembly.

When George had finished, the Admiral picked up a signal sheet and looked at it.

"Now, I've had a very brief report of your excursion into Constantinople. I would now like to hear a detailed account of what exactly happened. It says here that Mr al Mizri is dead, is that correct?"

"Yes sir," said George, suddenly saddened by the reminder.

"Pity, pity," he said, shaking his head. "I am very sorry to hear that. Please go on."

George nodded. He covered all the events from start to finish, and in the retelling of it he found it had become a little easier – as if it had now been firmly placed in the past. It was as if the more that he told it, then the more of a memory it became. Each rendition seemed to give him a feeling of absolution – a little like the absolution from a Catholic at confession.

Everybody was particularly interested in the German submarine commander. The loss of two allied battleships at his hand had put a price on his head as far as the Royal Navy were concerned.

"So, U-21 is holed up in Constantinople, that's going to cause us to rethink a lot of our present submarine strategy," mused the Admiral.

"She could certainly also pose a threat to our own boats in the Marmara, sir!" warned Roger Keyes.

"Yes, I can see that Roger," said the Admiral. "But we're being side tracked here. We can discuss that at a later date. Do carry on Torode. I believe that you were given a report when you left!"

"Mr Slade gave it to me, sir. Commander Sampson has it with him. It was wrapped in a waterproof tin to prevent it getting wet when I swam back to *E11*. He told me that it was vitally important."

Commander Sampson retrieved the package from the inside pocket of his flying jacket, and handed it across the table to the Admiral. The Admiral sat up in his chair.

"Ah yes, from what *E11*'s signal says, this could indeed be very interesting!"

The Commander in Chief opened it, unfolded the pages and started to read the document. His eyebrows rose, as his eyes flicked across the text.

"Good God! They are going to try and seal us in the Aegean by supplying sectionalised U-Boats to the Austrian port of Pola. The sectionalised parts will be transported down the Rhine on barges, and then overland by train. At the dockyard in Pola they will be re-assembled, fitted out, and the completed U-Boats will be used as a blockade. Can you imagine it gentlemen, a line of U-Boat's that our ships will have breach to bring supplies up to our men on the peninsula? That is probably how U-21 arrived here in the Mediterranean unnoticed. I do not for a minute think that she would have managed to breach the defences at Gibraltar. If we allow this to happen, any of our supplying ships could fall prey to their torpedoes, and for that matter, so will a lot more of our capital warships. It just goes to show how the importance of the submarine has grown since this war started. By them using a few U-boats, they can jeopardise this whole campaign. The mere threat of their presence, I think, proves this point. You can see the effect that Naismith and Boyce are having on the Turkish supplies in the Marmara, can't you!"

The report was several pages long, and he flicked through them one at a time.

"This second part of the report says that a German delegation will be visiting the Sultan's palace on August sixteenth, with the aim of signing a co-operation pact with the Turks to supply them with the German built submarines. Both the Sultan, and Ataturk himself, will be there in attendance. They intend to supply some these sectionalised units via the internal European railway system directly to Constantinople. What with those that will be sailing from Pola and these others coming out of Constantinople, we will be like the walnut in a nut-cracker. Gentlemen we have obviously got to disrupt that meeting, or at least cause the signing of any such agreement to be delayed for as long as possible. It also presents us with a chance to illuminate their top echelon as well. We need as much time as we can possibly get to enable our troops to take the peninsula. Once that victory has been achieved, then we will not be so pressurised, because we will then be able to eliminate the gun battery defences that line the Dardanelles and sail our task force through to attack Constantinople itself. Once the city has fallen, it will obviously make any treaty with Germany irrelevant. The sixteenth of August does not give us very much time gentlemen. I would like to hear a few of your ideas on how we can delay that signing of that treaty. Does anyone have any immediate suggestions?"

Commodore Keyes was the first to speak.

"Unfortunately, Slade now has only two other agents working with him, and only one of them is based in Constantinople itself. The other is upcountry at present. Maybe if we were to supply him with more agents and materials, he could come up with a feasible plan himself."

"That will take time Roger, and I don't want maybe's – I want a positive plan of action, because time is of the essence here," said the Admiral sternly. It was plain for all to see that Roger Keyes was not one of his favourite people on the Staff.

"May I suggest a joint service operation, sir!" said Charles Brodie, sitting next to Keyes.

"Go ahead, I am open to almost anything that is practical," said the Admiral, paying more interest this time.

"Well sir, what if a combined team of service saboteurs were to be sent into Constantinople. Slade could then act as their co-ordinator. He could provide them with a hiding place until the pre-planned attack. They could then make a covert attack on the Sultan's Palace, plant timed explosives, and retire without being seen. The explosives could be detonated by means of a time-piece to coincide with the meeting, once it is under way. Even if we don't manage to kill the Sultan, Ataturk, or any of the delegation, just think of the propaganda value to be had. You can almost imagine the headlines of the World's press – British infiltrate Turkish Capital, or Sultan Mehmet has nowhere left to hide. The resultant mayhem of such an operation could cause the U-Boat supply agreement to be put back by several months, sir. Months that might just allow us enough time to complete our objectives here."

"That is a good sensible idea, Brodie. This is the sort of thing that I need. I like the sound of your plan initially. We will have to finalise the nitty-gritty in a meeting with the Army Chief of Staff of course. They will be able to determine what we will need in the way of men and materials, et cetera. Has anyone got any other ideas in that direction? How many men we will need, what equipment will be required, how to get them out there, that sort of thing?"

"Sir!" said George, nervously raising his hand.

All eyes turned towards him, and he cringed in his chair, wishing that he had kept his mouth shut.

"Go ahead, Torode," the Admiral said.

"Well sir, having just come back from Constantinople for the second time, I have found that the best way of moving around in the city inconspicuously is by oneself, or in pairs. Any bigger group would immediately arouse the interest of the locals, who are generally a nosy bunch who always like to know what is going on. Getting such a small group there could be fairly simple if they were flown out to *E11*, just as I was flown here today. *E11* could then land them and their equipment ashore without too much of a problem. Maybe Mr Slade could arrange transport into the city?"

"That is an excellent idea. Roger, I want you and Brodie to liaise with Commander Samson over there. and come up with a plan to get a small sabotage team and their equipment aboard *E11*," said the Admiral. He turned back to George. "What else do you suggest?"

George's confidence was rising. "If you are intending to send a small force, it would be best to keep them at a safe house, or out of the way until the actual attack

444

takes place. Slade did have one safe property near the city centre on the European side, but he has had to abandon it because he is frightened that it may have been compromised after the capture of Karim and me. He told me that he has other houses around the city. He actually took me to one of them just before driving me to my rendezvous point last night. He also gave me a meal before setting off, so he would probably be able to feed the team until the actual attack. I think that three, maybe four men may be needed to get enough of the explosives and equipment into the target area. After an initial survey of the target area, a planned of entry could then be made. Once the explosives have been placed, it would only need one of the team to remain behind to witness that they have detonated, rather than have the whole herd of men there who are liable to be discovered in no time at all. I was able to move around the city with a fair amount of freedom. The only problem that I had was with the language, so one of the saboteurs at least should be fluent in the Turkish tongue if they are to stand any chance of success."

"Your knowledge of the city may also prove to be invaluable," said the Admiral. "I would like you to be part of this proposed team, Torode. I'm not going to order you, especially after your recent brush with death, but I will none the less ask if you are willing to go back once more as part of a team?"

"Yes sir," said George without hesitation. "But with your permission I would like to combine the mission with a secondary agenda, sir."

The Admiral looked puzzled.

"I would like to be empowered to arrest, and bring back for court martial, Sub Lieutenant Arthur Collenette, sir!"

The Admiral sat back in his chair thinking about what he had just said.

"I have just read the report about him. Nobody likes a traitor Torode, but why is this matter so important to you?"

George told the Admiral the story of the cliffs at Pleinmont, and of the death of Matthew Marquand. He related how Arthur's fictitious story had placed the blame on him. and then went on to tell about him of his suspicions that Arthur had killed his stepfather. He argued that he would like a chance to set matters right and bring to justice a liar, coward, murderer, and now traitor.

"As far as I am concerned young man, you can go ahead and arrest him, and if you are able, to bring him back here for trial, but this main mission must take complete priority above everything else. If catching this Collenette causes any hazard to the main mission, which is the attack on the palace, then it must be abandoned at once, do you understand?"

"Yes sir," said George.

"Then you have my authority to arrest Sub Lieutenant Collenette, and to bring him back for trial. I want the fact that this man is a traitor recorded in the account of these proceedings. Should you not be successful in arresting him, then feel assured that he will face justice after the war."

"Thank you, sir," said George.

"Good, then I want all of you back here at 1000 tomorrow with all of your ideas concerning this mission. By then I will have had a word with the Army. Together we can settle the fine details of the matter. Thank you all, gentlemen."

The assembly rose to their feet, and began to file out of the Admiral's day cabin.

Chapter Twenty-One

The Sultan's Palace

HMS E11 began to dive below the surface, her stern lifting slightly to send her bow deep into the darkness, disappearing through a bubbling cauldron of white foam. As the sea calmed over her, an eerie silence descended on the small group who were left behind, sitting in their rubber boat.

Despite the presence of his four companions, George Torode was experiencing exactly the same feelings of trepidation and abandonment that he had felt on his two previous missions, hoping that the outcome of this trip would be somewhat better.

Once they began to paddle the craft, attempting to head towards the shoreline, George quickly found out that his fellow saboteurs lacked any experienced in boat handling. An over-enthusiastic use of the paddles had quickly sent the small craft spinning one way and then the other, with very little headway being achieved. This time they had a small rubber boat containing the packs of explosives, weapons, and ammunition which was bobbing uncertainly behind them on the end of a length of manila rope. Seeing that some co-ordination was badly needed, and with him being the only sailor, George realised that he would need to take charge of the situation. First, he told them all to stop, and gave them clear instructions in how to paddle in rhythm. Then using one man to keep the stroke for the rest to follow, they set off tentatively once more. He sat at the stern using his own paddle as the rudder, hoping for signs of improvement. Despite a few initial mistakes, he managed to keep the rubber boat on a fairly straight course.

George reflected on his feeling of desolation, which oddly did not seem to be shared by any of his companions. He supposed that soldiers were often left alone in the field to fend for themselves, and must be quite used to such situations. Maybe it was just the isolation of being alone on the surface of the sea in the middle of the night that made him so edgy? Could this unease have been caused by the terrible experience on *C301*? His recent horrors might also be a major contributing factor, but this time, at least he had companions to share the mission.

Tonight, the Sea of Marmara was flat and even, with a cool breeze that provided some relief for the body heat being produced by their paddling. Once a steady rhythm was being maintained, George went on to explain to his comrades the importance of not making a splash with their paddles. He told them how sound travelled great distances across the surface of the water at night, explaining that there was the strong possibility of any sentries being alerted, and thankfully they all accepted his authority in good heart. He slowly sensed his fears beginning to ease, despite the fact that they were heading for the enemy coast once more.

All was quiet now, and the only water disturbance was in their wake. The four soldiers had learned quickly, and George settled down to guide the rubber boat towards the shore. The calm sea reminded him of the placid summer waters around his home in the Channel Islands. Summer evenings on Fermaine Bay came to mind again, when he and Matthew had continued to swim until it got dark. It had been along that shoreline to the south of St Peter Port that they used to construct ships in the last century, and there were still some smaller vessels were constructed there. Great sailing barques and clippers for the China tea trade were constructed right there on the stony beach. The shipyards that made them had long since disappeared, but the water around there was invitingly clear and still, just as it was here right now. Back in those salad days he had not arrived back home until well after twilight. His mother would invariably be angry, but only because of her concern for his safety.

Out here on the Marmara the sea seemed to hold the latent warmth on these semi-tropical nights. Looking ahead, most the coastline was hidden in darkness, but the faintest glow of a sentry fire could be seen on the higher ground, near the vicinity of the damaged bridge.

Then dreams of Gladys began to fill his thoughts with her pretty features smiling directly at him. He realised that he had hardly had a thought about her during his last mission with Karim, and that it had only been when he had returned to *E11* that he remembered that her photographic image was tucked above the trunking. He was still harbouring some doubts following his conversation with Basil Partridge. Would she be stepping out with young officers? He knew that he had no right to protest if she did, because of his own indiscretions with Maria in Malta, and with Mina in Constantinople. Would she still have the same feelings for him? When would they meet again? Would they ever meet again? After everything that had happened, would he have the same feelings about Gladys, if they did manage to meet? When would this bloody war be over, because it was certainly messing up everybody's personal relationships, forcing the men to be parted from those that they loved the most? He was very well aware that he would certainly never be here off the coast of Turkey, had it not been for the war.

These thoughts were replaced by hatred, as the image of Arthur Collenette suddenly filled his mind. He could see the sneering evil expression spread across his contorted features. It worried him how intense his feelings were. It was not exactly hatred, but such a deep and utter loathing for another human being, that it frightened him. To George, Arthur Collenette summed up everything that was vile and bad in this world. He was a murderer, a traitor, and a coward, and he wondered how he managed to live with himself. Then he realised that being evil must be the normal emotion for Arthur, and living with the despicable acts that he has committed was natural for him. His life needs came before everything. Decency and honesty were alien experiences, and so they never entered his mind. Just thinking about other people before himself would be something that he would never consider. He was selfish to the extreme – utterly selfish. Maybe that was the definition of evil – extreme selfishness. Maybe selfishness mixed with greed was the definition of evil? Arthur had always tried to put all of his own needs before anyone, and had stopped at nothing to make sure he got them. This was only achieved him by riding roughshod over everyone who stood in his way. Such egotism was a sin, and all sins have to be repaid in some way. He would eventually get what he deserved. God doesn't repay debts with money – he remembered his mother saying that adage. The other worrying thing that was troubling him was, that if it ever came to the moment when he was forced to fulfil his promise to Matthew – could he actually do it? Despite his loathing for Arthur, he seriously doubted that he could kill him in cold blood.

The operation he was now embarked upon had been thrashed out within the great cabin on board the Flagship on the day following his flight back to Murdos. George had sat quietly as Commodore Keyes and his staff had argued with the Army Chiefs of Staff over what was needed to achieve the main aim of the mission, when an army officer asked a question.

"What exactly is the stated aim of the mission precisely?"

George could not believe his ears, as the answer had been discussed non-stop for the past hour. No wonder the troops were bogged down on the peninsula, with duffers like this leading them. Heroes led by donkeys.

"Firstly, it is to land a small group of men covertly, to carry out an offensive action in Constantinople. Their main objective is to plant explosives with the purpose of eliminating as many participants as possible that will be attending the meeting between the Turkish Sultan, the despot Ataturk, and his advisers, along with the German Military Delegation. If the Sultan, or any of his major politicians, or indeed any of the Germans are killed, it will prevent the signing of the agreement for the Germans to supply the Turks with new submarines and other munitions," replied Commodore Keyes. "If indeed we manage to kill any of the major participants, it will also seriously damage the Turkish military high command infrastructure. Should the Sultan himself be killed, it will be a terrific blow to the Turkish troops and civilian morale. It will also unnerve, and cause a great deal of uncertainty amongst the general population. On our side, it will provide us with a tremendous propaganda coup."

"Isn't that what we are all here for, and why my men are in trenches over there on the peninsula – trying to eliminate Turkey from this war?" the colonel persisted. "Are we not trying to link up with the Russians, to pass them supplies so that they can attack Germany from the east?"

"Yes, of course, but as in the trenches of Flanders, we have currently reached another impasse. Your men are dug in, and are now facing an enemy who are equally very much dug in. The Turkish sappers have dug their trenches so close to our own that it has become too dangerous for us to bombard for fear of hitting our own men. This situation has continued for some weeks now. Be honest Colonel! We are not achieving any significant successes, are we? Therefore, we cannot allow the Turks to obtain any more German munitions to strengthen their offensive capabilities. With this tabled plan, it is hoped to strike a decisive blow, and bring about a radical change in our fortunes. The action of just a few hand-picked men can achieve far more in a few hours, than all of your thousands of men stranded on the Peninsula over these past months."

"The recent landings on the sixth of August at Suvla Bay were designed to split the Turkish lines. The peninsula should have been ours in a matter of days," the colonel persisted once again.

"From the latest information we have the ANZAC forces are still stuck on the beaches, and they are finding the formation of a bridgehead extremely difficult. The slaughter taking place over there shows how they too have met with another solid wall of resistance. Their casualties have been absolutely appalling so far. Anything that we can do to alleviate that situation should be welcomed. The greater the turmoil and discord that we can create at the Turkish nerve centre, then the better it will be for our troops to achieve a final victory."

After a great deal of discussion, it had eventually been decided to send five men, one of whom was to be Ordinary Seaman George Torode. With him would be two explosives specialists from the REME, a young officer from the Royal Sussex Regiment, and an exotic Asiatic gentleman who claimed that he was familiar with the layout of the Royal Palace. He had simply turned up at the initial briefing, accompanied by an army captain who introduced him as Mustafa Dalan Bay, a Turkish businessman. He would be acting as their interpreter, and apparently until recently, had been serving in Constantinople as one of Mr Slade's agents.

The Royal Sussex officer was a young lieutenant named Peter Ramsbottom from Chichester, in that county. He had graduated at Cambridge, where he also gained a blue as a wing-forward in the University XV when they had beaten Oxford in the Varsity Match of that year. He was a tall, heavily muscled, physically fit man of twenty-two years. With his short black hair and rugged features, he would have looked more at home in a blacksmith's forge than in an army uniform. His matter-of-fact accent hid a sharp inquisitive mind that was quick to evaluate, appraise and tackle any problem that presented itself.

Corporal Jan Sullivan from Plymouth, a diminutive man of twenty-eight years, who had quickly earned nick-named Jan Sullage-van after they had seen him eat his meals straight out of a tin using just his field knife and his fingers! Many would have said that he had the manners of a pig – if it were not an insult to the porcine breed. His rustic West Country accent sounded like he had grown up on a farm somewhere to the west of Dorchester. He referred to each of them, including the young officer, as my luvver, or my 'andsum. Yet his small stature hid a human dynamo, that hid the tremendous reserves of strength and stamina he possessed.

Private Dave Priest was an orphaned Londoner from Stepney. Unlike his name, he swore like the proverbial barrack room trooper, and dropped aitches with a carefree abandon. Most of his conversations were embellished with Anglo-Saxon oaths, as if they were a standard part of the English language. He was a slim, gangly, youth of twenty who was, and by a very large margin, easily the least intelligent of the three soldiers. However, what he lacked in academic ability, he more than made up for in his skill with explosives. Just as an artist performs miracles with paint, so Priest could create magic with amatol and torpex.

During the thirty-six hours of training that had followed, the selected five had been forced to get to know each very quickly. Their training exercises took place on a stretch of beach on the northern side of the Murdos anchorage, situated out near one of the isolated farms along that stretch of the island. Their instructor was a burly sergeant from the REME, who strutted about in a military manner, swagger-cane under his arm, bawling orders, ever quick to leap on any mistake.

"By priming your explosive in that manner, sir, you could very easily blow away your wedding tackle!" he said to Lieutenant Peter Ramsbottom. "Your missus wouldn't be very pleased with you, now would she, sir?"

"No sergeant," replied the chastened young Lieutenant.

"… and nor am I pleased, sir – now unrig that charge, and re-assemble it in the correct manner."

Although the sergeant was unrelenting in his attempts to force them to reach his high standards, he was also just as quick to dole out praise to anyone who began to show signs of reaching those dizzy heights.

"Well done lad – well done indeed. You might just come back to us in one piece if you continue to improve like this."

During those hours they had together, they essentially learned how to live and work as a team. They seemed to have blown up everything in the immediate vicinity, having removed a very large boulder from the edge of a farmer's field. Created craters that would fill with the next rain to provide the farm with a dew pond. Then they had used their explosives to divert a small stream down to keep the pond constantly filled. They had felled a tree, and demolished one wall of an abandoned barn. The acrid smoke of their explosives hung low in the windless air, wispy like the gossamer threads of a spider's web floating in the twilight rays of the sun.

The heat of the day had been oppressive. Coal, smoke, and the exhaust fumes from the oil-fired ships down in anchorage blended themselves to create a dirty fetid haze that hung permanently over the island. It reminded George a little of the *Levante* cloud that had hovered at the top of the rock in Gibraltar. This static haze served to trap the suns heat, creating a green-house effect that caused sweat to pour from every inch of a man's skin. Their uniforms clung to their backs, the material showing the dark patches of the moisture. Muscles ached from dawn to dusk from the never-ending practical exercises and assault courses, yet in those two days they had managed to form themselves into the basis of a raiding party.

The unknown member of the team was Mustafa Dalan, who had been Mr Slade's man based in Ankara. It had been he who had supplied the British agent with weekly updates of the current civil and political situation within the Turkish interior. He was a bona fide businessman, who ran his own import/export business, specialising mainly in coffee and teas. Apparently, he had responded positively to Slade's request that he should head the political translation part of this operation. In his business enterprises he had dealt with the Turkish royal households, and had visited several of the palaces in the process. George found him easy to talk to, and was extremely intrigued when he had learned of his own involvement with Slade. He was another diminutive unobtrusive man, only just five feet three inches tall, but he had distinguished features, with greying temples against otherwise jet-black hair. He was thirty-nine years old.

George was easily the youngest member of the team, and at first he felt a little shy in their company, but was soon made to feel that he was one of the team. Once they had found out that he was a crew member of *E11*, he was quickly treated more as an equal.

"You wouldn't get me down in one of those things. Give me a nice muddy trench half filled with water any time my luvver," said Jan Sullivan.

"Fuckin' deff traps – that's wot they are," added Dave Priest, sagely.

Their training had been all too short, simply because there was insufficient time for more. Commander Sampson's squadron had been mobilised to transport them all out into the Sea of Marmara to rendezvous with *HMS E11*. In all, six of the Airco DH2 bi-plane observation aircraft fitted with floats had been deployed. One aircraft was used to carry each of the men along with his weapons. The sixth was to transport the explosives, some extra weapons, and the smaller second rubber boat. There was already one rubber boat aboard *E11* that would be used for the men. The flight was escorted by three of the latest British fighters that had recently arrived here. The Bristol Scout's looked resplendent in their latest camouflaged livery.

On the evening of the fourteenth of August, the aircraft took to the air together, like a swarm of flying ants on a summer's day, crossing high over the Turkish lines above the Peninsula. As a token gesture, the Turkish anti-aircraft batteries had fired a bit of flak up at them, but none of it came remotely close. Soon the crystal-clear waters of the Marmara lay spread out below them, and the escorting fighters waggled their wings, banked hard to the right, and returned to their base, their pilots waving good luck as they flew for home.

For George, this flight was every bit as exhilarating as his first, but he was very glad that there had not been the same interest from any of the German fighters. For the briefest of moments, he wished that he'd joined the Army Flying Corps, or even the Fleet Air Arm, but his thought was quickly dispelled when he realised that his eyes were nervously searching the skies all around. The continual pressure every time a pilot went aloft must quickly drive them towards the edge of sanity, he thought. The incident with the Fokker had been both terrifying and thrilling at the same time, but it had left him impression that there was always something lurking behind a cloud, waiting for its chance to pounce. The absolute freedom of being able to soar above the clouds and fight the enemy with the wind in your hair seemed somehow very noble, even romantic, but that pleasure came at a very high price, because it was also a war fought very much on your own, and often in near freezing conditions. It was invariably a one-to-one situation, a gladiatorial fight to the death, and that took a special sort of nerve. Just like the gladiators of the Roman arena, if you were not good enough on the day, then you died. There would be no thumbs up or down at the end, because if fate had decided that it was your turn to die, then one could expect the most horrific of deaths. If you were not hit by bullets from your foe, then your aircraft could be damaged. You were then faced with two to three minutes of absolute terror as your machine plummeted earthward with the knowledge that you were totally impotent to save yourself. There were no parachutes taken on most of the operational patrols, and so very few aviators survived these crashes. If you were unlucky enough to have your engine catch fire, then you could expect to be roasted to a cinder crisp on the way down. George had heard stories of pilots who had leapt out of their cockpits, rather than watch their own flesh being burnt from their bones. This constant threat had to be endured every day, by every pilot.

He then remembered the close-knit camaraderie aboard the boat, and the amicable cohesion that bound them all together so that they acted as one body. He knew then that he wouldn't seriously want to change his situation, he was quite happy with his lot being in the Trade. For all the hardships and dangers involved in the operation of a submarine, it was more than compensated for by the pride he felt at being part of the legend that Martin Naismith and *E11* were creating here in the Marmara.

HMS E11 stood stopped in the water awaiting her new passengers, as each of the aircraft landed in quick succession on the clear calm sea. One by one they taxied up to discharged each passenger and his equipment, before moving away and taking off immediately to head back to base.

The explosives, rubber boat, and weapons were struck down below as fast as the crew could pass them. On completion the strong-backs were quickly replaced in the hatch opening, and the outer casing hatches quickly secured. Finally, the external water-tight torpedo loading hatches were hammered shut. Naismith breathed a sigh of relief when it was reported to him that his boat was in all respects ready to dive. To be caught on the surface in the vulnerable state of being unable to dive, was not a position he wanted to be in any longer than was necessary.

Down below, the newly arrived team were busy unpacking and checking their equipment in the confined space of the Forward Torpedo Room.

"How do you feel, now you're down a submarine?" George asked the two soldiers.

"It's a bit crowded my luvver – kinda cramped. A bit like being a sardine in a tin," said Jan Sullivan, laughing at his own attempt at a joke.

"I said they were fuckin' deff traps, didn't I! I feel like oive bein' nailed in moi own fuckin' coffin," added Dave Priest.

Mustafa Dalan caused a lot of interest when he came aboard. As soon as Brassington found out his name, he was rechristened Mustafa Phagg.

On their transit north towards the pre-arranged landing point, they all attended a briefing. Naismith presided, and George noted that there was a lot less room in the wardroom, than with his previous mission. The two junior soldiers had to stand in the passageway, where they listened to the instructions that might make the difference to them returning alive, or not.

"You will all be landed tonight at 0030 hours. That will be very early on Sunday the fifteenth of August. I have been informed your target has to be destroyed on the sixteenth, although I have not been told what that target is! All being well, if you hide the boat ashore, you can use it to return on the following evening. God willing, from midnight on the sixteenth, but if do not return within one hour, which will be 0100 on the seventeenth, I shall return to the same spot the next night at exactly the same time, and wait another hour. If you fail to appear after that then I am afraid that you will be on your own, and you will have to make your own way back as best you can. It's going to take a full half an hour to inflate that monstrosity that you call a boat, but hopefully it will be man enough to carry you all ashore. The small rubber craft will easily carry all of your equipment. Slade will be waiting at the same rendezvous that you used before Torode." He turned towards Lieutenant Sidebottom, "I suggest that you let Ordinary Seaman Torode guide you there. Are you OK with that, Torode? How about you Ramsbottom, are you happy to let young Torode here lead you until the initial contact has been made?"

George nodded, and Peter Ramsbottom confirmed that he was OK with the arrangement. Naismith continued.

"It's 2046 now, so I suggest that you all try to get a couple of hours sleep. Has anyone any questions before we close this briefing."

There were none, so Naismith wished them all good luck, and they moved off to try and find a corner in which they could lay down their heads to rest. George did not manage to sleep and nor did the three army men, which only left Mustafa, who surprisingly managed to achieve the full state of slumber. He had snorted like a bull elephant seal during the mating season, and questions were asked by the crew as to how his sinus had survived intact. Torpedo-man Mayne said that he had heard quieter flocks of geese.

Now here they were, sitting out here in the Sea of Marmara in the middle of the night. *E11* had disappeared into the veil of darkness. The men were positioned, two on either side of the boat, with George sitting at the stern steering. He looked ahead towards the direction of the bridge where he could see glow of a least one fire. The sentries were obviously still there!

"Keep your voices very low from now on. There are Turkish sentries up there near the railway line. Try and keep your strokes together," said George, for what seemed the thirtieth time. "That's it – In – Out – In – Out."

The paddling became synchronised once more. It was definitely something that they should have practiced more of during their two days training, but there had not been time. When he heard the gentle sound of the waves lapping against the stones on the beach, it came as a welcomed relief for George. He jumped out of the boat and reached over and grabbed the bow line, holding the craft tightly against the beach until the others had clambered out. Together they managed to untie the second boat, unload it, and pull them both up onto the higher dryer ground. Then the boxes of explosives, weapons and equipment were stacked. Both of the boats were then carried up into the nearby vegetation. Tucking them down in between two huge clumps of tamarisk, they were covered with greenery to hide them from immediate view. To George it looked more like a Guy Fawkes bonfire than a camouflaged boat, but it would have to do.

"OK, let's divide up the load and get going. Torode, I want you to lead the way from here until we make contact with Mr Slade, and his car," said Peter Ramsbottom, taking back his leadership duties now that they were back on dry land. "Come on Priest, let's get this gear sorted, and be on our way."

"There are sentries up there, sir," said George.

"How can we get past them?"

"If you follow me sir, I will take you up past the stone pillars, where we will climb up a rocky stream bed. I managed to come down that way a few nights ago without any difficulty."

"Then lead on," said the officer.

Each of the men picked up their own weapon, and shared out the explosives and other equipment. They then made their way along the beach and eventually reached the bottom of the chine. George held up his hand, halting the column of men. Peter Ramsbottom came up alongside him.

"What is it?" he whispered.

George pointed up the hillside, to the right-hand side of the damaged bridge.

"We're going to have to be really careful from now on, sir. I just saw a sentry patrolling along the line up there."

Keeping in close to a mass of vegetation, George led them carefully to the now familiar stream that was trickling down the chine towards the shoreline. Turning uphill, he began leading the team up the narrow watercourse until they were actually beneath the damaged section of the bridge. There was a lot of blasted rock strewn all around, and long lengths of twisted distorted metal lay in awkward confusion on the grassy slope. Looking up, George could see that the repairs were already underway, and alarmingly they were at an advanced stage. The stone pillars themselves had been partially rebuilt, and a new box girder framework stood in readiness to bridge the gaps. George crouched down and gathered everyone around him, quietly explaining in a hushed whisper how he intended to proceed.

"As we go up this stream, we will pass beneath the sentry's fire and it is just possible for them to spot us, so absolutely no talking, and keep yourself as low as you can. We will ascend one at a time. I will go first, and once I reach that rise above the level of the railway, then follow me up one at a time. I suggest that Mustafa follows me, because if I am spotted then he might be able to talk his way out of the problem. See that outcrop of rock up there at the top of that rise – that is your aiming point. Once we are all up there, we will be out of sight of the sentries – and after that it will be easy climb to the upper ridge. Mr Slade's car is parked on the road just over the crest. Keep your eyes on the route that I take, and try to follow it exactly."

George looked up at the sky, glad for the half cloud cover. A weather system looked like it was coming in from the northwest. He set off, keeping a wary eye on the sentry fire as he made his way carefully up the streambed. The nearest fire to him seemed quite a bit closer than a few nights ago, and was going to be more dangerous to get by.

As he had reached half way point, one of the sentries suddenly stood up. George froze like a statue, before slowly lowering himself down into the recess of the water course. The edge of the stream gave him cover from where he could clearly see the man silhouetted by the glow of the fire. It was plainly evident that the man was answering a call of nature and relieving himself. George remained still until the figure had disappeared from view, and then he rose dripping wet, and continued onward and upward towards the ridge.

He reached the safety of the outcrop without any further difficulty, and looking back he realised that he could still plainly see one of the sentry's fires below him, but alarmingly there was another that was partially screened by trees. It was too late to warn the others of the danger. The Turkish sentries had obviously moved their position slightly since he was here last. Their fire lit some of the stock pile of repair materials, and there were some tents nearby. Maybe it was a labour camp?

He decided that as the others arrived here, he would send each of them onward up over the crest, and out of sight to meet up beside the road. Once they were all there, it would be a relatively simple task to just walk down the road to meet Mr Slade.

Peering back down the course of the stream, the damaged bridge was faintly silhouetted in places by the Marmara beyond. After an intensive search for more dangers, he could vaguely make out the next figure setting out to join him. His anxiety level rose as he seemed to be taking his time, and climbed very slowly. George was willing him to go faster, but he knew from experience that caution was the wisest way to get up that hillside safely.

George suddenly felt a keen need to relieve himself, and as he stood and did so, he tried very hard to keep the next climber in sight, which was not easy. The next man should be Mustafa, but from this distance it was too dark to be sure. The spatter of his urine on the grass around him created a steaming cloud in the starlight, when he suddenly heard the noise. His senses, already honed sharp, were now on high alert. The sound of voices gradually grew in intensity from somewhere below, off to George's left. Buttoning his fly quickly, he flung himself back down onto the ground on the edge of the rise, drawing his revolver. He peered into the darkness, searching for any intruders. Then he saw them passing in front of the flickering light of the second sentry fire. Two more sentries had appeared, walking from the labour tented camp area near the first fire, heading along the rail track towards the damaged section of the bridge above the stream. If they carried on as they were, they would be directly above Mustafa and could not fail to see him. From the soldiers, he rechecked on Mustafa's position, – and could see that from the way he was still moving slowly up the streambed, he had obviously not seen or heard them. If things continued as they were, Mustafa was definitely going to be spotted.

George felt the frustrated impotence of clearly being able to see the danger there before him, and being absolutely powerless to do anything to prevent it from happening. His gaze returned back the fire-lit area and he could see the Turkish soldiers clearly now. They were about thirty yards away from Mustapha, and both men had a rifle slung over their shoulder on a leather strap. They were carrying something! A water flask! Ah! They heading down to the stream for some water!

It was dark down in the streambed, but the hillside had a ghostly sheen in the semi-starlight. George was praying that the shadowed area in that deeper part of the chine would provide enough cover to hide Mustafa. Please don't make a sound Mustafa.

It always seems to happen. Just when you one thinks that things are going to work out OK, those same fears actually happen. Mustafa's foot must have dislodged a rock, sending it clattering down onto others in a loud clackety-clack-clack. A howitzer shell exploding nearby could not have made a more obvious noise in the stillness of the night. The soldier's rifles were off their shoulders in an instant, and they were holding them out at the ready, as their eyes searched the chine below the bridge for the source of the disturbance. Suddenly one of them pointed down to the stream.

"Surada – o adam – surada."

His companion saw what he was pointing at, and both men brought their rifles up against their shoulders, into the firing position.

"Isminiz ne? Nerelisiniz?"

Knowing that his silence would bring instant death, Mustafa had the sense enough to stand and raise his hands.

"Ben Mustafa Dalan Bay," he called up to them. "Ben Stamboul – Ne istiyorsunuz?"

He had asked them what they wanted, and the rhetorical question had stunned both the sentries for a moment. Mustafa further confounded them by asking how they were.

"Nasilsiniz?"

The confusion in their voices could be heard, as they discussed the situation with each other. Mustafa pressed home his advantage.

"Yangin var – Yemek ne var?"

After him asking if there was anything to eat at their fire, the voices of the sentries changed, as they clearly re-appraised the danger. The situation quickly became less tense. The soldiers had obviously assumed that he was a peasant making his way home, who was trying to cadge a free meal from them. The two soldiers descended the slope towards him, obviously intent on checking that their assumption was correct. As they reached his position, they still held their rifles levelled at him. They asked what he was doing.

"Ne istiyorsunuz burada?"

Ignoring the question, Mustafa asked for tea.

"Cay var mi."

"Cay yok," they replied, stating that there wasn't any.

Mustafa went on the offensive again.

"Cay istiyorum."

The soldiers were starting to lose interest in this idiot demanding tea at this time of night, but before they could say another word two unseen hand's, grabbed their hair, yanked their heads back viciously, and slitting their throats from ear to ear. They both fell to the ground with blood gurgling in choking exhalations as their lives ended. Dave Priest and Jan Sullivan suddenly emerged out of the darkness holding bloody knives in their hands. The death of the sentries negated the danger, but George knew that when the bodies were discovered it would mean that extra security would be employed in the area. It may make their return awkward.

"Well done Mustafa," whispered Peter Ramsbottom sarcastically, as he arrived at his side. "Let's get these bodies hidden."

****

An hour later and they were all safe in Slade's car, heading towards Constantinople.

"I did not expect to see you again so soon, George," said the agent. "I never imagined that it would have been so quick after your last adventure. I have only just received the instructions for this mission, so you will get all the help that my organisation can give you."

"Second Lieutenant Ramsbottom is in charge of the operation, Mr Slade," replied George, indicating the young officer, who was sitting in the passenger seat beside him.

"Hello, Ramsbottom, welcome to Constantinople," he said, smiling at the Sussex man. George continued the introductions as the car bounced along the rutted road.

"Merhaba Mustafa Dalan Bey," Slade said, recognising his compatriot. "We will talk in English while we're all together old friend. It is always good to have reliable people to work with."

"Were there any comebacks from Turkish security following my last visit, Mr Slade?" asked George.

"The Turkish militia somehow found the old safe house on the European side, George. I thought that maybe they would. It was Karim who had rented the place, so it was only a matter of time before they arrived. Luckily, only one of my men was there. Unluckily for him he was arrested, and after six hours of torture in the Military Intelligence Head Quarters, he was executed. I know that he did not give anything away, because if he had we would all have suffered the same fate by now. He was a very brave man. You will all be coming back to my own house in Scutari. There's plenty of food, and whoever is unlucky enough to not get a bed can sleep on the chaise-longue. I have a servant who will help you with anything you need around the house. His name is Agamemnon. I call him that because his father comes from Athens, but his mother was born in a small village near the site of the legendary Troy. He is as honest and true as they come, you can trust him with your life. Later today, once you have all had a good rest, we will begin the reconnaissance of the Sultan's Palace. I have been informed that the attack will take place later tonight, when you lay the explosives for the meeting tomorrow – is it not?" he asked, seeking confirmation.

"Yes, I would like to do a quick reconnaissance to familiarise myself with the lay-out of the palace, Mr Slade. Then we can go in later tonight."

"Once we reach my house you can all grab a few hours' sleep, but we will have to have an early breakfast, then we can go out in my car to a couple of spots that I know, from where you can get a good overall view. There will be no need for everybody to come."

The drive into the city went well. When they arrived, it was well after three in the morning. They drove in through a pair of open gates, that led on into a courtyard. The headlights lit up a magnificent white two-storey cube of a house. On the ground floor there was a low balustrade wall, that lined the veranda surrounding the house. The main entrance was guarded by two round pillars, with a large ornate wooden door. It may have been an optical illusion, but the sides of the building appeared to gently bow outwards. The front façade was filled by tall floor to ceiling windows in the baroque style, all symmetrical, with a small matching balustrade along the base of each. High above, a superb cornice ran right around the roof.

"Cor," said George. "Do you actually live here Mr Slade? It looks like a palace."

"That's exactly what it used to be, George. The Sultan's friends and visiting Ottoman dignitaries used to be quartered here. There were even some apartments on the upper floor, that used to be the harem. It was located over on the far side of the building."

"Are there any of the women still there?" he asked hopefully.

The resultant laughter made George wish that he hadn't asked such a stupid question.

"Sorry George, wish I could help you. The palace is rented out now as a business centre. I acquired it indirectly through one of our people in the Lebanon. Come on in, and I'll get you all settled."

Once inside, Slade showed each of them to a room, leaving them to sleep off what was left of the night, but unfortunately, with all of the excitement of the past few hours' full slumber was not possible.

****

The Turkish Sultan was staying at the Beylerbey Palace, which stands over on the Asiatic shore of the Bosphorus. It was the usual summer residence for the royal household. The palace and the surrounding village which bore the same name, translated literally to mean Lord of Lords. It had been originally built for Sultan Abdul Aziz in 1861, but now it was the home of the deposed Sultan Abdul Hamit II, and has been in residence since his return from his Salonican exile, where he had been sent in 1913. This old Sultan had ruled Turkey with an iron hand, until he was deposed by Enver Pasha (Ataturk) in 1909. He had now been replaced by the younger Mehmet V, and his entourage as the head of State. A post that was no more than a figure-head, a puppet of the true Turkish leader Ataturk. The royal household had always taken residence here during the hot summer months, due to the cooling breezes that came wafting down the Bosporus from the Black Sea. It lay about four miles north east of Scutari on the Asian shore of the waterway, and had a private access to the cooling waters to enable the royal house-hold to bathe.

Slade, Mustafa Dalan, Ramsbottom and George, sat in the car viewing the grounds of the palace from a road that was situated on a steep hillside, high above the palace. It ran up behind the stands of cypress, olive, and oleander trees that filled these slopes with green. Just off one of the hair-pin bends there lay a space just wide enough for a car, and as he pulled. Slade warned them not to take too long. Now that they a good view of their target, they could see that the building itself was a three-storey building, imposing, but certainly not ostentatious judging from the exterior appearance. The grounds were extensive without being wide-spread. In the two corners of the grounds that abutted the Bosporus to the north and south, were situated small marbled buildings, which Slade said were the swimming changing rooms. The palace was similar to several other grand buildings that George had seen in and around the city, and having seen the interior of one, he knew that the outward stark appearance belied the opulence that lay within.

Through their binoculars they could see quite a bit of activity. Judging by the number of khaki uniforms that were dotted about the grounds, it appeared that the royal household were very well protected. Below them, there were more soldiers guarding the main entrance. Then Lieutenant Ramsbottom spotted the soldiers at the gate, who were staring up in their direction with binoculars. He informed Slade.

"We must hurry. There will be a patrol coming up here soon," said Slade. "Judging by the number of soldiers at that main entrance, I don't think that will afford you an easy entry."

Mustafa Dalan reached into the pocket of his jacket, and pulled out a folded sheet of paper that provided a description of the palace.

"The Beylerbey is divided into two very separate parts. Firstly, we have the Selamlik where the Sultan lives, and second, we have the Harem, or the women's quarters. Underneath the Selamlik, down in the basement are the kitchens and other services, plus the living quarters for all of the servants. The Staterooms and the Imperial Apartments are all on the upper two floors. I have taken the liberty of looking up this information from the books in your library, Slade Bay. There are twenty-six elegantly appointed chambers, which includes six grand salons for visiting heads of state. There is a magnificent split staircase, leading upwards from the reception hall, that divides at the top into the Selamlik and the Harem. The grounds are extensive as we have seen, and they include not two, but three Kosks. These are like small pavilions built in marble and stone. The Mermer (marble) Kosk, the San (yellow) Kosk, and the Ahir (stable) Kosk, which houses the Royal Stud. Also, there are two more smaller Kosks down along the Bosphorus shoreline, which are mainly used as bathing apartments during the royal picnics and swimming excursions. Those are the ones that we can see in each corner of the grounds. A marble wall, that is surmounted by a high wrought iron fence provides the water-front area with security," finished Mustafa, finally running out of information.

"Well that's a good start," said Peter Ramsbottom. "I must agree with you, Slade, I don't think we will get anywhere near the place from the front gate, and both sides will likely to be guarded in the same stringent manner, which just leaves the western side that faces the Bosphorus. These Kosks that are near the shore Mustafa, you say they are they like beach huts?"

"Very grand beach mansions would be a better description, Ramsbottom Bay," he replied. "They are made of marble, with the most elaborate of curved roofs. There is one at each end of the palace frontage. One is for the men and the other for the women."

"Are there any plans or drawings of the palace available, Mustafa?"

"Yes, but only as a general plan, nothing detailed. They could be copied without difficulty, and of course they are in Turkish, so they will need to be translated."

"Good. Do you know if either of the beach Kosks will be occupied at night?"

"Not as far as I know. I do not expect so, as I imagine they would be empty for most of the time. Servants would clean them after each visit, and close them up until they are required again."

Mr Slade had been listening to their comments.

"If you are planning on going in from the Bosporus side, then I know a small track not very far from where we are right now. I will take you there right now if you would like. It would provide you with a good launching place. The guards down at the gates are getting suspicious, so we should move."

The car drove off, and after a few hundred yards they reached the end of a track, where the sandy shingle stones of the shoreline could be seen through the window. Looking southward, much further down and across the waterway, they could see the European shore of the city with the rising silhouette of the Topkapi Palace, standing on the hill at the entrance to the Bosporus, with the giant dome of Hagia Sophia to the right. From this northern extremity they could just see the Beylerbey Palace through the trees by using their binoculars. Sure enough, as at the front, there were also a lot of guards positioned along the side of the perimeter, but Ramsbottom quickly noted that there were very few along the side that faced shoreline. Several soldiers could clearly be seen patrolling along a pathway on the northern side of the building, so the western face along the Bosporus certainly looked to be their best access option.

"Mr Slade," said Ramsbottom. "I've just had an idea! Is it possible for us to drive back to the rendezvous point to pick up our rubber boat?"

"What now!" he exclaimed.

"Yes! We could then use it to make our approach on the palace from the Bosphorus itself during the early hours, and once ashore we could take over to one of those beach houses. We could place all of our equipment in one, and use it as a base."

"I like that idea, Peter," said Slade. "But I am sure that the landing area around the railway bridge will be swarming with soldiers after your little adventure with those two guards last night. We would certainly be spotted in broad daylight. As you do not need the boat until much later tonight, why don't we leave it until after dark, when we can go back and retrieve it with a degree of safety? We could be back here in the city by midnight?"

"Good idea, Slade, I wasn't thinking."

"We will take three men. They should be able to carry the smaller boat without too much difficulty. I will arrange for a truck to take us, because it probably won't fit into the boot of my car."

So, their plans were made, and before they attracted any more attention to themselves, they decided to leave the area and return to Slade's house.

****

The drive back went without incident and they arrived there to find that the other two army men had been busy cooking. The whole place was filled with the smell of herbs, garlic and aromatic spices, many of which George failed to recognise.

Dave Priest and Jan Sullivan had certainly not been idle. They had lit the charcoal grill, which sizzled and spat as semi-charred meat protested loudly as it lay on the metal bars. Agamemnon was darting about, trying to assist them, pointing out where the various items that they required were located. A bowl of salad already adorned the centre of the table, alongside a mountain of flat unleavened bread towering on a plate.

"Just in time," said Jan Sullivan. "We've been following this Turkish recipe book, and although we could not read a word of it, the pictures inside are fairly self-explanatory. It was Agamemnon here who got us started, and helped with the translation, leaving us to finish off," he said proudly.

"Judging by the juice running down your chin, you've done plenty of sampling Jan," said George.

The West-countryman grinned from ear to ear.

"I can't go dishing you up a load of rubbish, now can I my luvver?"

It was a delicious meal, locally known as Sis Kebab, comprising pieces of lamb that had been speared on to a skewer with tomatoes, onions, and grilled over the charcoal. The salad was a mix of tomatoes, aubergine, cucumbers, lettuce, coriander, and celery dressed with lemon, olive oil, and yoghurt.

Once they sat down, the cook's health was drunk with a bottle of Raki, the local anis flavoured spirit. Slade showed them how to drink it, by mixing it in equal parts with water, which strangely turned the liquid a milky white colour. The Raki was definitely an acquired taste, and George found it rather strong, but quickly found that it complimented the Turkish food perfectly.

Agamemnon appeared at the end of the meal with a tray of Kahve, the strong aromatic Turkish coffee. Everyone agreed that it had been a thoroughly enjoyable meal. Good food, good drink, and good company, but the individual thoughts of the impending expedition had kept them rather sober and quiet. On completion it was decided that Mr Slade would drive the truck with Peter Ramsbottom, George and the two soldiers back to get the smaller rubber boat.

The drive out of the city had gone without incident, and they arrived at the roadside hide-away site to park just before 2130. George led them all up the hill, and walked along the crest before beginning the descent.

Strangely there were no sentry fires visible at the same sites of last night, but George knew that any lack of caution could prove fatal. He took a wide arc around the possible danger area, before finally descending down towards the beach. Once there, it was just a quick walk along to where they had hidden the rubber boat. It didn't take them long to find it, as it stood out like a hayrick.

"You didn't make much of a job of hiding it," commented Slade. "I could have spotted that without much difficulty. You are lucky the sentries have missed it."

Thinking of the lack of sentries, Peter Ramsbottom decided to carry the boat inflated, rather than let the air out, and then have to re-inflate it when they got back. Carrying the boat between them proved easier than envisaged. They were all sweating profusely by the time they arrived back at the truck, and the boat was bundled into the back. The two soldiers sat in the boat, while the rest squeezed into the cab.

Slade then drove back very carefully, it had taken longer than they anticipated, and as they entered the courtyard, George looked at his watch, it was 2348 – they were running a little late. Mustapha was waiting, and as they could not use the truck, which would cause suspicion, they soon realised that they could not all get into Slade's car with the rubber boat. So, it was decided that he would do it in two runs, but the boat would have to be deflated and taken on the first run. While Slade returned to collect the second group, those with the boat could use the waiting time to inflate it in readiness.

As the car drove down the gritty track, the hard tyres crunched loudly over the stones. Sitting in the car it had sounded like a firework display. Surely any passing patrol would have been able to hear them! By the time that they had all arrived at the launch site it was 0107.

On arrival Slade told Sullivan, Priest, and Mustafa Dalan to start inflating the boat with a stirrup pump, while he went back for George and Ramsbottom.

George and Ramsbottom quickly loaded the explosives and weapons into Slade's car, and they were soon back with the rest of the team. Mustafa and Slade began unloading the explosives, stacking them on the shoreline beach in readiness to be loaded into the rubber boat. The weapons and ammunition were placed on top of the pile.

It took them another forty-five minutes to fully inflate the rubber boat, and by the time they had it loaded and launched, it was well past two o'clock in the morning.

They had all been sweating by the time the boat was ready, and it proved difficult to get it into the water. It had needed their combined strength to launch it. Peter Ramsbottom allowed them the time to get their breath before instructing them to enter the water, and to swim with one hand, whilst holding onto the craft with the other. Once the boat began to move away from the shore everything went eerily quiet, making hardly a ripple on the surface of the ancient waterway. Slade stood and watched them safely off on the start of their mission, after telling them that he would pick them up a five o'clock that same morning.

There were other vessels that were passing less than one hundred and fifty yards away, but Peter Ramsbottom knew that by them keeping close to the shadows of the shoreline, they would remain undetected. Only few lights reflecting from over the European shore, hardly providing any light to navigate. A few swirling eddies disturbed the mirror-flat calm, as their swimming strokes moved them slowly forward.

The craft ran parallel the beach, and the lights of the Beylerbey Palace quickly became visible ahead. The rubber boat was much easier to use on the water, gliding almost effortlessly across the surface as they continued south. As they began to near their goal, Peter ordered them to turn, and manoeuvre the craft in towards the shore.

"OK George, guide the bow around and head us towards the palace. Aim for those two tall cypress trees to the right of the building," whispered Peter Ramsbottom at the bow.

George could just make out the trees, and directed the bow over towards the beach. His arm strained under the pressure to keep it there against the tidal stream, as slowly, they neared the shallows.

"Right men, I can see the Kosk," said Peter Ramsbottom. "We're going in. As soon as we hit the beach, I want everything out of the boat, and taken into that nearest Kosk. Keep low and no talking from now on. Good luck everybody!"

The craft ran silently aground up onto the stony shore. Dangling legs quickly found the firmness, and stood up erect. They pulled it in under the concealment of an immature willow, its hanging fronds dangling languidly down into the water.

Once Peter Ramsbottom was satisfied that the boat was hidden, the two privates and George began carrying the explosives ashore, stacking them on the dry ground above the watermark. Peter Ramsbottom and Mustafa Dalan carried all the weapons over towards marble paved promenade. Once everything was ashore, Peter gathered them all in readiness to move off. It was only a few paces to reach the marbled promenade and the protective wrought iron railings set into a knee-high marble wall. They were just about to start carry it into the grounds when a guard suddenly appeared around the far corner of the Palace, and everyone froze like statues. All eyes followed the soldiers every movement, until he had at last disappeared from view, when Peter urged them forward once more. By keeping everybody close to the protection from the shadows, they managed to cross the fifty yards of open ground to reach the path that led to the Kosk. It quickly loomed up out of the darkness, and stood behind a tall marble wall, that shielded it from the Palace. With it being so distinctively private, Peter Ramsbottom had guessed correctly that this was the women's bathing Kosk.

The front door was locked, but after a quick search Jan Sullivan soon found an open window, and his grinning features greeted them, after he had unbolted the entrance door to let them in. It didn't take too long to get themselves, and all of their equipment, inside. Although not large in size, the interior was very well appointed. Walking across the luxuriant pile of the carpets, felt more like walking on a quilted bed.

It was dark, but faint illumination from some security spot-lights lights situated in the palace grounds, allowed them to make out some of the sumptuous furnishings. Gold lacquer framed mirrors hung from the walls. Crystal chandeliers dangled from the ceiling, and bulging cushions covered ornate pieces of furniture. Silk embroidered fabrics were artistically draped down the walls, and each of the doors had, what appeared to be, gold handles.

"Blimey, wot a fuckin' place," whispered Dave Priest, staring around in wonder.

"Yes my luvver, and this just the shed where the Sultan keeps his bike," whispered back Jan Sullivan. "Sorry, his wife."

"Quiet you two. Priest, come and help get these explosives ready. Sullivan and Torode, do a quick search of the rest of the rooms. Make sure that we are alone," said Ramsbottom. "Mustafa, keep watch at the window, and let me know if anyone approaches."

Jan and George picked up a Webley revolver each, and quickly began to move around the confines of the Kosk. Beyond the main room, there was a small passageway with doors that led off on both sides.

"You do the port side, and I'll do the starboard, "whispered George.

"That's my left side, ain't it my luvver?" replied Jan, the enamel of his teeth flashed in the darkness.

"Yes," George hissed, as he clasped the handle of the door. Throwing it open and raising the revolver in one swift motion, he was greeted with a tiny squeal of fright. He almost fired, but his instinct told him this was no armed guard!

"Come out," he ordered.

His demand was only met with another terrified whimper. It sounded like a woman. Jan was at his side in an instant, with both men standing behind the protection of the doorpost.

"Go and get Mustafa, Jan, tell Peter, and I'll keep her covered."

He returned seconds later, with the rest of the group following behind. They were all bristling with weapons, ready to meet any eventuality. Peter Ramsbottom came up to the doorway, standing at George's shoulder.

"There's somebody in here, sir. It sounds like a woman," said George.

"Tell her to come out, Mustafa," ordered the officer.

As Mustafa made his way to the front of the group, a woman's voice whispered out of the darkness.

"Nerelisuniz – Isminiz ne?"

"She is asking who we are, and what we want," said Mustafa to Ramsbottom.

"Let's all go in together, no shooting unless I say so. On the count of three, ready! One – two – THREE."

The woman's scream was quickly stifled as the men rushed into the room. A hand was clasped over her mouth before she could give it full voice. They noticed an ungainly mound that was moving under the bed-clothes beside her, obviously a second occupant. Jan whipped back the sheet to uncover a young man, completely naked, cowering in fright.

"He's fuckin' brave ain't he!" said Dave Priest.

"You too would be very afraid Englishman," said Mustafa Dalan. "If he had been discovered by one of the Sultan's staff, he would be strangled, or beheaded within the hour. If she is married, then she would be stoned to death tomorrow morning."

"Why?" asked the Londoner incredulously?

"Because he is a commoner, and she is from the harem. The laws of Islam are very strict. She is probably one of the Sultan's older daughters, or maybe one of his younger wives."

"No fuckin' woman's worth losin' your fuckin' head over. There would be no fuckin' way I'd chance that, just to get my fuckin' leg over," he finished.

The hostages were tied up with strips of silk, torn from the sheets of the bed. Both of them were stark naked, cringing in a corner with their hands secured behind their back. Another strip tied a gag into their mouths.

"Come on, get moving, I want all these explosives primed and ready in ten minutes," said Peter Ramsbottom. "We are not staying here any longer than is necessary."

They were ready in eight, and everybody prepared themselves for the assault on the palace.

"OK, first team, Priest and Sullivan. I want you to plant all of the secondary diversionary charges, and booby traps. Place them where they will be tripped by any troops that may come against us, should we be discovered. I'll lead the second team as arranged, with Torode and Mustafa, and we will plant the main charges. We will all meet back here just as soon as you have finished. Does anyone have any queries, or see anything in the plan that they don't understand?"

Taking the silence as a 'No', the young officer led them to the door. Scanning the darkness for any movement that might indicate a guard, he sent the first group out on their way. They dashed off across the open grass, quickly melting out into the night, and becoming invisible.

"Right, we'll head for the main part of the palace. Mustafa, you know where the meeting is going to take place, so once we're inside, I want you to lead the way. Ready, Torode?"

George nodded, the butterflies in his stomach made his breath come in short, sharp gasps. He took a long deep breath as he steadied himself. Grasping his revolver, with one of the packs of heavy explosives in the other hand, he just wanted to get moving, the waiting was always the worst bit. He began cursing himself for volunteering for another mission that may get him killed.

"Follow me," said Ramsbottom, as he left the shelter of the chalet.

All of the nervous tension evaporated just as soon as they got going. Moving stealthily from shrub to shrub, they used some thick clumps of foliage to conceal their advance towards the palace. Mustafa pointed to the line of railings that partitioned off the servant's area from the grounds. They could make out a small gap in them, indicating to where the stone stair-case down to the basement was located.

"We enter down that set of steps, where you will find an entry door at the bottom," he said.

The steps were difficult to see in dark shadows, and after they had run across the divide, Peter nearly tripped as he went down. Sure enough, at the bottom there was a door, and mercifully it was not locked. They entered into the black interior cautiously, taking extreme care to be quiet after quickly discovering that they had entered the scullery, where all the dishes were washed. There were pots and pans sticking out from work-tops, and on the tables, as they threaded their way through the small room. At the far end, their way was dimly lit by the dying embers of a fire that heated water for domestic use. Two of the opposite walls were lined with marble sinks, each with a wooden draining board. The shelves above them sagged under the weight of copper cooking utensils, as they tip-toed through into the kitchen area.

It was here that they consulted Mustafa's plan of the palace. At the far end of this area there should be a staircase, leading up directly to the next floor. That should be the main entrance hallway, and they would have to check for any palace servants who may be stationed there. Moving swiftly onward they passed a set of wooden preparation tables, and a huge iron range, before they found the staircase. Climbing the stone steps, they reached a closed door. Peter slowly turned the handle, pushed it slightly ajar, and peered through the crack.

Sure enough, this did indeed lead into the main hall. After checking every corner, his eyes scanned the staircase at the far end – all were deserted. Peter opened the door fully, his eyes alert, searching all around as he moved towards the huge stairway. Halfway up, on reaching the mezzanine level, the staircase split left and right, obviously leading to the two segments of the palace. He could not see beyond that, but all being well, the conference room should be at the far end of that landing to the right, he thought.

"Be careful not to knock into anything," he warned the others. "We will all go up as quickly as we can."

The lighting in the hall was very subdued with the corners bathed in shadows. The only light source came from four flickering oil lamps, each standing on a small table that lined the wall. They provided just enough light to negotiate their way towards the set of stairs. The team ran up them two at a time, each man carrying his large pack of explosive, and they were soon standing on the landing. It was an enormous space, with carpeted passageways leading off in both directions. Immediately beyond them, there was another staircase that led up to the top floor. They turned left, walking hurriedly below a line of six huge glittering chandeliers, hanging like inverted icebergs in the Labrador currant.

Peter led them on, moving swiftly down the passageway before reaching the double doors to the conference room. Cautiously, he opened them, and silently mouthed that it was all clear. The other two men quickly moved inside, and he quietly closed the doors behind them.

Like everything they had seen so far, the conference room was huge, and standing in the centre was a giant elliptical mahogany table that gleamed like a mirror. Twenty-four ornate chairs were positioned around its edge.

"OK – Torode, under the table, start to secure the first charge on the underside. Mustafa – you guard the door. I'm going to rig the fuses, and set the timer. Let's get these bloody things planted, and then get out of here."

George went down onto his hands and knees, dragging the explosive package beneath the table. Reaching into his pocket he took out a screwdriver and four screws that he had brought especially for this purpose. Lying on his back and supporting the heavy satchel with one hand against the underside of the table, he proceeded to screw the canvas webbing to the underside of the table. He repeated the job twice more with the other two bags. Two minutes later, Peter Ramsbottom slid in alongside him carrying a timepiece with two wires attached by wires to two detonators. They repeated the job with the two other satchels.

"Well done Torode, that looks nice and secure – This is set for 1200 – I'll put the timer in that second bag, as I fit the detonators into the charge. You go and wait with Mustafa by the door."

George did as he was told, and scrambled out from under the table. They were soon joined by Peter.

"All quiet, Mustafa?"

"Yes, sir," he replied.

Peter opened the door, and quickly retraced their steps to the landing at the top of the stairs. They went straight down into the hall, and then down again into the kitchen and scullery area. Their eyes were used to the darkness by now, and they quickly found the stone steps outside that led upwards into the grounds. A final careful check of the area, before each of them ran like racehorses for the Kosk. As they entered, George leaned back against the inside wall, regaining his breath before and releasing a long sigh of relief. Maybe this mission will not be like the others, he thought. Everything has gone well. The most dangerous stage of the operation was finally over. All that they had to do now was to swim back, and get picked up by Slade.

Jan Sullivan and Dave Priest had not arrived back yet, but that was only to be expected. They were busy rigging trip wires, connected to their booby traps, and setting other diversionary explosives. They had also been charged to lay a series of secondary timed explosive charges, that would detonate five minutes after the main charge went off. This time period had been designed to prevent the guards from reaching the conference room, and thus decrease the chances of the Sultan, and any of the Germans, surviving the blast.

"Check the two prisoners, Torode," ordered Peter.

George went into the bedroom where they had left them tied up, but to his horror the room was empty. The silk strips were lying on the carpet. His heart missed a beat. Dashing back to the others, he informed the officer.

Peter Ramsbottom's face looked extremely concerned.

"We need to get out of here as soon as possible, but we'll have to hang on for another few moments, and wait for Priest and Sullivan to get back."

They ended up waiting a further five minutes. It seemed an eternity. Finally, Peter made a decision.

"I think it will be safer if we waited outside under cover of those bushes, down by the promenade. When the other two return, we can call them straight over, and then we can all set off immediately. If the guards have been alerted, they will head straight for the Kosk," he said, having thought things over during the wait.

They approached the door and opened it cautiously, but Mustafa who was in the lead, closed it again immediately.

"Guards!" he whispered.

Several armed soldiers came running around the side of the building, dashing across the lawn, and heading towards them. They began spreading out, trying to surround the Kosk before seeking any cover. Ironically, it was at that very moment that Priest and Sullivan re-appeared from the other corner of the Palace, and ran straight into them. They were immediately challenged, but instead of raising their hands, they drew their pistols and fired several shots as they ran hell for leather towards the Kosk.

George watched Jan Sullivan as he instantly killed the nearest two of the guards. Dave Priest was firing at anything that moved, as he ran ever faster towards the beach house. Jan followed his example by increasing his pace in his dash for cover. From the Kosk, the three men began firing, attempting to provide covering fire for them.

Shots from the guards began ringing out, which started as solitary cracks, but quickly grew into a fusillade. The Turks seemed to be everywhere at once.

Suddenly more flood-lights came on, illuminating the palace grounds as if it were day. It enabled the defenders to see exactly where the enemy were, but the glare destroyed their night vision, and made the sighting of targets more difficult. George was using his Webley revolver, and carefully taking aim he hit one of the running soldiers, who fell like his foot had hit an obstacle and tripped. He fired again, but only succeeded in wounding a second guard. Beside him, Peter Ramsbottom levelled his weapon, firing from the doorway, as he tried to provide more cover for his two men, but more guards rounded the corner – there were far too many.

Jan Sullivan went down first. His body was sent flying forward, tumbling and rolling into a heap on the grass. As he lay still, George could his body jerking, as more bullets thudded into him. It made him feel sick.

Dave Priest almost made it back to the doorway, before he too was hit. He suddenly stopped running, sank to his knees, with his eyes levelled on George and Peter Ramsbottom standing before him.

"Oh fuck!" was all he said, before falling forward onto his face.

Peter Ramsbottom slammed the door shut, moving over to the window where Mustafa was firing his revolver. All of the glass panes suddenly exploded inwards, as all of the guards' fire was directed towards them. The heavy door produced a sound like a drum roll, as bullet after bullet thudded into the woodwork, the frame started to splinter under the hail of fire. The exchange was incessant.

Mustafa was the first to be hit, when he suddenly fell backwards with a black hole in his forehead above his right eye.

Peter Ramsbottom saw him fall, but continued firing from the window, when a grenade exploded directly outside the door, the blast throwing the door and his body backwards. He lay on his back with blood pouring through his splayed fingers, which he was holding over his face. George dashed over to help him, and as he moved past the door, another grenade blast caused everything to go black.

Chapter Twenty-Two

Dardanelle Sinking

Through the dreamy ethereal strands of his subconscious, George Torode could hear voices. They were very faint at first – far off in the distance – possessing an almost spiritual quality in their tone. Sounding to exist somewhere out beyond that tangled morass that was once his memory, a floating tangible trace of reality. Their lucidity waxed and waned with the tides of his perception. Deep in the canyons of his mind, basic logic told him that he must be asleep, but surely that was because everything was so dark? The fact that he was thinking like this surely proved that he was not asleep – or maybe dreamworlds work subconsciously?

Alert!

His natural defences had detected danger; there was something, somewhere within the labyrinth of his cerebral cortex, that was trying to warn him. Beware of voices!

In the confusion of his mind, he was desperately trying to re-assemble his vague disjointed recollections. Attempting to focus fully on this hidden danger.

I have to concentrate on the source of those voices, to be able to comprehend what they were saying to me. It all sounded garbled, utter gibberish. Nothing was making sense. There was no coherence, format, or language.

Then they faded; disappeared into the void of stillness and silence, and George felt his mind relax for the first time since first hearing them. He felt himself drifting towards oblivion, but there was something niggling that disturbed his reasoning, and preventing him reaching the safety of obscurity. Slowly all of his troubles dissolved, and he finally succumbed to the warmth and comfort that surrounded him.

He returned to semi-consciousness, having no idea how long he had lain dormant, he felt himself walking the thin divide between sanity and fantasy. The irrelevance of time made him feel secure, as he lay in suspended animation, adrift in the luxury of ignorance.

Then the voices suddenly started up once more, destroying his solace. They were louder this time, but remained equally unintelligible. His brain was struggling in a cloud of uncertainty. Reason told him that they were not a dream – they were external, beyond the confines of his body.

It was quiet again now! Was there someone playing games with him? Where had they gone? The silence challenged him with the main question – was he awake, or was he dreaming!

Then a rhythmic squeak evoked some reality, sounding much like a wheel that needed oiling, it directed his attention in trying to determine its source. It was so annoying.

Then the voices started again. Very faint at first, far, far away, dancing on the edge of audibility. Here they come again – get ready – concentrate this time!

Relief! He could definitely hear footsteps this time. Someone was walking on a hard surface. Was it concrete? No, they were muffled – more like heavy shoes walking on a wooden floor. Coming to this analysis pleased him, because with it he had made a transition, crossing the no-mans-land that lay between dreams and conscious thought. Feeling pleased that he was thinking analytically, it could only be a good thing. What were the voices doing! Concentrate! They had disappeared again.

If this was a dream, it was developing into nightmare, because everything was black, he could not see anything. It was frighteningly real, like no other experience he had ever had. Why can't I see anything – am I blind? Maybe I am dead, and my body is lying in limbo! It certainly felt as if his body was floating on a cushion of air. He had been told by his mother just before she delivered his younger brother that an unborn foetus is suspended in an amniotic fluid filled sac, but still is capable of hearing external sounds. He was certainly feeling warm and comfortable right now, which provided him with a sense of well-being, but why was everything so dark?

From far off he could faintly hear the burbling of more voices. Maybe if he tried to get nearer, he could investigate the them better. His first attempt at movement was immediately curtailed by an acute pain that shot through his body, encouraging him to lie still. Something was very wrong.

Deciding to investigate, he initiated an exploration of his body, sending out his hands to venture towards their extremity. Try as he may, only one would obey, and moving that brought more acute pain.

Maybe if he were to force himself – and try much harder! Each attempt brought agonising pain, but he became encouraged because each shot of pain served bring consciousness closer. He finally gave up, as mental exhaustion prevented further effort. As his body relaxed fully, a feeling of nausea sent him swirling back down into the abyss of oblivion.

He was back again, his mind struggling to retain some degree of certainty. His nagging questions reappeared – why was everything so dark? It was nice to know that the pain faded if he lay still. Lying still, he could both hear and feel his own heartbeat. That proved that he was not dead. What a relief.

Checking again, his pulse seemed to beating at a normal rate, but why was it that his whole body ached so much? It wasn't in a specific spot – it was everywhere. Lying still was OK – bearable – until he attempted to move. So, he decided to remain still.

I feel warm and comfortable, he thought, but I am worried about this pain, and not being able to see.

After a while he detected a vaguely familiar smell, as it invaded his olfactory senses. It reminded him of something, he had smelled this before. Where had it been? His brain searched for the connection. It startled him at first, because it was an almost nostalgic aroma from his recent. By inhaling too deeply through his nose brought chest pains, so he went back to breathing normally. He should know it! It was on the tip of his tongue. It would be just a matter of time before he could put a label on it –

carbolic soap, or methylated spirits. Yes, that was it – Carbolic acid. He felt smugly pleased with himself, and could actually sense his lips creasing into a smile of satisfaction.

A sudden vision of Haslar RN hospital flashed into his mind. He remembered experiencing that exact same smell at the time that he had awoken following his rescue from *HMS C301* in the English Channel. He remembered smelling it prior to hunger overtaking his every other thought, but the idea that he may be in a hospital now stayed with him.

Another possibility was his Mother's scullery, which always smelled like this on a Monday morning – wash days – it was always a hot steamy affair. No, this smell had definitely been in Haslar hospital when he had awoken there. So, was he in hospital again? If so – where was he? He, didn't feel any threat here, but there was something that was trying to warn him. Dismissing the apprehension, he smiled again. Ouch!

"It ne George Torode – It Ingliz."

He was fully alert! That voice had just said his name! Yes – he had definitely heard it. The shock had increased his heartbeat, he could feel it racing. Every sense he possessed was on a knife edge – seeking an answer to what he had just heard. He could still clearly hear the jabbering voices – they were all around him right now – twittering like a cage full of canaries. The pronunciation of his name had sounded strange – heavily accented. Only foreigners have accents – unless you come from Scotland!

George could feel an influx of adrenaline begin to flood through his body, and raise his defences. The voices were certainly not English! His brain struggled with the problem for a few seconds, before the answer hit him like a sledge hammer – TURKS!

He was wide awake now – and he opened his eyes – but it was still dark! What was happening? He became very frightened that he could not see. Physically he could sense that his eyes were open, but his eye-lashes were brushing against something – it was still dark? Nothing! Why could he not see? Was he blind?

Gripped by this terror, he tried to sit up, but the piercing pain shot through the top part of his body, forcing him back down onto the mattress. That was a pain that he was definitely able to pinpoint – it was in his ribs, and left shoulder – but why couldn't he see?

Knowing that he could move his right hand without too much pain, he sent it up towards his face. It managed to reach some bandaging that was firmly around the upper part of his head.

What was wrong – why can't I see? Am I really blind? This has to be a Turkish hospital? The thought of being blind in an enemy facility brought terror.

His sudden movements caused the voices to become excited. A deeper, more dominant voice appeared to come much closer, saying something unintelligible. Then he felt a firm reassuring hand press his shoulder, and gently removing his hand, easing it back down to the mattress.

He could hear the same voice turning away, addressing remarks to the other voices. How many of them were there for goodness sake? There were some consensual murmurs, and then more chattering before George heard the footsteps fading away.

He could tell the difference in sound between a wood, stone, or tiled floor after the *C301* incident at the Haslar Military Hospital. It was amazing what one concentrated on in hospital.

In the ensuing silence George became very afraid, almost to the point of hysteria. His heart rate was fast, and his breathing came in short panting gasps. A thousand questions queued up for answers.

He tried to go through what he did know. He was in a bed – that much was clear. He could feel the bed covers with his free right hand, but why couldn't he move his left arm? He was in enemy territory? He was unable to see, and it was agony to attempt any form of movement. George reckoned that those were very good reasons for feeling frightened.

He laid there, desperately trying to recall what had happened over the past few days. Eventually the threads of the mission came back to him. In his mind he gradually began to piece together the events at the Sultan's Palace. A sudden vision of Mustafa, with the ugly red black hole in his forehead made him wince. Then he remembered Lieutenant Ramsbottom, with bloodied hands covering his gory face. After that, he could remember nothing. Everything was a blank. Was that last night? What was it now – day or night? How long had he been lying here? Just how badly hurt was he?

In the absence of any answers, he tried another exploration of his injuries with his free hand. Although it was painful, he checked his thighs and trunk for damage, finally discovering the reason that he could not move his left arm was because it was in a sling, and his head and eyes were both heavily bandaged. Below his waist around his thighs, the rest was out of reach, he could sense that for some reason his legs had been tied together. Whether it was a splint, or they had been tied for security reasons, he could not tell. He felt reassured by the fact that he could wriggle both sets of toes – that was a good sign. His hand gently found his private parts, and he breathed sigh of relief at finding everything in place. After this encouragement, he tried moving other parts of his body. His right foot moved without too much pain, but with it being tied to the left, any major movement was impossible. His left foot moved, but only with a pain that shot right up to the top of his thigh.

Just as he was finishing the exploration the voices reappeared, and he feigned unconsciousness. He could hear several people shuffling around the bed, and once again the more dominant voice spoke to him,

"Gun aydin, nasilsiniz George Torode?"

He could not help flinching on hearing his name, aware that the movement made it impossible for him to carry on pretending to be asleep.

"Ben Doktor Balyan – sen niz Scutari Hastahane," the voice continued.

George recognised the name Scutari. He had been there with Mina, when she had helped him to escape on his first operation. Another of the words he recognised was, doctor! The desire to have some of his questions answered overcame any further attempt of pretence.

"Where am I? How badly am I hurt? Can anyone here speak English?" he said, all pretence gone in his thirst for answers.

There was a silence, then a halting, accented voice spoke.

"This Scutari Hospital. You take bad shock on body – left side. Left arm and leg are bad bruised, not broken. Ribs, left side, bad bruise also. Bomb blast burn face and eyes. Not know how bad eyes are. Doctor Balyan takes good care of you. It three o'clock – afternoon. You, unconscious yesterday morning."

At least George now had some of his questions answered, but he still felt very apprehensive. The next voice to speak nearly sent him back into shock.

"Hello George. I have been wondering how long it would take you to wake up. We only want to get you well enough to stand you up in front of a firing squad, on crutches, or in a chair if we have to. This time you will get what's coming to you."

The gloating tone in the voice was unmistakable – its snarling assurance turned his initial apprehension, into a bowel-stirring fear. It was Arthur Collenette!

George became determined that Arthur would never know just how scared he actually was. So, with as much bravado as he could muster, he replied sneeringly, "Still cohabitating with the enemy, Arthur?"

"At least I'll still be alive at the end of this war," said Arthur. "Unlike you and your friends."

With that, George thought about the other members of the mission. He knew that Jan and Dave had definitely been killed. He had watched them fall, as each had gone down in that hail of bullets. Mustafa could never have survived, having taken that bullet to his head, but Peter Ramsbottom might just have made it through.

"Did any of my mates survive?" he asked.

"No, George. I have to admit that you are the luckiest bastard alive, but I'm afraid that now your luck has finally run out. Before too long, you'll be wishing that you had died along with those other losers, that came with you. Oh – by the way, the little bomb that you planted was found shortly after you were captured, so nobody one was hurt. Some of your booby-traps did go off, which managed to kill two soldiers, and injure several others; that was all you managed to achieve. The Sultan is fit and well. I hope that your pathetic pyrrhic victory was worth the lives of your four friends. The more I witness the Allied cock-ups in this war, then the more convinced I become that I made a good move in changing sides."

The cruel vindictive tone of his voice sounded arrogant. George decided that they were the words of a resentful coward, who was trying to understand his own weaknesses, and to justify his treasonous actions.

He remembered his frustration in the Papandross Stable Yard, as he had looked up at the window that had framed Arthur, and he was now experiencing that same impotence to effect a change to his situation. The fact that he could be blind was probably the most terrifying thing of all, and he was not completely certain that he could actually stand up unaided. He felt very vulnerable, and totally at the mercy of this cold-blooded psychopathic killer.

"Get some rest now George, regain your strength, because you're going to need it once we start to question you. You had better tell them what they need to know this time – or your whole world is going to be filled with pain."

The party of Turks around his bed departed, thankfully taking Arthur Collenette with them, and leaving him alone to his thoughts.

So, all of the team had all died in the assault on the Palace. How come he was the only survivor yet again? He knew that the others had had just as much chance of living as he had, because they had all fought just as hard as he had. It could have been any one of them lying here, and me who was dead. It just went to prove his recent theory that life really was just a lottery? Maybe it's a bit like cat lives – you only get so many chances in a war, and the others on the team had already survived many more dangers than he had – they had used up all of their lucky breaks. Then he realised that he had had more than his own share of lucky breaks. After listening to what Arthur had just said, his own luck might be running out. If only his body was in better shape, then he could at least make an attempt at an escape. He just hoped, above all else, that his eyes weren't badly damaged. It was the possibility of being blind that frightened him the most. Without his sight, he would be totally helpless in a foreign land.

It seemed to be an eternity that he lay there waiting for something to happen, so he decided to try and get an idea about his immediate environment. At first, he tried to make sense of his surroundings by just listening, trying to get some idea of the layout by identifying the sounds about him. The footsteps had all gone off to his right. That must be the entrance to this ward?

Just then he heard the sound of water being flushed away, way off to his right. The footsteps of the person who had used the washroom, faded into the distance. That probably meant that both the ward entrance, and the sluice were in that direction – over to his right.

As he listened, he could hear faint sounds of breathing and coughing around him, which meant that he was in a communal ward, and there were there were other occupants in the adjacent beds. He was apprehensive, unsure about attempting communication. They probably wouldn't be able to speak English anyway. By continuing to listen carefully, he thought that he could identify at least four other patients in the ward by the depth of their breathing, or by each type of cough. Not being able to see was extremely frustrating, so he gathered his courage, and finally spoke out aloud to his unseen roommates.

"Is there anyone in here who speaks, English?"

"Woi, can't yer speak t'e Turk? He who knows 'is enemy 'as t'e advantage. Wasn't t'at w'at Napoleon said – or was it, Alexandra t'e Great! Cum ter t'ink of it. It moight even of been t'at queer fella, Julius Caesar."

The reply took him aback at first, and he couldn't believe what he had just heard. It was a broad Irish brogue, and he knew from the slow drawling accent that the owner was from the south. Lieutenant d'Oyly-Hughes came from the north, and his accent was much more abrasive, and faster in its delivery.

"Who are you?" George enquired.

"Patrick Eamon O'Connel of His Majesty's Irish Regiment of Guards, at yer service," said the Irish voice.

"Mine is George Torode. How did you manage to get here, Patrick?" George asked.

"Probably, by t'e same way as yerself, George. Oi was captured be'ind enemy loines. We were tryin' ter blow up an ammunition dump t'at 'ad been located by t'e aircraft. I cawt a packet in my leg and was brought 'ere by ship t'ree weeks ago. Since oive bin a prisoner, oi've developed t'is terrible coff. Oi must 'ave cawt it at t'e prison camp 'ospital back in Gallipoli. Now I don't want to go on abowt moi wound, but it is a bit 'igher t'an moi leg – tis up in t'e cheek of moi bum actually. It's been playin' 'avoc wit' t'e sanitary arrangements. At foist I taut I was pissin' t'roo moi 'hip. Oi seemed to be 'avin' t'e bedpan every 'our, wit'out fail. T'ings are improvin' now mind yer and I can move moi leg quite a lot better. T'e bedpan is 'avin' a rest, so I expect t'ey'll send me back off ter t'e prison camp shortly – tat shud improve moi coff no end," replied the voice.

George was glad to hear his own tongue spoken again and the conversation he had just given him an idea.

"Is this ward for wounded prisoners of war?" he asked.

"T'at it is George. I can see t'at t'ose bandages are no obstacle to an active moind like yaws…" his voice was cut short by a hacking cough.

"Feckin' coff," he spat. "Did yer know t'at t'is is t'e 'ospital t'at Florence Noit'ingale tended t'e wounded durin' t'e Crimean War?"

"No, I didn't," said George. Then suddenly feeling concerned about his own injuries he continued. "How bad do I look, Patrick?"

"Yer 'ave a few bandages around your 'ead, and some on yer left arm, but ot'er t'an t'at yer look pretty good. T'ere seems to be an appendage cumin off each corner and t'eres no 'oles in t'e middle, so I would say that yer going to be OK, but oime no doctor moind yer."

George smiled to himself, he was quite taken with the cheeky remarks of the Irishman.

"'Ow did yer come to be 'ere, George?"

George's defences were immediately raised. It was instinctive. Maybe his experiences of the past months had at least taught him something. This man opposite him could have been planted by Arthur, and he was trying to pump him for intelligence. Despite being a killer, Arthur Collenette was not stupid, and he would use any ruse he could to obtain what he wanted to know. He didn't answer immediately, trying to form an answer without revealing any actual information.

"I was taking part in an operation behind the lines like you, Patrick. There was a loud explosion, and the next thing I knew was waking up in here."

"Who was t'a queer fella who's just left yer, George? 'E sownded English, but 'e wuz wearin' a Turkey uniform. D'yer know 'im?" asked the Irishman.

"Yes, I know him," said George. "He is a traitor named Arthur Collenette, and you will do well to stay away from him."

"W'at sort of operation were yer on, George?"

The alarms bells started ringing in George's head.

"Why do you want to know that?"

"No reason, dear boy. No reason. Oi've told yer about moi shoitin' problems, t'would be noice to 'ave somewun around who 'ad a few shoitin' problems of t'eir own. T'en we cud be in t'e shoite toget'er, so ter speak. Maybe it would take moi moind off moi problems. Oi wuz just makin' conversation – nut'in more. I t'ought t'at talkin' about it moight make it easier fer yerself. I 'eard t'at Art'ur fella say t'e rest of yer group were killed, t'at's roight isn't it?"

George said nothing more, but the silence didn't stop Patrick's questions.

"'Ow did you get into Constantinople t'en George, as it's well over a 'undred miles from the front lines, as the crow floies?"

Again silence.

"'Ave yous fallen asleep, George?"

He must have taken the silence for a yes, as his enquiries stopped.

As he lay there, George could hear Patrick's terrible hacking cough, inhaling hard as he fought for breath. The Irishman could not fake that, but he would not put anything past Arthur. George felt sorry for him, as he suspected that he may have contracted tuberculosis.

After an hour, someone had returned to his bedside, and they began to remove the restrictions from around George's legs. It felt wonderful to be able to move them independently, albeit very carefully. Once they had finished, whoever it was disappeared, and it seemed hours before anyone else approached his bed.

It was in fact the morning of the next day before someone finally woke him. George recognised the tone of the voice. It was the same Doctor that had been here yesterday. What was his name – Doctor Dalton, Baltan – no – Doctor Balyan – that was it!

He was here now, gabbling away in Turkish, but George was on his guard this time, just in case Arthur was with him, or was maybe standing somewhere nearby. The Doctor stopped talking, and started fiddling with the bandages around George's head. Maybe this was the moment that he was going to find out if he was ever going to see again! George suddenly felt very nervous, and apprehensive!

He could feel the strips of bandage being unwound from around his head. Then, all at once they were off, and the newly exposed skin on his scalp suddenly felt quite cold. He could feel a down draught of air, that was probably being blown from an overhead fan. He remembered the rusty wheel sound, and realised its source.

With the bandages removed, his eyelids remained closed – it felt as though his lashes had been welded together, but he felt heartened that he could see some daylight through the skin of his eyelid – surely that must be a good sign!

There was something touching his eyelids. The Doctor's hands were brushing gently against his cheek, and George realised that he was removing two pads of cotton wool, one at a time. Someone had a wet cloth and started to bathe his face, taking extra care around his eyes. They were using a warm liquid that smelled strongly of methylated spirit. He could feel small rivulets running down his cheeks, over his chin, and down towards his neck. Someone dabbed at it with a towel. Whoever it was, they were being very gentle.

"Acik siz er, er – EYES. O-pen eyes, pliz."

George tried, but he could not force his eyelids apart, the lashes remaining stuck together. More warm water was gently applied, and cotton wool dried it off. He tried again. They opened suddenly, but he quickly closed them again – as the sudden glare of light was too painful. He turned his head away from the glare. Slowly, squinting, he tried again. They were open now, but his vision was clouded. His heart was pumping like the engine room ballast pump. Very slowly some of the blurry images began to morph into recognisable forms, and as he looked about the ward, he tried to focus. He blinked several times. The inner corners of his eyes began to feel sore, then unexpectedly they began to flood with tears, and he was unable to see anything. Someone began to gently wipe them again, with a soft piece of cloth.

Once the tears had stopped, he tried again, and found that the blurry images had begun to clear. The vague shapes began to take on a sharper definition. He could see a smiling, kindly face that was looking directly at him. Inquisitive eyes were carefully watching George's reaction closely.

"Gud – gud – You seez – yez!" said Doctor Balyan.

George could now see his mouth forming the words.

"Yes," said George, smiling with relief. "I can see you."

He smiled with satisfaction, before standing and heading off down the ward. Once he had disappeared, the man in the bed opposite smiled the broadest grin at him. He had an unruly patch of thick ruddy hair that badly needed cutting. George guessed that he was in his middle twenties, with bright blue piercing eyes that were looking straight at him. One of his legs lay exposed on top of the blanket, covered with a light bandage. He broke into a hacking cough.

"I could recognise that cough anywhere. You must be Patrick Eamon O'Connel," said George.

"T'at oi am lad, t'at oi am. Oim very glad t'at yaw oiys are OK."

"You look younger than you sound, Pat. I was expecting someone of at least thirty to own that gruff voice."

"T'e way moi backsoide feels at t'e moment, oi feel as if oim at least fifty," replied the Irishman.

The two men chatted, getting to know each other, sharing the common bond of language in a foreign land. There were three other patients in the ward. George was sure there had been more. and wondered where they had gone. When he had asked Pat, he was informed that there had been some Armenian slave labourers, who were considered to be less than human by the Turks.

"Is there any chance of us getting out of here, Pat?"

"Oi 'ave only just regained t'e use of moi leg George," he said. "So, oi seriously 'aven't bin able t'er git up and 'ave a look around."

"Well, we're going to keep our eyes peeled towards that end Pat, from this moment on."

The ward doors crashed open, and a nurse entered the ward and headed straight towards them, condemning them both to silence. George watched her. She was the matronly type, with a rounded, fuller figure. She wore a long flowing robe, with her dark hair brushed back, kept in place by a white scarf tied tight around her face – looking a little like a nun's wimple. A boy's public-school sickbay would have been a more appropriate setting for her, he decided. Through her loose robe, George could not help but notice that she had great voluptuous breasts, which bounced with every step as she approached his bed. Standing for no nonsense, she removed the rest of the bandages from his upper arm, bundling them up, to carrying them back down the ward to a waste basket.

Ten minutes later, she reappeared with a bowl of water with a cake of soap. George was subjected to a somewhat embarrassing, but none the less rigorous, bed-bath. During his ablution, her hands went everywhere, sparing no part of his anatomy. It was not intentional, but George developed a full erection. He blushed, but the nurse seemed quite unimpressed, and gave his stiff member a flick with her hand, before she strode off towards the sluice area. More tears filled his eyes.

"Oi can see t'at you're makin' a remarkoible recovery t'ere, George," said Patrick smiling, once the woman had gone.

It was very quiet during that night, and George lay awake for many hours trying to remember the sequence of events that had led him here. Across the ward, Patrick's snoring was frequently interrupted by his hacking cough. Finally, George fully managed to recall the mission, right up until the moment that he had gone to the assistance of Peter Ramsbottom. That was the point when sleep finally claimed him.

The following morning, just as the nurses were removing the breakfast bowls, the doors at the end of the ward burst open. A Turkish army officer entered, followed by two young soldiers carrying rifles. The soldiers looked about them in awed amazement, obviously never having been in a hospital before. Their boots clumped loudly on the wooden floor, as they strode arrogantly up the ward towards the George and Patrick's beds. One of the soldiers was directed over towards Patrick, while the officer came over to George's bed, with the second soldier.

"Get up immediately, and get dressed," he snapped.

"Why, where are we going?" asked George.

"Do not argue, up now!" repeated the man, obviously in no mood to discuss the matter.

The soldier levelled his rifle at him, raising the barrel in a jerking motion, indicating that he should rise. George pulled back the single blanket, and slowly slid his legs over the side of the bed. In attempting to stand, his knees gave way momentarily, and he had to reach over to hold on to the bed-frame for support. It was the first time that he had stood up in over three days. He regained his balance, and bending down he removed his clothes from the wooden cabinet beside his bed, and began to get dressed. He immediately noticed how dirty his clothes were, and they had several frayed holes in them, complete with singed edges.

Bending down to pull on his socks proved to be absolute agony. His ribs hurt like mad, and his head felt groggy as he tried to stand – he fell back down and sat there puffing.

Across the room, Patrick was being made to do the same thing, and George could see that he was going through a similar pain barrier. He noticed Patrick glance across towards him with an enquiring frown. All that George could do was shrug his shoulders, as he had no more of an idea than Pat about what was going to happen to them. Reaching down, and tying up his boot-laces, George finally stood up.

"Good," said the officer. "Now come with me. If you attempt to escape, you will be shot."

They were led slowly down the ward by the officer, with the two soldiers shepherding them from behind. As they passed the ward office, the matronly nurse looked up with an expression of concern on her face. George winked at her, as they went through the door. For just an instant she dropped her haughty demeanour to smile back. 'The Turks are human after all,' thought George.

They were taken down a wide staircase, and out into the courtyard at the side of the hospital building. George felt a great relief when he looked around to find no sign of a firing squad. The fresh air helped restore the senses of both men, and each took deep breaths to ensure that their recovery continued. Just to feel the warmth of the sun's rays against their skin was invigorating. Just ahead stood an open-backed truck, with more Turkish troops sat on each side. They looked down at George and Patrick with a curious interest, as they were provided them with their first view of their enemy.

"Get in," ordered the officer.

The troops in the back helped them climb up over the tailboard. It was very painful for George, and he was glad of the hand up. It must have been equally painful for Patrick, as he could hear him groaning as he tried to raise his leg over the tail gate.

Both were made to lay on the floor, where they had several rifles levelled at their chests. The engine coughed into life, the gears rattled, and there were a few jerks as the driver attempted to engage the clutch, before they finally moved off.

Then all at once, they were moving along a street, and Scutari was flashing past them in a receding perspective. The next minute they turned into a street that George thought he recognised, but then again one of these busy crowded streets looks very much like another. However, he was fairly certain that he had travelled along this one, when he and Mina had headed for the docks, and he whispered his thoughts to Pat.

"D'yer t'ink we're being taken back to t'e prison camp on t'e Peninsula, George?" replied Patrick, speculatively.

"I should think so, Pat. The Turkish Army HQ at Gallipoli will be our destination, unless I'm very much mistaken."

Sure enough, the truck entered the dock region and pulled up in front of a large Turkish transport. It was an old vessel with two slender cork-tipped type funnels. Her passageways and decks were overflowing with troops on their way to the front. On the fore-deck, a steam driven derrick was swinging the last of its cargo, a hundred-millimetre howitzer, over on to the fo'c'sle.

The tail gate was dropped before Patrick and George were forced off the back of the truck and escorted over towards the gangway. The dockside was awash with stevedores carrying their loads, taken from the back of trucks, up the gangways of the ships at the quayside. It was all one-way traffic.

Looking up, George could see the wing of the bridge was sticking out over the edge of the quayside. A figure stood there looking down at their arrival. It was unmistakable – it was Arthur Collenette. He looked splendid, bedecked in his dark blue Turkish naval uniform, still wearing the red fez.

As George caught his eye, he noticed the sadistic smile on his lips. Another wave of apprehension flooded through George, as to what the future really held in store for him. He remembered Mr Slade telling him, how the Turkish Army interrogators in Constantinople would use heavy metal hammers to break a man's legs to get him to talk. He shuddered.

He and Patrick were prodded up the gangway, and taken in through a maze of passageways within the ship. Then they were forced down a series of long vertical ladders into the most forward hold. The descent was agonising for both men.

Once at the bottom, they were made to stand against the after bulkhead, where they were secured by handcuffs to two vertical pipes. The two pipes disappeared through the sheet metal wall at shoulder height, which made it impossible for them to sit down. Once they had been shackled in place, their guard was reduced to one man, and they were left alone with their armed nursemaid.

Looking around, George could tell that this was the most forward space on the ship as the two sides narrowed considerably, and only the anchor cable hawse pipes stood between them and the pointed section of the bow. Every inch of spare space down here had been utilised, with many large heavy crates had been stacked from bulkhead to bulkhead. A narrow space of just six feet stood between these the rear of the crates, and the bulkhead to which they were secured.

"It doesn't look like we're going to be able to go anywhere, until we reach our destination, Pat?" said George, looking at the metal cuff that was cutting into his wrist.

"Oi don't t'ink t'at t'ey wud let us use t'e promenade deck, but t'is is going a bit over t'e top. Let's juist 'ope t'at t'ey will let us use t'e Kharrazi, coz oime in need a shoit roit now!"

After asking their guard to use the facilities, he disappeared up the ladder, quickly returning with his friend. One stayed with George, while Patrick was unshackled, and taken up to the toilets somewhere aloft. On his return, he was immediately re-shackled to the pipes beside George.

The two men looked around at confines of their incarceration. It was not a good place to be, as they were crammed in between this bulkhead and those crated munitions. Any light down here in the hold was seriously reduced, with just a solitary deck access hatch above them. A solitary glass section allowed some the daylight to penetrate their prison. It was uncomfortably hot, and they languished in the stagnant oppressive heat for another hour before anything happened. The sudden blast of the ship's siren sounded, reverberating within the confines of the hold, making both men jump.

We must be getting prepared to get under way, George surmised.

George looked up and eyed the stack of crates that rose some twenty feet above his head. If this cargo were ever to shift, then those heavy crates would come tumbling down, and if they were not killed, there would be little way to avoid them. If they were not crushed – they would be badly injured.

Suddenly the thump of the engines began beating through the rivets. George could hear the boom, boom, boom of the giant's heartbeat resounding through the bulkheads, before the constant rhymical swish of water at the bow gradually became the norm. They were underway.

****

The sea passage across the Sea of Marmara was utterly boring for both men, but it was also extremely painful. The time dragged, and the journey time seemed never-ending, with neither man having anything to do except stand and wait. The resourceful guards had provided a bucket for when they needed a toilet break, which obviously did not afford any privacy. Their time was filled with worried thoughts, mainly concerning the uncertainty about their fate on arrival. Their bodies ached beyond reason, becoming extremely sore and stiff after being made to stand for so long. Both men longed to be able to sit down to ease their aching muscles. It transpired that it was nearly twelve hours, before they detected a slight change in the constant rhythm from the engine room, an indication that they were slowing in speed.

"We must be across the Marmara, and be approaching the narrows into the Dardanelles at the northern entrance," declared George.

"Oh, fer t'e benefoit of a naval education," said Patrick, before breaking into another bout of coughing. "Oi wish oi could see t'rew iron loike yous can."

Another long hour passed by before the ship began carrying out a series of manoeuvres. Just ahead of them, beyond the piled stack of crates, the hawse pipes suddenly exploded into life with a rivet-shaking vibrato, as the anchor was dropped over the side. The reciprocating engines could be heard going astern for an instant, before everything stopped, including the engine, leaving them in total silence.

"It looks like we've arrived. Wherever that may be!" said George.

Nobody came for them, and a little while later a second guard appeared with a mug of coffee and a slice of bread, which he handed to them. Another hour passed and there was still no sign of them being moved. Both men were now feeling extremely weary, having been standing for nearly fifteen hours. George could feel his pulse in the bruised areas of his legs, and his upper body, protesting, demanding rest.

"Can we have a break?" asked George, of their guard.

The man looked at them blankly, trying his best to totally ignore them. He was playing a game of solitaire on the deck of the hold, his cards decorating the small space. George looked down at them, and he could see that there was a red ten that was available to go on a black jack, but their warder had not seen it.

A further hour passed before the swanky young officer's legs appeared from the hatch combing high above, to descend nimbly down the ladder. After several pleas from the two men, he allowed them to be unshackled, and to sit down on the floor. The guard was doubled, and their weapons were kept aligned on the two prisoners.

****

It was very early on that same morning that the ship had anchored, as it awaited orders as to when it could enter the harbour at Gallipoli to unload the men and supplies it was carrying, as there were other ships forming a queue, awaiting to do the very same thing.

Unbeknownst to them all, was the fact that they were being observed through a submarine's periscope. The lone predator had been stalking its prey in their wake, and the underwater menace was lining itself up for the first shot.

Lieutenant Commander Martin Dunbar-Naismith in *HMS E11* had radioed a report of his latest sinking's from their communication slot in the Marmara the previous night. They in turn had received an intelligence report that four merchantmen transports, a destroyer, and a gunboat were at anchor above Nagara Point. There had been lean pickings over the last couple of days, and the report was most welcomed, giving them all a real chance to get back into the action.

Naismith had driven *E11* at top speed on the surface overnight to enable him to keep his batteries fully charged. He had trimmed the boat well down, so they would be ready to dive at a moment's notice. As the first dawn light had blushed the eastern horizon, George Plowman was the look-out, and he had reported several vessels running hell for leather for the entrance to the Dardanelles, nearly ten miles ahead of him. The intelligence signal had proved to be correct. Naismith was perfectly aware that he had no chance of catching them, but he hoped that by travelling fast, before diving as late as possible, these ships would eventually present themselves as targets. Remaining on the surface as the dawn light blossomed, he headed south, straight into the Dardanelles themselves, and on past Gallipoli, heading directly towards Nagara Point.

Not wanting to make himself a target by remaining in view, he had dived in the early morning light immediately on sighting ships in the anchorage. Scanning the small fleet, as the hills on both sides of the channel became more detailed, he found it difficult to differentiate any vessels at first, due to the presence of an unusual low-lying mist. Back in England, during the late summer and early autumn dew-filled dawns, the colder air that rose from the ditches and deeper recesses caused a delay in the evaporation process. The result was the forming of a low-lying mist to hover just above the grass, producing very much the same effect as this on view this morning.

By him coming shallow, it pushed the head of the periscope up just enough for Martin to spot the first mast peeking out above the mist – and then another. Sure enough, there were still three of the four of the reported transports anchored here. Their escort destroyer, and the lone gunboat were anchored nearby.

As he watched, yet another transport arrived, which immediately dropped her anchor just over a mile from his present position. The accuracy of the intelligence reports were much better of late, but he knew that they were only achieved through the hard work of the aircrews, who flew mission after mission out into the Marmara, to confirm or refute reports of ship movements from Constantinople, where Mr Slade and his team worked tirelessly tried to provide daily sailing reports from Scutari. The intelligence branch analysed everything, and immediately transmitted their findings out to the submarines. Martin silently thanked heaven for the wonders of modern science. This new technology of wireless radio communication was proving to be invaluable. He determined to give Telegraphist Lohden a pat on the back for his new-found enthusiasm in the radio shack in providing the information.

At least this mist served to hide his presence from the gun batteries situated high on the cliffs above the anchorage. Leaving the main channel, he slowly made his way into the anchorage, like a cat stalking birds in the garden. As he did so, the newly risen sun began clearing the crest of the cliffs, its warming rays beginning the evaporation process, which slowly began to eradicate the protective mist. Fully aware that it would not be long before his periscope would be spotted, he suddenly had an idea. He decided that on his run in he would increase speed and deliberately let his periscope be seen, knowing that the feather of white spray would be clearly visible across the smoothness of these placid waters. He knew that the defensive guns up on the cliffs all around him would not dare to fire on him for fear of hitting their own ships.

He directed his small craft into the attack, and as soon as he raised the periscope, the alarm in the anchorage was raised almost immediately. Complete panic spread through the Turkish ships like a wild fire. Martin smiled, the feathers would begin to fly, because the fox was loose in the hen-house. Ships sirens began blaring, showing the panic that their presence was creating. The merchant ship stokers rushed down to their engine rooms, attempting to raise enough steam to enable them to weigh anchor and run for their life.

The two anchored warships had kept steam up, and so they almost immediately managed to sail forth in a brave gesture of defiance, like faithful sheepdogs standing against the hunting lion.

Martin, in *E11*, deliberately turned away with his periscope still raised to lead the warships back towards the main channel. Once he could see that they were in hot pursuit, he lowered it and went deep, immediately turning back to allow them to pass overhead. Coming back up to periscope depth he headed back towards the now unprotected transports. As he re-entered the anchorage once more, he scanned the mayhem. On the forecastle of each vessel, seamen could be seen dashing about, trying to open up steam to their capstans and windlasses to enable them to weigh anchor.

Martin selected the two nearest vessels, which also happened to be the two largest merchantmen. Both looked to be heavily laden, with ordinance and stores ready to be landed at Gallipoli. He fired two torpedoes, one at each vessel. Each torpedo hit their individual target, sending both vessels to the bottom in less than five minutes.

Moving on to the third target, Naismith fired again, but this time there was no explosion. Had he missed, or had there been a mechanical problem with their weapon? Either way, the vessel was still afloat, and he only had two torpedoes left. Should he fire a second at her.

Not dithering for a second, he reset his firing solution and sent another weapon on its way. It hit her square amidships, sending her down almost immediately. All of these ships were so heavily loaded that they sank very quickly. This third giant ship had turned turtle, rolling completely over in a boiling cauldron of bubbles and steam. His last view of her was with her bow section well under, her single propeller slowly revolving as it protruded out of the water.

Finally, the Turks realised that they had been duped, and both of the warships were now thundering back towards the anchorage at full steam. They sped straight past *E11*, heading towards the position of the first sinking. In the meantime, the newly arrived merchant ship had managed to weigh its anchor, and she slowly turned. Martin thought that she would run hell for leather out into the Dardanelles channel to escape destruction, but instead she began heading down in the direction of the Mediterranean. So he knew that she would not be going too far. The cunning fox had already anticipated their movement, and had maneuvered himself to cut off the northern escape route. She was crammed with troops, and was certainly worth his last torpedo.

****

Down in their dark prison, George and Patrick had heard the cacophony of the ship's sirens blaring, indicating a major alarm. They then heard the first huge explosion, followed shortly afterwards by two thudding explosive cracks which reverberated against the hull, as the second and third two torpedoes had hit the two ships. George recognized them for what they were.

"They're torpedo explosions, Patrick. I've heard enough of them through the pressure hull of *E11* to recognise that sound well enough!"

"Yous're from t'at submarine! Well, oi nevour. But wait a minit, does t'at mean t'at it moight be your mates actually attacking t'is vessel, George?"

"Yes, it would be, Pat," said George proudly. "My Skipper is the best there is."

"Well, t'at's very reassuring George, but may oi remind yer t'at we 'appen to be on t'e receiving end."

"Oh yeah!" said George reflectively. "I didn't think of that."

"Well, I t'ink t'at you'd better troi moi lad, because if your Skipper is as good as yer say 'e is, 'e won't give up until we're sittin' on t'e bottom."

****

Naismith certainly hadn't given up on the last transport. Having only just arrived at the anchorage, it had raised its anchor too quickly for him to get a final firing solution. Although he was slower, he pursued the ship down the Dardanelles, knowing full well that it would eventually be forced to turn and come back up. The merchantman would be fired at and sunk by the Allied guns if she continued beyond Kephez Bay – and those minefields down there are impartial. There were no other ports where her master could seek refuge, so there was no alternative for him, he had to return to where his tormentor was lying in wait. Patience is a virtue.

Sure enough, it was later that afternoon when the very same merchantman was sighted heading back towards them. Naismith was very well aware that he only had the one remaining torpedo, and he had already decided that this ship was well worth firing it. She was riding low in the water, and he could see troops lining the rails. As she approached, he went through the set-up routine, aligning the periscope on its heading before firing. It is called the deflection angle. As the large transport's bridge passed through his cross wire, he fired his last remaining weapon. It ran straight and true, striking the ship slightly forward of where Naismith had aimed it. A column of water sprayed up between the bridge and the forecastle, and her bow dipped alarmingly as she started to go down.

****

When the torpedo had struck, both George and Patrick were sitting on the metal deck of the hold, with their backs firmly pressed against a bulkhead. The torpedo struck just aft of the hold they were sitting in. The force of the blast threw the two standing guards across the two men's outstretched feet. It also dislodged the top packing crate from the stack in front of them, unseating it, causing it to come crashing down into the narrow space. It smashed the legs of one soldier before tipping forward to crush him to death. It narrowly missed the other soldier, but sent him sprawling backwards, knocking him out as his head hit the bulkhead. His rifle landed beside Patrick.

Just beyond the broken crate, both men could see a huge fountain of seawater pouring into the forward end of the hold, and felt the ship began to tilt forward. The water level rose very rapidly, forcing the stack of crates to move aft towards them.

George and Patrick needed no prompting to seize their opportunity. Patrick picked up the discarded weapon, but realised that their hands were still handcuffed. The stunned guard started to roll over, as he began to regain consciousness – his eyes widening in surprise as he saw that his charges were attempting to escape. Before he managed to get to his feet, Patrick shot him through the chest.

The crates were creeping ever closer, threatening to crush them against the metal bulkhead. Working the bolt action of the rifle, Patrick loaded another round into the barrel from the magazine. Holding up his hand, George told him to shoot away the lock. It worked, although the recoil was extremely painful. George did the same for Patrick's metal restraint.

There was no time to waste. After a quick search of the soldier's pockets they relieved him of several clips of ammunition before both men headed for the vertical ladder, carrying the rifle.

The water rose ever faster, cascading into the compartment in biblical proportions. The upper crates leaned alarmingly and began to topple. They crashed down, one after the other, into the narrow gap to their right. A mist of water spray filled their vision, rapidly reducing their visibility. Then a huge white surge burst in, flooding the deck, and washing away the body of the soldier they had shot. They scrambled up the metal ladder just in time. The huge crates bobbed and banged against the bulkhead below their feet. Both knew that they had to get out of this hold – and quickly.

483

At the top of the ladder, they reached the hatch housing that led out on to the upper deck. Already they could feel the bow tilting downward, and the angle was steadily increasing.

"Come on Pat, we've got to get out on to the upper deck," said George.

"'Oi must agree wit' yer, young George! Yer Skipper certainly does know 'is stuff. Oi can see why yous 'as t'e reputation t'at yous 'as."

"Shut up Patrick, and follow me."

George knew that it would not be long before this ship sank. They had but minutes to save themselves as they had emerged up into a water-tight metal cell-like compartment which had port holes. The clips on the water-tight screen door had been pulled into place from the outside, thus preventing their exit. They were trapped inside. Looking out through the small viewing-port, everywhere was utter panic and mayhem. Terrified wide-eyed soldiers were running everywhere. One of them glanced towards George, and noticing his plight, came over to knock off the retaining clips. Before he could express his thanks, the man had dashed away. Both men stepped out into open air for the first time in eighteen hours. George looked around, trying to appraise the situation, and look for a means of escape from the stricken ship.

"We should try and get over the side as quick as we can, Pat. We're in the Dardanelles, so the furthest we will have to swim is a couple of miles. Can you do it?"

"Oi'm not t'e world's best swimmer laddie, but t'is is not the toime to discuss my aquatic prowess – let's get goin'."

Walking across the main deck, there was absolute panic as men rushed about in confusion, each bent of self-preservation. They crashed into each one another, while others began fighting for the possession of a life-jacket. The air was filled with the acrid stench of the explosive, and a small dark haze hovered over the doomed vessel.

The bow was getting ever lower, causing the downward angle to steepen. Water started to flood across the fo'c'sle, and the anchor capstan had already begun to disappear. The ship's forward momentum had slowed to a crawl.

Terrified screams and shouts of pure panic were everywhere, as the Turkish troops realised their predicament. Their faces wore crazed expressions of impending doom, with eyes bulging in the abject terror of the situation. For most of them, it was the first time in their lives that they had ever seen water, and many recruited from the interior would have no idea of how to swim.

A group of seamen were frantically trying to turn out the davits, to lower one of the lifeboats. The fall ropes were paid out slowly, and the boat began to descend. As it reached deck level there was a stampede to get aboard, as it continued its descent. Finally, its keel just touched the surface, and it hung there, suspended over the rising water. There came a loud internal explosion which shook the whole ship, as the cold seawater reached the boiler expansion tubes. Huge plumes of black smoke began erupting from the two funnels. The explosion proved to be the death knell, rupturing through the hull amidships and condemning the ship to her inevitable fate. She started her slide to the bottom.

Men were now began leaping over the side, after throwing anything that would float before they jumped. Crossing over to the rail, George looked down at the flotsam littering the surface. He could already see many dead bodies, most floating face down. Many others were being seriously injured, or being knocked unconscious, by landing on those pieces of flotsam.

He noticed that the lifeboat had now been successfully lowered into the water. It was overfilled with soldiers, but nobody had thought to detached fall ropes, which were still attached to the ship. It was obvious what would happen.

"Come on Pat, let's make your way up towards the stern. We should stand a better chance from back there."

Nobody took any notice of them, self-preservation being the supreme thought. Everybody was equal in this situation, and the soldiers were scattering like ants. The level of hysteria grew into a blind panic, as the ship was visibly sinking beneath their feet. The death slide was well under way.

George and Patrick were climbing their way up the port wing, which was difficult against the steepness. As they passed under the second funnel structure, George knew that they had less than a minute before she would be gone. They brushed aside dangling ropes, and a loose fire hoses which had fallen from its stowage, to clamber over some major obstacles to where a dislodged a life-raft lay. It was jammed beneath some bracing guy wires supporting the second funnel. George knew that it would be the answer to get away, and tried to move it, but it was tightly jammed. So, the two men continue towards the stern, where they soon made arrived.

Several of the soldiers obviously had the same idea, as the poop deck was packed with terrified men. Everyone edging back as the water rose ever higher towards them. Many began climbing up onto the stern guard-rail, where they hesitated before they would finally be forced to make the inevitable jump. Most clung on like rats, not wanting to leave until the last moment.

George, could see that staying would be dangerous, and decided to return to make another attempt to dislodge life-raft. Looking forward towards the bridge, he could see that it was going under, as an angry maelstrom rose ever upwards towards them.

Steam and soot belched from both of the funnels, standing tall, like a pair of erupting volcanoes. George could see the smoke swirling upwards, gathering in an ominous black cloud over the stricken ship. The devils epitaph.

There came a sudden loud groaning, which revealed the forward funnel beginning to bend backwards under the force of water pressure, and they could hear the wire guy ropes snapping like twigs.

"Get here, Pat," shouted George, climbing up onto the metal rack which held the life-raft. Pat still had the rifle, the webbing carrying strap over his shoulder. George reached over and detached the bayonet, using it to cut away all of the retaining ropes that were holding the raft in place. The rising waters were approaching their position just as he finished. A tremendous crash announced that the forward funnel had fallen into the sea. George tried to ignore the danger as he continued with his task to free the float.

The ship shuddered as the death slide began to increase its momentum. The violent vibration became deafening. Loud explosive bursts of air erupted up through the deck, as huge internal pressures blasted out through the glass scuttles, venting like steam relief valves. Deck iron rivets exploded like deadly champagne corks, ricocheting off any remaining super-structure. She was breaking up as she went down.

Water now began pushing against the second funnel, and it too began to bend alarmingly, almost next to where they were working. Suddenly the raft was free! Pat and George hung on to it for dear life as the turbulent waters engulfed them. A Turkish soldier saw them, and seeing that the raft would give him a chance of life, he began wading through the turbulence towards them, but the water flow was too strong and he was whipped away in the boiling foam. The force of the rising water picked up the raft, lifting it clear, of its attachments, forcing itself away from the side of the stricken vessel. It was floating!

Once clear, it bobbed about like a leaf in a mill race, a slave to the foaming currents bubbling out from the sinking ship. Both men clung to the tiny structure for dear life.

Although he faced the imminent termination of his life, George became mesmerized by the macabre spectacle that was unfolding before him. Everything felt strangely surreal. He realised that this was what it was like to be on the receiving end of a submarine attack. This would be repeated during every sinking. Down inside the boat, he remembered the crew's elation, and the feeling of relief after hearing a torpedo explode. He knew that their cheers served to ease the ever-present tension that filled their lives. Out here this afternoon, he was experiencing the terror that they had created.

As their raft steadied, he and Pat managed to turn and observe in spell bound horror, the final moments of the ship.

The steel guy rope stays of the second funnel twanged, humming their epitaph as the force of the water engulfed it. A resonant howl that quickly reached a crescendo before the wires exploded. The loud cracks sent the wires flying back like elastic bands, cutting through anything, or anybody in its path like a razor edged bull-whip. The second of the great smoke stacks leaned awkwardly, the metal sheeting crumpling like a discarded blanket. There was a demonic wail as the whole funnel tore loose, twisting before toppling over like a felled tree.

Along the last of the near vertical decks, men were now falling, or being washed into the water. The sea surface was strewn with the black dots of their heads, as each man fought desperately for his life. The first of the heavily overmanned lifeboats suddenly disappeared out of sight, snatched down by the attached falls, like a trout taking a fly. On the raft Pat began to use his rifle butt as a paddle, in an attempt to get well clear of the ship. Just when they thought that providence was on their side, the downward suction caused by the mass of the ship, began to drag the craft back towards the swirling vortex. A giant swirling eddy, looking like the water disappearing down a plughole, appeared horrifying. The tiny raft spun and bounced like a fairground ride. It became a wild mustang, that was trying to throw them off. The ship had nearly gone, speeding down on her last journey, like a train entering the darkness of a tunnel. The two of them could only stare dumbly at the terrifying spectacle.

The remaining soldiers aboard, who had been too terrified to jump, were still desperately clinging to the stern rail, terrified by the approach of their death. They were riding the express train to hell, and every one of them screamed with the realisation that he was about to die. Loud metallic groans could still be heard emanating from deep beneath the water, as hull plates twisted and distorted. There was another burst, a violent hissing as the last of the pressurised air escaped, causing the surface to bubble and steam like a cauldron kettle. The ships death throes merged with the soldier's collective wails to form a hellish crescendo, as the stern disappeared from view.

There was a sudden silence, a macabre eerie stillness. Then came the plaintive cries of drowning soldiers, each pleading voice, a cry for help – a prayer for salvation – a sobbing epitaph.

Flocks of gulls filled the afternoon air with their avaricious caws. The surface of the sea was littered with flotsam and dead men, those still alive trying desperately to stay afloat. Each of the birds patiently eyed this unexpected bounty, waiting, ever greedy for their chance.

George had seen enough to last him a life-time.

"We should try to make for the European shore, Pat. Keep using that rifle butt as a paddle, and head in that direction," said George pointing the way.

"'Ow on Eart' do yer know which is t'e European shore, George?"

"The Asian shore lies to the east, and the European to the west. The sun rises in the east, and sets in the west. At this hour of the day, you can see that it has well passed its zenith, and is heading down towards the west," he said pointing. Then turning, he said, "So that over there has to be the east, and therefore that is the Asian shore. Directly opposite is Europe."

"T'ank you professor! Geography was never moi strong point at sc'ool."

****

Arthur Collenette had just been washed off the bridge as the ship continued its downward journey. He had been standing beside the vessel's captain, when the water had burst in through the screen windows, sending him for the screen door. The engulfing water pressure immediately forced him over the side. In his initial panic he tried to swim away from the ship, but quickly succumbed to the suction that was dragging him beneath the surface of the water. Even though he was wearing his life jacket, he felt his body being pulled ever deeper. His body was tossed and turned, and he started to lose all equilibrium. To his great relief he suddenly he broke the surface, and began sucking in huge lungsful of air. Just as his senses started to return, an ominous dark shadow filled his existence. Looking up, his face paled in terror as high above him came the falling mass of a funnel. It had broken away from its mounting, and was heading down directly towards him. It smashed into the water just a few feet to his right, and sank almost immediately. One second he was on the surface breathing normally, the next he was being dragged down under, his jacket snagged by something. As the funnel sank, so it dragged him down with it. All sound became muffled, his vision was filled with bubbles that glistened and sparkled as they rose up past him, back up towards the rapidly dimming light on the surface. The mass of metal continued past him, before his jacket finally tore itself away. The pressure on his ears was unbearable. Suddenly he could feel hands grabbing at him, jerky panicked movements that were frantic to find a purchase to enable somebody to ascend back to the air above. Arthur struck out, feeling the hardness of pliable flesh and bone beneath his pummelling fists. His hands hammered the man away, pushing him downward, stamping and kicking as the body passed below his knees. Another man's head banged against his knee, and Arthur raised his leg to stamped down hard, achieving some upward momentum.

As he slowly began to rise, through the confused shadows in the water, he could see the dark awesome mass of the sinking vessel rushing past him. His lungs were burning, pulsing, almost bursting in their demand for oxygen. Trying to claw his way upward through the water, his legs kicked frantically, as he realised that his body was still being dragged down by the descending current. The water currents spun him around, rolling him over and over destroying his equilibrium. He was unable to tell if he was upside down, or the right way up. It was at that moment that he thought that he was going to die, and realised that there was absolutely nothing that he could do about it. His thoughts began to dim, or was it just the lack of light at this depth? His oxygen starved brain was desperately fighting to retain consciousness.

Unknown to him, as the vessel passed on down below him, a huge pressurised air cloud came bursting out of one of the engine room deck hatches, which quickly blossomed into a huge mushroom of bubbles. It sparkled in the darkness as it rose upwards, grabbing him, filling his clothing and lifting him up on the blanket of air.

A chance at life! Oh, thank you, but surely it was too late! If only it had happened seconds ago, Arthur felt that he may have stood a chance! Often in the past, he had wondered how he would die. The thought of death had always terrified him, but strangely this wasn't too bad, it was a little like drifting off to sleep. It would all be over with very soon, and then there would be nothing but eternal peace. Blissful oblivion!

Something struck his head, shocking him awake. It was something hard and unyielding that had jolted him to his senses. He instinctively tried to yell, but his mouth filled with water, and he began choking and pushing away at the hardness. Suddenly he broke through the surface of the sea, coughing and spluttering as he gasped in the life-giving elements.

Daylight had never been so bright. Greedily, he sucked in more great gulps of air. One great inhalation was followed down by another mouthful of oily water, making him choke and cough uncontrollably, his eyes filled with tears. He desperately trod water, trying to keep his head above the surface, but it only served to send more water down his throat. He realised that he was drowning, and knew that he needed something to hold on to something until he recovered. Through his tears, his searched around for anything that would keep him afloat. The hard object that had struck his head had been a wooden deck grating. Although it would not support his full weight, he grabbed it, and pulled his body flat across it, gaining enough support until his coughing had eased.

With air in his lungs, he felt his strength return sufficiently to pull himself fully up onto the flimsy wooden platform, lying prone across it to spread his weight. If he kept still, it would supply enough buoyancy to keep him afloat. He was going to live.

He started to recover quickly, and after composing his thoughts, he raised his head and began to look around. A litter of debris and corpses filled the flat calm sea, noting that a few men were still managing to swim, but without any support, he knew that they would not last long. The lucky ones, like him, were holding on to pieces of wreckage. Three hundred yards away he could see a small life-raft with two men in it. There was something about the figures that caught his eye, causing him to look again. He squinted against the glare of the low sun to make sure. No, it couldn't be! He couldn't believe his eyes as he recognised who it was. George Torode, and that Irish bastard from the hospital at Scutari!

Hatred welled up from his stomach, like an eruption of bile laden vomit, as he watched their steady progress. It was those two men who now stood between him and respectability when he returned to Guernsey. He determined that they both had to die, making a vow that this time there would be no mistakes.

Chapter Twenty-Three

Crusader Castle

The hopes of making an escape for George and Patrick quickly begun to fade by the appearance of a steam pinnace, which they saw heading out towards the scene of the sinking from the direction of Gallipoli. To the north the sky was perfectly blue, the air clear and fresh in the afternoon, while over to towards the east a foul dark smoky cloud hovered over the grave of the ship. The boat's steady bearing indicated that it was heading straight towards them. They watch with a rising alarm as the boat's steady bearing made it seem as if it were heading straight for them. The thought of being re-arrested started to become a reality. Holding up a hand to shield the glare reflecting off the surface of the sea, the two men could see the white hats of the sailors manning the craft, standing out against the grey paint of the cabin structure. Their spirit began to when they noticed that one of the Turkish seamen, standing on the fore-deck, was holding a rifle in his hands. They could only be heading out to recapture them! How on earth had they known that they were trying to escape?

Then something strange happened, much to their great relief, the craft began veering off to port, heading eastward towards the scene of the sinking. As it closed, George could plainly see that the rifle the sailor was holding, was in fact a boat-hook. It wasn't being sent to recapture them after all – but heading over to pick up the survivors from the sinking. They both gave audible sighs of relief as they continued to watch the progress of the small vessel. It began to slow down to rescue the first wretched survivors. Two of the crew were standing in the waist of the boat, and could clearly be seen reaching down to haul the bedraggled figures up and over the side.

"Keep paddling Pat, but don't get the rifle mechanism too wet. We might need it at any time when we get ashore."

Patrick paddled slowly past a floating corpse, lying face down in the water. George noticed that the body had a rifle attached at an angle across the man's back by a webbing strap, with ammunition packed into his bandolier.

"Get us over towards that body Pat. He has a rifle and ammunition. Having two weapons may well come in handy when we get ashore. The rifle will come in handy as a second oar."

They reached out, hauling the body alongside their frail float, and quickly relieving the drowned soldier of his weapon and ammo, before letting him drift away.

"Right Pat, we can now paddle ashore together."

"W'at d'yer t'ink oive bin doin' all t'is toime, sturrin' t'e C'ristmas pud?"

It did not feel as if they were making very much headway until they stopped paddling to recheck on the situation back over at the sinking site. George estimated that they had paddled over half a mile, and they had placed a good distanced between them and the survivors of the sinking. The steam pinnace could still be seen in the far distance, dashing hither and thither from one bobbing head to the next.

'Any of those who were still alive in the water must be on the point of total exhaustion,' thought George.

The massed hordes of black backed gulls, that were circling overhead, knew that their turn was coming, as they surveyed the carnage below. They had been waiting patiently, knowing that the rewards were going to be plentiful. More survivors were picked up by the recovery craft, but for so many others it had arrived just too late. The surface of the sea had become mottled with the bodies of the dead.

On their small life-raft, George and Patrick were getting ever nearer the shore. Finally arriving close to one of the few rocky promontories that protruded out along that stretch of the channel. George started giving Patrick directions, as they negotiated their way through a series of submerged rocks. Although difficult, it was still too deep to attempt to wade ashore. The Irishman accepted his orders unquestioningly. After all he was only a soldier, and this was the province of the navy. Finally, they hit the stony beach, and quickly abandoned the life-saving raft to its fate, walking up onto a tiny stretch of the small beach, squeezed in between two huge rock formations. Both men sat down on a dry rock, with their rifles laid across their knees, as they slowly regained their composure. Patrick began coughing, and George reached over and patted his back, attempting to ease his discomfort. Having eaten hardly anything in the last twenty-four hours, both men realised that they were extremely hungry.

"Moi stomach t'inks moi t'roat's bin cut," said Patrick. "T'ere must be a farm around 'ere, w'ere we cud get some eggs, or somet'in better."

George could not disagree with him. The stress of having to stand for so long over the past twenty-four hours had drained much of the strength from them both, and he knew that they were going to need sustenance to fuel their long trek back across the peninsula. They were also going to need a safe place in which to recuperate. Their clothes were soaked, and they were going to need to find some shelter before it got dark. Once they were dry, they could begin to put some distance between them and this shore-line. The chance of re-capture was still a strong possibility all the time that pinnace was still visible, so they were going to begin their search for shelter right now.

Rising up behind them stood some significant looking hills. Both sides of the Dardanelles had high ground running along most of its length, as far as the eye could see. To get a better idea of their position, they knew that they were going to have to climb up that steep hillside behind them, to get a fresh view of the area. It was going to be quite a climb, especially with their wounds being so painful. Patrick's cough was also a seriously consideration. They would wait a while longer before setting off.

The late afternoon sun quickly dried their clothes enough, but after they had begun the climb, the material began to aggravate their skin. Patches of dried salt appeared that acted as a scourer and irritated their flesh. Both tried to ignore it, but the annoyance remained. On reaching a craggy ledge, they stopped for a rest, and took the chance to survey the area.

They sat and watched the lone craft far below them, as it continued with its task of rescuing the survivors. After twenty minutes it finished, and they watched as it turned to head back towards Gallipoli. No other help was being sent out, and anyone remaining alive out there had been abandoned to his fate. Besides the heavy amounts of flotsam, the surface of the waterway looked smooth and serene, but dark pool patches of oil marked location of the merchantman's grave.

After a half hour of rest, the two men struggled to their feet, and reluctantly resumed their climb. The early evening tranquillity provided them with some late sun warmth that took away the horrors of two hours earlier. There seemed to be very little activity taking place down in the channel. The surface of the water was now covered by gulls, but they could be seen taking off as one as a Turkish destroyer came ploughing into view at speed. They watched as it slowed to make its way through the scene of carnage. The two men turned back to the task in hand, and carried on up towards the crest of the hill.

Nearing the crest they began moving very cautiously, utilising any available cover before emerging at the top, where they made a joint decision that they would keep walking as far they could today before trying to find somewhere to rest for the night. They were going to need a good rest, because any attempt to try and walk on against the pain barrier could well make their injuries worse.

Surprisingly, as they walked along the crest, the view down in the channel was poor due to the fading light. So, after assessing their position, the two men began walking in a south westerly direction. The undulation of the hills placed extra strain on their legs. Just before it got dark, they were approaching the top of the next rise, when they spotted a distant building. It was the first sign of life they had seen since stepping ashore. Stopping to appraise the situation, they both agreed that it looked like a farm, and the possibility of food stirred their hunger. They gave reaching it their top priority.

The channel had completely disappeared as the climbed up towards the farm, but on reaching the higher ground the waterway came into view once more. The search-lights could be seen far below, and George could just make out a sharp turn, which he thought must be Nagara Point, and the much larger search-light beyond must be Kephez Point. Seeing these familiar landmarks gave him a much better idea as to the direction that they needed to take over the peninsula to reach their own lines. They were going to have to circle around the Turkish lines to do so. The farm however was their priority for now, and was definitely going to be their first stop.

The light had gone, leaving a starry night. As the approached the farm they began to employ some degree of stealth to get closer to the buildings. The bellow of cattle ahead proved their assumption that it was indeed a farm, which increased their hopes that they might find something to eat.

"Oi moight be mistakin, but isn't t'at one of t'em milky queer fellers t'at oi can 'ear. Imagin all o' t'at rich creaminess, Georgie boy," said Patrick, licking his lips.

The two men used the cover of a ditch, that ran along the edge of a deeply rutted track-way, to survey the collection of the once white-washed buildings. Very little of the paintwork remained, and some of the exterior rendering had crumbled, where sections revealed a dull red brick work exposed. It was obviously a farm, but certainly not a prosperous one. Despite the obvious display of poverty, their expectation of obtaining some food was high.

Crouching down at the side of the lane, they watched the main building through the long clumps of long grass that had managed to escape the attention of a scythe for a couple of years, as they began trying to assess where they would find any food.

The general layout of the complex was the familiar square, with the small herd of milking cows standing nonchalantly together at its centre. If this group of buildings had been a fraction different architecturally, and in a better state of repair, then this farm could have been located anywhere on Guernsey. George remembered the big farm called Le Gron in the parish of St Saviour that he, Matthew and Arthur had passed by on their way to the cliffs at Pleinmont Point on that ill-fated day.

Despite the dilapidated appearance of the buildings, the whole area was peaceful. Despite the dark, a battered cockerel was still scratching at the dryer patches of the yard, its beak stabbing in the dust. In the top branches of a tree behind the house, the raucous caws of rooks could be heard as they settled down to roost for the night.

A hundred yards beyond the group of animals that were ambling slowly around their water-trough; there stood a dilapidated two-storey farm house. Its tiled roof obviously able to provide some cover, enough to keep the interior dry, but the façade was badly in need of renovation. The flaking paintwork on the blue wooden shutters standing guard either side of the windows on the upper floor gave a mottled effect. One had lost a hinge, causing it to hang down at an oblique angle like the blade of a guillotine. Off to the right of the house stood a large hay barn that had been built in same red brick, its plastered walls faring no better than that on the house. A large set of double wooden doors filled the central opening, one of which stood slightly ajar. Both of these buildings were topped by sun bleached terracotta pan tiles. Across the yard there were two longer, but narrower, single storied outbuildings, perhaps stables, or milking shed, which served to form the final two sides of the square.

Some of the rather emaciated, rather lean, looking cattle were standing in the middle of a large slurry pool that surrounded the water trough. Their droppings had obviously mixed in with the trampled mud to produce a brown sludge liquid, to create a rustic odour that assailed their noses. The cattle were joined by more of the beasts, ambling out from the direction of the milk-shed, one at a time. Their legs and hind-quarters were splattered with mud and excrement. Somewhere beyond those buildings there were some unseen goats, which they could hear bleating.

On their way up the hillside, George had noted that the surrounding fields badly needed harvesting, and by the colour of the corn it had already turning to a dark dirty brown, showing that it was well passed it best. Maybe all the working men had been recruited to fight at the front? What a waste.

The whole demeanour of the place was one of decrepitude, and semi-abandonment. Over on the south side of the house Patrick noticed that there were several neat rows of fresh plants, growing in cultivated soil. Beyond that, there looked to be a grove of olive trees. Around the rest of the house the grass was long, sun-bleached, and running to seed.

A loud rusty creak, immediately brought their eyes back towards the milk-shed. The milking appeared to be over, as a lone figure emerged, carrying two full pails, hanging at each end of a shoulder yoke. It was a young girl wearing a scarf over her head, her skirt swaying as she walked straight across the yard towards the house. After navigating her way around the filthy lake, she continued on up the steps at the front of the house, entering the main doorway. She left the door open, and the two men expected her to come straight back out again, but after ten minutes she had not reappeared.

"We could lay low in that barn, Pat. We could get some sleep, and afterwards we come out and find something to eat from those vegetables at the back of the house!!"

"Oi cud eat t'e hind leg oft wun of dem cows over t'ere roight now, George. T'en oide c'ase it all down wit' a gallon of t'er milk, so oi wud."

"You would have to scrub some of the crap off the back end of those animals first, Pat. Well, let's just hope that we find something in the meantime. There are chickens running around that door in that barn, so they may well have nests over there – raw eggs is not my favourite though. The most important thing now is to find a hiding place, where we can rest up. We don't want to be spotted out here – or we're bound to be caught again for sure, and I don't think we will survive being recaptured, especially if Arthur Collenette has anything to do with it."

"Oi was 'oping t'at he'd gone down wid t'e ship."

They waited another ten minutes for the girl to reappear, but all remained quiet.

"Come on Pat, we'll use the edge of this wheat field as cover to get as near to that barn as we can. Then it can only be a twenty-yard dash to get through that big open door."

"Oi wud be able ter dash a lot faster if t'ere was a plait of 'am and eggs waitin' for me, George."

The two men slowly crawled their way along the empty ditch on their hands and knees, using the uncut wheat and clumpy stands of grass to hide them from the house. George welcomed the fading light. On reaching the corner of the field, their eyes scanned the complex once more for any sign of life. The only movement was from the tails of the cattle.

"Dat smell reminds me of moi Grandfat'ers roses," said Pat.

"Aren't roses supposed to smell sweet?" replied George.

"Oh, t'ey do w'en t'ey're picked George, but moi grandaddy used ter cover t'e flower bed wit' t'e 'orse shoite ter make 'em grow gud."

George shook his head and smiled. "He could probably grow a field of roses with that lake over there."

They made a last check of the area for human activity – nothing moved.

"OK Pat, I'll go first. Once I'm in the barn, give it one minute and if nobody re-appears, you dash across and join me – OK?"

Patrick nodded, raising his thumb, trying to stifle another bout of coughing.

"Oft you go t'en laddie, oi'll be wit' you in no toime atall."

George's heart began beating faster as he prepared himself; he scanned for any danger one final time. Taking a deep breath, he dashed out of his hiding place, bending low and carrying his rifle – running the twenty yards to the barn as fast as his feet would carry him, but it was more of a fast limp than a run as the pain in various parts of his body was excruciating.

He crashed into the door, quickly rounded it into the safety of the interior. Once inside, he leaned back against it with relief, trying to regain his breath. He knelt down and edged himself into the gap, holding his rifle at the ready, just in case someone had seen him.

Another thirty seconds passed by, and George turned back to towards back towards his friend. He saw Patrick's head pop up above the grass as the Irishman made a final scan around. George also glanced over towards the farm-house to make doubly sure. All was still at the house, everything appeared to be quiet.

Then, like a greyhound springing out of its trap, the Irishman came charging out of the long grass at the edge of the field of ruined crop. He pounded across the open ground, his serious limp seriously impeding his speed. When he was just five yards from the door his bad leg slipped on some excrement, sending him headlong and sprawling into the effluent laden slurry. His forward momentum caused a small bow-wave to form under his chin as he arrived at George's feet, with his rifle crashing against the barn door. He looked up to see the sailors grinning face.

"Still can't keep out of the shite, can you Pat. Your Grandfather would be very proud of you."

****

After a hot soapy bath, Arna, the girl who had been assigned to him was toweling Arthur Collenette down. She dried his back and shoulders, and as she bent down to wipe his legs, he looked down at the top of her back. Those blue-black bruises were the result his beatings. He watched her muscles as they flexed in her labour. She was trying desperately hard to bring her task to an end as fast as possible.

The comforting warmth of the bath water had slowly eradicated the terrors of earlier that morning. He loved the manipulation of her fingers as she caressed his scalp when washing his hair, which had helped greatly in easing away all of that tension. She soaped his chest and under his arms, pouring jugful after jugful of warm liquid over his skin to rinse away the suds. Her attentive caresses had caused a stirring in his loins, and his thoughts drifted towards more carnal comforts. As she dried his ankles and toes, he looked down, studying the outlines of her shapely form. He had to admit that she was a pretty little thing.

She looked up at him, hoping that he would be pleased, and that she would be dismissed. Black curls cascaded down around her cheeks, framing those almond brown eyes that threatened their conqueror with paradise, but Arthur knew that he did not need to conqueror her because she was his property. His slave, a personal possession, but he knew deep down that he still had not tamed her fiery spirit.

His smile of contentment slowly morphed into a cruel sneer, knowing that she had no choice but to obey him. She was his to command, completely! His to do with whatever he wanted – his own personal sex slave, given to him by the grateful Turks as a thank-you for his assistance and co-operation.

Before he had sailed on the troopship from Constantinople, he had sent her ahead to the Turkish Army HQ here at Gallipoli to prepare his quarters for his arrival. The Turks had provided him a pleasant suite of rooms situated within the old Caliph's Palace, who at one time was used to rule this outpost of the Ottoman Empire. It boasted cool marbled floors, and was lavishly furnished. He had two other elderly servants to do his bidding besides Arna, but he had already dismissed them for the night. He was here alone with Arna.

The Turks really were really stupid bastards, because they had actually seemed surprised when he had agreed to co-operate with them to avoid the firing squad. The silly bastards actually thought that he would have chosen death. Nobody in their right mind would willingly go to the firing squad, especially when given the chance to live. So, if they were prepared to hand out these little perks at the same time, then he certainly wasn't going to refuse them.

Looking about the room, he certainly had to give the Turks some credit – they knew how to live well. He also had to admit to himself, that this girl that they had given him had provided him with more pleasure and sexual satisfaction than any other female that he had ever known. Not that he could boast of many conquests, just a couple of embarrassing sticky encounters with some Portsmouth prostitutes, both of which had both been totally uncontrolled, and not at all rewarding. From those embarrassing experiences he had quickly realised then that he needed to be in total control the during whole sexual act. Without complete domination, sexually nothing happened for him. As a consequence, he had never really had a fully satisfying sexual experience. It had been one of those dark inner secrets that he had never dared share with anyone. In the Naval Training Establishment amongst his fellow trainees, he had made up stories to enhance his prowess amongst his peers, so that he outwardly appeared to be one of the boys. Back then he had not recognised his impotence, or maybe there was something in his mind that had refused to accept the fact. But after he had been given Arna that had all changed. He had discovered this latent potency that he never knew that he possessed. Certainly, he had never experienced sexual satisfaction like it before.

He clearly remembered the day when she had been given to him – and from the look on her face she had been absolutely terrified, cringing like a trapped animal awaiting its fate. The first sight of her quivering form had given him an immediate erection. It was that power he had over her that had caused the stirring in his manhood. After forcibly taking her on that first night, it had certainly been the first time in his whole life that he had managed to achieve a fully controlled ejaculation during intercourse.

His erotic thoughts rekindled memories of how he had thrashed her with his leather belt – to show her who was master. Deep down he knew that it had been the pent-up frustration of George Torode escaping from the Papandross household that been the real reason for his bout of sadism. She had provided him with a release valve – the excuse to hurt her – a form of therapeutic redemption. The inner excitement that he had felt as she had crawled and cringed before him, screaming and begging him for mercy, made him feel like a masculine superman that he had always imagined he was. On completion he had raped unmercifully – forcibly taking her broken body as she lay bleeding on the floor. Previous attempts at penetration had always ended in disappointment and failure, but when she lay there stretched before him like a limp rag doll, his immediate response was to hurt her more. He enjoyed seeing her cowering before him, delighting in her misery. He got a real charge of excitement from her nakedness and vulnerability. He was enjoying the power, as his arousal strained against the material of his uniform trousers. The sexual urge pounded through his veins, as hot as a lava-flow. This was wonderful – it was how he had always dreamed it would be.

The reflection on these recent pleasures was abrasively brought to a halt by a vision of George Torode, when he saw him trying to paddle ashore with that Irish bastard, whilst he had been left wallowing in the water for over an hour, having survived by just the merest whisker from the sinking. The pleasure that he was feeling had quickly reverted to his more familiar emotion of total hatred. If it hadn't been for George Torode, he would never have been on that ship in the first place, because he had been ordered to take charge of escorting the prisoners to Gallipoli. Doing so had almost cost him his life, and he shuddered as he remembered the terrifying experience that he had undergone in the water.

Immediately on arrival here at Gallipoli, he had gone straight to his quarters, shed his sodden uniform, and plunged his body into a hot soapy bath. If there is one thing that the Turks are good at, it's taking a bath. Arna had instructed the elderly servants to wash his uniform, saying that she would press it herself. It was left hanging out on a line at the back of the veranda when they had finished, and he had immediately dismissed the two servants. It would soon dry in the Gallipoli sunshine.

George had managed to escape from him once again. He really was the luckiest bastard alive. The General was certainly not going to be pleased when he reported to Army HQ, and he was not looking forward to facing him over the incident. Ever since his childhood, it had always been George who had been the one to spoil things for him. It had only been by him using his quick thinking and sheer bluff that had he managed to worm his way out of that silly episode down on the Pleinmont Cliffs. If George had died along with Matthew, then life would have been so much easier – and things were going to be easier again, he told himself, once George Torode was dead.

He thought about that night, long ago on Guernsey, when he carried out his plan to murder his new stepfather. He smiled, because his planning had been meticulous, and once he had finalised everything, he remembered feeling quite proud of the sheer ingenuity he used. He had planned the perfect murder. Remembering how he had cleverly lay in wait for the one man he hated above all others, and in that he included George Torode. The adrenalin rush he had experienced as he had stepped out from the between the hedgerow, his stepfather's only reaction had been one of surprise at seeing him so far from home. The stupid man had even turned around obligingly when he had asked for help to find the non-existent wallet that he had told him that he had just lost. The spade that he had carried all that way, had split through his skull as easily as cutting through a pumpkin. He remembered the thrill of triumph that went through his body. After he had killed that abomination of a man, who had dared to defile his mother, there had not been the faintest trace of a suspicion cast by anyone that he had had anything to do with it. His plan had been that absolutely perfect. It had only been George Torode who had seemed to possess a sixth sense. There had been no incriminating evidence, because he had washed the spade on the way home and dug it into the ground a few times, to show that it had been used in the garden before he had returned it to the garden shed. He had enjoyed the surge of self-satisfied and pride on a job well done. The only thing that still bothered him was how on earth George had managed to figure out the truth?

He could still feel remnants of the excruciating pain in his genitals, where George had kicked him when he had affected his escape from the Papandross household. Later that day he suffered the humiliation of being hauled before the General at Turkish Army Headquarters. The severe dressing down had been followed by a bone chilling warning as to what his fate would he if were to betray his new found paymasters. They had definitely become suspicious that he may have deliberately aided George in his escape. The embarrassment of it all had made him squirm in angry frustration. As if he would have helped that bastard. Now he envisaged that reprimand being repeated, but he could hardly be held to be

497

responsible for the ship being torpedoed, although he would be taken to task for allowing the two prisoners to get away. George Torode had a lot to answer for. He was definitely going to kill him once he was recaptured. He had to die, because Arthur knew that all the time that he lived, he would never be safe – and he would never be able to return home to Guernsey. He had to die because he was also the only person in the world who knew that he had killed his step-father.

Before returning to his apartment, he had sent half of his available reserve troops out to scour the countryside in an effort to locate them – they were out there now searching for the bastards. The peninsula was not that big an area, and it would only be a matter of time. Once they had been located, he would lead his men out to recapture them, and he would then be able to take all of the credit. He would take great pleasure in taking charge of the firing squad himself, and getting rid of the bane of his life once and for all.

"That will do Arna, go get my dressing gown," demanded Arthur, his voice expectant.

The girl padded barefoot across the Persian carpet towards the wardrobe. The graceful sway of her curvaceous hips stood out beneath her dressing gown, graceful like a lioness pacing in her cage at the zoo. She collected the garment. and walked back towards him. The half-opened front of her silky garment revealed her cleavage, her breasts standing out proud and firm against the fine material.

She had nothing but hatred for the man who stood before her. She detested him with all of her being, feeling an utter revulsion as she handed him the gown. This was a man who had betrayed his own country and to do that made him the lowest form of life. The way he degraded her made her feel dirty and showed that he had perverted sexual lusts. Her skin cringed under his touch; she knew that she would kill him if she ever the chance should materialise. Men like him would be exiled from her community, back in her home village. There would be no place for such as him in any decent Armenian society. He would have his throat cut, because there were only men of honour who lived there. They were all honest men, who treated their women with respect. She had learned from others that this animal was British, a traitor, who had betrayed his fellows and thrown in his lot with the Turks. He deserved to die for that alone. She would have cut his throat in his sleep a long time ago, but for the fact that the Turks were holding people from her village as hostages. She was under no illusions that such an act would not only result in her death, but also other members of her family. Her thoughts caused her to lose concentration for a moment and too late she realised that she was standing far too close to him. A sudden gasp escaped her lips, as she felt his hand touching the inside of her leg. Her eyes bulged with a mixture of panic and physical revulsion welled up within her. She tried to pull away, but his fingers dug into her flesh, causing her to wince. Frozen in her disgust and pain, his hand began an upward journey. Reaching her pubic hair, his fingers rough, as they probed their way into her.

"Lie down on the rug, Arna," his voice had an urgency, more a demand than a request.

Her legs were shaking in fear and a nauseous bile began to rise in her throat as he pulled her down onto the carpet. As she landed onto her back, his hands grabbed her knees, with his fingers digging cruelly into her skin, brutally pulling them apart. His excitement visibly increased; as his breathing became panting gasps. She could see his erection and the thought of what was about to happen made her feel physically sick. He towered over her, positioning himself, ready to enter her body. She closed her eyes, trying to shut out the horror, as she felt him beginning to thrust at her entrance.

Just then there was a sudden knock at the door, which made her give an audible groan with relief – it was certainly not an expression of passion. At first, he didn't seem to hear it, or such was his urgency that he chose to ignore it. A powerful forward thrust from his hips, evoked a scream that burst through her clenched teeth. It hurt her like hell! The bastard always took her with as much pain as he could possibly inflict. He seemed totally incapable of arousing her, or any woman for that matter. His rhythmic thrusts were like a stabbing knife, a hard-burning invasion of her very soul. His bodyweight was crushing her, making breathing difficult.

There was another knock at the door – louder and more urgent this time. She felt his hesitation. He had heard it this time and she could feel his immediate loss, as she silently thanked God for answering her prayers. The knock came again, prolonged and more insistent. The pressure eased from her, as he raised himself and stood up. An oath was spat in her face, as he grabbed his discarded dressing gown. She curled her knees up to her chest, with her arms encircling her legs. She listened as his footsteps cross the room and heard the door being yanked opened.

"Yes!" she heard him shout.

"Sir, your presence is required at Headquarters immediately," said an unseen voice.

"I'll be along shortly," replied Arthur.

"I have been told that you must come right now, sir," the voice persisted.

"Wait while I get dressed."

The door slammed.

****

"No, I am not joking – you really stink Pat. Since your clothes have dried, they seem to be smelling worse than ever," said George.

"Oi'm layin' down a sawt of camouflage odour, George. If t'ey are usin t'em dogs to try and sniff us out, t'ey won't foind me 'cause oi'll smell loike t'ose milky queer fellas out in t'e yard. T'ose doggies will t'ink oim a cow," replied the Irishman. "T'ere is t'e added bonus that it'll keep all of dem mosquitoes away."

"You smell more like your Grandfather's roses," said George. "The dogs might get a bit confused and cock their legs up to pee on you, eh."

Both men laughed as they lay on a pile of soft hay on the upper level of the barn. They had quickly managed to find that chickens had indeed been nesting up there and found some eggs. They had cracked them and simply poured the contents straight down their throats. It was not pleasant, but it had provided them with the protein that they lacked.

After their arrival in the barn, George had chanced a quick dash over to the milk-shed and had returned with the dregs of some milk that had been discarded in pail, which disappeared as just quickly as the eggs. This sudden rush of protein into their empty stomachs, combined with the physical fatigue of the journey caused both men to feel drowsy and they had both drifted off into a deep sleep.

George stood up, and peering out through a hole in the roof he could see a star filled sky, but they were beginning to disappear as the dawn was under way. Looking towards the house, there was a lantern glow in the window. Over towards the east the light silhouetted the hills. They had slept longer than he realised. Encouraged, he climbed down the wooden rung ladder to the ground level and went to the barn door to check if everything was quiet. Looking out, but was suddenly alarmed when he saw the young girl's outline filling in the faint glow from the open door of the farmhouse. She had a lantern in her hand.

"Shhh Pat," he whispered, raising a finger to his lips. "Someone is coming."

She had a nice figure, he thought. Guessing her to be about twenty, she was slender, without being thin. She reminded him a little of Gladys. As the thought flitted across his mind, he began to wonder what Gladys would be doing at this very moment! He knew deep down that he loved her still, but there was still the nagging doubt that she would have found herself another beau by now. Then an image of Mina replaced that of Gladys. Yes, he knew that he had loved her too! How was it that he could he love two women? Mina was dead, but he knew that he had certainly loved being with her during their short time together. In a way they had shared a far deeper relationship than he had ever had with Gladys and not just sexually. There were thousands of extra men in uniform in Portsmouth and after that love he had shared with Mina, he knew that he could not blame Gladys if she were to seek love elsewhere. Maybe when you are fighting a war, there was not a time to think about true love. With the real chance of being killed, maybe chance encounters were all one should expect during these terrible times. The chances of surviving out here in the Middle East were certainly small and maybe with the long periods between his letters, Gladys may have thought that he had been killed. Maybe he was using that as an excuse, after the guilt that he was feeling over Mina!

Closing his eyes, he sighed and returned to this present situation. The girl's voice could be heard calling to someone – or something. In her hand George could see a bone. Maybe there is a dog? It was lucky that it had not come into the barn. Alarm! A dog could give them away! It would soon smell them and probably bark. Patrick appeared at his side.

"Phhhew," whistled Pat through his teeth, as he joined him at the door. "Now oi know w'at all t'ose Turks are foighten for."

A dog appeared out of the darkness and she gave it some food. Then, without warning she stepped out of the doorway and began walking directly across the yard towards the barn. Both men scrambled to climb the wooden ladder as fast as their injuries could take them diving for cover under the pile of loose hay in the loft. They heard the barn door creak loudly below them and could hear her humming as she went about her business. Maybe she was looking for eggs?

George started to feel a little guilty at having eaten five. Maybe she was looking for the half pail of milk that they had drunk? He was trying to keep his breathing soft and quiet, but nearby he heard Patrick's lungs rasping like a steam train, when all of a sudden, his body was wracked by a loud fit of coughing.

The girl looked up, startled, hovering a second too long, before she sensed the danger and made a dash for the door. George was too quick for her, dropping down from the loft to block her escape. The sudden jolt on landing caused a terrible pain in his leg, but he managed to bar her exit. Both stood there like statues, staring at each other, her eyes flicking left and right, looking for an escape route. Every time she tried to move one way, George countered, preventing any attempts by her to dart past him. She swung the lantern at him, which he easily avoided. The impasse grew, so he raised his hands in a gesture of friendship and in a soft voice tried to calm her fear.

"It's all right – it's OK – we're not going to hurt you."

Patrick's coughing fit had stopped, but he was still breathing heavily as he climbed down the ladder. She was cornered now, trapped between the two men. Her eyes were wide, like a frightened rabbit, realising there was no way out.

"D'yer speak the English moi darlin'?" asked Patrick.

Her eyebrows arched and her facial features creased in confusion and uncertainty. What were these strange men saying to her? What language were they speaking? She had convinced herself that she was about to be raped – already having made the decision to surrender, rather than a fight them. Rape by the Turkish troops had become commonplace on the peninsula. She had heard that many of the women who had tried to fight back had been badly beaten and some had even been killed. It was the best to go with it, she had been told and hopefully the rapists would be satisfied enough to leave in peace.

"You'se can rest assured we're not goin' ter 'urt yer moi darlin'," said Patrick, in soothing tones.

She could see that they weren't Turkish soldiers, in fact she failed to recognise anything at all about them. Even their dishevelled clothing was odd. The one with the nice voice stank to high heaven and both of them appeared to have injuries. Were they soldiers?

"Oi t'ink oi'll 'ave t'is little darlin' eatin' out of moi 'and befor too long, George. Oi've always 'ad t'at effect on women."

"Maybe she can't resist that lavender water that I can smell on you, Patrick," said George and they both smiled at each other. What began as a chuckle, quickly blossomed into infectious giggles and finally into side-splitting laughter!

The girl couldn't believe her eyes. Her two erstwhile captors had tears of laughter running down their cheeks and were guffawing uncontrollably. She had not understood a word of what they had said, but her initial fear began to fade. As the giggles subsided, the two men looked up to see the girl staring at them in open mouthed astonishment. Seeing her bemused features was enough to start them off once more and they bent over in their uncontrollable fits of laughter.

Seeing her chance, the girl made to dash past George. He only just managed to grab the hem of her skirt and hold on. She squealed in her frustration, realising that she had failed. Patrick came up and made over much of telling George to let go and with his arm around the girl's shoulder, he gently soothed away her fears.

Half an hour later, saw them both sitting in the farmhouse kitchen, with a steaming cup of hot sweet apple flavoured tea clasped between their hands. The girl was busy at the range, frying eggs, lots of eggs, which she served with great wedges of flat bread. The contents of their plates disappeared very quickly and Patrick gave a hearty belch, patting his stomach approvingly.

"T'at was magnificent moi lovely," he said to the girl.

His bold inviting smile made her blush and her downcast eyes showed her embarrassment. George could see that despite the language barrier, she was becoming attracted to this Celtic rogue, as she leaned forward to fill his mug with more of the tea.

With his hunger sated, George began to feel human again and he could feel the warmth of the drink permeating the extremities of his body, he started to feel truly relaxed for the first time since they had left the hospital.

"Moi leg 'urts to 'igh 'eaven. Despite that kip we just 'ad, oim still feelin' weary and could sleep fer a week George, so oi could," said Patrick, yawning.

"Well maybe if one of us has a kip, then the other could keep an eye on the girl and then we could swap over," George replied. "Because it will not be long before the morning light is with us, when I think that we should be on our way. Travelling at that time will be much safer and if we run into any Turks, we can hide until they have gone."

"Oid loike ter kip wit' t'e little darlin' over t'ere, but oi don't know if my leg wud stand t'e strain. Youse can keep watch if youse loikes," said the Irishman, smiling as he stood, heading towards the staircase. "Cos oi'm defoinately goin' ter sleep furst."

The girl kept herself busy, mixing some kind of flat bread dough in a bowl at the table, which she then baked on a flat griddle that to the left of the oven. There was an iron fire grate positioned between the two that heated both. Gradually the smell of Patrick faded, thankfully replaced by the smell emanating from the bread. The Irishman's reverberating snores could be heard resonating through the house, occasionally interrupted by a hacking cough. It was a full hour before he finally re-appeared scratching his head and yawning more than when he had climbed up the stairs.

George took the occasional walk outside in the light, looking back over the hills of the way they had come. The town of Gallipoli lay over that way and if they were going to send any soldiers out to find them, they would be coming from that direction. Thankfully there was nothing in sight.

"T'at was a feckin' gud sleep George. Now it's your turn now moi boyo," he said, expelling a long blast of wind. "W'at toime d'yer t'ink it tis?"

"It's still quite early Pat, it must be somewhere around seven o'clock. By the sound of it you seem to have developed a puncture in your arse, but thanks to the attar of roses that you're wearing, we have thankfully been spared from the smell. I am hoping that bed doesn't smell as bad as you do!" said George, heading for the stairs. "Wake me in an hour, Pat and we will be on our way and keep an eye out down that hill, mate. If they send soldiers after us, they will be coming up from that direction."

Unfortunately for George, the bed upstairs did smell and despite several attempts to drift away, sleep was impossible. After less than an hour he finally gave up and went downstairs. He was surprised to find that the kitchen was completely empty and his friend was nowhere to be seen – and neither was the girl.

Strange, he thought as he looked out of the window searching for them, but the yard also appeared to be deserted. He went outside, the slopes of the hills around them had banished the shadows as the morning advanced. It was going to be a nice day.

Then just as he was about to return inside, something caught his eye. It had been just a flicker – or was it a flash? It was way down the hillside, almost below his field of vision, but something was definitely moving at the base of the hill. The morning light revealed the waterway, far far beyond and as he was searching the waterway, he saw the flash again. They were just crossing the ridge of that first rise, a series of dots from this distance, but clearly moving! He looked again – they were soldiers spreading out in a wide arc, heading up the hillside in their direction.

Where the bloody hell was Patrick?

As he re-entered the kitchen, he heard a grunting sound coming from the front room, which immediately caught his attention. He hurried across the kitchen and threw open the connecting door. Patrick and the girl were on the couch, in what could only be termed, a compromising position. The girl gave a startled cry, pushing down her skirt and trying to do up the buttons on her blouse. Patrick just gave a smug grin.

"You do pick yer moments moi lad," he said, a sly smile creased the corners of his mouth.

"So, do you, you stupid bastard. You're supposed to be keeping an eye out. There are a troop of soldiers on their way up the hill," replied George.

Patrick sprang up, grimacing as another pain shot through his leg and hurriedly began dressing.

"Oi know you're only a sailor George, but you only get troops in t'e cavalry. Tis a company, a squad, or a platoon t'at you saw, depending on 'ow many there are…"

"Just shut up and let's get going. I'll grab us something to eat on the way and you get that wine-skin over there. Fill it with water. We'll be hungry and thirsty again by this time tomorrow," said George, grabbing some of the freshly baked loaves and stuffing them into a hessian sack.

A wineskin container was unhooked from a nail on the newel post at the base of the stairs and Patrick filled it with water – they were ready to go. Standing outside the door, they both looked down the hill spotting the soldiers making slow but steady progress up towards them. Picking up their rifles and ammunition, the two men set off. Patrick turned and blew the girl a kiss. With glistening eyes, she gave a sorrowful wave.

They walked across the yard towards the barn, moving carefully around the edge of the stinking puddle and set off up the low gradient of the next hill and already they could see the crest of a further hill faintly outlined beyond. With full bellies and aching limbs, running was out of the question, but at least they now had the energy and stamina to keep up a good steady pace. That short break had done wonders for both men and the pain in their bodies was thankfully beginning to ease.

Soon the farm was far behind them, looking like a small cardboard model below them as they approached the crest. From where they stood, the filthy muddy pool was obscured by the barn but they also saw that the soldiers were just arriving, climbing up those last few hundred yards up towards the same buildings.

The two friends turned, making their way up and over the ridge, heading towards a line of trees that covered another line of hills to the south of them. Beyond the trees there was the glint of water. That should be the Mediterranean!

Patrick reasoned that these trees would prevent any silhouettes they may present from being seen, when those soldiers reached this point. That far line of hills looked to be much dryer and rockier than the ones they had just negotiated. George remembered how the topography on the peninsula changed from the northern Marmara side, across to the Mediterranean of the south. It all began to look very familiar to him, as it had only been a few weeks since he had moved through very similar terrain. Remembering the last time, he recalled how stupidly complacent he had been to get caught on the last stretch. Caution had to be their watch-word, and it would not happen again.

An hour later and they had made it to the top of the next hill and thankfully from there it looked to be downhill all the way to the Mediterranean. They found themselves walking along the bottom of a dry streambed, where water erosion had cut its way through a rocky outcrop, as it drained on down the far side of the hill. It was approaching midday and the strength of the sun had gone, as a rain cloud moved in from the south. This streambed, although free of water, was still had boggy patches. It had obviously rained recently. Great sticky clods of mud began to stick to the soles of their shoes, making them heavy and each step became painful. A rocky ha-ha rose up steeply on each side of them. High above them there was an extremely rocky uneven surface that prevented them from using any drier pathway. The constant effort began to sap their strength.

"Keep going Pat, we'll soon find somewhere where it's drier soon," said George. "We will have to get out from this streambed, because we are leaving tell-tale foot prints."

"Oi've got so much mud on moi feet, oi feel as if oi'm seven feet tall," said Pat, behind him.

Eventually they emerged out from the stream bed and climbed a small hillock, and from the top, the countryside ahead looked drier and a lot rockier, with scrubby vegetation.

Luckily the rain cloud passed overhead without them getting a drenching, but on the re-emergence of the sun it made them sweat profusely. A combination of a hot sun and dry sea breezes on this southern side of the peninsula created a much drier, almost desert-like environment. It was the same type of topography to be found on and around the beach-head of Cape Helles and Suvla Bay. As they continued, George could feel an inner hope begin to blossom, sensing that they were getting closer to the Allied lines.

"I don't think that we have too far to go now, Patrick," said George. "That's the Aegean Sea that you can see out there."

That afternoon more sporadic cloud appeared, and the dullness had thankfully reduced the temperatures. Their slow descent of the far side of the central peninsula spine of hills took much longer than they thought and by the time that they had reached the cliff above the Aegean, the light started to fade with the approach of the early evening. They turned and as they walked along the cliff-top they could see spots of bright light in the far distance. The lights had come as a complete surprise to the two men, because they had assumed that they were completely alone in this barren landscape. Those lights had to the cooking fires of small contingents of soldiers. It made George realise how vulnerable they still were and how careful they had to be from now onwards. They were getting close to their goal, but achieving it would only be obtained if they remained continuously alert. Although it would be dangerous on foot at night, they decided that they would carry on towards the Allied Lines, and hopefully by breakfast, they would be eating with the Allied soldiers on the new beach-head at Suvla Bay.

****

Arthur Collenette had returned from being on the receiving end of yet another severe reprimand at the Turkish Army Head Quarters in Gallipoli. The General was extremely angry, ordering him to go out to capture the escaped prisoners and not to return without them. He had been given command of a search party, that were already scouring the countryside for them. There had been a reported sighting and Arthur was given the position and told that failure would not be tolerated again.

Leaving the Gallipoli HQ, he had immediately set off with his sergeant translator on horseback to round up his men. Before they left, he went to his apartment with a spare horse, ordering Arna to get ready, and to accompany him.

He felt relief when he had caught up with his men, on discovering that they had sighted them early that morning. They had been sighted leaving a farmstead. He had studied the maps, which allowed him to assess where they had landed after the sinking. Yesterday evening his soldiers had quickly discovered the canvas covered cork float, so Arthur was aware of George's starting position. Using logic allowed him to assess the direction George and the Irishman would be heading and he sent his men off after them. The route led straight up the hillside towards the farm where they had been sighted. He, Arna, and the sergeant caught up with the soldiers half way up the hill.

Once they reached the farm, Arthur sat astride his horse, allowing his men a break after the strenuous climb. He had been hoping that the two fugitives would still be here, but his men had spotted them leaving earlier that morning. Sitting impassively aloof on his chestnut horse in the yard, his men began searching every building. He had brought Arna with him because he had an unfinished lust to wreak upon her body, after he had been disturbed by that messenger. He would not be denied, as his eyes flicked across to her sitting on the Arab to his left. Tonight, he would make her pay for his frustration ten times over. She sat with her eyes downcast, desperately trying to avoid giving him the slightest reason to abuse her again.

There was a great whoop of delight when his men discovered a girl in the farmhouse. Arthur had her brought out and questioned her through his sergeant. He quickly became irritated by her refusal to answer and stood over her, pulling her hair, twisting it viciously. Still no answer, so he reached down, ripping open her bodice, exposing her breasts, not sparing her blushes and beginning to enjoy the pain he was causing her. Since his capture and following his alignment with the Turks, he had quickly learned the technique of inflicting the maximum amount of pain, using the least effort. After ripping more of her clothes from her body, he began using his riding crop to beat her to a pulp, until the effort tired his arm. Still she would not answer his questions, but after more of the whipping she revealed that two men had been there overnight. Arthur didn't have to ask her anymore, because from his map he knew exactly where George would be heading. They were no more than two or three hours ahead of him.

The girl lay in the dirt sobbing semi naked in her distress. Now that he had finished with her, he told his men to carry her back into the house and to enjoy themselves. He was well aware that, with him being British, these men treated him with a degree of xenophobic suspicion, so by him giving them this little gift, he knew that it would increase his popularity.

Arna's face contorted in disgust, as she listened to the agonised screams of the girl that came echoing out into the yard. Despite the girl's initial denials that she had seen the two fugitives. Arthur had obtained everything that he wanted to know, but her initial reluctance to talk had annoyed him greatly. The delay in her replies had given George and O'Connell more time, allowing them to put more distance between them.

Arna closed her eyes in disgust, trying to shut out the mental picture of what that poor girl inside the house was going through. With each new scream, she could see the excited flicker on Arthur's top lip, as he listened. She had seen it before when he had beaten her with his leather strap. It was at that instant that she came to a definite decision. Despite all of the threats against her family and herself, she would kill this monster at the first opportunity. He deserved to die, even if it meant that her life would be forfeit. He was evil and she knew that her moment would eventually come. Maybe on this manhunt!

The girl had eventually revealed to Arthur that the escapees had been there just over two hours beforehand. He had made her point to the spot up on the crest of the hill where the two men had disappeared. A quick look at his map revealed that there would be time enough to catch them and allow his soldiers could have their fun with the girl before they moved off. He knew that they would be readier to obey him once their lust had been satisfied. George and the Irish bastard were heading up over the backbone of the peninsula, obviously heading for the Aegean shore to guide them back down to the Allied lines. By them taking the particular route they had, it would mean that they would be travelling along two sides of a triangle, so if he were to cut directly along that third side, he should easily be able to make an interception well before they ever got anywhere near safety.

There were wide smiles on the faces of his men, as each of them emerged from the house, buttoning up their uniform. They were definitely warming to Arthur. The discipline within the Turkish army was very strict and Arthur was unusually lenient – but only as long as he got instant obedience. They were used to obeying officers, as any disobedience usually brought death. That was why the army were taking so many casualties at the front, because their infantry was being sent on attack after attack against the enemy holding the beaches, while their machine guns were preventing any meaningful counter advance. Any soldier hanging back during an attack as they went over the top of a trench, was shot.

As a result of his generous nature, Arthur was becoming very popular with them, but any transgressor received the full force of his wrath. There had been other times, like now, when he would let them have a free reign. He seemed to turn a blind eye, even enjoying the moment while they vented their lust on the latest luckless victim. He would often walk in and observe the proceedings, urging them on, giving them verbal encouragement.

The girl's screams had ceased five minutes ago and Arthur looked at his watch, deciding that it was time to go. He sent off his sergeant to round up the last of the men. His NCO was not only his military link with these men, but also his interpreter. The last few soldiers began tumbling out of the farmhouse door, some still buttoning their trousers, while others staggered pulling on their boots. There was a lot of good humour and a jostling banter as they all made themselves ready to move off.

While the sergeant was forming them into ranks, Arthur quietly dismounted from his horse, and walked purposefully over into the house. He made his way through the ransacked kitchen, noting the floor was awash with smashed glass, sticky preserve, torn pieces of bread, broken earthenware and scraps of food, but as he looked around there was no sign of the girl.

A faint groan from the next room drew his attention and he slowly made his way through the door. He saw her lying on the floor of the main living room. She was completely naked, dirt, bruises and red wealds despoiled her olive skin. As he looked down at her and he could see her glazed eyes staring up at nothing. His sudden presence startled her, but she was unable to move her broken form. Her eyes, became more frightened now, followed his movement until he stood astride her outstretched legs. His hand slowly moved upwards to slip the leather strap of his holster and he withdrew the revolver. Her pained expression creased in puzzlement, if he was going to have his way with her, then why did he need the gun? The frightened bewilderment in her eyes swiftly changed into utter terror, as Arthur levelled the weapon directly at her head. She grunted against the bondage of pain as she attempted to move out of the way.

The men outside were formed up and ready to go. The crack of the gunshot caused a rustle amongst their ranks. Arthur appeared at the doorway and bellowed at the sergeant.

"Tell the men that the two fugitives that we hunt have raped and murdered a girl who lives here. Anyone who wants tells a different story will be executed without trial!"

The sergeant translated as he was ordered and predictably enough there were no challenges to the statement. Arthur remounted his horse. Arna looked at him with complete revulsion.

"OK sergeant, follow me," he said, holding the folded map in front of him and pointing towards the crest of the spine. "We're heading up towards the crest of that hill over there."

****

The night was long and surprisingly cold, and George and Patrick were still walking an hour before daybreak. They had already decided that they would check their position just as soon as it got light enough, but as the sky lightened it revealed the same dry craggy landscape, and no distinguishing land marks. The last of the lush green vegetation had disappeared after crossing the central spine and what growths remained were sparse, spindly scrub. George was happy as they approached the coast, knowing that all they had to do was walk south along the shore-line to reach the Allies, but it seemed to be taking a lot longer than he assumed. The two of them sat for a while, studying the coastline ahead. Far in the distance they could see two or three small promontories fading into the hazy horizon. Each of them thrusted out into the Aegean, as did others in the opposite direction, the protrusions created small rough stony coves. George did not recognise any of this stretch of the coast. Towards the south west, in the far distance, they spotted the ruins of an old Crusader fortress that stood out at the end of the longest promontory. George could see that the same narrow finger of land was in fact the end of a ridge that ran down from the hill into the sea. He could see the reason why those ancients had been it built the castle there, because there were steep precipices on three sides. So, it could only be reached along the top of the narrow ridge.

Beyond it, far out towards the horizon of the Aegean, they spotted a black silhouette – a ship! It had to be an Allied vessel and they sat and watched it for some time until it was near enough to recognise its lines as being that of an RN county class cruiser, obvious steaming along a patrol line that was some two miles or so from the shore.

So near yet so far, he thought.

Walking all night had taken its toll and over the last hours due to increasing pain, George and Patrick had frequently had to stop for a break. They both knew that they were going to have to hide once the day materialised. Later on, after dark, they would be recovered enough for make the final leg of their journey.

With the discovery of the fortress, it was the obvious place to rest up for the daylight hours, as it would provide them with some protection. Despite the early hour, as they descended that last dry dusty hillside, sweat began to dampen their clothes following the appearance of the sun. On the way down, they had to stop once more for another rest and after the two men had taken stock of their immediate situation, they scanned the vicinity once more. Patrick looked high up at the hills they had left behind. He was scanning along the high ridge, when something caught his eye. There was something that glinted high up on that far crest. It was on the far ridge, the one that lay beyond the one on which fortress stood. Flashes do not happen without human intervention – do they? There was someone up there.

The bright flash became erratic, unpredictable and general area became blurred, as if smoke was rising. The two men became transfixed, thinking that it was probably a cooking fire.

Two minutes elapsed when George realised that it wasn't smoke, but a cloud of dust. There were several men running down that slope, and as the sun fully lit the slope, they could see them with the naked eye, skidding downwards, running as fast as they dared. Behind them there were three mounted riders. They had to be Turkish soldiers and it was obvious that they were desperate to cut them off from their route back to the Allied lines. George and Patrick could see that they would not be able to beat them to the sea. As they watched their progress, both realised that they had been out thought and out manoeuvred. It was probably Arthur Collenette who was behind it! The Turks had obviously spotted them as well, because they suddenly altered their direction and began heading straight towards them and they were closing fast.

After thinking about their next move, George and Patrick realised that their best chance lay with their original plan of heading into that fortress. George knew that neither of them was not fit enough to try and evade the soldiers and so they both rose and began hurrying towards the ramparts of the fortress, which would provide them with their only hope of avoiding capture.

"It looks loike we're gonna 'ave ter stand our ground, George. Oi suggest we find a good position up on t'e castle battlements, t'ere," said Patrick.

So, both men began half running, half limping as they made their way towards the crumbling ruined fortification. They quickly reached the promontory on which it stood and turned south onto the narrow, flat, open area that led up towards the arched entrance. Patrick's head was turning right and left, taking note of the approach area, before his eyes flicked up towards the defensive walls. Most of the ramparts on this northern side of the castle were still intact and would provide them with good cover, but over on the southern side the masonry was crumbling into the sea.

George realised, that this time he would have to bow to Patrick's expertise. After all, as the Irishman had so often pointed out, he was only the sailor.

A quick look over their shoulder revealed that the pursuing soldiers had gained significant ground, and were only about half a mile behind them. The sound of an optimistic single shot being fired spurred them on.

It didn't take them long before they entered to the fortress through a stone archway, any doors had long since rotted away. They had only just arrived in the ruins, as the first of the pursuing soldiers rounded the far end of the promontory. They were hot on their heels, giving the two fugitives very little time to make any formative plans. They had to be ready!

The fortress architecturally was of a western design, rather than eastern. It was not unlike any of the hill top castles of southern Europe. Probably built by the army of Crusaders as part of retaking the Holy Land, and to consolidate the victories of the Christian army in this area, somewhen around the twelfth or thirteenth centuries. There was something about the place that made it appeared different from the standard western construction from that period. Maybe it was the light cream colour of the stone, opposed to the darker granite edifices further west. The crenulations were also much taller, giving it a somewhat exotic appearance. A quick look inside revealed that all the floors had long collapsed as the lines of holes high up along the walls showed where the wooden joists would have fitted.

Patrick led the way as they climbed a small set of stone stairs that led upwards towards the high point directly above the entrance. At the top of the steps they emerged out onto a wide rampart. Dashing to the front, they gazed out between the gaps in the tall crenulations, which afforded them a perfect view along the flattened top of the ridge. The Turks were almost half way along it, and running straight at them.

George quickly started to lay out his weapon and ammunition. Between them they only had the two rifles, and he quickly started to count the clips of ammunition. Patrick hobbled back down the steps and George watched him re-appear out below him on the open ground in front of the fort. He watched him as he purposely strode out towards the oncoming Turks, who were now running along to the promontory. They spotted him and some knelt down to fire their weapon at him. Unperturbed, Patrick kept walking. Every so many paces he would stop, and make a small cairn of stones, before continuing striding on in the same manner. After he had made four mounds of stones at equal distances, he quickly returned, running back as fast as his limp would permit. Spurts of dust began spouting up behind him. They could both hear the sharp cracks as the Turkish soldiers firing their weapons, but none were good shots, and nothing came remotely near. As Patrick panted his way the steps, George could see that the Turks had slowed their pace, and were now advancing much more cautiously. Having checked their ammunition, he found that they only had two spare clips each, besides the ones already fitted in the magazine of each rifle. Patrick still had his rifle with him as he arrived at the top of the steps.

George began wishing that he had taken more off that dead soldier in the water, but it was too late. Having noted that there were five rounds in each clip, plus what was left in the magazine of his rifle. Then he remembered firing at least one round at the guard. Ten rounds in those two clips and four in his rifle. That was fourteen shots. Patrick may have the same, which did not fill him with a great deal of confidence.

"Have you got any clips of ammunition, Pat?" he asked his friend, as he finally reached him. The Irishman stood puffing after his excursion. Patting his pockets, as if he suddenly realised that he would need bullets, a smile of relief broke across his face.

"Only t'ree clips, plus what oi've got in moi magazine of course. 'Ow about you?"

"Only two spare ones, plus four in my magazine. We will have to make every shot count. Don't fire unless it's a sure target, every shot has got to be a kill, or at least incapacitate, if we're going to have any chance of getting out of this alive," said George.

"Just maybe we's cud swim across to t'at next promontory once it gets dark," said Patrick. "But we 'ave these bloiters to deal wid foist."

Ducking down behind the protection of the wall, just above the gateway to the fort, they watched the steady progress of the Turkish soldiers. They were tentatively walking towards them with their rifles at the ready.

From up here, the two men had good panoramic views along the coast, in both directions. Steep sided cliffs adorned each of the promontories, with a calm sea below.

The Turkish soldiers were now just two hundred and fifty yards away, and still advancing towards them. Trying to count them, George made it twenty-five, while Patrick thought that he saw twenty-six. They had just enough ammunition to account for them, providing they were both very careful.

"You's moit 'ave t'ought t'at oi wuz taking a Sunday stroll in t'e park just now, George, but each of t'em poiles of stones are at fifty-yard intervals. You's can see the front loine of Turks are jost comin' up to the two hundred mark."

George nodded, feeling glad that Patrick knew his stuff.

Click-click – click-click – using the sliding bolt action to load, both the weapons were quickly ready for use. They had two of the very latest weapons, German Mauser eight-millimetre rifles. George took a sight on one of the advancing soldiers, but realised that he should wait for Patrick's order. The Irishman tapped him on the shoulder.

"Set yer back sight to two 'undred yards George, and oi'll tell yer w'en ter foire. We should get a certain 'it at t'at t'at range, and if t'ey don't stop, bring the range down by fifty yards for each round t'at you's foire."

George nodded and watched Patrick as he wound the back-sight mechanism, and imitated each of his movements.

"Roight, t'ey are about two 'undred and twenty yards away. Get yer rifle up 'ere. Rest yer left arm on t'e wall ter keep t'e barrel noice and steady. When oi tell yer, pull t'e butt 'ard inter yer s'oulder, grip t'e stock noice and toight. Get yer target in t'e soights, hold yer breath steady as youse gently squeeze t'e trigger. OK?"

George nodded once more, carrying out his friend's instructions. He remembered Leading Seaman Andrews on the firing range at Tipner – his orders had been very similar. When he had been at sea, he had often wondered what it was like to be fighting in the trenches. He was just about to find out, although this position was a little above the ground, it was probably going to be a similar experience. He could feel that his heart pounding in his chest, and he suddenly felt the need to relieve himself with the impatience of waiting for the enemy to get close enough. Quickly he rose, turned around and did so against a wall just behind their position.

"Oi youst ter feel loike t'at. Yer get used to it after a woile, George," was Patrick's only comment on his return.

Still the Turks came on – Two hundred yards – One hundred and ninety – One hundred and eighty. They were just about to reach the small mound of stones at one hundred and fifty yards.

Beyond them, George could see the three riders, way off in the far distance. One of them looked like a woman, and another was an officer, judging by his uniform. He wore a red fez. The two riders reined in, allowing more of the soldiers to walk past them, and head out towards the fortress. The third rider dismounted and came forward with the soldiers.

"Stan' boi, George. Woind yer back soit down to one fifty and get a bead on wun of t'em Jo'nnies. We bot' foire toget'er in about anot'er ten yards."

Both men made final adjustments to their position as they readied themselves. George picked out one of the leading soldiers, carefully taking aim on his upper torso, trying to remember all the things that Patrick had told him.

"Are yous ready, George?" whispered Patrick.

George grunted affirmative.

"Foire when oi count ter t'ree – Wun – Too – T'REE!"

Both of the guns exploded simultaneously and two of the Turkish soldiers fell. Their comrades in the immediate vicinity broke, running in search of cover, dispersing in every direction, seeking any hiding place in the sparse dry landscape. Most of them quickly found somewhere, but others were not so lucky, and began dithering, looking for anywhere that would get them out of the line of fire. Two more of them fell before they were all out of sight, and those that remained standing, panicked and fled as fast as their legs could carry them back along the promontory.

"Well dun, George moi lad. T'ats four Turks that won't be givin' us any more bodder. Now find yerself a target behind wun of t'em rocks. When you sees a Johnnie who is oiden, take aim on t'e top of t'e rock and when he pops 'is 'ead up – blow it off."

"No misses so far, Pat. That's not too bad for a tin canned sailor, eh!"

"Well dun moi bucko. We've got t'em pinned down gud, alroight. T'ey can't get around our flank eit'er, but we've just got ter make sure t'at we keep it t'at way."

Two bullets smashed into the stone wall behind them, but it was difficult for the Turks to fire their weapons without exposing themselves. In the next half an hour, three more of the soldiers met their end as they took aim.

The mounted officer at the rear began bawling orders, but he was too far off to waste a bullet on. His voice however carried to them on the light morning breeze, and it could just be faintly heard.

"Unless oi'm very much mistaken, t'at bastards shoutin' in English, so 'e is," said Patrick.

"Arthur – bloody – Collenette," said George.

"D'yer mean t'at traitorous bastard from t'e 'ospital back in Constantinople and on t'e boat – oi moight juist risk a round at t'at son of Satan."

He was too far away to risk a shot. If he ever came close enough, George vowed that he would put an end to him. As they both turned their attention back to the battleground, they saw Arthur turn his horse and ride off in the direction of the south-east.

"'E's runnin' for it," said Patrick.

"He's did that to me once before," said George sarcastically.

Patrick's gun exploded, and another Turk jerked, sprawling over to lie still forever. George squinted as he watched Arthur heading away from the scene, with the mounted woman behind him.

Chapter Twenty-Four
Showdown

It was four o'clock in the afternoon and the sun's rays were unmerciful. George and Patrick were both very thirsty, and had moved their position twice to take advantage of any shade. The water in the wineskin from the farm had disappeared earlier in the day, and each could feel his tongue beginning to rasp against the roof of his mouth. While Patrick had kept the Turks pinned down, George left their lofty perch and made his way down into the interior of the fortress to search for any water. It was probably a forlorn hope, but he was hoping that the interior might well have an area that any of the recent rainfall may have accumulated within the shadows, and not evaporated. He knew that it was a vague hope, but many of these old castles were built with a deep well at its centre, or they would encompass some sort of protected water supply.

After fifteen minutes searching through the dust and debris filled interior, he climbed a heap of crumbled remains of an inner wall. It was one of several piles of rubble, each had been compacted by the seasons of rain and sun. A fine dust blanketed the area like a desert. There was the occasional patch of struggling vegetation, managing to survive in the shadier areas of the dry stony soil. Above him, the sun continued to blast down, bleaching any trace of colour from the big blocks of stone.

As he made his way through the ruins, he could see the Aegean Sea spread out before him, stretching out beyond the top of the southern walls. The castle had been built on a gentle downward gradient, that continued on towards a sharp cliff-edge. Despite him being on the ground level here, he realised that he was still quite a bit higher than the crumbling remains of those southern ramparts. Down in that lower part of the fortification there were more piles of rubble that had banked firmly against those walls. Here, near the central keep, it was very dry and dusty.

Making his way along the base of the keep, there were several small lizards sitting sunning themselves before being sent scampering for the nearest crevice, as his shadow fell over them. He was becoming extremely doubtful that any water existed as he ventured deeper into the shaded areas created by the southern abutment walls. Towards the western edge there was some vegetation managing to exist that had appeared to have escaped the ravages of the weather. He climbed another heap of rubble, sliding the far side to get nearer to them.

Pain was his constant companion, and he took each step tentatively. After another fruitless search, he made an amazing find purely by accident. On inspecting one of the very last buildings in a line of buildings abutting of those southern walls, he found an entrance that was blocked by a mass of thick matted green vegetation.

He was about to discard it, when he thought that it seemed out of place, because all of the other buildings had very little growth around them, and none of the vegetation was green. Logically he put the general lack of growth down to the lack of water, but this area must have some form of irrigation to look so lush. Although it was not exactly flourishing, it was a lot greener than any plant that he had seen so far within the fortress. So, he moved towards it. As he neared, he noted that it was a thickly matted tamarisk bush that had completely covered the entrance. There must be some moisture to be so green, he thought.

He assumed that when it did rain, the water must naturally be channelled down here from the upper sections of the walls. If he could get through that tangle mass, and enter that building, there may be water in there! His pulse increased with anticipation, and he began tearing away at some of the branches, to slowly reveal a dark shadowed interior. He eased himself through the partial gap he had created, entering to find a huge stone rectangular block lying along the back wall, deep within the shadows. Further inspection showed it to be an old stone trough, and even more wonderful, although it was empty, the bottom was damp with traces of water.

Despite a thorough search, the lack of light in this room made it difficult to see any source. It was very dark, but he assumed that the stone roof above him formed the underside of the parapet on the southern wall. The only light that entered came in through that matted doorway where he had entered. It was pleasantly cool here in the shadows. He squinted, trying to adjust his eyes to the murky gloom, his hands feeling their way slowly along the trough, examining it for further traces of water. The far end stood in the deepest darkest corner. As he reached it, he looked up to find a tiny hole directly above him. When he looked upwards, its centre glowed like a lamp, lit by the sunshine above. Although the light did not penetrate down into this room, it revealed a hole there that must go all the way up to the parapet above. George examined it further. This trough had been purposely positioned under the end of a culvert, that was obviously meant to collect rain water from above, and diverted it down here.

He began to recheck the bottom of the trough, finding less than an inch of water, far too shallow for him to try and top-up the wineskin. He dipped his hand in and began sucking the moisture from his fingers. As he did so, the water rippled away and hit the end of the trough. As it did so he caught sight of another square hole. It was just six inches from the top edge of the tough, and as he moved in closer, he saw that just beyond the top rim there was another channelled section that had been cut into the stone. He could immediately see that it was an overspill from this trough, which runs along the channel on the back wall. Tracing it he saw it disappearing down through a hole in the floor. He re-examined the square hole at the end of the channel. The water has to be channelled down there somewhere. How could he get down there to find out?

He turned about, looking for a way he could follow his discovery downward, and caught sight of a stone block. His excitement mounted as he moved across the room, where he quickly discovered a series of steps that disappeared down into almost total blackness.

He carefully began his descent. His eyes grew accustomed to the darkness faster than when he entered the room above. He could see a series of large pieces of masonry that supported the roof, causing him to stoop to get past. Once he was below them, he could see the faintest gleam of light that coming in from the small hole from above. He had done it, he had traced the hole from the trough above! It was a much smaller room than the one above, and once his eyes became adjusted, he could see two more smaller stone tanks. Looking up, logically he could now see how the culvert channelled the water down here. From the parapet above, the culvert directed rain water down into this first tank, which was then over-spilled into the second. Any excess from both of these troughs would be directed out through a hole on the southern wall itself.

Closer inspection revealed the second trough to be half full of water. Elation!!

George quickly filled the wine-skin and drank his fill until his thirst was quenched. The water was cool and sweet. Refilling the wine-skin, he quickly made his way back up to Patrick.

For the Turkish soldiers trapped down on the killing ground in front of the castle, the day had turned into a living hell. They had been forced to lie prone, totally exposed to the direct sun. What water they had been left in their canteens had become hot and insipid, and most had them had drunk the dregs long since. Nearly every one of them had run out, and many could be heard yelling to their friends, begging for a drink. Two more of their comrades had fallen victim to the pinpoint accuracy of the fugitives up on the parapet, as they had tried to ease their discomfort.

Up on the wall, George and Patrick could hear the voice of the Turkish sergeant, as he began to hold a roll call. They had not a clue as to what he was saying, but it was obvious from the replies, that he was trying to ascertain just how many of his men remained alive.

On completion, the sergeant realised that he had lost a total of ten men, one of them being his younger brother, Yousif. He knew that he and his men were trapped here in an impossible position. Any movement away from their protection, would bring instant death. He also knew that by remaining where they were, he and his men were having to endure an agonising exposure to the sun. It was going to continue until the sun set on the western horizon, and even then, they would not be able to escape from their predicament until it got dark. He began to pray for sunset, and for the nightfall to come early. Its arrival would not only bring relief from their torture, but it would also give them the chance to make their escape from the snipers above them. He assessed that once darkness had descended, they would be able creep back out of range. At five hundred metres they would be fairly safe, and still be in a position at the landward end of the promontory to block any escape by these two fugitives. The sergeant had spent all day trying to appraise the strategic situation.

This torture had brought about by that arrogant British bastard! He had insisted that they go in and make a full-frontal assault. He had screamed that the two fugitives only had one weapon. They had two. A show of force would make them surrender, he had said. Collenette might be popular with the men, but he knew very little about military strategy. Bloody naval idiot – what did he know of field warfare? He had tried to argue the implausibility of such an action with him, but he had threatened him with execution. Then, when the action had got too hot for him, the coward had ridden off on the pretext that he was going to HQ to get reinforcements. He did not expect to see him, or his whore, again.

Poor Yousif! He knew that he would have to break the news to his mother, and that she would be heartbroken. He had been her youngest. As he looked out across the flat area, he saw his brother lying still, with a bullet through his head – he was unburied with the sun going down. He could hear the buzzing of the flies, that were crawling all over his face. Islamic law dictates that he be buried within the day. Anger gripped him, and he gritted his teeth against the injustice of it all. Yousif's death had to be avenged. If he couldn't kill the two men in the fort, then he would kill that English coward whom he held to be ultimately responsible for his brother's demise.

He raised himself up on one arm, shouting to his men, telling them his thoughts, encouraging them, trying to raise their morale. The bullet caught him in the right shoulder, smashing the ball joint socket into a splintered mess of bone and blood. He rolled over gasping in agony, his left hand trying to stem the onrush of blood. Almost too late, through his agony-wracked brain, he realised that he had rolled clear of his rock cover, and painfully strained to roll back just a spurt of earth spouted up where his head had just been.

"Shit – that's our first miss," George cursed.

"Oi 'it 'im t'ough, just before youse foired George – but yaw man owt t'ere is only wounded, so 'e is," said Patrick.

As the evening twilight brought some relief to all of the soldiers, the sequence of the day's events had developed into a strange situation with the two adversaries facing each other, yet both being at a complete impasse.

The first thought that George and Patrick came up with was to try and sneak past the soldiers and head off along the coast towards the Allied lines, but they realised that those remaining would do everything to prevent that happening. 'This was the same stalemate that must exist on a much larger scale in the trenches at the end of this peninsula,' thought George. He wondered if there had been any change in the Allied Army's fortunes since he had been away.

"It'll be noight soon George – w'at d'yer t'ink t'ey'll try ter do once it's dark and we can't see t'em?"

"My guess is they'll fall back out of range, and try to re-group. They know that they will still have us cut off, so at nightfall they'll just get back out of range, and wait until the cavalry turns up."

"Youse s'ould 'ave been int de army George, you'd 'ave been a sergeant in no toime atall. W'at oim tryin' ter say is w'at are weese goin' ter do once it gets doark?"

"We could try and make a run for it?" suggested George.

"T'ey will 'ave t'ought of t'at," replied Patrick. "T'ey will probably send sum men around t'e promontories on eit'er side of us, ready to pick us off, s'ould we be silly enough to try and swim across. We 'ave to troi and out t'ink t'em – we 'ave to act furst young George, t'row der furst punch, and beat t'em at t'eir own gayme. 'Ows about wees set up a crossfoire? One of us goes down t'ere, and usin' t'e steep soide of t'is 'eadland, we creep around der soide of t'em when t'e light goes. Once its doark and t'ey begin to move back, t'e one up 'ere foires at t'em. T'at should make um stampede onto t'e ot'er gun. T'ey'll be so scared, w'en t'ey can't run back, or forward, t'at we s'ould be able to cut quite a few down in t'e confusion."

"I think that you deserve those stripes on your arm and no mistake," said George, nodding approvingly and trying to mimic Patrick's accent.

Straws were drawn to decide who would stay and who would go down to the edge of the promontory. Patrick had drawn the short one, and so he grabbed his rifle and began to make his way down towards the cliffs on the eastern side of the castle. After using a breach in the walls to exit, it took him the best part of an hour to worm his way around the side of the Turks. He achieved it by descending the steep rocky slope, remaining well out of sight from the Turks above him, as he slowly made his way past them. During the time that he was crawling, the last of the daylight had disappeared and it was well past the last of the twilight when he finally arrived in position. Climbing up to the top level of the promontory, he made himself comfortable found a good position to fire from, and he began his wait.

As the sun set there was a strange light as the sun had set in the west, which George guessed might be an indication that the weather was about to change. The dark low cloud that hugged the horizon made it look very likely.

As darkness blanked definition, a faint light grew out towards the east where an almost full moon began to rise up over the hills, but the initial appearance had been semi-obscured by the low-lying cloud base. Patrick assumed that the Turks would want to move before it illuminated the promontory.

Patrick had managed to position himself one hundred and fifty yards beyond the prone forms of the Turkish soldiers and he had taken cover behind a large flat-topped boulder. From there he could just make out their humped forms, lying out on the open ground. If he wanted to, he could pick at least two more off from where he was, but that would alert them and mess up the planned ambush. Finding a small groove in the rock, he aligned his rifle in their general direction and waited.

The moon suddenly became totally obscured by the ever-thickening mass of silver edged cloud and Patrick readied himself, satisfying himself that he was more than ready to meet their retreat. As the full mantle of darkness descended across the ridge, he could still just see the faint outline of the walls of the fort silhouetted against the moonlit sea. He took another peek, but was unable to see the Turks now, then there was the slightest distortion, indicating that someone had already started to make his move. Patrick used lateral vision and he could see the light khaki of the Turkish uniform, almost spectral in the blackness. Then a momentary gap in the cloud allowed a partial moon to shine through and the area was suddenly lit up like act one of a play.

Crack!

The shot caused the soldiers to dive back down on to the ground, almost trying to dig themselves back into the dusty surface. George had kept them pinned down well, but knew that once the cloud covered the moon again the light would fade and that would provide the Turks with another chance to retreat. Patrick, not wanting to alert the soldiers of his presence until more were standing, had restrained from firing.

Fifteen minutes later it became darker once more. The Irishman could hear whispered calls from the unseen enemy. A minute later, the first vague spectre grew up from the rock-strewn ground. Then another materialised and another. Patrick's hand gripped the stock of his rifle. He could make out five figures. Then the unmistakable crack from George's rifle brought forth a high-pitched scream. The rest of the forms froze, standing transfixed for a couple of seconds before they broke and ran straight towards Patrick.

Aiming down the length of his Mauser, he had a clear view of the leading Turk by the light colour of his uniform. He let him come another fifty yards before he dropped him. His hand went through an automatic sequence of grabbing the small metal lever, twisting it upwards, pulling it back to make a quick ejection of the used metal cartridge casing. A reverse of the procedure and he was reloaded and on aim and firing once more. Another Turkish soldier toppled forwards into the dirt.

The stampede of men faltered as the second victim's hideous scream made the survivors realise that to proceed further would bring death, but also, they knew that to go back was equally unhealthy. The resultant confusion was complete and so was the hail of bullets from both George and Patrick.

Finally, the survivors ran obliquely, tearing panic stricken on past the Irishman, running frantically off into the night as fast as their legs could carry them. He had tried to count them, which proved impossible in the darkness, but was sure that there certainly were not more than six or seven survivors.

Once they had disappeared, he let out several long sighs of relief, trying to gain a release from the stress of combat. In the ensuing silence he stood up and began to make his way back towards the arched entrance to the fort. He called out to his friend, not wanting to be mistaken for a Turk.

"Well done moi lad, we certainly s'owed t'em t'e way 'ome, didn't we?"

"I don't think we should hang around though, do you?" George replied, seeking reassurance. "This is our chance to get away."

Patrick agreed and after they had refilled the wineskin with the fresh water, they moved off. They hadn't gone more than five hundred yards when Patrick stopped.

"Now t'at we've beat Jo'nnie Turk back t'ere, t'en t'ere's somet'ing else oi t'ink we s'ould settle before we go 'ome, George."

"What's that, Pat?"

"Oi t'ink we s'ould wait for t'at traitorous bastard, Art'ur bloody Collenette, to come back and do for 'im once and for all."

"But this may be our only chance to get away Pat. If we stay, there is a better than average chance that we will not come out of this alive," George could not believe that Patrick had just said that. In huis mind he could hear Matthew's voice telling him to get Arthur for what he had done.

"Oi knows t'at moi lad, but t'ere's goin' t'e be an awful lot of our boys w'ose goin' t'e die because of the information t'at bastard is givin' to t'e Turks. Oi t'ink we s'ould give it a troi, at least – fer t'eir sake."

George knew deep down that Patrick was right. The Admiral had given him the authority to arrest Arthur, so killing him would certainly be a legal act. He shook his head, realising that he had to agree with Patrick and quickly realised that they had to do it. So, they both turned and went back to the fort, and stopped at each body to check for weapons and ammunition. Most of the soldiers had full bandoliers, and pouches, not having a chance to return fire. They found several grenades and a satchel pack of explosive. They took two of the water canteens as well, as George thought they may be easier to fill than the wineskin. Carrying everything up to the fortified area above the gate, they stacked it into a pile. Then they went back down for more and started to rummage through the bodies for anything that would be useful. As they carried their final haul back towards the gateway, a shot rang out and chips of stone masonry spattered down on their heads.

"W'at der feck was t'at?"

"One of the Turks out there must only be wounded!" replied George shakily. "He must have been playing dead while we collected this lot. Let's go up and finish him off. That is if we can see him in the dark."

"Roightio moi lucky lad. T'will be one less Turk, t'at we 'aff t' worry about."

"Oi'll'ere go up t'ere and present 'im wid a target, so t'at yous can get a gud shot."

Patrick made his way up the stone steps as swiftly as his leg would permit and soon reached their former lair. The pain in his leg was excruciating, but he tried to ignore it as he settled himself down behind the crenelated defence.

Below him, still standing in the arched entrance, George loaded his weapon, taking a quick look out over the area immediately in front of him. There was nothing overtly visible, so he made his way around to the side of the gateway to be able to get a clear shot, should a target appear.

On the rampart, Patrick took off his shirt and proceeded to hang it over the muzzle of his rifle and then he stuck it up above the parapet, attempting to draw the Turk's fire. He was hoping that the Turkish soldier would reveal is position, so that George could get a shot at him.

Meanwhile down below, George had flattened himself, prone on the ground to balanced his rifle via his left elbow, his right hand gripping the stock, index finger poised on the trigger. His right eye trying to pierce the darkness. The stillness was deafening – nothing happened.

Ten seconds passed in total silence. Then suddenly, through the murky gloom, something stirred. It was no more a flicker in the darkness. George moved his rifle around slightly towards that direction, but it had gone – so he took aim on where it roughly had been. A vague light-coloured shape moved in the darkness, revealing his enemy. George lined up his sights and holding his breath, slowly tightened his finger on the trigger. Bang! – The shape jerked and all movement disappeared.

"Did yer get t'e bastard, George?" Patrick's voice was strangely loud and resonant in the stillness of the night.

"I think so," he called back. "Keep your eyes peeled, just in case."

They waited five minutes without any more movement. Another half an hour passed and nothing had happened. There were no signs of life out there on the open ground.

"We're going to have to check him out, Patrick."

Patrick tried another wave with his shirt, but it produced no response.

"I'm going out there to take a look, Pat. Make sure that you cover me, mate!"

As George stood up, he could feel the stiffness down his left side start to ease. His badly bruised leg was still paining him and he stretched it gingerly, hoping the fresh circulation would ease the pain. As he stood fully erect once more, the ligaments in his right knee gave way, causing him to lurch unexpectedly. As his hand shot out to prevent himself from falling, he grabbed the stone supporting the gate and he felt the wind of a bullet as it whistled past his ear. It thwacked into the wall inches from his head.

"Shit!" yelled George, "that was too close! He is still out there, Pat."

Then he heard Patrick's retaliatory shot, followed by a yell of glee.

"Oi got 'im t'at toime George! T'at's twice youse missed. Yous are losin' yer touch, sose you are."

George walked over towards the body of the Turkish sergeant. He was lying on his back, unsurprisingly very close to his dead brother. The blood around his smashed shoulder had congealed and the man had been forced to use his weapon with his good arm, using his dead brother's body as a support. His eyes were wide open, staring up at the moon. There was a bullet hole in the side of his head and he was very dead.

****

Arthur Collenette rode at the head of the small mounted column of troops. Arna was keeping up on her horse, riding at his right shoulder. Her eyes held her deep-seated hatred for the man. They were on their way back from the Peninsula Turkish Army Headquarters in Gallipoli, where Arthur had been forced to justify his presence without the prisoners. After giving an exaggerated account of cornering and trapping them within the Crusader castle, he requested extra men, along with a small artillery piece, to ensure their capture with the least possible loss of life. He was informed in no uncertain terms that there was a distinct shortage of men. Fighting at the front was reaching a crucial stage, but none the less he had been reluctantly allocated these fifteen extra cavalrymen. He had also been supplied with two packhorses, on which were harnessed a wheeled heavy machine gun. The gun mechanism had been tied along its back and the wheels had been removed. One had been tied on each side of the animal to even the load. The other animal was loaded with several boxes of ammunition.

As he left, Arthur felt more confident than he had at any time over the past forty-eight hours. Capturing George Torode would not only put an end to any dis-favour with his paymasters, but also end years of worry that George would talk, which would see him at the end of a rope.

On clearing the ridge, he looked at his watch. It was six o'clock in the morning, and he could finally see the fort far below them, stretching out into the sea in the morning light. It was a cloudy day and the sea looked dark, reflecting the change in weather conditions. None the less the rays from the rising sun gave the stone walls a golden hue, making it stand out sharp. Far out at sea, just beyond the defensive position, Arthur spotted the black silhouette of a British warship travelling at speed. From his training, he recognised it as a Royal Navy cruiser, one of the city class that was patrolling along this stretch of the coast. She really looked the part, an ocean greyhound, with the smoke from her four raked funnels raking back astern. A faint shudder of nostalgia swept over him, as he remembered the life that he had turned his back on, but it passed as his concentration quickly returned back towards the fort. After all, what choice did he have? He would be dead otherwise. As far as he was concerned, there had not been a choice.

George and Patrick were observing this new development from their position above the gateway. They had been taking it in turns to keep watch with a pair of binoculars they had taken from the dead sergeant, confirming the first visual identification of reinforcements. Through the lens George could also see the remnants of the decimated soldiers, as they ran out from their cover to meet Arthur and his new force. The range was about one thousand yards or so. There were just seven survivors that they could count. Not a bad result considering that they had only two rifles and a very limited amount of ammunition. The bodies of their comrade's still lay littered across the approaches to the fort. Looking down, George could count at least twelve corpses, the last being that of the sergeant, who had so nearly caused of his own death. If he had not staggered!

The variety of weaponry they had managed to salvage from the dead, would now prove its worth. One of the weapons turned out to be a Schneider-Canet sniper's rifle, which was fitted with a telescopic sight. Patrick was already cradling it in his arms like a midwife with a new born baby. He was considering the possibility of taking a long-range pop at the new figures.

While they were waiting for Arthur and his small band of reinforcements, Patrick began showing George how to rig up a booby trap. He jammed a hand grenade between two hard and fast fixed stones. Then he showed him how to tie a piece of string to the ring of the pin as a trip wire and how to slide the retaining pin until it was almost out, so that the slightest jerk would remove the pin fully. They had several grenades that they had removed from the dead.

They kept themselves busy and set up several of these death traps in and around the likely foxholes that the Turks might use as cover in front of the castle. Feeling more confident and pretty pleased with themselves, they both thought their chances of beating Arthur were better than last night. There was a fifty-fifty chance of beating him, and of still making it back to the allied lines. Despite the fact that they were just two men against Arthur's force, they reckoned it was they who held the advantage. With everything prepared, they had returned to their lofty perch above the arched entrance. Patrick turned his attention back to the precision rifle with the telescopic sight.

"Wud youse look at t'is little bewtie, George. T'is is one of t'em long-range pieces. Oi'll be able ter pick off a few of those Mustaphers well before they can get wit'in range wit' t'eir own rifles. Oi've just got ter get moiself positioned noice and comfortable loike."

With that remark, he found a crumbled part of the wall, where the top edge was only a foot above the rampart floor and after brushing away the loose rubble and dust, he laid his shirt across the jagged pieces of stone on the parapet. Then, very carefully, he placed the stock of the weapon on it and kneeling down behind, he seemed to take an age looking through the sight and making several minor adjustments to the back-sight. Finally, he appeared to be ready.

"T'at s'ould do it George. Pick up t'ose binoculars and tell me if oi 'ave any luck. T'is moight be our best chance of t'e day to plug his royal flatulence out t'ere."

Lying down behind the parapet, he snuggled himself in behind the rifle, as if he were cuddling his girlfriend on a blanket. George laid the binoculars on top of the parapet, the steady position allowing him to get a good view of the approaching assembly. He could see that the two groups were just meeting up and they had on the dirt track just over half a mile away. He counted the mounted figures and could see that there was a long file of fifteen mounted horses, followed by two packhorses. The two at the front were quite obviously Arthur and the girl. That meant that Arthur only had fifteen extra men – and that made a total of twenty-two with the seven survivors – which was less than he started with. He could see the seven survivors gesticulating with their arms and rifles, before they all started pointing towards the castle. Then his eyes centred on Arthur sitting astride his horse, as he turned and looked straight at him. The vision unnerved him for a moment. Was it possible that someone could emit evil?

"OK, ready Patrick," he said determinedly. "Arthur is on the horse to the left of the column, as we look at it."

"Roight, oi can just see t'e bastard."

It seemed a very long time, as George waited for Patrick to fire his weapon. He could clearly see Arthur waving his arm, as he began pointing towards them. By scanning his binoculars slightly to the right he could clearly see the woman sat astride a horse beside him – her presence puzzled him somewhat. The seven survivors were standing before him and all began to turn to make their way back towards their refuge. Finally, the newly arrived column began to follow them.

Through the telescopic sight Patrick could clearly see Arthur, high on his horse and he now had him firmly in the cross-wire as his finger slowly tightened on the trigger. Taking up the first pressure, he held his breath. The weapon was rock steady. Holding the sight firmly on Arthur's chest, his finger steadily closed. Just as he could feel the last pressure begin to give, another of the mounted soldiers rode up and crossed directly in front of his target – Crack – the weapon jumped in his hand. He realised the mistake just a fraction of a second too late.

George watched through his binoculars as the man fell from his horse directly in front of Arthur. Patrick would have got him if this chap had not gotten in the way. He relished the look of terrified surprise that appeared on Arthur's face. Then, as the real danger registered, total panic broke out, and the whole assembly ran for cover.

"Bastard," shouted Patrick, reloading the rifle. "Oi 'it t'e wrong fella – sorry."

From the way Patrick apologised, George wasn't sure if he was saying sorry to the chap that he had killed by mistake, or for his missing Arthur.

The whole column had broken ranks, as both the soldiers on foot and those mounted rushed headlong towards the refuge of covering rocks, every one of them frantically desperate.

George watched as Arthur reached out and grabbed the reins of Arna's horse and he could see him using his spurs and gallop towards the gully, but by the time they reached its protection, it was full of surviving soldiers. They were all forced to dive out of the way, as Arthur and Arna rode straight through them. Immediately behind them came the mounted troops, and George watched in amazement as any discipline disintegrated in favour of self-preservation.

The mayhem taking place behind that tall bank of rocks produced total panic. Terrified horses whinnied with fear and men screamed in confusion. One of the frightened horses reared up, its front legs pawing the air, unseating its rider. Soldiers were running into each other, trying to avoid being run down. Some of the horses bolted, running headlong to escape, forcing the others ahead of them to do the same. Two of them were the pack horses. The frightened animals charged right through the melee, stampeding through the gully to get away.

Arthur drew his and Arna's mounts to a halt, both of them quickly dismounting, only to observe many of his newly arrived horses throw their riders, and galloping away up the hillside towards the ridge. His heart sank as he also noted that two of the runaways were the pack-horses that were carrying the much-needed heavy machine gun and its ammunition.

Behind the rock, the whirling dust cloud began to settle as the animals and men, tried to placate each other. George watched the scene with some delight. He had seen those horses galloping away. The cargo of one had worked loose, and he watched the heavy machine gun and two wheels rolling over and over, down the steep incline towards the cliff edge. They sailed through the air to come crashing down, and smashing against the rocks below.

Strangely the whirlwind of choking dust thrown up in the panic had served to provide Arthur and his men with the cover they sought. Having reached the protection of this rocky gully, Arthur's terror had calmed, and in his trying to maintain some credence with his soldiers, he made much of grabbing his binoculars and climbing up on to a rock to peered out to assess the general situation around the front of the castle. He was sweating profusely, but at least he was safe. Despite his confidence returning, he noticed that his hands were still trembling. That had been too close for comfort.

It was an hour later and Arthur began to realise dire predicament that he was now faced with. Despite bringing all of these reinforcements, they were now in exactly the same standoff situation that had existed before he had left. The one thing that could have made all the difference was that machine gun and now that lay smashed to pieces at the bottom of the cliff. He was very well aware that he could not waste any more of the men by ordering another frontal attack – simply because there were not enough of them. There was one thing that he knew for certain, and that was he would not be going anywhere near to the fort himself. A tremor of trepidation passed through him, because he knew that he would have to account to the Turkish HQ for too many casualties incurred from that first attack and now he would have to explain the loss of the heavy machine gun and the horses. His only consolation was that the fugitives were trapped and couldn't leave, but how on earth was he going to capture them? Feeling frustrated, Arthur realised that his journey to the HQ had been a complete waste of time.

Up on the walls, George and Patrick had already reached that exact same conclusion and were making plans as to how to repulse another assault. The chief concern at that moment was the fact that both of the men were extremely hungry. They had not envisaged that they would have to spend another long hot day in the fort without any food, because following their decision to kill Arthur they imagined that the soldiers would have broken ranks and gone back to their headquarters. They now had to think of another plan.

"What about trying to make our way down the hillside tonight and then swimming over towards the next promontory in the darkness?" suggested, George.

"No, t'at won't work, George. Moi bet is Art'ur will cover t'at possibility boi t'is evening. I t'ink t'at he'll troi and call up yet more men and maybe anot'er artillery piece by tomorrow. If t'at shud happen, it will mean t'e end for us. Oive taught of ano'ter possibility 'owever."

"What's that?" asked George.

"Youse remember yesterday. W'en we came over t'e crest from the farm and we saw t'at wars'ip. Well, oi saw it again early t'is morning. Oi t'ink it must do t'e same patrol run at t'at toime every morning. 'Ow about we'se cloim down t'e cliff and swim out to it and t'en get picked up?"

"Yeh, that's very good idea and it's certainly worth a try, Pat."

"Well, oi t'ink wese s'ould swim out in t'e early hours," said Pat. "T'en weill be on station w'en t'e ship arroives."

"I am up for that Pat. But before we leave in the early hours, I think that we should rig up a nice big surprise for Arthur and his men. We can use that pack of explosives and any grenades we have left."

"Are youse quoite certain youse wouldn't loike ter be a sergeant in t'e Army?"

****

While Patrick kept guard, George assembled all the remaining equipment. Taking the wine-skin, water canteens and some of the webbing straps, before walking down into the interior of the castle. Finding the top of the cliff he began binding them together to construct a small float, that would act as a buoyancy aid to support them while they were waiting in the water, remembering how useful the inflated bicycle tyre had been that Mr Slade had given him. By the middle of the afternoon he had made a second serviceable effort by inflating the wineskin and tying some of the webbing around it.

As the sun rose through the clouds, they began to part, and the threat of bad weather evaporated only to be replaced by high temperatures. As the day grew hotter, even the usual aerial fly past of the avaricious gulls failed to arrive. From the cliff top, George could see them sitting out on the serene calmness of the inshore waters.

Patrick was glad to see that the Turkish soldiers seemed to have learned their lesson from yesterday and were keeping well out of the way, although he had managed to pick off one who had stuck up his head for far too long. Arthur's men never returned his fire, knowing that their weapons did not have the same range as the sniper rifle.

The stalemate lasted right through the heat of the day and continued on towards dusk. Then as the sun began to set, as Patrick had rightly guessed, Arthur sent three men along the crest towards the promontory to the east and another three to the west. The two friends watched the soldiers ran low and fast, heading towards their assigned positions. Patrick tried a couple of shots at them, but he missed. Once out of range of the Schneider-Canet, they slowed to a trot in making their way round to the promontories on either side of the fort.

"T'ere t'ey go, roight on toime, trottin' round to make sure we not goin' ter disappear in t'e middle of t'e noi't. Little do t'ey realoise t'at we're goin' t'e use t'e back door. W'at toime do yer t'ink we s'ould get inter t'e water George?"

"I reckon about three o'clock. We can then easily make the couple of miles out to the patrol line by sunrise. Just before it begins to get light, I think that Arthur will try and send some of his men into the fort before dawn breaks. I think that we should rig up our booby trap as I suggested and be well out of the way when it goes off," he replied.

"Booby traps are moi speciality dear boy, juist youse leave it ter me."

****

By midnight they had rigged the main trap and also a couple of smaller ones by attaching the trip wire to the pins of hand grenades. The main charge was the pack of explosives they had found out on the killing ground in front of the fort. It only weighed a couple of pounds, but they had buried it under a pile of stones, which would be enough to provide a terrible shrapnel effect that would kill anyone in the immediate vicinity. One of the trip wire grenades had been rigged to act as the detonator. All was carefully concealed by placing the canvas satchels and bandoleers over the pile and they hoped that it would remain unseen in the shadowed dimness of the dawn light.

Taking turns in sleeping as they waited in the coolness of the early hours until it was roughly three o'clock. Having no watch or timepiece between them, they had to guess the time from the moonrise. They simply laid down their weapons, and made their way down through the inner part of the fort. George was carrying the two swimming aids he had made under each arm. He led his friend through to the crumbling breach in the wall, that allowed them access out onto the cliff top itself. Making a quick search along the edge of the precipice, they both searched for the easiest way down. Before they began their descent, they felt an immediate up-draught of cold air rose from rising up the cliff face to meet them. It was an indication that the wind off the sea was freshening once more, which might make it more difficult swim, as a stronger wind usually increased the wave height, but it was too late to change their plan.

Despite scouring the cliff face for a good five minutes, both had trouble locating a way of descending the initial twenty feet, although Patrick had seen a clear pathway possibility further down. Below them, they watched as each wave arrived at the base of the cliff, watching it ride up to flood across the jagged rocks, producing a foaming whiteness. If the sea state got any worse, they may have to reconsider!

Finally, they gave up trying to find a way down, deciding that they would return back up to the parapet position, retrieve the rest of the spare strapping. Then they could tie them all together, and use it to lower themselves down that initial part of the rock face. Patrick was limping so badly that George told him to rest on the cliff top while he went back.

"Don't yous go trippin' that booby trap, George," said the Irishman.

As he approached the stone stairway, George took great care to step over the trip wires. A quick check out into the darkness of the killing ground revealed nothing amiss and it all seemed reassuringly still. He picked up every available piece of webbing that he could find quickly returning to Patrick at the top of the cliff.

Above them the sky had a silvery sheen as a layer of thin newly formed clouds raced across the moon. From their speed, it was clear that there was going to be a change in the weather. The sea state was clearly changing too, from the placid calm of yesterday, it was now showing this slight swell that was coming in to break against the cliff with ever increasing enthusiasm. Beneath the moonlight, the surface of the Aegean Sea had a pewter sheen, and the water looked uninvitingly cold. It was too late to change their plans, because there was no plan B. If Arthur was not going to show himself, then they were not going to be able to shoot him, and it was doubtful that they would have another chance of escaping.

Both of the men began tying the strips of webbing together. On completion George tied a line from the wine-skin float to his belt – just in case he should drop it on the way down.

"T'e sea looks loike wun o' t'em screens in t'ose new bioscope's down in Commercial Road in Portsmouth'."

George laughed. Funnily enough, that's just what it did look like.

"I didn't know you had been to Portsmouth, Pat!"

"I wuz down t'ere ter do moi demolition course George – Too many sailors for moi loikin' – pardon t'e expression."

They both spotted the dark split in the rock a little further along the cliff-top, revealing a possible descent point, providing they used the strapping rope to lower themselves down.

"Let's try over there, Pat," said George, pointing towards it.

They wedged one of the metal buckles attached to the end of the webbing into a sliver of a crevice in the rock until it was jammed in solid. Throwing the free end over the drop, both men headed for the edge. Patrick went first, and he had not gone three paces before a voice stopped them in their tracks.

"Don't move either of you, or I'll shoot you," said a voice out of the darkness.

Both the men froze – the order being spoken in English, told each who it must be. How the hell had he got here so quickly? They turned slowly, raising their hands.

"Good evening, George," said Arthur Collenette. "Do you know that you are so predictable? My men saw you two moving about up on the fort. I guessed what you would be up to, trying to make a run for it. We must have all covered that half mile in less than four minutes. When there was no shooting, it only confirmed my theory."

"This will put a feather in your cap, Arthur! Or should that be in your fez?"

"It's just a shame that you won't be around to see me wear it, George! You've been a thorn in my side for far too long, and now I'm going to finish off what should have happened a long time ago on Pleinmont Point."

"You really are a piece of shit, Arthur. Of course, this will not be the first murder that you've committed, will it? You killed your own stepfather on the Vale Road as well, didn't you? You're only a big man when you're holding a gun – or a spade on that occasion? You're especially brave when you have a small army to back you up."

"Those bloody fools are busy searching the castle for you both," boasted Arthur. "But I alone knew that you would come down here. By the time they have finished searching for you, both you and O'Connell will be lying at the bottom of that cliff behind you."

George and Patrick exchanged a worried look, thinking about the booby trap they had rigged, and of their own proximity to it.

Arthur carried on gloating, continuing with his egotistic diatribe. "… yes, I knew that you would try to escape down these cliffs. Don't worry because you'll soon be going down there, but not in the way that you intended. I'm going to make sure that you reach the bottom very fast."

Then Arthur's face creased into a puzzled expression, as if something was bothering him. His mind was pondering George's accusation.

"Yes, it won't hurt for me to admit to you now that I did kill my stepfather, George, but I have always wondered how you managed to figured that out?"

"After what you did to Matt and me on that day on the Pleinmont Cliff?" he replied. "It wasn't hard to work it out, Arthur. If you could leave us both to die without any conscience, then I knew that you were capable of just about anything. You may have fooled everyone else with your lies that day, but I knew you for the real cold-blooded murdering bastard that you are. The way you carried on at school about your step father when your mother had first started to get serious about him, the way you ranted and raved. Your hatred was plain for everyone to see. Most of us liked him, your stepfather that is, and we all felt happy for your mother that she had found some happiness after all her suffering. Everyone else thought that your accusations were totally unfounded. When he was murdered with no apparent motive, it all just fell into place. There was nobody else who had any reason, other than you. You deserve to be hung, Arthur Collenette."

"Quiet – that's enough. Now turn around both of you. This will all be over nice and quickly."

They slowly did as he bade, and George experienced once more the frustrated impotence of having to face death without being able to go down fighting. As they began to tur, the shock wave of the explosion hit them.

Up in the fort, the Turkish troops had charged up the stone staircase towards the rampart. The first man's shin hit the trip-wire, pulling the pin out of the grenade that was wedged under the pack of explosives. It had a short fuse, so apart from an uttered curse as he nearly fell forward, the soldier had no idea that he was living the last five seconds of his life. More followed him, even overtaking him as he had fallen. They began to fill the parapet above the gate, but not one of them survived the blast.

Down on the cliff top the shock wave blew the three men completely off their feet. George felt himself go spiralling over the edge of the cliff, his arms flailing, as he desperately tried to regain his balance. The world was turning upside down. and he lost all equilibrium. A sudden heavy jolt knocked the air from his lungs. There was a searing pain in his shoulder as his landed, and he could feel skin being scratched off his back by the abrasive rocks. His feet hit the rock, as he continued to skid downwards. Instinctively he reached out, trying to grab hold of anything that would prevent him from going right over into the void. The skin ripped from the palms and fingertips, as he clawed frantically for a grip. A protruding rock thumped hard against his heels, bending his knees into a bone-jarring halt. Stars and flashing lights flooded his vision. Nausea swept through him as his lungs fought for air. He felt faint, as his body began to slide down once again. Although it caused him excruciating pain, George managed to stop further descent by using his injured bleeding hands. His secured his feet on to something hard. Gulping air like a goldfish, his hand groped furiously for another safe handhold. Jamming his fingers into a crevice, he secured his position. He could feel the wet stickiness of his own blood running along his arm. A groan to his left made him turn.

"Oooh – Bejesus."

It definitely wasn't Arthur! Patrick had landed almost right next to him.

"Are you OK, Pat?" he gasped.

"Am oi dead, George? Is t'is 'eaven?"

George could just make out Patrick's outline in the darkness. He was being supported on the same narrow ledge as himself, which seemed to extend out slightly more from George's landing point. By careful probing with his feet he found the far edge, and managed to manoeuvre himself over until he was sitting next to his friend.

"Are you OK?" he repeated.

"Moi 'ead seems ter be workin', but oi 'aven't checked t'e rest of me yet."

"Come on mate, let's try and get you out of here. We've got a cruiser to catch and I don't fancy our chances if we stay here and wait for help."

They began to lever their aching bodies away from the rock in readiness for the descent to the bottom, but then an old familiar voice came from above.

"Stay where you are you two. It's not over."

Both men looked up towards the cliff top, seeing Arthur's form looming high above them, outlined against the moonlit clouds. Somehow, he had managed to remain at the top of the cliff. He stood there with his feet apart, staring down at them, his Mauser pistol held in both hands, pointing directly at them. George let forth a snort of frustration, they were both trapped once more. Would this nightmare never end?

"You two bastards have just managed to kill most of my men, but now you have run out of tricks? You have never been able to get the better of me, have you George? Unfortunately for you – now you never will, because this really is the end of the road for you."

They both heard the click of the hammer being cocked on the pistol, as the gun aligned on Patrick. There was a bright flash, and a loud bang as the weapon fired. To George's horror, he heard Patrick gasp.

"Oh, moi Gord, t'e kweer feller's really shot me, George," he said. There was a look of amazement on the Irishman's face.

Slowly his body slumped downwards, to sit in a crumpled heap on the edge of the drop. Below him there was nearly one hundred feet to the rocks below. George could just see the white water beyond him, and tried to move towards him to stop him going over the edge. The force of the fresh gusts wafting upwards, stirred the Irishman, and sensing the danger he was in, he leaned backwards. Patrick was OK and George was relieved. He looked back up towards Arthur to find that he was staring straight up into the barrel of the gun.

"Now it's your turn, George. Stand up."

The cocking hammer clicked once more. George closed his eyes, expecting an explosion in his head.

It never came – but following a hideous scream of pain, it was Arthur himself who came! The almost feminine scream of terror lasted as he came plummeting down the cliff face, straight towards him. George raised his hands instinctively to fend him off, and as he did so he caught the briefest glimpse of a girl, standing where Arthur had just stood. Then the full force of Arthur's body hit him, knocking him off balance, as his weight impacted like a sack of coal. The force knocked George back off the safety of his ledge, ripping his hand from his hold on the rocks, and forcing him to slide further down the cliff. Arthur's hands grabbed hold of his clothing, like those of a drowning man. The sheerness of the precipice was interrupted as another small ledge, and the two levelled off just before the sheer drop. George, more by instinct than judgement, managed to dig his heels in to stop himself going over the edge. The searing pain in his back and hands created an electric agony, as yet more of his skin was being torn away. Arthur was still screaming as his body careered on past George, heading over the edge. Without a second thought, George's hand shot out, grabbing his outstretched arm. His fingers closed around Arthur's wrist, but before the full weight of his body hit him, George's free hand was grasping for a good handhold. He felt his fingers gripping the rim of a protruding rock. The sudden curtailment of Arthur's fall caused his body to swing in an arc, almost wrenching out George's shoulder socket. Arthur crashed hard against the cliff with a loud sickening splat.

"Aaaargh," grunted George, as he experienced more pain than he had ever known.

Arthur's screams were brought to a sudden halt, as his head crashed against the hard rock-face. The impact burst open his forehead, sending blood gushing freely down his face. His feet were dangling below, with nothing between him and the foaming rocks far below. As he looked down, Arthur's eyes opened wide in terror, suddenly realising the full extent of his predicament. He looked up into George's agonised face, and realised that he was being held – suspended. Looking back down, he gave a dreadful whimper of fear.

Seconds passed, and the adrenalin in both men eased, as they began to assess their predicament. Arthur could see that George was in a great deal of pain. Blood was running freely down his arm, down onto his own gripping hand. He could see that George was supporting them both with his other arm attached to a hold on the rock face. Both were silent, as they took stock of their situation.

Through his pain, George became confused when he looked down and saw the glint of a steel dagger protruding from Arthur's back. Had that girl stabbed him? Why? He realised that she had to have been the cause of his unceremonious fall? Arthur had the knack of making enemies, and he felt very grateful for her intervention.

The terrible strain on George's arm brought his concentration back to the present. He suddenly realised the irony that this tableau presented. An exact repetition of that day so long ago on the Pleinmont Cliffs, but with Arthur replacing Matthew. Beads of sweat began to run down his face, as George remembered that day. It was almost as if revengeful Matthew had created the situation as he looked down from above.

There was the same extreme pressure on his muscles, as he looked down towards Arthur. His lower lip was quivering, and his water filled eyes were wide with terror. George was experiencing more pain than he had ever known in his life – as he said through gritted teeth.

"Well this is a turn up for the books, Arthur. Wasn't it about this time, when I was holding Matthew like this, that we saw you running away along the cliff-top at Pleinmont – surely you remember that?"

As if to make the point, George jerked his arm.

"Agggh," screamed Arthur.

Arthur's face was a picture of pathetic terror, crying and panting he started mumbling gasps.

"Can you now imagine just how Matthew and I were feeling, Arthur. You were running off and deserting us – remember! You went off leaving us with no chance of rescue, and no hope of us both coming off that cliff alive."

George's anger was reaching a head, as he viscously twisted Arthur's arm again, enjoying another scream of fright.

"I was going for help – honestly, George."

"Then why did you tell all those lies, Arthur?"

Silence! He said nothing. George thought about his promise to Matthew, and was toying with the thought of whether to just drop him there and then. He knew that this murdering piece of shit deserved to die, because just a minute ago he who was going to shoot him. He looked down at the blood that covered Arthur's face, as he began pleading for his life.

"Please don't do it George… Pleeeease."

'He has to die,' thought George.

He decided that he would do it on the next breath – just let him go – it would be that easy, and it would all be over. Just let him drop down on to those rocks. It would be justice for Matthew!

Below him, Arthur was now blubbing uncontrollably, sobbing like a child, crying that he was sorry, and begging him for mercy. George tried to steel himself, remembering Matthew's face as he fell away from him. Arthur had to die, and that was that. Then as a mist filled up-draught hit him full in the face, he heard Gladys' voice. She was saying that he had to forgive, or it would destroy him. George shook his head. No, he had a promise to keep. He gritted his teeth, and tried to become more resolute. He would do it after the next breath.

The next breath came and went, and the next, and then a third. George became angry with himself because he realised that he couldn't do it. God knows that Arthur deserved it! Tears of frustration welled up with his inability to carry out the deed. After all this time, it should have been so easy… the bastard has had it coming… but he just couldn't bring himself to do it!

He remained still for a moment, trying to make sense of his thoughts. He felt his arm beginning to go numb, just as it did that day holding Matthew. He did not have long left.

The damp wind, blowing upwards from the base of the cliff had a strange effervescent effect. It's refreshing caress soothed away all of his tangled emotions. It was as if it was massaging away his anger, and calming his troubled vengeful spirit.

Seconds later, and George had come to terms with the situation. He was thinking hard about what to do next, as he looked down at Arthur's wet pleading eyes. At that moment he realised that he did not hate him – he just pitied him. He knew now that if he had let him go, then that act would made him as bad as Arthur, because that would have made him a murderer as well. That realisation was enough for him to confirm his decision.

"Get your other arm ready Arthur, I'm going to pull you up."

Arthur's snivelling gratitude made him feel sick.

"Come on Arthur – before I change my mind – make sure you're ready."

"Yes – thank you, thank you. I won't forget this George. I promise I'll help you get back to the Allied lines – honestly. You won't ever regret…"

"Shut up Arthur, just concentrate on what I am saying. On the count of three, you reach out with your free hand, and grab this ledge that I'm on."

"OK," panted Arthur.

George readied himself.

"OK – One – Two – THREE."

George pulled with all his might, and Arthur's hand landed with a slap on the stone lip of the ledge near his boot. As Arthur began to take his own weight, George helped to pull him further up onto the ledge. As he did so he inadvertently knocked the dagger from Arthur's back, causing him to scream in agony, but he continued hauling him up. On reaching the relative safety of the ledge, Arthur grunted his thanks as he pulled himself up onto his knees.

George lay back groaning from the effort, absolutely spent, before turning over on to his side, gasping for air. Every muscle in his body ached, both of his hands were a gory bloody mess, his back must look the same as it throbbed with pain. He had lost a lot of blood which had fused his shirt material to his skin. Most of his clothing was soaked with his blood. Both of the men were panting heavily, as each slowly regained their strength.

George tried to make sense of the decision that he had just made, realising that he had actually saved Arthur. After all this time – after all these years of hatred and bitterness. After his promise to Matthew to avenge him – when at the point of fulfilling that commitment, he had not been able to do it?

He knew that Arthur was not a human being like everyone else, so it should have been something that was easy. After all nobody would turn a hair at putting down a mad dog. Why had he…

Arthur's heavy gasps had gone quiet, which created the ominous stillness. Something was very wrong! His sixth sense was screaming in alarm. The hairs on the back of his neck were raised, as he suddenly realised that there was an unseen threat. A screaming silence! He spun himself over, ready to face whatever!

George turned and his eyes flicked around towards him, immediately raising both of his arms instinctively in self-protection. Arthur was standing over him with a large rock raised up above his head. There was an ugly, maniacal grin etched across his bloodied face.

"You will never learn will you, George!" he snarled.

George lay totally helpless, he could do nothing, in such an awkward position on the ledge. If he tried to move out of the way, he was going to topple off the ledge. Fear flooded shot him, as he watched Arthur's face muscles tense in readiness to bring that rock smashing down on him. He started to curse his decision, when he saw the expression on Arthur's face suddenly change.

A second beforehand, George heard a heavy clunk of a rock, as it bounced off of the large one that Arthur was holding high. His shrill scream followed the bones in his fingers being smashed. Arthur blurted out another cry of pain, swearing in surprise. George looked up at him, seeing his features contort in pain, the rock began slipping from his grasp, falling down on to his shoulder. That stone that had hit him had been no bigger than a cricket ball, and George had no idea of where it came from.

In front of him Arthur staggered as the rock fell down towards his feet, as he struggled to keep control. He was totally unbalanced as his foot stepped backward to avoid the rock, but it missed the ledge, causing his body to arch backwards as his body weight carried him over into the void. As he went, he threw the rock away to try and save himself, but it was too late. Arthur disappeared over the edge. George's hand instinctively reached out to save him, but was too late. Arthur's screaming wail followed him all the way down to the rocks below, where it was abruptly cut short.

George looked up towards the top of the cliff, catching sight of the girl as she turned and disappeared into the darkness. He just sat there and began to examine his damaged hands.

"Yer want ter be careful who yer 'ang around on cliffs wit' moi lucky lad," said a croaky weak voice out of the darkness to his right.

"Patrick!" George gave a great joyous cry of relief. "I thought you were a gonner and no mistake."

"T'ere's anot'er ledge just over here moi lad, it's part of the one you're on. It goes on downwards. Oim 'urt pretty bad t'ough. T'at bastard 'as shot me t'rou t'e left shoulder George and it 'urts loike billyoh."

"Who threw that stone? Was it you, or that girl?"

"Oi know t'at it wasn't me, cos oi can't even raise moi arm. I t'ink it was t'at girl who stabbed 'im, so oi guess t'at it was 'er who t'rew t'e stone. Good t'ing for youse t'at she did."

"OK mate. We won't be having any more trouble from Arthur. Let's see if we can get down the rest of this cliff safely, and swim out to that cruiser like we planned."

"Now t'at he is gone, we's cud walk it ter the next promintory. We cud go back up and get a couple of ter weapons. T'ere are just t'ose a couple of Johnnies over on t'e far ridge to get rid of. Moi bet is t'at t'ey will 'ave run for it boi ter toime we get t'ere."

"No. I don't think that either of us is in any fit shape to walk anywhere Pat. It is over ten miles to the front lines, and we cannot guarantee that we will be able to get through them without being shot. We have a much better chance swimming those couple of miles to get picked up by the cruiser as we planned."

He ran his hand down to his belt, breathing a sigh of relief when he found the line was still attached. "The inflated float will keep you from sinking Pat, and I'll pull you along. We seem to have lost the other one."

Patrick agreed with him, and they slowly and carefully made their way down the rest of the cliff. George left Patrick sitting at the water's edge nursing his wounded arm and shoulder, while he searched around the swirling waters in the early dawn light to find a way through the rocks to be able to get out into the open water. It was while doing this that he came across Arthur's broken body. Even in death there was that sneering, arrogant expression on his face. He was lying unnaturally awkward, trapped between two large protruding rocks. Broken rib bones had erupted through the skin of his chest, giving his body a grotesque appearance. Just beyond him there was the deep water that they needed, and floating there was the other float. He managed to retrieve it.

He made his way back to Patrick, and began tying the webbing of the float around him, and the other to himself before finally making their way out towards the deep water. Both men waded out and launched themselves, swimming out into the Aegean. George took a last long look back, seeing the waves breaking over Arthur's inert form. Determinedly, he turned to face back towards the open sea.

Together, he and Patrick swam painfully out the two miles towards their objective. George's injured hands and back stung unbearably in the salty water, but after twenty minutes everything appeared to go numb. Patrick tried to assist him by using his one remaining arm, but excruciating pain forced him to stay still. After an hour and a half both men stopped, held on to their float, and waited for the cruiser. Fortunately, from then on things started to go according to plan, although the increased wave height proved to be irksome.

The cruiser appeared on time, arriving within fifteen minutes of the time that they had expected. The bridge lookouts aboard the warship had quickly spotted them in the early dawn light. Had the weather been any worse, then it might well have been a different story. They were picked out of the water by the cruiser's sea boat a little after six o'clock that morning.

The cruisers captain had been amazed when it had been reported to him that there were two men swimming in the water over two miles from the shore. He had brought the great warship around, heeling hard over to starboard, as he reversed his course to investigate the sighting. Once the sea-boat had come back alongside, it proved to be very difficult to get Patrick out of the boat, and there had been a few failed attempts to get him up the scrambling net that had been rigged down the ships side. George found it unbearable to try and grab hold of the rope netting, the fibres digging painfully into the raw palms of his hands. The crew finally settled for a canvas harness attached to a rope block and tackle, in which the Irishman was hauled up via a small davit. Due to the lack of skin on his hands, George was raised in a similar manner. Even with him just holding on to the rope edge of the harness caused him to grit his teeth. His torn flesh sent needles of agony through his upper limbs. It was like literally like grasping broken glass.

Finally, both men swayed on the iron deck. George looked back towards the shore, as the first rays of the sun lit the old Crusader castle. There was a faint wispy pale of smoke that rose ominously from the tower, as he finally realised that their adventure was over.

Chapter Twenty-Five

C'est La Vie

The familiarity of just being aboard a Royal Navy vessel once more gave George an immense feeling of security, and one of utter relief that he and Patrick had finally made it to safety. All of the dangers had disappeared. The last half an hour in the water had been touch and go, because while they both were being supported by the float, George's whole body was a temple of pain, and he could feel his strength seriously waning. He knew very well that he would have drowned had the warship not seen them.

Down in the sick-bay, while the sick bay attendants cleaned his wounds, George's mind drifted back over their escape, realising just how lucky they had been to be sitting here. Had it had been just been fate that had reared its head once more in his favour? After all, things could have gone either way. It was even stranger to think that had it not gone the way that it did, then it could be Arthur Collenette who survived. He became convinced that it had been pure chance that they had made it, and that it had nothing at all to do with an intervention of some supernatural being, such as a guardian angel watching over him. It had simply been fate.

If that bullet hit Patrick a fraction of an inch to the right, he would be dead. If that girl had not thrown the rock at Arthur, George knew that he too would be dead. It is fate that decides the outcome of everything, life itself was just a series of chance happenings, and once again it had settled in their favour.

Although he had not actually killed Arthur himself, George felt that with his death, it fully discharged his promise to Matthew. The pledge that he had made to his friend so long ago, had finally been honoured, but it worried him a little that he had been unable to kill Arthur. Did that mean that he was weak, or lacked fortitude? Then he realised that his reticence had been because he had always held the hope that Arthur was not as evil as he was. That he may change. It was a normal human quality to refrain from the act of murder. Arthur was certainly evil and had certainly deserved to die, but was it right that he should have to do it in cold blood? Had it been a face to face encounter, then the old primaeval survival of the fittest outcome would have resolved the encounter, but to kill him someone in cold blood was just not in him. Maybe that was a positive quality!

Once the sick-bay team had patched up George, he asked for permission to go and speak to the Captain, while Patrick remained down in the sick bay, to have his bullet wound attended to. He was taken up several metal ladders, which took some time due to the terrible pain in his leg. Finally, he stood before the ship's commander, who was sitting at his desk in his day-cabin.

George briefly related the story of their escape, but the Captain seemed to be totally disinterested.

"You are not unique young man," he said. "We have often rescued members of the army who have got themselves into difficulty off the shore. So, get yourself back down to the sick-bay, and let the medics fix you up."

Not allowing himself to be dismissed in such a cursory manner, George then went on to explain about the strategic importance of his mission, emphasising to the Captain that the Admiral would want to be informed of his return. The senior officer became peeved that a junior rating had the temerity to suggest to him what he should, or should not do.

George hated the huge class divide that existed between the upper and the lower deck within the service, knowing how the so-called upper classes were immediately selected for a commission with the least qualifications.

He patiently tried to explain to the officer that the Admiral needed to be made aware of his rescue, and his persistence finally got its reward, because the Captain called for his telegraphist, before making out a signal for transmission to the C-in-C and ordering him to send it immediately.

Even then he was put down in no uncertain terms.

"This had better be true, or you will regret it."

By the time that George had made it back down to the sick-bay, the Wireless Office had received an almost instantaneous reply, ordering the Cruiser to abandon its patrol and to return to Murdos at the best possible speed.

On reading the reply, the Captain's demeanour became a little more convivial towards George, but he retained the imperious aloofness. It was the class system rearing its ugly smugness – the public school against the village school – the gentry against the artisan – it existed everywhere, and has done for over a thousand years.

During the transit back to the anchorage, George remained in the sick bay, where they attempted to ease his discomfort and treat his damage his skin. His palms, elbows, and his back were all badly damaged. His palms were the worst, appearing as red raw inflamed flesh. A lot of the epidermis had been almost rubbed away by that rough stone, during his slide down the cliff. His back was a series of red patches where his vertebrae protruded, the skin had been grated off, giving him needles of pain. His arms were a series of simple abrasions. Cooling ointments were applied, before bandages covered the wounds to prevent infection. He was told that he would be sent to the hospital ship on arrival at Murdos, where the doctors would carry out a better diagnosis of his wounds.

Over in the next berth, Patrick's face was pallid, looking physically drained of all energy. The bullet remained in him, the Naval Surgeon said it would be difficult to remove, and that he would leave it to the specialist teams aboard the hospital ship to perform the operation. The medics worked hard to make both of the men as comfortable as possible, until they could be transferred.

An hour and a half later saw the Cruiser passing through the two head-lands that afforded entry into great circular harbour at Murdos. After making its way slowly through the throng of vessels, the warship finally dropped anchor close to the Flagship.

As they had made their way into the harbour, George had looked out through the scuttle in the sick bay, feeling terribly nostalgic as he could just see *HMS Adamant*, over on the far side of the anchorage. He could just make out several of her dark, low-lying charges nestled alongside, and some of the submarine crewmen working hard to get their boat ready for their next patrol. Thinking ahead, he knew that he would need to go back aboard her once his wounds had been attended to, as all of his naval kit lay in a locker aboard that depot ship. He remembered also the present he had bought for Gladys, because it would be so nice to give it to her after so long.

That in turn reminded him of good old *E11*, who would be still out on her patrol in the Sea of Marmara. The only possessions that he had that were still on board was his cap, that was stuffed up above the pipes, and the small framed photograph of Gladys. At that very moment he only had the clothes that he stood up in, which were the things that Mr Slade had given to him prior to setting off on that fatal mission.

An hour later, and a messenger appeared to inform George and Patrick that they were going to be transferred across the harbour to the HM Hospital Ship Guildford Castle, where the medical teams were on stand-by, waiting to treat their wounds more effectively.

A companion ladder had been rigged down the side of the Cruiser to enable them to make their way down into the motorised cutter, for the journey across the harbour. It was extremely painful exercise for both men, and it took rather a long time for them to get into small boat. As they cast off, they passed under the bow of the mighty flagship that flew the Admiral's pennant from its fore masthead.

George leaned back against the gunwale in the sunshine, although in great pain, he rather enjoyed the ride. After leaving the claustrophobic confines of the sick-bay, being out in the open air became a freedom unsurpassed. Beside him, Patrick sat somewhat subdued, having received an injection of morphine to help ease his pain.

Lying on the surface all around them, the filth within the anchorage was as bad as ever. They passed one of the huge rafts of rotting material, surmounted by several squabbling gulls. The utter repugnance of the smell had not changed either, being a mixture of effluent and rotting cabbage. Before George realised what was happening, the towering white ships side of the floating hospital loomed high above, like the chalk cliffs along the south coast of England. George craned his neck back, noticing that there were lots of bandaged men leaning over the guardrails, staring down at their arrival.

This maritime hospital had been especially converted for her important task from being an ocean-going liner. She boasted the very latest medical equipment that could be found in any top hospitals anywhere in Britain.

He heard the cutter's engine going astern as it drew alongside a large wooden pontoon, which had been especially positioned to accommodate the smaller craft that ferried the wounded back from the land battles. It enabled them to berth safely, and transfer their charges without them having to climb any ladders. A wide gangplank had been rigged from the pontoon, up towards a large open doorway cut in the side of the vessel. The gentle slope made it easier for the stretcher bearers to access the vessel.

Once aboard they were registered, and checked in. A medical attendants helped them down the stairways towards the initial assessment area that were located near to the operating theatres. Once they had completed their second examination that day, the two men had been parted, each being sent to their respective specialised treatment areas. Within the confines of such a large ship, it was difficult to believe that she was afloat.

Patrick's examination revealed that the bullet wound was worse than at first thought, and that he would have to undergo emergency surgery to remove it to allow the damaged tissue to recover. Arthur's bullet had entered in a downwards trajectory, through the top of his left shoulder, passing dangerously close to his lung and damaging his clavicle. What he needed more than anything was a good period of rest, along with some good wholesome food. Soon after arriving he was made ready for the theatre.

In these high temperatures, any wound quickly turns septic, which in turn allows more dangerous infections to enter the body and cause many more problems. It was little wonder that Patrick had been unable to swim out from the shore earlier that morning.

George wondered how he had managed to swim those two miles, dragging his inert floating body. He was sent to a ward specialising in skin wounds. His recently applied dressings were removed, and he had undergone a whole hour of having the wounds cleansed by one of the medics. More, deeper fragments of stone were extracted before medical salves were applied, and his hands were finally redressed. His back was thoroughly cleaned and bandaged. He was then allotted a bunk in one of the many wards, and told to rest.

The following day, after a second examination of Patrick wounds, the doctors discovered something that George had feared – he was suffering the initial stages of consumption. The Irishman was immediately sent up into an open-air convalescent ward, located high within the upper superstructure of the huge ship. It was the tuberculosis ward, where each morning the wheeled metal beds were pushed out onto the uppermost deck, so that the patients could breathe fresh air – or as fresh as it ever managed to get within this hell hole. It was going to be a very long time, if ever, before Patrick would ever be fit again for active duty. Although he had guessed his condition, the news still came as a shock to George.

His own diagnosis proved to be slightly better, although not by much. His upper leg was severely bruised, and it had what the naval surgeon suspected, was a suspected hairline fracture of his femur. To repair this problem his leg was placed in plaster. An examination of his facial scarring from the blast revealed that, although the hard scabbing made it appear to look much worse than it looked, it was in fact the natural healing process trying to repair his damaged skin. The surgeon told him that in six to twelve months there should be virtually no facial disfigurement. He was very relieved to receive the diagnosis from the opticians that his eyes were both in good condition, but when the surgeons examined the terrible abrasions that he had suffered on both of his hands and his back, George became worried when one of them had whistled through his teeth, and shook his head disbelievingly. There was obviously something very wrong that was giving him a cause for concern!

The surgeon tried to be as gentle as he could, as he probed the terrible abrasions. Yet more tiny pieces of stone were removed from deep within his raw flesh with tweezers, which evoke more bleeding. Not only had some of his skin been rubbed away, but he had also lost some of the muscular tissue. The one positive thing was that when he swam out to meet the warship the seawater had cleaned his wounds which had prevented infection. Afterwards they had to be carefully cleaned once more and redressed them, which George had found even more painful than when it had first happened. Later he had been informed that, although they too would eventually heal, he would bear the scars for the rest of his life. The healing process was going to take a long time, and the surgeon had added that he would be experiencing pain for the next year, before things would start to improve. Along with his leg in plaster, his back, and hand wounds were all heavily bandaged. It became very difficult for him to move, or to be able to find any position where he could fully relax.

There were many huge wards aboard the Hospital ship, each one filled by hundreds of bunk beds, and each bed filled with a wounded soldier. The severity of their wounds could be pinpointed by the number of bandages. Some of the men could walk, while others were recovering from the amputations of their limbs. As George limped his way through them towards his own bunk, he witnessed to some terrible injuries. It was evidence of man's inhumanity to man, in all of its gruesomeness.

There was one major advantage of him being allotted this particular bunk, and that was that it lay direct under an open scuttle, and was therefore a lot cooler than being amidships, where the heat seemed to congregate. Some newly installed rotary fans were spinning tirelessly overhead, which distributed the hot air to everyone. George sat down on the edge of his bunk, because he was unable to lie, due to him being so heavily bandaged.

"It looks like you have been in a war mate," said a cheerful voice with a strong antipodean accent.

"You should see the other bloke," George replied.

"He must be a gruesome sight."

George smiled to himself. Thankfully there was still somebody who had a sense of humour, because he had noticed that an overpowering air of pathos existed, mainly due to the fact that many of these wounded men knew that they would not be making it home. He turned awkwardly towards the voice to see a young smiling fair haired soldier, who was lying on the top bunk next to his. Looking at him, George could see that his left leg had been amputated below the knee, but otherwise he looked to be well.

"Looks like you have done your bit too," George replied.

"Yeh. That has really pissed me off. Before this lot kicked off, I was picked to represent South Australia in the two hundred yards sprint. I don't think that will be happening when I get back home – do you?"

"No," said George, feeling sorry for the young man. "But least you are going home mate. There are a lot of men here who would willingly change places with you."

"Yeh, I suppose you're right there, mate," said the young man reflectively. "The name's Harry Roberts of the Australian 10th Battalion, late of Adelaide, South Australia. I ran the fastest two hundred in the whole of 1914, but unfortunately I couldn't outrun a Turk bullet."

"Good to meet you Harry," said George. "I am George Torode from Guernsey in the Channel Islands. Late of His Majesty's Submarine *E11*."

"Are you off that British submarine that was in all of the headlines?"

"Yes, I was," said George.

"I read all the reports on your exploits when we were in Egypt. Your captain got the Victoria Cross."

"Yes, he did," said George. "I got the Distinguished Service Medal as well. In fact, the whole crew were decorated."

"Well done mate. It's good to meet you. I don't suppose that I will be winning any medals now."

"No, I don't suppose that you will, Harry, but at least you will survive this war and I expect that the army will supply you with a false leg, so that you will be able to get around. It will take some time for you to get used to wearing it, but with a strong determination like yours, I know that you will get there. You could possibly use your athletic expertise to train youngsters to achieve the things that have been denied to you."

"I never thought of that, George. Maybe I could," said Harry. "You certainly have a bright outlook on life."

"The only alternative is death Harry, and I have seen far too much of that over these past few months. I am just thankful to be here, and not lying out there in some ditch with a bullet through my head. I might still have two legs, but the doctor says I will never have the full use of my hands again. If you give in and fail to stay positive, then self-pity creeps in and takes over your mind. That will gradually bring your spirits down and eventually it will destroy you."

Harry Roberts looked back at George thoughtfully. He nodded his head.

"I very am glad that you turned up today, George. You certainly have lifted my mood. Thanks for that."

"You are welcome mate. Keep the old chin up, and everything will turn out right. Now if you forgive me, I need to get some sleep. So, I am going to try and get my head down for a while."

"OK George. See you when you wake up, as I am not planning on taking any world tours in the near future."

As soon as he attempted to lie down, George made the mistake of trying to lie on his back. It produced the most unbearable stabbing pains he had ever felt. So, he sat up before attempting to lie on his side, but the pain in his plastered leg made that difficult. Even lying face down caused pain. So, he sat on the edge of the bed once more, and even then he felt a pain in his buttocks, making the experience uncomfortable.

"Can't you sleep, George?" asked Harry. "I can see that lying in any position is painful for you. They have some deck chairs down by the ward office. Go down and ask them if you could try one."

"Thanks Harry, I will do that."

Sure enough, Harry was right. A deckchair was placed beside his bed, and with two soft pillows positioned behind him, in spots where his skin was still intact, George was finally able to relax.

That night he slept well, although falling off to sleep had taken some time to achieve. In the morning he awoke refreshed and ate a good hearty breakfast of bacon and eggs. One of the sick-bay orderlies had cut up his food for him and fed it to him.

Later that morning, the Naval Surgeon Commander did his medical rounds of the ward. When he finally reached George, he told him that everything that could be done for him had been done, and that only time would reveal just how much use of his hands would be available to him in the future.

Once the medical rounds had been completed, there were two naval officers who entered the ward. In the lead, George quickly recognised Commander Charles

Brodie, along with one of his staff lieutenants. He watched them as they went into the office to make enquiries of the Petty Officer Sick Berth attendant. The PO turned and pointed over towards him, and the officers headed in his direction.

"Hello Torode," said the Commander, as they arrived at his bedside. "I have come to take a statement from you, if you have recovered enough to make one."

"Good afternoon, sir," replied George. "Unfortunately, I am not going to be running about for a bit, but I feel pretty good considering everything that has happened."

The young lieutenant came forward with a notebook.

"This is Lieutenant Challen. He is going to write a full account of your recent adventure. So, just make yourself comfortable, and just tell us everything that happened from the moment that you and your team left *E11*, right up to this present moment. Once we have it all written down, I have to get it typed up, and go and report to the Admiral what has happened. If you could be as accurate as possible, with times and dates et cetera, then it would help me. So, go ahead when you are ready."

George spent the next hour going over the raid, bit by bit, along with its ultimate tragic failure. He related how he had awoken in a Turkish hospital, his meeting Patrick, and of how Arthur Collenette had taken them as prisoners aboard the ship to Gallipoli. How the sinking of their transport had led to their escape, and of their stand at the Crusader castle. He informed Commander Brodie of the death of Sub Lieutenant Arthur Collenette, and of how he had nearly killed both Patrick and himself. He ended by relating how they managed to get picked up by the patrolling cruiser. Finally, he repeated the diagnosis from the doctor, and how he would be out of action for some time. The lieutenant wrote it all down verbatim, and on completion Commander Brodie stood up.

"That is a remarkable account, Torode. Well done on your ingenuity in getting back safely. I shall report back to the Admiral in due course, later today. I am sure that he will be the first to wish you well in your recovery. If you see your Irish colleague, O'Connell, please pass on our thanks for his significant contribution. It is good to know that such men as you two, are out there giving their all. With this kind of dedication, we can only expect a final victory. Goodbye and well done."

With that, the two officers turned towards the exit and disappeared.

****

The following day George was escorted up to the upper deck, and was sat on a chair under the shade of the huge spread of the rigged white awnings that covered the whole area. Later that afternoon, just as the sick berth attendant was about to help him back down below deck, George asked if he could go up, and visit Patrick.

He had already discovered that his ward was on the highest deck, and to get there he had to be helped up a metal ladder. His ward was actually positioned just aft of the funnels. When George finally got there, he was amazed to see that not one, but hundreds of deck chairs and beds positioned outside on the deck. Men were sitting there in the shade of the spread awnings, where Patrick and his fellow TB sufferers would be able to get plenty of fresh air. With him being positioned so high above the water, it permitted the air to move more freely, and George immediately felt cooler.

"George – over 'ere."

He immediately spotted Patrick with his good arm raised over in the corner, his deck chair placed against a metal screen. He waded his way through the mass of men, his heart sinking as he heard Patrick coughing before he reached him.

"Hello mate, how are you feeling?"

"Oim foine, considering," he said. "But t'e food 'ere's terrible. Oi cud do wit' anot'er plate of t'em eggs loike t'at young lady at t'e farm cooked fer us. Oi wunder 'ow t'at little gal is doin'?"

Another hacking coughing bout took his voice away.

"Moi bludy coffin' doesn't get any better, but on t'e broit side, moi arse is defoinately on the mend, Georgie boy. T'ey 'ave cleaned it up really gud, and oim shoitin' abilities are much better."

"I can at least smell that you have had a wash, Pat. It's a big improvement on that rose manure that you infested the bed with at that farm."

They both laughed at the memory.

"T'at feckin' bullet t'at t'e kweer fella, Art'ur, shot me, nearly put an end to me, George. Just a quarter of an inch away from moi lung, so t'was. T'e world weel a happier place widout 'im in it."

George nodded his head in agreement.

"I have been asked to pass on the thanks from the Admiral's staff for your help in getting back to safety Pat."

"T'at's noice of t'em. We certainly showed 'em, didn't we George?"

"We sure did mate. We held off a small army. Do you know what is going happen with yourself?"

"T'e powers t'at be are sendin' me off to Malta on t'e very next transport, George. So t'is will 'ave to serve as our goodbye."

"They will have you fixed up in no time, Pat. They have a large military hospital there. Think of all those nurses waiting for you!"

They talked for another half an hour before one of the sick berth orderlies came up to tell George that he had just five more minutes, because one of the Surgeon Commander wanted to see him in his office.

"Oim sure t'at t'ey'll 'ave me as roight as rain in no toime at all," Patrick said, as George stood to go. Another series of coughs interrupted him for a while. "We'll bot' be off on anot'er adventure before you's knows it my Bucko. Once t'is war is over wid, we'll 'ave ter share a glass of the black stuff on O'Connell Street in Dublin. Did yer know t'at t'ey named t'at street after me?"

"No, I didn't," said George, then seeing the cheeky smile on his friend's face, he realised that he was having his leg pulled.

Both of the men were fully aware that sharing a pint was not going to happen. Patrick would be lucky if he lasted another year, and George's heart went out to the big Irishman.

"You just wait Pat. You'll be home tending your Grandfather's roses before you know it," replied George. "This time, try and keep out of the shit!"

They had laughed at the memory the remark stirred. George couldn't shake his hand, as both of his own were still heavily bandaged ,and stinging like a nettle rash. He gently lay his arm on his friend's good shoulder, both knowing that they would probably never meet again. After going through so much together, it seemed impossible to think that they were going their different ways.

It was with a heavy heart that George made his way back down to his own ward on the deck below. He was getting very frustrated, as trying to get anywhere with his leg in plaster was proving to be very difficult.

Arriving back in his ward, he found that another batch of casualties had arrived. To fit them all in, the medics had begun laying out camp beds between the metal bunk beds. There must be well over a hundred extra berths, and it looked like everyone was filled by a new patient. George guessed that many of them were going to be sent to Malta on that same transport as Patrick. Soldiers were being given priority, because once they reached the British Military Hospital, they would quickly be able to fix up those men with superficial wounds and those worst cases of dysentery and get them fit and ready to return to their respective regiments. George had been told that dysentery was a major concern over in the trenches, and on the beach-heads. Without treatment it was fast overtaking the Turk bullets to become one of the main causes of death.

George noted that there were a lot of amputees up here, who were obviously convalescing, waiting to be sent home. The surgeons must be working overtime down in the theatres. Some of the men with more horrific injuries would be left behind, especially those whose life expectancy was not good, and they would remain here until either their condition improved, or they died. Some of them had suffered grotesque facial distortions and ugly burns, where blood-stained bandages hid their disfigurement. None the less George noted that the bandages failed to hide the terror that still existed in each man's eyes. There were so many men who looked to be near death. They made George feel fortunate.

It was obvious that this war was going to change the lives of many thousands of men before it ended. It was only just over a year old now and still there was no end in sight.

Tired war weary lack-lustre eyes followed his progress, as he slowly threaded his way through the beds. Blood-stained bandaged heads turned slowly as he walked by. George's own eyes were searching for the Commander's Office, where he was due to meet the Surgeon Commander.

"Got any baccy, mate?" asked a wounded Corporal, from an Infantry regiment, his voice a husky whisper. He was lying on his back in one of the new camp beds. "I'm absolutely gaspin' for a fag."

George could see from the position of his bandages that he had been shot through his upper body, and he could clearly hear a rasping rattle as he breathed. A cigarette would not do him any good. The man's beggar eyes widened bright with hope.

"I don't think that the Sick Bay Tiffy's allow any smoking in here mate. I'm sorry pal, but I don't smoke," he replied, and carried on his way. As he moved on, he could hear the man swearing his disappointment.

The sign – Surgeon Commanders Office – stood out in bold black letters on the door just ahead of him.

George poked his head through the open door, and saw a Petty Officer sitting at a desk.

"Ordinary Seaman Torode, to see the Surgeon Commander," he said.

"Ah! There you are! Go straight in, he has been waiting for you."

The Commander looked up and indicated to a chair as he walked in. George sat carefully, waiting until the doctor finished reading the open file on his desk. He folded the document, and looked up at him.

"Let me have another look at your hands," he declared, and began to remove the bandages that were covering them.

George held them out as he inspected them, turning both over to closely inspecting the palms. The naval doctor looked him squarely in the eye and declared that despite all the attention he had received, his hands had become infected, and were swollen and red as his blood fought to contain the infection.

"I am not going to pull any punches young man. Both of your hands have become poisoned, following the loss of so much skin from your palms. It was probably the heat that caused the infection, and even with all these heavy bandages, it is easy for germs to flourish in these conditions. We will clean them again now, and replace the dressings with something lighter. The good news that I can give you is that your back will eventually heal, but it is going to be months before things are anywhere back to normal. The plaster on your leg can be removed in five weeks' time. If these dressings are not changed, and your wounds cleaned on a daily basis from now onwards, there is a very real possibility that you may have both of your hands amputated. We don't want that to happen, do we? So, I am going to have you evacuated on a ship that has a doctor aboard. He will change your dressings, but unfortunately it will not be heading straight home. There is one leaving tomorrow that is heading for Alexandria. After you get dropped off there, you may have to wait a couple of weeks for another ship that is heading home, but you will eventually get there. We must keep your hands clean – so we have to send you home via hospitals – what do you say to that?"

George felt a stab of fear, he certainly did not want to lose his hands. Secretly he had been hoping that he would still be here when *E11* came back from her patrol in the Marmara, but he was not willing to stay here at the expense of his hands. The Surgeon Commander could see him dithering.

"I can understand your reticence young man. Your crew-mates will probably miss you as well. But if you remain out here in this heat, then the chances of your hands recovering are virtually nil. You have done more than your duty. Get yourself home and recover – get fit again – and maybe then you can re-join the fight. We need young men like you if we are going to win this war."

Reluctantly George agreed. The Commander told him to rest until he had made the arrangements to have him transferred aboard the next ship heading outward with a doctor.

He was escorted back to his own ward, thankful to be back under those moving air of the rotary fans. Ten minutes later there was disturbance from the entrance, and he saw Commander Brodie once more. He approached George.

"Hello Torode. I hope that your injuries are starting to heal. Everybody on the Flagship is very glad that you have made it back alive. It was very unfortunate that all the others in the raiding party were killed. I have recounted your story to the Admiral. He sends you his congratulations on getting back to us against all the serious adversaries that you have had to face. Although the mission was a failure, he wanted you to know that the explosion that you caused did indeed delay the signing of the arms treaty between the Turks and Germans. So, your friends did not die in vain. He also wanted me to tell you that you will be mentioned favourably within his formal report of the mission. I would like to add my own congratulations to his, on a job well done. Once you are healed, and you manage to get back on active service, I want you to come and see me Torode. I can use your talents on my staff. The

Surgeon Commander tells me that he is sending you home. Use the time to get yourself back to fitness, and I will do all that I can to ensure that you remain within the Trade."

He reached into his pocket and removed a card, which he handed to George. It was a personal identification card with the Commanders home address on it.

"When you are fit, write to at this address Torode, and I will get you back into the Trade." With that the Commander said goodbye and withdrew.

The next day George was called to the Surgeon Commanders Office once more.

"I have just been informed that there is a merchant transport heading for Alexandria in Egypt, the day after tomorrow. I have booked you a passage aboard, as they also have a doctor embarked. Once you reach Alexandria, you will find that there are lots of ships that will be heading for home, usually via Malta. So, you should not be holed up there for too long. Report to the Port Office when you arrive, and hand them this letter. The Harbour Master will either transfer you immediately to the next ship that is heading home, or he will send you to the British Military Hospital there to await the next ship. They will look after you there. I am going to send a Medical Attendant with you now, who is going to help you pack your kit in readiness for your departure. Just remember that each of your hands will have to be cleaned, and the dressings changed on a daily basis. You must make sure that they use only new clean dressings. Remember that, and we will not have to amputate. I am very glad to have met you. Have a safe journey home."

Once they had travelled across the harbour to *HMS Adamant*, the packing of his kit went well. The Medic had to do everything for him, but he was able to make sure that nothing was missed, and that everything went into his kit bag. Then they made their way back to the Hospital ship, where George cleared his bunk area and then made his way over to say goodbye to Harry Roberts. The Australian was sad to see him go.

"If you ever get out to Australia come and see me, George. I live in Adelaide. While you have been away, I have been thinking about your unusual name. Out near where I live in Adelaide, we have a builder by the name of WC Torode, who has built many of the civic buildings in the city. Is he a relation?"

"He probably originates from Guernsey, Harry. The name is only found on the on the Island. There was a lot of emigration out your way in the middle of the last century."

"It's a small world and that's a fact. I hope that you get home, and that your wounds all heal, mate."

"You are right there. Remember what I said about training the youngsters Harry. You will achieve all of your hopes and dreams through them. Goodbye."

George made his out towards the pontoon.

Looking back over his time out here in the Aegean Sea, George thought of how transient service life was. He had become good friends with so many people over the past couple of months, most of whom were now either dead, or were lying badly injured aboard this hospital ship. He felt glad to be going home, but he knew that in making that decision, it was going to put an end to his big adventure, and he felt extremely sad at not being able to say goodbye to his crewmates. He felt cheated that he would not be there to see the boat return. His one consolation was that he still had left Gladys' shawl, so at least he would still be able to give her the present when he got home.

George sat with his kit bag packed in readiness, waiting to catch the launch across the harbour to join the Royal Naval Transport named *SS Levante*. The name brought to mind the cloud that hugged the top of the Rock of Gibraltar on *E11*'s journey out here. That seemed so long ago. The Surgeon Lieutenant had redressed his hands, before allowing him to proceed.

He reflected on the words of Commander Brodie. He had said that it had just been bad luck that the others had been killed. So that word luck had been bad for those who had died – so it must have been a piece of good luck that he had lived! He realised at that moment that God had nothing to do with his coming through the mission, unless Luck was another pseudonym for God! A supernatural deity had done nothing to help him, and certainly had not prevented any of the misfortunes that he had suffered.

He remembered seeing several of the Allied soldiers in dusty camp on the Murdos hillside on their knees praying for deliverance from the fighting over on the peninsula, prior to those initial landings – but many of them had been killed. A fat lot of good praying did them – had they died because God had not answered their prayer? If a God had not been on their side, then they must just have had bad luck. Was it God, or bad luck that the wards on the Hospital Ship were filled with wounded men, many of whom were not going to make it home. George could not deny that he himself had silently prayed on occasions – but now he had the proof that he had survived by luck – and certainly not through any God's intervention. As children we are taught to pray during our informative years, and now at the age of nineteen, he had discovered that it was all a complete waste of time. Religion was a fallacy, a set of rules that governments used to keep the population under control. If God had answered any of those soldier's prayers at Cape Helles, then the death toll would not be nowhere near as bad as it is. Many religious people must be praying that this conflict will come to an end, but there was no sign of it happening any when soon. In fact, the hostilities seemed to be escalating, with no end in sight. Was God ignoring all of their entreaties as well?

He was beginning to see that religion was a way to keep the populace living in the eternal hope that things would get better. That is, he decided, the reason why people prayed – hoping that things would get better, and to give those hopes a destination, they sent them up to their God.

George knew that most of the wars in history had been caused by the confrontation between different religions, or the clashing of religious factions. He started to wonder if he was becoming cynical. It was ridiculous that people fought over the most trivial aspects of the same religion. Catholics fighting against Protestants was a prime example. One country that supported one creed, could declare war and fight another using the opposing faith. England standing against the might of the Spanish Armada came to mind. When two different religions were involved, it was a case of one invisible deity being considered better than the other invisible deity, and anyone who denies the fact will be killed. Religious intolerance the cancer of the human race. Trying to endorse his theory, George thought of the Crusades. Both of the Crusades had been bloodbaths. Both sides believed that they had the right of God on their side, which gave them licence to butcher the unbelievers. To let good decent men to be slaughtered, or horribly maimed, should not be the action of a loving benevolent God. Religion, and all divinities, were simply a creation of people's minds, and has been since time immemorial.

Just then the launch came alongside the ship, collected and took him across the harbour, where he was helped up the companion ladder to board the *SS Levante*. He was taken to an upper deck cabin, where he found that he would be sharing it with three other wounded men, who were also being sent home under the care of a doctor. He immediately noticed that they were all Australian pongo's. Each of the injured men had been confined to their bunk, being unable to move around unaided. Every one of them had a least one limb amputated. Despite him trying hard to start a conversation, George found that each man's thoughts were of surviving long enough for him to see his homeland again. George settled in, and decided to rest as much as possible.

On the twenty second of August the *SS Levante* weighed anchor, and sailed from Murdos. As the ship manoeuvred its way towards the entrance, George made his way out to the railing, and watched the ships as they passed by. The *Adamant* was way over on the far side of the anchorage, and he felt a twinge of regret that he would not see her again. He felt some relief to be finally leaving this hell hole, and he remained there watching the island grow smaller and smaller, until it finally disappeared over the horizon. He hoped that he would never see it again.

Once he did manage to start a conversation, George's three companions endorsed his scepticism about the state of the war on the Gallipoli Peninsula.

One was an artillery sergeant from New South Wales, whose whole gun crew had all been killed, but who had remained at his post and continued to load and fire his weapon single handed, until he passed out from his wounds. He had lost the sight in one eye, and had a heavily bandaged left leg. His left hand had been amputated, something that made George more determined to follow the daily dressing routine. Later, when the sergeant had staggered across the cabin to make his way to the toilet, one of the others told George that he had been awarded the Military Medal for his action.

The second was an infantryman from Western Australia, who had been blown up by a hand grenade. He had suffered severe shrapnel wounds, and was in serious danger of losing his sight. His breathing was belaboured, having had his left lung punctured, and it was obvious that his right leg had been amputated.

The third was an Australian Army cook whose field kitchen had been hit by a shell. The blast had destroyed his left arm, and the skin on his face and upper body had been terribly scalded. George could see that the man was in permanent agony. He was undergoing a similar series of bandage changes, just like George. Never the less, from all of the terrible injuries that George had seen aboard the Guildford Castle, he realised that he and his companions were among the lucky ones.

George hated to see this waste of good men. Each and every one of the injured men aboard that hospital ship had given their everything towards an Allied victory, only to be cruelly maimed with life changing injuries. He began to realise that despite all of these magnificent selfless efforts from every branch of the Allied force, that the capture of the Gallipoli peninsula was not going to happen. The question that had to be asked was – were the Allies going to be faced with this same scenario on the Western Front?

Once the ship had berthed in Alexandria, George said goodbye to his companions, and as instructed had reported to the Harbour Master. He was told that there were no ships heading to home for at least a week, and so he was assigned to the hospital of the Military Camp outside of the city to await orders. He ended up being stuck there for over month, becoming increasingly frustrated as there were lots of ships travelling between there and Murdos, but apparently none that were heading for Malta.

On that first full day ashore, it had been even hotter than in Murdos. The camp was terribly unhygienic, with dug latrines and simple tent accommodation, but George made sure that he attended the medical call every day to get his dressings changed. The lack of any facilities made the time drag unmercifully, so remembering the words of Commander Brodie he began a regime of staggering around the camp perimeter to strengthen his leg muscles. The thing that George found most awkward was keeping himself clean, so he began asking the doctor, when he removed his bandages, if he could go and give himself a strip wash before he redressed them. Even when he did manage to wash, the plaster on his leg got wet, and he then had to go out into the sun to dry it. This soon become his normal routine, but he could not hold a razor, and so had started to grow a beard. Then he found that there was a barber in the camp, and he went and asked him to trim his new growth.

The news from Gallipoli seemed to go from bad to worse. After spending a month of purgatory in the camp, and with no sign of a ship, he was extremely glad to be transferred to the British Military Hospital in Cairo. He was told that he would be informed when one would be heading home. Once there he kept up his training regime by walking around the grounds. It was much healthier place, which was being run been run by the Army Medical Corps. The hospital was located within a large stone building, with brick-built accommodation. At the beginning of the Gallipoli Campaign, it had catered for the many Antipodean troops, who seemed to be arriving on an almost daily from Australia and New Zealand, prior to them being deployed on towards Gallipoli, or Palestine, but these days the place was being swamped by those same troops returning with horrific wounds, where the medical corps was trying to get them fit enough to be able to head back to their respective countries.

At the BMH Cairo, the daily routines were a lot stricter than back in the camp at Alexandria, and George was not one to enjoy regimented regimes one little bit after the relaxed discipline enjoyed aboard *E11*. He kept himself remote from all of the bullshit and square bashing, because thankfully, his medical condition precluded him from attending the daily parades and drills.

Thinking about his submarine caused him to wonder if she had arrived back safely, after her patrol in the Marmara. She must be back by now he surmised. Would they have been sent back to Malta to enjoy another spell in Horlick's pension? Maybe there would soon be a ship heading for Malta? Just maybe they would all be there when he reached the Island.

It was while he languished in Cairo that his leg plaster was removed. In the heat it had begun to itch unbearably, and it felt so good to feel fresh air tickling his skin. He sat in the sun all morning trying to give his white skin some normality.

It was just a day later that he learned of the imminent arriving of an RN Cruiser that was possibly heading for Malta. He managed to find out that the cruiser, *HMS Suffolk* had docked in the harbour at Alexandria for a two-day call to load fuel and fresh provisions. This was the very same cruiser that had rescued Patrick and himself from the sea off the Crusader castle. Thinking about that period, he wondered how poor Patrick was faring. Having a difficult disease like TB in that fumed filled hell hole was not the best environment for a positive recovery. Hopefully he was now in Malta! In having found out that the *Suffolk* was heading for Malta, George went to see his ward officer, and asked if a passage could be obtained. To his great joy a passage was indeed granted, and he managed to get a ride aboard an Army lorry running from Cairo up to Alexandria.

Riding along the dockside, he was impressed by the magnificent sight of the Royal Navy cruiser with her ensign flying in the breeze. It served to restore his pride in the service. He and his kit were helped aboard by two members of the crew, where he was transferred straight down to the sick bay. Three hours later the ship sailed. He breathed a sigh of relief to be leaving Egypt and be a step nearer to his passage home.

Whilst being ashore in the Army establishments, George noted that he never given a tot of rum each day. When he made enquiries, he was told that he was under twenty-one years of age, and did not qualify. He now realised how lucky he had been to get one aboard *E11,* and how the rules had been bent to accommodate him. However, he really enjoyed the surface cruise through the eastern Mediterranean, and after three days the ship entered the magnificent defended harbour of Valetta.

Again, he was immediately transferred ashore to the British Military Hospital there, before *HMS Suffolk* was refuelled to sail back to Murdos with the dispatches for the Admiral, and Army Staff.

To his disappointment E11 was not there, and after many enquiries neither was Patrick. After hoping for a quick onward journey George was left ashore to languish for another three weeks. He considered going ashore and paying a call on Horlicks at his Pension, but he knew that it was a long way, and that his leg might not hold out. After dithering about it, he thought that all of the good times, like those he had enjoyed there with his crew mates, and that they should be remembered as they were. Any attempt to recreate those days never brings them back. However, he did manage to catch an omnibus up to the Kingsway, where with the use of a walking stick, he managed to reach the parapet that overlooked the harbour. His heart leapt as he looked across the water towards the old fortification of *HMS St Angelo*, with the old ironclad *HMS Egremont* still lying in the creek below its towering walls. He remembered *E11* tied up alongside her.

He was utterly spent by the time he returned to the hospital, the pain in his leg had become absolute agony, a fact that made him realise that his recovery was going to take longer than he realised.

At the end of that third week the Battle-Cruiser *HMS Inflexible* entered harbour. She was stopping over on her way back towards Gibraltar. George quickly made enquiries and managed to get himself a passage on board. The three weeks he had spent here in Malta had proved to be beneficial because some of his injuries were just starting to show the first signs of improvement. He had continued to walk determinedly around the grounds of the facility several times a day, despite the aches and pains. He had also managed to sit in the sun, which he was finding rejuvenating.

Immediately on joining *HMS Inflexible*, he was again sent straight down to the sick bay, where he was employed assisting the Petty Officer sick berth attendant – not that he could use his hands to any degree of usefulness. He was beginning to be able to bend his fingers a little without them bleeding, and those sore patches on his back were now a series of thick scabs.

It proved to be another long week of them transiting through the very hot conditions of the western Mediterranean. On departure from Malta the cruiser transited along the North African coast close to Algiers, where a shimmering heat haze hid the city from view. Soon the towering Atlas Mountains rose proudly off to port, as they began their passage across the Alboran Basin.

At school in Mr. Jeffrey's class George had heard the stories of the Barbary Pirates, who had operated out of the ports along this coast. The primary reason for these Corsairs attacking the merchant shipping was to capture European men and women to sell into the slave markets of the Ottoman Empire. Horatio Nelson had been an officer aboard one of the ships that were sent to quell their activities, but the activity was not finally eradicated until the French invasion of Algiers in 1830.

At the end of each day George went up to the upper deck, once the heat of the day had begun to fade, to enjoy the cooling breeze. Then on the third evening, as he scanned the horizon, he recognised the towering edifice of the Rock, silhouetted against the backdrop of a beautiful sunset. They docked in the harbour two hours later under a twilight star filled sky. The harbour at Gibraltar was as busy as ever, with ships from all the Allied navies represented. Across the bay, the lights of the Spanish port of Algeciras could be seen twinkling in the darkness.

George was drafted ashore the following morning to join the shore establishment *HMS Cormorant*. Two rating from *Inflexible* were detailed to assist him with his kit. Once there, he was sent on to the British Military Hospital to await his next passage, which he hoped was going to be the final leg of his journey home.

It was very frustrating for him because today was the eleventh of November, and it had been over two and a half months since he had left Murdos. The latest news from Gallipoli was absolutely dispiriting. The Turks had not been moved back one inch, and the state of impasse still existed, with the steady list of casualties growing every day. The futility of continuing the operation was becoming a matter of controversy at home. George thought of the huge financial expenditure that had been made. It made one wonder how all of that military might had failed, and how there had been so much manpower wasted. He felt depressed after reading the news report. What an absolute bloody waste it had all been. So many good men had died for nothing. Mina's beautiful face suddenly filled his mind, and he wondered what his future would have been had she lived.

It was on the second day that he was in Gibraltar that the weather began to deteriorate. The sun and clear blue skies were quickly replaced by a blanket of grey cloud. The temperatures plummeted and George felt the first chilly fingers of winter for the first time since his departure from Portsmouth earlier this year.

George used much of his spare time to replace many of the diesel soiled items of his uniform clothing within his kitbag. A new white cap replaced his old beaten brown stained original, that was probably still jammed up in the pipe work aboard *E11*. He had paid a local laundry to thoroughly clean and iron his best uniform, and it was returned correctly pressed, with eight horizontal creases in each leg. With the arrival of the cold weather, he needed to change from the usual uniform white front, worn during the summer months, into his navy-blue knitted sea jersey. Wearing it was much warmer, but it was also very itchy against bare skin. He ventured out into the town to buy himself two new short armed vests that he could wear beneath it without being seen above the neck line. Once his he completed the replenishment of his kit, he felt much better, and his spirit began to look ahead to his arrival home.

His hands had lost a lot the swollen puffiness, a good sign that the infection had been eradicated. They still looked bad however – but the red rawness of the exposed flesh had turned pinker, and the surface of both had a hardened crust. His bandages were still being replaced each day, but they were now thinner, which made them much lighter. He found that he could actually use his finger-tips a little, but they still gave him sharp pains if he tried to grip anything too hard.

At the end of his second week on the Rock, he was informed that all of the sailings that were heading home from Gibraltar had been suspended due to the sighting of several German U-boats in the Western Approaches. This had been ordered because, ever since the sinking of the Lusitania back in May, the Germans were conducting a campaign of unrestricted submarine warfare. Ships were being kept in port, and a new ship collective system was starting to be employed which would seriously reduce the chance of them being attacked. It was known as the convoy system. It had been unusual for enemy submarines to appear in the south west approaches, as the U-boat commanders had to either breach the boom defences lying across the channel at Dover, or they had to make the long journey around the top of Scotland to reach their patrol areas. With this new convoy system, the navy sent escorting destroyers, which seriously reduced the U-boats chance of success.

George could imagine how uncomfortable life must be aboard one of those boats in those cold forbidding seas of the Eastern Atlantic. He certainly did not envy them. It went to show how these small craft were influencing the strategic planning of this war.

It was not until the start of the second week of December that any sailings were resumed, and George heard that a troopship was to be included within this new convoy system, whilst being escorted by several armed warships. He made enquiries and was thrilled when he had been given passage aboard. The troopship was returning to Portsmouth with soldiers who were due home for leave, and it was due to arrive there on the 20th of December. She was sailing in company with an oil tanker and four merchant vessels who were all due to arrive home for Christmas. The ships were to be escorted by the destroyer *HMS Scourge* and two others, as yet undesignated.

George had enjoyed his first visit to the Rock, but he was certainly not sorry to leave this time. During his incarceration in the BMH, along with the onset of the cold weather, the place had lost much of that initial excitement. The town and harbour presented a depressing sight in the dismal December gloom. He remembered that there had been three submarines here on that first occasion, and now *E15* was a burned-out wreck lying on that muddy shoal in the Dardanelles, with her crew either dead, or prisoners of war.

As the giant vessel was about to pull away from the quayside, George stood expectantly at the rail of the troopship *The Men of Harlech*, looking down at the dockside as the gangway was removed, watching the group of stevedore's struggle to remove the huge berthing hawsers from the steel dockside bollards. He was just very thankful that this was it – the final leg of a very long and tiring journey. The ship was full of pongo's, and despite George searching, there were no navy, other than the crew of the Troopship. Unfortunately, with the date of their arrival being so near to the Christmas period, he realised that it would preclude him from being able to get out to Guernsey for any leave that was due to him, as the ferries did not run over the holiday period, but he was looking forward to seeing Gladys.

****

On the voyage home, the convoy were forced to take a series of huge avoiding courses due to U-boat activity and George finally entered Portsmouth aboard The Men of Harlech on the 24th of December 1915. It was another of those grey cheerless mornings, as the line of vessels steamed into the harbour, passing between the Round Tower and Fort Blockhouse at the entrance.

Seagull sentinels hovered overhead noisily overhead, squawking their annoyance to the world, as they negotiated the freshening south-westerly winds that were blowing in off the Solent. Through the overcast blanket of thick cloud, a watery sun failed to lift George's spirits. Portsmouth presented a rather lack-lustre appearance, as the natural harbour began to expand before him.

Transiting inward past Fort Blockhouse, the Alma Mata of the submarine service, George again wondered what *HMS E11* had managed to achieve on her last patrol. Had she carried out a third mission, or was the Gallipoli campaign completely over and done with? He started to recall all of the faces of his shipmates. The Skipper, Martin Dunbar-Naismith. The First Lieutenant, Guy d'Oyly-Hughes. Lieutenant Robert Brown, the navigator. Coxswain James Doyle and Chief Jupp, the Engineer. George Plowman, the signalman. Lohden the wireless operator. Good old Brassie, Baxster, Maine, Basil and all the others. They had all been great mates on a great boat and he earnestly wished that he was still out there with them. His mind travelled back to his early days of training in Fort Blockhouse with Fred Chapman. Poor old Fred, he was lying within the shell of *HMS C301*, somewhere on the bottom of the English Channel.

Just beyond the bow of the trooper, he could see the Gosport chain ferry crossing perilously close. He watched the faces of the alarmed passengers, as she increased speed, sent scurrying over towards the Hard by the angry booming blast of the ship's siren. George moved from the port guardrail, crossing over to the starboard side to watch as the ship approached her berth at the northern end of the South Railway Jetty. The powerful steel bulk of a Royal Navy battleship filled the southern berth.

Looking to the north, the harbour spread out towards the mudflats below Portchester, with the line chalk cliffs rising in the far distance. Their crest was being obscured by the low-lying cloud.

On the dockside the sight of all the bright multicoloured bunting accompanied by rows of union flags fluttering resplendent in the breeze did little to lift the gloom of the day. On the quayside there was a smart Royal Marine brass band oompahing through several patriotic tunes, as the bulldog efforts of the dockyard tugs shouldered the bulk of the troopship alongside the dockside wall. The crowd were all dressed for the weather, with heavy top coats with a variety of headwear. Children clung to their mother's skirts in bewildered uncertainly, confusion etched on their faces.

Looking around at the other ships that were littering the harbour, some were tied alongside at the berths further to the north, while others were riding out the wind shackled to buoys on the northern fringes of the harbour. George noted that many of the ships had been repainted in the new weird looking two-tone dazzle patterns, that was meant to confuse enemy submarines and baffle the range finders of the German capital ships. The last coat of paint that George had given *E11* had been a navy-blue and grey camouflage effect. He wondered who was doing the painting now!

Lying beyond the Semaphore Tower lay the industrial might of the Royal Dockyard, where black smoke belched from the hundred or so red brick chimneys of the foundries, forges and machine shops, all fighting to keep pace with the incessant demands of the Fleet. Giant cranes carved huge semi-circles in the sky, lifting enormous marine components, crates of stores and in the case of The Men of Harlech, her gangway into place.

As the berthing ropes were being secured, George looked over at the Seventeenth Century Number One Basin noting the small fir tree had been tied to the Main Top Masthead of *HMS Victory*. Seeing it there served to remind him that it was Christmas Eve and all around him there was an air of expectant excitement abounding amongst the soldiers that were lining the rail. Each of them knowing that he was going home for Christmas. Happy times in the arms of his family. The prospect of leave seeing their loved ones compensating for all the hardships they had endured during these past months.

George patted his pocket where the letter from Commodore Roger Keyes was located, knowing that its contents guaranteeing he would be granted two weeks convalescent leave immediately on joining the Royal Naval Barracks at *HMS Victory*. Unusually for the navy, there were two *HMS Victory*'s, one being the barracks where he had joined and the other the preserved hulk of Nelson's flagship.

He had already discovered that there would be no passenger ferries heading over to the Channel Islands until after the holidays, so he knew that going home was not going to be an option. What was he going to do with fourteen days leave? The thought of spending it in one of those huge accommodation blocks within the barracks filled him with despair. Just what was he going to do? He certainly wanted to see Gladys again and the chance of seeing her in the flesh today was the foremost thing in his thoughts. He had rewrapped her present last night and used a sheet of brown paper he had bought in Gibraltar, tying it up with some white silk ribbon. He had been pleasantly surprised by the dexterity of his fingers, although they had ached afterwards. Yes, he was quite excited by the prospect of giving it to her personally this very day, but he had to admit to himself that over the past ten months, his feelings towards her had become confused. Basil Partridge's prophetic words had remained with him all of this time, having created an uncertainty ever since he had spoken them – would Gladys still be his? His brief, but traumatic relationship with Mina had also had a cataclysmic impact on his life knowing that it would be something that would be a part of him forever. Following her death, he had experienced such loss. Being with her was one of the most significant moments in his life, thinking it had been his ultimate transition into manhood. From that short relationship he felt that he could face the world head on. On his journey home from Gibraltar, he began to wonder if his love for Gladys had been a youthful infatuation of a naïve young man on a ferry – who was leaving his Guernsey home for the first time? After all, everything had all happened very fast. Had that really only been a year ago?

He did remember her kiss though. That had made a huge impact on him, but was one kiss enough to fall in love with somebody? Despite him only spending just over a day with Mina, he knew that he loved her passionately. Had she lived he would have chosen her and would definitely have gone back to find her after the conflict. So, does one innocent embrace with Gladys provide a man with enough emotional impetus to want to spend the rest of their life with her? He was not sure.

With Mina, it had been such a roller-coaster of emotions. They were the cause of all the doubts that he was having now about Gladys. He had tried to tell himself that his liaison with Mina had just been a chance meeting between two people in the turmoil of the war, having been thrown together by circumstances. Their paths would probably never have crossed in peacetime, but George harboured a deep certainty that their union had certainly meant more to him, than just a casual kiss. It was everything that he had ever wanted from life.

Maybe every experience that one has in life comes from chance happenings, very much like his theory about fate. Everyone of one's life events happened by chance, just as it was with fate deciding who lived and who died during this bloody war. There was no predetermined course for life that had been laid out by some supernatural being – he now knew that to be a fact. Everyone's life is controlled totally by fate – so that was very probably the same with relationships!

George hadn't had a chance to write to Gladys before he had sailed from Murdos – as his heavily bandaged hands had not allowed him to pick up, or even hold a pen. It had also been over three and a half months since he had received any mail from anyone, which had probably been due to the fact that nobody knew exactly where he was in the world. There might be lots of letters for him lying in various postal locations around the Mediterranean. By now his parents must be getting worried that something bad had happened to him and he resolved to send them a letter today and post it when he went ashore.

What would he have said to Gladys in a letter anyway, even if he had been able to write one? Maybe when he went to see her today, the ambivalence that he was feeling towards her would finally be settled one way or the other, but he knew that he would definitely have to go and see her. He had to know what fate had in store for him.

After thinking of his parents, he began thinking longingly of the peace and security of his home on Guernsey. Over there on the Island there was none of these complications that had filled his life ever since his departure for the war. If the ferries had been sailing, he would have loved to have gone home to see his parents, brothers and sisters and friends for the Christmas holiday, but he had more chance of landing to the moon than he had of getting home.

The one bright thing from all of this was that he had not had a chance to spend any of his pay since *E11* had left on her second war patrol. With him being incarcerated in hospital his wallet had begun to bulge with notes. So, he was contemplating going ashore and taking a room in a pub for the holiday period.

Looking over the guardrail once more, he peered down at the crowds below on the quayside, where there were squeals of delight as some of the women spotted their men and children began to scream with excitement, waving their arms as they recognised their father. There were the hopeful cheers from other men who were craning their necks, searching with expectant eyes, trying to spot that one recognisable face. George was very well aware that there was nobody down there who would be looking out for him.

Just an hour later he was in the naval barracks, *HMS Victory*. After transferring some essential kit into a smaller canvas bag, he left his large kit bag in the baggage store with the request that it be transferred over the harbour to Fort Blockhouse for him for when he joined there after his leave. When he was issued with his leave pass, the Petty Officer writer informed him that he was to report back for duty at Fort Blockhouse on January the seventh of 1916. That meant two whole weeks of leave. He made his way into one of the messes, and wrote his letter home.

So, with his bulging wallet in his pocket, he had decided that he was going to have himself a splendid Christmas. After all of the hardships he had endured, he reckoned that he deserved it. Perhaps he could afford to have a week in a cheap hotel down in Southsea! From there he would be able to see Gladys every day! The dream of Gladys coming to visit him in his room appealed to him very much.

He headed towards the main gate with his canvas bag on his shoulder. His hands were just usable, if he was very careful. His leg felt so much better, although if he put too much strain on it the tell-tale ache appeared. The scabbing on his back had flaked off, leaving circular pools of pink skin down his spine. He reached the kerbside just outside and took a good look at the first civilian Englishman since leaving these shores for foreign climes all those months before. It was the old newspaper vendor, who had his pitch adjacent the gates. Off to his right, George looked down towards the harbour, where he could just see the hanging sign of the Dog and Duck public house. He shuddered at the memory.

"Read all about it – French relieved of Allied Army Command – General Haig to take over the Western Front – Read all about it! Gallipoli campaign falters once more. Troops evacuated from the beaches. Read all about it."

George had had no news of the war since leaving Gibraltar and he went over and bought a paper. All of those enthusiastic predictions of breaching the Dardanelle's to directly attack the city of Constantinople had gone. We had lost!

Reading further, things were no better over in Flanders. This was about to be the second Christmas of the war and there still no end in sight. If anything, it was getting worse and we actually seemed to be losing the conflict. By reading through the report of the Gallipoli fiasco, he found out that *E11* had returned from her patrol safely, as had *E14*. If that had been from her second patrol, or even her third, it did not say. He carefully read a report about the ANZAC evacuation with some concern. Apparently, the troops of those two embryonic southern nations had suffered terrible casualties.

Carrying the rolled-up newspaper and with the canvas bag over his shoulder, he strolled down towards The Hard actually walking past the Dog and Duck public house. It looked to be very full. I wonder if the busty barmaid still works there, he thought, but he did not feel the slightest inclination to go in to find out. Poor old Fred Chapman – he had been such a good friend. He remembered meeting him at the bar in there. That was now history and so much had happened to him since then.

On seeing a red post-box, George took out his letter home, and posted in through the slit. Then reaching the corner at the bottom of the road, near the Dockyard Gates, he turned left and began walking along the waterfront area known as The Hard towards where he hoped that he could catch an omnibus down to Southsea. The walking that he had persevered with on the way home seemed to have helped him because, although there was still an ache, his legs felt stronger, but today this would be the longest that he had walked for some time. He had already decided to take an omni-bus part of the way.

As he walked, the sound of a puffing steam-train attracted his attention. It suddenly emerged from a raised embankment and viaduct over the road and into the Harbour Station building. It was obviously under great strain from its heavy load, because it was producing great plumes of grey and black smoke, speckled with red sparks erupting angrily from its stubby funnel. Seagulls wheeled away from the dark acrid fumes, squawking their disgust, as they headed for the clearer air out in the middle of the harbour. The engine did not actually enter the Harbour Station, but continued along the elevated branch line that ran out on wooden piers over the water towards the southern end of the Dockyard. Thirty rumbling wagons followed along behind, all filled with the essential war supplies that were needed by the great battleship that lay berthed just astern of the Troopship the Men of Harlech, that he had just left earlier that morning. Dockyard railway cranes, stood waiting on the quay like giant herons fishing at the water's edge, each ready to transfer the contents of the wagons aboard the great vessel.

George hurried across the road to catch an omnibus that had stopped near to the Harbour Station entrance and he felt the pain in his leg increase with the effort. Stepping aboard, he surprised to find that the ticket conductor was a woman. He had never witnessed this phenomenon, and being curious he watched the girl with interest as she efficiently dispensed the tickets. He had certainly heard reports that women were beginning to take over men's places in a lot of public sector jobs, releasing more men for active service – but this was the first time he had actually encountered it in action.

"Where to, my luv?" she enquired.

"Osbourn Road, please," said George, pleasantly surprised by how pretty the girl was.

After sitting down, he noticed that the driver of the vehicle was also a woman. She drove with hunched shoulders and determined concentration, which was probably why they had made such painfully slow progress down towards Southsea. The bus took a very winding route, picking up and discharging passengers with great regularity.

George soon began to get bored with the journey. So, he began observing the passing populace disconsolately, feeling a remoteness from the humdrum everyday happenings of domestic life here in England. For the past ten months he had led a completely surreal existence, which had been so far removed from this urban normality. He had returned from a mad world of death and destruction, to a place where people went shopping for Christmas and arrived home each evening to find a meal waiting for them on the table. His world had been both fearful and terrifying, where the men who had shared those dangers were thankful that they were still alive at the end of each day. Looking out at these tranquil scenes felt strange, but he definitely liked to being back here in a life of normality.

George knew that his experiences in Turkey would were always going to be imprinted in his memory and that they would always form a huge part of his life.

Looking out through the glass window of the bus, he saw a man quickly step back from the edge of the kerb as a heavy lorry passed by very close, just missing him. He had just witnessed the perfect example of his theory about fate. It must happen to everybody, every day here on earth, he thought, no matter where you were, or which god you worshiped. After all the risks that I have lived through in this war, my chances of dying must have been just like that man there, who had been nearly run down by that lorry. He had been lucky that he had not been killed, just the same as with me! I could have been hit by a lorry as I crossed the road to catch this bus. I could have been blown up by those mines that we had to transit through in the Dardanelles. Maybe when a man serves in a war then it makes his chances of being killed appear more obvious, but here in Portsmouth those same dangers exist. When will my time eventually come? George began to wonder if he was going to survive the war, or if his own death was imminent. Only fate knew that. All he could do was to live his life as well as he could.

Looking out of the window once more, he noticed that everyone they passed seemed to be carrying a heavy bag full of festive fare. Some had brightly wrapped parcels, another hugged a huge plucked fowl and a third had a Christmas tree. Everybody seemed to be determined to enjoy the coming holiday, or what passed for a holiday during the restrictions, caused by the deprivations the war created. He could see holly and mistletoe adorning shop doorways and coloured paper chain links brightened their interiors. Passing by the front window of a butcher's shop, he could see facade covered with hanging fowl of every breed and size. Plucked capon's, turkeys and duck hung in white regimental lines like the rows of hammocks in the barracks. Carol singers stood on street corners, providing musical cheer to passing strangers in the dreary weather. All that was needed to make it appear like the perfect Christmas card scene, was a blanket of snow. Everything seemed so natural and so very reassuringly ordinary, far removed from the high action drama of the Eastern Mediterranean. George felt glad to be home.

He decided that he would get off the bus near the King's theatre. Sitting down for so long was making his hip ache and he felt the need to stretch his legs. He decided to walk the rest of the way, knowing that it was not too far. After stepping down onto the pavement, he placed his new cap on his head at a jaunty angle, picked up his small bag, and tossing it up onto his shoulder he watched the omni-bus jerked away to the sound of an over-revved engine. Tossing the bag up without thinking had hurt his hand reminding him to take greater care. His hands were still lightly bandaged. The sick bay aboard the troopship had given him a lot of bandages, and two small tubs of cleansing cream. He was going to have to do all of his own dressings while on leave.

His cap tally bore the legend *HMS E11* and as prepared to cross the road it had already attracted a few looks of admiration from passing civilians, followed by muffled murmured remarks behind him. After the foggy cloud of bus exhaust smoke had cleared, he adjusted his silk and lanyard, patted the medal-ribbon of the DSM sewn on his chest.

Looking about him, George could see several public houses and tried to decide if he would go for a drink, or not. No, it was too early. Across the road was the Kings theatre and he could see that the matinee performance queue was just beginning to go in. He walked on past the pubs and glanced up at the bill poster, advertising a good-looking variety show. He smiled to himself as he remembered how back to Gibraltar, the crews of various warships had sung rude versions of the songs that had been made famous by some of the stars that were performing here this very afternoon. We'll all go back to Oggieland. He smiled as he remembered those sailors singing in the Universal bar.

"Hello, Mister George," said an unseen voice.

Surprised to hear his name, George stopped, his head turning, searching around for a familiar face. All he saw was a sea of strangers in the queue. Then, looking down, he recognised the diminutive face of Gladys' maid, peering through a narrow gap between two gentlemen dressed in heavy overcoats. She elbowed her way through, followed by an equally small soldier. Finally, they both stood before him, hand-in-hand.

"You're 'ome then!" she said, stating the obvious.

The queue moved slowly onward towards the kiosk. Both she and her soldier friend took a side-step, crabbing sideways to keep their place. George found himself sidling along with them.

"Er – hello there," replied George, feeling a little awkward, as he could not remember her name, or even if he had ever been told it.

"Are you off to see, Miss Gladys?" she enquired with smugness showing through a knowing smile.

The queue moved again, so did the three of them.

"Er – Yes I am," he said, finding the question oddly personal.

Her face assumed a look of self-righteousness and George could see that she was enjoying the moment dying to impart something that he did not know.

"It's not really my place to say and I don't want to be the one to tell tales, but I think you might be wastin' your time," she continued.

"What do you mean?"

"Well – It's not for me to say, really…"

"Come on – you called me over here – out with it – what do you mean?"

The door of the theatre loomed.

"Well, she's bin walkin' out with a Naval Officer these past few weeks, so she 'as," said the girl a little too quickly.

George stood silent for a second, while he digested the new information. Basil Partridge's words hit him like a tidal surge. He looked back at the maid, who started to turn as her boyfriend pushed his money through the small window of the ticket kiosk to purchase their tickets. The two of them were just about to go into the theatre and George determinedly kept a smile pinned to his lips and politely thanked her, saying that he hoped that they enjoyed the show.

After walking a hundred yards George stopped, becoming overwhelmed by a mass of conflicting emotions that suddenly choked him. Strangely enough, he did not feel betrayed. He was trying to decide if he was hurt – or if he was relieved by this news, knowing that he certainly did not have the right to feel betrayed by Gladys, because he had done the very same thing with Mina? With Mina, he had used the war as an excuse for his betrayal and knew now that he would have to grant her that same privilege? It was just life, he decided. C'est la vie, as they say on Guernsey. Fate.

He had come here today to try to court Gladys, so would he try and make her change her mind! Could he win her back? Did he want to win her back? Was it a challenge to his masculinity? After thinking about all of the various aspects, he realised that it was the war that had come between them and that it was too late for both of them. They had both moved on. Maybe if he had not been away for so long their relationship may have stood a chance. The war was to blame for that. In another lifetime, if the country had been at peace, then he may well have ended up marrying Gladys. Would that have made him happy? Who knows! Sometimes one is forced to make instant decisions, especially in a time of such uncertainty. It was clear that Gladys had made one of her big decisions – just as he had made one when he had met Mina – and yet strangely enough, he felt no regrets. Gladys may well have thought that he had died – having not heard from him for so long – and to be honest she had nearly been right. Her father may have been a deterring factor! Life changing decisions have to be made from so many external sources.

The one thing that he was absolutely sure about was that he had to see this thing through to the very end and at least give Gladys the chance to speak for herself. He became absolutely certain that he had go to see her and make sure. After all, this story might just be a figment of the maid's fertile imagination. It was only fair.

He felt terribly nervous as he walked up Osborne Road towards her house. He stood hovering outside her gate, looking up at the front door. Then taking a deep breath, he lifted the latch, and walked up the path. His knock was bold and it was Gladys herself who opened the door – probably because it was the maid's day off. They both stood staring at each other, seemingly shocked by their physical nearness. He felt strange, but as he looked at her, he realised that the thrill he had experienced on that walk on Southsea Common was no longer there. She looked prettier than ever, but with her beauty came the realisation that any love that had existed between them had gone. He imagined that he could see a mutual response mirrored in her eyes and they both looked away at the same moment, unable to maintain eye contact. George broke the silence.

"Hello Gladys – I'm home," said George, rather lamely.

She showed the same awkwardness. Her lips creasing into a polite social smile, but her watery eyes looked sad.

"Er – Hello George. It's lovely to see you again."

Her voice sounded sincere, but her nervous demeanour didn't make him feel that she meant it. There was a pregnant pause, as the awkwardness between mounted. Was she going to ask him in?

"I just wanted to see you – I have only just arrived back in Portsmouth from the Mediterranean this morning."

She noticed the bandages on his hands.

"What has happened to your hands?"

"I damaged them a bit out in Gallipoli. They are getting better every day."

He thought he noticed a fleeting expression of regret flickering across her face. She seemed to be on the verge of tears and took a deep breath.

"The rest of you looks very well, George. I've been following all the exploits of your submarine in the newspapers. You are all quite famous you know."

This remark was followed by another uncomfortable silence.

"I see that you have won a medal," she said, searching for something positive to say.

George patted his ribbon proudly. Then, in an attempt to retrieve his pride, he took a deep breath and said, "I can't stay Gladys. I have only popped around with a little present for you for Christmas. I hope that you like it, as I have got to get back to the ship," hoping that his white lie sounded acceptable.

Finding nothing else to say, he said, "Have a merry Christmas, Gladys."

He passed over the present he had bought for her so long ago, smiled, turned and headed back down the steps towards the front gate.

"George!" she cried.

She dashed down the steps after him, grasping his arms. Tears filled her eyes as she looked at him.

"George, there is something I have to tell you…"

"It's alright Gladys, I know…" interrupted George. "I met your maid on my way here and she tried to explain the situation and tried to warn me not to come. Look, I don't blame you Gladys and I wish you all the happiness in the world. Honest I do."

Before she could speak, a voice from inside the house reached them.

"Gladys – where are you, darling?"

A man wearing a Naval Lieutenant uniform appeared from behind the half-closed door. George looked ruefully at him, then back to Gladys.

"Sorry," she whispered.

George gently touched her arm and at that moment he experienced that same maturity that he had felt with Mina. There was no anger, no envy – just a regret for something that had been, and now was no more.

"Goodbye, Gladys."

It was with a reflective air that he walked back down Osbourn Road, continuing onwards until he reached the Queens Hotel. The great green expanse of the Southsea Common stretched out towards the Solent, with the black silhouette of the Isle of Wight looking menacing beyond. Each step that he took away from her door, seemed to ease any tension within him and by the time that he reached the hotel's entrance, he felt strangely relaxed and calm. What was he going to do next?

Standing on the pavement, just outside the doorway he noticed an advertising placard that caught his eye. It displayed the delights of a menu for a Christmas Dinner being served by the establishment. George read through the tempting list and although it was outrageously expensive at ten shillings and six pence, he decided that he would go in and book it. After all, why should he not treat himself? He deserved some luxury after all the hardships and deprivations that he had endured. Why not splash out a little and salvage what he could from Christmas.

He decided there and then that he would take a room in a Southsea pub for the week, he did not know which one yet, but at least he would be able to enjoy a Christmas dinner sitting here in some degree of comfort. He pushed open the door carefully with his elbow and walked into the hotel foyer. At the reception desk stood a tall stout man wearing spectacles, looking resplendent in a morning suit. He wore a grey cravat, with a pearl stickpin holding it in place. His eyes opened wide in surprise as George approached, as an expression of repugnance spread across his face.

"Can I be of assistance – er, sir?" he said imperiously.

"Yes please," said George. "I would like to book one of your Christmas Dinners, please."

"Are you absolutely sure?"

"Yes," said George, beginning to detect the air of pomposity emanating from the man.

The man coughed disdainfully and added, "We do not admit men in uniform."

George looked past him into the lounge bar. It was full of Naval Officer's, who were all in uniform.

"What about them, then," he said, nodding towards the bar.

"Oh – but they are all gentlemen," replied the man in a self-righteous tone.

The anger that George had expected to feel when he had met Gladys, now made itself known, as it welled up within him. The class system was everywhere and he directed his anger towards the stuffed shirt behind the desk. He had felt like hitting him, but successfully restrained himself.

"Then it is a great pity that I can't say the same for you, eh?" he retorted, turning and slamming the door shut behind him. Ahead of him Southsea boasted literally a hundred hotels and public houses, so why was he standing here outside this palace of class pretentiousness. He was going to find himself a nice comfortable pub and enjoy this Christmas – c'est la vie.